Molly

TERESA CRANE was born in Hornchurch, Essex.
She had always wanted to write, and has been
doing so professionally for seven years. She
began with short stories, which were published
in *Woman*, *Look Now* and other magazines, and
then wrote her first novel, *Spider's Web*. *Molly*,
which is partly based on Teresa Crane's own
family history, is her second novel. She has
already completed her next novel, which will be
published by Fontana in 1984, and is beginning
another.

TERESA CRANE

Molly

FONTANA/Collins

First published as *Molly O'Dowd* in 1982
by Victor Gollancz Ltd
First issued in Fontana Paperbacks 1983
Fourth Impression April 1985

Copyright © 1982 by Teresa Crane

Made and printed in Great Britain by
William Collins Sons & Co. Ltd, Glasgow

PROLOGUE

It was finished almost before it was begun: the wet air sang with silence after the brutal blast of gunfire; blood ran in the gutter with the rain.

Molly O'Dowd crouched in her doorway staring in stunned disbelief at the two bloody, shattered bundles that had been such a short time before her youngest brother and the boy she was to marry. In the mud of the road Cormac, the brother closest to her in age, moaned and writhed, his leg shattered; not far from him another wounded man struggled to a sitting position nursing a blood-soaked shoulder. Apart from these – the debris of violence – the street was empty. Not a door nor a window opened; the whole village might have been dead.

"Not Sean," Molly whispered through furious, streaming tears. "Dear God, not Sean—"

From the direction of the police station came a shouted order.

Molly stepped into the street and Cormac's head came up sharply. "Get away, Moll!"

She ignored the words as she ignored the tears and the advancing red coats. She knelt beside him in the mud. If there were nothing she could do for the two she loved most in the world, it was at least some comfort to try to help Cormac. But as she calmly ripped the hem of her skirt to staunch the awful flow of her brother's blood she could not stop the question that burned on her tongue like acid.

"How did Sean come to be with you? How?"

Cormac shifted his gaze, glassy with pain, away from her face.

"Father," she said with bitter certainty, "wasn't it?"

Cormac closed his eyes, the gesture an admission.

"And how did he do it?" the girl asked quietly, her reddened hands busy about his leg, her eyes, silvered in the growing morning light, upon Sean's and Danny's obscenely sprawled bodies. "What did he say to bring my Sean here to die for nothing? Isn't it enough that his sons are as crazy as he?"

"Leave it," Cormac said tonelessly, wincing. "Leave it, Moll—"

But the girl's tongue ran on. "Did he sing a fine patriotic song? Did he talk of O'Dowds who have perished for Ireland? Sean doesn't—" she swallowed "—didn't hate the English any more than I do. What is he doing here?" The soldiers, weapons levelled, were almost upon them. She sat back on her heels and wiped the tears from her face with a bloodied hand. "And where," she asked the drifting, dove-grey clouds in a voice that made Cormac flinch, "was our brave father when the shooting started? *Where was he?* It should be *him* dead, not them. It should be him."

Her wounded brother did not answer, but steeled himself for the ungentle touch of the soldiers.

Seamus O'Dowd watched his only daughter gather her few belongings into a meagre pile on the kitchen table. The silence between them had lasted since the deaths of Sean and Danny six weeks before. He had argued, cajoled, threatened. At one time he had even unbuckled the wide leather belt that had so often been used to bring the girl to heel, but she had stood silently before him, frail and childlike, her great blue-grey eyes – the image of her dead brother's – fixed upon his face with an expression of mixed contempt and hatred, her lifted head and straight, uncompromising mouth defying him. What could he possibly do to her worse than had already been done? Later he had tried to talk to her; always his tongue had been a weapon as effective as any he possessed: persuasive, eloquent, provocative, a tongue to talk the dead to life and to cut the living to the heart. And Molly, as the words flowed unheeded about her, had wondered when her Sean had begun to listen to this voice? And why hadn't she noticed, hadn't she guessed, the fatal influence her wild, attractive family, their tongues as quick as their tempers and their laughter as ready, were having on the man whom she loved for his gentle nature, for his very contrast to the passionate, exhausting men with whom she lived? She had watched her father's vivid, handsome face as he talked. "Coward," said her eyes. "Coward! Where were you when they died?" She had turned and left him then without a word. After that he seemed to accept her silence, to ignore her as she ignored him – believing, Molly was certain, that she would eventually come round. It was not in Seamus O'Dowd to believe that a woman could truly hate him.

Without her brothers the house had been like a morgue! Danny dead; Cormac in the hospital of an English gaol; Patrick her eldest brother, who had escaped in the confusion of that bloody morning in Kilcarrigen, God only knew where. Those shocked and empty weeks had been a nightmare, the only relief coming with the news that Patrick had left the country and was safely on his way to America. But long before the first grief eased or the passionate rage at the terrible and irredeemable waste died, Molly had known she would leave. She had made her plans quietly, spoken to no one, gathered her small resources.

Now she laid her little stock of much-darned but clean and neatly pressed clothes upon a shawl spread over the table, drew together the corners and tied them firmly. Then she straightened to meet her father's eyes. He was leaning in the doorway, the light firing his crop of curly hair to ruddy gold, leaving his face in shadow.

"You're leavin' then?" He did not sound surprised.

She nodded and broke her silence at last. "I am."

She lifted her bundle and stood waiting for him to move. She could not leave until the doorway was clear. With her wild hair, gypsy black and curly as her father's, and that deceptively fragile look that comes from years of not-quite-adequate nourishment, she looked, from a distance, little more than a child still. But in the thin, pearl-skinned face the blue-grey eyes were very far from childhood, the stubborn set of the straight mouth and the wilful line of the jaw telling more of truth than the narrow shoulders and thin, childish hands. At eighteen Molly O'Dowd was a woman grown.

"You'll be goin' to Patrick?"

She did not answer.

"I'd thought of it meself."

She had guessed it and, for this reason – and others – had made different plans. As things stood she had little more time for her brother than she had for her father. His hand, after all, had been as firmly in that wild and ill-conceived fiasco that had cost them all so dear. She waited in silence for Seamus to step aside and let her pass.

"Don't go like this, girl," he said softly in the warm, winning tone he knew so well how to employ. "It would have broken your mother's heart to see you leave so, with no word of kindness. . . ."

That was too much. "I doubt," she said clearly, "that 'twould be me that broke her heart. I thank God she didn't live to see Danny blasted to kingdom come in Kilcarrigen village street—" Her breath choked in her throat at the picture the words brought to mind and she stopped abruptly. Handsome, heedless, laughing Danny had always been their mother's favourite. "Let me go, Father," she said after a moment. "We've nothing to say to one another."

Still silhouetted against the light he shook his head.

"How can you say that, Moll? You're me daughter, me only daughter. At least tell me where you're going."

She shook her head.

"Not to Patrick, then?" There was a hard edge now to the mellow voice.

"Let me go," she said again. Something in her voice alerted him. He pushed himself from the doorpost and straightened.

"England," he said. The word was an imprecation.

She said nothing.

"I'll see you dead first."

"You'll have to," she said, simply. "For you'll stop me no other way. I've made up my mind. Sean and I decided long ago, to go to London—" She looked at her father, studying him, her dark, arched brows drawn together, asking a question to which she could find no answer. "What did you say to him, Father?" she asked at last, very quietly. "What in heaven's name did you say to persuade my Sean to carry a gun to Kilcarrigen? He isn't – wasn't – one of you. He never was. I couldn't have loved him else. We were to have a different life, a new start. Peace. Something to work for, something to build." She looked slowly and with clear, seeing eyes around the squalid, sparsely furnished room that had been her only home. "A decent place to bring up our children, an education for them—" She could not go on, her struggle for calm lasting for several seconds before she asked, "Why did he go with them? He'd never held a gun in his life."

"He went because he wanted to." Her father was no longer looking at her.

"No."

"And I tell you that he did."

She shook her head, stepped closer to him, tilting her head to study his face before voicing the suspicion that had kept her all these weeks from speech lest she scream it at him. "You wouldn't have told him," she asked, deceptively calmly, "that you wouldn't give your permission for your darlin' daughter to marry a man who didn't measure up to her brothers?"

Silence. Beyond the door a bird sang.

She stepped back from him. Her face, always pale, was bone-white. "How could you? *How could you*? Why didn't you just kill him where he stood, and me too?" She was clutching her bundle as if it were life itself; tears she would not allow herself to shed roughened her voice. "Why, oh why can't you understand? Hatred is no answer, Father. It never has been. Killing begets more killing. What is the use of it all—What has ever been the use? How can you ask a woman to bear children simply to perpetuate that hatred and die in their turn? I am not my mother. I'll not see it happen to my children. There has to be an end. But the end is not here for me; neither is it with Patrick and you in America. Leave me to find my own way, Father. Go to Patrick. Nurse your wrongs together. Just be certain that you never look too hard for the real reason why Sean and Danny lie rotting in the churchyard. For if you find it you'll surely kill yourself." She had shouted herself hoarse and short of breath. She dumped her bundle back on the table for a moment, clutching at it to stop the trembling of her hands, breathing in deep and jerky gasps.

Her father had stepped at last from the doorway, his face of a hue to match his hair, his powerful hand lifted to strike her.

She stood her ground and watched him come. "If it makes you feel better," she said, her voice edged hard with contempt. But the blow died in mid-air. The colour receded from the handsome

5

face and an expression close to bewilderment took the place of fury.

"The soldiers killed them," he said, "the English soldiers." The echoes of his voice hung in a questioning silence.

She stared at him, her own anger draining in face of the dreadful uncertainty in his eyes. "I know that," she said more gently, "I know it. I was there, wasn't I? But it wasn't only them, Father. You did it together, you and the soldiers. Don't you see that? You can take pride in the fact that they died for a cause — comfort, even. I cannot. I see only the waste: their lives, and mine; children unborn. And for what? Nothing has been gained. What I cannot forgive you for is that Sean knew it. You goaded him to Kilcarrigen and he died for nothing."

There was a moment's pause as she awaited her father's comment but he said nothing.

"I have to go," she said lifting her bundle and swinging it up into her arms. As she did so something fell out and slapped onto the floor at her father's feet. A book, battered and dog-eared from much reading. Before she could move he stooped to pick it up, riffled through the pages. Finally he turned to the frontispiece with its hand-written inscription.

Molly watched him in silence. The book was her treasure, a memento of a friendship she would never forget; the only true friendship of her short life. It had begun when an English girl named Mary Livingstone surprised a small, fierce trespasser on her father's lands. From such an unlikely beginning had come a friendship that would have a profound effect upon Molly. Gentle Mary opened to her a world that until then she had not known existed. For two long summers the girls had spent hours together, stolen hours in the cave-like, sun-dappled shade beneath the old willow that had become their hiding place. From Mary, Molly learned of a way of life for which her own soul yearned: a life of peace and comfort, of books and music, a life where each day was not a brutal struggle to survive, a hand-to-mouth affair with ragged arrogance and bitter pride its only support. But more valuable by far, she learned practical skills as well. Mary had been delighted to discover in the wild, uneducated Irish girl a burning will to learn and a sharp intelligence that made teaching her a pleasure. And so, under the curtaining willow Molly learned to write and figure and read. The book her father now held was Mary's parting gift on the day she had left Ireland with her family to sail to a new life in India. Molly knew large chunks of it by heart, had lived through it many times. Alice and the White Rabbit and all those other characters created for a much-loved child from one man's joyous and witty imagination had figured in her dreams, had peopled a world she could not now conceive of being without.

Her father traced the written signature with his finger and lifted his head. "This is her doing," he said. "She it is who caused the rift between us. She had no right—"

"No, Father. Though 'tis certain that she taught me to think for myself, and I can only thank her for that. Don't blame Mary, Father. Blame me, blame yourself, blame us all. Things are as they are and cannot be changed. I'm going to England and I will not be stopped. I want a decent place to live, places to go, books to read. I never again want to be hungry. And I never again want to hear the sound of gunfire, nor to shake with fear at the sight of a soldier or a policeman."

In the silence that followed, each of them came finally to recognize that the gulf between them was unbridgeable. At last, as if in defeat, her father asked quietly, "How will you live? Have you money?"

"Some. Enough, I think, at least to get me there. Sean and I had saved a little—" She paused awkwardly. "– I'll be all right. I'll find work." She held out her hand for the book, avoiding his eyes. "Goodbye."

He closed the small volume and laid his large hand palm-down upon the leather cover. "I'd like to keep it."

She lifted startled eyes to his, flinched at the look on his face.

"I've nothing of you," he said. "Nothing at all. I've seen you with this often – it would comfort me to keep it."

She had come too far to be defeated now. "Keep it." She smiled crookedly. "I'll buy a better one when I'm rich," she said and left him with no further farewell, standing solitary in the middle of the beggarly room staring blindly at a book he could not read.

PART I

Autumn 1898

CHAPTER ONE

EUSTON STATION IN the early afternoon was Bedlam on a Sunday. Carried along unresisting by those in a greater hurry than herself, Molly was swept by the stream of humanity and its luggage past the ticket barrier and on into the great station hall. She staggered as a case carried by a burly man caught her painfully behind her knees. The man tutted impatiently and glared at her as if she were at fault. She hesitated then, a small and uncertain figure, her bundle clasped to her chest, her eyes wide upon the noisiest confusion of human activity she had ever seen.

As the crowd around Molly's still figure thinned a little, she became more aware of her own unkempt appearance. The overnight trip as a four-shilling deck passenger on the steamer *Kerry* and the subsequent long, tiring train journey from Liverpool had done little for her looks. Her hair was tangled and salty from the windy rough crossing, her face and hands were dirty, her already shabby skirt and shawl were sea-spotted and smeared with grime from the train. Dressed so, she knew she appeared drab and incongruous amongst the fashionable, and even the not-so-fashionable people who swarmed through the station hall. Nearby stood two girls about Molly's own age. They were dressed almost identically in smart, wasp-waisted suits with sweeping skirts and puffed leg o' mutton sleeves that narrowed elegantly to the wrist; the ruffles at their throats and cuffs were snowy white, contrasting with the sober colours of their travelling clothes; their upswept hair was set off with saucily-tilted boaters trimmed with flowers, and their small hands were genteely gloved. Indeed, if there were one thing that Molly had noted from the moment she had stepped onto the dockside at Liverpool it was that no woman but she was without a hat or gloves. She tucked her bare hands beneath her shawl, aware that one of the girls she had been studying had noticed her and said something, giggling, to the other who stared most rudely. Molly turned away, a flush creeping into her cheeks. She was tired, she was hungry and rather more than a little scared, though this last she would not have admitted, even to herself. She squared her shoulders and looked around. Some distance off a notice proclaimed the Ladies' Room; putting her faith in the saints that the term 'Ladies' might not be too strictly applied she headed determinedly in that direction.

When she emerged from the cloakroom with at least some order brought to the chaos of her undisciplinable hair and the worst of the journey's grime wiped from her face, she was walking as briskly as everyone else.

Once through the astonishing Doric arch that guarded the station entrance, she took breath and hesitated for only a moment before marching straight-backed to the row of horse-drawn cabs that lined the road outside. The leading driver, dozing in his high seat, sensed her approach, lifted a bowler-hatted head and briskly raked her from head to foot with eyes that weighed, measured and found her wanting. Girls in country homespun and their brother's battered hand-me-down boots did not hire cabs. By the time she reached him he had determinedly gone back to sleep, but gritting her teeth she stepped past him to the second vehicle, whose driver had a more friendly aspect. Like his companion, he looked her over and dismissed her as a fare; but at least he smiled.

"Yes, love?"

"I wondered—" she said, appalled at her uncertain tone, "I—want to go—to Regent Street." At that moment it was the only name she could think of. "Would you be kind enough to tell me the way?"

" 'Course. It ain't far. Just down ter the corner there, see? Turn right and a little way up the road you'll come to a crossroads. Turn left an' there you are. Easy as fallin' off a cart. You can't miss it."

She could barely hear his words above the awful din of the traffic, but it was beyond her to ask him to repeat his instructions. Smiling her thanks she left him and started in the general direction of his waved hand. With every step she took the level of her panic rose. She had not thought, had not dreamed, that London could be like this. She had spent the whole of her life in a village of a few hundred souls, had never until now been further than the nearest small market town. Her preconception of London, formed from conversations with Mary, had been of an elegant and only slightly larger version of that town; not for a moment had she been prepared for the overwhelming size, the infinity of streets and buildings, and above all this multitude who pushed and jostled and passed her and each other with no glance, no courteous word, no curiosity. The constant movement of people and horses, the spin and clatter of wheels dizzied her. Cabs and carriages and open-topped horse-drawn omnibuses rolled in an endless, confused, slow-moving stream; carters shouted and cursed as pedestrians wove in and out of the traffic dodging wheel and hoof with admirable and life-preserving skill.

Molly turned the corner and let herself be carried on towards the crossroads. Where she should go from there she had no idea; that part of the cabman's instructions had been lost to her. She simply hoped with a fervour close to prayer that the traffic would ease a little before she had to cross the terrifying road.

At the corner she stopped and looked around her, holding her own as best she could against the current of the crowds. Poised on the curb, she assessed her chances of getting across the road in one piece; then like a swimmer taking a deep breath and diving into turbulent water she stepped into the moving stream, dodging an advancing omnibus as if she had been doing it all her life.

If London was not quite as she had imagined, Regent Street was; it at least did not disappoint her as so often the subjects of long-held dreams do. Mary and she talked so often of London, of this street with its shops and arcades, its fascinating windows, the bustling, fashionable life of its pavements, that Molly had once or twice wondered if her usually truthful friend might not be exaggerating. But now she knew differently; she had never seen such splendours.

For a while tiredness and uncertainty were forgotten. Here indeed was the stuff of dreams, separated from her by only a sheet of glass. Beneath the shadowing awnings she dawdled, hardly aware now of traffic or people, bemused by the sparkle of the artfully displayed treasures, watching the comings and goings. She smelt the perfumed warmth that gusted through the swinging doors from the brilliantly lit interiors and shivered suddenly as a cold wind blew on her back. In her dreams of the future she had almost forgotten that she had not eaten for hours, nor slept since the night before last. On board the *Kerry* she had preferred to stay on deck in the clean if stormy air rather than be prisoned in the nauseous and overcrowded shelters provided. But now evening was advancing; she had to find lodgings, a place to eat and sleep. The very thought of bed seemed to bring to painful life all the until-now-ignored effects of her long journey; her neck and shoulders ached relentlessly, her bones felt brittle with weariness. She had walked the length of the west side of Regent Street and had emerged into Piccadilly Circus where the confusion of traffic was even worse than it had been outside the station. The odd, triangular-shaped Circus was jammed with every conceivable kind of vehicle, while above the turmoil winged Eros poised, expressionless and on the whole ignored. People hurried past, intent upon quitting the draughty, darkening streets. So many people, and all apparently with somewhere to go. Suddenly Molly felt a loneliness she had never known before, and it was hard to learn it here in the noisy and uncaring chaos of a city that seemed, with advancing darkness, to become more hostile every minute.

She lifted her head and drew a breath that lifted her narrow shoulders. First things first. A bed for the night, something to eat.

Tomorrow she would start her new life. Tomorrow would be better.

The clerk, impeccably dressed, eyed the small, untidy figure before him and raised a supercilious eyebrow.

"Out! We don't buy off the street."

Molly lifted a challenging head. The hotel vestibule was warm and smelled invitingly of food. Beyond a burnished swing door she could hear the clink of cutlery and the hum of conversation.

"You've a rule there that suits the both of us then, for I've nothing to sell."

It had taken a great deal of resolution to walk from the dark street into this shining area of light. In the mirrors that lined the walls she could see reflections of reflections: herself with gypsy hair blown wild again, a haphazard smear of dirt down one thin cheek, looking absurdly out of place in this oasis of enormous potted palms and highly polished brass. She had lost count of the number of inns and cheap hotels she had tried; London, it seemed, was not the easiest place to get a room. Almost desperate now for the rest, she had abandoned her original hope of finding cheap accommodation and had come to the reluctant conclusion that for this one night she would have to pay rather more than she had planned.

She planted her bundle on the floor at her feet and dropped her purse onto the counter before the clerk, making sure that it landed hard enough to make it clink.

"I'd like a room, please. Just for the one night."

For a long moment he looked at her, every cynical experience of street girls and their money in his pale and slightly protruding eyes. Then, without looking at it, he pushed the purse back to her.

"We don't have any rooms." His eyes were hard and mortifyingly sure of themselves.

She was scarlet to the roots of her hair, nearly choking in her rage.

"That isn't," she said calmly, "what it says on the door."

He leaned across the counter, resting on his two hands. A drift of sweet-scented hair oil wafted on the warm air. "What it says on the door is not for the likes of you. Out. Before I call someone to put you out—" his hand hovered above a shining brass bell.

Fighting to suppress her temper and clinging to the shreds of her dignity she picked up her purse and bent to the bundle. She had more sense than to attempt to fight a battle lost before the first shot was fired.

She did not have it in her to risk such a rebuff again. She tried no more palm-decorated lobbies. She wandered instead into the narrow side-streets, almost too tired by now to notice or care about the hazards of the badly-lit passageways and doorways. London's night-streets never emptied; they were peopled always by a motley army of homeless souls to whom the law of the land denied the right to rest. Among these vagrants Molly attracted little attention; she was just another pair of wandering feet.

Exhaustion dogged her heels. She turned one corner, then another, leaned against a wall for a moment, rubbed her tired eyes. When she lifted her head it was to see, in the faint bloom of light from a dirty uncurtained window, a small sign hung crookedly across a doorway, advertising rooms to let. She hesitated. The house front was grimly dirty, its entrance a door at the end of a long, dark alley with an unevenly tiled floor, indescribably filthy; but the time for qualms was long past.

Molly knocked on the door, but receiving no answer, opened it carefully and peered inside. She was stunned by the savage squalor of the room, and her breath caught at the smell.

"Well?"

Molly gasped when she spotted the man who had spoken. He was hunched like a bundle of rags, the meagre fire in front of his tattered chair casting a sickly glow onto his face. It was one of the most unpleasant faces Molly had ever seen: his narrow cheeks were unshaven, his thin grey hair was plastered across his dirty scalp.

"What the 'ell do you want?"

"I—" Molly shook her head. Panic, a sour sickness rose from her stomach to her throat. "Nothing. A mistake. I'm sorry—" and she fled, unashamedly frightened, her feet clattering on stone slick with slime, her breath painful in her chest.

It was an hour or so later that, almost at the end of hope, she at last found something close to what she was looking for. In a quiet lane hedged with many-storied houses she came upon a sign in a neatly lace-curtained window. Molly, with a whispered prayer, knocked loudly upon the front door. It was some moments before it opened, and then by barely a crack. A woman's voice, hard and suspicious, snapped, "Who is it?" A knife-edge of light fell across the step.

"Please—" Molly could not keep from pleading, though the desperation in her own voice disgusted her, " – your notice says you have rooms to let—?"

The door opened a little more, and a face appeared, the bubbled blonde hair lit from behind like a halo.

Molly resisted the temptation to put a foot in the door. "I have money," she said wearily. "I can pay. In advance if you like."

"Is anyone with you?"

"No." Would she never open the door? "I'm alone. Please. I need a bed for the night."

There was an endless moment's pause.

"You'd better come in."

With the door safely shut behind her Molly found herself in a short passage, cream painted and with stained lino floor. A narrow flight of stairs led off to the right. Molly made to move forward, but the woman, who seemed fairly to fill the passage with her black-bombazined girth, held up a remarkably white and delicate hand.

"Just a minute, dearie." Her cheeks were rather too pink for nature and the smile she levelled at the girl did not match her narrow, avaricious eyes. "In advance, you said?" The pale hand cupped itself, waiting, and Molly was suddenly aware of a painfully stupid mistake. Why had she not separated a few shillings from her precious hoard?"

"How much do you want?" She dropped her bundle and turned from the watching woman as she reached for her purse.

"One and six to you, dearie." The woman shuffled closer, peered over her shoulder. The chink of coins sounded very loud.

"That's very expensive."

"It's also very late." The inference was beyond doubting and the situation not open to argument. Molly turned, the coins in her hand, the purse held firmly by her side in the folds of her skirt. The woman took the money. She was smiling again, this time with a degree more warmth.

"This way, then, dearie. I'll show you to the room. I'll bring a cup of tea if you like. I'd just made a pot for meself."

The room was not large; neither was it warm. With wardrobe, washstand and massive iron bedstead there was hardly space to move without banging knee or elbow. Molly thought that no room had ever looked so fine or so comfortable. The woman left for a moment then reappeared with sheets and a pillowcase.

"You make up the bed, dearie, and I'll go and get the tea. Comfortable, the bed is—" She sat on it herself, bounced a little, and the bedstead, stout as it was, groaned. "You'll get a good night on this all right."

"I'm sure I will. Thank you."

Molly shut the door behind her and had to use her last remaining strength of will to prevent herself from falling onto the unmade bed and sleeping for a week, just as she was. Smiling with the pleasure of the thought, she leaned against the door and swung forward with it nearly stumbling out onto the landing. She pulled it, hard; but it would not shut properly, nor was there any sign of key or bolt. Odd that it opened outwards; there were marks on the door jamb where the hinges had been changed. Molly was suddenly wide awake again. Thoughtfully she made up the bed, gratefully accepted the tea, bade her well-paid hostess goodnight and listened as the heavy footsteps receded down the stairs.

When all was still she unwrapped her much-travelled bundle and with no great degree of regret began to rip up her second-best skirt to fashion a make-shift rope with which to secure the door.

In the darkling hours of morning she was wakened from a stone-sound sleep by a tug on the bedstead. She lay quite still in the darkness. The door-handle was wrenched again, harder this time and Molly, her breath held, willed the knotted material not to give. From beyond the door she heard a muffled curse, quickly hushed: a man's voice. Then the hissing of a woman. The door moved again, but anchored as it was to the heavy bed it would not open. There was a furious whispering, a sharp retort. Molly made a great and noisy to-do of turning in the bed and the sounds stopped dead. Moments later the stairs creaked, and then there was silence.

—

CHAPTER TWO

FOR A COUNTRY girl it was no great effort to wake with first light. Molly lay for a moment listening to the clatter of cart-wheels on cobblestones; the world outside was astir. Within the house all was still, and in a matter of moments she slipped from the bed, gathered her belongings and, boots in hand and with her heart thumping loud enough to wake the whole of London, loosened the knot from the doorhandle. She opened the door a crack: the windowless landing was dark; all the doors were shut and the rooms beyond them silent. The door swung a little, creaking, and she grabbed and held it, the silence rushing in her ears as she strained to detect any sign of disturbance. She slipped like a wraith through the shadows to the top of the stairs, freezing as a board groaned beneath her bare feet. Somewhere near a man coughed, bedsprings creaked. At the foot of the stairs the intricate pattern of coloured light thrown by the stained glass in the front door urged her on, and she moved soundlessly forward. As she set her foot upon the top stair a door near the landing was thrown open and a man's voice boomed out, "What's this, then?"

She had never in her life moved so fast. She was down the stairs in one flying leap, and then struggling frantically with the bolt on the front door. The man was starting heavily down the stairs behind her. The bolt crashed back, catching her fingers, and then she was out into the cold, early-morning street.

She ran until her breath gave out, though she knew the likelihood of pursuit to be slim; the man on the landing had been in his nightshirt, unlikely apparel for a chase through a waking neighbourhood. When finally she stopped she was panting painfully, and her feet hurt. She bent to pull on her boots, then straightened to look around her. She was in a narrow, winding lane, tiered high with windows and rickety balconies. From a doorway blank and irritated eyes watched, blinked, closed again in sleep. Peace was hard enough to come by. Stamping her feet firmly into her cold boots she set herself to walking, shivering, in the sharp dawn air.

Several random turnings later she emerged from the maze of cramped and dirty streets into a wider cobbled thoroughfare in which there was already considerable activity. Several market stalls were set up; men and women called cheerfully to one another. Near to where Molly stood was tethered an old horse, his rough hide steaming in the chill air, jaws working contentedly in his nosebag while an enormous darkly handsome young man unloaded fruit and vegetables from the cart. As Molly stopped, leaning for a moment on the wall, cheeks bright with cold and exertion, the young man looked up and, smiling cheerily, called out, "Mornin'."

"Good morning to you," Molly replied, watching as he swung a huge sack effortlessly from the cart to the ground.

"Lookin' for something?"

She nodded, returning his smile. "Breakfast."

"No problem. Down the street a ways, see?" He pointed. Molly saw a steamed-up window, a low, dark doorway, "Old Mother Randolph's place. Best breakfasts in Whitechapel." He ran his eyes over her appreciatively and winked.

"Thank you."

"Don't mention it. Try the pork pies."

She did, the rich and meaty pie and dark, sweet tea giving rise gradually to a sense of confidence and well-being that she had not experienced since she had stepped on board the *Kerry*.

A girl was waiting on the tables, a bright-eyed beauty with expressively arched eyebrows, a wry mouth and a mass of blonde hair. Her tongue was as sharp as her movements as she threaded swiftly around the tables, balancing cups and plates like a music-hall artiste, avoiding outstretched hands and deflecting suggestive compliments with equal ease. It was a game regularly played, part of an early-morning ritual, Molly realized, listening from her quiet corner and watching with admiration as the girl flitted, smiling, around the room, bestowing upon each admirer an equal share of pungent charm, never favouring one above another and ready to slap hard at a too-persistent hand. Well-worn jokes were bandied back and forth with a gusto enhanced by familiarity; everyone, it seemed, knew everyone else, and first names were the rule. These were the market traders, Molly guessed, up since midnight and waiting for the profitable day to start. An outsider, she sat quietly nibbling at her second pie, cheered by the friendly atmosphere.

. Deciding on another cup of tea, Molly waited until she could catch the handsome waitress's eye and then lifted a hesitant hand. The girl smiled and nodded and came across the room towards her. As she passed the table next to Molly's, around which sat a particularly boisterous group of young men, a ruddy-faced lad with a shock of fair curls reached blithely for her waist. He was obviously as surprised as anyone else when she failed to dodge him and, more by luck than judgement, found herself sitting on his lap. The roar that followed nearly brought down the ceiling.

"What're you going to do with her now you've got her, Tiny?"

"You've got more of a lapful there than you bargained for, you silly bugger—"

"Look out—" a smothered explosion of laughter, " – here's Johnny. You couldn't have come at a better time, John. Maggie's taken a fancy to Tiny—"

Molly's eyes followed the others' to the door, where stood the man who had directed her to the best breakfast in Whitechapel. The breadth of his shoulders filled the doorway and he had to bend to enter the room. He was laughing with the others but his eyes upon Maggie were hard and questioning and there was a dangerous tilt to his head.

Only slightly ruffled, Maggie detached herself from a now scarlet-faced Tiny and nodded to the newcomer. "Mornin', Johnny."

Molly was aware that the atmosphere of the room had changed subtly. Chairs scraped upon the tiled floor, someone cleared his throat, and lurking now beneath the surface of good humour was a faint charge of violence. Tiny's hand, almost unthinking, was still fast upon Maggie's wrist. Under Johnny's cool gaze he released the girl hastily. For a fine-balanced moment nobody moved.

"May I have another cup of tea, please, and a pie?" The soft, Irish voice, practised at breaking silences more dangerous than this one, was perfectly composed. "Coming up, love." The murmur of voices rose and the moment had passed. Molly, aware of covert glances, dropped her own gaze to the table and concentrated resolutely upon preventing the rise of blood to her cheeks. She was therefore unprepared when the chair beside hers was dragged backwards by a large hand and Johnny, all six feet and some inches of him, settled himself with a certain amount of care upon it.

"You've got some gall for a little 'un," he said, grinning.

She lifted clear eyes, refused to pretend misunderstanding. "I've a brother who looks just like that when he's about to start a fight—"

The grin widened. "Can't say I wasn't thinkin' of it."

"Well, I like my breakfasts peaceful, thank you. If I want a circus I'll pay for a ticket."

He laughed. He was looking at her in open appraisal, taking time over his assessment of the delicate transparency of her skin, the wilderness of curly hair, the shadowed lavender of eyes that would not waver from his, though a faint colour warmed the bones of her cheeks.

"You'll know me, I should think," she said with the asperity of embarrassment, "if we should bump into one another again?"

Behind him Maggie was making her way towards their table, a tray of toast and tea expertly balanced. When she reached them she thumped the tray on the table and reached for a chair.

"Time for me own breakfast. Might as well eat with you as on me own." The softness in her eyes as she looked at Johnny gave the lie to her uncaring tone. He did not look at her, but continued to stare at Molly.

Maggie poured the tea. "Don't mind 'im. 'Is mother never taught 'im manners."

Johnny sat back on the perilously swaying chair, his hands spread on his knees. "Not long off the boat, then, eh, Irish?" he said with a certainty that might have provoked her.

She shrugged. "Four o'clock yesterday morning."

He picked up his cup. "That's what I thought." His bright, dark eyes watched her as he drank. "Ever bin to London before?"

She shook her head.

"What you plannin' on doin'?"

Molly, unwilling to admit even to herself that she had no clear answer to that question said tartly, "I'm planning on drinking my tea."

Johnny gave a shout of laughter, slapped the table with a hand the size of a carpet beater. "By Christ, I like you, Irish. That I do."

Maggie leaned forward, her elbows on the table, her lovely face cupped in her hands. "Gawd, girl, you must 'ave *some* idea?"

"I thought – perhaps—" Molly stopped. The truth was that until now all her energies had been channelled into getting herself to London. Exactly what she might do when she got there had been something for later consideration. "I have to find work, and somewhere to live," she said, and even in her own ears her voice sounded rather less than confident. She was watching Maggie; she did not see the speculative light in Johnny's eyes.

Maggie sucked crumbs and butter from long, none-too-clean fingers. "That's easy, duck," she said, off-handedly. "Go into service. Work an' lodgin's both, that way."

"No." The sharp finality of Molly's tone startled them. "No," she said again more quietly, "that's not what I had in mind at all. I was thinking—" memories of the bright glitter of the Regent Street windows crystallized suddenly in her mind, " – I thought perhaps I might get work in one of the big stores—?"

"Hah!" Maggie exclaimed with pure disgust. She sat back inelegantly, her hands on her knees, shaking a bright, knowing head. "What in Gawd's name makes yer think that bein' a bloody slavey in a posh shop's any better than bein' in service? You just try it! Take it from one as knows, love. Shop work's bleedin' murder. Workin' six in the mornin' till eleven at night, at the beck an' call of any bugger that's got sixpence to spend, fined 'arf yer wages if yer so much as dare to try to take the weight off yer feet fer a minute – an' better digs to be found in the work'ouse, I can tell yer. It's a mug's game, that. Shops is fer one thing, and one thing only: spendin' brass. Preferably someone else's. I'm tellin' yer – you'd be better off in service."

Molly looked down at her small, grubby hands that were nursing her half-empty mug, her mouth set in a stubborn line.

Johnny moved his chair a little closer. "Ease off, now, Maggie. Can't you see she's made up 'er mind? She's no one's skivvy. Right, Irish?"

Molly nodded, trying to ignore the chill of apprehension that was creeping through her. She felt suddenly, desperately, lonely. She lifted her chin. "I'll find something."

"Well, 'course you will," Johnny said encouragingly, his smile friendly, "there's a million places. Sweatshops where you can sew yerself blind fer pennies, or take the skin off yer fingers makin' boxes. Factories where you can choke yerself ter death makin' Lucifers—"

"I can read and write. Figure, too," Molly said doggedly. "That'll help."

Johnny's sardonic eyes took apart, stitch by stitch, Molly's shabby, much-darned skirt and shawl. "You can?" His disbelief was palpable.

Molly saw no reason to justify her claim. "Yes."

Maggie laughed as she began to gather the dirty crockery from the table. "Readin' and writin', eh? There's a thing. There's a lot o' call fer that kind o' thing round 'ere, love. I don't think." Someone across the room called her name. "I'm comin'," she yelled. "'Old yer bleedin' 'orses. Will I be seein' yer later?" This last was addressed, casually, to Johnny, but there was an intensity in her eyes that belied the tone.

Johnny ignored her. He had rested his chin on a massive fist and was regarding Molly thoughtfully. "I'll tell you straight, Irish. I'm worried about you. Wanderin' the streets of Whitechapel at five in the morning with no more idea than a new-born babe in a brothel." He shook his head, slowly and soberly. "You're bloody lucky you 'aven't 'ad your throat cut. Or worse."

"Johnny, I asked you—"

"Shut up, Maggie." It was said conversationally. Bright colour stained Maggie's cheeks. Johnny jerked his head in a dismissive gesture. Maggie slammed cups and plates noisily onto the tray and walked away, moving between the tables with a defiantly provocative swing of her hips that brought several appreciative glances but impressed Johnny not at all.

Molly sat in miserable silence, her earlier feeling of well-being completely evaporated. Dismay and discouragement nibbled at the edges of her mind.

"Tell you what," said Johnny, his voice breaking her unpleasant reverie. "There's a chance – just a chance, mind – that I might be able to 'elp you out. Just temporarily, like. If you're interested, that is?"

She lifted her eyes to his broad, sharp-eyed face. "Help me out? How?"

"Ma Randolph – she owns this place – is a good friend of mine. Owes me a few favours, know what I mean? Now, I 'appen to know that Ma's lookin' for another girl, to give Maggie a bit of a hand. Sharp kid like you'd be just the ticket, I shouldn't wonder. How about me havin' a word in 'er ear—?"

Molly looked around her unhappily. "Work here?"

"Why not? Just till you get yerself sorted, o'course, find somethin' better, like—?" His handsome face was intent and sympathetic. He smiled.

"Well, I—" Molly looked down at the table, her heart sinking. Where was the difference between working here and going into service? And yet – what else, at the moment, could she do? Could she turn down any offer of help?

Johnny leaned forward. "Just while you get yerself settled, eh? It wouldn't be as bad as yer thinkin', Irish. Me an' the old lady, we're like that—" he held up two crossed fingers " – she'd treat you right, knowin' you were a friend of Johnny Cribben's." He paused and watched her, letting her own fears work on her. "Better think about it Irish," he added softly. "You can thank yer lucky stars you fell among friends. They ain't easy come by in this part of the world. You got any goin' spare?"

Molly bit her lip. The thought of setting off alone into the unfriendly streets of this unknown city to hunt for work and lodgings suddenly appalled her. The warmth of the room and the cheerful atmosphere offered comfort and safety, for a while at least. Just, as Johnny said, until she found something better.

There was a shout of laughter from across the room, obviously in answer to something that Maggie had said. Johnny grinned his wide, pleasant grin. "Look at Maggie there. Nobody's drudge our Maggie, eh? I ask you – does she look hard done by?"

Molly had to laugh. "That she doesn't."

"Well, then, what's yer worry? Give it a bloody try, eh?"'

She hesitated for only a moment longer. "All right, I will. Thank you. Just till I can save some money and get myself straight—" The decision made, right or wrong, was like a weight lifted from her heart.

"That's the girl!" He stood up and took her hand in his. "Come an' meet Ma. She's an old cow, sometimes, but her heart's in the right place!" he said, and, shouting with laughter, pulled her in the direction of the kitchen.

CHAPTER THREE

IT WAS LESS than a week before Molly discovered her mistake, and during that time she learned many things very quickly. She learned that her employer, a tall, rake-thin woman with sharp, deepset eyes and the shadow of a moustache above her thin-lipped mouth, was a greedy shrew with a raucous voice and a bitter heart. Molly learned that beneath the surface cama-raderie of the men who frequented Ma's eating house lurked a ready, almost casual violence that could maim, or kill, upon the slightest provocation. She learned, too, that Maggie would do anything – up to and probably including murder – for Johnny Cribben, and that the girl was a compulsive thief. Dishonesty was second nature to her: she overcharged customers and pocketed the difference, gave the wrong change whenever she thought she could get away with it, smiling and wheedling her way out of it if caught; tucking the money into an already well-filled wash-leather purse beneath her mattress when she was not. She would steal anything she could get her hands on and even boasted of her skill. "I'd 'ave the gold from the buggar's teeth if I could," she said, laughing at Molly's startled face. Molly took to carrying her own precious if meagre store of coins in a purse that she strapped around her waist, next to her skin. She strongly suspected that Maggie's off-hand and careless friendship would be no protection against the girl's long, thiev-ing fingers.

The days were long: they were up at four to help in the kitchen, spurred on by Ma's caustic tongue. The eating room opened at four-thirty. Molly, dressed in a cast-off dress of Maggie's, belted tight and with several inches cut off the bottom, soon learned to hold her own with the customers – not for nothing had she lived eighteen years with a houseful of brothers – and though the work was tiring and the surroundings less than pleasant it was a relief at least to know with certainty that her next meal was assured, and that she had a roof over her head. She worked hard, refused to be provoked by Ma Randolph's ways, and battled homesickness, resolutely putting from her mind all thoughts of the green hills and soft skies of Ireland. If a Whitechapel eating house was not quite what she had envisaged in her dreams of the future, she at least had her independence. And she would not be here for long, she told herself as she rested her aching back upon the pallet bed in the attic room that she shared with Maggie. She wrinkled her nose at the greasy smell of food that hung about her hair and skin; no, not for long. She was grateful to Johnny for helping her – grateful, too, for the fact that he had quite obviously taken her under his protection; while his huge form was anywhere around – and it quite often was – she had no trouble with the men of Whitechapel. It did not occur to her at first to wonder at that.

It was late one afternoon that, after climbing the narrow stairs to the attic, she was surprised to discover upon her bed a pile of clothes – tawdry things of scarlet and black and emerald-green from which, when she picked them up, lifted a faint, unpleasant smell of sweat and cheap perfume.

"These must be yours." She made to toss them to Maggie.

Maggie was sitting on her own bed with an open box beside her from which spilled a cascade of glittering trinkets. She was wearing a gown of red satin that was trimmed with rhinestones and left her beautiful shoulders bare and exposed her white, swelling breasts almost to the nipples. Molly had seen her so before, on the evenings she was meeting Johnny Cribben. Maggie slid a bright ring onto her finger and held her hand out, spread, to judge the effect. "Oh, no. Johnny left 'em fer you. We're off up West tonight. Oh – there's shoes and stuff over there. Can't 'ave you tricked out like a fairy queen in that navvie's footgear, can we?" She gestured scornfully at Molly's small, battered boots.

"But—"

" 'E said," Maggie walked to the pile of clothes and sorted through them, pulling out a dark-blue silky bombazine dress trimmed with heavy cream lace that looked at least a little less tastelessly gaudy than the others in the pile, "that 'e thought that this'd do you nicely." She tossed it to Molly, shaking her head, "but if yer want my advice, then take one o' the others. Yer likely to get lumbered with more than you can 'andle in that."

Molly stood with the dress in her hand, her small face a picture of incomprehension. "Maggie what are you talking about? I'm not going anywhere. I'm tired. I want to—"

"Well, it ain't a case of what you want, is it gel? It's what Johnny wants. An' tonight 'e wants you with us. So, was I you I'd act a bit nippy. Come on, try the green. You'd not look 'arf bad in green, I reckon."

Molly shook her head. In the silence Maggie looked at her, her face very hard. "You ain't goin' ter cause trouble now, gel, are yer?"

Something very close to fear was creeping through Molly. "Trouble? Of course not. It's just that—"

"Good. 'Cos if you are – yer on yer own. I thought I'd better warn yer. I ain't crossin' Johnny fer you . . . don't think it. Do as yer told and we're all 'appy, see?"

"There isn't any reason for anyone to cross Johnny! Why should he want me to come out with you tonight? I mean – it's very kind of him—" her voice was uncertain " – but—"

"Kind? Johnny? Jesus, gel, what you on about? Johnny don't know the meanin' of the word. Ain't you realized that yet? You surely don't think 'e makes 'is livin' on the market? That's a front, gel. A blind. You want yer throat cut?" Maggie's scathingly blunt question, Molly realized in sudden horror, was perfectly serious.

"Of – of course not."

"Then get yerself sorted, and quick. Johnny was 'opin' to leave it a couple of weeks – break yer in slowly, like. But one of 'is girls 'as got 'erself cut up by 'er fancy man – an' I wouldn't want to be in '*is* shoes either," she added with malice. "So tonight's the night. Get dressed. Like I said. Try the green."

"'Avin' a bit 'o trouble, are we?" Johnny Cribben's soft voice, his sudden appearance in the doorway, shocked both girls to silence. He stood, massive and unsmiling, his hard eyes taking in Molly from tousled head to shabby boots. He was in a superbly fitting dress suit which emphasized his good looks and his size. His stiff-collared shirt was blindingly white, pearls at the cuffs, a diamond pin in his pale-grey cravat.

Maggie dropped a ring on the floor and it rolled noisily in the silence across the wooden floorboards. "No trouble, Johnny. Honest. She was just going to get dressed."

"Well. So I should 'ope." The quiet words raised the hairs on the back of Molly's neck. She realized suddenly, seeing the cold cruelty in the hardened line of his mouth, that it was not simply Johnny Cribben's size that kept tough men at arm's length from him.

"Please—" she said, struggling stubbornly to keep her voice from shaking " – I think that I should rather stay here. I'm very tired, and—"

His hand was clamped about her wrist. After her first, reflexive jerk away she stood quite still, watching him as steadily as she could manage, knowing that to struggle would be as pointless as it would be undignified.

"Where's yer manners, girl?" Johnny asked softly. "I'm askin' you out to meet some of me friends. Toffs they are, too, some of 'em. Now you wouldn't want to disappoint them, would you? Or me, neither, for that matter?"

"Well?" he twisted her wrist sharply and she gasped.

Maggie turned her back on them, making a great and noisy show of searching in her box of worthless baubles.

Johnny's hand tightened further. For her life Molly could not prevent herself from crying out with the pain of it.

"Now, Irish, what's it to be? A good time or a beatin'? One good turn deserves another – didn't you know that? Don't tell me you thought I was actin' out o' the goodness of me 'eart?"

Molly, from past experience, was nothing if not a realist. "All right. I'll come," she said softly, hating him.

He grinned, his boyish good looks returning with his temper. "That's better. Now," he reached for the blue and cream dress and threw it at her – "get this on, an' quick. Don't bother with the other gear. It ain't right for you." He poked a finger beneath her chin and forced her face up, looked into the blazing, silvered eyes. "You ain't bad lookin' under all that tat, girl. You'll go far, shouldn't wonder, with yer Uncle Johnny. Might even give you a try meself one day. But no trouble, understand? Or no one's ever goin' ter be able to look at that pretty little face of yours without shudderin'. An' don't think I don't mean it."

She stood, trembling and rubbing her wrist until the door

closed behind him. In the quiet his going left, Maggie shrugged wearily. "Don't say I didn't warn yer. Stupid little cat. E'll be in one 'ell of a mood tonight now. Come on, fer Christ's sake. Get ready."

She watched as, still shaking, Molly struggled into the blue bombazine. It fitted as if it had been made for her, nipping in her slender waist and flaring softly over her hips. To her astonishment it was demure to the point of girlishness with a square, lace-trimmed neck and small puffed sleeves – and though the bodice was uncomfortably tight, at least, Molly thought looking at Maggie's almost bared breasts, it was decent. Surely with flamboyantly beautiful Maggie beside her no one would even notice her? She began to feel a little better. She slipped her feet into a pair of worn and soiled velvet slippers, and in the dim, fly-specked mirror looked with astonishment at the effect. She saw reflected a tiny, graceful figure whose wide, shining eyes and oval face, still flushed with anger and humiliation, were strikingly framed by the wild, dark curling hair above the demure cream lace of the dress. She looked like a beautiful and disturbingly unchildlike child.

Maggie shook her head. "I told yer that yer should've worn the green. George is goin' ter love yer. Rather you than me. Come on."

The low-ceilinged, velvet-draped room was airless and over-crowded, uncomfortably hot from the warmth of too many bodies, scented with the sickly smell of hair oil and perfume. In a hidden corner a piano played, almost indistinguishable background to a babble of slurred and lifted voices, the clink of glass, much laughter. In an ante-room, through a wide arch and behind a half-drawn beaded curtain, gaming tables had been set up; young men with intent and feverish eyes watched the dice and the cards, the bright, bobbing ball as if their next living breath depended upon them, while at their shoulders, mostly ignored, girls with bright, avid faces urged them on. Strewn casually upon the green tables was more money than Molly had ever seen in her life before. She was sitting amidst a noisy crowd of men and women around a table set in a candle-lit, heavily draped alcove that opened off the main room. During the uncomfortably silent journey in the cab she had formed her strategy: play along with them – not that in the circumstances there was much else to be done anyway – get through this evening; tomorrow she would leave. Nothing this side of Heaven would prevent her. To have attempted openly to defy Johnny would have been lunacy; remembering his brutal grip, the light in his eyes, she had no doubts on that score. She must appear docile, lull him into believing that she had given up, was perhaps even enjoying herself. . . .

So now she sat, submissive, trying to ignore the clammy hand that her companion rested possessively on her arm, and trying equally hard to still the wild and surprising dizziness in her head. Lemonade she had asked for, and her partner, tittering, had said delightedly, "Lemonade! Of course, my dear, of course. How splendid! Lemonade!" Molly had looked at his pink and vapid face with absolute dislike and said nothing. When they had joined the group at this table, true to her plan she had smiled and quietly acknowledged the introductions, not attempting to move away from the portly bald-headed man who had with exclamations of delight caught her with damp, soft hands and pulled her down to the seat beside him.

The drinks had arrived. "Lemonade," chuckled her elderly mentor. "Drink up, my dear, there's a good girl, drink up." In the heat of the room the clear, sparkling liquid had seemed like nectar; she had drunk two glasses before she realized that her 'lemonade' was coming out of the same bottle as Maggie's champagne; but by that time there was already an odd, almost comforting unreality about the room and its occupants. The fat, pink, sweat-sheened face of the man beside her receded a little and blurred. She could not hear what he was saying. Did it matter? She nodded and smiled, and he looked pleased. His pudgy fingers walked up her arm, slid under the puffed sleeve of her dress. She pulled away, and was aware of a punitive gleam in Johnny's eyes from where he sat across the table. But far from being offended her admirer laughed happily and took his hand away.

"Oh, there's a nice little Miss—" His small, pale eyes glittered in folds of flesh. "What a good little girl she is—"

"You've certainly found one for George," said a young man

with a cultured voice, hardly any chin and a diamond as large as a pea on his finger. "Quite taken he is from the looks of it. I hope she's tougher than she looks."

"Shut your face, Toby," Johnny said pleasantly, "and mind yer own."

Molly furrowed her brow, trying to concentrate. George had moved closer, crushing her into the corner with his soft bulk.

"Here we are, little one. More lemonade." He held a brimming glass to her.

She shook her head. "No. No, thank you."

He pouted. "Oh, come now. Mustn't be a naughty girl. Do as Daddy says," he smiled, his eyelids drooping almost sleepily over fierce and maleficent eyes, "or Daddy will have to punish you—" His fingers moved up on her leg, found the soft flesh of her inner thigh and pinched mercilessly. Her gasp of pain opened the small eyes wide and sweat stood on his forehead.

With a head suddenly miraculously cleared Molly reached with shaking hands for the glass.

"There's a good girl. That's better." He watched her as she sipped it, then was distracted by a commotion on the other side of the table where the young man called Toby had tipped a glass of champagne down the plunging front of a girl's dress and was attempting now to lick it dry while the girl, with no great conviction and much loud laughter, struggled and squealed and almost slipped beneath the table. Maggie and the young man who had claimed her when she first arrived, Molly noticed with naïve surprise, had disappeared. Molly took the opportunity to try to slide a little further around the corner of the upholstered seat, away from George, but at her first movement his hand gripped her arm painfully and he hauled her back. She sat rigid. No one at the table took any notice of them, all eyes but Johnny's were on Toby's efforts with the champagne. George's fat hand moved from her arm to her breast, swathed tight beneath the smooth material of the too-small bodice. His eyes held hers as he probed and rubbed and pinched, hard and feverish. Johnny watched, smiling, daring her to protest. She trembled and tried not to resist the awful, pudgy hands. Beneath their handling she could not prevent the hardening of her breast, the rising of her nipple.

33

"So," said George suddenly, pouting and pinching harder, "not such a good girl after all, eh? Wicked to let a man touch you so. Wicked. Do you know what they do to wicked little girls, eh? Oh, yes, you know. Whipped, they are, whipped soundly. A good birching does wonders for a naughty girl like you—"

Across the room a curtain was drawn aside and Maggie and her young man re-entered the room. Maggie's hair was down and tangled to a bird's nest, the bodice of her dress was torn and stained with wine. She was laughing open-mouthed, her head thrown back, an invitation. As they came into the room her companion pulled her to him and kissed her savagely, his fingers gesturing obscenely behind her back. Comments, cheers and encouragement flew, the most explicit, so far as Molly could hear, seeming to come from the women. Maggie, barely capable of standing without support, lifted her arms and began to wriggle out of her dress. Then the sight of her was blocked from Molly's eyes by George's bloated, soft-skinned face as he leaned close to her, whispering. Nausea took her; she turned her head from him, pressing her hands to her ears. He caught her wrists and dragged the shielding hands down, whispering, whispering – telling of what he would do to her, of how he would punish such a naughty little girl, of how he would make her take her clothes off, bit by bit, and fold them neatly, as a good girl should before he—

The red rage that rose suddenly within her was irresistible and overwhelming. For the first time in her life, Molly, had she thought about it, might have understood what sent her brother Patrick flying into a fray with no thought of injury or consequence. Her outraged, furious lunge took the man completely by surprise, sent him back with a painful thump into the table, which rocked perilously, scattering glasses and bottles. With fingers crooked and hardly knowing what she did, she went for his face, scratching and tearing. Beyond the blind haze of fury she heard shouts, and some laughter. George tried to roll away from her, his arms across his face to protect his eyes. He was screaming, the sound high and womanish. The girl on the other side of him scrambled out of the way and George fell after her onto the floor. Molly was off the seat and past the prostrate figure, heading for the door, before Johnny's huge hand landed on her shoulder and with overpowering strength spun her round to face him. His other hand caught her a stunning, head-rocking slap across her mouth before she could raise her arms to protect herself. She staggered, was prevented from falling by his massive grip. He raised his hand again, but before the blow could fall other hands caught them both and pulled them apart.

"All right, Johnny, that'll do." A well-dressed man with a florid, clean-shaven face and wrestler's shoulders lifted a single, menacing finger. "No trouble. Not inside. You want to kill her, you do it when you get her home. Not here. You know the rules."

Johnny tensed for a moment against the restraining hands, then relaxed, and the two men who held him let him go, watching him warily. Maggie, clutching the remnants of her scarlet satin to her, had struggled through the crowds and now appeared at Johnny's side, her eyes uncertain and frightened. Molly, dwarfed by her own captors, who still held her, stood breathing heavily, her eyes on Johnny, her small face entirely expressionless, her heart pounding with terror.

George, ignored by all, staggered feebly to a chair nursing his bleeding face. "Bitch!" he moaned, "little bitch! Get me a doctor, someone – a doctor."

"Shut yer face," someone said unfeelingly. "It's no more than you deserve."

"Get me a cab," Johnny spat out. "Maggie, get your things. You—" he stabbed a threatening finger at Molly, his eyes barbarous with rage, "you'll never forget the day you made a fool of Johnny Cribben."

With the last of her desperate courage ebbing and leaving behind it only the appalled and icy weight of fear, Molly did not for a moment doubt his words.

The journey back to Whitechapel was a nightmare as contemplation of what she had done and its likely consequences churned in her stomach and filled her mind with terror. At Ma Randolph's, however, there was a momentary reprieve. At one of the tables in the empty, darkened dining room sat a young man with a cheery grin and villainous eyes. Before him was spread a gleaming treasure-house of gems and jewellery.

"Thought you'd never get 'ere, Johnny boy. Worked like a charm, your plan. Share-out time. Come an' get it!"

Maggie, her fright forgotten, perched on the arm of his chair, her face avid, her long fingers stirring the glittering stones.

Johnny hesitated for just one moment. "Give me a sec to get this under lock and key," he said then, his hand firm on Molly's upper arm. The other man's eyebrows lifted sardonically, but Johnny turned away, pushing Molly hard in front of him. "Upstairs, you."

Almost dragged from her feet by his violence, Molly stumbled down the dark passage and up the stairs to the attic where, with another savage push, Johnny sent her flying through the door to sprawl on the floor.

"I won't be long, Irish," he promised softly. "Think on this while I'm gone: I'm goin' ter make you wish you'd never been born."

From where she lay on the floor. Molly heard the door shut, heard the emphatic click of the lock that she knew was too strong for her to break, heard his quiet footsteps fade down the creaking stairs. She did not for a moment make any move to rise, but laid her head wearily on her crooked arm, fighting rising tears, unable to control the violent trembling of her body. For some minutes she lay so before she dragged herself to her feet and went to the washstand. There was water in the bottom of the jug, and she splashed her face with it, wincing as it mixed with the blood from her cut lip. When she was finished she turned and leaned against the stand, her arms crossed tightly over her breast, panic stopping the breath in her throat as she looked around the prisoning attic.

She had to get away. She had to. She had no doubt that Johnny would kill or maim her. Her eyes moved to the tiny dormer window. It was high up on the sloping wall and she could see out of it only by standing on her toes. She dragged Maggie's bed across the floor, flinching at the noise, and climbed up onto it. Beyond the window was darkness: an infinity of wet roofs stretching past the small light of the flickering candle she held to the dirty glass. It was impossible. Even supposing that she could squeeze through, the danger out there on the slippery, decaying roofs with their loose tiles and rotten timbers would be almost as great as the danger she faced from Johnny.

Almost as great.

Anything, surely, would be better than doing nothing, than simply sitting here, waiting—?

She flew to the corner where her bundle and her discarded clothes lay. It would be lunacy to scramble around out there in the tight-fitting bombazine. Anyway – she threw the thing from her in a spasm of disgust – it had brought her quite enough trouble for one day. Dressed in her old homespun she tied the laces of Danny's heavy boots together and slung them around her neck. She'd be more surefooted without them. Then she checked that the knot of her bundle was secure and slipped it over her arm. Running to Maggie's bed she climbed on to it and forced the window open. The opening looked alarmingly small. With only a fraction of a second's hesitation she pushed the bundle through. It fell onto the slates a foot or so below the window, slid into the gully beyond. From somewhere below a gas lamp threw a faint, yellow light that glinted upon wet slate and cast shadows so deep they might have been bottomless holes. About to follow the bundle, she stopped suddenly, drew her head back in and stood for a moment in desperate thought, battling a conscience that under the circumstances was ridiculously tender. But then she bent and, slipping her hand beneath the mattress, drew out the bag that contained Maggie's ill-acquired 'savings'. Feverishly she knotted the long cord into a loop and slipped it around her neck, tucking the bag firmly into her bodice before turning back to the window.

There was one dreadful moment when she thought that she would never make it: head and shoulders through, the heavy material of her skirt bunched around her hips and jammed her firmly in the narrow opening. She struggled fiercely, succeeding only in making matters worse, and then subsided, panting and sweating in the chill air. The roof below the window was smooth and unbroken; there was nothing she could catch hold of. Her feet off the bed, she hung for a helpless moment like a carcass on a butcher's hook. She inched forward, willing herself not to struggle. Balancing with one hand on the roof, she reached the other to her jammed skirt and eased it through. The window frame scraped her skin, but she hardly felt it; her whole being was intent upon her agonizing, inch-by-inch progress. The pressure about her hips lessened, and she wriggled out a little further. The skirt caught; she pulled frantically, heard the material rip and then, unbelievably, she was through, falling awkwardly upon the slates, banging her shins and bruising her elbows. But she was free!

She stood up carefully and reached for her bundle. Although the wet slates were cold and razor-sharp on her bare feet she knew instinctively that to put her boots on would halve her chances of survival – the worn soles would be too likely to slip, their very weight might go straight through the weakened fabric of the ancient and dilapidated roofs. So, still barefoot, and with pounding heart, she crept out along the shadowed gully that ran away from the window and into the unyielding darkness.

That hazardous journey across the roofs of Whitechapel, short as it was, was a terror beyond almost anything else that had happened to her. Sick with fear, her ears singing with the expectation of the shout that would mean her flight had been discovered, she slipped and scrambled from one steeply sloping roof to another, clinging to chimney stacks that were often no more firmly based than she was herself, hunting desperately for a skylight or a window, breaking into a cold sweat whenever she came close to a precipitous edge. The wet, cobbled streets and alleys below, occasionally lit by a pool of lamplight, but more often in darkness, beckoned with a dizzy magnetism that almost paralysed her. Life and limb depended upon small, sweat-slick fingers, trembling legs and an overwhelming determination.

There must be, there must surely be, somewhere, a way down?

She found it at last in a derelict building at the far end of the street in which the eating house was situated. A skylight hung open, swinging on one rusty hinge: but between her and the gaping hole that would lead her to safety stretched an area of decayed roof untouched and uncared-for for what must have been fifty years. The clouds were clearing. As they scurried darkly across the sky, in the fleeting moonlight Molly saw gaping holes, rotting beams.

Very carefully, on hands and knees, she began to crawl towards the opening. The timber beneath her creaked in protest, a slate slipped from beneath her hands and slithered downwards. She froze. The broken skylight was only feet away. Through it, in a shaft of moonlight, she could see stairs – her way down to the street and safety. She felt the structure of the roof bow and give beneath her. She scrambled forward, and then her hand was on the worm-eaten wood of the frame. She dragged herself to the edge, rolled into the opening and without stop for thought, for there was little else she could do, let herself drop.

Moments later, her legs still trembling violently, she was in the street. She paused for just a moment to pull on her boots and check her bundle and the precious leather bag, then she was off, running into the rain-drenched shadows as if the devil were behind her.

CHAPTER FOUR

IT WAS PERHAPS fifteen minutes later that she heard the
distressed wailing of a child, the weary remonstrance of a
woman's voice, the sound of a sharp hand on tender flesh and a
howling yelp of pain. Molly had stopped running minutes
before; both her breath and her strength had given out. She
had no idea where her blind dash had taken her, nor how far
she had come. Some minutes after stepping into the street she
had, more by luck than judgement, left the maze of alleys and
narrow streets and entered much wider thoroughfares, with
here and there the odd gas lamp to illuminate them. She
slipped like a shadow through the patches of light cast on the
pavement by the dingy windows and open doorways, intent
simply on getting as far away as possible.

Ahead of her the child's voice lifted again, crying hopelessly.
In the pool of light beneath a lamp she saw a small family
group – mother, baby, several dirty children ranging in size
from toddler to perhaps eight or nine years old – standing
around a small boy who lay, sprawled and sobbing, on the
ground. The mother was thin to the point of starvation, her
straggling hair hanging untidily over a young-old face, her
bony arms struggling to hold the baby to her hip.

"Stop grizzlin' fer Chrissake, and get *up*, Tommy. We'll git
ahselves locked aht if we don't 'urry—"

Molly stepped forward. "May – may I help?" Her voice was
uncertain, and her motives not entirely selfless. Johnny was
certainly looking for her by now. Looking for a lone girl
wandering the streets. "I could carry him a little way if you'd
like, if one of the others would carry my bundle. . . . It isn't
heavy."

Several pairs of eyes turned her way; solemn, interested,
surprised, suspicious.

"No, thanks," the woman said shortly. "We can manage."

Tom, still on the wet pavement, wailed again. "I wanna be carried—"

"Please." Molly turned huge, desperate eyes to his mother. "I could carry him quite easily. Are you going far?"

"To the Refuge at Allgit," she said, studying with knowing eyes the small figure, the pale, marked face and dirty scratched skin. "They'll feed us if we get there in time, an' there'll be beds, too, if we're lucky."

The thought was overwhelming. "I've nowhere to go," said Molly with sudden, weary honesty, "nowhere at all. If I came with you I could carry the little boy and we might all be the better for it . . . ?"

The woman's defeated eyes showed some trace of sympathy. "What's the matter, love, thrown yer out, 'as 'e? The best of 'em come to it, sooner or later." She grinned bitterly and indicated the silent, watching children. "Thank yer lucky stars yer on yer own."

"Yes," Molly said, flinching from the look in the older girl's eyes.

The woman shrugged and hefted the baby higher onto her skinny hip. "Well, please yerself. Come if yer want. Sal, take 'er bundle an' 'elp 'er with Tommy."

The girl, her pigtails bobbing, hauled the sobbing child to his feet. "If yer bend down," she said to Molly, "you can give 'im a piggy back. It'll be easier."

Molly obediently crouched and Sal heaved Tommy into place on her back, then picked up Molly's bundle. The others, led by their mother, were already trailing dispiritedly up the road.

"Who runs this – Refuge?" Molly asked, settling the little boy firmly upon her back, his legs dangling through her crooked arms.

The girl looked at her, puzzled, and shrugged. "Dunno," she said. "Jus' some ladies. Ladies what do – good works—" The corners of her mouth turned down in a completely unchildlike expression that combined acid derision with an uncomprehending resentment. "Still, their soup's good, I'll say that for 'em."

41

Molly smiled. "I think I'm rather more interested in the bed."

Sal turned and started off after the others. "Don't bank on it," she said pessimistically, lifting one narrow shoulder. "Beds is 'ard come by round 'ere. They'll be full." And on that cheerful note they set out for Aldgate.

The Aldgate Refuge for the Destitute and Homeless was an enormous, depressing and tumbledown building that had once housed an indoor market. It was cold in the warmest weather, draughty as a barn, dirty no matter how hard the volunteers who ran it worked. Together with the destitute and homeless there lived rats, mice, cockroaches, spiders and numerous dispossessed cats and dogs. But to many of those who turned up at its doors, night after night, for a bowl of soup and a bed, it was the only thing that stood between hopelessness and total despair. Lady Margaret Wharton, who had founded the Refuge, and who, with friends and volunteers ran it now, knew this; it was the only thing that prevented her from giving up the unequal struggle altogether. Certainly there was a limit to what one small group of women could do, but each night they did it, doling out soup, bread, and help where they could manage it, providing shelter and at least some semblance of comfort. For her efforts she endured the animosity of a great part of her own class, was perfectly aware and even understood the grudging resentment of some of those who accepted her charity. But the Refuge went on.

When Molly and her companions arrived, the children's mother, who had spoken only in monosyllables but who had at least told Molly that her name was Gertrude, looked dismally at the great closed door and said simply, "Too late."

"What?" Molly swung the sleeping Tommy off her aching back and into her arms.

"Too late. Door's shut."

"Shut doors," Molly said with the determination of desperation, "can be opened. Sal, will you take your brother for a moment?"

"S'no good." Gertrude leaned tiredly against a grimy, windowless wall. "They on'y shut the door when they're full."

"Well, we'll see about that." Molly stepped to the door and hammered on it with her clenched fist.

Nothing happened.

She assaulted the worm-eaten door again. "Is anybody there?"

Moments later the door swung open to reveal a young, well-dressed woman, her smooth skin glowing in the light of the lamp she carried.

"I'm sorry," she said uncertainly, "I'm afraid we're shut for the night."

"Please," Molly said, putting out a hand to the closing door, "we've children with us, hungry children."

Tommy, stirring in his sister's arms, gave a providential snivel. The girl in the door hesitated.

"If you could just find them a bite to eat, a corner to sleep in?" begged Molly, sensing an advantage.

The girl shook her head. "There isn't a bed left. I really don't think . . ."

"What is it, Sarah?" the voice, crisp and well-modulated, came from the shadows behind the girl.

"A family, Lady Margaret. Two women and some children—"

"Well—" a figure appeared, tall and thin, the sombre darkness of her dress relieved only by a snow-white collar and cuffs, the latter being pulled up to her elbows in business-like fashion, "Let's have a look at them."

Molly stepped back to let Margaret Wharton survey the group, and the woman's thin face lit with a wry smile. "Hello, Sally. And little Tom – crying as usual, eh? Here, give him to me," she said, relieving little Sal of her brother's weight. She turned to Molly. "Here's a face I don't know."

"She 'elped me carry Tommy," Gertrude said, as if that were all the explanation required.

The thin, kindly face smiled again. "Well, in you come. We can't leave old friends standing on the doorstep, can we?"

"But Lady Margaret—" the girl called Sarah exclaimed softly. An upraised hand stopped her protest.

"We'll find somewhere. Come along."

The great vaulted hall smelled of soup and unwashed bodies.

Beds and mattresses took up the greater part of the floor space; men, women and children lay or sat upon them, the hum of their voices and the occasional shriek of the youngsters echoing to the high, girdered roof.

Lady Margaret led her charges to a table around which were set several rickety chairs and a long splintered bench.

"There. Sit yourselves down and Sarah will see to some food for you. I'll go and organize beds."

By the time they had finished eating most of the occupants of the hall had settled down for the night. The lamps had dimmed and the noise died to a few whispers, mutters, snores. Lady Margaret, her finger to her lips to enjoin quiet, led Molly, Gertrude and the children through the rows of beds and mattresses to an archway that gave onto a dark corridor lit by a single lamp. At the end of the corridor she opened a door into a small room into which had been packed, beside the large bed that obviously belonged there, several comfortable-looking mattresses, complete with pillows and blankets.

"Cor," Sal said expressively.

Gertrude said nothing. She was already settling the baby on the bed.

"But this is your own room," Molly said with quiet certainty, "isn't it? Where will you sleep?"

The woman looked at her in some surprise, then a kindly smile curved her lips. "Why, bless you, child, I'm too busy to sleep," she said firmly. "I've a soft enough bed to go to tomorrow, never fear. Don't worry your head about me. Good night, and God bless. Sleep well."

Fully dressed and totally undisturbed by the hubbub around her as the children noisily disputed who was to sleep in which corner, Molly dropped onto the nearest mattress and slept like the dead.

In the early hours of the morning she awoke, stiff, sore and thirsty. She lay for a moment, uncertain of her whereabouts, puzzled by the aches and pains that assaulted her. Then, as memory returned, she lay staring into the darkness listening to the sleeping breath of the children around her. For a long time she stayed so, trying to think, trying to plan, battling against her ever-growing thirst. A tiny window high up in the wall above the bed where Gertrude, the baby and little Tommy were sleeping, showed the pale yet lightless sky of pre-dawn. At length, her throat as dry as sandpaper, Molly crept from beneath the thin blanket and slipped out into the corridor.

The lamp was still burning, its faint and flickering light throwing shadows onto the stained and dirty walls. Beyond the arch at the end of the passage burned another lamp, equally dim. Molly walked quietly towards it. If she could find herself a glass of water she might be able to get back to sleep.

In the vast hall all was still; the sleepers, in their only escape from a brutal world, lay sprawled and silent. But in a small alcove by the side of the archway stood a table, upon which burned the oil lamp whose light Molly had seen; and sitting, elbows on table, head in hand, apparently absorbed in the open book that lay before her, was Lady Margaret Wharton. Next to the book stood a full jug of water and a glass.

Molly hesitated, shy of disturbing their benefactor, but her thirst overcame her qualms and she tiptoed to the table.

"Excuse me. I wondered—"

The woman's head jerked up in shock, one of her elbows slipped from the table. She had been sound asleep.

"Oh, I'm sorry, I'm truly sorry. I didn't mean to startle you—" real distress sounded in Molly's softly accented voice.

Margaret Wharton looked at the small, woebegone face and smiled. "It's all right, my dear. I'd just dozed for a moment."

"I only wanted to ask if I might have a glass of water. . . ."

Margaret Wharton smiled. "Help yourself, child." She watched as Molly poured the water and drank it down in one grateful gulp. Something about the sensitive face, the intelligence in those astonishing eyes, woke her interest.

"I don't know your name?"

"Molly O'Dowd." Molly poured more water and drank it, slowly this time.

"You're Irish?"

Molly nodded.

"Have you been in London long?"

Centuries. The curly head shook. "A week or so."

Margaret Wharton sighed. "How on earth do you come to be here so soon? Did you come with no money?"

Molly's hand crept to the bodice of her dress. "Oh, no. I've money. But—"

The woman at the table watched with clear, tired eyes from beneath straight brows. "But you're in some kind of trouble?"

The girl did not answer. Margaret Wharton reached out and lightly rested a strong hand upon her wrist. "You don't have to tell me if you don't want to" – the first and golden rule she had learned in Aldgate – "but I'd help you if I could, if you'd let me."

Molly leaned against the table, staring down in sudden misery at its scratched and battered surface. Her shoulders were slumped. "I don't think you can."

"I could try."

Molly turned sharply from the upthrown light of the lamp and made no answer.

"With advice if nothing else," the voice persisted.

The idea took root slowly. Lady Margaret watched as some small light of hope kindled behind the blue-grey eyes. She patted the corner of the table in an invitation to sit – there were no other chairs but the one in which she was sitting herself.

Molly pulled herself up onto the table, settled herself like a child with her feet dangling and her hands folded in her lap. "I don't know where to begin."

The watching woman steepled her fingers before her and laid her lined cheek upon them. "From the beginning," she said, her voice warm and inviting.

By the time Molly's tale was finished the window was washed with morning and the outside world was beginning to stir.

As the girl's voice died Margaret Wharton sighed softly. How many times had she heard this story in one form or another? And how many times would she be called upon to listen to it again? She looked up at the earnest little face above her; at least, thank God, this one by a combination of luck and courage seemed to have escaped the worst and was not beyond helping.

Molly looked at the thin, thoughtful face, and in her lap her fingers crossed so tightly that they ached from the pressure. Around her neck Maggie's wash-leather bag seemed to weigh a ton; she felt as if it were glowing, red as sin, through her bodice.

"So—" the woman smiled her worn and kindly smile, "we have to get you away from here before this – Johnny – discovers your whereabouts?"

"Yes." Wonderful thought.

"That won't be as hard as you might think. This part of London is full of tuppeny ha'penny thugs like your Johnny. Once away from here he won't be able to find you. His arm is not as long as you think it, never fear. Your mistake was in coming to this part of London in the first place – oh, I know," she held up a hand as Molly opened her mouth to protest, " – it wasn't your fault, you knew no better. How could you? But there are more – respectable—" she smiled again as she emphasized the word a little " – places. Places where Johnny Cribben's rule does not run. The easiest thing, of course, would be for me to try to place you in service—" Molly's head came up sharply at that, " – but I gather you've set your heart against that?"

"I have." The stubborn, damaged mouth was set defensively.

"I see." There was a short silence. "You say you read and write well?"

"Yes. And figure, too."

"Had you considered office work?"

Molly shook her head. "I wouldn't know where to start."

"You could learn. Times, my dear, are changing, thank Heaven. The days when a woman could earn her living only as a teacher or a skivvy or a prostitute will soon be behind us. It is no longer considered scandalously eccentric in the business world to employ intelligent young ladies. If you learned to operate a typewriter—"

"What's that?"

Lady Margaret suppressed her smile. "It's a machine that prints words clearly and much faster than handwriting."

"And women work them?"

"They do." Lady Margaret did not miss the gleam in the girl's eyes. "You like the idea?"

"Indeed I do. How would I learn?"

"You'd have to take lessons at a business school. You say you have some money?"

"Yes. A little. Sean and I had saved. To be married. I've enough, I think." There was no thunderbolt; Molly breathed again. To her own ears the jerky sentences rang with untruth, but Margaret Wharton's expression did not change. She leaned back in her chair.

"Well, as it happens, I think that I might be able to do something for you. You need first of all somewhere to live, somewhere where you'll be safe and reasonably comfortable while you get yourself started.

"You know of somewhere?" Too much to hope for, surely?

Margaret Wharton nodded. "I think I do, yes. The woman I have in mind usually takes young gentlemen, but I'm certain that if I asked her—" she was rummaging amongst a pile of papers on the table, " – ah, here it is, yes: Linsey Grove, Upton Park. Ellen Alden is a widow with a son who is not, unfortunately, strong; her father once worked for my family. Ellen does a lot of good work for the Refuge. I remember that she mentioned last week that their last lodger had left. So providing the room is still vacant—" She reached for pen and paper.

"Oh, that would be so kind." Upton Park. A faint vision of green: trees, and grass. Surely with a name like that it must be a little more like home, less like the decaying ant-heap that was the East End?

Lady Margaret held up a warning finger. "No special treatment, mind. If I know Ellen, her rules are rigid and not to be broken. She is a woman of very high Christian principles. She may even at times appear a little harsh. But you'll find no cleaner nor more comfortable home than hers. You'll be in good hands." Margaret Wharton grinned suddenly in a most unladylike way. "I doubt even your Johnny Cribben would take on Ellen Alden at her best." She sobered. "Once you're settled you should be able to obtain a place in a commercial school or college – I believe there are quite a number in that area. Or if the fees are too high you could go to night school and work during the day. Would you be prepared to do that?"

"Yes. Oh, yes. Anything."

"Good. Then after you've had a wash and some breakfast come back to me here; I'll have a letter for you to take to Ellen and instructions as to how to get there."

Molly slipped from the table. With the resilience and optimism of youth she felt as if a door, tight shut against her, had been opened to show her the world. "Thank you so much. I'll never forget it."

Lady Margaret patted her hand. "Gently, now, gently. You've a long way to go, and it won't be easy. This is just a start."

Molly, as she ran to a breakfast of none too fresh bread and sugary jam, thought she had never heard such a happy phrase. Just a start . . .

CHAPTER FIVE

WITH THE CLOUDS and rain of the previous day entirely cleared, Upton Park greeted her with golden October sunshine that gilded the marching rows of undistinguishable houses and lit smoke-darkened brick and tile with a deceptively mellow glow. Sitting in the train, Molly had swiftly relinquished the hope that Upton Park's nature might suit its name, since the view from the window had soon relieved her of such a misconception. Street after featureless street had slid past, the avenues straight as lines ruled on a map. Long and narrow strips of garden ran to the railway embankment, the degree of their cultivation varying enormously, from shabby wildernesses of nettles and weeds to ordered patches that marched with military precision from neat back yard to tiny, tended vegetable plot; the small houses stood wall to wall, shoulder to shoulder, like an invincible marching army. Yet the scrubbed doorsteps and shining, red-tiled paths pleased the eye and the tiny privet-hedged gardens gave at least some illusion of privacy to the lace-curtained windows and porched doors, though there were many roads where both doors and windows opened straight to the pavements with no pretension to seclusion.

She stood now in a wide, busy thoroughfare that was flanked with shops and business premises of all kinds, amongst which were more than a few public houses.

"Paper, lady?" The urchin's voice, sharp and unexpected, made her jump.

"No, thank you." The boy turned away. "Oh, wait, though. Yes, I will take one."

The child held out a paper in a grubby hand, took her money and with a cheeky grin wandered off into the crowds calling.

Molly hitched her bundle further up her shoulder, tucked the paper under her arm and, armed with Lady Margaret's somewhat vague directions, marched into the busy afternoon streets.

More than an hour and several mistaken turnings later, she at last found Linsey Grove. By this time she was hot and untidy and, to her own irritation, was beginning to feel almost as great a vagabond as she looked. Linsey Grove was a short street, lined with dusty plane trees, the houses a little larger and better kept than some she had seen in her wanderings today: the paths were swept, the gardens tidy. She found number twenty-six – a well kept house even amongst its respectable neighbours – and after only a second's hesitation pushed through the heavy brown-painted wooden gate. The porch was shining clean and decorated with brightly glazed brown-and-green tiles, the heavy knocker was polished to rival gold, and the slanting afternoon sun glittered upon the leaded stained glass of the front door. She brushed herself down, pulled her wretched untameable hair back behind her ears and, as an afterthought, dumped her bundle almost out of sight beside the porch before she knocked twice, hard, on the door, then folded her hands demurely around Lady Margaret's letter and waited.

It was a full minute before sound and movement beyond the coloured glass bespoke an answer. When the door opened it was to reveal a tall and angular young man with thin, sandy hair and pale, weak-looking eyes whose hesitancy clearly spoke of lack of confidence rather than unfriendliness and whose face the moment he began to speak flushed an uncomfortable scarlet.

"Y–yes?"

She smiled, with intention, the most charming smile she could manage. "Mr Alden?" – as close as she could come to Margaret Wharton's clear-vowelled, well-modulated voice, the soft consonants of Ireland deliberately hardened. She suspected from the way that he screwed his eyes up that, looking into the sun, he could make out few details of her appearance.

"Y–yes?"

"I wonder, is Mrs Alden at home? I have a letter for her. From Lady Margaret Wharton."

"N – no." The young man's large, bony hand was rubbing with nervous movements on the shiny paint of the door. "N – no I'm afraid she isn't. C – could you perhaps c – come back later?"

Her heart sank, and her feet throbbed painfully. Beyond him

she could see polished lino, shining wooden banisters, and through an open door a clean and comfortable kitchen. She sighed tiredly, let her shoulders droop dispiritedly, bowed her curly head a little. "Oh dear, how disappointing." Her voice was a breath from tears. "Have you any idea how long she'll be? I've come a very long way. . . ."

The young man fidgeted uncomfortably. "I – I'm not sure. Not long, though. At l – least, I shouldn't think s – so."

She lifted a brave little chin, watched him with wide, artless eyes and let the awkward silence stretch on. The sun gilded her wild curls, glinted gold dust on long, tangled lashes; she looked fragile and forlorn. Some emotion, totally unfamiliar, stirred within Samuel Alden's breast. He was not used to small, helpless-looking females.

"P – perhaps," he said to his own astonishment, "you'd l – like to c – come in and wait? I c – could make a c – cup of tea?"

"Oh, no, I couldn't possibly put you to that trouble—" She opened her wide-set, sun-silvered eyes; Sam fell into the lavender depths and drowned.

"It's n – no trouble. Honestly. P – please—" He stepped back, inviting her into the hall with a shy and awkward gesture. With a feeling of indescribable relief, and totally unaware that in her efforts to gain some respite for her aching feet she had inadvertently sparked the beginnings of devotion, Molly picked up her bundle and stepped across the shining red doorstep.

The house was almost obsessively neat and clean, the furniture polished to a miraculous shine, no single picture or ornament out of line, no speck of dust, no smear or grubby mark daring to besmirch paintwork or wall. After the dirt and squalor of Whitechapel it was another world; the very air smelled clean. Molly followed her guide along the hall and into a kitchen that looked as if no human agency could be responsible for its immaculacy.

"P – please sit down." Sam's pale eyes had widened in a surprise he had not the art to conceal; here in the cool shadows of the kitchen and away from the glare of sunshine he saw clearly for the first time the patched homespun, the battered boots, the marks of violence about the small, vivid face. Molly laid her precious letter upon the scrubbed table and faced him squarely;

let him look. He flushed under her slightly defiant gaze and turned to the black kitchen range that, polished to a steely sheen, ran almost the length of one wall. Molly sat down and watched him in silence as he filled the kettle and set it on the hob; seeing the house, and the son, a strong picture was forming in her mind of the woman, Ellen Alden. Letter or no letter, first impressions would count.

"Excuse me."

Sam turned. In his every movement, in every aspect, he was awkward: his hands seemed too big for his thin wrists, his shoulders stooped, his fine sandy hair fell untidily across his eyes, his face looked very pale and shadowed, as with ill-health.

"I wonder if I might tidy myself a little?" Molly looked down at her spread, dusty skirt and added with beguiling honesty, "I wouldn't give myself houseroom looking like this."

He stared. "You've c – come about the room?"

She nodded.

Sam was aware of an odd mixture of emotions: pleasure, doubt, something, for him, close to excitement. "M – Mother usually only takes gentlemen."

"Yes. So Lady Margaret explained. But she seemed to think that her letter—?" Molly gestured towards the envelope, letting the sentence hang unfinished in the air.

Sam ducked his head in a kind of nod. "P – possibly, yes." And for the first time he smiled, a fleeting, wry twitch of his long mouth that irresistibly brought an answering response from Molly's. "L – Lady Margaret's the only p – person I know who c – can make M – Mother do something she doesn't really w – want to—" The kettle had begun to sing. "If you g – go through there," he said, pointing to a small door leading into a lean-to beside the kitchen. "I think y – you'll find everything y – you need. T – tea will be ready soon."

"Thank you. I'll be only a couple of minutes."

She scrubbed her hands and face sore in an enamel bowl of cold water with soap that seemed to be made of sandstone and inspected her broken lip in a damp-speckled mirror that hung on the wall. The swelling had gone down considerably, though a faint shadowing bruise marked the pale skin around it. She wetted her comb and tried to slick her rebellious hair down,

53

whispering an imprecation that owed a lot to brother Cormac as it sprang inevitably back to its accustomed dark halo of curls. She brushed at her dusty clothes, rubbed the towel – in the absence of anything else suitable – across her boots, and thus prepared re-entered the kitchen where Sam was pouring the tea. As he lifted his head to smile shy acknowledgment of her return they both heard the sound of a key in the lock, and for a fraction of a second Sam froze before carefully placing the teapot in its little flowered stand and turning towards the door.

"Sam? Sammy!" The voice was authoritative.

"Here, Mother," he said opening the kitchen door.

Molly stood, small and composed, her back so far as was possible to the light, her hands clasped before her as Ellen Alden swept in, as tall and spare as her only son, but with none of his ungainliness and the poise of a woman who knows herself to be completely in command of almost any situation. As Ellen eyed the small stranger in her kitchen with arid surprise, Molly thought that in her youth Mrs Alden must have been a striking-looking woman; her skin was dark, her thin, high-bridged nose dominated her face. But her lips were narrow and almost bloodless, drawn constantly to a straight and uncompromising line, and her eyes were not friendly as she waited with icy composure to be informed of the patently unacceptable reason for this intrusion.

"M – Mother, th – this is—" Sam stopped in confusion, stumbling more than ever over his words, " – a y – young w – woman from L – Lady Margaret—"

Dark brows rose, unimpressed and questioning.

"I have a letter." Soft voice, downcast eyes. Molly picked up the envelope and held it out.

"So." Ellen Alden held the long envelope in her hand and looked at it, the inscription written in Lady Margaret's bold and scrawling hand seeming to cause some softening in that hard face. She laid the letter back on the table and lifted her hand to draw a long hat pin from her hat, then remove the hat from her smooth dark hair. Sam stepped forward and took the hat from her, helped her carefully from her long black coat.

"I've t – tea made, M – Mother."

"Thank you, Sam." Molly, intercepting with some astonish-

Ellen, unkindly, allowed the defeat that showed in Molly's eyes to last a moment longer than necessary before she added, "However, since this comes as a special request from Lady Margaret—"

Had she seen the look of pleasure that lit Sam's face she might instantly have reconsidered. But she did not; she was watching Molly.

" – I am willing to give you a trial. Shall we say a month?"

Molly relaxed suddenly, her tight-clasped hands easing their grip; the smile she bestowed upon Ellen was brilliant, beautiful, and entirely wasted. The dark unfriendly eyes did not change.

"The rent is four and sixpence a week." Molly's eyes widened a little, but she did not protest. "You may use this kitchen for an hour each evening. The bath is there—" She pointed to the door leading to the outhouse. "You may use it once a week, on a Thursday evening. Sam and I are always at Chapel on a Thursday. There are, you understand, certain rules that I shall expect you to abide by."

"Of course."

"The door is locked at ten each evening. Including Saturdays." She paused, waiting for argument. Molly said nothing. "No male visitors at any time, of course. Females you may entertain at certain times in your room providing you give me notice."

"I don't know anyone," Molly said quietly. "I don't expect I'll be having many visitors."

Mrs Alden ignored the interruption. "Lady Margaret mentions the possibility of Commercial College or some such thing?"

Molly nodded.

"Very well. A month, and we'll see. Come, I'll show you the room."

They climbed the stairs in silence and Molly followed the woman into a large bow-windowed room in the front of the house. It had the same air of ordered cleanliness as the other rooms Molly had seen; the furnishings comprised a bed, a deep armchair, a table covered in a heavy, dark-red cloth that matched the bedspread and the curtains, a wardrobe that looked big enough to live in and a washstand with jug and basin. Molly added in her mind's eye the touches of personal habitation, noted the blaze of an afternoon sun in the window, the dusty leaves of a plane tree outside, and thanked the star that had led her to this room.

"I'll leave you, then, to—" Ellen eyed disparagingly her scruffy bundle " – unpack. At the end of the street is a pie shop. You'll no doubt need some supper."

"Thank you."

Ellen inclined her head and turned to go. "The rent is due each Friday," she said before she closed the door, "promptly, if you please."

"I could give you a month in advance."

"That won't be necessary," the woman said sparely. "A week will do, payable tomorrow." Molly waited for the firm click of the lock, then pulled a ferocious and childish face at the closed door. But the sight of the golden, sunlit room – hers, all hers, while she could pay the rent – more space and more comfort than she had ever had in her life, lifted her spirits and sent them soaring. With an overwhelming feeling of happiness she threw herself backwards onto the bed and lay, arms spread wide, luxuriating in the feel of the sun on her face through the glass, the rainbowed glory of it in her half-closed eyes.

A month – Ellen grimly marched back down the stairs – if the baggage can manage to stay in one place for that long. A little gypsy if ever I saw one. One foot out of place, just one, and out she goes, Lady Margaret or no.

Upstairs, the object of her doubts rolled from the bed, took the looped thong of leather from about her neck and began to count Maggie's money.

CHAPTER SIX

MOLLY SLEPT LIKE the dead and woke in the early morning thinking herself in her mother's kitchen. On a sudden wave of unexpected misery she turned her face to the pillow, defenceless in that unguarded moment between sleeping and waking, unable for her life to control a surge of unhappy homesickness. Nothing about these surroundings was familiar. Molly clamped sharp teeth into her lip: in her inner, childhood ear her mother, dead now for two years, sang softly as she cooked breakfast in a warm, untidy kitchen, her husband's cap and jacket thrown across a chair, her sons' boots lined up against the stove for warmth . . .

Molly sat up, pushing her mass of hair from eyes that burned and blurred and, finally, cleared. This room was her home now, and a great improvement it certainly was on the attic in Whitechapel. Her life was her own, win or lose – that was above all what she had wanted; there was little to be gained from tears now.

She scrambled from the bed, wrapping her shawl over her nightdress against the early chill, and scuttled on bare feet to the window. In the small grate the embers of the fire that Sam had lit for her the evening before were stone-cold and grey; she shivered. Sounds floated up from downstairs: voices, the clatter of plates. She opened the draped, dark-red curtains, letting the light seep into the room, lap the dark furniture, creep across the rose-patterned carpet. Outside a milk cart rumbled down the street, pulled by a shaggy, patient horse; a few people hurried past below the window. From downstairs she heard Sam's voice raised in farewell to his mother; the front door slammed, his footsteps clicked on the tiled garden path beneath her and she stepped back from the window. To be seen at the window in her nightdress would hardly be the best way to start her residence at number twenty-six.

She washed swiftly, scrambled into her old clothes, keeping her eyes firmly from the sight of herself in the mirror, then reached for the newspaper she'd bought the day before. She turned the pages until she had it folded back at a large advertisement proclaiming, "GRAND SALE. TALBOT AND CO., LTD. DEPARTMENT STORE. PRICES SLASHED. BUY NOW."

She found her stub of a pencil, tore off a clean edge from the paper and began figuring.

Quite some time later, with the morning light stronger, she was still at it. Before her on the tablecloth was spread Maggie's money – nearly seven pounds, more than she had dared to hope – and her own hard-saved few shillings. Her scrap of paper was covered now in neat writing and a column of figures. She added them up again. For a costume, three flannelette blouses with detachable collars and cuffs – "very smart" proclaimed the advertisement – a pair of shoes and two pairs of gloves she had committed one pound nineteen shillings and sixpence ha'penny of her precious hoard. She went back to the newspaper. "Smart felt hats in brown, Beaver and Navy, trimmed with Stylish Bows." She had seen enough to know that a hat was essential to a well-dressed lady. At 2/11d, down it went on her list. She hovered for a moment over corsets, "special, white, 3/6½d". Frowning a little she studied the high bosom and nipped waist of the girl in the advertisement whom she intended to emulate, and then the corset joined the list also. A wool skirt and cloth jacket were next. She calculated again, tapping the end of her pencil on small, strong teeth. Then she turned to the back page of the paper where were the columns of personal advertisements; she skimmed the teachers of pianoforte and singing, the offers to improve her handwriting or her memory and stopped at "J. Marsden. School of Business Studies. Typewriting, Shorthand and Bookkeeping taught. Competitive Rates. Highly Recommended." There followed a list of fees. Molly did a little swift arithmetic and then added the sum of thirty shillings to her expenditure. Taking out the amount she would need to live on for four or five weeks she was left with just about thirty shillings. She should save that for emergencies, she knew. On that she might eat frugally and pay her rent for another month, supposing her plan took longer than she was expecting. Or, if the worst happened, thirty shillings would pay her fare back to Ireland, or to America, to Patrick.

She turned back to the Talbot advertisement; at the foot of the page in discreet but slightly more fancy lettering ran the legend: "Special. Ladies' Silk Shirts. All Colours. 7/11d. Reduced from 15/9d. Also, Exceptional Value: a Few Black and Navy Silk Broche and Satin Skirts. 19/6d. Much Below Normal Price."

She looked at it very thoughtfully for some time, picked up the pencil, fiddled with it, laid it down and began to gather together the stacked piles of money before taking herself downstairs to enquire after the whereabouts of Talbot and Co., Department Store.

The small figure in the mirror, ridiculously unfamiliar in the grey tweed skirt and jacket and soft white flannelette blouse, twirled and swayed and dipped her curly head; then muttered a descriptive and unladylike Irish curse as the smart little black hat slipped sideways and finished at a gay but unfashionable angle over one eye. She should have bought a hat pin. Why hadn't she thought of it? She straightened the hat, pulled a few provoking curls foward onto her cheeks and, her temper restored, smiled at her reflection. She could barely breath in the contraption of a corset; her feet in the dainty, pointed kid shoes already hurt; the stiff detachable collar of the shirt rubbed painfully upon skin not used to such restriction – and she had never, never seen herself looking so astonishingly lovely; had never, indeed, dreamed that she could look so. The dark blue bombazine had made her look a pretty, wayward child; in this outfit she was a smart, self-possessed and very attractive young lady. She stopped smiling and rearranged her expression into one of cool composure. Her silvered eyes reflected the gentle colour of the tweed, her full breasts and tiny waist were shown to perfection by the fitted jacket. She turned and walked to the window, trying not to wince as her toes cramped and pinched in the shoes, then she turned and glided back towards the mirror with a dazzling smile. "Mr Marsden?" she asked in her new, Margaret Wharton voice, "my name is Molly O'Dowd." She stopped, frowning ferociously. That wouldn't do at all. She must look efficient, businesslike – she lifted a fine-drawn curve of eyebrow, lowered the arched lids a little. "Mr Marsden? My name is Molly O'Dowd—" That was better, much better. For a moment she studied intently the girl in the mirror, her eyes moving from pointed toe to discreetly feathered hat, looking for anything that might connect this genteel, sober, smartly dressed young woman with the ragamuffin who had stepped from the *Kerry* onto Prince's Dock ten days ago, or, worse, with the girl who had scrambled dazed and terrified across the wet slates of Whitechapel. . . . There was, so far as she could tell, no hint of either. Excitement stirred, causing her stomach to churn uncomfortably and her heartbeat to increase within the awful confining corset. It was begun, the new life. And – she turned to the bed upon which her other purchases lay – there could be no turning back now. For alongside the black wool skirt and sensible cloth jacket lay a soft, sheer silk shirt the colour of forget-me-nots, like a jewel against the dark bedspread, and a navy broche silk skirt trimmed with satin. And the man at the ticket office, she reflected with wry certainty, won't accept *them* in payment for a return ticket. She had added to her wardrobe two pairs of stockings, a small bag, which had cost her one and sixpence, and an umbrella for half a crown. Apart from the thirty shillings she was now hoping to venture upon Mr Marsden, she had barely enough money to live on for four or five weeks. After that she must earn her keep.

She picked up the bag and umbrella, for the sky outside was overcast, laid in passing one caressing finger upon the lovely blue silk of the blouse, regretting faintly the down-to-earth flannelette, then left the room, shutting the door firmly behind her. Her new clothes rustled gratifyingly around her as she descended the stairs and marched along the empty hall to the front door. As she opened it she heard a sound behind her. Ellen Alden had come to the kitchen door and stood wiping floured hands upon an immaculate apron.

Molly inclined her head, smiled gently and shut the door with quiet care behind her. If she had needed any reassurance it was there in the unguardedly astonished eyes of her landlady.

With neither thought nor care for painfully tight shoes she set off in search of Mr John Marsden, Teacher of Shorthand,

Typing and Bookkeeping, leaving Ellen Alden to wonder if Lady Margaret Wharton might not have been so mistaken after all.

It had been by no means a good day. John Marsden rubbed a hand through his thinning, grizzled hair and consigned to perdition all idiotic, simpering, giggling women; pretty or plain, clever or dim, they were all the same. Not one of them with the straightforward good sense of a man. Thank God in Heaven he'd never married. He couldn't have stood it.

He sat down, breathing heavily and wheezing painfully. God damn this chest that made him good for nothing but playing nursemaid to a bunch of schoolgirls. Damn the bloody weather that was sending raindrops sliding like dreary tears down the windowpane, reminding him that November and its discomforts was nearly upon him. He eyed, savagely wistful, a full pipe rack that stood on his desk; and damn the damned doctor who had convinced him that tobacco, his only vice, might well kill him.

As he reached for a pipe the front door bell rang loudly. Who in Hell was that? He hadn't another pupil till four o' clock – that stupid Miss Denby who had a tendency to tears when he shouted at her.

A few moments later the door opened.

"A young lady to see you, Mr Marsden." His housekeeper eyed the still-empty pipe repressively but refrained from comment.

John Marsden watched the small, tweed-suited figure that the housekeeper had ushered in, noted the unsmiling composure, the still, gloved hands that did not fidget with the small bag they carried, the level blue-grey eyes. Not as bad as some, anyway. At least she didn't look as if she'd burst into tears when he told her that the world of business was not waiting with eager open arms for pretty, brainless, unqualified young ladies. She appeared quite undisturbed by his regard; he had the suspicion in fact that she rather enjoyed it. As the door closed behind the housekeeper she said in a low, musically accented voice, "Mr Marsden? My name is Molly O'Dowd. I saw your advertisement in the newspaper—"

He nodded. Molly, slowly, began to count to ten. If the

wretched man did not offer her a seat by the time she had finished she would leave. Not even in the days of cast-off boots had her feet hurt her so.

"Sit down, Miss O'Dowd."

With no outward sign of relief she walked steadily to the chair across the desk from his and sat down, of necessity bolt upright; her new corsets were like steel. Grateful for the cover that the enormous desk provided she slipped swollen and agonized feet from the constricting shoes. Whether she would ever get them back on again was open to question; but the immediate relief was so intense that she could not for the moment bring herself to care. Gravely she looked across at a craggy, bad-tempered face, the cheeks sunken with ill-health, bloodshot eyes overhung with brows so thick they appeared to frown even in repose. He showed no inclination to question her; the only alternative to an afternoon of silence appeared to lie with her.

"I wish to train for office work," she said. "I have absolutely no previous experience, but I read and write well and have a very good head for figures. And I don't mind how hard I have to work. I wish to learn typewriting and book-keeping. I should like to learn shorthand as well, but I don't believe that I have the time. I could perhaps take a course in that later. Your terms, according to the paper are ninepence for an hour's lesson, is that correct?" A slight movement that might have been a nod. "I thought we might come to a special arrangement for—" she paused "—something a little more intensive than usual. I should like a lesson each day for a month. I can pay thirty shillings, no more."

John Marsden sat back in a creaking, high-backed chair, steepling long, bony fingers. "You're in a hurry, are you?"

"I am." She saw no reason to prevaricate. "I have to find a job within five or six weeks."

"And you think that by some miraculous formula, some effortless waving of a thirty shilling magic wand I can provide you with one?" He noted the spark of temper in her expressive eyes, the sudden sharp lifting of her chin, but when she spoke her voice had not changed.

"I think nothing of the kind. I hope that if I work hard—and if you are a good enough teacher—" she did not give herself time to wonder if she should have resisted that temptation " – I might find myself with the qualifications to obtain an office job. If not—" she made a small movement with her head and her little hat tilted slightly " – I'll have lost my thirty shillings and I'll have to try a shop or a factory."

He did not for the moment speak. The girl sat straight and slight as a blade of grass, waiting.

"Typewriting," he said thoughtfully, "and bookkeeping."

"That is what your advertisement says."

"It is," he agreed, peacefully; then shot out, "Add threepence three farthings, elevenpence ha'penny, one and nine and twopence farthing."

"Three and twopence ha'penny." The answer came with no apparent thought.

"What is a third of two pounds ten and six?"

"Sixteen and tenpence."

"Show me your hands."

She carefully removed her gloves, held up small, narrow-boned hands.

"Do you play the piano?"

She hesitated, considering a lie, but discarded the idea as impractical. A piano stood in the corner of the room; any claim might be expected to be substantiated.

"No."

He smiled for the first time, a shadow of a twitch of the lip. It might have been missed had she not been watching so closely. "Good. These parlour musicians tie their fingers in knots when it comes to a typewriting machine. A lesson a day, you said, for a month?"

"Yes. Could you teach me in that time?"

He nodded slowly. "I might. If you work like the Devil."

"I will."

"Thirty shillings?"

She nodded. "That's all that I can afford," she said frankly, then added with firmness, "I should expect at least two hours a day for that. Your advertisement said ninepence."

He got up and walked around the desk. Smoothly she hooked her toes into her discarded shoes and drew them beneath her skirt. At least her feet had stopped throbbing. Mr Marsden rested upon the desk, fingers drumming reflectively, eyes upon the far wall.

"I'll tell you what I'll give you for thirty shillings," he said at last, "an hour and a half's personal tuition each day followed by an hour by yourself practising on one of my machines. How does that sound?" He had suspected that she might be very pretty indeed when she smiled, and now his opinion was confirmed. "I guarantee nothing," he added sternly. "If you have no aptitude, both time and money will be wasted, you understand that? You might as well apply to the laundry in Green Street right now."

"I understand."

"Can you start tomorrow?"

She nodded.

"About this time? Right. Three o'clock tomorrow afternoon. Now I suggest you put those silly shoes back on your feet before you leave. Or you'll likely get very wet feet."

Molly could smile about that, even as she hobbled through the rain towards Linsey Grove; she was not dissatisfied, something about John Marsden had inspired her confidence. He would do his best for her, she was certain of that. The rest was up to her.

The first thing she heard when, with a proprietary air, she turned the key in the lock of number twenty-six was Sam's cough. She had noticed it last night, a shallow, irritating catching of the breath in his throat, which seemed to be made worse by his attempts to suppress it. As she shut the door he appeared in the hall, flushed and a little breathless but no longer coughing.

"Good afternoon, Miss O'Dowd."

She smiled, "Good afternoon."

He was blocking her way. They stood for a moment, awkwardly, before he stepped hastily aside. "Sorry." The thin skin of his face was scarlet.

She stepped past him to the foot of the stairs.

"Do you usually get home this early?" She had to say something, could not leave him there with that odd, expectant look on his face, without breaking the silence.

"No. No, I don't. But Uncle said—" He stopped, gestured

helplessly. " – It's the d – damp. It seems to make my cough worse. It gets on his nerves, I think."

"You work for your uncle?" She could think of nothing but the haven of her room and shoeless, corsetless comfort.

"Yes. He has two shops in the High Street. I – I help him." She nodded, her duty done, turned to the stairs. "I must say—" he spoke in a rush, one hand half-lifted as if to stop her movement. Wearily she turned. His eyes, milky-pale, were fixed on her with an expression that in her present mood she found vaguely irritating, it somehow inferred a responsibility she had no wish for " – I must say that you're – looking very n – nice."

"Thank you." Her smile was genuine, but nothing could keep her from mounting the stairs. His eyes followed her.

"I lit the fire," he called, "I thought you might be cold."

She paused in the dark at the top of the stairs. "You're very kind. Thank you."

"Don't—" he coughed, smothered it " – mention it."

The kitchen door opened. "Sam? Who's that you're talking to?"

Sam's cough overcame him. Beneath its cover Molly gently closed the door of her room.

CHAPTER SEVEN

THE LESSONS WENT well from the start. Molly was an apt pupil with an unflagging determination to learn, and John Marsden was impressed. In the first week their relationship was established, the teacher appreciating the girl's diligence and the strength of will that drove her, she reacting to his acid tongue and short temper not with tears and tantrums but with an asperity that matched his own and even won his grudging admiration. A couple of days after she started her lessons he offered to lend her some books to study at home, and was startled at the speed with which she read them and the amount of information she absorbed.

"You ought to be learning shorthand," he said, watching the bent curly head as she ran a finger down a column of figures, adding them almost as fast as he could himself.

She nodded without taking her eyes from the paper, said quietly, "I know. But I haven't the time. Later, perhaps."

She was painfully aware of the passing of time, of every penny spent and every moment wasted – as any time spent away from John Marsden and his typewriting machine seemed. She borrowed more books, devoured them, asked questions. During the second week she agreed with eager thanks to his suggestion that she might like an extra half hour's practice at the machine each day.

" – though you must be nearly down to your knuckles already?" John Marsden allowed himself one of his rare, craggy smiles.

Molly conserved her money like a dying man his breath. She limited herself to one meal a day which she most often cooked for herself in the evening once Ellen and Sam had finished in the kitchen. On Wednesdays and Fridays there was a street market near the Marsden house through which she had to pass on her way home. On these days she bought hot pies for a penny and had bread and jam for supper. So absorbed was she in her enterprise that the Aldens rarely saw her. She paid an extra three ha'pence a day for the privilege of a fire early-lit as the evenings closed in and the weather grew colder; her time indoors was spent huddled around it, her face flaming, her back like ice, her nose in John Marsden's books.

Her speed on the typewriting machine picked up considerably. Her nails broke, her fingers grew sore, then hardened.

Sometimes in the evening she heard Sam Alden's cough; often he 'happened' to be in the hallway as she passed in or out of the house. On these occasions she was contented to smile and greet him, but rarely stopped for more than a word. She was quiet in her room, tidy in the kitchen; an altogether well-behaved model of a lodger. Ellen Alden's stiff dislike tempered a little and Molly found herself on odd occasions offered a cup of tea or a slice of her landlady's excellent cake. But always, she noticed with a smile, when Sam Alden was away from the house. She had no objections to that; she could not but be aware of the way he looked at her, of the efforts he made to waylay her, for however brief a space of time – she simply hoped that his mother had not noticed also. She had herself no desire to encourage these attentions. It was not just that she was busy and often tired, nor that she had no wish to antagonize Sam's formidable and protective mother. Almost without her being aware of it some part of her beneath the occupied exterior still mourned her dead. At the core of her there was still a wretched grief, hardly acknowledged except as a leaden weight to be carried with her, unabated as yet by time or distance or frantic activity. Against the death-sanctified image of dark and gentle Sean what chance had poor, stooping Sam with his weak, sensitive face and his stutter? She hardly noticed him. Set against his mother's good will – for Molly had no illusions as to whom she had to please in that house – Sam's feelings did not rate highly in Molly's priorities. She worked and she planned and she pored over the situations vacant columns in the newspapers and the days raced on.

Halfway through November it became obvious that the weather was set for a cold, wet winter. Gas lights flickered wanly in the streaming streets as Molly hurried in her flimsy shoes through rain-shimmering, featureless avenues of houses to

Linsey Grove and her fire. She steadfastly refused to spend money on omnibus fares and walked everywhere, though, as her fashionable shoes squelched soggily on her feet, she had to admit that this might be false economy. It wouldn't be long before she would have to buy herself a new pair of shoes.

On the corner of the Grove, beneath the awning of the pie shop and outlined by the light that glowed through the steamy window, Molly came upon a swarthy man playing a barrel organ, the lilting, musical-box tune at odds with the driving rain and the wet, empty streets. A despondent monkey huddled, shivering, on top of the bright contraption, a tin cup in the tiny hand. Molly had not eaten all day – nor, to be honest, much the day before – and she was looking forward to a steaming-hot plate of pie and mash to eat before her fire. She looked at the barrel organ man, who looked no less thin and ill-fed than his monkey, and was struck by his dark face, knife-sharp and strangely proud in the gas light. She wished she had a penny to spare, but the smell from the pie shop was beckoning and she hunched beneath her umbrella and hurried past him into the warmth of the shop. She could not afford sympathy, she thought wryly, any more than he could afford pride. She stood for a moment, shaking her umbrella and stamping the worst of the water from her sodden shoes. Then she turned and cannoned straight into the waiting figure who had moved hesitantly up behind her.

"Oh! I'm sorry—" She stopped. "Mr Alden! I'm sorry, I didn't see you—"

"It was my fault. Really it doesn't matter—" The usual painful flush of colour was lifting to his face.

Molly shook the rain from her skirt; the hem was sodden and dirty. "Wretched weather!" she muttered, more to herself than to him.

"Yes. Yes, it is." He did not move but stood uncertainly beside her. She stepped towards the counter where stood half a dozen people wating to be served. Sam followed her. She smiled at him absently, began hunting in her bag for her purse. Sam coughed; not his usual, breath-catching rasp but an embarrassed clearing of the throat. She looked at him expectantly. He was scarlet to the roots of his sandy hair.

"I wondered – that is—" Molly waited politely. " – M –

Mother's out tonight," he said, starting again. "She's gone to visit a friend in West Ham. I waited – well, I hoped – that perhaps y – you might – eat with me. Downstairs. In the kitchen."

Excuses scrambled in Molly's mind, none of them good enough. A satisfied customer moved off and the queue moved forward; as the door opened a wintry blast was let in and the barrel-organ music lifted above the seated customers' conversations, as the door shut again.

"I don't think," she said carefully, "that I should."

"Why not?" He had the stubbornness of the weak; having made the initial, impossible effort he was not going to be brushed aside so easily.

Molly chose what seemed to be the incontrovertible answer. "Your mother wouldn't like it."

"She needn't know." The reply was too quick; he had had that one planned. The queue moved forward again.

"There wouldn't be any harm in it. W – where's the sense in you eating on your own upstairs and me downstairs? Please, M – Miss O'Dowd, I would like it if you w – would—"

She had her purse out now. "I really shouldn't. I have a lot of work to do this evening—"

"Oh." Something in his face forewarned her; she lifted questioning eyebrows. "Well, I should have t – told you. I'm afraid it won't be very warm in your room yet. I haven't lit the fire. I w – was going to do it when I got back—"

She looked at him in exasperation. He looked away like a child caught in a lie, afraid to find anger in her eyes.

"You needn't pay your three ha'pence of course," he muttered and was surprised at her sudden shout of laughter.

"All right. You win. I'll eat in the kitchen. But you must light my fire first, and as soon as we've finished eating I must go up and do some work."

His smile was marvellous to see. He bought the pie and mash, refusing absolutely her offer to pay for her share. As they left the warm shop and stepped into the November darkness the barrel-organ still battled gallantly against the sound of a rising wind. Molly's purse was in her hand; she hadn't had to pay for her own supper.

"Here." She held out a coaxing hand to the monkey. "Come here, then." He scuttled forward. His master's handsome face was stony. Molly dropped two pennies into the cup, smiled at the sound and was rewarded by the antics of the little creature as it leapt delightedly onto its master's shoulder, shaking the tin. The dark face lit with the smile of a gypsy prince and the man bowed, courteously, from the waist.

"What made you do that?" Sam's voice was serious; the question was not a casual one.

She shrugged. "I'm an idiot." She only half-regretted the two-pence squandered.

And Sam, who had never done anything on impulse in his whole life, turned quickly into the rain to prevent himself from reaching for her hand.

Molly sat in a small armchair by the range and toasted her wet toes. The bottom of her skirt steamed as it dried.

Sam laid the table, one eye on the small figure by the fire.

"How are your l – lessons going?"

She was staring into the glowing cave of coals, relaxed, her mind travelling its own road. "Well, thank you," she answered absently.

"You'll be looking for a job soon?"

"Yes."

"Around here?"

She shook her head and leaned back in the chair. "No. In London, I think. That's where I'd rather work. Mr Marsden said—" She paused. Sam looked at her in question, and she shrugged deprecatingly. " – He hinted that he might know of someone who would help me. An office in the City. But I'm not banking on it. 'Tis—" almost without thinking she corrected herself " – It's by no means certain."

Knives and forks clattered as Sam took them from the drawer. She went back to her still contemplation of the fire, unaware of his eyes upon her.

"You must be lonely in London? I m – mean, you must miss your home—?"

She jumped. He had come very quietly to her side; his blunt question cut unexpectedly into her reverie. For one second, had he been capable of seeing it, her face and her unguarded eyes answered with the truth before with a flashing smile she said, "Oh no, I like it here. I'm quite settled."

"But your family? You must miss them sometimes?" He knew that she never received any letters, nor so far as he could tell did she ever write any. He knew, too, that his questions had gone further than good manners would allow; but his need to know more of this self-possessed girl with her pearly skin and wide, spacious eyes lent him an unusual courage. From the day that she had turned up on his doorstep in her pauper's clothes, her eyes cool as springwater, the almost arrogant lift of her head in such sharp contrast to her rag-bag appearance, Molly O'Dowd had never been far from his thoughts. He woke in the morning simply happy to know that she was in the house. At work the thought of her hovered just beyond the daily drudgery of Uncle Thomas's stock lists and takings, his profits and losses. At home he waited for her quick, light footsteps, listened for the sound of her unmistakable, lilting voice. The strange confusion of his feelings, the extraordinary effect that this unknown girl exerted upon him were entirely new to Sam. In his over-protected twenty-five years of life his only relationships with the opposite sex had been with a mother who alternately bullied and indulged him and with his cousin Lucy whom, it had long been accepted in the family, he would one day marry. Plain, dull Lucy. She was her father's only child; Uncle Thomas needed someone to take over the shops and if the brutal truth be told neither had any expectations elsewhere. It had until now seemed a satisfactory arrangement for all concerned. But in the past weeks Cousin Lucy's company had grown more tedious; Sam found himself making awful comparisons. Molly's bright, intelligent face, her swift and graceful movements, the impression she always gave him of being half a step ahead of the rest of the world made his cousin seem like stone to quicksilver. Now the spark that lit a dull world was here with him, hovering for a moment before she flew about her own affairs. She was looking at him composedly, his impertinent questioning about her family seeming not to have disconcerted her in the least.

"Family? I haven't any. Only an old uncle in Dublin who was as glad to see my back as I was to see his. I doubt he'll leave me any fortunes." She did not exactly know why she had lied;

except that to do so was easier. Anyway – she looked up to the mild, oddly innocent eyes above her, pale in the lamplight – what else should she do? Tell him of her family? Try to explain insupportable injustice and oppression and the blind and bloody hatred that it spawned?

Sam would not understand a word. How could he? What would he think, she wondered, had she said, "I have a brother shot dead by your soldiers, another in an English gaol, one who escaped by the seat of his breeches and a father who will no doubt one day hang, if he survives for it."?

She turned from his watching eyes towards the table, the subject closed, appalled to discover that she was having to battle an unexpected rise of crushing homesickness.

They ate almost in silence, Sam having questioned as much as he dared, Molly so wrapped in her own thoughts that she hardly spoke at all. When they had finished she left him sitting at the table and climbed the stairs. The fire, lit half an hour before, was burning brightly. She drew closed the curtains, dragged the chair towards the hearth, and picked up the book she had been studying, propping it upright on her knee to read it. Between her eyes and the page, insistently rose a vision of green hills, the quiet movement of water, laughing, volatile faces, quick to anger and as quick to tenderness. She moved the book a little further from her; it was John Marsden's book. She would not give it back to him marked with tears.

The days flew by and her precious month was nearly gone; the day inevitably came when there were just two lessons left, and her purse was distressingly light. On the Thursday afternoon of her last week she was sitting in the tiny, cold room that John Marsden had allocated to her for typewriting practice, when he walked in, pipe in one hand, a letter in the other.

Molly looked up. He was taking his time. He opened the letter, laid it upon the desk, spread the creases with his fingers, looked at her from beneath lowered brows and puffed ferociously at his pipe.

"I trust you're free next Monday morning?"

"Very," she said drily, wrinkling her nose.

"Good. Then you will present yourself at precisely eight in the morning at the offices of Josiah Richmond and Company, Bishopsgate, for the purpose of being interviewed and assessed by one—" he consulted the letter " – Mr Owen Jenkins. Who—" he added repressively, as delight lit her face " – does not, apparently, approve of employing young ladies."

Her smile faded. "Then why?"

"Mr Josiah Richmond happens to be a good friend of mine. A very good friend. Oh, no," he held up a hand as she opened her mouth, "you won't get the job on the strength of that, I promise you. Josiah is a hard-headed business man. You'll have to prove your worth before he pays you a penny. And you've a task ahead of you there, my girl, because he relies almost entirely on his Mr Jenkins' experience and advice. I've got you the chance. It's up to you to make the most of it. And in the unlikely event of your satisfying the said Mr Jenkins—" only the twinkle in his eye belied the sternness of his words and tone " – you have a permanent position with Josiah Richmond and Co. at the princely – or should it be princessly? – sum of twelve and sixpence a week. Office hours are eight till six, and until one on Saturdays. Needless to say, Mr Jenkins absolutely insists on punctuality."

"Oh, Mr Marsden, thank you! Thank you!" Molly wisely restrained herself from jumping up and throwing her arms about his neck. "I won't let you down. I promise I won't."

He puffed at his pipe, smiled one of his rare, craggy smiles. "Between you, me and that typewriter, Miss O'Dowd, I didn't for a moment think that you would."

CHAPTER EIGHT

As was to be expected, Monday turned out to be both as bad as she had feared and much better than she had dared to hope. Having woken ridiculously early to the miserable, sulphurous yellow light of late November she was so anxious not to be late that she arrived at the office half an hour before anyone else and had to hang about in the clammy cold, her hair and clothes festooned with glimmering beads of moisture, until someone arrived to open the door.

Her first impression of her place of work somewhat dismayed her. Whatever she had expected (and she was not certain herself what that was) it had not been a series of gloomy and rather dirty rooms lit constantly by the yellow glare of bare electric light bulbs, crammed with chipped and battered office furniture, the walls and ceilings painted a particularly depressing shade of mushroom, the few tiny windows opening onto a narrow, ill-lit alley. She was happily surprised however by the attitude of her fellow workers; she had been prepared for some hostility to the introduction of a female into their until-now exclusively masculine world, but on the whole her reception was very pleasant, the inevitable interested and curious glances reasonably well hidden. There was some little embarrassment about the toilet facilities; since there was only one lavatory, and since Mr Richmond had not yet come to a decision regarding the employment of other females and had no intention of squandering his money on further conveniences until he had, the arrangement had been made for Molly to use a toilet on the second floor of the building in an office that already employed several girls. She thanked the pink-faced lad who had been given the task of passing on these details and asked if he knew when she was to meet Mr Jenkins.

He pulled a fearsome and sympathetic face. "Right now, I'm afraid," he said and led her along another inevitably mushroom corridor to a door with the name "Owen Jenkins" emblazoned upon the frosted glass. Outside the door he stopped, his eyes on Molly, his hand poised to knock. "You're sure you don't want to change your mind?" he hissed below his breath. "People have come out of this room in pieces before now—" But before she could reply he brought his knuckles into sharp contact with the glass.

Within moments of entering his office Molly's preconceived notions of Mr Jenkins had been confirmed. Owen Jenkins did not simply have his doubts about young ladies working, he positively and obdurately disliked them. The office manager was a tall, thin-faced, austerely handsome man with a hard, narrow mouth and disappointed eyes. His person, like his office, was immaculately tidy, his voice light and almost toneless. Before his uncompromising and unfriendly gaze Molly felt herself shrivel like paper consumed by a flame. In the corner of the room were a small table and a chair, and on the table a typewriting machine and several sheets of paper. With teeth clenched so nervously that they ached from the pressure she settled herself to the test.

She need not have worried; despite Mr Jenkins' thinly veiled disapprobation she passed, and she knew it, with flying colours; he could not fault her. He examined her work with an eagle eye, spoke in his fast, expressionless voice and then catechized her sharply upon what he had said, invited her opinion on several matters and then dismissed what she said with unsmiling dispatch. She held her nerves and her temper in check, spoke quietly and courteously, refrained, though she was never afterwards sure how, from throwing the inkpot at him. When she, battered but far from broken, finally emerged from the battlefield into the mushroom corridor she knew she had not let John Marsden down, and the thought gave her pleasure; though not as much pleasure as the discovery that she was not actually to work for Mr Jenkins but in one of the outer offices with a senior clerk, Mr Vassal, whose main attitude to Molly seemed at first one of mild confusion, but whose quiet and kindly nature was some antidote to the abrasive Mr Jenkins. She spent the afternoon learning her tasks and responsibilities, trying to remember names and faces. By the end of the day she was exhausted but not at all unhappy, her head like a child's kaleidoscope of shifting patterns and impressions. As she donned her coat to leave a group of young clerks passed the open door of the office, among them the lad who had taken her to Mr Jenkins. He smiled as he caught sight of her and lifted a cheery hand.

"G'night. See you tomorrow."

She nodded. "Good night."

She belonged. Mr Jenkins or no, she belonged.

She went to sleep on the train and nearly missed her station.

By the end of the week she had made absolutely certain that not even Mr Owen Jenkins could give any good reason for refusing to employ her, and on Friday afternoon she was summoned into his office to hear her fate.

With hands not quite steady she brushed down her skirt, rubbed at but could not erase the inkstain on her finger, received a vague but kindly smile from 'her' Mr Vassal, and went. Fifteen minutes later, after an interview in which Mr Jenkins left no doubt in either of their minds that he was certain that, sooner or later, his poor opinion of women in general was bound to be confirmed in her even though she had managed to avoid it so far, she emerged with the security of a permanent position with Josiah Richmond and Co. and a conviction that Mr Owen Jenkins was quite the most exasperating and unpleasant man she had ever come across. His inference that her continued employment with the company was due as much to John Marsden's influence with its founder as to her own abilities did nothing to temper this feeling. However, for the moment at least, her predominant emotion was one of triumphant happiness. She had surmounted the first hurdle.

Later that afternoon she received her wages. Twelve and six. As good as a fortune. Last night she had had sixpence ha'penny left in her purse . . .

In the weeks that followed Molly worked hard and settled happily at Richmond and Co. despite Mr Jenkins and his iron-bound regime. Although the lack of anyone of her own sex in the office precluded any close friendship, she was on pleasant terms with most of her fellow workers. She particularly liked old Mr Vassal, liked him and pitied him, for his bumbling and sometimes downright incompetent ways earned him no favour from Owen Jenkins, whose contempt would not always be confined to the privacy of Mr Vassal's own office. Molly took more and more upon herself; sometimes she wondered a little grimly if she were not doing more than Mr Vassal, but she did not truly mind. All of her efforts were made worthwhile by her growing feeling of independence; each Friday evening she laid the money for her rent on Ellen Alden's kitchen table, and never without a wave of pride. She was saving, too; not much, but saving nevertheless. She was not herself certain why she scraped and saved in order to add a few coins each week to the growing pile that she kept in an Oxo tin at the bottom of her wardrobe; but when her shoes finally fell to pieces on her feet and she had to dip into the red tin to buy new ones she was furious and lived on scraps for a week, determined, penny by penny, to replace it.

The month of December was tediously wet and foggy. Sam's cough was racking; she noticed that he was often at home. They had seen little of each other since that awkward evening they had spent together, and such contact as was made was usually with Ellen present or, as before, on landing, hall or stairs.

Ellen's attitude to Molly was pleasant enough. If the girl paid her rent, kept herself to herself, was clean and tidy, there was no particular reason why she should not stay. If the unfortunate, gypsy hair and the pale oval of her face were a little too extravagantly inviting of attention it was hardly the girl's fault, any more than a hare lip or a club foot might have been. She did not, as Ellen had first feared, flaunt herself; on the contrary, as she worked longer and longer hours the eyes grew more tired-looking, the face thinner, that sudden, flashing smile was less in evidence and the pearly glow of skin faded a little.

As Christmas approached and the dark cold nights grew longer Molly discovered books again. She borrowed them mostly from Sam who was delighted to oblige – or bought them second hand from a stall in Liverpool Street, and devoured them night after night and all day Sunday. She hated the empty thought of the coming festive season so, typically, she absolutely ignored it, burying the thought in her fantasy world of books, telling herself that she had all that she needed there. Sam introduced her to the local lending library, where for a ha'penny she could borrow any book she liked. She was delighted, and so was he, for even his mother could not object to an occasional excursion to the library, and although their conversation on these occasions was almost entirely on the impersonal subject of books, it was better than nothing; at least he could watch the animated face as she talked, laugh when she laughed.

Christmas crept inexorably closer; it would not be ignored, though Molly obstinately did her best. One Saturday afternoon she arrived home to find Ellen and Sam preparing to go on a Christmas outing – they were taking the tram to Stratford Broadway to look at the decorations and shops, to visit the Christmas bazaars – and Ellen, softened by the season and encouraged with unusual subtlety by Sam, suggested that Molly might like to accompany them.

There was nothing in the world that Molly wanted to do less. She had been working all morning, had come in tired and cold and with a novel she had bought for a penny from the second-hand stall outside the station. It was wet outside, and almost freezing.

"I—" She hesitated, aware of clear pleading in Sam's eyes, of dawning displeasure in his mother's. "Thank you," she said, "I'd love to come. If you'll just give me a minute to change my jacket. This one's wet—"

Cursing herself she ran to her room. As she took the dry jacket from the wardrobe she stopped for a moment to look sadly at the forget-me-not silk shirt and beautifully cut satin-trimmed skirt that hung beside it. What had possessed her to buy such things? They had never been worn. Nor, she reflected sourly, were they ever likely to be – in no good temper she slammed the door shut, watched herself in the mirror as she struggled into the jacket.

Damn Stratford Broadway in the rain! Damn Sam and his wretched mother! Damn Christmas!

She stopped, staring at herself, one arm awkwardly half-in a sleeve. Christmas. What was she going to do? Midnight Mass. Irish voices lifted in golden song, her father's soaring exultantly above all until she thought she would burst with pain and pride. Christmas dinner; always Christmas dinner, no matter how hard the times. Since that evening in the kitchen with Sam her homesickness had been buried, defeated by hard work and by her own refusal to take note of its existence. But Christmas . . !

Sam and his mother were going to Uncle Thomas, everyone in the office had been talking of their Christmas plans almost ever since she had joined them. Everyone with somewhere to go; everyone but her. What would she do?

She shoved her arm roughly into the sleeve. "Sleep!" she said savagely to her reflection. "That's what you'll do, my girl. Sleep!" and the thought of a day's undisturbed rest almost cheered her.

Stratford Broadway, even in the drizzle, was a sight for sore eyes; against her expectations Molly was both impressed and delighted. They wandered along pavements thronged with crowds of happy Christmas shoppers, cheerful even in the rain. The shop windows were an enchantment, the magical essence of Christmas, candled and cribbed, dressed with greenstuff, smooth laurel and sharp holly. In one window a great cathedral cake, a miracle of spun sugar and snowy icing drew an awe-struck crowd. "Ooh, they won't *eat* it, will they?" asked one youngster unbelievingly. Even further down the wide street came the sound of carols, enthusiastically played by a brass band; people sang as they walked, a girl in Salvation Army uniform shyly held out a collection box. Sam put his hand in his pocket and with obvious pleasure, beneath his mother's approving smile, dropped a penny in the box.

"A very happy Christmas to you, Sir, Ladies. And God bless you."

He ducked his head, pleased, his eyes sliding to Molly's face. "Are you glad you came now?" She hadn't fooled him.

There was no need to ask. It was impossible not to be affected by the atmosphere. Molly's despondency had slipped from her; her wide eyes were shining with the reflection of the rain-reflecting Christmas lights, her face glowed like a child's. Sam, as he had on the night of the hurdy-gurdy man, experienced a dangerous urge to reach for her hand; he moved around to the other side of his mother and took her arm.

They strolled down the Broadway, deafened by the rattling trams, smiling at the horse-drawn vehicles, ordinary carts dressed to carnival in festive decorations. They bought hot chestnuts and Sam and Molly laughed like children as they jumped them from hand to hand trying to peel them.

It was as they crossed the road by the station that in the midst of laughter Molly saw a pair of sad, young-old eyes, rat's tail hair, a thin, grimy face. The little girl, inadequately clothed and with boots on her stockingless feet two sizes too large that made Molly wince to see them, was carrying a tray of odds and ends, calling inaudibly against the noisy crowds. Pushed and buffeted she was ignored by most passers-by, except as a nuisance to be avoided or cursed. Molly took out her purse. Ellen looked at her with dark, astonished eyes.

"What on earth are you doing?"

"Here—" Molly beckoned to the child, holding out two pennies. The enormous, hunger-drawn eyes fixed upon the money. "I'll take—" she searched among the worthless oddments, " – this." She held up an absurdly ugly statuette, a plaster thing, chipped and badly painted, of a small boy and a dog. "Is this enough?" she said, holding out the twopence. The damp, dirty head moved in affirmation. She dropped the coins on the tray and straightened to find Ellen and Sam looking at her as if she had taken leave of her senses.

"And what," asked Sam's mother in a tone of immutable disbelief, "do you intend to do with that?"

Molly felt a nerveless, uncontrolled happiness rising. Oh, it had been so very long since she had felt so. "I intend," she said very seriously, "to give it to Sam for Christmas," and solemnly she held it out to him. For a nonplussed second he was caught between her apparent sincerity in offering the awful thing and the expression of outraged disbelief on his mother's face. Then he caught the smouldering light of mischief in her eyes and a grin wide enough to split his cheekbones spread across his face.

"And I," he said, managing in the middle of a crowded pavement an extraordinarily adventurous imitation of a bow, "would be pleased to accept it."

Their sudden laughter rang so loud that passers-by turned, smiling.

"Sam! Miss O'Dowd, please—" but the occasion and the atmosphere even overcame Ellen Alden's sober nature and she could not but smile with them. It was that smile which tempted Sam to his mistake.

"Oh, Mother, wouldn't it be nice – I mean, couldn't Miss O'Dowd come to Uncle's with us for Christmas. It doesn't seem right to leave her on her own——"

Molly flinched, her laughter frozen hard upon her lips. Ellen Alden's laughter might never have been; suddenly still, she regarded her son with suspicious and forbidding eyes. Molly turned sharply away to study, unseeing, a decorated window. Sam's mother watched the colour lifting in the delicate profile, had a sudden vision of her niece's blurred and unbecoming features.

"No," she said in a tone which defied argument. "I'm afraid that wouldn't be possible, as you should know. Your Aunt Maude has quite enough to do."

"But——"

Ellen held up a stony hand. "I'm sorry, Sam." She inclined her head to Molly. "Miss O'Dowd, it isn't possible." Her voice was icy.

" 'Tis no matter." Molly broke in before Sam could protest, making a miserable situation worse. "Truly, 'tis no matter." She was unaware that her accent had become more pronounced. "We never made much of Christmas at home."

The pleasure had gone from the afternoon; the crowds jostled and pushed, the lights were suddenly tawdry in the rain, and though Sam, stubbornly clinging to the ridiculous statuette that Molly had given him, tried once or twice to start a conversation, they were all too quiet on their way home. And more than once Molly caught Ellen Alden's thoughtful eyes moving from herself to Sam, alive with vague suspicion.

On the day before Christmas in honour of the season, the staff of Richmond and Co. were told they were to be given a whole hour off; the office was to be closed at five o'clock. An atmosphere of raggedly suppressed excitement built all day, an atmosphere in which Molly felt she had very little share. She smiled and returned seasonal good wishes pleasantly enough, but her heart was not in it. When the hour to leave had arrived she quietly cleared her desk, smilingly wished everyone a happy Christmas and walked with heavy heart into the dreary wet night.

*

82

Number twenty-six was empty when she at last reached it, having fought her way through merry crowds of last-minute shoppers and early-start revellers to get there, empty and cold and utterly devoid of life. Nothing of Christmas here; she scowled and told herself defiantly that she did not care. She lit the ready-laid fire, piling on the coal until the bright and comforting flames leapt in the chimney, sheaves of sparks flying into the darkness. It was not until then that she noticed, lying on the table, a clumsily-wrapped parcel with a sprig of holly tucked awkwardly into its folds. Sam. His the forethought that had laid the fire ready for a match, his the almost endearingly inept touch in the inefficiently wrapped parcel. She picked up the package, and the paper fell away to reveal a book, brand new and smelling tangily of leather. She held it to the light and smiled; the only book that could truly have cheered her, the book that she remembered from clandestine happy lessons with Mary Living-stone, the book she had mentioned just once in passing to Sam as being the book she loved most, and had laughed as she'd said it, thinking to make light of a silly passion for a children's book, expecting scorn. But Sam's inner ear, sensitive to every tone of her voice, had recognized the truth, and here in her hand was *Alice's Adventures in Wonderland*, a beautiful edition bound in dark-blue leather with tooled, gold lettering on the cover and heavy, shiny pages that crackled as she turned them, their golden edges glittering in the moving firelight. The pictures were protected by leaves of fine tissue which rustled beneath her fingers; serious, straight-haired Alice followed the white rabbit, spoke solemnly to the Mock Turtle, stamped her foot at the pack of cards. It was the loveliest book that Molly had ever seen. She took her present to the fireside, settled herself into the chair, opened the book.

"Alice was beginning to get very tired of sitting by her sister on the bank . . ."

Her Christmas was saved.

CHAPTER NINE

THE LAST NEW Year of the century came in on a blast of brutally cold weather; the water froze in the pipes, the bleak, black-iced mornings made it hard to creep from bed, the sharp wind cut cruelly through clothes that were never intended to withstand such Arctic temperatures. Halfway through January Molly developed a cough that almost rivalled Sam's; the man in the chemist's shop tutted in a fatherly way and gave her some linctus, which she took when she remembered it, which wasn't very often. There was, she could not help noticing, some considerable strain between Sam and his mother; it appeared that over Christmas something had happened that had not pleased Ellen Alden, although Molly had no inkling as to what it might have been. She sensed, however, that Sam was avoiding her, guessed that he was under some duress from his strong-willed parent and made no move that might make his – or her own – life more difficult. She managed gracefully to thank him for his present at a time when Ellen was out of earshot, and detected the gratitude in his eyes for the thought. The previous, slight softening of Ellen's attitude towards Molly was gone; there were now no extra cups of tea, no friendly pieces of cake, and Ellen and Sam had almost always finished their meal and pointedly moved into their sitting room by the time Molly came in at night.

As January drew to a close her cough grew steadily worse and the cold weather showed no sign of a break. It snowed; not the soft and pretty flakes of fantasy but nasty, stinging, wind-blown particles of ice that flayed the face and caused one to slip on the hardened ground. Molly began to experience little, stabbing pains in her chest when she hurried or got out of breath, and the cold seemed to make her permanently tired. For two nights running she had not had the energy to shop for food and again she plodded miserably home, climbed thankfully into bed without eating and slept through an uneasy, dream-filled night to awaken next day with a foul mouth and a head that splintered each time she coughed or set foot to the ground. She paid another visit to the chemist, was given powders for her headache and trudged to work. On the fourth day she lifted a head that felt as if it were filled with molten wax to find Mr Vassal's eyes fixed worriedly upon her.

"Are you feeling unwell, Miss O'Dowd?"

She cleared a throat which over the past few hours had become painful to the point of closing.

"A little."

The kindly glance took in the hectic colour, the fever-bright, heavy-lidded eyes. "You should not have come out today with the weather as it is. I think you should ask Mr Jenkins' permission to leave early. I can finish up here alone—"

Molly opened her mouth to protest, but subsided without speaking. She felt awful. Her joints were stiff, her skin dry and sore. The thought of bed, of warmth and quiet and darkness, was a vision of Heaven.

She made her way to Mr Jenkins' door and knocked.

There was, as always, a small, significant pause before the quiet voice said, "Come."

He looked up as she entered, his eyes questioning. "Yes?"

"I'm sorry to bother you, Mr Jenkins." Her voice cracked and she cleared her throat painfully. "I'm afraid I'm feeling very unwell. Mr Vassal suggested that you might allow me to go home."

The eyes raked her, turned back to the pile of papers on his desk. "Did he indeed?"

She bit her lip, detesting equally him and the weakness that had brought her here.

Owen Jenkins picked up a pen, made a small mark alongside a column of figures, then looked back at her. "You presumably felt well enough to come to work this morning?" the question was coolly polite.

"Yes." Her answer was neither; anger and resentment boiled in the one word.

He raised sardonic eyebrows. "It has always been my contention that women make more of such matters than do men. I suggest, Miss O'Dowd, that you go back to your work. Tomorrow is Saturday. If you are still – unwell – then I suppose you may take the morning off." He returned to his work, the interview, such as it was, at an end.

Molly passed the rest of the day in a haze of discomfort and pain. Her throat grew worse; it was painful to swallow or to speak, impossible to eat. Her head throbbed viciously; her chest hurt when she drew breath. Mr Vassal watched her struggle until five o'clock before saying with a vehemence totally unlike his usually indecisive tone, "That is enough, Molly. Home, at once. I insist."

She seemed only barely to grasp what he was saying.

"But—"

"But nothing. Off with you. And don't come back until you're better. If Mr Jenkins wants to know where you are I'll tell him. Now off you go."

The bitter air hit her like a physical blow; flakes of snow whirled in dizzying dance past her unfocussed eyes. She plodded down the dark street in the direction of the station, hardly knowing how to put one foot before the other, her teeth clenched against the hammer-blows of pain that shattered her head at every step. She leaned for a moment in a doorway, gasping for breath. Her chest felt as if a slowly constricting band of iron had been forged around it. For a frightening minute the dark world was bright as brilliant flashes of colour lit her mind and her body flushed with fever. Then she was back in an unbearable misery of cold and darkness, shivering, with the station, the train and home seeming limitless miles away. She felt tears rising, forced them down, something like panic moving in her. Part of her mind was still clear enough to know that she was ill. Really ill. She must get home. The Aldens would get a doctor. She would be safe if she could just get to Linsey Grove. . . .

She struggled on, turned blindly into Bishopsgate. There she had to stop again, leaning against a wall, fighting with desperation to regain her breath. The wind gusted, invincibly cold and laden with stinging pellets of ice. She knew beyond doubt that she could not make it as far as the station. As she stood there a horse-drawn omnibus drew up beside her. The open, wind-whipped roof was empty, the lit interior looked crowded, but not to capacity. The windows were steamed against the cold, the yellow glow of the lamps a pool of comparative comfort in a comfortless world. " – West Ham, Plaistow, Upton Park Station, East Ham Town Hall—" the conductor called as the car came to a halt.

She could not move another step. Thankfully she stumbled onto the bus and sank onto a seat, out of the wind at last.

"How close do you go to Linsey Grove, Upton Park?"

The man shook his head. "No idea, luv. Never 'eard of it. Upton Park Station do you?"

She nodded, paid for her ticket. As she laid her burning face to the cold, running-wet glass of the window the world tilted and swayed wildly around her. Her skin felt as if it had been burned, every nerve-end raw; it was all she could do to breathe. She set herself to survive the nightmare. The vehicle jogged and jolted, stopped and started, time contracted, expanded, spun in frightening circles inside her head. . . .

She jumped awake, panic-stricken at the conductor's call; she had missed her stop. No she hadn't, she was here; this was it. She came to her feet like a sleepwalker and pushed with the other passengers along the body of the bus and out onto the street.

By the time she realized that the freezing, sleet-blasted street was totally strange to her it was too late – the omnibus had gone, and she was alone.

Jack and Charley Benton strode, heads down into the wind, broad shoulders hunched to their ears, towards home and a good hot supper. They were both big men, hardly an inch between them for height, Jack perhaps the stockier of the two. They walked fast and easily, hands in pockets, caps well down over their eyes. It was Charley who almost fell over the small figure that stumbled from the shadow of a high wall obliquely across his path.

"Hell's bells. What's this?" He regained his balance easily; the girl with whom he had collided staggered away from him and grabbed at a lamp post to stop herself from falling. She clung to the post muttering, her odd, silvered eyes gleaming in the light.

"Drunk? By God, she's drunk!" Charley laughed, preparing to step past her and go on his way. "Tight as ninepence! Can't say I blame her, mind. One way to keep the cold out—"

"Wait." Jack put a restraining hand on his arm. "I'm not so sure she *is* drunk."

He stepped forward. The girl hardly seemed aware of him. Her eyes were upon him, but with no focus; burning with fever they looked through and beyond him, dazed and frightened. Her face was peony bright, the sockets of the light, feverish eyes bruised and shadowed. She was trembling violently.

"The lass is *ill*."

As if in confirmation of his words she coughed, but Molly neither saw them nor heard them. Her head was a mass of raging pain, her throat raw and swollen against her ragged breath. She coughed again, convulsively and as she doubled under the tearing force of it had to let go of the post. Suddenly, uncaringly she pitched into darkness.

She came from a cave of confusion into gentle, quiet light; the light of a glowing fire in a twilit room. She felt incredibly frail, shatteringly weak, almost as if her body no longer existed, as if only nerve remained to awake. She knew this room; she had seen it before, through a blaze of fever, when a tall man with an impatient voice had forced something sharp and painful into her mouth, had felt her wrist and her back and the hard cage beneath her breast with cold, efficient fingers. The bitter taste of medicine was still in her mouth. She had seen this room too, night-shadowed, though never in total darkness; always there had been the faint glow of the fire, the tiny flame of a night-light on the table. And always on those dark occasions she had been aware of a reassuring presence; never had she been left to fend off her fears alone, always there had been a warm, motherly strength that had tethered her firmly when, after the fever, the chill weightlessness of her body had tempted her to drift away. A warm strong hand had held her then, prevented her from slipping into the peaceful dark. There were faces, she thought, that belonged to this room, but she could not for the moment bring them to mind. It didn't matter. She was happy to lie, unmoving, half-asleep. She could hear voices from beyond the door, hushed talk, quiet laughter, the subdued clatter of living.

As with the room, the voices, with their slight, strange accent, had a familiarity; they too belonged to that odd, timeless emptiness that seemed to have taken some part of her life. Where was she? How had she got here? She had not the slightest idea, nor could she bring herself greatly to care. She was warm, comfortable and safe; and she could feel within herself the first stirrings of returning life. That was enough. And with a deep, sighing breath she fell back to sleep again.

When next she opened her eyes the fireside chair was occupied; a girl sat, straight-backed, her smooth head bent over a complicated spider's web of crochet, the hook slipping through the threads with delicate and practised speed, slender, bony hands flying in constant motion. Despite the long, soft, brown hair that was coiled in a tidy bun on the nape of her neck there was a look of boyishness about the figure; her face was spare-boned and serious, her body not soft nor rounded but athletically slim and straight. Molly watched her from beneath lowered lashes, struck by the grace of the sloping shoulders, the bent head. Then she became aware of someone else; a young man was seated on the floor on the far side of the chair. Molly could only see the top of a head of brown-blond hair and one strong narrow hand, undoubtedly male, flung across the girl's knee. As she watched the hand reached for the yarn and tweaked it, teasing; the girl slapped the hand away hard, though she smiled indulgently.

"Nuisance! Haven't you got anything better to do? Go and find someone else to pester—" The broad vowels and stressed syllables had no origin in London; they were northern, Molly guessed, though she could not place the accent exactly. Neither of the two by the fire had noticed that she was awake.

The young man stretched and came to his knees, his face towards Molly. Her half-closed lashes flickered and lifted as the shadowed light moved on a sharp-cut, smiling mouth, sparked blue in the clear-arched, heavy-lashed eyes. His hair was the colour of dark honey, thick and feathered like a child's; his skin was brown and smooth over strong, fine bones. Beside him the girl looked ordinary, almost plain. He had an arm across her shoulders, coaxing, and was about to speak when his eyes strayed above her head to Molly's corner and he paused.

"Well I'll be – our sleeping beauty's back with us from the look of it—" echoes of the north in his voice too.

The girl in the chair turned sharply. When her eyes met Molly's her face lit with a smile and she laid down her work.

"Go fetch Mam, Harry."

She came to Molly still smiling, a little shy, her brown eyes searching the wan face.

"Hello. Are you feeling better?"

Molly moved her head on the pillow. "Yes. Thank you—"

The girl held up an admonishing finger. "Lie still, now, Dr Adams said you'd be very weak when you woke. Harry! I asked you to go and tell Mam."

Harry was standing at the foot of the couch, his head on one side, his smooth-chiselled features alight with sympathetic interest. He was undoubtedly the most beautiful person Molly had ever seen.

"Harry!"

"I'm going." His voice was slightly husky, pleasant to the ear. With a swift grin he turned and left the room.

The brown-haired girl perched on the edge of the couch beside Molly. "I'm Nancy Benton. That was my brother Harry. Do you remember anything? Do you know where you are?"

Molly shook her head helplessly.

"You're in our house in West Ham. Jack and Charley; they're my brothers, too—" her smile widened, " – we've a houseful of men – found you wandering in the street. You were very ill. We were afraid—" she stopped. "Are you certain you feel better?"

"Truly I do. I'm sorry. I must have put you to a lot of trouble." Molly was warmed by the girl's obviously sincere concern, by the look in the kind dark eyes. "How long have I been here?"

"Since late last Friday. It's Wednesday evening now—"

"Five days!" Molly struggled to sit up, all her languor falling from her. Her job! Her room! The movement started her coughing, and she was horrified to discover that she had not the strength even to lift herself to her elbows. She dropped weakly back into the pillows, her eyes filling with tears.

"Oh please don't. Don't cry. You mustn't upset yourself—" The girl clasped her hand in a firm warm grip, " – you *must* rest.

The doctor said so. You're not to fret."

"Well, well. What's this then?" Another voice, very like Nancy's but with the accent stronger. Molly remembered this voice from the far reaches of a painful night, her hand, too, recognized the firm, roughened touch that took the place of Nancy's. This was the strength that had held her when her own had been vanquished, this the will that had supported hers in the battle against peaceful, tempting darkness. The eyes were darker than Nancy's, almost black, and the face marked with the years and with hardship; but in line and feature and lift of bone here was the beauty she had just seen in Harry, but tempered by time and without the arrogance of the young man's face.

"Tears now?" A work-hardened hand brushed gently the damp curls from Molly's forehead; Sarah Benton smiled at the frail girl whom she had watched over as she would have one of her own, whom she had coddled from the moment Jack had carried her, a helpless, failing child, into the house. "Harry said that you were feeling better?"

Molly, disgusted at her helplessness, simply could not stop the tears of weakness that rolled down her face. "I am," she whispered, sniffing. "Yes, I am." She blinked, ashamed of the silly tears, aware of their eyes upon her. "My name's Molly," she added more calmly. "Molly O'Dowd."

Harry leaned over the back of the couch, his face solemn, "How do, Molly O'Dowd. Pleased to meet you." His eyes were warm and glittered like the summer sea in sunshine. "Welcome back to the land of the living. Once or twice there we thought we'd lost you. When our Jack brought you in you looked like a drowned kitten—"

She managed a watery counterfeit of a smile. "I really must get up. There are things I must do. I have to contact the office. Please—"

"Later." Sarah held up an authoritative hand as Molly opened her mouth to protest. "Anything that needs doing the lads'll do for you. And the first thing is to contact your family, they must be going wild with worry. If you'll tell us your address Jack'll—" she stopped. Molly was shaking her head, the tears still running, sideways, into her hair.

"I don't have any family."

Nancy looked truly shocked. "None at all?"

"Not here. Not in London." Too much to try to explain.

"Is there someone else we should get in touch with?"

She gave them both Richmond's and the Aldens' address; the irrational panic was still churning in her stomach. "I must owe a week's rent if I didn't get home on Friday night." The tear-drenched eyes were huge in a face that had thinned pathetically.

"Our Jack'll see to it for you. Don't worry about it. I doubt they've put your things into the street just yet." Sarah Benton patted and smoothed the pillows.

Molly managed another wobbly smile. "I wouldn't be too sure of that."

"Well if they have," Harry was grinning from ear to ear, "I expect our Jack'll see to that too."

Somewhere in the house a door slammed and a child's treble called, "Mam? Mam!"

"That's our kid." Nancy stood up, smoothing her skirts, "It's all right, Mam, I'll see to him. I'll come and see you later if you like?" she said smiling at Molly.

"Yes, please." Looking into the smiling, boyish face a feeling of happy warmth washed over Molly; a family, a home, and herself for however short a time part of it. The tears had stopped. She touched Sarah's hand, "I don't know how to thank you."

"You can thank us by being a good lass and doing as you're told so that you get better. We don't want all our trouble for nothing, do we? Now—" Sarah said, standing up briskly " – something to eat, I think. Out you go, Harry, leave the lass in peace. She needs to rest."

Later Nancy came back to sit with her, bringing her crochet work, pulling her chair up next to the couch. Neither of them said much; Molly lay drowsily on her pillows, happy simply to have the other girl's company. Sometimes when she opened her eyes she found Nancy watching her. They smiled as their eyes met and friendship grew quietly as a flower in the tranquil room.

About an hour after Nancy had joined her she heard an outer door bang, the sound of booted feet and men's voices, swiftly hushed.

Nancy lifted her head. "Jack and Charley," she said, "They'll be glad to know you're feeling better."

"They were the ones who found me?"

Nancy bit through a strand of yarn with sharp teeth. "Mmm. They were on their way home from work – they work together in the docks. You walked right into them, I think."

"I don't remember."

"I'm not surprised. You were in a terrible state."

They fell silent for a moment listening to the noises in the room next door, then Molly asked, suddenly shy, "Do you have any more brothers that I don't know about?"

"Lord, no." Nancy smiled Harry's wide, unselfconscious smile. "Thank goodness. The ones you've heard about are quite enough, believe me. Jack's the eldest – he's been sort of head of the family since Dad died five years ago – then there's Charley who's—" she thought for a moment " – twenty-three in a few weeks' time. Then there's Harry, you met him earlier, he's twenty-one, then me, then our kid, Edward. He's a lot younger, not six yet. He was born just before we came to London—" It seemed to Molly that something in her tone had changed, but before she could recognize the new note in Nancy's voice there was a rap on the door.

Nancy put down her work. "Yes?"

The door opened a little way and a head appeared, surprisingly close to the top of the door; more dark blond hair crowned a broad and ruddy face. "It's me. Can we come and see the invalid? Mam says she's woken up."

Nancy looked at Molly. "This is Charley. Can you stand it?"

"Of course."

Molly's eyes widened as the two came into the room. They were giants; two pairs of wide shoulders, six-foot dockers' frames that seemed to fill the small room. Jack in particular gave the impression of a rock-like strength. They both stood a little awkwardly at the foot of the couch.

Charley grinned. "You're looking better than you did."

"And a sight better than I'd have been if you'd not found me. Thank you."

"Don't thank me. It was Jack realized you were bad. He brought you home. Mam and Nancy did the rest."

The luminous eyes transferred their gaze to Jack. "Thank you," she said again.

"Don't mention it, lass." His voice was deep and quiet and had in it something of his mother's calm authority. "Mam says you've some errands for us to run?" He was smiling. He had neither Harry's startling beauty nor Charley's merry expression, but the blue eyes were there, an inheritance, apparently, from a dead father, more peaceful in his face than in either of his brothers' and it seemed to Molly that though this one had less of beauty he had more of strength.

"I don't want to put you to more trouble."

"It's no trouble."

Molly let her head drop back into the pillows and smiled. The thought had occurred to her that Saint Patrick might well have been somewhere in the streets of West Ham last Friday night.

CHAPTER TEN

IT WAS TWO weeks before she was strong enough to get up, and during that time she became an unquestionably accepted part of the Benton family, her couch the centre of the social life of the household. No one passed the door without popping in to speak to her, to bring a book or a magazine, to tell of the day's incidents. As her strength returned she was happier than she had been for months. Nancy, quite openly delighted to have a girl of her own age in the house, became her special companion and would make a point of hurrying home from her work at a nearby dress factory to be with Molly. The boys, each in their own way, did their best to make the little stranger feel at home: Harry teased her and made her laugh; Charley treated her with the same easy and open friendliness that he apparently showed to the rest of the world; and Jack, though a little more reserved than the others, was kind, considerate and above all practical. It was he who wrote the letter explaining to Mr Vassal what had happened. He, too, who visited Linsey Grove, told the Aldens what had happened, paid the rent and brought back their good wishes, which he relayed with just enough of Ellen's repressive lack of enthusiasm to make Molly smile. When she talked worriedly of repaying the money, both for the rent and for the doctor's bills, he waved her aside.

"Not now, lass. Later'll do. When you're back on your feet. We're not short of a penny or two at the moment, with us all working. Settle with us later, when you're ready."

She had another friend, too, the biggest charmer of the whole family, as she discovered the day after her awakening. Edward, the baby of the family, known to one and all as "our kid" had eyes of velvet brown like his mother's, which sparkled with the mischief of an indulged and loving child. His smooth, still-baby cheeks were peaches and cream, his hair a mass of fair curls that would, no doubt as his big brothers' had, darken as he grew up, but that at present had the glint of new-minted coins. He soon discovered that the interesting stranger who was occupying his mother's front room was not the kind of grown up who objected to pet spiders in matchboxes, or bullseye-sticky fingers, and became Molly's fast friend. After the quiet daytime hours with Sarah, Molly came to look forward to the slam of the door that told of Edward's return from his lessons, though there could be no denying that his company could be tiring; he would ask a question, answer it himself and change the subject all in one breath. Often, when the child was occupied at the table or stretched on his stomach on the hearth rug turning the pages of a book her lids would close and she would drowse.

One evening in the second week of her recovery she did just this, to awaken later to find Harry in the chair and no sign of Edward. Harry was watching her with vivid, smiling eyes. In his hand he held a small bunch of violets.

She blinked, still half asleep, "Where's Edward?"

"I threatened him." He grinned at her suddenly wide eyes, "With twopence."

Molly laughed. She must have slept for some time; from the room next door came the sounds of the family, home for the evening. There appeared to be some kind of heated discussion in progress; she heard Jack's voice, and Charley's, rather louder than usual, raised and vehement.

Harry leaned forward and laid the small bunch of flowers into her hand. They were cool and soft and full of the gentle promise of spring. She lifted them to her face, for a moment unable to speak. Then she said in a whisper, "I'm always saying thank you."

"That must be why we do things for you. Because you say thank you so nicely."

The raised voices lifted again: Charley's, Jack's somewhat quieter, then Nancy's, sharp and irritated. The door opened, and Nancy marched in, still speaking over her shoulder to the others. " – and if I have to listen to another word about Keir Hardie *or* the blessed Labour Party I shall break something. Over your thick head, probably. I'm sick of—Oh, hello, Harry. Didn't know you were home." Her eyes moved to Molly and the violets. "Oh, aren't they sweet!" Her laughing eyes flitted back to her brother. "Did you bring some for me?"

"As a matter of fact I did," Harry said. "But I met Nelly

Morris down the road, so I gave them to her instead. One of these days, my girl," he added sternly, "the wind'll change and you'll stay like that."

Nancy rearranged her face into a more normal expression and dropped into the vacated chair. "Why don't you go out and practise your razor wit on them?" She jerked her head towards the open door. "Charley's on his soap box again. Been down to the King's Head, I should think."

Harry put together pious hands and lifted his eyes to Heaven. "The Lord preserve us from Charley, Keir Hardie, Will Thorne, the Trade Unions, Organized Labour, the minimum wage—" He stopped, running out of steam and looking at Nancy. "What else?"

"You," she said succinctly, and Molly giggled.

" – He'll be back—" said Charley's voice through the door " – Hardie'll be back, you'll see, and then West Ham'll know what it is again to have a Labour Member of Parliament."

"Charley Benton." Mam's voice, quiet and cutting. Harry and Nancy looked at each other, recognizing that tone, hilarity rising in their eyes. Charley would be for it now. "That's enough. If you can't behave in a civilized manner at my table I'll thank you to leave it."

"But Mam—"

"But nothing." The voice had become even quieter. There was sudden silence. Nancy stifled a giggle.

Then Jack said, his voice level, "I've nothing against Hardie, you know it. If he did decide to stand for us he'd have my support. It's the others, Charley, that worry me. That bunch of lunatics you meet at the King's Head. Talking revolution. Talking blood. It makes no sense, lad, can't you see that? It can only mean trouble. It'll be bad enough if there's war in South Africa – there'll be real blood spilled then – but as for those bloody silly hot-heads you've got yourself in with—"

" – If you ask me war in South Africa'd be a godsend to the working classes of this country! I hope the bloody Boers *do* have a go! Because every gun and every soldier that's sent to South Africa's one less to send to Liverpool and Wales!"

"Think on, lad! You're talking civil war—"

"Well happen I damn' well am, yes. Happen a bit of spilled

blood's what this country needs! We sure as hell aren't getting anything for the asking—"

"That – is – *enough*." Sarah's tone this time was not to be ignored.

There was a small silence, then muttered apologies, the movement of feet and chairs. A moment later came the fierce clatter of crockery, the sharp, decisive sounds of a woman wreaking her displeasure upon the inanimate objects around her.

"I'd better help Mam." Nancy stood up, lifting exasperated eyes to heaven. "Men!"

Molly lay back wearily on her pillows. Charley's angry violence had stirred unhappy memories.

"Something wrong?" asked Harry from the fireside.

She shook her head, slowly and tiredly. "It's just that I hate to hear Charley talk so easily of spilling blood. Ireland has known enough of that to last the world a hundred years. If Charley had ever seen what bullets and bayonets can do to flesh and bone—" sickeningly clearly in her mind rose a vision of a wet and bloody street, of her young brother lifted from his feet and slammed against a cottage wall by a hail of machinegun fire " – I don't think he'd speak so."

"You make it sound—" Harry paused "– as if you'd seen it?"

"I have."

In the silence the glowing cave of embers in the fireplace collapsed, sending up a shower of sparks. Molly turned her head from the sudden glare of light and found Harry's brilliant eyes fixed upon her, wide, glittering, oddly intense.

"Daft thing," he said, leaning forward to retrieve the crushed violets from her fingers, "you've spoiled your flowers. Perhaps I should have given yours to Nelly Morris too?" and with one long finger he gently wiped the tears from her cheeks.

In her time with the Bentons that discussion in the kitchen was the closest thing Molly heard to a row; and at that there was no noticeable rift between the brothers once they had got over their tempers. They were a close family. Charley's bout of unfortunate revolutionary tendencies was treated in the same way as "our kid's" mischief or Harry's apparent refusal to take anything seriously; the other Bentons tutted and shrugged and

98

hoped that sooner or later he would grow out of it.

Soon Molly began to spend part of each day out of bed and on the Saturday following the argument was sitting in front of the fire, a rug over her knees and a letter in her hand when Harry came in carrying a tray on which was balanced precariously a teapot that slurped hot tea from its spout every time he moved, two cups, milk and sugar.

"There," he said pulling a small table forward and laying the tray upon it. "Mam said to tell you she'd be in later with some cakes. The others are out. Except for Nance, and she's in the bath, so I'm to keep out of the scullery." His eyes lit on the letter and he smiled, "Reading it again?"

A faint colour rose in her cheeks. "It was so good of him to write and reassure me. He's such a nice man." Mr Vassal's letter rustled in her fingers. The relief of knowing that her job was safe had done almost as much for her as the last bottle of Doctor Adams' undrinkably awful medicine. The fleshless, insubstantial look had left her; the elfin face was alive again; the tangled, matted hair had regained some of its gloss.

Harry poured the tea. Molly sensed that beneath the long sweep of lashes he was watching her. For her own part she had neither tried to deny nor to analyse the enjoyment that simply looking at him gave her; the smooth dark skin, the jewel-bright eyes, made such pleasure seem natural.

He laughed. "I wish I could say as much for my chief clerk, the old so-and-so." Harry worked in the offices of a sugar factory in Canning Town. "Miserable old—" he pulled an expressive face.

"You shouldn't lead him such a dance. . . ." Molly had heard enough to guess that Harry was not, despite his agile brain, the perfect employee.

Harry snorted. "What else is there to do? What a life! Up at six, off to work, scribble, scribble, scribble; home again. Christ! –Sorry—" the apology was automatic, the expression, for Harry, sour. "There's got to be something more than that, hasn't there? I sometimes wonder if our Charley's new friends aren't right. At least they've got something to fight for, something they believe in. What the hell do I believe in? Nothing, that's what. I sometimes wish—" His voice trailed into silence. Molly sipped her tea; there was a pause.

"Molly?" His voice had changed; it was soft, oddly coaxing.

She lifted her head. "Hmm?" He was not looking at her, his narrow fingers played abstractedly with the fringe on the cushion of the chair.

"What you said the other evening."

"Yes?"

"What happened?" The straightforward question caught her off guard. She stared at him, her face a white flame of distress. She turned her head.

"I don't want to talk about it."

He put his cup down with a clatter, stood and strode to the window, standing with his back to her, looking through the heavy cream lace of his mother's curtains to the street outside. He took a deep, sighing breath, as if he could not get enough air into his lungs. "At least, obviously, *something* happened—" He threw back his head, flexing the muscles of his neck and shoulders. She watched the straight, graceful back, unblinking. "—Something apart from scrawling stupid, meaningless things on damned bits of paper all day and every day." He paused, then said abruptly, "We had an Irishman in the factory last year. I liked him a lot. We got quite friendly, though he didn't stay for long. He was a Fenian. He'd been hunted for a year through all of Ireland by the police and the soldiers before he got away and came to England. They were still after him, I think." His voice had in it such a sudden wild tension of longing that Molly's blood ran cold.

"And you found that – exciting, did you? And romantic, perhaps?"

He turned, his head set arrogantly, his face defensive at her tone. "Not entirely. But I can't deny that I'd like to know what it feels like to feel so strongly about something that you'd lay down your life for it. . . ."

"Other people's lives."

She saw his mouth tighten, but he said nothing.

"People who feel that strongly," she said bitterly, "and talk about it, tend to lay down lives other than their own. Don't be fooled, Harry. Jack was right about that. You want to know how I know about such things? I'll tell you. My brother Danny, who was like you in many ways I think, went out on just such an exciting adventure—" the lit blue eyes blinked at the violence embedded in the words " – and died, terrified, on an Irish street, smashed to pieces by the bullets of the soldiers who lay in wait for him. My Sean—" how could it still hurt so? " – Sean lasted perhaps three seconds longer. The bullets pinned him to the wall like knives. I know. I was there. When we found that the soldiers were waiting I tried to warn them – and only got there in time to see them die. . . ."

"Don't." Harry was across the room and kneeling by her side. "God, Molly, stop it. I'm sorry. I didn't realize—" He took her hand; she had clamped her teeth into her lower lip and was sitting curled into herself, remembered agony in her eyes. He lifted her hand and laid it to his cheek. "I'm sorry, lass." His fingers were hard about hers, the skin of his face warm and smooth; his breath on her hand, despite her misery, sent a wave of physical pleasure through her.

She snatched her hand away. "It's all right."

"No, it isn't." He looked exactly like Edward, the penitence in his eyes mixed with the certainty that she could not stay angry with him for long. The bloody visions in her head receded, the tension draining from her in the warmth of those eyes.

"You'd better get up, my lad," she said. "You're going to look some kind of fool if your mother comes in and finds you on your knees. She'll think you're—" Her tongue had run ahead of her; she stopped abruptly as she realized what she had been about to say.

He picked up the thought with delight. " – That I'm proposing?" He jumped to his feet with an easy and relieved change of mood. "Ah, but she knows me better than that, lass. She knows that if I were ever daft enough to pop the question it would be with champagne, not a cup of tea! She also knows that, at the moment—"

" – the world's too full of pretty girls," Molly said, finishing the sentence for him, laughing now, the pain almost gone, "I was right. You're just like Danny."

He looked at her smiling, "Except that he was your brother," he said softly, "and I'm not." And before Molly had the chance to weigh the significance of that he had thrown open the door to his mother and her plate of cakes.

A week later Molly was up, her recovery almost complete, and gradually she began to pick up the threads of life again. It was not without regret that she said goodbye to her couch at the Bentons' and prepared to go back to her room in Linsey Grove, yet neither was she entirely sorry to be on her own again, to have time to think, to assess the change that had overtaken her life; for change there had certainly been. She was no longer alone; now she had friends. At the Bentons' urging she had happily promised to spend her Sundays with them, so there would be no more long and lonely days to be filled only with reading. Outings had been promised for the spring and summer – Epping Forest, the seaside; and Nancy, unusually demonstrative, had hugged her as she had left the house, saying, "Don't make it just Sundays, Moll. Come and see us whenever you like." When quiet Nancy made a friend, it was for life.

"That would be lovely."

The undisguised pleasure in the light, clear eyes made more of the words than the simple polite response sounded; and Molly, too, was aware that Nancy was her first friend since Mary Livingstone.

It had been already arranged that Jack should take her home on Sunday afternoon, but Molly could not deny her pleasure when Harry had announced firmly his intention of accompanying them. So these two escorted her to Linsey Grove where Molly felt a mild lift of affection at the sight of Sam's quiet pleasure at her homecoming, and a much stronger feeling of amusement to see that even Ellen Alden was susceptible to Harry's charm. Sam hovered, fidgeting, in the background, his presence overshadowed both by Jack's solid strength and by Harry's slighter grace. To Molly he looked thinner and more awkwardly angular than before, and she sympathetically attempted to draw him into the conversation, but his stuttered monosyllables and obvious, painful shyness defeated the attempt and before long he excused himself and left them.

Later, when Jack and Harry had gone, and Molly, a little tiredly, climbed the stairs to her room, it was to find the fire ready-lit and, on the red-clothed table, a tiny vase of snowdrops from the garden; heralds of spring and as kind a welcome home as any words, stuttered or no.

CHAPTER ELEVEN

As THE LOWERING, ash-grey skies of winter lifted and the buds of spring hazed green about the bare, pen-drawn line of twig and branch, Molly felt herself improving with every day. The brightness had returned to her face, her step was brisk again. She went back to Richmond and Co. and was greeted with pleasant fussiness by Mr Vassal and a cool lack of enthusiasm by Owen Jenkins whose attitude conveyed with no doubt whatsoever that her weakness in falling prey to illness simply confirmed his original poor opinion of her.

But not even Owen Jenkins could depress her now. The weeks flew by, the year advanced, the sun rose higher and days lengthened. No longer did she leave home in bleak darkness and return long after night had again closed in on the world; spring drew fresh green from the earth, painted a high, pale sky. And for Molly, a country child who had seen the blazing beauty of every season many times over in the bright hills and soft valleys of Ireland, no season had ever seemed as lovely as this city spring which in truth barely changed the physical face of the world in which she now lived, but which for her sang in the air and in her own blood with equal vigour. She felt herself alive and happy, as if she had emerged herself from the earth into sunshine, as had the spring flowers.

Sundays lit the week like a beacon; and after the first few weeks she was too honest to try to pretend that it was simply her delight in the company of the whole Benton clan that made these days so precious. It was the possibility of seeing Harry, of being near him, watching him, arguing, laughing. Not that she did not love them all. Her affection for Sarah would never waver, she looked on her as a mother; Nancy was a friend whose companionship she cherished; Edward with his cherub's face and mischief of the devil in his eyes she loved dearly. Charley treated her as he did Nancy, with a warm and sometimes patronizing brotherliness – he was courting now and his attention was for the moment concentrated wholly upon a young lady who did not, unfortunately, appear to be over-impressed by it. Only Jack seemed a little reserved with her, and Molly found herself wondering if he approved of her as wholeheartedly as the rest of the family seemed to; for though his quiet smile and few words were never less than civil, of all of them he was the only one in whose company she sometimes felt a little awkward and ill-at-ease, an outsider again, although she was certain this was never his intention. Catching the intense blue of his eyes upon her she once or twice wondered if Harry had spoken of what she had told him of Danny and Sean, if, perhaps, Jack misunderstood and in his capacity as head of the family he saw in her a threat. She hoped not.

She never mentioned her family at all, and no one questioned her; in fact as week followed week the thought of them dimmed and she discovered that even the aching memory of Sean was easing, as the bright colour fades from a pressed flower. She felt it happening, and after a while understood why; Harry again. She faced the thought squarely and finally on a Sunday morning in April when she had arrived at the Bentons' to discover that Harry had stayed with a friend overnight and would not be coming home at all that day. She was totally unprepared for the way in which the light seemed to seep from the day at the thought of the long hours without him. There had been other times when he had been out, and when he was at home he did not always spend his time with her; but on those other occasions that he had been expected home she had, half-unconsciously, been able to listen for his returning step, his lifted, laughing voice, and then simply to know that he was there had been enough. To discover his absence unexpectedly and to endure it for the whole day was like a physical blow; a complete week, a lifetime to wait before she would see him again. The strength of her own disappointment astonished her.

That afternoon as she walked with Nancy through the April gardens of West Ham Park she was singularly quiet, but as it happened, the customarily observant Nancy noticed nothing. Nor for her part did the quite frequently unobservant Molly notice that her friend had little to say – although later, when the time came for Molly to walk to the bus stop to catch the evening bus home she was startled from her own preoccupation when Nancy excused herself from walking with her, as was their habit, on the grounds that she was going to church. Molly opened her mouth to question this unusual circumstance, then noticing Sarah's raised and expressive eyebrows and Charley's smothered grin, to say nothing of the defensive colour that had risen in Nancy's fine-boned face, she shut it again, unwilling to embarrass the other girl.

That evening Molly sat for a long time in her bow window watching the sun as it dropped in a glow of apricot from the sky and she admitted at last to herself that her feelings for Harry were neither purely friendly nor in the least brotherly. As the short evening spent its light and darkness shadowed the streets below she tried to bring to sensible order emotions that were an absurd tangle of elation and desperate misgiving. She could no longer deny the enormous physical attraction that Harry exerted upon her. She could call to mind now, as clearly as if he were in the room, the texture of his skin and hair, which always made her want to reach and touch it, the set of his head on the wide, strong column of his neck, the strength of sweeping bone beneath the dark skin, the bright arrogant blue of his eyes within the shadowed, almost girlish lashes. Even his flaws for her simply enhanced his attraction; his mouth, a little too hard, a little too selfish, the sudden, flaring temper that reminded her so much of her own father – as did the occasional self-centred blindness that made him seemingly unaware of the feelings of others. What mattered beyond the warmth of his smile, the light-muscled strength of his body? She was surprised at how much she knew of him; the way he moved, the way he sat, the various tones of his voice, all were stored in some mysterious memory of which until now she had been hardly aware herself. Above all she was astonished at her own reactions to the thought of him, at the restless stirring of her nerves, the until-now unknown feeling of physical weakness that swept her. Nothing she had felt for Sean had been like this; his presence had been a comfort, a reassurance and a promise for the future, there had been no spark of danger, no hurt, no threat of harm as somehow she sensed in Harry. In him was a restlessness that would not be stilled by love; of all things, Molly was certain of that. As night slipped unnoticed through the window and filled the room about her with shifting dark, Molly brooded upon the almost obsessive excitement in Harry's voice when he had spoken of his friend the Fenian; she remembered the usually shaded and often lazy eyes wide and lit with intolerable excitement in that split moment before her own distress had reached him as she spoke of the deaths of Danny and Sean. She could have found Harry's like at any clandestine meeting of her father's. Not so beautiful, perhaps, and hardened by vastly different circumstance, but the same, and she knew it. She pulled a wry face at the irony, and shifted in her chair, suddenly aware of stiffening muscles and a chill in the air. It was full dark now, and becoming cold; her fire had died to glowing embers.

She drew the curtains, pulled back the bedclothes and began to step from her clothes, folding them carefully as she always did, shivering as the cold air crept to her skin. Down to her drawers and corset she reached for her voluminous nightdress. The flash of her movement in the mirror caught her eye; she stood for a moment, the nightdress in her hand. Faintly she could see her own reflection, white skin, white clothes, wide eyes silvered by the dying fireglow. Almost without volition she dropped the nightgown back onto the bed and walked without taking her eyes from her reflection to the long mirror, where, slowly and deliberately, she unlaced the corset, stepped out of the drawers and stood naked in the dim light, staring at herself, a fierce excitement rising in her, warming her chilled skin as she stared at the stranger in the bloodily fire-lit glass.

The stranger stared defiantly back.

For moments she stood so before, shivering and with sudden angry movements, she dragged her nightdress over her head and hurried into the cold bed.

It was a couple of weeks later, during the planning of the promised outing to Epping Forest, that Nancy's secret came out.

It was early May. The weather had warmed and settled and Charley announced triumphantly that he had arranged with a friend to borrow a horse and cart that would carry all of them and a picnic to the glades of Epping the following Sunday.

"The Forest!" Edward's eyes looked as if he had seen a vision of Heaven. "All *day?*"

"That's right, our kid," Charley said, swinging him round with easy strength. "Coming?"

"Mind the lamp, Charley," said his mother mildly. "You'll brain the child. And how many mouths am I supposed to be feeding on this famous day out?"

Charley sat Edward on the table, perched beside him, counting off on his fingers.

"Well, there's you and our kid, Nancy and Molly, Jack and Harry, me, Bill'll have to come of course, since it's his cart and—" he paused.

"And?" his mother asked, smiling.

"Well, I did wonder if Annie'd like to come—" Charley's patient courtship of Annie Melhurst had over the past couple of weeks finally shown some signs of success. His not altogether altruistic motives for organizing a day in the wilds of Epping Forest dawned on them all at about the same moment and there were several broad grins in evidence.

"Not that you've asked her yet?" asked Sarah, straightfaced and innocent.

"As a matter of fact – I did – well, mention it to her—"

"And?"

He grinned. "Count her in. Wait till you meet her, Mam, you'll love her."

"So that's—" Sarah counted " – nine?"

"That's right."

"I hope it's a big cart."

"Big enough to take another half a dozen. Anyone want to invite anyone else?" The question was casual.

"I might." Nancy's voice, very small, drew every eye in the room to its bright-faced owner. "That is, I don't know if he'll—"

"*He?*" Harry was staring at her in astonishment. "He who?"

"He who she's been going to church with every Sunday, thickhead," Charley was shouting with laughter. "Hell, Harry, you're blind as a bat sometimes. He who walks her home from work and leaves her at the corner so that he doesn't have to face her wild brothers. He who—"

"Charley, that'll do " Sarah's eyes were sympathetic upon her daughter's unusually rosy face. "I don't hear anyone tormenting you about your Annie. What do you think, Nance? Would he like to come?"

"He might. I'd like to ask him. I've been meaning to bring him home, but it's difficult; he's rather shy, and—" She looked at Charley, who snorted and was silenced by a glance from his mother.

"Well, I think you're right, this seems as good a chance as any for him to meet us all, if he can stand it. So that's ten, with Nancy's young man. Let's hope the sun shines."

Molly smiled absently, her eyes upon Harry as he leaned forward teasingly to his sister. A day, a whole day in the forest. What did it matter if the sun shone or not?

As it happened the sun did shine, spasmodically, but enough to deck the day in brightness and to further lift spirits that were already flying like kites in a spring wind. They gathered at the door, waiting for the cart: Molly, Sarah, Edward, Jack, Harry, Nancy and her young man, two enormous picnic baskets and a pile of cushions and blankets. Charley had already left to collect the cart, his friend Bill and his even more important friend Annie. Edward was beside himself with excitement; he talked incessantly of Charley's promise that he should ride on the driver's bench with Bill, dashed backwards and forwards from the doorway getting under everyone's feet waving enough of an assortment of bats and balls to stock a shop. Molly smiled at him, herself aglow with happy excitement. She had lived on penny pies for a week and on the proceeds had bought herself a new straw boater decorated with a wide scarlet band and a bunch of shining cherries, and the unrestrained approval of the assembled Bentons – especially Harry's – as she had walked through the door with the early summer sunshine had given this special day the right start. Nancy too had a boater, hers garlanded with marguerites, the same flower that she wore in the lapel of her dark blue jacket. She looked more soft and feminine than Molly had ever seen her; she had done her often somewhat severe hair differently and her cheeks were flushed becomingly. As they stood at the door Molly took the chance covertly to study the young man who was the obvious cause of her friend's transformation. Joe Taylor had surprised Molly when she had first met him; the immediate impression he gave was of cold and rather humourless severity. He was slight-built and had a thin, regularly featured, rather handsome face. He rarely spoke, had a somewhat forbidding smile, and Molly could not rid herself of the feeling that although he was with the excited group in no way was he a part of it, that he viewed the proceedings as frivolous and lacking in dignity. Then she shrugged her hasty judgement aside. It was hardly fair to jump to such conclusions; the Bentons could be a little overwhelming under calmer circumstances than these.

"They're here! Here they are." Edward's shriek echoed and re-echoed down a street lit with scudding sunlight and drifting cloud-shadow. Around the corner plodded a great black-and-white carthorse with enormous silk-fringed hooves and a mane gaily plaited with ribbons exactly the colour of the cherries on Molly's new hat. Behind him rolled the cart, a wide farm-wagon brightly painted with fruit and vegetables, the flat platform sides overhanging the wheels, the driver's bench high in the front over the body of the cart. Three grinning figures were perched on the bench: the driver – who could only be Bill, an enormous figure in flat cloth cap and a jacket of the loudest check Molly had ever seen – and Charley, who had his arm around the waist of a girl as tall and thin as a bean stick and who had a face like a flower and a mop of bright red hair.

"Well, well," Harry said softly, admiration in his voice and in his eyes as he looked at Annie Melhurst. "Looks as if our Charley's done it this time. That 'un'll keep him in order right enough."

When the cart had rolled to a halt outside the door, there was a flurry of introductions and squeals of excitement. Charley swung tall Annie as if she had been a child down from the driving bench and sat her in the corner of one of the two long benches that had been set along the sides of the cart, then vaulted down to join her. He reached a huge hand and hauled Nancy up beside him, nodded in friendly fashion to Joe who with neat and economical movements swung himself over the tail of the wagon and settled himself straight-backed next to Nancy on the end of the bench. Jack had already set Edward beside the driver and before he climbed up beside the child he lifted Molly onto the other bench in the corner opposite Annie and helped Harry to steady Sarah as she climbed a little stiffly into the cart. Then up came the baskets, the blankets and the cushions which were distributed amongst the passengers to stuff down between themselves and the hard wooden sides of the cart. Harry was the last to swing aboard, pulling up and fastening the tail of the cart behind him before he settled himself next to Molly. He wriggled for a moment, as if in discomfort, put his hand behind him and with apparently enormous effort brought out a huge turnip which he looked at with comically astonished eyes.

"Tell you what, Bill—" Harry said to the driver who turned grinning, " – I'm damned glad you're not a fishmonger."

The roars of laughter that greeted this were out of all proportion to the joke. Jack, smiling, turned from his perch on the driving bench, counted heads and baskets, asked "All set?" then waved a hand. "Off we go."

As the cart jerked into motion Harry reached a casual, steadying arm around Molly's shoulders. Ignoring Nancy's knowing, happy eyes, Molly smiled.

The day stretched ahead of them like a promise.

They rode laughing through the streets to London's forest, following unknowing in the wake of lords and ladies, kings and queens, huntsmen of bygone days; and no company before them could have been gayer. Talking, laughing, even sometimes singing, they made their swaying way through streets that became less familiar as they moved further from home, their merriment drawing smiling glances from passers-by. Even Joe Taylor unbent enough, Molly noticed, to pass a civil word with Harry; and as for Charley's Annie, by the time they had gone a mile they all felt as if they had known her all their lives. She had the readiest tongue that Molly had ever heard, and a down-to-earth wit and infectious laugh that was impossible to resist. Charley beamed, obviously gratified, his arm around Annie's shoulders, unable to get a word in edgewise and loving every moment of it.

When they finally reached Epping there was a lively argument as to how far into the forest they should venture, and where to stop. In the end Bill guided the creaking wagon down a rutted track and a little way into the woodlands before rolling to a halt in a fair-sized glade unoccupied by any other Sunday picnickers.

Their voices died and even Annie's laughter was muted for a moment. Above the lacework of fresh leaves the sunlit white clouds raced across a watercolour sky. The grass was soft and lush and a little damp; in the near distance a sea of gentlest blue lapped to the roots of the ancient trees: bluebells, thousands of them, scenting the air and easing dust-filled eyes with their colour.

"It's lovely! Oh, it's lovely," Nancy said very softly.

"Right, everyone," Harry said briskly, "Let's get ourselves sorted. Come on, Moll, down you come. Hand the basket out, Mam—"

In no time they had established themselves beneath the wide-spreading branches of an oak tree, the blankets laid out, cushions scattered, the baskets hidden on the shady side of the tree. Sarah set herself comfortably, her back to the tree, and reached for her knitting.

"That's me settled. You youngsters do what you like – back here to eat at one."

"Cricket!" Edward swung his bat around his head, to the imminent peril of anyone near him, "Come on, our Jack, you promised. Bill, too—"

"Let's all play." It was Annie, her pretty face alight with mischief. "There's plenty of room." She looked at Charley who had opened his mouth to speak. "We can go for a walk later, Charley," she said equably, reading his mind like a printed page. "After lunch. The kid wants to play cricket."

They played cricket; or rather their own particular version of the game, for nearly two hours. Except for Joe, who was out first bowl and declined to bat again, the male members of the party could not resist showing their prowess and the ball flew skittering through leaves and branches, bouncing off trees, losing itself wilfully in brambles and nettle patches. The girls, refusing with one voice to have a partner run for them, lifted hobbling skirts and ran like hares between the makeshift stumps. Edward, in his element, made up the rules as he went along, was out three times before he finally and with reluctance relinquished the bat. Their voices echoed through the woodland like children's, and Sarah, watching them, smiled.

At last, still laughing and dishevelled, they threw themselves down beneath the tree where Sarah had laid the picnic and tucked into cold meat and cheese, pickles and hunks of buttered bread as if they had not eaten for a week – which, in Molly's case, thanks to the now-abandoned boater, was not far from the truth. They washed down the feast with cider and lemonade and then, the edge taken from their appetites, nibbled at cakes and fruit, enjoying the dappled sunshine as it glittered down through the canopy of branches above them.

"Why does food always taste so much better out of doors?" Nancy leaned against a log, her eyes closed. On the other side of the tablecloth Bill, Jack and Charley were engaged in their own conversation.

Annie plucked at a blade of grass. "Because you don't have to do the washing up afterwards," she said absently, one ear tuned to the men's conversation, the beginnings of a frown on her expressive face. "What're you nattering about over there?"

They did not hear her.

" – and the only way to prevent that—" said Bill, smacking a huge fist into his open hand, " – is to organize. Charley's right there, you know, Jack. If it wasn't for the dock unions you wouldn't have—"

"What!" Annie was on her feet in a trice and marching with a flash of petticoat on the three reclining forms. "What's that? Unions? I should think so!" She buried a none-too-gentle hand in Charley's mass of hair and pulled. "You wanted a walk? We'll go for a walk. Now." Charley scrambled painfully to his feet, willy nilly. She poked him in the chest with a long bony finger. "Unions indeed? On a day like this? Let me tell you, Charley Benton, that if you take me on there'll be less of this Union lark!"

Bill smothered an explosion of laughter. Charley kicked him.

"Come on," Annie said, smiling like an angel and took his arm, laughing into his reddened face, "let's see if the trees look the same on the other side of that path—"

As the others, smiling, watched their retreating backs through the trees Joe Taylor cleared his throat awkwardly. "I thought," he said formally to Sarah, "that, if you wouldn't mind, Nancy and I might also—?" he looked to the spot where Annie and Charley had disappeared; Annie's laughter still drifted back to them through the dim reaches of the woodland.

"Of course, lad. Off you go." Sarah reached comfortably for her knitting.

As he and Nancy left Jack stirred.

"Coming to find that bird's nest, our kid?" Edward, cake in hand, scrambled to his feet. Jack's eyes moved to Molly. "Would you like to come with us?"

Molly was caught. "I—" she stammered, not looking at Harry, " – I—think perhaps—" in the silence the birds sang very loud, " – perhaps I ought to stay and help your mother clear away the picnic—?"

"Rubbish." A strong hand caught hers, lifted her to her feet. Harry's eyes gleamed in sunlight. "I thought you said you wanted to pick some bluebells?"

"I—" she hadn't mentioned the bluebells. "Yes, I did, but—" Her heart was pounding.

"Well, come on, then. Mam won't mind, will you Mam?"

Sarah, smiling, shook her head.

Harry bent and picked up the discarded boater. "You'll have to put this on, though. You can't go buying a hat like this and not wear it." He settled it on her head, laughed as it bounced on her massed, coal-black curls. "The prettiest hat for the prettiest girl." He was warm and vital as the afternoon itself, his hand in hers was the happiest thing she had ever known. "If we aren't back in three days," he said solemnly to his mother, "send for Sergeant McIntosh."

"You behave yourself."

"I always do. Don't I?" He drew Molly towards the path that ran into the woods in the opposite direction from that taken by the others. "Well, almost always."

If Molly could have stopped the world she would have done it at the moment when the voices of their companions died behind them and the forest sounds – the birdsong, the rustle of their slow footsteps in last year's leaves were the only things to be heard. She had not dared to hope, had almost forcibly stopped herself from thinking about the possibility of such a situation:

herself and Harry wandering alone through the sweet-smelling early summer's afternoon.

He bent his head to look at her.

"You're very quiet. You aren't mad with me, are you?"

"Mad?" The thought had not crossed her mind.

"For telling fibs about the bluebells. For making you come with me—?"

"Oh, no." She did not care how eager she sounded, could not anyway prevent it. "I wanted to. I just didn't want—" she stopped.

" – to go bird's nesting with Jack." In the shadows beneath the trees his skin stood very dark against the white of his shirt, the blue of his eyes.

She ducked her head, flushing. "That's right. 'Tis awful of me I suppose." As always in times of stress the Irish in her voice sang louder than usual.

"Awful?" He laid an arm across her shoulders, pulled her to him as they walked; her curly head did not reach his chin. "I don't think so—"

They strolled in silence down the forest paths, each extraordinarily aware of the other, of the still beauty of the woodlands, pierced by the shafting gold of sunlight.

"'Tis a miracle," said Molly at last, her quiet voice a shout in the still air, "that such a place should exist so very close to London—" she turned and tilted her head to look at him, almost unaware that they had stopped walking.

He did not answer; his eyes, very serious, were on her pale, upturned face; with the slightest pressure of his arm he turned her to face him. As he bent to her mouth she reached eagerly upon tiptoe to him. His lips were as she had imagined them: hard and warm and sharply demanding.

Then as suddenly as they had come together they stepped apart, Harry still holding her hands. Above them in the branches a bird sang, piercingly sweet; someone, far in the distance, called.

"Molly," he said and smiled, white teeth against brown, smooth skin. "Dear little Irish Molly—" There was excitement in his eyes, painful urgency in his hands. She moved to him again, metal to a magnet.

Unnoticed the small straw hat fell into the bluebells, the bright cherries winking in the sun.

When, with the dipping sun painting the laced treetops with fire, they returned some time later to the picnic spot, they were guided by challenging voices. Everyone was there, and to Molly's relief too absorbed in a heated discussion to throw more than a cursory glance in the newcomers' direction as they joined the group, though it seemed to Molly that Jack's piercing gaze seemed for a moment longer than most to rest upon her wild hair and heightened colour, the grass-stained boater she carried in her hand, before he returned to the fray.

"Do you really believe, then, that these Boers could defeat the British Army?" The question was more interested than out-raged. "With no properly organized army of their own? The newspapers call them a rabble—"

"The newspapers are wrong." Joe Taylor's well-modulated voice was calm. "The Boers might be bull-headed but they aren't stupid and they aren't cowards. They are convinced they have been wronged, and they believe that God fights beside them."

Charley, lying on a blanket with his head in Annie's lap and a tall stalk of grass between his lips, laughed. "Seems to me I've heard that before. Fat lot of good it'll do them when the bullets start to whistle."

Joe took no notice of the interruption. "And if they are forced to fight," he continued earnestly, "they'll be fighting for their homes, their families, their land, their survival as a nation – at least that's what they believe. And they're probably right. That'll mean a sight more than cannons and fancy uniforms."

Nancy reached up a hand and drew Molly down beside her; Harry squatted on his heels behind them, his face suddenly intent and frowning.

"Joe's brother's just come back from South Africa," Nancy whispered. "He's a missionary there. He thinks there's going to be a war—"

Bill rolled onto his stomach, plucking at the tufts of grass. "Hellfire, you're surely not serious? There isn't an army in the world could beat the British at the moment. Look at India—"

" – the Sudan—" Jack put in.

" – Aldershot—" Charley said, grinning, and was rewarded by a sharp clip with a bluebell from Annie.

"They aren't an army." Joe's voice held the patience of a man talking to children. "They don't pretend to be an army. They are just men, like you and me; husbands, fathers, brothers, who have been pushed too far, men who have a tradition of self reliance, self defence. They are hard men, they have to be for the life they lead; their commandos won't be easily defeated. They have pride and courage."

"And we don't?" Harry's sudden voice was raw with anger, jarring amongst the reasonable tones of the others. Nancy and Molly turned with one movement to look at him. Colour burned on his cheekbones. He was looking at Joe Taylor with anger sparking every line of his face. "Is that what you're trying to say? Well, let's wait and see about that. I'll tell you this for nothing. If those bloody Dutch farmers attack the British settlers they'll regret it. They won't know what's hit them."

There was an awkward silence. Joe, whatever his opinions, was a family guest; Harry's angry tone had verged on the insulting.

Joe said deprecatingly, "I'm not saying they're braver. I'm saying that they know the country, that it is, after all, their home, they will be fighting literally on their own doorsteps."

Jack nodded. "That'd make a difference, I grant you. But they're on their own, Joe, aren't they? They've no one to call on for any kind of help. They wouldn't stand a chance, surely? Don't they know that? When you think of our manpower—"

"Joe obviously thinks," said Harry, his voice hard, "that the British Army won't be able to deal with a few ragged-arsed Dutch farm boys. Does the Government know this, Joe? P'raps you should offer them your services?"

The tone was too much for Nancy. "Perhaps *you* should since you know so much about it," she flashed angrily.

He eyed her stonily. "And perhaps I will."

"What do I have to do," asked Annie mildly, "to break up this bun-fight? Throw a fit?" She moved her legs and tipped Charley onto the grass. "If you must argue about something why don't you argue about something sensible, like who gets the last of the cider?"

"No argument," said Bill, the jug in his hand, "I do."

Charley, still rolling, grabbed his legs. "That's what you think." As Bill tried to kick Charley off, Annie leaned forward and grabbed the jug neatly, sat hugging it and laughing as the other two rolled over and over in the grass.

Molly looked at Harry. He pulled a self-conscious and apologetic face and lifted his shoulders in a shrug, his quick temper dying; but the light of battle was still in his eyes. Molly sighed.

Nancy said, anger still in her, "What makes you so damn' patriotic all at once?"

"That'll do, Nance." Jack's voice was easy. "It's not worth fighting about."

Charley and Bill were still wrestling, only half-laughing; a flailing bundle of arms and legs, they rolled back and forth across the clearing, a danger to anyone or anything within yards of them.

"Right." Still holding the cider jug Annie unfolded her long body and stood up. "That'll do, I think." And marching up to the wrestlers she poured the dregs of the cider indiscriminately over both of them. The ensuing pandemonium restored everyone's good temper and by the time, in the dying evening light, they had packed up and climbed once more aboard the cart, the high words and talk of war had apparently been forgotten.

They were quiet on the journey home, their high spirits muted by tiredness. Edward rode in the wagon this time, his head in Sarah's lap, asleep almost before they were out of the forest. Annie leaned into Charley's shoulder, humming, her eyes soft on the child's sleeping face. Nancy and Joe sat in quiet conversation, they might have been alone together. Molly sat close by Harry, the nearness and warmth of his body lighting her senses. She did not need to look at him. Everything about him was printed indelibly within her; she knew every line of his body, every expression on his face. As they settled for the journey he pulled her to him, drew her head to his shoulder. She caught Nancy's smiling eyes and grinned back. As full darkness overtook them she felt his firm, stroking fingers on her neck, ached to turn her head and kiss him.

The trip was too short by hours; she could have stayed all night just so, ignoring the hard bench and the jolting of the cart, aware only of the man beside her. They went home by way of Upton Park; Jack directed Bill to Linsey Grove and they rolled to a gentle halt outside number twenty-six. Stiffly Molly sat up, careful not to disturb small Edward; soft goodnights and thank yous were spoken. Harry swung himself down from the cart and lifted her lightly after him. They stood by the gate for a moment, acutely aware of the others' watching eyes.

"Goodnight, little Molly."

She smiled, aching. Wasn't he going to kiss her?

"I'll see you next week."

She nodded. In the downstairs window of the house a curtain twitched. With a swift movement he bent and dropped a light kiss on her cheek before turning and vaulting back onto the wagon.

"Off we go, Bill."

She watched them move off into the darkness. As she turned at last and walked up the path, the street door opened.

"Did you have a nice day?" She could not see Sam's face in the darkness. His voice was quiet.

"Lovely, thank you." Her cheeks burned from the sun, her shoulders and back ached agonizingly from the jolting of the cart, her mouth felt bruised.

"Would you like a cup of tea?"

Oh Sam, Sam, you and your tea . . . ! "No, thank you. I'm very tired." Next Sunday seemed a full month away. But it would come.

With echoes of the day still singing in her bones she wearily climbed the stairs to her bed.

CHAPTER TWELVE

THAT WAS A summer not to be forgotten. As May became June and June, July there were other outings, usually with some or all of the family, occasionally – and these were the highlights of Molly's life – alone with Harry. They went to Southend and ate cockles in the rain, took the train to Brighton where red-headed Annie got sunburned to a cinder. They often took the steam-ferry across the river at Woolwich and spent the day wandering the Kentish lanes, arriving home tired and famished and feeling as if their feet were worn down to their ankles. Bill and his cart took them to Epping again, though for Molly no other trip to the forest ever quite came up to that first one. Charley and Annie were with them on almost every trip. Nancy and Joe occasionally joined them, as did Jack, Edward and Sarah. It had been tacitly accepted in the family since that day in the forest that Molly and Harry were 'walking out', though no one – including Harry – ever put it into so many words. As for Molly there were times when her growing infatuation for Harry almost frightened her: it was the lodestone of her life. When they quarrelled, which they did – not frequently but with sometimes quite destructive passion – her misery infected every aspect of life; when they were happy together nothing could disgruntle her; the world was a rainbow. By the middle of the summer she was going to the Bentons' straight from work on Saturday, returning to Linsey Grove on Sunday evening. Ellen Alden's insistence upon doors locked at ten-thirty was too much of a stricture when there were music halls and circuses to visit, parks to walk in, hung with shadows on a warm summer's night. At last Molly's lovely silk saw the light of day; how had she guessed that the shimmering material would be just the colour of Harry's eyes? Sometimes their Saturday evenings would be spent at home with Sarah and Jack playing cribbage for ha'pennies and with a glass of port to enliven the proceedings; though these were evenings in which Nancy and Joe never took part, for Joe, it was apparent, strongly disapproved of such activities as unbecoming to a Christian family, and more and more Nancy was being drawn into his world: a world of good works and relentless rectitude, ruled by a strict if commendable code of behaviour that seemed to Molly to take no account at all of human failing. Nancy's relationship with her undoubtedly worthy young man intrigued Molly but she could not for her life discover the common bond that held these two together. They hardly ever touched, never held hands, nor looked at each other as Molly considered that lovers should. That Nancy truly loved this oddly cold, sparely handsome young man was in no doubt; the efforts she made to please him spoke volumes in proof of that. Yet they never laughed, as Molly did with Harry, as Charley did with his Annie, never bought silly, affectionate gifts nor shared a private joke. And sometimes Molly thought that she caught a look in Nancy's eyes that did not become a twenty-year-old girl in love; an odd, haunted, unhappy look which verged sometimes on desperation.

But nothing during those happy months could worry Molly for long. As the talk of war in South Africa grew more persistent she ignored it; if Owen Jenkins were particularly unpleasant she shrugged, smiled like summer sunshine and thought about something else. At Linsey Grove she sang in her room, smiled a lot, skipped through the house like a child. Ellen Alden softened a little since she too approved of Harry Benton, though nothing would have made her admit it. Sam, his Christmas row with his cousin Lucy patched up, his cough eased by the summer sun, moved like a shadow through a life that seemed to belong to everybody but him. In a drawer in his room, buried beneath his winter pyjamas, was an ugly little statuette of a boy and a dog.

As August approached the paving stones burned through thin-soled shoes, doors and windows were opened to street and garden, the trains were uncomfortably hot.

One Saturday afternoon Harry declared his intention of allowing Molly to decide what she wanted them to do for the rest of the day. He laughed at the way her great shining eyes lit.

"Within reason, mind, lass," he said, wagging a finger. "Visits to the palace are out. My best suit's at the cleaners."

"Oh, Harry. Could we go to the West End? To look at the

shops?" Not since her arrival in London had she been back to Regent Street. "Just to look."

"What a smashing idea." Annie was on her feet, reaching for her hat. "Moll, you're a bloody genius. Why didn't I think of that? Not—" she added, hauling lazy Charley to his feet with a wide grin, " – that I go along with this 'just looking' lark."

They strolled, arm in arm, from Piccadilly to Oxford Circus and back again, Annie on top of her form, the young men delighted to have what they considered to be the two prettiest girls in the street on their arms, Molly somewhat preoccupied. Everywhere she looked she saw a forlorn figure in too-big boots and a patched and ragged skirt. She had felt badly enough then; looking back now she knew in mortification how pathetic she must have appeared.

They stopped for tea and cakes in a large tea shop; and Molly was perfectly aware of the special attention Harry received from the pretty waitress, and was equally aware of his flattered reaction. She kicked him under the table, to Annie's uncurbed amusement. They visited one of the larger departmental stores and wandered from floor to floor inspecting with a casual air goods that would have cost all their earnings collectively for a year. Charley bought Annie an emerald green scarf and Harry picked for Molly a pretty lace handkerchief to go, he said, in the pocket of her blue silk shirt.

" – you can wear it tonight, Moll," said Annie enthusiastically.

Molly looked at her blankly. "Tonight?"

"Tonight. Me sister's do. – Oh, Charley!" she groaned, turning on him, almost stamping her foot in exasperation, "you didn't tell them!"

"I did!"

"You didn't," Molly and Harry said in one breath. "What do?" added Molly.

"It's me sister's birthday. Her twenty-first. She's havin' a party and you're all invited. Oh, damn it, Charley, you should have remembered." Annie's face was colouring to match her fiery hair. "You *promised* you'd tell them."

Charley looked uncomfortable. Harry grinned.

"Sure, it doesn't matter," said Molly soothingly. "It isn't too late. We know now. And we'll come, won't we Harry?"

Harry nodded.

They were back out on the hot pavement now.

"I'll have to go home first," said Molly, looking down at her Saturday clothes. "I'm going to no party dressed like this. Not when I've my best hanging in a wardrobe in Linsey Grove."

"Right." Harry was brisk. "Here's what we do. Charley, you and Annie get on home. I'll take Moll home from here; she can get changed and we'll come straight on to you from there. How's that?"

"Fine." Annie already had hold of Charley's hand and was towing him into the crowds, "See you later, about eight."

They reached Linsey Grove just after six; the evening sun was full on the closed door and firmly shut windows. As Molly opened the door a blast of hot air hit them. Molly stopped short. "They must be out," she said awkwardly. "I didn't know. . . ."

Harry shut the door and the slanting golden sun filled the hall with prisms of coloured light; amber rose and green splashed upon the walls. "That's no problem," he said. "I'll wait in the kitchen. Mrs Alden won't mind. And if she does," he said, grinning suddenly, "I'll smile nicely and she'll forgive me."

"One of these days," said Molly, already swinging around the stairpost and up two stairs, "you'll rely on that once too often and get the shock of your life." Laughing, she leaned across the banisters to kiss him lightly. He lifted a light-limned face, his swift-moving hand catching her hair and forcing her head down hard. She felt sharp teeth and tongue, tried to pull back and was held. The dazzling sunlight was liquid gold. She closed her eyes, drove her mouth from her position above him hard down onto his. His free hand lifted to her breast, his fingers moving unerringly to her nipple, strong through the thin material of her blouse, and her mouth opened helplessly to the shock. It was Harry who finally, letting go of her hair, stepped back with a jerky movement.

"You'd – best get changed," he said in a voice nothing like his own, looking into eyes that blindly begged and took no count of hurt. The wall was at his back, the light stabbed into his head.

The girl on the stairs straightened, the wild look dying; he saw ment the look that Ellen Alden bestowed upon her anxious son, and with aching memories of her own mother and laughing, handsome Danny to assist her, knew beyond doubt that Sam, unlikely as it might seem, was doted upon. She watched the young man as he poured tea for his mother, sugared it carefully, placed it on the table before her as she slit open the envelope.

There followed a long silence during which the ticking of the kitchen clock sounded thunderous.

At length Ellen Alden lifted forbidding eyes from the paper before her and studied Molly quite openly, her gaze missing nothing, not the patched and threadbare clothes, nor the boots, nor the evidence of violence on her face. Neither did she miss the promise of beauty in that thin, tired face, the curves of the small body beneath the ragged clothes.

"Lady Margaret suggests – asks, even, that I should take you as a lodger," Sam's mother said at last, bluntly. "She assures me of your good character, despite outward appearances, and takes responsibility herself for your good behaviour."

Molly breathed a small prayer of thanks to the woman who had made such a decision on such short acquaintance.

"She talks of the charity and duty of a Christian—"

The word charity brought blood to Molly's cheeks.

"I can pay," she said, shortly.

"Yes. She tells me that also." The reply was cool, the slightly raised eyebrows next to insulting.

Ellen Alden looked back at the letter. Every instinct urged her to turn this ragged, self-possessed urchin away, back into the streets where she undoubtedly belonged. Yet the personal connection with Lady Margaret Wharton, however tenuous, was something that meant as much to her as almost anything else in her life except her son. Supposing, through offence – for the letter was couched in terms of a personal favour – that the connection should cease? Ellen Alden was far from being a stupid woman. She knew how much her position of strength in the hierarchy of the women of the Chapel depended upon her personal acquaintance with Lady Margaret.

"You know that I usually take gentlemen? That I have never even considered taking a young lady?"

"Yes."

the fingers of her small hand grip firmly the smooth wood of the banisters. Then she turned without a word and ran swiftly up the stairs.

She entered a room aflame with sunshine, the hot silence of the house humming in her ears. She leaned for a moment on the door after she'd closed it behind her; head back, eyes closed, breathing deeply, she was fighting herself. She could still feel the pressure of his mouth on hers, his hand violent in her hair, on her breast. She pushed herself to her feet and marched with a semblance of anger to the wardrobe. She was appalled at her image in the mirror; her cheeks flamed; her eyes were lit as if by a lamp. She threw the blue outfit onto the bed, still fighting the unreasoning anger, flung the curtains across the window, scrambled feverishly from her clothes, and in drawers and camisole top – fashion or no she had discarded corsets during the heatwave – hurried to the washstand. The water that was left in her jug was lukewarm but nevertheless refreshing. She splashed her face and neck and reached for a towel; she did not hear the door open. As she turned, water dripping, towel in hand, Harry stood in the shadowed doorway, a strange, oddly helpless expression on his face. Sunshine fell across the carpet in a bright slash where the carelessly drawn curtains did not meet; the rest of the room was filled with warm rose darkness. She did not move as he came into the room, shut the door behind him and leant on it just as she had herself a few moments before. Neither spoke. She watched him: like a stalking cat he crossed the room, unsmiling. Her hands loose by her side, she remained where she was, perfectly still, the towel dropping to the floor. He reached for her shoulders and with some force he drew her to him and kissed her.

"Let me see you?" he said, softly. "Just let me see you. I won't touch you, I swear."

The warm silence rushed around them. She watched the muscle throbbing in his jaw.

"Please?" he said. But neither his eyes nor the tone of his voice pleaded. She battled him in silence, begging him to go; obdurately and just as wordlessly he refused. "I just want to see you," he said again, the words a breath on the heavy air.

She bent her head, drawing slowly at the ribbon in the low

neck of the camisole. Unlaced, it hung open; she could do no more. He pushed it aside with one long, brown, careful finger. She traced the pattern of the carpet with her eyes, unable to lift her head. With firm hands he slipped the top from her shoulders and she stood naked to the waist, her breasts painful beneath his eyes. Still she could not look at him.

"Please." This time the pleading was there in his voice.

She stood like a doll as he slipped the drawers over her narrow hips and down to her feet, his hands never once touching her skin. He knelt back on his heels.

"Look at me."

She would not.

"Look at me."

She lifted her eyes; shame and fear and unbearable excitement shadowed her face.

"You're beautiful," he said. "Bloody beautiful."

She shook her head.

His vivid eyes ran over her slowly from head to foot; she felt them as she would have felt his hands.

"I love you," he said. The first time he had ever mentioned the word. "Christ, I really think I love you."

He came up onto his knees as she stepped to him; his face was in her soft belly, her hands buried in his thick, feathered hair.

From the street came voices, the impatient click of the gate. Molly had never seen anyone move so fast. Harry was on his feet and noiselessly across the room almost before her own mind had registered what she had heard. He did not look back from the door. She heard his swift flight down the stairs, heard too a fraction of a second before she heard Ellen's front door key in the lock, the kitchen door click quietly shut.

By the time she heard Ellen's and Sam's voices, surprised, as they walked into the kitchen and found Harry there, she was almost dressed.

CHAPTER THIRTEEN

Sᴀʀᴀʜ Bᴇɴᴛᴏɴ ᴡᴀᴛᴄʜᴇᴅ them all, that summer, with toler-
ant affection and some few misgivings. She watched Annie wind
Charley around her bony little finger, torment and tease him,
order him from here to Christmas and back; but she saw too the
look in the girl's eyes, the contentment in Charley's face, saw
him weaned from dangerous company and was satisfied that
these two were nothing but good for one another.

About her daughter's happiness she was not so certain and, as
none knew better than herself, with good reason. If Molly had
noticed Nancy's not-quite-hidden unhappiness, Sarah felt it in
her own heart and knew as mothers always know that she could
do nothing to ease it. Joe Taylor's uncompromising attitudes did
not make him an easy man to like. Respect, he commanded; and
no one could complain of his behaviour, which was at all times
rigorously well-mannered. But there was little warmth in the
man; and he gave the unavoidable impression that his cold and
logical decisions, once made, would never be tempered by
circumstance. The thought disturbed Sarah. And while the
others walked and picknicked, laughed and teased, kissed and
quarrelled, Nancy and her Joe went soberly to church, talked of
heavier matters than next week's outing or the latest music hall
song, and Sarah found herself wondering, not for the first time,
at the caprices of human nature.

But if Nancy's romance was a low-key affair, the same could
in no way be said of Harry and Molly. Sarah watched the flame
that grew between these two and was torn between the simple
pleasure of seeing them together and the worried conviction that
nothing so fierce could last. And her worry was more for Molly
than for her own indestructible son. She wondered, watching
them, if the girl were not perhaps blinded by bright eyes and
laughter. Harry had not changed as Charley had; he was still the
same restless, unpredictable and occasionally ruthless spirit.
The strength of will that drove Molly had all of Sarah's

admiration, but she was certain that the girl had not yet discovered that it had no true parallel in Harry. That their temperaments were very similar was irrefutably true, but Harry had never felt the need for self-discipline, and that was a chasm between them that apparently neither had yet noticed. Yet even taking into account these differences, it was hard to believe, watching them together through the bright summer, that anything could come between them.

As summer drew into the last autumn of the century it was becoming more and more likely that Joe's prediction of war in South Africa would be fulfilled. As the Boers, grimly patient, awaited the African spring grass that would feed the horses and oxen of the commandos, the British, too, slowly gathered their scattered reinforcements. Argument raged in Britain as in Africa, and feelings ran high. To any suggestion that the British Government's handling of the situation in the Transvaal, their uncompromising demand for the vote for British Nationals in the Boer Republic might be regarded in some quarters as high-handed and provocative, Harry, together with most of the rest of the nation, was scathing.

"A lesson's what they need, and it's what they'll get. A few stretched necks."

"The Empire's safe, then," Molly said drily and with no smile from her place on the arm of Harry's chair. "For hanging's something the British Army needs no lessons in."

"Irish rebel talk." Harry slipped an arm about her waist, not noticing the sudden coldness in her eyes. "Just wait till you see the lads in their uniforms, then you'll sing a different song. Nothing like a uniform for impressing the girls, eh, Charley?"

"Your brother," said Annie to Charley, her eyes on Molly's rigid face, "can be as thick as last night's cocoa. It's a good job you're pretty," she added to Harry in a tone as unfriendly as any that Molly had ever heard her employ. "Come on, Moll. Let's go and help Sarah with the tea. The company's better in the kitchen."

At five o'clock on the eleventh of October 1899 the ultimatum issued by Paul Kruger to the British ran out and the Boers of the Transvaal and the Orange Free State moved on Cape Colony and Natal. Despite forewarnings the British were far from prepared, with only 15,000 regular soldiers ready to take the field in South Africa, and the 47,000 reinforcements under the command of General Sir Redvers Buller still on the high seas. The Boers wasted neither time nor advantage; before breath could be drawn the news came: Ladysmith, Kimberley and Mafeking were all under siege, and the army that was the pride of an Empire had been boxed like chickens into crates. Popular pride was outraged, and the call was for Boer blood; but it was mostly the blood of Britain that spilled on the warm and thirsty soil of Africa at the outset, and as the war correspondents reported, their words, however carefully chosen, told of disaster, of engagements lost by lack of military forethought, won by the marksmanship and resource of the well-mounted, mobile Boer commandos. And patriotic temper and outrage began to build to a fever pitch.

During a bout of cold weather at the end of the month Molly caught a chill and was immediately and uncompromisingly ordered to bed for the weekend by Sarah.

"You get on home, my lass. Look at you. Just remember what happened last winter. You've got to look after yourself. Here—" she thrust a small bottle into the girl's hands, "lemon and honey with a drop of brandy to help it along. I doubt your landlady'll have anything. Harry, get along with you; get the lass home."

And Harry, gratifyingly concerned, did. He saw her to the Aldens' gate, kissed her sympathetically. "Do as Mam says, now. And look after yourself."

She nodded miserably. "I'm sorry. I've spoiled the weekend."

"Don't be daft." He lifted her chin with his finger, kissed her small red nose. "It isn't the end of the world. I'll have a night out with Ben and the lads. I did have a few friends before I knew you, you know."

She leaned her aching head upon his shoulder, stifling misgivings. Harry's friend, Ben Samson, she knew as a likeable utterly reckless young man whose attitude of total irresponsibility tended to put at risk anyone within a half-mile of him. His influence upon Harry was not exactly a tranquil one. "I expect you'll enjoy that," she said, and then smiling goodbye went into the house and to bed.

*

He did enjoy it; enough to make him want to repeat the experience rather more often than Molly cared for, though she had more sense than to say so. A couple of weeks later he went out with Ben on a Friday night and swore, groaning, on the Saturday that he'd never go near the man again.

Molly laughed at the pale face and bruised-looking forget-me-not eyes. "Serves you right," she said heartlessly. "What on earth did you get up to?"

"God knows. I think we must have finished up with a tot from every bottle in the place – wherever it was – and there was Ben, fresh as a daisy and ready to start again. He's got the constitution of a carthorse, that one. I think he's done it this time. I'm dying."

The room was empty. Molly slid from the arm of his chair into his lap, her arms loose around his shoulders, her face in the hollow of his neck.

"Ouch!" His hand came up to her head, forced back her laughing face with its sharp white teeth and kissed her.

"You aren't dying," she announced with some certainty a few moments later, and was tumbled sharply to the floor for her pains. But despite her laughter his drinking bouts with Ben worried her.

All through November tidings of the war were called on street corners, and the newsboys did brisk business even though all the news was bad. The sieges were unbroken, the Boers' hit-and-run tactics harried and defeated the relief columns as they marched in uncompromising military order through a wide and wild countryside that was totally alien to them. Molly ignored the war stubbornly, refused to discuss it, turned on Harry in an anger born of fear when he spoke with enthusiasm of the reported valour of the British troops defending Ladysmith, Mafeking and Kimberley.

"'Tis the other side of the world," she snapped sharply. "What has it to do with us? Can you think of nothing else? Is there nothing closer to home worth noticing?"

And indeed there was; for at the beginning of December came a pleasant if not altogether unexpected event – Charley announced, as happily as if no such thing had ever occurred before, that Annie had agreed to marry him. The occasion was marked by a party that went on till four o'clock in the morning at which time Ben, standing astride the open garden gate with one foot on each gatepost and an upturned, fortunately empty, chamber pot on his head, brought the festivities to a close with a very unofficial version of 'Rule Britannia'. Charley kissed Annie to loud applause, Nancy and Joe were seen for the first time in public to hold hands, and Harry, drawing Molly into the cold darkness of the garden, asked in mock anxiety if she thought proposals might not be catching?

She tilted her head to look at him in the darkness. "I hope not," she said.

"Oh?" He was startled, slightly stung.

"I don't want a share of Annie's proposal," she said softly. "If I'm to have one at all I'll have one of my own, thank you."

The shouting and singing by the front gate had died into cries of goodnight and a few last, laughing words of advice for the happy couple.

"I see." He bent his head; his lips teased hers. "Fussy in Ireland, are we?"

"We are," she said firmly.

A quick gust of December night-wind rustled the leaves around them, roughened their party-warmed skins. Molly shivered. He wrapped his arms about her and spoke into her hair, his voice suddenly totally sober. "I'll make a terrible husband, you know. Terrible." He was not joking.

From inside the house came the sound of Jack's voice, calling Harry.

Molly smiled into Harry's shirt. "Do you call that a proposal?"

He laughed with one of his quick swings of mood, stood her from him at arm's length. "Oh, no. Didn't I once tell you I'd do it in style?"

She nodded. "You did."

"And so I shall, lass, see if I don't." His voice was serious again, the drink-flushed, high-boned face gleaming in starlight. "Just give me time."

Jack was bellowing, impatient now, from the back door. "*Ha — arry.*" There was clearing up to be done.

"As much as you like," said Molly softly, tempting fate beyond forbearance. "As much time as you like."

Molly was given an unexpected treat that Saturday morning: Mr Jenkins was away on business and Mr Vassal had a niece getting married and was anxious to be away; so it was that Molly got to West Ham a couple of hours earlier than usual.

The day was cold; a gusting, swirling wind tormented the last of the fallen leaves. Molly held on to her hat as she battled around corners, her skirts plastered dangerously around her legs and ankles. Knowing that Sarah and Jack were away in Yorkshire caring for Sarah's sister, who had been taken ill, and that Charley, inevitably, would be round at his Annie's, she was looking forward to a quiet afternoon around the fire with Harry, Nancy and Edward. At the thought of the promised warmth and comfort she quickened her steps; as she rounded the last, gusty corner she heard her name called excitedly. She stopped, lifting her head, her blinking eyes stung by the dust-laden wind. Edward, his blond curls tossing like unseasonal buttercups in the breeze, his face alight with an excitement beyond the blustery weather, was dashing towards her. Behind him, her face a sudden picture of apprehensive dismay, was Nancy. Molly did not see her; her eyes were upon the child as he raced to her, shouting above the wind.

"Molly, Molly! Guess what!"

She caught his hands and swung him round, laughing. "What? What's happened?"

"Edward!" Nancy's voice, harsh and urgent, was nevertheless nearly lost in the wind. "Edward, don't—"

"Harry's going to join the army! With Ben. They're going to fight the Boers—"

She released him so suddenly that he almost fell. He stumbled, righted himself, looked at her in surprise. He'd never seen anyone look so queer.

"Edward!" His sister, usually so gentle, grabbed his arm roughly and yanked him to her side. He looked from Nancy to Molly, his lip trembling.

Nancy stared at Molly, watching the white flame of rage kindle in the wide-set grey eyes as Edward's words finally registered in a brain made unreceptive by shock. "Molly, oh, Molly, love, I'm sorry. He shouldn't have told you like that. We weren't expecting you. Not yet. It didn't occur to me that we'd meet you. I should have told him not to—"

"What has he done?" The sharp question cut across her friend's words; and Nancy knew that it did not refer to Edward.

Miserably she said, "He was out with Ben and the others last night. He came back—" She stopped.

"Drunk," Molly supplied expressionlessly, the clenched fury in her eyes the only life in a bone-white face.

Nancy's shoulders drooped. "Well, you know how – Molly, you have to talk to him yourself. It isn't fair on either of you that you should hear it from me."

"Where is he?"

"At home." Nancy jerked a head back over her shoulder.

The wind buffeted them, their skirts streamed out like dark funeral banners. Without a word Molly walked past them and away down the street towards the Benton house. Nancy watched the rigid back with pain in her eyes.

Edward, his dampened spirits recovered, swung on her hand. "Come on, Nance. You said you'd buy me a cake."

Very quietly Molly let herself in through the back door. The frozen shock that had clutched her was loosening gradually, being replaced by a more painful burning anger; she could barely breathe as it spread through her veins, pounded in her ears. The scullery was empty, as was the living room beyond, empty and warm from the lit range, the December darkness through the small window throwing gloomy shadows around the unnaturally quiet house. She pushed open the front room door; the fire was laid, ready but unlit in the black, polished grate; the window rattled in the wind; the air was chill and slightly damp. Harry was not there.

From the room above came a stirring, the vaguest creaking movement.

She climbed the dark stairs noiselessly, pushed open the bedroom door.

He sat upon the side of the bed, his brown and honey head bowed to his hands; despite the chill he was wearing only trousers and his feet were bare. The bed was rumpled and untidy and the room smelled unpleasantly. As the door swung back against the wall he straightened, wincing, the brilliant eyes for a moment unfocussed, the face bleached of colour. He looked very sick. She slammed the door and watched him flinch.

"What's this I hear?" Her voice was soft, ineluctably hard, "Going for a soldier, are we?"

He could not look at her. He ran long fingers through thick and tangled hair. "Who told you?"

"What does it matter who told me?"

"You must have known I might."

"I did not." Every quietly enunciated word dripped an acid disbelief. "Have you taken leave of your senses?"

He did not reply, but rubbed the heels of his hands hard into his eyes. The buffeting wind outside was carrying rain now, hurling it against the window pane like showers of pebbles.

He stood up, his eyes steadier, his head lifted. She felt the defending rage slip from her; she ached to touch him and was afraid that he knew it. This time it was she who turned away. She walked to the window and stared sightless at the streaming glass. She felt him come up behind her, braced herself against his hands on her shoulders.

"Molly, you have to try to understand."

She did not turn; her voice was even and expessionless. "Understand? I understand. I understand that you and Ben Samson found a message at the bottom of a whisky glass last night. I understand that the man's a lunatic and that when you're with him you're no better. What's the plan? Are the two of you going to relieve Mafeking double-handed? For God's sake, Harry, are you a child to get yourself talked into such a thing? Do you even *know* what you're doing?" She turned to face him at last, no longer caring to hide the tears. "A soldier, Harry? You? A murdering, red-coated bastard of a soldier—?" Her voice choked in her throat.

He stepped back from her, staring, then laughed suddenly, the sound sharp and harsh. "And I thought you were worried about *me*."

"I am!" She had known her mistake as she spoke, but had been powerless to stem the bitterness. "How can you doubt it? I love you, Harry, I love you; you know it. I'd give my blood for you if you needed it, every drop. How can you think of throwing it all away? This war has nothing to do with us; there is no threat to us in it, win or lose. Why should you risk your life—and worse? Why?"

"Because," he said, and it was as if every ounce of energy he possessed were in his eyes, willing her to understand, "because I can't spend my whole life pushing about bloody stupid bits of paper and counting bags of stinking sugar. I *can't*. Because there's got to be more than this." He gestured at the tiny room. "Ben says—"

"Ben says! Ben says?" Her voice was threaded with fury. "What the Hell does Ben know about it? Do you know what soldiers do, Harry? Have you thought about it at all? They kill! That's what soldiers are for. To *kill*. And not just each other, either, don't fool yourself about that. What do you think South Africa will be like, Harry? What do you think is happening there? Rows of smart little toy soldiers marching up and down to fife and drum with brave flags flying? They are fighting across a land where people *live*. Do you think there is never a woman or a child who gets in the way? Never an old man who can't move fast enough to get away from the bullets? And do those brave soldiers care, do you think? What do you think they do to Boer women who have information they need? Ask them nicely for it? Think, Harry, *think*! Have you seen what happens to a man with a bullet in his stomach? Has Ben? Are you ready for that?" She saw it then, through the tears; the fear in his eyes, quickly mantled; remembered his stance when she'd entered the bedroom and knew beyond doubt that he had thought of these things and was afraid. She took his hands, clinging like a child. "Please, Harry, please, please. Don't go. Let Ben go alone if he's so set. Don't go, don't leave me. I couldn't stand it. I couldn't!"

He gathered her, sobbing, into his arms, rocked her gently until the spasm of weeping had passed. In the silence the sound of the rain that was now drumming steadily on the window filled the room. As she calmed she became aware of her hot, wet face on the smooth and cool skin of his chest. She closed her aching eyes; his fingers trembled in her hair, on the nape of her neck. Though her sobs had ceased the tears still ran, sliding down her cheeks as the rain slid down the window, and she as powerless to stop them.

He drew her to the bed, sat her upon it like a child, crouched before her and held her hands, the bright lines of his face lifted to her in the gloom. "I want you to understand."

"You don't have to go," she said stubbornly, sniffing. "No one can make you. You don't have to go."

"I promised Ben. We said we'd join together."

"But you haven't actually signed on yet?"

He shook his head.

"Well then."

He bit his lip, shook his head again, indecision in his eyes. "I promised."

She sensed a balanced irresolution, some softening of his determination; leaning forward she kissed the straight mouth, pulled him to her. Off-balance he tumbled onto the bed beside her, his lips still on hers, and suddenly his hands were on her breasts, moving across her belly, fumbling with her clothes. Her body was like wire strung taut and singing; she helped him, trembling, with the buttons of her jacket, then her blouse, baring her breasts for him, holding and caressing the honeyed hair as his strong tongue found her nipples. She was still breathing in odd, sobbing gasps. He pulled away from her and sat up, burying his face in his hands in a violent movement.

She lay still, watching him; his shoulders were bunched as if against pain.

"You'd better go," he said, and even through the muffle of his hands she sensed the dangerous edge to his voice.

She calculated and accepted the risk; something she never later forgot. "No."

He turned in mixed anger and pleading. "For Christ's sake, Moll. This won't help. You have to leave me to make up my own mind." His eyes ran over her breasts, lifted to the pale light of her face in its frame of wild black hair. She neither moved nor spoke; her die was cast and she would stick by it. She watched the rage and frustration growing in his eyes and a small flame of fearful excitement flickered within her.

"If you won't go," he said at last through clenched teeth, "then I will." He stood, towering above her, his every move a shout of anger, his face a blaze of violence.

In between one breath and another she ceased to care, ceased almost to remember what had brought her here, was aware of nothing but the aching hunger and thirst that the sight of him inflicted. Following an instinct older than anger, she moved, sliding her body further onto the bed until she lay, her arms loose above her head, her body relaxed and supplicating, her eyes, silvered with excitement and fear fixed upon the man's face.

Despite the cold a faint sheen of sweat glistened on his skin. He tried to move, tried to force himself from her, but might as well have been nailed where he stood. Still he remained obdurately standing, refusing to touch her. He caught the sharp gleam of her teeth through her parted lips, bright in the dim light. She moved slowly, languidly beneath his angry eyes; her hands lingering over her own breasts, touching lightly the raised and reddened tips; a dark sweep of lashes drifted over shining eyes. Choked by an undefeatable wave of love and fury he reached for her.

He would not lift his head, nor turn. He lay on his stomach, his forehead hard upon his crossed arms, the strong curve of his back outlined sharply in the grey light from the window. She lay on the pillows beside him and watched him quietly, wanting to touch him, to soothe the knotted tension of his muscles, knowing beyond any doubt that she could not. She was drained and aching; blank fear walled part of her mind. Yet there was a kind of happiness. No matter what he decided, no matter what he took from her now, he could not take the feel of his body, the sound of his wild voice as she had known it in the last few minutes. Part of him at least was hers.

The silence stretched on; she made no move to help him. Something within her was dully certain that she had lost.

He lifted his heavy head at last, in the shadowed eyes some look of peace. "We'll get married," he said quietly. "Now. Before I go. Ben'll have to wait."

She felt as if a hot blade twisted somewhere inside her. "No."

He moved impatiently. "Don't be daft, lass."

"No. I won't do it. Don't ask me."

He was staring at her now, angry disbelief growing in his face.

"You don't have any choice. You're not trying to tell me that you don't want to marry me?"

"You know I want nothing more. But I won't marry a soldier. I will not." The total and tired lack of emphasis on the words added to their force. She turned her head away. "If you go with Ben – if you wear that uniform – you'll not see me again."

He sat up jerkily, swung his legs to the floor. "Don't talk such bloody rubbish."

"*You don't have to go.*"

"I do! I do! Christ, woman, can't you understand that? We shook on it, shook hands on it. In front of the others. I gave my word—"

"I'm surprised," she said, slithers of ice suddenly in her voice, "that you didn't mingle blood like true brothers in adventure."

"Bitch." The dread was there again, unacknowledged, gnawing. What had he done? She was right, and he knew it in his soul. To kill or be killed. Why hadn't he thought of that the night before when, in face of Ben's gay eloquence it had all seemed so different, so much a game? To defeat the fear he spoke rougher than he intended. "I won't ask twice. Stop being so bloody awkward. You've no choice, I tell you. We can get married in a couple of weeks. The Boers can wait that long, and so can Ben. You can stay here with Mam and the others till I come back—"

As he spoke she was dressing calmly, obstinately suppressing the trembling of her hands and body. "No," she said again, flatly. She felt sticky and uncomfortable; empty.

"Moll, for God's sake—" The misery in his voice stilled her for a moment, then she steadily continued dressing. He watched her helplessly. "Don't force me to a choice—"

She did not answer, reached for her jacket. Her silence maddened him, made him tremble. "If you go through that door you don't come back. I warn you." He took a deep, shaking breath. "So now it's your choice, not mine. I'll marry you—I want to marry you—I love you for Christ's sake—" she turned sharply from him, not to show the spasm of pain that caused "– but I won't leave Ben in the lurch. I can't."

Something blazed in the space behind her eyes; perfectly calm she walked around the bed. "Don't come near me," she said, "in your fancy red butcher's uniform. I'll spit on it. I wish you joy of your killing." And with the air between them acrid with bitterness she left him.

She had not truly believed he would let her go. Against all reason she listened for his voice calling her back, strained her ears for the sound of his running footsteps above the rain. Back in her room she huddled over her fire, too hopelessly miserable for tears, waiting for the knock that would tell her that he had come.

But the wet and endless day turned to winter's night and there was no sign of him. Not the next day, or the next. She ate nothing, hardly slept; she snapped back at Owen Jenkins and was sharply reprimanded for it. She did not care. A week passed, then another.

Then Nancy came, Ellen Alden announcing her arrival late on a dark evening.

Molly had heard the knock on the front door, but had long ago given up listening for the sound of Harry's voice. When the sharp rap on her own door came, she jumped.

"Yes?"

Ellen Alden stood there unsmiling, "A visitor for you."

Her heart leapt to her throat and she half-stood. Nancy's eyes as she came through the door took in the stance, the half-expectant excitement. "It's me, Molly," she said gently.

The door closed behind her and the girls were left in the flickering light of the gas mantle, looking at each other.

"Does Harry know you're here?" One last chance – he might have sent his sister, asked her to come.

Nancy shook her head.

"Then why have you come?" The sharpness of misery; Nancy bit her lip.

"I'm here because I can't bear to see you two doing this to each other. Molly, you can't let him go like this, without a word——"

"Go?" Her heart had stopped beating entirely.

"He's leaving the day after tomorrow. For South Africa."

Nancy's own face was drawn with a sense of loss. She said into the silence, "He loves you, Molly, you know it. Oh, I know he's a bit – hasty sometimes, a bit selfish. Aren't we all? But he loves you. And I was so sure you loved him——?"

Silence.

"I was hoping I could persuade you to come home with me. To see him before he leaves?"

The pain grew worse. "No."

"Oh, you're as bad as he is! Is your blessed pride worth—"

"Pride?" Molly turned on her, blazing. Nancy stepped back. "Is that what you think? You think *pride* is stopping me? Don't you know that I'd go on my knees to him if I thought it would make any difference? Don't look to my pride, Nancy, for the cause of this misery, look to his." She measured the other girl with her eyes for a moment, then said more calmly, "I'll tell you what stops me, what lies between me and any man, Harry or no, who of his own free will takes up arms against another. Two young men, dead in the street. No. More than that. Dozens of young men. Hundreds. Thousands. And all with someone to love them. Those two were just my own, so it hurts more. I've lived through a war of sorts all of my life. I've seen—" She stopped, something close to panic moving in her eyes. "It is wrong to impose your law with a gun. *Wrong!*" She smashed a hand painfully on the table. "How will Harry do it?" she whispered painfully, "how?"

Nancy let the whisper die into the shadows. "I don't know about such things," she said quietly, "I only see two people apart who should be together. Come home with me. He leaves the day after tomorrow."

"If he wants me he must come for me. But not while he wears that uniform."

Nancy shook her head sadly. "Never, then," she said with certainty. "Won't you even write to him?"

Molly shook her head. Nancy turned and walked to the door; she stopped with her fingers on the handle. "When he's gone – will you come and see us sometimes? Mam asked me specially to ask. We all miss you. Our kid's always asking where you are."

Molly cleared her throat. "I expect so. But not yet. Not just yet."

Nancy nodded and left her.

In the end against her own better judgement Molly spent Christmas with them, but for her it was not a success. The sight of Charley and Annie, Nancy and Joe, turned a knife in her no matter how she tried to deny it. Harry had been gone for a fortnight; no one offered news of him and she did not ask. Pressed to join them for New Year she refused gently.

"But Moll, it's special this year. A new century." Nancy caught her hand. "I hate to think of you on your own."

"I won't be on my own," she lied, "Sam and his mother have asked me to join them."

Perhaps the wish was father to the thought: on the day before New Year's Eve Sam accosted her in the hall.

"We – M – Mother and I – wondered if you'd like to s – see the New Year – century in with us?"

"Aren't you going to your Uncle's?"

He shook his head, grinning suddenly. "N – not even mother can stand Uncle Thomas twice in one week. We spent Christmas with them."

She hesitated.

"Please," he said, and she smiled.

"All right. What time shall I come down?"

And so it was Sam who kissed her shyly upon the cheek – after he had saluted his slightly less austere than usual mother first – and wished her with no sense of irony or forboding a happy and peaceful new century. Around them the bells pealed wildly their oddly ambivalent message – for bells can ring warning as well as celebration – and as the last moment of 1899 died and the hand of the quietly ticking clock slipped past midnight and into another hundred years, the changes had already begun.

CHAPTER FOURTEEN

JANUARY WAS NEVER a good month for Sam. The cold weather invariably aggravated his bad chest and the grey skies and the thought of the long months still to struggle through before spring relieved him of a little of the burden of his cough depressed him. January 1900, to begin with, was no different from any other. He suffered and tried to suppress his cough, suffered and knew no way of suppressing his mother's overbearing ministrations. He took with meek patience his doses of the Grand Old Remedy recommended by Mr G. T. Congreve in his book on Chest Diseases and Consumption – Ellen Alden's Bible at this time of the year, and Sam's bane. He did as he was told as far as he was able, wrapped himself against the cold, tried to resist the drained tiredness that so often overcame him, and quietly bought a new handkerchief each time he had to throw one away because of the bright spattering of blood that was becoming noticeably more frequent. He found it difficult to eat; he knew he was getting thinner than ever. His mother bullied and cajoled him, demanding of his Uncle Thomas, to Sam's mortification, that his duties in the shops be made lighter.

"It's time he gave you an assistant. After all, you aren't just any employee. One day—"

"Mother!"

"One day," Ellen repeated sternly, "when you marry Lucy the shops will be yours. Maude was talking of it at Christmas. Though I must say that you didn't seem to be doing much about it—"

"Mother, I don't think I want to marry Lucy." His voice was mild, uncertain; he hated the sound of it. "I don't think I should."

She ignored him. "I think it's time we made some definite plans. I'll talk to Maude about it."

"Mother—" He broke off, coughing into his handkerchief.

His mother's handsome face darkened, her clear, strong-marked brows came together in an expression he knew all too well, one work-hardened finger lifted, jabbing the air between them. "Now, you just listen to me, Sam Alden. Not a word – *not a word* – do you hear? Are you going to be a messenger boy all your life? Don't you want to make something of yourself? You're fond of Lucy, you know you are. A man should be married. What do you want – that Lucy should go off and find someone else for Thomas to hand the shops to? Over my dead body. She may be plain as a broomhandle, but if you dangle her much longer I warn you she'll likely go looking – and her father's money will make up for lack of other things, you may be sure of that. There'll be plenty to take advantage of such opportunity—"

A wave of tiredness overcame Sam. He tilted back his head, his breath wheezed painfully. His mother's voice rattled in his head like coins in a tin. He closed his eyes. "I'm going next door for a minute. That wretched boy has broken the fence. I warned that woman there'd be trouble if he did it again—" her voice faded down the hall.

Sam flinched as the door slammed, finding echoes in his aching body. He sat still for a moment, savouring the silence, letting thoughts of his mother, Aunt Maude, Lucy drain from him and calling up quietly that image he saved for his few private moments. He was worried about Molly. She had not been looking well lately; the unhappiness in her eyes hurt him when he saw it. He knew that her trouble had something to do with her young man, that gay and graceful Harry whom he had met last summer and in whom he had recognized ungrudgingly a fit mate for his beautiful Molly. He had seen the look in her eyes when Harry was near, heard her sing, watched her bloom through the summer, changing from the elfin waif who had first knocked on his door to an assured and lovely girl. But now the visits to the Bentons had almost stopped and she spent long hours upstairs on her own. She hardly spoke except when spoken to; dark shadows smudged her eyes. He was certain she was losing weight. Sam had seen the bright, glittering tears that had stood in her eyes at midnight on New Year's Eve, had understood without rancour even as he had for the first time kissed her smooth, pearly cheek that his were not the lips she had been thinking of in that moment. He thought of Harry's challenging laughter, the arrogant lift of his handsome head and admitted to himself that he could hardly blame her—

As if his thoughts had conjured her to him he heard the sound of a key in the lock and the street door opened. Not Ellen. She had barely had time to get started yet. He waited for the sound of light footsteps in the hall. None came. He walked to the kitchen door and opened it. Molly was standing by the front door, leaning upon it, her head back, her eyes closed. She looked exhausted and miserable, frail as thistledown. His already-sore chest tightened painfully. He stood and watched her for a moment. Her teeth were caught hard in her lower lip and her breathing was light and shallow. Remembering how ill she had been this time last year he started forward anxiously.

"Molly? Is something the matter?"

Her eyes flew open and she pushed herself from the door, straightening her body and coming to life in that split second that she realized she was observed.

She laughed. "Matter? Not much. I've lost my job, that's all." The bravado did not quite cover the distress.

"How on earth did that happen?"

She shrugged, walking slowly to the foot of the stairs. "My own fault; it was bound to happen sooner or later, I suppose. I'm afraid I was extemely rude to one Owen Jenkins. A mistake that I have a strong feeling that my father would have been proud of. Mr Jenkins was only too pleased to point out, in front of the whole office, that he had always held women to be temperamentally unsuited to the responsibilities of office work, and that now I had so obligingly proved him to be right I might take myself off and never darken his office door again. Whereupon I gave him – also in front of the assembled staff, I'm pleased to say – my own opinion of himself, his office and his prejudices, and left."

"I'm sorry," he said awkwardly.

"Oh, it wasn't all bad." The lightning grin that lit her eyes soon died. "Bits of it I quite enjoyed."

"What will you do now?"

She shrugged tiredly. "Look for another job, I suppose."

"In an office?"

"Perhaps. Or a shop. I don't know." She didn't sound as if she greatly cared. Her hand was on the banister and she leaned her head upon it. The shadows were back in her eyes. "I'm a bloody idiot," she said.

All the months she had put up with Jenkins' sardonic dislike, and now, now of all times, she had lost control of tongue and temper and predictably harmed no one but herself.

"Come and have a cup of tea."

"Thank you, but no. I'm very tired. I'll go straight to bed, I think."

He divined her need with sure instinct. "I'll bring you a cup if you like; you don't have to stay down here and talk. And we've some nice honey. Let me bring you a couple of slices of bread and honey – you must eat."

Disconcertingly the wide lavender eyes clouded with tears. "You're very kind."

He felt strong, suddenly, and protective; never in his life before had he been anything but the recipient of help. He realized suddenly that he had not coughed, nor stuttered, since his mother had left the house.

"You go on up," he said firmly, "the fire's lit. I'll bring you a tray."

It was Sam who, a few days later, answered the summons of the doorbell to find Jack and Nancy Benton standing on the door-step. One look at them told him that something very bad indeed had brought them here. Nancy's thin face was swollen and patched red with crying, her dark eyes dulled with misery. The man's strong face was drawn tight to the bone, his brilliant eyes, so like his brother's and usually so calm, were fierce with pain. He wasted no time in greeting.

"Is Molly here?"

"Yes. She's in her room. I'll call her."

Jack's great frame pushed almost angrily past him, his eyes already lifting to the stairs. Nancy, gentler even in her distress, put a hand on Sam's arm.

"I think it would be better if we went up." Her voice was hoarse; crying had drained it.

"All right." Sam closed the door, watched their heavy tread up the stairs. His own heart was pounding painfully.

His mother came from the kitchen, her sharp eyes going immediately to the stairs. "Who was that?"

"Friends of Molly's." He tensed himself to listen; the murmur of voices, Jack's mostly.

"A man? You've let a man up there? Now you know the rules—" His mother made for the stairs.

"*No.*" Sam barred the way. "Something's happened. Something really bad. It's Harry Benton's brother and his sister. She'd been crying." He sucked nervously at his lower lip. " – I think he had, too."

Jack and Nancy were upstairs for a very long time. Then, at last, Molly's door opened and Sam heard footsteps on the stairs. Ignoring his mother's warning glance – for no matter how curious Ellen Alden might be there were certain conventions to be observed – Sam leapt for the door, almost upsetting his chair as he went. He met the brother and sister at the foot of the stairs – Nancy was crying unrestrainedly, sobbing within the circle of Jack's arm. Jack looked as if the hounds of hell were at his bones.

"She wouldn't let us stay." Jack's voice was completely flat, worn out. "Wouldn't come home with us either. Can't say I blame her, there's not much there for anyone at the moment."

"What's happened?"

"Harry's dead. He volunteered for South Africa. Died on the ship on the way out. Fever."

"Jesus." Sam's shocked word was almost a prayer.

Nancy said, trying to hold her sobs, "They had a fight before he went. She wouldn't even see him to say goodbye. Oh, God, she looks so awful. Please, Sam, take care of her; she won't let us do anything—"

"I will." Something in his tone drew Jack's attention from his own grief. For a moment the inward-looking eyes regained awareness and he studied the thin, flushed face of the man who stood awkwardly before them, his sensitive mouth tightened to a pain not his own, his pale and usually indecisive eyes firm with a desire to help.

Jack nodded brusquely, hesitated for a moment, his eyes lifted to the door at the top of the stairs, then he shepherded his crying sister to the door.

Sam let instinct oust manners and let them see themselves

out. He went up the stairs at a pace that left him gasping. He stood outside her door for a moment, regaining his breath, then, without knocking, entered the room.

Molly sat like a shadow in the chair by the fire, perched on the edge of the seat, her head down, her body bent over her crossed arms as if in dreadful pain. She was rocking very slightly, making no sound. At the opening of the door she lifted a face blind and bloodless with shock; her eyes were ash-grey, sightless and unfocussed. Sam had the awful feeling that she could not see him.

"Molly," he whispered, stepping forward, "Molly, I'm so sorry."

She stared at him as if she did not know him.

"He's dead," she said in an unrecognizable voice. "They said Harry's dead. Harry. Harry. Harry." She spoke his name to the rhythm of her rocking. Sam had never seen or heard anything so terrible.

"Molly," he said again, desperate to stop the awful movement, the dry, rhythmic voice. "Please don't. Please, Moll—" He felt absolutely helpless.

He saw her shudder, felt in his own bones the effort she made; the rocking stopped and she fell silent. In the street outside flakes of snow were falling, the first of the winter. They drifted past the window in pretty, aimless, ever-changing patterns. She watched them with empty eyes.

"He never even got to South Africa," she said at last, her voice a little closer to normal. "He never even got there." – Harry, laughing, gleaming in sunlight – "He died of fever."

"So his brother said."

– Harry, honey-gold and arrogant, kissing her with warm, hard mouth—"He would have hated that. Hated it," she whispered, aware that she was rocking again but powerless to stop herself. – Harry, blazing with anger, her own voice bitter; "Don't come near me in your fancy red butcher's uniform. I'll spit on it. . . ."

"Oh God," she said, "oh, my God." The tears she had believed would never come suddenly rose in a blinding, scalding flood. Death was for ever. For ever. She felt as if she were bleeding. She heard his name, over and over, did not realize that her own voice spoke it. She could not sit still, she stood up, moving her head blindly, trying to escape the insupportable knowledge that she would never see him again, never hear him—

"Molly." Her own name pierced the blackness, the single word spoken as much in pain as she had uttered Harry's.

"What shall I do without him?" she asked, lost. "What shall I do?"

She felt gentle arms around her, laid her face on the rough tweed of Sam's jacket. She was crying now, crying as if she would never stop.

Sam held her to him as if he could somehow will the pain from her.

"I'll take care of you," he said, the first time he had ever spoken those words to a soul. "Don't worry, I will. I promise."

But he knew that through her own wild sobbing she had not yet heard him.

"You're mad! Stark, raving mad!" Ellen Alden stormed around her kitchen like a tempest, unable in her angry incredulity to remain still. Sam stood by the table, an even more hectic flush than usual on his thin face, stubbornness in every line of him. He said nothing.

"To marry her! *Marry* her! A penniless Irish beggar? She'll be the death of you, do you know that?"

"Mother, I won't argue. I've made up my mind. I've asked Molly to marry me and she has agreed."

"I should think she has," sneered his mother.

Sam plodded on. "If you absolutely refuse to accept the idea then we'll have to leave, find somewhere else to live."

"So it's come to that, has it? She's put you up to this, hasn't she? Coming between mother and son. It would serve you right if I did throw you out. You'd starve together in the gutter if I did. Which is no better than she deserves. What about Lucy? You'll break her heart—"

"Oh, Mother, no. N – not that. Lucy thinks no more of me than I do of her, and you know it. She j – just couldn't be bothered to find anyone else, to s – stand up to her father and mother." He struggled angrily, knowing his stutter was getting

worse. "Lucy's that idle that she'd starve to death if her m –
mother didn't cook her dinner. What kind of wife would she
make?"

"And what sort of wife will that flighty Irish piece make, do
you think? Oh, I was sorry for her, I don't deny that, her Harry
dying and all. But she's got over it pretty sharply, hasn't she?
Only weeks since we heard. What kind of girl could do that?
She's marrying you on the rebound, that's what." She stabbed a
finger at him, certain of an irrefutable point. "On the rebound."

"I know that." His voice was quiet.

"What?" His mother was struck to stillness by the shock of his
words. "Now I know you're mad. I'll have you committed—"

"I've made her see that it's for the best."

"Best for her," his mother hissed.

"Maybe. Anyway, there it is. M – Molly and I are getting
married. The only question is, do we stay or do we go? That's up
to you."

Ellen did not for the moment answer; she watched her son
with a lowering anger that would normally reduce him to a jelly.

"Very well," she said at last, deceptively mild, "let me put it
another way. Does your Molly know what she's getting in this
bargain?"

"What do you mean?" He was wary.

For answer his mother turned and strode to the dresser. She
opened a drawer, rummaged in it, then came back to the table.
"This is what I mean." The anger was almost gone from her
voice; only pain was left as she dropped onto a table that
gleamed with cleanliness a bloodstained handkerchief. "I took it
from the dustbin. You didn't tell me. Have you told her?"

He felt a dizzy rushing in his ears. The stains looked much
worse than he remembered: dark and forboding.

"No," he said. "I haven't. And you won't either."

He lifted his eyes from the disgusting, crumpled piece of
material to his mother's drawn face. "If you do I'll g – go. I
swear it, Mother. And you'll n – never see me again. Never."

For the only time in his life he saw his mother collapse before
his eyes. Her shoulders slumped, she would not look at him. "Do
as you like," she said. "You're over twenty-one, supposed to be a
man, God help us. I can't stop you."

He turned and walked to the door, hesitated there.

"I w – want us to be happy," he said, knowing it hopeless. "All of us. Together."

He closed the door on silence.

On the last day of February 1900, a cold day with a hard frost in the air, Molly Meghan Teresa O'Dowd became the wife of Samuel John Alden at the tiny chapel in Green Street before a small gathering of his friends and relations. The bride might have been made from the ice that frosted the world outside; her dress was not whiter than her small, bleached face, nor the inexpertly embroidered flowers around its hem more lifeless than her eyes. Yet she smiled at Sam as she spoke the words that bound them, held his hand, as if for comfort, as they left the rather ugly little building. If she missed the grandeur and ceremony of her native church she did not mention it – though in any case an odd circumstance checked the wedding with a gaiety of which, under other circumstances, most of the dour congregation would not have approved; as the couple came into the crisp February air and made their way back to Linsey Grove where Ellen, concerned as always with outward appearances, had grudgingly laid on a meagre wedding breakfast, all over London, all over the country, the bells began to ring. Thousands of miles away the town of Ladysmith had been relieved; the tide of war had begun to turn.

PART II

Autumn 1900

CHAPTER FIFTEEN

SAM ALDEN LEANED for a moment against the front gate of number twenty-six, battling for breath and fighting a painful spasm of coughing. The weather was dry and warm for late October; the dust that lifted and blew in the gusty wind stung his eyes and aggravated his sore chest. With the sun low to the south, the early afternoon was golden and mellow. Irresistibly he was reminded of the first time he had seen Molly – small, determined, dirty and, he had thought then, the most beautiful girl he had ever seen. He still thought so.

The painful grip on his diseased chest relaxed a little and his breathing eased. He wasn't well, he knew it; knew that never before at this time of the year had his troublesome chest been so bad. He saw in the mirror each day the shadowed hollows of his face, the pallid transparency of his skin, felt the awful, drained weariness that defeated him more and more often and that, combined with the constant and now quite open warfare that existed between his wife and his mother, wore him down, tired him to death. His long mouth turned down at the apt phrase.

Not long after their marriage Sam had fallen very ill indeed; he had been aware, as he lay fighting for breath and drained of strength, that his life had been ebbing from him as surely as water drains through parched ground. But the sight of Molly's pinched and lifeless face, the ominous look in his mother's eyes as Molly's pregnancy had at last become impossible to conceal had been the goads to make him fight on. Slowly he had pulled himself back, had even gained a little ground, so that by the early summer he had been feeling better than for some time. He had, as never before, followed to the letter the doctor's instructions, taken every drop of medicine and tonic prescribed – and several that Ellen had found advertised in the chemist's besides. He'd rested for long hours upon the day bed that Molly had made up in the sitting room of number twenty-six, the room that by arrangement with Ellen was supposed to be the couple's own. Regrettably, during those first, lethargic months of their marriage and the trauma of Sam's almost fatal illness Molly had had neither the strength nor the particular desire to stand up to her dominating mother-in-law, and during that time precedents had been established that now Sam no less than Molly resented, but that no amount of fierce argument on Molly's part nor reasoning on Sam's could change, among them the fact that Ellen took it as her inalienable right to walk into the younger Aldens' rooms at any time she thought fit, and without knocking. In consequence in the eight months of their marriage, Sam and Molly had had hardly any privacy at all, and this, compounded with the inevitable antagonism that had grown between the two women as Molly had slowly recovered from the shock of Harry's death and become more herself again, had made for a turbulent and contentious atmosphere that tightened the nerves and would have made quarrelsome the most peaceful nature. And Sam had to admit that neither of his women had exactly that.

Ellen's bitter outrage when she had come to realize that not only could the coming child not possibly be Sam's, but that Sam had known of Molly's pregnancy from the start, had only been surpassed by her furious and indignant disbelief at the discovery that neither Sam nor Molly had any intention of playing the world's game of pretence that might have been expected of them. Molly flatly refused to juggle with dates, to speak of premature births, to agree to go away for a few months at the appropriate time so that the actual date of the birth could be respectably blurred; and Sam, to his mother's scandalized horror, backed her up. The child, he insisted, would be his, whatever the world – or his mother – chose to say of it. It was nobody's business but their own. And when, at the beginning of September, a crumpled, fierce-tempered, bawling scrap had struggled through Molly's agony to life, no blood-father could have felt a more amazed and genuine surge of feeling for the screaming little bundle that was placed in his arms than did Sam for Daniel Seamus Alden. Molly, totally exhausted by that last unbelievable effort that had brought her son finally to the light, had lain back on her pillows and watched in astonishment the look on Sam's face as he had cradled her son.

"He's b – beautiful," Sam had said softly, "beautiful as his m – mother—"

In that moment Molly had perhaps come closest to truly loving him.

And Ellen Alden, her mouth set to an embittered and acrimonious line, had stalked from the room with no word, her rigid back a warning of things to come.

That had been almost two months ago. Two months of Hell. Molly's strength had returned rapidly; and, with pregnancy and childbirth behind her and little Danny now to protect and defend, it was with a new Molly that Ellen had found herself contending. Every scrap of the stubborn willpower that had so characterized her before had returned. Whatever ascendancy that Ellen might have enjoyed during Sam's illness and before Danny's birth had gone; but not without a bitter fight. And poor Sam, his nights broken by the baby's crying, his days made nerve-wracking by the dissent of the women, slept less and coughed more, knowing all the while that the cold threat of winter was creeping closer.

Now he leaned tiredly against the gate and listened to the sounds of battle that drifted to him through the open window of the house. He could make out no words, but the harsh and wrathful tones of his mother's voice and the softer yet somehow more fiercely violent sound of Molly's told their own story.

Sam sighed and closed his eyes for a moment, unable to summon the energy to interrupt them. "Go and get some rest, boy," Uncle Thomas had said sympathetically a little earlier, listening to the rasp of his nephew's breath and seeing the signs of strain in his face. "We're slack today. I'll finish up here." The strangest outcome, in Sam's opinion, of his rebellious action in marrying Molly had been a great improvement in his relationship with Uncle Thomas. Through Lucy's somewhat surprising hysterics and Maude's indignant fury, Thomas had remained, while still firmly beneath his own women's thumbs, placidly approving of his nephew's sudden – and only – assertion of independence. "Rest" he had repeated, in his eyes that shadow of worry that Sam had come to recognize in those who cared for him, "that's what you need."

Rest. Not much chance of that by the sound of it.

Sam pushed open the gate and started up the path just as the front door flew open and Molly, clutching baby Danny, erupted from it, her face a blaze of rage. None too gently she thumped Danny into the perambulator that stood by the porch, and the baby, who already showed signs of a considerable will of his own, yelled angrily.

" – and take the brat with you!" came Ellen's suppressed and vicious voice, held down so that the neighbours should not be given too great a treat. "Good riddance to the pair of you!"

"What's g – going on?" Sam could not resist the paroxysm of coughing that rose suddenly to his throat.

Molly turned, startled. "Sam? What're you doing home at this time?" A flash of concern replaced the fury in her face as she heard the racking cough and noted the handkerchief pressed to his lips, the way he hunched his shoulders and turned from her as he coughed. Leaving the screaming child she flew to him, "Are you ill? Oh, Sam—"

He shook his head, wiped his mouth carefully and with practised deception, keeping his head turned until he was certain there were no tell-tale stains to be seen, said, "I'm all right. I've been coughing a bit, th – that's all. Uncle Thomas sent me home. To g – get some rest—" His long, expressive mouth twitched. Molly, with a sudden, affectionate gesture, laid her curly head upon his chest.

"I'm sorry, Sam. Truly I am. But you've no idea what she's like when you're not here. You just don't know. I believe that she'd harm the baby if she could—" She sensed shocked dissent in his sudden movement and she caught his arm fiercely, "She *would* I'm telling you. I'm afraid to leave him for a moment—"

Sam shook his head gently. "You're exaggerating, Molly dear. You mustn't l – let things get out of proportion."

A spasm of irritation crossed Molly's face and the anger smouldered again, hardening her momentarily softened mouth. By the front door the child screamed enragedly, determined to regain his mother's attention.

"W – were you going out?"

"Yes." Molly marched to the pram, tucked the baby in firmly and rocked him to silence.

"Where were you going?"

"I don't know. Out. That's all. Just out. Anywhere, to get away from that—" Molly jerked her head towards the house.

"Perhaps you should. A w – walk might do you good, and little Danny too. It's a lovely afternoon. Here—" leaning surreptitiously on the porch for support Sam put his hand into his pocket and pulled out a half-crown and a couple of shining shillings, " – take this. Perhaps you'll see something in the shops, some l – little thing that you'd like. A present from me."

"Oh, Sam?"

"I'd c – come myself if I felt a bit better. Perhaps tomorrow?"

"That would be nice." Molly stood on tiptoe and kissed his cold, thin cheek, trying not to flinch from the sick and fragile feel of him, trying as she had tried every day in the last months not to compare it with the memory of Harry's vital warmth.

"At least you'll get some peace with me out of the way," she said honestly.

He walked to the gate with her, held it open as she man-oeuvred the great, easy-sprung black perambulator – Uncle Thomas's surprising birth gift – through it, watched her as, without looking back, she marched to the end of the road and turned the corner. Then, after a moment's hesitation he went into the house to his mother's anxious and reproachful min-istrations.

At first Molly took no note of where she was going. Her blood still boiled in her veins, her mind, whenever she thought of Ellen, was almost blanked out with fury. Danny was asleep, lulled by the rocking movement of the pram; Molly slowed her steps a little. With nowhere particular to go there was little point in travelling at the rate of a cavalry charge. She tried to turn her mind from her latest virulent exchange with her mother-in-law, her temper not in the least improved by the fact that in this instance at least one of her charges – that she, Molly, had been the cause of the deterioration in Sam's health – might have in it some grain of truth. She remembered him as he had stood there on the path just now. She had been shocked to see him: he had looked ill, worn out. It saddened her to see him so. Poor ailing, kindly Sam, who asked for no more than affection and a little peace and quiet. Through the desolate emptiness of the time since Harry's death she had taken for granted Sam's quiet presence, his unswerving and total devotion that seemed more than grateful to accept in return the only thing she had been able to offer: a mild fondness tinged with pity. If Ellen's charges were in the least true – and she could not in her heart entirely deny them – then she was sorry. She would not deliberately hurt Sam for the world, though she knew too well that in impatience she often did so.

She turned a corner, aware that she was walking a familiar route, but for the moment unheeding. She peered into the pram. Danny was sleeping peacefully, the curls that strayed from beneath his bonnet gilded like flame in the sunshine; she had almost become resigned to the fact that the hair that had started as wispy blond was slowly but unmistakably turning to her father's bright marigold hue. "My little Irishman," Sam called him, laughing at the soft downy hair and bright blue eyes; but it was a gentle half-truth and they both knew it. It was not from his mother's family that Danny had inherited those eyes.

Her footsteps slowed a little as a thought that had been fluttering at the back of her mind suddenly presented itself fully fledged and ready to fly; and she knew where she was going, where she had been heading from the time she had left Sam at the gate. There were others who, if they wished it so, might be said to have some claim upon Danny. Indeed, Molly's only consolation in her bitter feuding with Ellen came from the fact that the woman she detested was no blood relation to the son that, to her own surprise, she adored. Danny had a grandmother who, so far as Molly knew, did not know of his existence. Molly had had no contact with the Bentons since Harry's death. Twice Nancy had come to the house during those awful days after the news, and once Jack, on his own. Each time she had not been able to bring herself to see them. Neither had she told them about or invited them to her odd, dreary little wedding, an event that now seemed to have happened to some stranger, in another life. At the time she had not been able to endure the thought of seeing an echo of Harry in other eyes, hearing him in other voices. But since the baby's birth it had occurred to her more than once that her treatment of Sarah, to whom she knew she owed her life, had been less than kind. Should she not be told that her dead son had left this fragment of life behind him?

Should not she and Danny be brought together, now, before such an introduction, through the passing of time, became impossible? After the fraught and unpleasant atmosphere of the house in Linsey Grove the thought of the Bentons, their affection, their laughter, their total lack of malice was irresistible.

The baby stirred; small hands, like the petals of a flower, opened and closed again. A small, sick flutter of misgiving stirred in Molly's stomach. It came to her suddenly that she had, unconsciously, held this last refuge in reserve; what if she were not, after all, welcome? In the circumstances nothing could be taken for granted.

There was certainly only one way to find out.

She began to walk a little faster, the pram rocking smoothly before her, its momentum carrying her along, the springs creaking rhythmically in time to her quickened footsteps as she trod the painfully well-remembered route to West Ham.

Her determination took her as far as the top of the Bentons' street and there it faltered.

Park Road, to a stranger's eyes, was no different than fifty others in the district, but to one who knew it as Molly did it was unmistakably and achingly familiar. The sight of it brought a tumble of memories that constricted her throat and burned sharply behind her eyes. Her footsteps slowed, dragged. Several doors, including the Bentons', stood open to the unexpected late afternoon warmth; windows were wide, their lacy curtains barely moving in the soft air. Curious eyes watched, one or two smiles and nods of recognition – and inquisitive interest – brought a stiff response from Molly. Her hands were clamped hard around the handle of the pram, as if her life depended upon their grip. By the time she reached the Bentons' front gate her courage had left her and she knew with certainty that she was making a dreadful mistake. The thought of the words that could, in absence of charity, be used against her jangled already in her ears. But she had been seen, and recognized; it was unthinkable now to do anything but follow through her impulse.

She pushed the big pram through the gate and up the short path that led to the open door; she could see no one, but from the back of the house came the sound of voices, Nancy's and Sarah's.

Carefully she lifted Danny from the pram, brushed and straightened his dress and bonnet. The baby stirred, squeaked, went back to sleep again. Molly stood within the familiar, shadowed doorway and strained her ears. Still just those two voices, Nancy's and Sarah's. Her fast-beating heart calmed a little; the women she could face. It came to her, surprisingly, that Jack's voice had been the one she had suddenly dreaded to hear. She stepped quietly across the room where she had first opened her eyes after her illness and seen Harry teasing Nancy by the fire, and opened the door into the back room. From the adjoining scullery came a sudden clatter of crockery and Nancy's voice, raised as Molly had never heard it before, edged raggedly with tears.

"Don't keep on about it, Mam. Please. I've made my mind up. I've got to tell him. Got to."

"I know that, lass. All I'm saying—" Sarah stopped in mid-sentence, her widening eyes fixed upon the small and uncertain figure who had appeared in the doorway.

Nancy turned.

"I'm sorry," said Molly into the silence, "I didn't mean to startle you. The front door was open—" The baby, clutched in her arms, mewed in discomfort; she had to make the physical effort to relax, to hold him less tightly.

Sarah's eyes had gone straight to the child, but Nancy was looking at Molly, her thin face alight with astonishment and dawning delight. "Molly!" she said, and the welcome and warmth in that single word was the final release for Molly's threatened tears. Unable to wipe them away she stood speechless and sniffing as with one accord the two women rushed to her, embracing, exclaiming, words tumbling disjointedly like marbles from a child's pocket. Danny, infuriated by this unaccustomed disturbance, let rip an earsplitting shriek, and Molly found herself handing him into Sarah's competent arms as naturally as if she did it every day. With her arms free she was able to return Nancy's hugs and surreptitiously mop away the tears that were such a confusing compound of happiness and pain. Sarah was crooning softly to Danny, her quiet voice lifting and falling around the girls' excited exclamations, her eyes intent upon the tiny face.

Nancy paused in her torrent of questions, none of which Molly had had opportunity to answer properly anyway, and looked at her mother and the child.

"Is it a girl or a boy?"

"A boy. Danny."

"He's beautiful. Beautiful! Look at the colour of his hair—"

"From my father."

Sarah lifted her head and asked, almost steadily, "And his own father?"

Molly hesitated for only a fraction of a second. If the truth were to be told, it had to be now. "He has Harry's eyes, I think," she said simply. She heard the quick intake of Nancy's breath, saw Sarah's cradling arms gather the baby closer to her, and knew with relief that her instinct had been right.

After a moment's quiet Nancy bustled to the table and picked up the teapot. "Sit down, Moll, for Heaven's sake. I'll make a cup of tea."

Molly sat carefully, her eyes still on Danny, unable yet quite to meet Sarah's. "I'm sorry I didn't tell you," she said awkwardly, "sorry I didn't come. It was just – I couldn't. I couldn't." She ducked her head.

"Don't fret, lass. You've come now. That's all that matters. "Here –" with a small, regretful smile Sarah relinquished the little warm bundle. "It's his Mam he wants. Make yourself comfortable while our Nancy makes the tea. Then we can talk. We've a lot to catch up on—"

Nancy appeared in the doorway with the empty teapot in her hand. "You've come back in time for the wedding," she said happily. "You'll come, won't you?"

"Oh, Nancy, how lovely. Of course I'll come. When is it? Where are you going to—?" She knew as she spoke that she had misunderstood. She stopped abruptly.

Nancy shook her head, set the pot on the table as if it were glass; colour had risen furiously into her face.

"Not me," she said steadily, "Charley and Annie. They're getting wed next month."

Molly looked from one to the other. "Is something wrong?"

Sarah opened her mouth. Nancy said sharply, "Nothing that won't wait till later." She leaned forward and indicated the wedding ring on Molly's hand. "We haven't heard all of your news yet—"

The sound of Jack's arrival, half an hour or so later, was completely covered by the sound of the women's voices. He stood for a moment in the doorway unobserved, watching them. Molly saw him first; Nancy followed the direction of her startled and rather apprehensive gaze and thumped to her feet.

"Jack, oh Jack, look who's come. It's our Molly. And—" she hesitated " – and Danny."

He seemed even bigger than Molly had remembered him, but his square, strong-boned face was the same, and his sun-streaked hair. Oddly, he did not smile, and though he spoke to Nancy his calm blue eyes held Molly's.

"She's right welcome," he said quietly, "she knows it. And the little lad too." Of all the younger Bentons Jack had retained most of his northern origins in his speech; his 'right' still came out almost as 'reet'. Harry, born mimic, had almost totally assimilated the speech of his adopted home. Only in fun had he dropped back to the broad accent of his childhood. The sound of it now stopped Molly's heart for half a beat. She stood up. If he would only smile.

"Thank you," she said.

His serious gaze shifted from her face to the bright head of the child and back again, his expression giving no clue to his thoughts. Molly stepped forward nervously, holding the baby tentatively towards him, unable completely to subdue the slight trembling of her arms. Jack was the undisputed head of the family; she needed, without absolutely understanding why, his approbation, his acceptance of herself and of her son. Always in the past she had been uncomfortably aware of a slight reserve between Harry's eldest brother and herself, something akin to coolness that she could only interpret as disapproval, perhaps even dislike. A year ago her reaction had varied from mild defiance to an elaborate carelessness; now she knew that she needed his friendship. For a long second she stood with the child in her shaking, extended arms, unaware that her eyes spoke the plea that her tongue would not. Jack made no move to take the baby, and with sinking heart she was certain she had lost. Then he lifted an enormous hand, touched the bright soft head gently with a calloused and not very clean finger.

"Nay, lass," he said, his voice thick, "I'll not take him. Likely I'd drop him." He smiled for the first time, the slow, lovely smile he took directly from Sarah. "I doubt he'd take kindly to that. Or you, either."

Molly could not yet return his smile; there was another hurdle to be crossed first. "He's Harry's son," she said, flatly, un-emphatically, hearing the note of defiance in her own voice, unable to prevent it, willing her eyes to remain steady on his.

Jack nodded. "I guessed so."

The front door banged.

"Charley!" said Nancy, happily.

"Good God Almighty! Little Moll!" Charley's delighted grin over Jack's wide shoulders had them all laughing; the odd tension of the preceding moments was broken. "Come on out here, girl, where I can get at you. Bloody scullery's not big enough for me and Jack together." He caught her, baby and all, in a bear hug. "Wait till I tell Annie. Just wait! She'll throw a fit!"

In the hour that followed Molly was happier than she had been in months; but time flew and the baby whimpered, then yelled in good earnest.

"My bedroom," said Sarah, expertly divining the reason for his indignation. "You can feed him there in comfort."

Edward, who had come in some minutes before and who was eyeing Danny with a mixture of fascination and distrust asked, "Why's it go to eat in the bedroom?" and Molly, as she climbed the stairs, heard his small, plaintive voice behind her, "but *why* does the baby have its tea in the bedroom? Can I have my tea in the bedroom? When, Mam? When can I—?"

When she returned to the kitchen some little while later she glanced a little guiltily at the clock, then said, "I really must go. Sam will be worried."

Jack stirred in his chair.

"I'll walk with you," said Nancy quickly, "I can bus back. It isn't late."

"Why don't we all go?" Charley asked cheerfully, but he was quelled by a meaning look from his mother.

"You'll come again soon?" Sarah asked as she kissed Molly's cheek.

Molly nodded. "I promise. You'll get tired of seeing me, that you will."

Charley was looking down at the tiny, milky scrap in the pram, an expression of wonder on his face. "Hell fire," he said quietly, talking almost to himself, "Annie and me could have one like that by this time next year."

"Then I'd advise you both to get as much sleep as possible before it happens," Molly said drily, "for you'll certainly get none afterwards."

"Annie wants six," Charley said, thoughtfully.

"One at a time, I hope!" Molly said, and then she and Nancy left the others still laughing; but the smile soon died from Nancy's face leaving it, as before, strained and unhappy-looking.

The big pram bounced in front of them; Danny, replete, was asleep. Molly stayed quiet, waiting for her friend to speak, but for some time she did not and they walked through the cooling streets in silence. Yet as they walked both were aware of the renewal of their old companionship, of the bond between them that past events might have strained but had certainly not broken. The light was failing rapidly now, though the sky to the west above darkly silhouetted rooftops and chimneys was washed with the faint rose-gold of the aftermath of sunset. As they passed a piece of desolate-looking waste ground across which, despite the deepening dusk, children still ran and called, their voices echoing along the canyons of the surrounding streets, Nancy said abruptly, "There was a bonfire here on Mafeking Night. And fireworks."

"Did you come?"

"Yes. With Charley and Annie. And – Joe." Molly did not miss the infinitesimal hesitation before she spoke the name. "We didn't really want to go at first, but the others talked us into it – you know what Annie is – and they were right. I was glad afterwards, that we went. It would have been a shame to miss it. I've never seen anything like it – people were singing and dancing in the streets, there were bonfires on every corner. It's a wonder London didn't burn down. The greatest celebration ever held, so they say.''

A few more steps in silence. Molly considered her next words carefully and decided that she could be nothing but blunt.

"How is Joey? Do you still see him?"

In the short pause before the other girl answered, their footsteps rang loud on the grimy pavements. "Yes, I still see him. He's fine. He'll be going with his brother soon, out to Africa. As a missionary. And schoolteacher."

The air was turning chilly; Molly fussed Danny a little, pulling the blanket up, tucking his tiny hand beneath it, lifting the hood slightly to protect him from the night air. House doors were shut now, and windows bloomed yellow light. As they passed one Molly glanced at her companion's face. Nancy was staring ahead of her with the lost look of an unhappy child.

"Nancy, what is it? What's wrong?"

"Joe's asked me to marry him. He wants me to go with him to Africa." It was said quite flatly.

Molly stared. "What? But I thought—"

"I said no." Nancy continued, as if Molly had not spoken. "But he doesn't understand. He thinks – he's certain that I'll change my mind. And I won't. I can't. But he won't listen, won't believe it. Oh, God, I didn't want this. I didn't! I just wanted us to be friends—" The edge that Molly had heard in her voice when she had been talking to Sarah was back, wrung with unhappiness, a breath from tears. They turned the corner into the long road that led to Linsey Grove, and their pace slowed.

"I can't say I understand any better than Joey does," Molly said at last, with honesty. "I would have said that you loved him, that you wanted to marry him—"

"I do!" It was a cry from the heart.

"Then for Heaven's sake—?"

"I can't! That's all there is to it. I can't. Oh, it's my own fault, I know. I should never have let things go this far. I tried not to. But I couldn't help it. I love him. I didn't mean to, but I do. I couldn't stop myself."

Molly was close to exasperation. "Why on earth should you try? Nancy, you aren't making any sense. Unless it's that you don't want to leave home, go to Africa – I can understand that—" But Nancy was shaking her head vehemently. "Well, what, then? Do you mean that you think that Joey doesn't love you?"

Nancy took a deep, wretched breath. "He loves me. He says he does, and I believe him. Oh, not – wildly, I know that. It isn't in his nature. But he does love me."

"Well, then—"

It took a visible effort for Nancy to calm herself, but when she spoke her voice was composed again. "I told you. Joey wants to be – is – a missionary, a teacher. He is dedicated to that. He is so sure, so certain. He sees things in black and white, there are no shades in between. There is good and there is bad. He holds every soul responsible for his own actions, and weakness, to Joe, is the same as wickedness; there are no excuses for either." She shrugged, helplessly. "I can't marry him. It would be dishonest. I can't."

They had turned the corner of Linsey Grove. Molly stopped walking so suddenly that Danny woke and stirred protestingly.

"Holy Mary!" Molly's voice held the vehemence of disbelief. "What are you talking about? You're surely not trying to tell me that you won't marry Joey Taylor because you don't think you're good enough for him? Saints above, Nancy, don't be ridiculous." Her voice had risen, disturbing the baby. "Be still," she said to him, "no one's talking to you."

Nancy was shaking her head; in the gleam of lamplight Molly could see the shine of tears.

"You're crazy," Molly continued. "The man's known you long enough. Don't you think he's able to judge? He says he loves you. You love him. Isn't that enough?" Awful echoes of herself and Harry; the thought roughened her voice. "If you ask me about who's good enough for who, I'd say the boot's on the other foot entirely. If Joey Taylor gets you he'll be a lucky man, and I'll be the first to tell him so."

There was an odd little silence. "Oh, Molly," said Nancy, her voice shaking.

Molly looked at her, her heart sinking at the tone of those two simple words. "Tell me," she said very quietly, "Tell me what you haven't told Joe. Perhaps it will help."

"Nothing will help. Nothing. But I'll tell you anyway. You should know." Nancy was leaning into the deep shadows of a dusty privet hedge. A little way down the road the light from the front door of number twenty-six streamed down the path and touched the gate, a bright, waiting finger. A horse and cart clopped sedately across the end of the road and was gone; a dog barked.

"Edward," said Nancy in a clear, tired voice, "isn't my brother. He's my son."

There was no disguising the shock. Molly stared blankly at the pale blur that was Nancy's face. "Your son? But – he can't be—"

"He is." The figure beside her was rigid, the voice expressionless. "He's the reason we left the north, came to London. Can you imagine the tongues? Not even Mam could face them, strong as she is. Right friendly were our neighbours –" bitterly she broadened her accent, " – who'd 'a thowt it, eh? A gradely lass like ower Nance. Ee, I feel reet sorry fer them Bentons—"

"How old were you?"

"Fourteen."

Molly chewed her lip. The splash of light on the pavement outside number twenty-six broadened and brightened as the door was opened. A shadow danced, and footsteps sounded on the tiled path to the accompaniment of a quickly suppressed cough.

Faintly came Ellen's voice, sharp and impatient. "What on earth do you think you're doing now? Sam? Sammy! Come back in here at once. You'll catch your death."

"Just a breath of air, th – that's all." Sam's voice was weary. The two girls saw his thin, stooped figure appear, leaning on the gate.

"If you're looking for your precious Molly," said his mother's voice with relentless hostility, "then you're wasting your time, I'll tell you that for nothing. She'll be back when she feels like it and not before. She'll not give you a thought until she wants something."

Molly sighed. "God Almighty," she said in a conversational tone, "I swear I'm going to kill that woman one of these days. With my bare hands."

The tension seemed to have drained from Nancy with her confession; surprisingly she managed a smile, "You'd better go."

"I don't want to go. I want to talk to you. You're making a mistake, Nancy, surely you are? If Joey loves you he wouldn't let something that happened so long ago and while you were still almost a child come between you, would he?"

Sam had seen them. The latch rattled and the heavy gate swung open; Ellen's voice followed him, harsh as the call of a crow. He peered along the dark street.

"Molly? Is that you?"

"Yes. I'm coming."

"Is there someone with you?"

"Nancy Benton."

They waited as he came towards them; Molly fought down a sudden raging impatience, a desire to walk away, to deny his right to interrupt.

"Miss Benton." He held out a cool, thin hand. "How n – nice to see you again. Will you c – come inside?"

"No, thank you. I really have to go. It's getting late."

"Thank you for walking Molly home." Sam's voice was slow and careful; Molly's irrational exasperation died; he was trying to control his stammer. She almost reached for his hand. She had hoped, for his sake, to bring up the subject of her renewed friendship with the Bentons in private, and gently; a sudden confrontation had been no part of the plan. By the gate she saw another shadow; Ellen had come out of the house and was craning her neck to see whom Sam was talking to, shading her eyes against the light of the street lamp with her hand.

Nancy was turning from them. Molly caught her arm, but Nancy shook her head. "I'm all right, Moll. You can't help. No one can. I have to make up my own mind."

"But you're wrong about Joe," Molly said, doubting her own words even as she spoke them. "Surely you must be."

"Perhaps. Anyway," she said, her voice was falsely bright, "right or wrong I've a bus to catch."

"I'll walk you to the stop," Sam said.

"Oh, no—"

"Please. I'd l – like to. It's only round the corner." He turned to Molly. "Shouldn't you get the baby inside? It's a b – bit cold."

Molly nodded.

"Sam? Who's that with you?" Ellen's peremptory voice.

Sam did not reply. "I was worried about you," he said to Molly gently.

"I'm sorry." She did not sound it and she knew it. She made an effort to soften her tone. "I went to see the Bentons. I hadn't planned to, I just went on the spur of the moment. We got talking, and I didn't realize—"

"Sam!"

"I won't be a m – minute, Mother. I'm going to w – walk Miss Benton to the omnibus."

"You don't have to, Mr Alden, truly you don't."

"But I want to. The w – walk will do me good. And it's the least I can do after you've come all this w – way to see Molly home." He waited while Nancy bent and kissed the silent Molly's cheek. "I'll see you later, dear."

Molly nodded and watched them down the street, aware even at this distance and without looking at her of Ellen fuming at the gate a short distance down the street. Firmly she kept her back turned. Let her fume. She could hear Nancy's light voice as she replied politely to some comment or question of Sam's, then the two turned the corner and were gone.

Ellen, her lips clamped as tight as a sprung mantrap turned from the gate, marched up the path and through the front door, slamming it shut behind her, leaving Molly to follow as best as she could.

Molly stood for a moment alone in the darkness, in her mind a picture of Joey Taylor with his cool, uncharitable eyes, his humourless self-discipline, his uncompromising views on human frailty.

Poor Nancy.

CHAPTER SIXTEEN

"DON'T TELL HIM," Molly's practical, Irish voice made the solution sound unquestionably simple.

Nancy, standing by the window, smiled faintly and shook her head but did not reply.

"For heaven's sake, if it'll upset him as much as you think, what good will it do him to know? Oh, I know it might be—" she paused, delicately, " – a little difficult. But you could manage it if you really wanted."

Nancy turned from her contemplation of the wet street and came to the chair where Molly sat nursing Danny. She touched the tiny face thoughtfully with a long, thin finger.

"You know as well as I do that I can't. I don't believe for a minute that you'd do it yourself. Oh, I'm not saying it would be impossible to hide the truth. In some ways Joey is very innocent. I could deceive him. But that's it, isn't it? What would be the point? What kind of marriage could be built on deception?"

"Perhaps you're wrong about him. Perhaps he will understand. God above, Nancy, you were a child. A child! You didn't know what you were doing—"

"I wasn't forced." Her voice was cruelly strained; she averted her face.

"So you said. You also said that Edward's father was a grown man, a friend of your father's. A man you had loved and trusted for years, as one of the family. A man who had known you since you were born. How can you possibly take any of the blame on yourself? How could Joey see it so? Edward's father took advantage of your trust and your innocence. It was worse than rape. Worse! No one could blame you."

"I blame myself," Nancy said quietly, "Joe will blame me. Perhaps Edward, too, when he finds out."

"Nancy. You've your life ahead of you. If you're sure you want to marry Joey, then do it. Life's too short and too – uncertain – to let a chance slip away." There was an edge of bitterness to her voice. "We all do stupid things sometimes. I can see no reason why we – and others – should be made to suffer for them for the rest of our lives."

In the silence that followed the sound of the rain beating on the pavements outside filled the room. The weather had broken, the Indian summer was over and the clouds were so heavy that even at four o'clock in the afternoon a lamp burned on the small table by the door.

"When are you seeing him?"

Nancy looked up. "Tonight."

"And he expects your final answer?"

"Yes."

Molly reached for Danny's shawl. "Well, you know what I think."

Nancy helped her gather together the baby paraphernalia that was spread about the room. "It isn't that simple, Molly."

Molly stilled her busy hands and looked into the dark, unhappy eyes. "I know it."

Impulsively Nancy threw her arms about her, hugging her awkwardly, baby and all. "Oh, Moll, I'm that glad to have you back. Must you go? Can't you stay to tea?"

Molly shook a curly head. "I ought to be home for Sam when he finishes work. It's Saturday—" she grimaced self-derisively, " – we're going to awful Aunt Maude's." Nancy lifted surprised eyebrows. "Oh we do, you know, keep up the silly pretence of happy families. Once a month we visit, and tonight's the lovely night. Dear, bitchy Lucy will spend the evening inferring with every other sentence that there's someone not a mile from her who's no better than she should be, Aunt Maude and Ellen will sit there with faces sour as lemons scoring points off each other; and poor Sam will get more and more tongue-tied until he can't get a whole word past his teeth without coughing his heart out. Uncle Thomas will retire to his corner and say nothing at all. Then when it gets so bad that I can't stand it any longer I'll give Danny a shake and get him to yell good and loud and we'll make that our excuse, regretfully, to leave.

Nancy, in spite of herself, laughed. "You make it sound such fun."

Molly stood up. "You don't know the half of it," she said, and for the first time Nancy took note of a certain, fine-drawn hardening of the vivid, flower face, of a new expression in the wide-set eyes.

"Come tomorrow," said Nancy impulsively, "to tea. And bring Sam. Mam won't mind. It isn't fair to keep leaving him out. He ought to come to meet us, and soon. I think he's rather nice."

"So do I." Molly's voice gave nothing away. She tucked Danny into the pram that had been brought in from the front path when the downpour had started, pulled the hood up to its furthest extent, snapped up the waterproof cover. "We'll come if you'd like. If you're sure."

Nancy laughed a little shakily. "Who knows, we might even be celebrating?" And Molly, straightening, looked at her friend with sinking heart. Somewhere in Nancy's voice, in her eyes, beneath worry and uncertainty, burned a flame of hope; her common sense, her knowledge of the man she loved, had not quenched that flame, nor even truly dimmed it no matter how hard she tried to pretend that it had. She, who had all along asserted that Joe Taylor, once he knew the truth, would repudiate her love, did not in her heart believe it. And Molly, who had in kindness argued otherwise, did.

The thought followed Molly to Linsey Grove, lay beneath the surface of her mind all through the evening, making the miserable, edgy occasion even worse than usual, and was still hovering when, thankfully, she shut the bedroom door behind her and flopped onto the bed, leaving Sam to tuck the baby into his crib.

"Uncle Thomas likes you." Sam's colour was a little better this evening and he had coughed very little.

Molly grinned suddenly, like a child. "That's more than you can say about your Aunt Maude. Or Cousin Lucy, come to that. She thinks I've bewitched you; turned you from a handsome prince into a frog. Or something."

Sam blushed. "Don't be silly. Cousin Lucy doesn't care twopence. She never did."

"Ah, that's what you think."

Dramatically Molly threw her arms wide, the effect only slightly marred by the fact that she was lying flat on her back. "Heartless brute! Secretly she was dying of love for you. Dying!"

She clutched her hands to her heart and used the exaggerated, declamatory tones of the stage. "You can tell just by looking at her. She's fading away. Disappointed passion has rendered her the very shadow of her former self—"

Sam could not but laugh at this description of the pudgy and unimaginative Lucy. "You're t – teasing," he said gently, sitting on the bed beside her and touching her hand lightly. "I told you, Lucy never cared about me. T – truth to tell I think I irritate her. What she cares about is not being married, about having the b – bother of looking for somebody else." The words were absent; he was looking down at her with sober, loving eyes. "I do love it when you laugh like that, when you tease me. N – no one's ever done it before. You're very good for me Molly. You m – make me happy, just to look at you. R – remember that, won't you?"

Molly smiled a little and moved her head on the pillow, embarrassed by the intensity of his gaze, aware suddenly of the warmth of his body beside her.

"I'm sorry things are so difficult for you here. I w– wish—" He stopped.

Molly squeezed the hand that he had put in hers. "Don't be daft. It doesn't matter. I'm all right. It's you who suffers most, I know that. And I do try, truly I do." She pulled a face and added honestly, "But not hard enough, I know. It's difficult. But perhaps we'll settle, your mother and I. Perhaps it won't always be like this."

He watched her face and forbore to say that time, that she so took for granted, might not be so kind to him. In the dim light his face was shadowed in planes and angles, the touch of his big-boned, thin hand was gentle. On impulse Molly lifted the hand to her lips, kissed it, bit the thumb lightly, nibbling with sharp teeth. He was trembling suddenly.

Molly half closed her eyes and as the lamp glimmered on blood-red curtains, out of nowhere, like a blow, came memory and pain. In this room, in the hot, scarlet glow of sunlight through those same curtains Harry had undressed her, had seen her naked. She moved restlessly, trying to suppress the thought, hating herself, unable to prevent the wildness in the blood that was not, had never been, for Sam. Tentatively Sam touched her breast. She could hear his breathing; harsh, difficult. She turned her head and closed her eyes. He would not kiss her, he never did. Neither would he take her, as Harry had, in blind strength and the certainty that she was his. His body would not command hers; always he was awkward, a little ungraceful.

And for her there would be no release, except in the tears that so often followed, sliding helplessly down her cheeks and soaking her pillow in the silent darkness.

Gently she lifted her arms and guided his mouth to her breast.

From the moment she stepped through the Bentons' front door the following afternoon, Molly sensed disaster in the air. Nancy was nowhere to be seen. Jack's face as he rose to greet the newcomers did not come easily to a smile, and Sarah's face was strained. Charley had gone to fetch Annie – also invited to the tea party – and the only one unaffected by the obviously uneasy atmosphere was Edward who, ignoring Danny, greeted Molly a little coolly, then announced cheerfully to Sam that Sam bore the same name as his – Edward's – favourite pet mouse, and wasn't that funny? Sam agreed solemnly that it was and pronounced himself delighted at the honour, agreeing with pleasure to Edward's suggestion that he should meet his namesake after tea. It was noticeable to all but Edward that Sam's stutter, so pronounced when he was speaking to the others that it had made the introductions an agony, all but disappeared when he was talking to the child. Edward, happy to have found an audience at last in an adult world that seemed to have been acting a little oddly today, perched himself upon the arm of Sam's chair and embarked upon a lecture on the delights of keeping mice, and was amazed, while taking full advantage of the unusual circumstance, that no one made any attempt to stop him.

Molly put up with the peculiar silence, upon which the child's confident voice was superimposed like a painting on glass, for as long as she could before leaning to Sarah and asking quietly, "Is Nancy all right?"

But she chose the wrong moment; Edward had inconveniently paused for breath, and the question rang in the ears like a bell. Sam looked puzzled; Jack's already sombre face darkened. Edward's brown, intelligent eyes moved from one to the other.

"She's got a headache," he said clearly. "She shouted when I made a noise."

"Where is she?" Molly was looking at Sarah.

"Upstairs." Nancy's mother made a small, helpless movement with her hands, obviously inhibited by the presence of the child and of Sam.

"Would it be all right if I popped up to see her, do you think?" Molly was already on her feet.

"I don't know. I'm not sure if—"

"Let the lass go. It'll likely do our Nancy good to have a visitor," Jack said, then looked up at Molly. "Try to get her to come down. Likely her – her headache'll get better if she makes the effort and comes downstairs. Charley and Annie'll be here soon."

On the dark stairway Molly paused for a fraction of a moment, trying not to remember the last time she had climbed these stairs, then she was on the tiny, lightless landing and calling softly.

"Nancy?"

There was no reply. Molly moved to the door of Nancy's room, a boxroom, little more than a large cupboard, and tapped lightly upon it.

"Nancy? It's me. Molly."

Silence.

Molly pushed open the door; Nancy was standing by the window, her back to Molly, her neat, smooth head and slim shoulders outlined sharply against the light that filtered through the draped net curtains.

"Nancy—"

"Please go away, Moll. I'm all right. I just don't want to talk to anyone. Not now." Nancy's voice was austerely composed. She did not turn round.

Molly paused, half-in and half-out of the room. "Jack thought you might feel better if you came downstairs. Charley'll be here soon with Annie."

Nancy shook her head.

Molly stepped across the threshold and closed the door softly behind her. There was very little space; a narrow bed, pushed right against the wall, and a small wardrobe took most of the available room. A mirror hung on one wall, reflecting silvered light, a pile of books was stacked on a battered shelf next to a small vase of flowers. Nancy's figure was as inanimate as the rest of the furniture; like a statue she stood, rigid and still.

"You told him," Molly said at last.

Nancy moved her head in a tiny gesture of protest, took a sharp, controlled breath. "Yes."

"And—"

"He was – shocked," Nancy said drily, the understatement bitter. What single word could describe the brutal cruelty of Joe's reaction to her stammered confession? It had been worse than anything she had imagined. His voice still sounded now in her mind, clipped and intolerant. She had listened, defenceless, to the awful words he had used, had flinched from his cold anger and had not been able to answer it; for the things he had said had been, in the strict sense of the word, true. Taking no account of age, of circumstances, of innocence, or of love, she *had* acted the part of harlot, she *had* borne a bastard, had hidden her whoring from the man who had courted her in good faith and virtue. The betrayal, he assured her, was beyond forgiveness, either here or in Heaven. She had been reduced to begging, and he had turned from her in disgust. Now she looked across the ranks of familiar roofs and chimneys and saw nothing; had seen nothing, or so it seemed, since her last sight of his face, blazing white, a sickness in his eyes.

That the sickness was more in him than in herself she had not recognized.

Molly was quiet. She had read enough into the tone of Nancy's simple sentence not to have to question further.

In the street outside there were voices, laughter. Charley and Annie were coming down the path.

"Come downstairs, Nancy, love. Please do. I'm sure you'll feel better if—"

Nancy turned and Molly fell silent. The thin face was the colour and texture of ivory, the eyes set deep into bruised and painful sockets. The awful composure did not, would not, break.

"Not now. Later, perhaps."

Molly wanted desperately to console; but the girl who faced her exuded a chill self-containment that dismayed and discouraged her. "I'm sorry, Nancy," was all she could manage. "Truly sorry. But it isn't the end of the world. You mustn't think so, however badly you feel. You will get over it. You will. Nothing hurts for ever." She moved awkwardly to the door. Nancy still said nothing, but at least nodded faintly when Molly urged, "Do try to come down later. You shouldn't be up here on your own, it isn't good for you. You know how we all love you. We'll help if you let us—" the last words were very soft and the door closed quietly upon them.

Nancy looked across her shoulder at the shut door for a brief second before turning back to her dry-eyed, sightless gazing across the regular grey ranks of the rooftops.

CHAPTER SEVENTEEN

"No more," said Ellen with dismissive conviction, "than you would expect from dockers." She invested the last word with such absolute contempt that Molly's fork clattered to her plate and she opened her mouth to protest, the quick red banners of temper flying in her cheeks.

Sam forestalled her. "Not dockers, Mother. S – stevedores. Jack and Charley Benton are stevedores."

Ellen sniffed. "Stevedores. Dockers. What's the difference in a fancy name? Not a pin between them that I can see."

"There's all the difference in the world. S – stevedores work the ships, not the wharves. They're skilled men. That's the d – difference."

Ellen ignored him. "Brutes, all of them. Drunken, idle good-for-nothings. The streets around the docks aren't fit for decent people to walk in, and you know it. There's no excuse for it." Ellen's mouth snapped shut, her last word uttered, and there an end.

"That isn't f – fair, Mother. You don't know anything about it." Two pairs of eyes turned to him, Molly's astonished, Ellen's outraged. Sam's own glance could not sustain his mother's, but he would not be intimidated to silence. "All right, some of them are rough, yes; they have to be to survive. But idleness is forced upon them by the system." He flushed at his mother's disbeliev-ing snort. "It's true. M – men walk for miles to be told there's no work for them; and when there's no w – work, there's no money. Jack says that's treating m – men like animals. And if you do that you can't blame them if they don't always act like so-called d – decent men. And he's right."

"I see." Ellen's voice was acidly quiet. Molly glanced at her from beneath lowered lashes; two patches of colour burned in the older woman's sallow cheeks. Ellen Alden did not take kindly to being contradicted at her own supper table.

Sam ploughed on with more stubborn persistence than tact, his head bent over his plate.

"If you put men in cages, force them almost literally to f – fight for a few hours' work, make no provision for them or their families wh – when the work isn't available, what can you expect from them? The calling-on system is corrupt; it gives too much power to too few, and they abuse it. A man's livelihood, his right to work, is put into another man's hands; it leads to preference, to b – bribery—"

"Cages?" Molly had only just managed to swallow a mouthfull of hot pie. "What do you mean, cages? Jack and Charley don't work in cages, do they?"

Sam almost laughed. "No, of c – course not. The cage is what they call the place where the casuals have to wait to be taken on. But I told you, the B – Bentons aren't casuals. The stevedores are more or less permanently employed. Better paid too."

"Then what business is it of theirs what happens to others?" asked Ellen brusquely. "Do they think they know better how to run the docks than men who have been doing it for generations? I daresay they've managed well enough till now without Jack Benton's free advice. What would he have them do? Pay men to stand idle? What a very good idea—" her voice was heavily sardonic " – for the dockside publicans."

"Oh, Mother—"

"Don't 'oh Mother' me. What do you know about any of this, tell me that?"

"What J – Jack tells me."

"Exactly. And he's not about to say that his precious docker friends are a bunch of lazy, drunken bullies is he?" asked his mother with sour sarcasm.

"Jack doesn't try to pretend they're angels. He just says that the system is wrong. It's t – too open to abuse, and it has to be changed. The dock authorities don't care; why should they, as long as there's labour there ready when they want it? No, reform has to come from the m – men. And that's why Jack's come round to the Union side—" It had been mention of the Stevedores' Union that had first provoked Ellen's wrath.

"*Jack's* joined the Union?" The exclamation came from Molly Ellen for the moment apparently being struck dumb by the unique experience of having her son actually stick to his guns in an argument. "But it's Charley who's the Union man, not Jack. He had no time for them at all."

"He's changed his mind—"

Sam got no further before his mother recovered her tongue as she further lost her temper. "And yours with it, apparently. Well, that will be quite enough, thank you. This is my house, Sam Alden, and my table and you'll please remember that. I'll have no Union talk here. Not from anyone, leave alone my own son! The very idea! Unions!" She spat the word out like a pip. "They make contented people miserable; they stir up trouble where there was none; they dangle ridiculous hopes and expectations before those who did very well without them; they cost people – the very people they say they care so much about – their jobs and their homes. They cause nothing but discontent and disruption." She stabbed a bony finger into Sam's helpless face, and went on, "The men who run our industries are the men who made this country great, make no mistake about that. The mines, the railways, the mills – yes, and the docks. They know what they're doing. Your Jack Benton's precious Unions would be better employed in helping them rather than hindering. But no, they say, every man is entitled to the same as his master. What rubbish. There are those who'll work and those who won't. Those who'll save and those who'll squander. You can't change human nature. Pity the poor miners, they say. Well, I say this: if a man doesn't like his work in the mines, let him leave and look elsewhere for a livelihood. No one forces him to be a miner. And as for the Unions inciting trouble, encouraging people to gang together against those who pay their wages – well, it's always been my feeling that if a man—" the faintest scorn accentuated the noun as she looked at her son square in the face " – wants something, then let him fight for it himself and not rely on others to do it for him. It's easy enough to be part of a crowd; it takes neither strength nor courage. The weak and the idle may be thankful for charity; they should not expect anything else by right."

Sam's shoulders drooped. He looked down at his plate and played with his food. "You're very hard, Mother. You m – make the world sound like a jungle."

"It is only thanks to me, Sam," his mother said with cutting clarity, "that you haven't discovered that for yourself. I forbid, absolutely, any further discussion on this subject at my table."

"Pretending they don't exist won't make it so," pointed out Molly, rejoicing for once in the advocacy of sweet reason. "The Unions are not going to go away just because you won't talk about them."

Ellen turned withering black eyes upon her more usual adversary. "And discussing them gives them more dignity than is their due. The world would be turned upside down by these people: Socialists, Anarchists, these mad Suffragists who try to pretend that women are interested in politics. I've no time for any of them. And I'll thank you, Molly, to remember upon whose charity you and your child live and obey me in this."

Molly smiled, a derisive downward turn of her soft mouth; a knife may strike stone so often that it is blunted, and charity was a word cast at her so often by her mother-in-law that the insult did little beyond adding slightly to the grudge that each bore the other. Sam was rather thinner skinned. With the blood rising again in his pallid face he began to rise clumsily to his feet.

Molly put out a gently restraining hand and shook her head. "Leave it, Sam. It really doesn't matter," she said quietly, and was amply rewarded by the flash of fury that she saw in Ellen's eyes before she applied herself quietly to what was left of her pie.

Later that night, lying beside Sam and with little Danny snuffling in the crib on the other side of the room she asked thoughtfully, "Did Jack really say all that? About the docks and the casuals and the Unions and all?"

Sam moved beside her. "Yes."

"I'm surprised. A year ago he gave the impression that he was positively opposed to them. Charley was the Union man—"

"Charley's an Annie man now," Sam said, smiling into the darkness at his own small joke, "and no one else is allowed even the smallest slice, so f – far as I can tell."

"But Jack of all people! I wonder what changed him?"

"Oh, no, Moll, you've got it wrong. J – Jack was never anti-Union. It's the extremists he's against. He's made friends with th – the man – Ben Tillet's his name I think – that led the strike a few months back."

"Wasn't that broken by blacklegs?"

"Y – yes, it was."

"Well, now," said the practical Molly, "that sounds more like an argument against the Union than for it?"

Sam subsided. After a while he said, almost to himself, "J – Jack's a very clever chap, you know. I like him." He stopped as he caught his breath and coughed painfully.

Molly winced. "Do you need your medicine?"

Sam was gasping for breath. "N – no. Thanks. I – I'll be all right."

But long after Molly slept peacefully beside him he lay staring into blind and silent darkness, listening to the rattle of his own breathing. And fighting desperately that gnawing fear that never, lately, seemed far from the surface of his mind.

"Mam?"

Sarah lifted her head, her fingers still busy with the needle, and looked at Edward who was with great relish wiping out the last of a cup of last night's gravy with a hunk of bread. "Hmm?"

"Does the Queen eat bread and dripping?"

Molly, sitting quietly in the corner with Danny asleep on her lap, smiled. Sarah considered. Nancy, opposite Molly across the hearth, continued to fiddle absently with the long fringe of her shawl, her blank eyes fixed unblinking on her own restless fingers.

"Well," Sarah rested her work for a moment on her lap; she was embroidering a blouse, a lovely thing of cream and russet and deep red-gold, for Nancy to wear at Charley's coming wedding. Nancy had hardly looked at it. " – I don't expect she does, no."

"Not even for tea?"

Sarah shook her head. "I wouldn't think so."

"That's silly. If I was Queen I'd eat bread and dripping all the time. For breakfast, too. Will we be having bread and dripping at the wedding?"

Molly laughed aloud this time and the baby stirred. Nancy did not look up. Since the break with Joe a couple of weeks before she had swung confusingly from introverted quiet to a kind of frenetic gaiety that, alien as it seemed to her nature, was more disturbing than the unhappy silences. Her family, nonplussed, watched helplessly and waited patiently for her to heal. Molly sometimes wondered, looking into those damaged eyes, if she ever would.

Sarah picked up the blouse again. "No, lad, I doubt that we'll be eating bread and dripping at the wedding." Her voice held the faint exasperation of a mother who isn't certain whether or not she is being teased.

Edward, noisily, finished his bread and licked around the edge of the cup, then slipped from his chair and came to stand at Sarah's knee, wiping his greasy fingers on his trousers and watching, fascinated, the glittering, jewel-coloured thread and the flashing needle. "What do they do with it then?" His bright head was on one side, the small angel-face was solemn.

"What?"

"The dripping," supplied Molly, laughing from her corner, quicker on the uptake than Sarah. "He wants to know what the Queen does with her dripping if she doesn't eat it. Right?" she enquired of Edward, who nodded.

"Well *I* don't know—" Sarah stopped, seeing from the too-familiar set of the small pink mouth that that would not do at all; if some satisfactory answer were not forthcoming then Edward would pursue the question all afternoon. "I suppose they use it. To cook with. Or perhaps they give it to the servants. Cook's perks."

"What's perks?"

"Perks is treats," said Molly in dreadful imitation of a cockney accent, "somethin' ter make yer eyes sparkle."

Edward chuckled and sidled over to her. His early antipathy to Danny had declined now that the baby had become less of a novelty in the house and was consequently slightly less fussed over. And Molly's special, friendly twinkle was still for him, even with the little intruder asleep on her lap.

He leaned heavily on her knee, to see if she would push him away. She didn't, and he smiled up into her face. "What's your favourite treat?"

Sarah watched the little group as Molly pretended to consider the question, her wide, white brow furrowed ferociously. Here was a different girl from the one who had stood, pale and half-defiant, in the kitchen doorway a few weeks before. She had lost that fraught and high-strung look she had possessed then; she had put on a little weight, and laughed almost as easily as she used to.

"Humbugs," she said. "Those great big minty ones. And wallies out of Mr Simpson's stone jar."

Edward shrieked with laughter. "What, together?"

"Of course not, tinker." She tweaked his nose with her free hand. "The humbugs for dinner, with roast potatoes, and the wallies with winkles for tea." She laughed aloud at the child's disbelieving face, then said, "What about you, Nancy?"

Nancy jumped. "Pardon?"

"Treats. What's your favourite?"

"Oh—" she shrugged " – I don't know. Nothing really."

Edward, overconfident of his elders' indulgence, pulled a face, and used a phrase he'd heard more than once at school and had been dying to try out. "That's a bit of a bloody silly thing to say, isn't it?" he asked with simple clarity.

There was a moment's slightly stunned silence during which all eyes turned to Sarah who, after regaining her breath put a rapid end to the proceedings with a sharp slap and even sharper words. As the resultant furore died away up the stairs, where the miscreant was marched to the punishing seclusion of the bed-room he shared with Sarah, Molly looked at Nancy.

"The choice of words might have been a bit unfortunate," she said quietly, "but he wasn't far from right, was he?"

Nancy averted her eyes and did not answer. She knew that it was more than an answer to a child's silly question that Molly was referring to.

Molly leaned forward. "Nancy, you must stop this. You must. You mope around the house, won't go anywhere, won't do anything. You'll make yourself ill. You'd feel so much better if you'd try. So you lost Joey Taylor; good riddance I say. He wasn't good enough for you; wasn't worth the breath to tell him so—"

"It isn't that." Nancy's voice was small, seemed to come from some distance. "Not just that."

"What, then?"

Nancy brought her eyes to Molly's face. "The things he said.

The words he used. I hear them, in my head. Almost all the time."

"Oh, Nancy—"

"I can't help it. I try, but I can't. Sometimes I try to shut them out with noise, but they don't go away, no matter how much I talk or laugh, they're always there. So then I sit and listen. Because they're true, those things he said. All true."

"What!"

"They're true," she repeated.

Molly was staring at her in dawning, horrified understanding. "What did he say?"

Nancy did not answer.

Molly carefully laid her sleeping son in the deep armchair and knelt before the other girl, taking her hands.

"Nancy, what did he say?",

Nancy battled with herself for a moment before saying in a voice completely devoid of emotion, "He told me that I was a whore. He said I had no business associating with a decent man, tempting him to sin. He said that my body had been defiled, degraded, that what should have been pure was—" she swallowed, " – dirty. Disgusting to him. And through my own fault."

A bright mist rose somewhere behind Molly's eyes and she shivered. Seldom did this kind of blinding fury possess her; never before had she felt it on behalf of someone else. Had Joey Taylor been in the room she felt she would have torn him apart with her bare hands. So great was her rage that she could not for the moment speak.

Nancy continued in the same, strained voice, "Harlot, he said. Deceitful, shameless Jezebel. Am I?" For the first time she looked directly into Molly's face. "*Am* I?"

Molly came up onto her knees in one movement as she flung her arms about the girl. "Oh, Nancy, Nancy, how *dare* he say such things? Wickedness to say them, wickedness to believe them. He's the one, not you. You hear me? Devil take him, he's no more love or life in him than a stone. Less. I pity him, that I do. He deserves nothing, and he'll get nothing. I hope his cold-hearted God keeps him warm in his old age. 'Tis certain no one else will. Sanctimonious, narrow-minded—" Her invective ran out with her breath; she took another, added more calmly, "Don't think of it darlin', don't think of the things he said. You're worth a thousand Joe Taylors. You're good, and you're kind. And listen to me—" she pulled fiercely away, held the bigger girl's shoulders with hands made painfully strong by emotion, " – you just look at your Edward—" Nancy flinched from the pronoun, but Molly repeated firmly, "*your* Edward. He's beautiful. You can be nothing but proud of him. You can't regret a lovely lad like that, Nancy. You *can't*."

Nancy wrenched herself free and buried her face in her hands, the sobs shook her beyond any consolation.

And behind the concealing door Sarah, in the darkness, sat tiredly down on the bottom step of the stairs, bowed her head and wept also.

CHAPTER EIGHTEEN

THE DAY THAT red-headed Annie Melhurst became Mrs Charles Benton was one that remained in many memories for a long time.

The weather was, for November, kind, though the pale sunshine held little actual warmth and the scurrying wind that ruffled wedding finery and nipped sharply at exposed ankles carried in it the cutting edge of approaching winter.

Inside the cold church, and in the odd, self-conscious atmosphere of such occasions the two families gathered, strangers divided rigidly by the line of the centre aisle – like two armies, Molly thought suddenly – drawn up to face each other across a battlefield. Speculative looks flicked, as if casually, from feathered hat to buttoned shoe; glances clashed and slid from each other like silently crossed swords. If the matter were to be decided on simple numbers, then the Bentons were outclassed. Molly, her black hair reaching tendril fingers up and around the upswept brim of her little hat, which sported the curled ostrich feathers known popularly as 'Kruger's Ticklers', cast a woman's lightning glance over the gathering: Annie's side of the church was already filled to capacity, while the Bentons, including Molly, Sam and little Danny, managed – thinly spread – only to take possession of the first two or three pews. But then numbers were not all, not in any battle, and if the Bentons were outnumbered they yet had heavy armaments to balance that; Molly knew that there was not a soul in the church who did not believe – whether they would openly admit it or not – that Annie had 'done very well for herself'. In these class-conscious days even the separate classes had their own clearly recognized divisions, and the Melhursts – a seemingly enormous family from Canning Town whose way of life, according to Annie, embraced a kind of happy-go-lucky shiftlessness that did not admit to the necessity, or even the desirability of a steady job – were streets removed from the hard-working and respectable Bentons. Today, however, the Melhursts were putting on their very best front. An almost truculent air of scrubbed and shining respectability issued from their side of the church. Someone – and looking from the corner of her eye at Annie's formidable mother, Molly had not much doubt who that someone was – had persuaded, bullied or threatened even the most distant and careless cousin into his best; and the peacock shades of choker and scarf, the rakish angle of cap and hat, the extravagance of feather and fur made the Bentons look not only few in number but a little dull besides.

In the body of the church someone coughed, and the sound echoed to the lofty roof; murmurs and whispers and subdued giggles bespoke a restless and excited congregation. In the front pew sat Charley, bolt upright in the place of honour, awaiting his bride with eyes half-closed against the glare of candles and his normally ruddy face totally colourless. Even the back of his neck, encased in a collar so stiffly starched and tall that it looked as if any sudden movement might decapitate him, looked sick. The spectacular festivities of the night before, in which half the young male population of West Ham had joined, had left him looking more like death warmed up than an eager groom; and neither the buckets of ice-cold water that Jack had obligingly poured over his head, nor the swallowing of enough Cockle's anti-bilious pills to make him rattle had much improved matters. It was not just the tall starched collar that was keeping Charley Benton's head unnaturally still this day.

His best man and older brother was in better shape, though Molly thought she noted a certain pallor that indicated that he too had enjoyed the celebrations. Behind Jack and Charley, Sarah sat beside Nancy and Edward, her statuesque figure encased in tasteful blue alpaca trimmed with fox fur, her hair swept fashionably up beneath a wide-brimmed hat. Beside her Nancy looked slender to the point of fragility, her small, neat head and arrow-straight back completely still. She was dressed in the colours of autumn, the blouse that Sarah had made her toning exactly with her stylish, slightly severe russet suit, a small brown boater set at a firm angle upon her smooth, folded hair. Somehow the sight of her sobered Molly; there was an unnatural tension in her stance, a line to her set, downturned mouth that twisted Molly's heart. She was still watching Nancy when the crash of the organ brought her back to the occasion as Annie appeared at the church door.

Charley, standing now at the altar with Jack, squared his shoulders. In a whisper of lace and flowing silky white Annie passed upon her father's arm, her head high, her eyes fixed on Charley's broad back. She carried a great trailing bouquet of fragrant white flowers, the green fronds spilling gracefully from her hands almost to the hem of her dress. Beneath the veil her red cloud of hair glinted in the light of the candles. The lovely, sharp lines of her face showed clearly through the mist of lace. Rose, the eldest of her many sisters, followed, a fair, solid girl in lemon and green with a wide flowered hat and a worried expression. As they reached the altar the sound of the organ died and there was an excited rustling hum from the congregation, which quieted as the rector lifted a solemn eye and after clearing his throat twice to attract the groom's attention from the tall vision in white that stood beside him, began the service.

To Molly, used to a more lengthy and complicated ceremony it all seemed over almost before it had started; suddenly Charley was slipping the ring on his Annie's finger. Molly saw a flutter of lace in Sarah's lifted hand, but across the aisle the display was nowhere near so discreet; Annie's mother was openly crying. Molly blinked, aware of a flutter of as-yet-unidentified emotion; then as the new husband's big hands lifted the fragile barrier of lace from his wife's face and he bent to kiss her, Molly knew suddenly that what she was feeling was shamefully close to envy. She fought it down; it wasn't only Charley and Annie who deserved better from her than that. Sam's big-boned hands were folded quietly about a battered prayer book, his golden wedding ring gleaming dully in the candlelight.

Mr and Mrs Charles Benton turned from the altar and led the way out of the church. Annie, as she passed, caught Molly's eye and winked happily. Molly, her wayward emotions back under control, smiled back.

Then they were out in the chill, sunny air. Charley and Annie climbed aboard the little shining ribbon-and-streamer-decorated trap that had been hired, complete with a white pony whose harness rang with tiny silver bells and a resplendently uniformed driver, to take them at the head of a motley procession of vehicles – from farm wagons to little coster carts – through the streets of Canning Town to Alfred Road and the party that everyone in the neighbourhood had been looking forward to for weeks.

The wedding celebrations encompassed almost the whole street. Doors stood open up and down the road, neighbours who had not come to the church, but who had no intention of missing the party, crowded the pavements waving and shouting as the little jingling trap spanked past. In Annie's house almost every stick of furniture had been cleared from the parlour and a large and battered piano had been installed. The food had been laid out next door; roast meats and pies, jellies and trifles; while in the kitchen the men broached a much-needed cask of beer and the first, thirsty gulps went almost without swallowing down throats dry as the Sahara from a day's abstinence. Some way down the street, in the house of Annie's Aunt Hilda the older members of the family were gathering; every chair in the neighbourhood had been lined against the walls, and elderly aunts and uncles settled themselves comfortably, the talk already turning to births, deaths and marriages. Those with younger legs who were unlucky enough to get caught were sent scurrying along the road for a plate of goodies and a glass of claret; "a big one, mind, save you going again—"

In such a family atmosphere, Sarah, Nancy and Edward, together with Molly and Sam were left for a short while as a small island isolated in a sea of good-natured greetings and laughing, back-slapping reunions. But not for long; Annie exploded from the crowd, her long dress trailing, her eyes brilliant with laughter and happiness, threw her arms about her new mother-in-law then hugged Nancy with the mock-dismayed exclamation "*Another* sister! As if I haven't got enough already! Come on, all of you. Mum and Dad are dying to meet you." She kissed Molly and gave Danny a finger to grasp. "We've got plans for you, too, little monkey," she said, "we're not going to have you spoiling your Mum and Dad's fun." and with her free hand she caught the flying curls of a passing sister who stopped, willy-nilly, with an injured shriek. "Betsy, take Moll to Aunt Hilda's. There's a cot there," she added, smiling to

Molly, "in a nice quiet little room. You can feed him there too if you like."

"Oh, Annie, how kind—"

"We aim to please," Annie grinned. "Couldn't have our Moll missing all the fun could we? Don't worry. The old'uns'll be downstairs. They'll listen out for him."

Molly followed little Betsy to Aunt Hilda's. With the baby settled comfortably upstairs she spent a few busy moments before a dingy mirror in one of the other, empty, bedrooms. It had been a long time, she realized suddenly, since she had enjoyed this kind of excitement. She stepped back and smiled a little into the mirror, not dissatisfied with what she saw. Her sweeping dark-blue velvet skirt nipped her tiny waist fashionably small; the matching little bolero jacket cast glints of blue into her wide, blue-grey eyes; the high-necked, softly frilled blouse beneath it complemented perfectly the small face above it. Her hair, as always, resolutely went its own way regardless of her efforts and stubbornly resisted being smoothly unswept as it should, but beneath the little hat with its curling feathers, the effect, she told herself, was not altogether bad, even if it were not strictly fashionable. Happily she slipped down the stairs and along the street to Annie's house, where she found Sam, Sarah and Nancy awaiting her with her first glass of claret.

Edward was nowhere to be seen. Children seldom stand on the same ceremony as their elders and he was out in the street kicking, punching and rolling in the gravel as if he had known his companions all of his life. As Molly joined the group so did Charley, kissing his mother and sister and slapping Sam on the back. Sam looked a little tired, but then, thought Molly with sinking heart, he almost always did. Nancy's high-boned face was unusually flushed, and her dark eyes were shining. Excitement – and the claret – had shaken her from her usual cool detachment. Yet still, to Molly, there was something disturbing in the way those bright eyes wandered ceaselessly about the room, never resting for long on one face, never giving away the thoughts behind them. As Molly watched, Nancy tilted her head, and with a kind of defiant finality in the movement drained her glass. Sam, smiling, proffered his, scarcely touched, and with no hesitation she took it and tossed it back.

Over the heads of the crowd Molly caught sight of Jack's earnestly-bent head. He was talking to a group of equally serious-faced men. Unreasoning exasperation stirred in her. She lifted her glass and drained it. Sam, with an apologetic glance in her direction, drifted to the outskirts of the group around Jack. Molly reached for another glass of claret.

Afternoon turned into evening in a noisy, hot, jangling haze. She spoke to people whom she did not know, and half the time in the hubbub could not hear a word of what they said in return. She laughed a lot, her smoke-blue eyes jewel-bright behind their sweeping lashes, and her glass seemed to empty and refill with remarkably little effort. She found herself to her own surprise extremely popular with the younger male members of the Melhurst clan. In Annie's house someone's uncle was well settled at the piano, upon which the empty beer glasses were lined up like skittles. The room was hot and crowded; a young man grabbed Molly and swung her into a stumbling attempt at a waltz. Laughing, she held him up as long as she could, then deposited him in an empty chair. Before she could make good her escape, however, the piano crashed discordantly again and she found herself dancing in a fast whirling circle partnered by an elderly man who wheezed and panted and declared to all who would listen that he could dance all the youngsters under the table, see if he couldn't. Later, still breathless, she joined the surge of people who swept along the street to the house where Charley and Annie were about to cut the wedding cake. There was no sign of Sam in the crowd. Nancy was standing near the table, half-leaning against a tall young man who had his arm about her waist. The speeches were delivered, the cake cut, and to roars of approval the bride kissed the groom, very thoroughly. In the hubbub Jack fought his way to her side with a slice of cake and yet another glass of claret. She accepted both with appreciation. He then stood in a silence so awkward that it almost tempted Molly to ask what on earth he had found to talk so volubly about to the menfolk. However, a moment before she was driven to such impolite lengths he did manage finally to ask was she enjoying herself, and was Danny settled happily? She said yes, rather shortly, to both questions, her irrational irritation exacerbated by the twinge of guilt she felt at not in fact having looked in on the baby for a while. Before either of them could say more a tall and buxom girl with blonde hair and china-blue eyes and a neckline that drew the gaze of every man in the room, sidled up to Jack and said in a small baby-voice that grated Molly's nerves like a file. "So here you are, you naughty boy. I've been looking *everywhere* for you. Come an' dance, darlin'. You promised you would."

The colour in Jack's darkly weathered face deepened painfully. "I'm talking, Dolly—" His voice had that oddly helpless note of a strong man faced with a woman he does not quite know how to handle.

"Don't worry yourself on my account." Molly was brusque, "I was going anyway." And beneath Dolly's china-blue, calculating gaze she turned on her heel and left.

Jack's question about Danny had for the moment put thoughts of Sam's whereabouts from her mind. She had fed the baby earlier, but had not checked on him since. She slipped along the cold, dark street to Aunt Hilda's and there, in the little room upstairs, she found them both. Danny was sound asleep in the cot; Sam lying neatly on top of the small bed that occupied the other half of the room slept also, his thin face shadowed, his breathing difficult. The sight sobered her. She pulled a thin blanket over him. He sighed and stirred but did not wake. Quietly she left them, shutting the door gently behind her and leaning for a moment, listening. The sounds of talk and laughter drifted up from below. In the dark garden, Edward and his new friends, taking full advantage of their unaccustomed freedom were shrieking like banshees. She wondered for a moment if perhaps it would be best after all to wake Sam and the baby and take them both home. She gave a slight, rebellious shake of her curly head. They were safe and comfortable and she, for the first time in an age, was enjoying herself. She went back to the party.

Some time later she found herself part of a group of young people that included Nancy and her tall young man who was by now quite comically unsteady on his feet. The talk was loud, the laughter louder, and the noise altogether deafening. Molly found herself watching Nancy. Something had changed in the thin, boyish face; the light in the dark eyes was reckless, the smile too ready. Her long brown hair had come unpinned –

deliberately or by accident wondered Molly? – it hung, straight as rain, down Nancy's back, swinging as she moved, making a shining, silky shawl for her slender shoulders. In her hand was yet another empty glass. Then Molly became aware that she was not the only one to be watching Nancy. A tall, compellingly ugly young man with dark, diamond-sharp eyes and a crooked, unkind mouth stood still as a drawn figure, leaning against the wall. He watched her steadily for some moments before pushing himself gracefully from the supporting wall and moving through the crowd to Nancy's side. He slid an arm around her waist and detached her with no difficulty from her tipsy young escort.

"Come on, sweetheart. They're dancin' down the road."

Nancy looked up at him, her eyes wide and intensely focussed upon the unsmiling, arrogant face, her body tensed against his arm. Then her lashes swept downwards and her head drooped in an oddly submissive gesture. He smiled then.

Alarm bells rang in Molly's mind. Dangerous. This one was dangerous.

"Nancy—"

"Dancing!" The whole crowd was seized by the word, swayed as one towards the door, and Molly found herself swept along with them. Nancy, within the confident circle of the strange young man's arm did not look up at Molly's call.

They surged down the street to the house where music pounded through open door and window. Someone had produced a banjo; the music changed tempo suddenly, irresistibly. It was country music; intemperate, hand-clapping, foot-tapping rhythms that infected them all. With a whoop they were off, galloping, swinging, stamping their feet. Molly found herself whirled off the ground, passed from one to another, laughing breathlessly. Out of nowhere a chain was formed and hand to hand, left to right, they wove and swung. Faster and faster. The weaker spirits dropped out and leaned, panting, against the walls, clapping and calling encouragement to the others, including Molly, who danced on as though bewitched, as though they would never, could never stop. She caught a glimpse of Nancy whirling wildly with the man with the face of a bandit, her hair tangling them both in a silken, flying net, then she lost sight of them as she herself was drawn back into the weaving, dancing line. She lifted her eyes dizzily, missed a step and almost stumbled as there, swinging towards her, head and shoulders above the crowd, his honey hair wild, his brilliant wilful blue eyes fixed upon her, came Harry, alive again and laughing.

The music receded, something thumped terribly in her head. Reality faded. He came to her, caught her in strong hands. She relaxed to an awful, exhilarating vertigo, closing her eyes against the spinning, splintering lights. His body was warm and hard as rock; to feel it against hers brought her alive, when she had not until that moment realized that she, too, had been dead. She laid her face into his strong neck, breathing him, her lips on smooth, warm skin. The banjo had died almost to quiet, the excitement had drained at last to a lulling waltz. Hard hands, possessive almost to the point of pain, would not release her, nor did she want them to. And it was Jack who held her, hardly moving. She knew it, had known it all along. For long, suspended moments they remained so, vividly aware each of the other, of breath and blood in unison. She could not lift her head to look at him. He had set her on her feet with savage care, stood now with his face resting lightly on the damp mass of her hair, his eyes closed. They moved, bemusedly, to the distant sound of the music. They were not alone in such indiscretion; hardly anyone could now be said to be truly dancing and some sly hand had turned down the lamps. He held her hard to him with that perilous and irresistible strength that she remembered so well in other hands; hands that, like these, were scarcely aware of their own power. Time stopped. The world withdrew. With no volition they found themselves near the door; which of them first moved towards it would have been impossible to say. They slipped together down the narrow, darkened passage, through a tiny scullery and into the frosty, star-brightened back yard. She it was who stopped, just beyond the door and slipped quietly and inevitably into his arms, her face lifted for his kiss, and it was he, long minutes later, who broke away, shaking like a girl.

"Molly—" His voice was split ragged between longing and shame. The sound broke the spell. The feel of his mouth was still on hers; she knew enough to know that she would not easily forget it.

A few houses away Sam struggled for breath beside the baby

he had cared for and protected as his own. From the house behind them several voices were raised in an eager shout, a few practised flourishes on the piano bespoke new entertainment.

"Christ, Molly—" This time the pain in his voice twisted like a knife in raw flesh, shocked her awake. She lifted a hand, laid it lightly to his mouth. Words not spoken were easier to live with. The feel of his lips on her fingers was like physical pain.

"Don't say anything. Please don't." Would he understand? Would he?

His arms were still around her. He bowed his head; she saw his powerful shoulders hunch. She stood on tiptoe, wrapped light arms about his neck, barely touching him. Her kiss this time was long and soft, an admission, a pleading, a million words and not one of them uttered. Then she stepped back. The brilliant, ice-blue stars behind his head blurred and ran.

"I'm not Harry," he said, desolate.

"I know."

"And Sam—"

" – is your friend. I know that too." She lifted helpless hands, let them fall, turned and fled from him, leaving Jack Benton alone in the empty frost-lit yard, suddenly, shockingly sober and with a hole blasted in his painstakingly engineered defences that would take more than he possessed to make good. In a few unguarded moments he had squandered the iron control of a year.

He swore in a shaking voice and thumped his hand bloodily into the brick wall.

A stupid thing to do but, for him at any rate, better than tears.

CHAPTER NINETEEN

HE HARDLY SPOKE to her, barely it seemed even looked at her, would not be alone with her. In the weeks that followed Charley's wedding Molly saw less of Jack than she had before. When she did see him he was the same as he always had been; coolly friendly and impeccably polite. She might have preferred it if he had been otherwise. Jack, she told herself bitterly, was never impolite to anyone. He would treat a stranger so. She tried not to think of him, tried even harder to tell herself that she didn't care what he thought of her. Yet she could not forget those short minutes from the time he had swung towards her, eager and alive as ever Harry had been, to the time she had left him in the clean, cold darkness of the starlit yard. Those moments seemed imprinted on her mind as firmly as the feeling of his warm strength was imprinted upon her body. She knew what it would be like to have him love her. The thought hardly seemed to leave her. It made her days wretched, her nights unbearably restless. She looked at his closed, austere face and felt certain that she knew what he was thinking; of her, and of himself also. For she had no doubt, knowing him as she did, that his judgement of them both would be as harsh. He would see betrayal and treachery where she saw none; for him there would be guilt, the humiliation of shame, where for her these things had no place at all in something as simple and natural as their coming together in that moment had been. He it was who was spoiling it, making of it something to be ashamed of. She held imaginary conversations with him, reasoned, argued, all but pleaded – and grew even more frustrated that her defence of herself and of him never actually reached his ears. As the weeks passed she told herself it didn't matter, that she didn't care – and still when she saw him the set of his head, the width of his shoulders brought a treacherous churning to her blood.

In the first days she had hoped, against hope, that he might come, just once, to see her – to talk, to give her all the reasons that she already knew why they must forget what they had both learned of each other. But eventually, listening to common sense, she gave up hoping for his knock on the door, his voice in the hall.

When it finally came she was completely unprepared for it.

She opened the door to him in the mid-afternoon darkness of a dreary December day. The sight of him took her breath with surprise. Behind her she heard – and ignored – Ellen's door clicking softly open.

He stood self-consciously, strong colour staining his high cheekbones, his hands bunched into awkward fists about his rolled-up cap. He was in working clothes, his jacket was shabby and his boots marked and dirty.

"I need to speak to you," he said with no preamble.

Molly stepped back, opened the door wider. He followed her into the sitting room, dwarfing the doorway with his bulk, and she was aware in the darkness of the hall, of Ellen's eyes on them both. She shut the door with a sharp, unnecessarily decisive movement. Her heart was pounding.

"I'm sorry to bother you like this," he said, his voice gruff.

She shook her head. She had to tilt her head right back to look at him; his eyes were tired, dust streaked one side of his face. Yet the strong and healthy glow of him, even beneath the grime and weariness of the docks, lit the dim, unloving room like a lamp.

"It's our Nancy," he said without moving towards her.

She blinked. Nancy?

Jack ran his huge hand through already untidy hair. "I'm sorry. I know I shouldn't have come. But I couldn't think of anyone else the lass might listen to. I can't tell Mam, Christ knows. Charley and Annie are that wrapped up in each other they don't see anything that's not under their noses. And anyway, she'd not heed them any more than she does me—"

"Nancy?" Her voice was leaden. "What's wrong with Nancy?"

"You haven't noticed anything?"

"I've barely seen her." The table was between them now, the world had shifted back into perspective. Jack was a tired, obviously worried young man. And Nancy, the closest thing that Molly had had to a sister, was in some sort of trouble. "She's been going out a lot. I thought it was an improvement. I mean, she seems to have made some friends—"

Jack's sudden movement as his hand hit the table had in it a raw violence that brought her heart to her throat. "Friends? Jake Aster and his cronies? As soon make friends with a pack of rats." He forced his voice to calm. "He's vicious, Molly. He's a killer and a thief and God only knows what else. What does his kind want with my sister?"

Molly remembered a fierce, heartless face, a crooked mouth. "He's the man she met at Charley's wedding?"

"Aye, he is. And it's his good luck that I didn't see them together earlier." He wrapped his arms around himself, as if to contain his own violence. "It's sure as Hell that Charley didn't know he was there. A mate of some of Annie's kin it seems. Jake Aster dancing at Charley's wedding; Judas, there's a joke. I tried to tell Nancy then, I've tried since. She won't listen. That's why I've come to you. I'd not have, Moll, believe me, if I'd not thought it important—" For the first time his eyes acknowledged that there was something more between them than Nancy's problems, " – but there's a chance she'll listen to you. Make her, Molly. Make her listen. Make her understand. He's out to hurt her, nowt more. He doesn't give a tinker's cuss for her. He'll destroy her—"

"Why should he want to do that?"

He turned from her and walked to the window, stood staring out into the clouded light.

"Jack? How do you know so much about this Jake Aster? How can you be so sure he means Nancy harm?"

The silence lengthened. Molly gnawed her lip; she sensed more here than simple brotherly concern for a girl fallen into bad company.

"You know him?"

Jack nodded.

"How well?"

"Well enough." It was like pulling a tooth.

"From the docks?"

"Aye." Something in his low voice brought the hairs on the nape of her neck to separate life.

She watched the still back. "You can't stop Nancy from going round with someone just because you don't like him, Jack. I can't say that I liked the look of him much myself. But, well, it's Nancy's business, isn't it? It's her life. I don't see how we can interfere. And if he cares for her—"

"*Cares for her?*" Voice and movement were slow as he turned from the window; Molly flinched from the expression on his face. "Jake care? He doesn't know how. Did you not hear what I said? He's a killer. A cold-blooded killer."

She stared at him. "I thought you meant—"

"I meant just what I said. He has killed with his bare hands. He has his dirty fingers in every rotten racket in the docks. He's a pimp, an extortionist, a thief who'd steal the blood from his own brother's veins. A gutter rat. And he has his filthy hands on my sister. I just don't know what's happened to Nancy, Moll. She's changed. It's like talking to a stranger. She won't *listen* to me." The violence of frustration threaded the words.

"You and this man—" began Molly, questioningly.

"– hate each other's guts." The language and the tone were so unlike the Jack she knew that she stared. "Jake Aster's got the wharves tied up like a Christmas parcel – he decides who'll work and who won't. And anyone who doesn't like the way he runs things'll likely wake up in a dark alley with their kneecaps smashed, or under a fallen crate with a broken back. But not us. We've kept him off the ships. You need skilled men in those holds; skilled men with a lot of muscle. There's no place for the likes of Aster."

"You fought him?"

"We did."

"I once heard you preach against violence to Charley. I thought you meant it."

"Aye, I did. I do. Violence as a means to an end I'll have no part of, it's no answer to anything. But when it comes to vermin like Aster, that's a different thing, lass. That's self-defence. Survival. What do you think it's like inside those dock gates? A Sunday school outing to Southend?"

"Of course not. But—"

"But nothing. With a bastard like Jake Aster you thump him before he thumps you, and that's that. Now he has a grudge, against me and against Charley, but mostly against me because

I organized the men against him and the scum he leads. Grudges come hard with Jake. They stick."

"And you think that's why he's taken up with Nancy? To get back at you?"

"Nothing's more certain. I've seen him and his women; he likes them fast and flashy and loud as they come. Where does Nancy fit in there? Yet she doesn't seem to care. I've tried to tell her, tried to explain. I don't understand it, by God I don't. What's wrong with her, Moll?"

"Joey Taylor," Molly said, wondering at the short-sightedness of men. "That's what's wrong with her. The things he said. She's brooded on them, until she believes them." She perched on the arm of a chair, fiddled absently with the fringed antimacassar.

"What did he say?"

"It wouldn't help you to know."

"There's another neck I'd like to break."

Molly tipped her head back and looked up at him, half smiling. "For a peaceful man you're surely after wreaking havoc today."

He did not smile back. "It's our Nancy," he said simply.

"I know. And I'll help if I can, I promise. If you think she might listen to me then I'll try. Though I don't know how much good it'll do."

"Not a word to Mam."

"Of course not." Molly stood up.

"Thanks." They stood looking at each other. Jack made an awkward gesture with the hand that still held his cap. "I'd best be off then."

"Yes."

He stepped closer; for a second her breath checked in her throat, but he did not touch her. "You have to make her see, Molly. I know the man. He's a bastard."

"He's also very attractive. Have you thought of that?"

He didn't like that. "You think so?"

"I know so. Any woman would."

He shook his head in perplexity. "You've got me beat. All of you."

"You don't do so badly yourself."

He had half-turned towards the door before the significance of that caught him. "What's that supposed to mean?"

She watched him. His face was suddenly brick-red.

"If you're talking about – what happened – at the wedding—" she let him struggle, made no attempt to help, "I thought – that is, it seemed best not to mention it."

" 'Least said, soonest mended'?" Molly's voice was dry.

"I don't know what came over me to act so. It wasn't the drink, at least—"

"You don't think it was," she finished for him.

He was looking at her with something close to anger in his eyes. "You make it sound cheap."

"No," she said shortly, " 'tis you who are doing that." For God's sake, asked a voice in her head, what are you doing? Who needs to fight with him?

"I'm sorry if that's how it seems. I'm no great man with words." He spoke stiffly, stepped to the door. "But I've apologized. I don't see what more I can do. It's best we both forget it."

"If you say so."

The air between them rattled with unspoken words.

"I'll be off, then."

She nodded.

At the front door he put his cap on, lifted a hand and left with no goodbye. When she shut the door and turned it was to see Ellen standing in the shadows at the end of the hall, malevolence drawing her face sharp as a knife edge.

Molly went back into her room and slammed the door, hard.

Nancy turned her head, looked into the fire. "I know what he is. What they say he is." The bruise on her cheekbone throbbed in the warmth of the flames.

Molly lifted expressive hands. "Then in the name of God what are you doing, Nancy? He's not your kind and you aren't his. You know it. Why do you go with him?"

The neat head moved impatiently. "My kind? His? Don't talk rubbish, Molly. How would you know? Ask Joe Taylor who my kind might be."

"Oh, Nancy!"

They fell silent. In the grate the fire crackled and spat; a coal rolled onto the hearth. Molly scooped it up with a shovel and a poker and settled it back on the glowing heap.

"I know you're trying to help. I know what Jack must have told you. But you have to understand – there's nothing you can do, nothing you can say that will change me. Jake's cruel. I know it." She was rubbing her hands on her upper arms, a little ceaseless, nervous movement of which she seemed hardly aware. "Worse than cruel. He's arrogant and brutal. He terrifies me. But I can't stop. Don't ask me why. I can't. Maybe Joey Taylor was right about me after all—"

"No!"

"How do you know? How do any of us know what we really are?"

Molly watched her worriedly; there was something terribly disturbing in the thin, bruised face, something that was not Nancy Benton at all. "I think you're mistaken, Nancy," she said softly.

"I don't care." Nancy lifted dark, intense eyes. "I don't care, do you hear? And it isn't your business. Nor Jack's. I'll find my own road."

"And you don't mind how much you get hurt following it?" asked Molly, knowing the answer, "or how much you hurt those who love you?"

"No, I don't."

In the hearth the cave of coals finally collapsed and sent a blast of spinning, glowing sparks streaming up the dark chimney.

Christmas was in the air. Sam came home one evening, coughing. The advancing winter was unkind to him; there were dark rings under his eyes, hollows beneath the bones of his face.

"Are you tired?" Molly strove to keep the impatience from her voice. Tired again?

"A little."

"Would it be best for you to go to bed? Early, I mean?"

"Well—" he looked at the vibrant life of her, felt his own small strength ebb.

"Why don't you? You'd feel better for a good night's sleep."

"What will you do?"

"I thought I'd pop over to the Bentons'. I promised Sarah a pattern. I have it here, and she's waiting for it. Danny's fast asleep. Would you mind?"

It had been a week since she'd seen Nancy. Or Jack.

"I don't like you going out alone at night." He tilted his head wearily to the back of the chair. "You know I don't. Why can't you leave it till tomorrow? It's bitter out there."

But she was already slipping into her coat, reaching for her hat. "Don't be silly, dear. It's hardly the middle of the night. I've been cooped up here all day, I could do with some air. The bus stops at the end of Linsey Grove. And Jack'll see me to the stop at the other end. I shan't be late." She paused, ready and impatient to be gone. "If you're sure you wouldn't like to come with me?" He shook a tired head. She dropped a kiss on the fine, straight hair. "See you later. Get a good sleep."

He closed his eyes on the sound of her departing footsteps. As the front door clicked firmly shut his mother's voice called from the kitchen.

"Sam? Sam, why don't you come in here and sit with me? It's nice and warm and I've got the kettle on—"

It was fully half a minute before he could muster the breath to answer her.

At ten o'clock Molly stood up. "I really should go. Sam will worry."

Sarah, sitting ramrod-straight in a fireside chair, smiled a small, strained smile. "Thanks for coming, lass. And for the pattern. It's just what I wanted."

It had not been a good evening. For the last hour there had been little conversation; any step in the street outside warranted a pause, a sharp expectant look at the door. It had never happened before that Nancy had not come home from work; no matter how her habits had changed lately always she came home before going out. Tonight there had been no sign of her, nor any message. Sarah had spoken of the bad winter service on the roads, wondered aloud if the girls had been kept behind to work some extra Christmas order; she had checked, at regular intervals, her daughter's supper spoiling in the oven and had finally subsided into anxious silence. Molly wondered uneasily how much, despite Jack's efforts, Sarah knew, how much she guessed, about Nancy's new friends. Jack himself, sitting for the best part of the evening in the corner with his newspaper, had said nothing of Nancy; but both women were aware of the throb of the muscle on the side of his jaw, the listening lift of his head at any sound from outside.

"I'll walk you to the stop." He stood up now, moving towards the kitchen for his jacket and cap.

"Thanks." With her coat half-on Molly stopped. They all heard it. Nancy's voice. A man's laughter.

Jack was across the room and at the door in one bound. His mother rose from her chair, her hand pressed hard to her breast. "Jack!"

He stopped, stepped back from the door. Outside, footsteps sounded unsteadily on the path. As the door opened Sarah sank back into the chair. Molly, close to her, put out a reassuring hand. Jack straightened, his face like granite, stared at his sister as she, with chin high and her split mouth set in a defiant line, closed the door behind her and leaned on it, facing them.

"Nancy, oh, Nancy—" Sarah's voice, fretted with tears, was all the sound in a full minute.

"What's he done to you?" Molly made a move towards her, but like the others was restrained by the total rejection of their concern that was implicit in Nancy's stance.

"I'm all right." The quiet voice was slightly slurred. "Just leave me alone. It looks worse than it is." As if for the first time, she seemed to taste the fresh blood on her mouth, she lifted a hand to wipe it away, smearing it across her cheek, a ghastly splash of colour on her colourless skin. Her hair was blown wild and tangled about her shoulders, her skirt was stained with mud and vomit. The smell of gin, sickly sweet, hung about her. "I'm all right," she said again.

"You look it, by God." Jack's voice was raw. "Christ Almighty, you look it."

"Jack." Sarah said, her eyes on her swaying daughter, "that's enough, we'll talk tomorrow. Let the lass to bed. She looks as if she needs it."

"She looks," said Jack, viciously and without thought, "as if she's had it."

His mother's hand cracked hard against his face before he or anyone else could move. Molly's hand went to her mouth. Nancy turned to the door, her forehead pressed hard to the wood, her eyes tight shut. Jack stood like a breathing statue, the mark of the blow bright on his face. Sarah was trembling.

"I'm sorry, son," she said. "I'm sorry. But I'll not have such—" She could not go on.

Very slowly Jack's massive, bunched shoulders relaxed. He spoke to Nancy's rigid back.

"You can tell him, our Nancy—" he emphasized the two words grimly, "that it's working nicely. Wouldn't he give his right arm to see us now?"

"I don't know what you mean." The words were muffled.

"You know as well as I do what I mean. You know what he's doing. And you know why he's doing it."

Nancy was shaking her head, back and forth, shaking, shaking, a steady, desperate denial. Sarah was crying silently, her face buried in her hands. Molly put a comforting arm about one who had comforted others so often.

Nancy turned at last, her head still stubbornly shaking, her hands flat on the door behind her for support. She looked sick; there was a bruise on her forehead, her mouth was blurred and reddened. It had not been a blow that had drawn blood.

"I'd better leave," she said into the silence.

"Aye," Jack said savagely, "you better had."

"I didn't mean – never wanted – to hurt you all like this—"

Jack stepped to her. She flinched as he took her ungently by her shoulders. Her face was sheened with sweat.

"Hurt us?" Jack shook her. Molly had never heard his voice so hard. "Think on, our Nancy. When they talk about you down at the docks, in the waterside pubs—" he saw the look on her face " – oh, ay lass, they do talk you know. How in Hell do you think I found out what was going on? When they tell their filthy jokes about Jake Aster's new bitch, Benton's the name they use. Benton. Mam's name. Charley's name." He lifted her almost clear of the floor. "My name. So think on this. You stay with him, you keep clear of us—"

"Jack, no!" Sarah's voice was agonized.

"Yes, I say. And either way, our Nancy, you tell that bastard this: if it's a fight he's been after, he's won. If I see his ugly face I'll break his bloody neck." He let go of her and stepped back. Nancy stared at him, biting her lip. "God knows," he said in a suddenly shaking voice, "what's happened to you to bring us to this."

"Leave her alone, Jack. Leave her now. She needs help, not abuse." Molly stepped between him and Nancy.

Nancy warded her off with upraised hands. "No. He's right. I'm sorry. But I don't want your help. I only wish I did."

Almost steadily she walked to the kitchen door, stopped a couple of feet from Sarah. "I'm truly sorry, Mam."

Sarah shook her head, unable to speak. At the look in her mother's eyes Nancy's face crumpled and tears came at last as she fled the room, leaving a deathly silence behind her.

CHAPTER TWENTY

A MONTH WENT by, and a miserable Christmas had come and gone before anyone heard again from Nancy. Jack had fallen into a bitter and black mood that cast a pall across them all and in the Benton household Nancy's name was never mentioned. Poor Sarah suffered in silence. She would not speak of her daughter, not even to Molly, but the pain was in her eyes. It was one early day in January when the silence was at last broken.

The day was foggy; a wreathing blanket of yellow smothered trees and houses, pressed to windows, muffled the sounds of the streets. Molly, holding a Danny whose ever-increasing size and weight made him more difficult for her to handle every day, gazed into the shrouded street, thankful for the glow of firelight that lit the room behind her. Ellen was out and the house was preternaturally quiet. She laid her cheek against the soft, bright head as the baby dozed on her shoulder. She moved gently, swaying, crooning to him in a sing-song voice.

Beneath the dripping, fog-swathed branches of the plane tree the muffled figure of a child paused, looked at the number on the gate and lifted her eyes doubtfully to the house. She hesitated, her hand on the gate, obviously debating whether to enter, then scurried up the path. Molly laid the almost-sleeping Danny in the little day crib by the fire and went into the hall in time to see a crumpled piece of paper pushed through the letter box. Puzzled, she picked it up and took it into the light to read. From the street outside came the sound of running footsteps, swiftly smothered by the fog.

There was an address on the grubby paper, printed in pencil, the letters oddly formed and distorted: "16, Old Dock Rd. Silvertown. Upstairs." Underneath were scrawled the words "for God's sake help me. N."

Molly stared at the thing. She had no doubt whatsoever as to its sender. The desperation embodied in the scribbled scrap of paper appalled her. She had to get it to the Bentons at once.

Surely even Jack, faced with this, could not refuse to help his sister?

The baby stirred in his cot. Outside the fog was thickening with every moment as early darkness closed upon the crowded streets; and as fires and ranges were lit heavy, soot-laden smoke rolled from the chimneys to mingle with and sink through the choking atmosphere that already had people coughing into their scarves and mufflers. Not even for Nancy could she take the baby out in this.

Where was Ellen? In such an emergency even she could not refuse to help, surely?

She ran to the window, strained her eyes into the infuriatingly blank wall of fog, glared into the murk as if willing Sam or Ellen bodily to appear. From the street came a happy, tuneless whistling. The boy next door – an urchin of ten who was the only person Molly knew who detested Ellen Alden as much as she did herself – tossed his satchel over the hedge of the house next door, followed it with a skip and a jump and still whistling disappeared up the path.

Of course. Mrs Johnson, next door. She was a motherly, obliging woman who had happily looked after Danny before in an emergency. Molly flung on her coat and gathered up the protesting baby, muffling him against the fog.

It took an interminable time to get to Park Road. The foggy streets were chaotic with traffic jams that made it quicker to walk than to take the horse-drawn omnibus. The sense of urgency that drove her, half-running through the streets, was unabated when she turned the corner of the Bentons' road. But when she reached the house her heart sank. The windows were dark; no glimmer of light showed. She flew down the path and hammered on the door; the sound of the knocker echoed emptily. No one was there. She stood on the shadowed step for a moment longer before burying her chin in her collar and her cold hands in her pocket and setting off for Jesse Street, where Charley and Annie lived.

Jack was there. She heard his voice as Annie opened the door. Annie, flaming head silhouetted against dull yellow gaslight stared at her in astonishment. "Molly! What the blazes are you doing here? Is something wrong? Come in, love. Gawd, what a night—" She ushered Molly into a small, cozy room. Two pairs of surprised blue eyes were turned upon her; Jack and Charley, awkward in the confined space of the little, cluttered room, scrambled to their feet.

"I went to Sarah's—" Molly began. She was breathless, and her bare head was netted with beads of moisture.

"She's visiting. She'll be back in an hour or so." Jack waited.

"What's up, love?" Annie asked quietly.

Molly was watching Jack. "I – I've heard from Nancy. At least, I think – I'm sure – it's from Nancy."

Jack turned away, his face like granite.

"– She's in trouble, Jack. Asking for help. Please! Look at it at least—" She pulled out the note and held it out. Charley took it, glanced at it in silence, then passed it to Jack who, after a momentary hesitation, took it and stood for a long time, studying it. When he lifted his head his eyes were chips of ice in a face harsh with anger. "Get your coat, Charley."

"I'm coming too," Molly said. The resolution had formed as she had run through the wreathed and dripping streets. Nothing was going to shake it.

"Don't be daft, lass. You don't know what—"

"I'm coming. Nancy sent the note to me. She might need me. You'll not stop me, Jack Benton." Stubbornly she held his blazing eyes with her own. "If you try, I'll just follow you. I'm coming."

Jack caught the coat that Charley tossed to him from across the room, held it for a moment, watching her. "Fair enough," he said at last, quietly, "there's no time to argue. But stick close, lass. If Jake Aster's around this'll be no social visit."

Old Dock Road was as quiet as the grave; and about as enticing. The black and ugly terraces of houses edged the narrow pavements, crowding together in hostile, fog-wreathed silence.

Somewhere, very faintly, a piano played; a thin, jangling, nervous sound.

"Number Sixteen," Molly said, with an effort preventing her voice from dropping to a whisper. "It must be on that side."

The street was a dark funnel of swirling mist patches. For a moment the air thinned and Charley, counting along the houses, said, "That'll be it, I reckon. Just beyond the lamp."

"Right." It was almost the first word Jack had spoken since they had set out.

The door of the house, one of a three-storied row of six, opened directly down three steep stone steps to the pavement, along which ran dilapidated and rusty iron railings that leaned at a wild angle to the wall. There was neither bell nor knocker.

Jack lifted a fist like a hammer, and sound thundered through the house.

Nothing happened.

Charley rattled the door. "It's bolted from the inside. There must be somebody there."

Jack knocked again, hard. Molly glanced nervously over her shoulder. They seemed to be making enough noise to waken the dead. As she opened her mouth to say so a weak light moved beyond the dirty glass fanlight above the door, yellowing the fog, Making of it something solid and oppressive over their heads.

" 'Oo is it?" A querulous voice, old, bad tempered.

Jack hammered on the door again. "Mates of Jake's. Open up."

"All right, all right. Keep yer 'air on." A bolt was rattled back and the door opened a crack. " 'E ain't 'ere." A bald head appeared, small, crafty eyes, an unshaven face that looked as if it had not seen soap and water for a week; the old man peered suspiciously into the foggy gloom, "You'll 'ave ter come back later."

"No." Jack's hand was on the door, pushing inexorably, his solid working boot planted itself in the widening gap, "We won't."

Something in the voice, in the hard eyes, encouraged discretion. The old man stepped back from the door and it opened wide. He was small – only a couple of inches taller than Molly herself – his dirty shirt overhung patched and filthy trousers. In his hand he carried an oil lamp that smoked and smelled and filled the hall with leaping shadows.

"What d'yer want?"

Molly, silently, indicated a dark stairway that rose from the corner of the hall.

Jack jerked his head at the man who held the lamp. "We've come to see the girl. Show us."

The man shook his head. "Jake won't like that. No one's allowed up there."

"Jake," Jack said quietly, "isn't going to like a lot of things. Show us." He moved threateningly and the old man backed away. ":No need fer that, Mister."

He led the way up the stairs. The passage above was lit by two wall brackets; he put the lamp he was carrying on a small table beside a solid-looking door and fished in his pocket for the key. Jack's face in the guttering light was stone white.

As the door swung open Nancy lifted her head and looked at them; and for one moment there was nothing but terror in her eyes.

"Jesus Christ," Charley said thickly.

"Get a cab, Charley." His brother's voice, scraped raw with rage, was still quiet. "Quick as you can."

Charley stood stock-still for a moment, staring, then he turned and clattered, cursing, down the stairs.

Molly was on her knees beside Nancy, holding her hand, stroking it, whispering.

"Oh, Nancy, Nancy dear—"

The girl's dazed eyes lifted from Molly's bent head to her silent brother who stood by the door.

"Jack? *Jack?* Her voice was strained with incredulity, the fear of hope. Her bruised face and tangled hair, the angry welts on her body hardly hidden by the dirty robe that was her only garment were not the only signs of ill-treatment; she was paper-thin, her eyes dark holes in a haggard face. "I didn't think you'd ever come."

In two steps Jack was by the bed, had lifted her bodily and crushed her to him, his face over her shoulder a sharp-boned delineation of pain, his eyes closed.

The old man by the door moved, sly as a weasel.

"Jack!" Molly flung herself forward, too late to prevent the man's escape but at least quick enough to foil his obvious intention of slamming and locking the door behind him. With surprising agility he ran for the stairs.

"Leave him," Jack said, setting Nancy carefully on her feet.

"He can't stop us now. Charley'll be back in a minute. Come on, lass, we're taking you home."

Like a child Nancy allowed herself to be ushered down the stairs to the front door, but when Jack opened it and rolling yellow fog drifted like poison into the hall she shrank back.

Molly tightened her arm about her. "Come on, darlin'. It's all right. Charley will be here with the cab—"

They left the house, not bothering to close the door behind them. Jack was on the pavement, his hands held up to help Nancy down the steep stone steps, when the voice rang out.

"And where the 'Ell," Jake Aster asked pleasantly, "do you think you're goin'?"

He was leaning against the lamp post, a nebulous figure half-obscured by drifting fog, his teeth gleaming like an animal's as he smiled. There were men standing at his back; Molly saw the wet shine of a blade, the solid hefting of a cudgel. A bald head and old, crafty eyes caught the edges of the pool of light cast by the lamp. The old man grinned at her.

Jack's hands dropped to his sides and he turned slowly to meet the other man's bright and baleful gaze.

"Seems you thought I was away from 'ome," Jake said thoughtfully. Then, after a pause, threw in, "Seems you was wrong."

The old man cackled, some of the others grinned. Jake pushed himself upright with easy grace. "An' I thought you loved me, Princess. Disappointed, I am. Disappointed." He was shaking his head sorrowfully, his eyes narrowed upon Nancy.

Nancy shivered. Molly stepped closer, slipped her hand into the other girl's. Jake smiled fiercely. He studied Molly, deliberately offensive, from head to toe. "Bit on the small side fer a big lad like you, Jack, ain't she? 'Ow do you manage? Use the kitchen table, do yer?"

More laughter. Molly felt her cheeks burn; Jack neither moved nor spoke.

"Well, look at that, will yer? Cat's got 'is tongue. Not like you, Jackie boy, not like you at all. Quick enough ter speak out when you've got yer gang at yer back, eh? Quick enough ter stick yer bleedin' fingers into other people's business, too. Well, you ain't got so much to shout about now, Big Jack, 'ave yer? 'Ow d'yer like yer sister, eh?" His voice dropped to a caressing murmur; "Shame really. Jumped the gun you 'ave. Another week'd 'ave done it nicely. Never mind, mustn't be greedy. I've 'ad me fun."

Jack stirred; the light glittered on the drops of moisture that had formed on his hair and skin. Jake's thin, brigand's face sharpened with pleasure as he watched him. He was tall as Jack, but slighter; his hair was long, straight, gypsy-black. He stood like a dancer, limned in light in the shifting mist. "End of the fuckin' road, Jack Benton," he said softly. "I've 'ad yer sister, and now I've got you. You won't stand in Jake Aster's way again—"

One of his companions pushed forward, a burly man who carried in his hand a long, shining knife. "Come on, Jake, cut the cackle. Get on with it." He made a deft pass with the weapon, smiling widely. "I bin lookin' forward to this fer a long time. You ain't the only one with a grudge, you know. This sod got me thrown off the wharves."

Jack shifted his weight slightly, ranging himself as best as he could before the two girls. Something caught Molly's eye; she let go of Nancy's hand and moved very carefully towards the railings beside the steps.

The man with the knife danced closer, light on his feet despite his bulk. Jake Aster watched, the wolf-smile on his lips. When another of his companions would have joined the advancing knife-wielder he held up a barring arm, shaking his head slightly. Jack watched the coming man intently. The man showed yellow teeth, cut a silver arc in the air inches from his intended victim's face. The watching men murmured, laughing. The man moved again; Molly's heart almost stopped as the knife, flickering in the lamplight, sliced the space where a second before Jack had been standing; so fast was Jack's movement that it blurred the eye. The blade, shaken free from a suddenly helpless hand flew into the air and Molly heard a nerve-grating crack as bone broke beneath Jack's hands. The man he held shrieked, fell to his knees as he was released, clutching a grotesquely dangling arm. But he had served his purpose; the violence of Jack's movement had taken him across the pavement and within reach of waiting hands. Jake Aster jerked his head and half a dozen men, two of them wielding heavy clubs, leapt forward and their weight bore Jack, fighting savagely, to the ground.

Molly reached for the broken railings.

Jack was hauled to his feet. Blood seeped from his cheekbone, his mouth, matted his thick hair. Distantly through the fog came the click of a horse's hooves on the cobbles.

"Get that little 'un," shouted Jake, just as the heavy railing came loose in Molly's hand. She turned, swinging it like a flail, and more by luck than judgement caught the man who was advancing on her clean and hard across the chest. With a bellow of pain he backed away.

"Take 'er," snapped Jake, his tone vicious. "Fer Christ's sake, man, you goin' ter let a bit of skirt stand you off?"

Jack stopped struggling. "Let her be, Jake. It's me you're after. I'm here. Let her alone."

Molly, her back to the wall, swung the iron rail in a lethal swathe before her, watching her would-be attacker with wary and defiant eyes.

"Try it," she said, "if 'tis a broken head you're after."

Jake threw back his head and laughed. "Irish, is it?" He walked to just beyond rail-swinging distance and regarded her with his head on one side. "Well, all right, Kitty-o, we'll come to you later. It'll be my pleasure."

"Leave her!" Jack made one violent, wrenching attempt to free himself, then stood still, recognizing the futility of it, pinioned as he was by four men.

Jake walked to him, silent and balanced as a cat. "Shut up, Benton," he said quietly, "no one's askin' you." His hand crashed hard against Jack's already damaged mouth.

Jack spat, very accurately, blood and spittal and a piece of tooth.

"Son of a bitch—" Jake's arm was raised again; then Charley hit him, coming out of the foggy darkness like a thrown stone. Jack's face split into a wide and bloody grin. Molly swung her iron bar and caught someone a satisfying crack on the back of the head before she grabbed for Nancy's hand. The dark bulk of the hansom loomed beyond the light.

" 'Ere, 'old on," an aggrieved voice said from the driver's box, "I ain't 'avin' no part in a rough 'ouse—"

Charley, using one opponent as a club to beat off another, swung closer to the cab and leapt onto the seat beside the cabbie. "Won't be a minute, mate," he said, cheerfully, and above the tumult Jack's voice rang like a bell.

"By God, if any bastard takes another step I'll slit Aster's bloody throat—"

In one hand he held the long, razor-sharp blade the burly man had dropped, in the other a huge handful of straight black hair, held excruciatingly close to the scalp. Jake Aster was nearly on his knees, his head drawn painfully back, his long throat open, defenceless, to the threat of the knife that no one there doubted that Jack would use.

"Tell them." Jack jerked Jake's head brutally. "Tell them, Jake."

Jake in reply gave his captor an instruction from the gutter so explicit that Molly held her breath; the point of the knife drew blood from the stretched throat and Jack twisted his other hand until it seemed that Jake must choke. The effect was the required one: the men – two were already on the ground; the big man with the smashed arm was sitting on the curb cursing monotonously – gathered beneath the lamp post, none of them unscathed, none of them ready, in the face of the iced blaze of Jack's eyes, to risk Jake Aster's life; or their own.

"Get in the cab," Jack said to Molly and Nancy. Molly nodded swiftly, pulling Nancy towards the vehicle. The bedspread had dropped from the girl's shoulders and been trampled underfoot; she was shivering violently.

" 'Ere, I don't know abaht this—" the cabbie half-stood in his seat.

Affably and with a hand like half the side of a barn Charley pushed him back. "Take it easy now, squire. There'll be five bob in it for you." The cabbie opened his mouth to argue, looked at the breadth of Charley's shoulders, the blithe grin, and changed his mind.

By his hair and the scruff of his neck Jack dragged Jake to the door of the cab.

"In," he said.

Jake made no move. His eyes, contemptuous, were on the knife. "Sod you," he said, "use it."

The glinting blade lifted, the needle point held steady as a rock just an inch from his right eye. "Say that again, lad," Jack said savagely, quietly. "It'll be a pleasure."

Nancy, in Molly's arms in the cab, moaned a little and turned her head; her face was slick and shiny with tears that ran as if they would never stop.

Jake took a long, uneven breath. He had dealt with men enough to know true threat from bluff. Awkwardly he climbed into the cab.

"Tell your pack of hounds to stay put," Jack said.

Jake lifted his voice. His eyes did not move from Jack's face. If looks could kill, thought Molly, Jack would not have lasted one second. "Leave it, boys."

The cab pulled away, rocking and bumping across the uneven surface of the street. Nancy was sobbing into Molly's shoulder; Molly, her hand stroking the other girl's hair soothingly, watched the two men on the seat opposite. Their hatred of each other was almost a tangible thing. It howled through their eyes, concentrated itself in the lethal gleam of the knife Jack held. Neither spoke. Ten long minutes passed, Molly guessed, before Jack lifted a hand and rapped on the flap that communicated with the driver's seat.

"All right, Charley. This'll do."

The vehicle rolled to a stop. Dense fog still drifted through silent streets. Almost all transport, it seemed, had finally been halted by the weather.

Jack leaned across and unlatched the door; it swung open. "Out," he said to Jake, but the dark head stayed rigid, in his face the finality of death. He had no doubts as to what he would do in Jack's place.

"What's the matter, Benton," he asked, "don't you want the ladies to see the blood?"

"Don't tempt me. Just get out of my sight." There was a sick weariness in Jack's voice, and Jake finally slid along the seat, watching all the while the knife in Jack's hand. Then he was out and standing in the road.

"Shut the door," Jack said tightly.

In a darkness lit only by the hansom's own lamps Jake's eyes shone venom through the closing door, and then Jack was calling to Charley. The cab lurched forward. Through the window Molly watched the slim, still figure as it receded into the murky darkness, then turned back to see Jack, with a gesture of disgust, toss the knife into the corner of the seat and lean his head back on the scuffed upholstery, his eyes closed. Up on the box Charley was talking cheerfully to the driver, encouraging him as he grumbled his way slowly through the shrouded streets. Within the confines of the cab's interior there was nothing to be heard but Nancy's quiet sobs until Jack at last sighed, as if waking, and turned his head to find wide grey eyes fixed upon him still.

He attempted a smile, a tired grimace. There was blood on his face. "Tha did a reet fine job there, lass," he said, broadening his accent, "I'd wish ta 'ave thee at me back in all me fights."

She could not smile back. "It isn't over. Is it?"

"No," he said simply. "It isn't."

They finished the journey in silence; to find that the shocks of that night were far from over.

Annie was at Sarah's. Unable to wait alone she had, understandably, taken the tale to her mother-in-law and they had shared the vigil together. Annie it was who opened the door to them, whose eyes went not immediately to Nancy, but to Molly.

"Sam's here," she said. "He's bad, Moll, real bad."

"Sam?" Molly stared stupidly, as if she barely recognized the name.

"He came looking for you. He had to walk. The buses had stopped. With his chest, in this weather. He was taken bad—"

Molly was past her and into the back room before she could say more; Sam was propped in a chair, the colour of his face ghastly, the front of his shirt patched with blood, fresh stains on old, his cough the bark of death. He could not speak; there was nothing that Molly could do but take his hand and hold it tight.

The doctor who had been called to tend to Sam took one look at Nancy and ordered her upstairs to bed. When he came down from seeing her he spoke quietly to Sarah in the scullery before attending to Jack's cuts and bruises. On his way out he asked Molly to accompany him to the front door. On the doorstep he turned.

"I've left instructions with Mrs Benton regarding your husband. The sooner he's got to his own bed the better. What possessed him, Mrs Alden, to wander the streets on a night such as this I cannot imagine. He must, surely, know that he is a very sick man?"

Molly rubbed her forehead with a weary hand. "Shouldn't he be in hospital then?"

"There is nothing," the man said quietly, "that a hospital could do for him that his own bed wouldn't do better. I repeat, I cannot think what he was doing on the streets tonight in such a condition."

Molly's mind had been slow to register not the words he had spoken but the emphasis in his voice. She lifted her head. "What do you mean? What condition?"

The doctor looked at her with eyes that had seen too much suffering to allow themselves to care deeply. "He is dying, Mrs Alden," said the doctor. "Almost certainly, dying."

CHAPTER TWENTY-ONE

POOR SAM TOOK a week to die. Dazed and unhappy, Molly nursed him through sleepless nights and endless, painfilled days while Ellen watched her every movement with dark, venomous eyes. The impulse that had carried Sam out into the lethal foggy night, that had finally destroyed his damaged lungs, she blamed entirely upon Molly. Molly, at first, in exhausted anguish, was inclined to agree with her, until Sam himself, on the third day of his illness, gave her cause to think differently. He had lain, propped on his pillows, watching her as she tidied the room.

"M – Molly?" Every word he uttered was punctuated by the ugly rasp of his breathing. "C – can I ask you something?"

She came to the bedside. "Well, of course. What is it?"

Sam's thin fingers were picking nervously at the counterpane, his bright-boned consumptive's face turned suddenly from her.

"Sam?"

He took a deep, rattling breath. "Did Jack—" he coughed, recovered himself. "Did Jack c – come here sometimes? D – during the day, I mean? To see you?"

Silence sang between them. "Who told you such a thing?" No need, truly, to ask.

"M – mother m – mentioned that – he came here sometimes." He lifted tired eyes to her face at last.

"Once he came. About Nancy. That's all." She could not keep the desperate anger from her voice.

He flinched. "O – of course. I'm sorry." He was painfully flushed.

"Oh, Sam, dear—" She reached for his hand and held it tight. Now she saw how the canker had grown in him. Now she understood. He had come home to an empty house, Danny left with a neighbour, his wife gone, once more and with no explanation, to the Bentons. And in his mind the malicious, poisoned seeds planted by his mother. Had she realized, Molly wondered bitterly, that those seeds would kill the one she loved most in the world? "Jack's your friend," she said, "your true friend. You know that, don't you?"

His face relaxed. "Of course." He lay in silence for a moment, his cold hand still in hers. "Molly, will you get something for me? In the chest of drawers. The t – top drawer. The little s – statue. I'd like to have it here, where I can see it—"

.She opened the drawer, lifted out the chipped and ugly statuette she had bought from the beggar-girl in Stratford – how long ago? Two years. A century. "You've still got this?"

"Put it on the table." He was smiling. For the life of her Molly could not. "Th – thanks. I think I could sleep a little now."

As, almost blindly, Molly left the room she almost walked into Ellen, standing at the door, openly listening. They stared at one another for one long, hate-filled moment before Molly pushed past Ellen and ran down the stairs.

Between that moment and the time when, in the early hours of the morning, Molly threw her coat over her shoulders and ran, terrified, for the doctor, the two women said not one word to each other. Sam drifted, and sank, and reached a hand desperately to Molly. She held it for hours, until her own was numb, willing her living strength into the frail, failing frame of the dying man, making impossible bargains with the saints and devils who peopled her mind. The baby was next door with the Johnsons; the house was itself deathlike, the atmosphere thick and silent. Ellen's face was blank with grief and bitterness; and still she shed not one tear.

Molly for her part would not, could not, give up hope entirely; she refused to accept what was plainly before her eyes. The crisis would pass. It would.

But it didn't, and as she fled down the silent street and pounded at the doctor's door she knew it to be a wasted effort. As they climbed the stairs they could hear Sam's voice, a stranger's voice, strangled and harsh.

"Please, Mother. P – promise me—"

Molly pushed open the door. The pale, shadowed eyes moved to her, as did the dark and unforgiving ones of his mother.

"I'm sorry," Sam said to Molly; his last words to anyone. A few moments later, choking in blood, he was dead.

The rest of the night passed in a daze of unreality. The doctor was sympathetically efficient. Death and its attendant ceremonies was no stranger to him. He insisted upon administering to Ellen, after a rather worried look at her rigid, grieving face, a small draught to 'calm her nerves'.

"It will help her sleep," he said to Molly, "it might ease her a little. And now, young lady, what about you?" He had fetched Mrs Johnson from next door; the murmur of their voices as they tended Ellen filled the house at this strange hour with more life than it had held all day.

Molly shook her head. "No, thank you. I'm all right."

"How long is it since you slept?"

She lifted a vague, impatient hand, "I'm – not sure."

"Or ate?"

She shook her head.

The doctor tutted. "It won't do, my dear. You've a child to consider, as well as yourself, you know. Life goes on. You may not believe it at the moment, but it does—" words he had obviously spoken – how many times? Kindly meant, totally meaningless. Molly looked past him into the darkness beyond his head, the sound of his voice lost before it reached her ears. Sam was dead. Quiet, kind Sam. She saw him as he had been on the day he had first opened the door to her – blushing, tongue-tied. She saw him, laughing, on Stratford Broadway in the glow of the Christmas lights. She felt sad, tired, worn out. But she knew in her heart that even in this Sam had lost; her grief for his death was not as it had been for Harry. And that saddened her more. Poor Sam. She refocussed her eyes upon the doctor's face. He was holding something out to her.

"There's a good girl. Drink it up."

She took the glass obediently, drank a little. "Thank you."

"I'll be back in the morning. About eleven."

She saw him to the door, stood for a moment leaning against the jamb, her head bowed, her mind an utter blank.

Upstairs quiet voices rose and fell; Ellen's, occasionally strident, foremost of them. The hall swung a little, dizzily, around her. Her eyelids were lead. With the dregs of her strength finally draining from her she walked back into the sitting room and almost fell onto the chaise longue. Within seconds, with her head pillowed on her arms, she was asleep.

She woke to noise – shattering, destructive noise.

She lifted a dazed head. The fog had gone, driven before the rain that dashed against the window and streamed from the gutters. The light was cloud-obscured; it could have been any time, morning or afternoon. From the room above came another crash. She pulled herself to her feet. Her mouth was sour, her head throbbed; she had woken with the dark knowledge of Sam's death possessing her mind.

Through the ceiling came a quiet, monotonous voice.

Molly went out into the hall, stood at the foot of the stairs, listening. It was Ellen's voice, that vicious monotone, the words unintelligible, punctuated by violent crashes. The stairs creaked under Molly's careful feet. At the open door of the room she had shared with Sam she stopped, paralysed. It was a battleground. Every stitch of clothing, every article that she owned was shredded, smashed, thrown to the floor. The very sheets on the bed had been ripped apart. Paper was everywhere, manic confetti, pages ripped and scattered, from her books. Just inside the door lay the ruined blue leather cover, the pages gone, the copy of *Alice* that Sam had given her destroyed. A glimmer of blue silk – forget-me-not blue, the colour of summer skies, the colour of Danny's eyes – caught her eye. She bent and picked it up. The blouse hung in ribbons from her fingers.

Ellen turned. The grotesque stream of obscenities stopped. In her hand she held a mirror, a small hand mirror that Sam had bought Molly for her birthday, the frame of silver decked with plump, laughing cherubs.

"Harlot!" Ellen brought the mirror down with frightening force on the edge of the dressing table. Splinters of light flew in the dark room. "Filthy whore!"

There was nothing to reason with here. The dark face was wild, distorted with hatred. Molly sent a prayer of thanks to Heaven that Danny had not been sleeping in this room. His cot stood splintered in the corner. Ellen's voice lifted to a shriek; in her hand still glinted the shattered mirror.

"Get out of my house! Out! Get to the gutter where you belong." With a sweep of her arm she emptied the dressing table of pots and bottles and oddments; they flew, spinning, into every corner.

"My things—" said Molly, stupidly.

"Yours? You've nothing. You came with nothing. Go the same way. Starve, damn you! Out!" Ellen advanced threateningly. The thickness of a wall away her only son lay still and silent.

Molly turned and ran, there was nothing else to do. Down the stairs, out of the door and into the freezing, streaming rain. She slammed the door behind her, struggled desperately to get the perambulator through the gate, flew to the Johnsons' door.

"She's gone mad," she said, gasping, "mad." There was no need to explain further; through the upstairs window Ellen could be seen and heard, raving, her movements violent.

"I'll get the doctor," Ernest Johnson said.

"Yes, please."

Danny was screaming, furious at the upset, at his mother's jerky, frantic movements.

Molly tucked him tight into the pram, "I've got to get him away. If she comes after us—" She lifted her head to find Mrs Johnson's eyes fixed upon her, their expression torn between concern and scandalized delight at this turn of events.

"Where will you take him, dearie? Where will you go? I'd offer you a room here, but—" She glanced half-fearfully through the rain at the house next door.

"It's all right, thank you, Mrs Johnson." Molly was astonished at the sudden calmness of her own voice. "I've friends to go to. They'll help. I'll leave the address—" She scribbled on the used envelope the woman handed her. "Perhaps you'd give that to the doctor, in case he needs me?"

She turned the pram. Through the window Ellen had seen her; with a crash that shook the house to its foundations she threw the window up and leaned into the rain screaming, shaking her fist.

Molly stood for a second, drenched to the skin, looking up at the woman in the window. Ellen's hair dripped dark rat's tails around her livid face. She fell silent; then she lifted a pointing finger.

"I curse you," she shouted clearly above the rain, "you and your bastard brat. Curse you. No good will ever come to you from us, from Sam and me. You hear me?"

Molly was walking away, as fast as she could manage, her shoes squelching on her feet, the pram bouncing on the rain-sluiced pavement.

As she turned the corner of Linsey Grove for the last time, above the rain and the baby's squalling anger she could still hear Ellen's curses. They followed her, it seemed, for a long time after she was certainly out of earshot.

CHAPTER TWENTY-TWO

"When the new King gets crowned," Edward said, "will he be the King of Wales?" He was sitting on Annie's best chair, thoughtfully swinging his short legs.

Molly laughed and flicked the duster at him. "Of course not, silly. Whatever put that into your mind?"

"Well, he's – he was – the Prince of Wales, wasn't he?" he asked with the indefatigable logic of a seven year old. "So why isn't he going to be the King of Wales?"

Molly tousled his hair.

"Well, what *is* he going to be, then?" Edward had long since realized that Molly was one of those grown ups who didn't mind persistence. "What will he be called?"

She considered for a moment.

"I suppose – King of England, I think."

"But what about Ireland and Scotland and Wales? Isn't he King of those as well?"

"Oh, yes. And a lot of other places besides – India, Australia, bits of Africa, half the world, so they say."

"Well, then—"

The front door slammed and Annie's quick footsteps tapped down the hall.

"'Lo, Moll, Edward—" She paused in her swift advance and eyed the duster in Molly's hand. "Now, Molly, I told you that you didn't have to do that—" she began mildly.

"I like to do it. It keeps me busy and it helps at least a little to repay you and Charley for what you've done for me. Kettle's on."

"Thank Gawd for that," Annie said, kicking her shoes off. "But, honest, Moll, I don't want you to think you've got to—"

Molly turned, smiling, hand on hip. "I don't. Truly I don't. But while I'm here on my own for the best part of the day I might as well make myself useful. What else should I do? Sit in the corner and suck my thumb?" Edward giggled. Molly pretended to dust his ears, still talking to Annie. "I'll be able to give you some rent soon, when the money that Mr Ambler, Sam's solicitor, told me about arrives. A couple of weeks he said. And then, when I get a job, I'll see about getting some rooms of my own." As she walked into the tiny kitchen across the hall to make the tea Annie flopped into a chair, her legs outstretched, bony toes wriggling painfully.

"Stay as long as you like," she called. "I'm just sorry we've no better room to offer you. That box room's not much more than a cupboard."

Molly came back with the tea on a tray. "Don't be silly. It's fine. You know I can't thank you and Charley enough."

"Oh, shut up and pour." Annie grinned. Always she looked as if she were on the point of laughter.

"I will pay you," Molly persisted, "as soon as the money comes."

"If it makes you feel better." Annie thoughtfully stirred three heaped spoonfuls of sugar into her tea. "Handy, that little bit Sam left you."

"Yes. Poor Sam. Penny by penny he must have saved it. It's certain that his mother knew nothing of it."

Molly had neither seen nor heard from Ellen since the day of Sam's funeral, when each had rigidly ignored the other. As far as Molly could see it was unlikely that their paths would ever cross again, and she was happy to have it so.

Annie lay back in her chair. "D'you know I ache all over? That bloody laundry's going to be the death of me, I swear it. Still, it's better than the dye shop; thank Gawd I'm not working there."

"Oh?"

Annie fanned a hand in the air. "Talk about depressing. Black, black, black. Nothin' but. Coats, dresses, skirts, suits, the lot. Even sheets. Sheets! People want them to hang out of the window on the day of the funeral. Everythin' black as Newgate's knocker. Funny, ain't it?" She took her tea and sipped it meditatively. "What did the old girl do for us? I mean, really do? Did she care that I sweat my life away in a stinkin' laundry? Would she have cried if Jack or Charley'd got themselves clobbered by a crate? 'Course not. When big Bill Shepherd down the road died in that accident at the sugar works, did she send flowers? Like 'eck. Yet look around you. People are cryin' in the streets. Cryin'! The whole bloody country's gone into mourning – shops, houses, whole streets, draped in black. Looks as if God 'Imself 'as died."

Molly nodded. "I suppose it's just that she's been around for so long. There aren't many alive who can remember the country without Victoria on the throne. And though we all knew it had to happen sooner or later, it's still a shock somehow. The paper says that every King and Queen in Europe will be at the funeral. That'll be a show." Molly gathered cups and saucers onto the tray. "I'll just wash these up, then I'll walk Edward home. Supper's on the stove. If Charley comes in before I'm back help yourselves. I'll eat later."

"Righto. Come on, Eddie, get your coat on." Annie began to help the boy with his outdoor clothes. "By the way, she called to Molly over the clatter of crockery, "wasn't it today you were going to see your John Marsden?"

There was the tiniest pause. "It was."

"What happened? Any luck?"

Molly appeared at the door, a cup and a teacloth in her hand. "He said that he'd help if he could. But." She smiled wryly.

"But, but, but," Annie said. "Such a little word."

"He says there are dozens – hundreds – of girls like me, looking for work, local work, because of home commitments. And next to no jobs for them. The typewriting machine has not yet arrived with a bang in West Ham. Or East Ham. Or anywhere else east of Liverpool Street."

"I expect Sarah'd take Danny for you if you wanted to try in town again."

"Yes, I expect she would. And it still might come to that. But it isn't what I want. I want something that will fit in with looking after him."

"Is that all? Don't ask for much, do you?"

Molly pulled a face. She was still absently rubbing at the cup she held.

"I've been thinking."

"That's dangerous for a start."

"Oh, Annie, do listen for a minute." Molly sat herself on the table, discarded the cup and cloth and frowned at the wall.

"I'm listening, but you aren't saying anything," Annie said, injured, after a short silence.

Molly spoke slowly. "John Marsden – and he should know – says that most local businesses, especially the small ones, are miles behind the times. Out of touch. Plain old-fashioned. A lot of the girls he's trained are now in the same position that I am: they want office work but they find themselves faced with opposition and prejudice about employing women. Especially round here." She smiled suddenly, that quick urchin grin that Annie was glad to see was much more in evidence lately than when she had first come to them. "Now don't you think it's time someone came to the rescue of those poor, silly men who've still got clerks perched on high stools writing everything out by hand, who won't have a typewriting machine near the place, let alone a *woman* in the office? Do you think it's right to leave them so deprived?

"So what do you think you're going to do about it? Wave a magic wand?"

Molly jumped from the table. "No. Better than that. I'm going to see John Marsden again. Tomorrow. Come on, Eddie me lad. Time for home."

"An agency?" Charley, his feet propped on the fender and the smell of his scorching slippers acrid in the air regarded Molly with surprise. "What kind of agency?"

"An employment agency. For young lady office workers, full- and part-time. Heavens, Charley, you'll cook yourself."

Charley moved a quarter of an inch further from the blaze. "Hold on a minute. You'll have to do better than that. You know your Uncle Charley's a bit thick sometimes. I thought you told Annie there aren't any jobs?"

"That's right."

"So you're starting an employment agency for unemployable young women. Sounds like a good idea."

"If you don't hold your noise I'll not tell you."

"I'm holding it. Honest."

"Sooner or later," Molly began, "things have got to change around here."

"And you're going to change them single-handed?" put in Charley with a grin.

"Let's say – I'm going to give them a hand, yes. I'm going up every staircase, down every alley, through every door with a name on it. And I'm going to make all those little men sitting on their high stools see that they can't possibly go another day without that invaluable, indispensable—" she paused, running out of words.

"– unbelievable—" Annie supplied.

"– essential—" Charley shouted in his best music hall voice.

"– asset to every businessman—" Molly ploughed on grimly.

"the typah – writingah – machinah!" Charley finished happily.

"The lady typewriter," Molly corrected, trying not to laugh. "And it isn't funny. Not *that* funny, anyway."

Annie leaned forward. "Are you serious? Do you really think that you could convince them?"

"Why not? It's worth a try, isn't it? I'm not a bad talker." She pulled a face at the rude noise Charley made, "I've had experience and can demonstrate myself the speed and efficiency of the machine. It's bound to come; and there must be enough people close enough to considering it already to make it worthwhile trying to influence them."

Her seriousness had sobered the other two.

"But what if you do convince them?" Charley asked. "Then what happens?"

"We organize the right girl for the right job. For a small fee, of course."

"You mean you and John Marsden!" Annie exclaimed, suddenly getting the drift of Molly's plan. "Well, damn me, you're right, Molly. It *isn't* funny. It's a bloody marvellous idea. And I suppose that if some of the smaller places only want a girl for one or two days a week—"

"– then we can supply her. You've got it. And that girl can finish her week elsewhere; the office saves money, the girl gets a full week's wages. And I thought of a kind of pool, too, for firms who don't want a permanent typewriter to draw on, but who'd like some work done each week. They pay us a fee – much less than it would cost them to employ someone full time – and we pay the girls. Everyone's happy. And if a girl employed through us needs some time off, or is sick—"

"— you'll supply a substitute. My Gawd, Molly, what an idea! You didn't come up the river on the last tide, did you?"

"You two," Charley said with expressively lifted brows, "are beginning to sound like a ventriloquist's act. Neither of you've managed to finish a sentence yet."

"Come off it, Charley. We've got a genius in our box room. A blessed genius!"

"Except," he pointed out with masculine obstructiveness "that Molly hasn't set foot outside the door yet. You're acting as if the whole thing's set up. How does your Mr Marsden feel, Molly? Is he as enthusiastic?"

Molly hesitated, balanced finely between optimism and the strict truth.

"He thinks it's a good idea," she said finally, nicely placed between the two. "But he can be a crotchety old thing."

"So what are the arrangements? Between him and you, I mean?"

Molly fidgeted a little. "Well, I can't say exactly that we've made what you could call arrangements—But he did say that if I can prove to him that the scheme will work he'll be delighted to join me in what he keeps calling 'your little venture'. I'll venture him, see if I don't. I'll talk myself into every office between here and the East Ham Town Hall. He'll be crying for me to stop."

"And so will they. Owch!" Annie's pointed toe had connected sharply with her husband's shin.

She leaned her lovely face to Charley and poked a long finger into his chest. "Well, I think it's a fine idea. Takes something, you know, to think up a scheme like that. Anyone can use brute force and ignorance to blast their way through life." She prodded him again.

"Watch it, my girl." Charley reached and gently caught her wrist, pulled her close to him. "Just because we're wed doesn't mean you can say what you like, you know. I'm still bigger than you are."

Annie laughed, a world of warmth and meaning in her eyes and in her voice. "I know you are."

Charley buried his face for a second in the soft, fire-gilded hair. "Little cat."

Molly stared at the fire. Never once had she and Sam been this casual, this close, this happy. She mourned him quietly and sincerely, but she could not pretend to any violent grief. And somewhere, deep in her, she was aware that she relished and revelled in the freedom his passing had brought her; she could not deny it. Out of the blue she had another chance – with, she felt, slightly better odds this time on winning – to do something on her own. Her feelings for Jack were so confused that it was beyond her to sort them out. He had made no move towards her in the time she had been staying with Annie and Charley; the constraint between them was as great as ever. At best she could only assume that his emotions were as mixed as her own, and that possibly he had guessed more of Sam's reasons for braving the fog that had killed him than was comfortable for a tender conscience. But, she told herself with some defiance, she was not going to waste tears on something she could not change. She wasn't ever going to waste anything ever again. Not time, nor opportunity. This time she would keep some control over her own destiny, prove to herself, and to others, that she could stand on her own two feet. And if there were times, in the dark, quiet hours, when the thought of Jack whispered in her mind and in her body – impossible never to remember those moments at the wedding – there were, too, times when his obstinate self-control, his stiff-necked sobriety convinced her almost that those moments she remembered so well must be an illusion, a fantasy brought about by wedding flowers and claret.

Charley and Annie were talking quietly, seriously now. A name caught Molly's attention, brought her sharply from her reverie.

"Jake Aster? More trouble?" Her stomach had contracted painfully at the name. She still saw, in dark dreams, that graceful, threatening figure, felt the malice that sang in him for Jack.

Charley shrugged. "Talk, that's all. He has to, doesn't he? It's all over Silvertown and the docks that we took him apart and he couldn't stop us. And the stories get wilder as they go. There's plenty glad to see Jake done down, if only with a story. You can't expect him to take it all lying down, can you?"

"What's he been saying?"

"Oh, threats is all. And that's how it'll stay. There's nothing he can do." He looked from one solemn face to the other, wide grey eyes to green. "Don't worry, the pair of you. Jake Aster can't touch us."

Molly had never in her life been inside the dock gates; but she was not short on imagination. She saw huge warehouses, dark corners, long empty wharves, black, swelling water. "Are you sure?"

"'Course I am. Now, come on lass, make yourself useful before you make your fortune and move up West. Pop the kettle on, eh? If I don't get a cuppa soon I'll be off down the pub for a beer." He glanced slyly at Annie, but for once his volatile wife did not rise to the bait.

"Be careful, Charley," Molly said softly. "Be very, very careful."

Molly could not decide which was worse: the hard pavements she walked, the hard chairs upon which she was kept waiting for hours on end, or the hard look in the eyes of a man who was not about to be convinced that a chit of a girl, however persuasive, knew more about running his business than he did.

She walked her feet sore, talked her throat dry, learned to use sweet words and reason, to control her temper in the face of the most obdurate ill manners, the most flat and dismissive refusal to listen to what she had to say.

And, at first, it seemed as if it all might be for nothing.

She marched upon the Barking Road, Stratford Broadway, East Ham High Street, North and South. She visited small offices and large ones. She scrambled over piles of lumber, got coal-dust in her shoes, slipped and stumbled across the uncertain surface of many a stable yard. No concern was too big or too small for her attention. She was listened to, argued with, sometimes laughed at, and occasionally propositioned. She carried with her an old typewriting machine that John Marsden had lent her and which Charley fitted into a stout wooden box with a carrying handle. She swore, to Annie, that one arm was getting longer than the other. She had bad days, and very bad days. She had the occasional success. The money Sam had left her dwindled; her determination sometimes did the same; but she kept going, kept smiling, saved her tears for her chill, empty bed at night. One or two firms she visited were in fact already considering employing a typewriter and her demonstration convinced them. The first time it happened she had to restrain herself from running, singing, down the street; it felt as if God and His angels had come over to her side. Considerable interest was shown in her idea of a 'pool' for smaller firms who might not wish to employ a girl full-time, though since this was something that could only be organized once the agency – which in a fit of sarcastic humour she had named 'The Venture Employment Bureau' – was well on its feet, it was an interest upon which she could not immediately capitalize. Each day she left Danny with Sarah and set off like a mad prospector searching for gold; her equivalent of pick and shovel in the heavy box by her side, banging her legs uncomfortably as she walked. In the long hours she spent waiting in other people's offices she amused herself by furnishing, in her mind, her own office . . . a splendid haven of deep carpets and expensive leather furniture to the door of which the world would one day beat a path.

Such daydreams served at least to soften harsh reality. She spoke of them, laughingly, to Sarah and Nancy one night and was delighted to discover that Nancy, whose slow recovery from her ordeal had been almost as agonizing to those who watched it as for her who experienced it, was interested in, even enthusiastic about the Venture project. On the day that Nancy asked if she might be allowed to help with the agency work Molly, aware of the happiness in Sarah's face, assured her that her assistance would be most welcome. It was the first time that Nancy had shown any interest in anything, and it seemed to indicate another step in her recovery. Only the bitterness deep in her eyes did not change.

As the weeks slipped by and those first, drudging days of effort began at last to pay dividends, Molly's hopes began to appear a little less pretentious. As word of her activities spread, people did start coming to her. By late spring she knew that in the Venture Employment Agency she had a service for which the demand was only just beginning, and with the groundwork done she was ready to advertise. But she could not, she knew, do that while she was still working from Annie's kitchen table. One bright spring day, therefore, she visited John Marsden, dressed to kill, armed and ready for the battle she was certain was about to be joined.

"I need a room," she said flatly. "An office."

There was a short silence. In two years John Marsden had changed not a whit; he was cantankerous as ever, still looked permanently as if he had lost a shilling and found sixpence. He glowered from beneath craggy brows.

"Do you indeed?"

"I do. And if we're to be – partners –" she said, emphasizing the word, "in the Venture Employment Bureau then I think it's time you put four walls and a ceiling in it, to match my worn out feet and laryngitis. Seems only fair to me."

John Marsden leaned forward, unsmiling. "And to me. Congratulations, girl. I never thought you'd do it."

Molly felt as if someone had pulled the chair from beneath her. The man's lips, under his grizzled moustaches, twitched. He reached into a drawer in his desk and tossed her an envelope.

"Here."

"What is it?"

He turned his eyes to heaven in quick exasperation. "And she calls herself a business woman! Your commission, girl, your commission. Working for nothing, are you? We've had so many firm offers I'll be running out of girls."

"We'll put that in the advertisement!" Molly exclaimed. "Let me think . . . 'Qualified Lady Typewriters' – no – 'Qualified and *Efficient Lady* Typewriters Urgently Needed for – for Reputable Employment Agency'. How does that sound?"

He nodded.

She jumped to her feet.

She had done it. On her own. Her own simple, commonsense idea, her own efforts. The work was hard and carried with it in the beginning quite as much disappointment as success, and the rewards were small. But nothing could daunt her now; she was ready to work herself to a shadow to make a success of the agency. Above all she was happy; happier, she sometimes thought, than she had ever been before in her life, even with

Harry. And shivered as she thought it, wondering if she were tempting the gods.

"And where do you think you're off to in such a hurry?"

"To the offices of the Stratford Express."

"Not so fast, not so fast." He stood up, grumbled his way out from behind the desk. "Don't you want to see your own office first? It's been ready for a week."

CHAPTER TWENTY-THREE

CHARLEY BENTON STRAIGHTENED his back painfully. The day had been hot, the evening was sticky; his shirt lay where he had flung it earlier across a barrel, one of a stack alongside a warehouse wall. He reached for the garment and struggled into it, sweat and dirt making the operation both difficult and uncomfortable.

"Christ, I'll be glad to get home tonight. Anyone seen Jack?"

"Saw 'im earlier on, down on number two. They're loadin' the South American – the *Carlotta*." His companion swung a dirty jacket over one shoulder. "Comin' fer a pint before the off?"

Charley shook his head, not without regret. "Sorry, Ted. I promised Annie I'd give our Jack a message for Mam. She'll skin me if I don't do it."

The other man chuckled. "That's what I like to see. A man boss in 'is own 'ome."

"Garn!" A third man, who had been sitting on the ground, his back to a barrel, his legs stretched out before him as he made the most of a few minutes' rest in the sun after a hard day, scrambled tiredly to his feet and slapped Charley good-naturedly on the shoulder. "Take no notice, Charley. 'E's jealous, is all. 'E'd give 'is eye teeth to be ordered about by your Annie!"

Another small group of men – stevedores from Jack's gang – trooped together along the quayside, their heavy boots clattering on the wood. The sun, though low, still shone benignly, gilding the rippling water with gold, warming metal and stone, drawing into the air the smell of tar and of oil; the strong tang of cinnamon lifted from the bales stacked further along the water-front.

"Evenin', Ted. Charley."

"How's things, Charley boy?"

"Fine thanks, just fine. Seen Jack, have you?"

"You've missed 'im again, mate. 'E's gone back to the *Carlotta* lookin' fer you. You must have missed each other somewhere along the way." He made to move on.

Charley caught his arm. "Looking for me? On the *Carlotta*?"

The man turned a sweat-streaked dirty face. "Yeah. You. You're 'is brother, ain't you?"

"Aye, but—"

The man shook his arm free and moved on, calling over his shoulder. "Me an' Jack 'ad to see one of the officers earlier on, about the stowing – dangerous cargo and all. When we was coming back a kid stopped Jack and said as 'ow 'is brother Charley'd been lookin' for 'im all over, an' 'e'd see 'im back on the ship. So Jack went off. That's all I know –" His voice echoed hollowly in the empty, pillared space of the warehouse.

Charley watched the retreating backs with a frown, then turned and walked on out of the dim, shadowed building and once more into the bright, sea-smelling air. His footsteps bounced back from the high walls that edged the landward side of the wharf. They were faster now, a little urgent.

He had sent no message to Jack.

The *Carlotta* was berthed at an isolated point at the far end of the docks, perhaps a quarter of a mile away. Charley was almost running when he reached her. He took the steeply sloping gang-way at some speed, his long, experienced stride taking in a dozen wide wooden slats at a time. On the deck he stopped, his sun-bleached head lifted.

There could be no mistaking it; pungent, acrid, the faint smell of smoke.

The wide space of the deck was empty, the working gear cleared and tidily stacked, ropes coiled, the paraphernalia of a seagoing vessel neatly stowed. The *Carlotta* had two great hatches, one closed and well-battened down, the other, the one they were loading, was open, chains and ropes running down through it from the enormous crane that overhung the ship's decks from the quayside.

It was from this open hatch that faint, living tendrils of smoke drifted and coiled into the clear evening air.

"Jack?"

No reply; no movement but the slight lift and fall of the deck beneath his feet. The fragile ribbons puffed and drifted, almost invisible. He should raise the alarm now, without delay. But Jack. Where in hell's name was Jack? He ran to the unguarded edge of the hatch and peered into the dimness of the enormous hold. It was a cavern of shapes and shadows; the smell of smoke drifted strongly to him, but he could see no flame, and neither, yet, was the smoke very thick.

"Jack? Jack, lad, are you there?"

He heard the faint footfall behind him a fraction of a second before Jake Aster slammed hard into his back. But that split second was enough. Before the man hit him he had half-turned, stepped a little to the side, and the murderous intention of his attacker, to knock him over the edge and into the smoking hold, was at least partially frustrated.

The knife Aster held spun noisily across the deck. The two men stared at each other, breathing heavily. "I got one of you bastards," Jake said quietly. "Now I'm going to get me the other—"

From somewhere below came a faint cry: Jack's voice, Charley was certain. With a roar he launched himself upon Aster. Taken by surprise the slighter man could not withstand the violence of the charge. He teetered for a moment on the edge of the hatch, hugging his assailant to him, trying to retain his balance. With an immense effort Charley broke his grip, and with a cry Aster toppled helplessly backwards into a darkness that now rolled with dense smoke. But in falling he unbalanced Charley; the big man staggered and slipped over the edge, landing on hands and knees on the flat of one of the packing cases. Pain shot up his left shin, taking his breath, jolting his stomach unpleasantly. A billow of turgid smoke rolled over him and he choked, cursing. Somewhere in the far reaches of the darkness around him a tiny, angry flicker of light flared and died and flared again.

He scrambled to his feet.

"Jack? *Jack!*"

A slight answering sound, a smothered, choking cough. Charley dragged his neckerchief from his throat and tied it around his nose and mouth, then balanced himself for a moment before he jumped into the narrow alley that led between the huge cases. His shin jolted again. There was, so far as he could see, no sign of Jake Aster.

"JACK, WHERE ARE YOU?" He had to lift the protecting cloth from his mouth to shout; the acrid taste of smoke was on his tongue, in his throat.

He strained his ears; faintly he heard it. "Here. Port side." Pain-filled, short-breathed words, not so very far away. Charley blundered through the veiled dark. The fire had been set in more than one spot; glimmers and flashes lit the gloom, dancing shadows appeared above him, leaping like demons on the underside of the deck above.

He found his brother at the end of the gangway formed by stacked lumber on one side and rows of crates on the other. He had pulled himself painfully upright; in the faint glow of the fire one whole side of his face looked to be an open, bloody wound. When Charley, too stunned even to curse, held out a hand to help him, Jack flinched away.

"Chest—" he gasped. "Broken ribs – I think. – Get out, Charley. – Get out. – Explosives."

Not far from them fire cracked, something slipped and flared. Charley's eyes were streaming, the air scorched his throat and lungs as he breathed.

"Back to the hatch," he said coughing, "I'll haul you up."

Jack shook his head; he was almost doubled up, only the stacked timber prevented him from falling. "Can't."

"Bloody can." With his teeth clamped into his own lip at the revulsed shudder of agony that went through his brother's body as he did it, Charley bent, pulled Jack forward and over his shoulder and stood in one movement. Jack's body gave one outraged convulsion and went limp, his arms swinging. With sweat rolling down his face, stinging his eyes, plastering his hair to his smoke-grimed skin Charley staggered towards the promise of the open hatch.

It wasn't far. Above him, dangling through the hatch, was the loading gear; chains, cables, ropes. And on one side the thing Charley had most hoped to find; a long rope, hanging free and running independently through a pulley just above the level of the deck.

He lowered his burden; Jack doubled up, coughing excruciatingly. Not so very far away something moved; slithered, like a wounded animal.

Charley wrenched a piece of planking from a crate, tied it with a few swift, skilful movements to the end of the rope; tied directly around Jack's body it would crush his already damaged chest.

"Explosives," Jack wheezed. "*Get out, Charley.*"

"Not without you. Get your arse off that deck and on to this." Charley coughed viciously. "*Hurry!*"

Jack pulled himself upright, clung to the thick rope.

"That's the ticket. When you get to the top just hang on. I can – follow – up the chain – pull you over the top—" It was becoming impossible to breathe.

In the distance, at last, an alarm bell rang.

With all his strength Charley began to heave on the end of the rope. Painfully slowly Jack lifted, rising through the smoke towards the blessed patch of blue sky above. Behind him, twisted into the fire sounds, Charley heard a wheezing, anguished blasphemy.

The makeshift swing spun as it rose, slowly one way, then the other. Jack slipped a little, grabbed for the rope: the shock ran into Charley's fingers.

Then at last the strain on his arms was released. Jack had pulled himself onto the side of the hatch; he lay now exhausted, half-in-half-out of the hole, his legs dangling in smoke.

Charley let go of the rope and jumped for the thick chain that dropped into the hold from the wharfside machinery. With the heavy links under his hands he turned at last and looked at the man who was dragging himself to his feet just yards away. Jake Aster's body was twisted, his face a scream of hatred and pain.

Charley started up the chain. A moment later he was in the relatively clear air, swinging across the gap, dropping to his knees on the warming deck and dragging Jack up and away from the hole, which looked as if it led down to Hell. He half carried his brother to the rail, away from the smoke that billowed from the hatch. Along the quayside men ran, shouting and waving their arms. A clatter of hooves, and a fire engine swayed around the corner. Charley propped Jack over the rail, grabbed a rope and turned to go back.

"Charley! No!"

"I'm not going back down there. But he's just under the

hatch. I can't leave him there, Jack. I can't. If he can manage I'll try to pull him out."

"I told you, there's a case of—"

But Charley was gone, running back through the rolling smoke, throwing himself on his stomach beside the hole.

"Aster! Can you hear me? I'm dropping a rope. Try to get it round you. I'll pull you out. But quick!" His voice was all but lost in the animal roar of the fire.

There was no reply. Blistering heat lifted, singeing Charley's skin and eyebrows.

"Aster!"

A gust of wind swirled. The smoke sucked, eddied, cleared for a fraction of a second. Below him Jake Aster stood, leaning on a wooden crate, his figure drawn in fire, his face the most terrible thing that Charley Benton had ever seen. And the last. For in that moment a detonation lifted the other hatch, blasted fire upwards, rocked the *Carlotta* at her moorings.

Charley was flung backwards like a rag doll tossed aside by a child's hand.

Jack was left clinging to the rail, totally untouched by the explosion, screaming his brother's name.

The news of the fire and explosion on the *Carlotta* ran through dockland and beyond like fire itself; and it lost nothing in the telling. By the time Molly, riding home in a packed omnibus after working rather later than usual, heard the story, the casualties were running into dozens.

"Sabotage," said one man, squashed beside her, "bound to be. Them ruddy Boers, shouldn't wonder."

"Or the Irish," said another, gloomily.

"Accident, I heard." A man perched on the edge of the seat opposite Molly was chewing something noisily and talking around it. "Me brother's in the docks. Trucker. 'E was there when it 'appened. Explosives 'e said. An accident."

The pavements were crowded with home-going workers, the pubs were doing a roaring trade. Her fellow passengers had now embarked upon a lively discussion of the war in South Africa. Molly reflected wryly that on a normal evening no one would say a word to his neighbour, scarcely an apology if he stepped on his foot; but given a disaster to break the ice people who would not usually greet one another would talk like old friends. The bus creaked laboriously on, swaying and jolting.

Molly tried to subdue the faint unease that the news of the explosion had awakened in her. It was ridiculous to worry. There were thousands of men working in the docks. The odds against Jack and Charley being involved in this explosion, or whatever it was, must be enormous— But when she turned the corner of Park Road, forboding struck hard. A group of women stood talking by one of the gates, obviously having come straight from their kitchens. All still had on their aprons, one of them brandished a wooden spoon as she talked. Two men stood with them. As Molly's sharp footsteps approached they turned, looked, nudged each other. As she came closer they fell silent, and one of them called, "Have you heard anything, love?"

"Heard anything?" Molly felt sick. "What about?"

"Oh, dearie me, don't you know? The Benton boys. They was caught in the explosion in the docks."

Molly heard no more; she was running, skirts gathered to her knees, flying to the gate, up the path.

Nancy had seen her coming, was standing at the open door. She was very pale, but composed. She had heard the news an hour since and had had some time to recover a little.

"Nancy? Nancy, what happened?"

"We aren't sure. Come in, Moll. Get your breath. There's some tea in the pot—"

Molly shook her head. "No. Thank you. Tell me—"

"Jack and Charley are both hurt," Nancy said quietly, "that's all I know."

"You don't know how badly?"

"No. They aren't dead. Or they weren't an hour ago. That's all the man could tell us. He came to fetch Mam and Annie. They went off to the hospital." Her lip quivered, she took a breath, holding hard to her composure. "I've heard nothing since. I stayed to take care of the baby and to wait for you and for our kid. He's gone from school to supper with a friend. I hope to God no one tells him before he gets home." Her voice shook despite her efforts. "It may not be as bad as it sounds," she added, with no great conviction.

"What happened?"

"They don't know exactly. But—" The expression on her face almost warned the other girl what to expect.

"What, Nancy? What is it?"

"A man was killed in the explosion on the *Carlotta*." She paused, then said, flatly, "Jake Aster."

"What!"

"Jack was working the ship. Charley wasn't. No one knows how he came to be there—"

"Jake Aster. Oh, Nancy."

Nancy turned away, leaned her crossed arms upon the mantelpiece above the empty grate. After a moment she said, shakily, "Would you go to the hospital for me, Moll? Find out what's going on? God knows when Mam or Annie will be back, and I'll go mad if I don't hear soon."

"Of course. If you're certain you wouldn't rather go yourself? I could stay and—"

Nancy shook her head. "No. I can't let anyone else tell our kid. Not even you. You know how he feels about Jack and Charley. He'll likely need looking after. He's mine," she added – the first time that Molly had ever heard her say it so – "even if he doesn't know it. Besides," she said, attempting a small, strained smile, "that great lummock of a brother of mine would rather see you than me any day, daft pair that you both are. Give them my love if—" she paused painfully " – if you're allowed to see them."

Molly kissed her swiftly on her smooth, cold cheek. "I will, I promise," she whispered, and was gone.

The hospital smelled as only hospitals can; of disinfectant and urine, of an indefinable sickly odour that had no counterpart in the outside world. Molly's boots clipped sharply on the floor of the long cream-and-green tiled corridor down which she had been directed. Her mind, as it had been for the whole of the journey, was blank of all but a fierce, talisman determination to believe that all would be well.

Ahead, heavy swing doors swept shut, creaking, behind a hurrying, uniformed nurse. Before they had stopped their movement Molly had reached them and was peering through the thick glass. In the corridor beyond was a row of straight-backed chairs set against the wall. One lonely figure sat, head and shoulders bowed, fingers twisting in her lap, her statuesque figure slumped to dumpiness.

Sarah.

She did not look up at yet another pair of hurrying feet tapped through the swing doors and approached her. Only when the feet stopped directly in front of her did she lift her head tiredly.

Molly's heart stopped. She dropped to her knees beside the older woman, took the cold, nerve-wracked hands in her own. At the look in Sarah's eyes she had almost relinquished the hope that she had stubbornly held to ever since she had heard the news. One, or both of them must be dead. Still holding Sarah's hand she seated herself on the hard chair beside her.

"Jack?" The voice sounded like someone else's.

Sarah shook her head. "No. He's all right. At least he will be, so the doctor says. Broken ribs, he's got, and he's been badly beaten." Absently Sarah touched the side of her own face in the place where her eldest son would bear a scar for the rest of his life.

Molly closed her eyes, floated for a second on a golden flood of relief. Then, remembering, her fingers tightened on the hand she held.

"What about Charley?"

Sarah's head shook again; but differently this time, slowly from side to side, tears running silently down a face already marked by earlier weeping.

"He's dead?" Molly whispered.

"No."

"What then? For God's sake, Sarah, what?"

"He's blind. My Charley's blind."

"Blind?" Molly repeated the word stupidly, as if she had never heard it before.

"Mrs Benton?" Neither of them had heard the rustling approach of a nursing sister in a uniform so stiff that it looked as if it could stand alone.

Molly stood up. The sister, a middle-aged woman with

243

a severe mouth, looked her up and down in repressive enquiry.

"I've come to see Jack Benton," Molly said bluntly, ready to roll up her sleeves and fight for the right.

The woman shook her head briskly, neither a hair of her head nor any corner of her starched white headdress stirring as she did so. "Impossible, I'm afraid."

Molly stepped forward; her head did not reach the sister's officious shoulder. "I—"

"Sister Marlow?" A big, genial-faced man had come into the corridor from a nearby door. He fixed bright, intelligent eyes on the group, read at an experienced glance what lay behind Molly's belligerent stance, the hopeless droop of Sarah's shoulders.

"Yes, doctor?"

"A moment." He looked kindly down at Sarah. "Your son Jack is fairly comfortable now, Mrs Benton. You may see him again for a few minutes, later. Your daughter-in-law is with your other son in a room just along the passage there. A remarkable girl, if I might say so. She'll be a great strength to him I'm sure. If you feel up to it I'm certain they'd be glad to – they'd like you to join them. Your son is awake; it is remarkable that apart from his eyes he is unscathed. Both your boys have the constitution of horses, Mrs Benton. They'll get well, I assure you. Now, Sister Marlow will take you to Charley."

Sarah rose heavily to her feet. "Thank you, doctor."

Molly turned to this new adversary. "I've come to see Jack Benton," she said grimly.

"You're a relative?" His gentle voice made her own belligerence gauche.

"No," she said more quietly, "a friend. My name is Molly—" she hesitated " – Alden."

"Ah, Molly . . ." He smiled, understanding in his eyes. "If I'm not very much mistaken, Mr Benton has been asking for you. Unless, that is, he has more than one – friend – by the name of Molly?"

"Then I can see him?"

"Of course. But only for a very few moments. And I must ask you not to tell him of his brother's blindness. He isn't strong enough yet. His brother, it seems, almost certainly saved his life; it will do him no good to learn of the cost before he is well enough to bear it."

*

Jack's marked, bloodless face was of a colour with the bandages that swathed his head and with the bleached sheet upon which his big hands lay motionless. His eyes lit when he saw Molly.

Very gently she laid a small finger on his lips in a perfectly natural gesture. "Quiet now, my love. No need to talk. I'm here." She felt the movement of his lips beneath her finger, saw his small smile of happiness as she settled beside him, his hand in hers, the blue eyes – so very much like Harry's – fixed upon her face as if he could not bear to look away. She sat so until he slept, and was there still when he woke. In the weeks that followed she spent every spare moment by his side.

They were married in September, just seven weeks after the explosion on the *Carlotta*. Seven months later two-year-old Danny Benton, to everyone's delight and to his own slightly aggrieved astonishment, was presented with twin sisters. The birth was premature, and very difficult, but within days Molly was up and about again. Within a few weeks, with Sarah's grandmotherly aid, she was back at work as if the Devil were behind her. Marriage or no marriage the world still waited to be conquered.

PART III

Autumn 1906

CHAPTER TWENTY-FOUR

MOLLY RUBBED EYES strained by the failing light, pressed her fingers hard into them to ease their ache. In the book laid before her on the table long columns of figures danced and blurred. Through the open scullery door – not for the first time that afternoon – came the sound of the children's voices raised in one of those monotonous wrangles that tempt any adult within earshot to put a stop to them with a slap.

"They were!"

"They weren't!"

"They were!"

"They couldn't have been."

"Big as your head."

"I don't believe you. And Kitty doesn't, either, do you, Kit?"

"Well, I—"

"Oh, of course you don't. He's telling lies again." This in Meghan's clear, flat little voice brought about a short and ominous silence. Molly drew a breath, debating the possibility of putting her fingers in her ears and ignoring her contentious offspring. Meghan was an impossible child; at four and a half years old she looked like a fairy, had a will of steel and a mind as sharp as a new-honed razor.

"I am not!" Without being able to see him Molly knew exactly the look on her son's face at that moment: the thin, fair skin brick-red with temper, the cherub's mouth pouted and furious.

"You are!"

"I'm not, I tell you."

"Yes you are."

Danny knew that in a battle of sheer persistence with his sister he could only come off second best. He tried a new tack.

"You're just jealous. 'Cause I went hop picking with Aunt Annie and Uncle Charley and you didn't. I was having the best time anyone ever had and you were stuck here. Serves you right.

Who'd want you? They took me because I'm grown up. And – you're – a – baby." These last words a slow, calculated insult, said in the tone of a man very sure of his ground.

"I'm not!" Meg's voice rose to a shriek.

"You are!"

"I'm not!"

"Oh, yes you are. Baby, Baby Bunting – Baby, Baby Benton—"

Molly, thunder in her face, straightened her aching back and threw down her pen. The chanting in the scullery broke off in a scuffle and a sharp yell.

Kitty's small, distressed voice – "Danny! Oh, Meg—" was almost entirely lost in the sounds of battle.

In two angry steps, Molly was at the door. The two children were rolling under the scrubbed pine table – the scullery was so tiny that there was no other floor space clear enough for such activity. Katherine, known to them all as Kitty, twin to Meghan in birth, yet astonishingly opposite in looks, temperament and manner, stood saucer-eyed. When Molly appeared, Nemesis personified in the doorway, Kitty shrank back for all the world as if she had been personally responsible for the fracas under the table.

"Meghan! Danny! What in Heaven's name – Stop it, at once! At once, do you hear me?" Molly reached under the table and none too gently hauled the two children out and onto their feet. "What an exhibition! What on earth is it all about?"

"He was telling lies," said Meghan with an uncompromising stubbornness that Molly could only recognize and regret. "He said that when they were hop picking they had apples as big as my head. And then he called me a baby."

"So you decided to show him what a perfect little lady you were by rolling under the table punching and kicking like a guttersnipe?" asked her mother tartly. "I'm not stupid. Nor deaf. You're as bad as he is. Worse. Now then, You—" she caught tall Danny by the ear and marched him to the chair at one end of the table, "sit there. And you—" she picked up Meghan, feather-light, and swung her onto the opposite chair, "there. And don't move. Either of you. Until the clock chimes quarter past. That's ten minutes. If I hear one sound – *one sound* –

before that, it's straight to bed with no supper and no waiting up for Daddy. Do you understand?''

Meghan, scowling down at her still-pudgy baby hands nodded. Danny sat rigid and glared at his sister. Kitty, in the absence of specific orders, climbed upon a chair half-way between them both, her gaze fixed upon her mother's face. For a moment Molly's hand rested upon the fine, mousy hair and she came closer to smiling than she had all afternoon. Meghan bestowed one disgusted look upon her twin then looked back at her hands.

Molly, her concentration shredded, went back to her books. She added the same column three times, unsurprised to discover that she achieved a different answer each time, before with an exasperated sigh she laid down her pen again. The strained silence in the scullery had given way to small, scuffling sounds, smothered explosions of laughter. Molly visualized the wildly swinging feet and ferociously pulled faces. At least it was quieter than the earlier roughhouse. She rested her chin on her hands and looked gloomily around her. In such poky surroundings who could blame lively, strong-willed children for getting on each other's nerves? She understood only too well how they felt – she was sometimes tempted to a good scream herself. The little room in which she sat, the only one downstairs apart from the scullery, was cluttered with furniture, badly lit, too hot with the fire burning and too cold without it. A rabbit hutch, she thought, bad-temperedly. She and Jack had lived in this house since the day they had married. At that time it had not seemed so bad; it had been convenient, and cheap at a moment when their resources had not been great. It was just around the corner from Sarah, and not far from the small grocer's shop that Annie and Charley had taken with the money subscribed for Charley by his workmates in the docks after the explosion on board the *Carlotta*. But it had never crossed Molly's mind, either then or later, to regard it as their permanent home. Yet here they still were. It was impossible. More, it was ridiculous. Although work lately was not easily come by Jack was rarely idle, and anyway with the money she was earning from the agency they could easily afford to move somewhere more spacious. Somewhere like The Larches. She would have to speak to Jack soon. John Marsden was waiting for her answer. Why had she left it so long? She took a deep breath and dropped her face into her cupped hands, screwing up her tired eyes. Because logic and sense were useless weapons against a man's pride, she answered herself. But tonight she would try.

In the kitchen the clock struck the quarter hour. Seconds later she felt a touch on her skirt and opened her eyes to find Kitty standing beside her, her quiet, brown-flecked eyes fixed upon her, her hand resting lightly on her knee. In the doorway stood the other two – handsome, difficult, self-willed – yet in both their faces a vulnerability and trust that would have melted a heart stonier than Molly's. With one arm she encircled Kitty, the other she lifted in invitation to Meghan. The little girl flew to her, nestled to her side. Over the two heads Molly smiled quietly at her son, who came and leaned on her chair beside her.

"Look at that," she said, nodding down at the girls, "two little apple-heads."

Meghan giggled into Molly's lap. Danny laughed. "They really were ever so big, the apples we had. You ask Aunt Annie. Some of them you couldn't hold in your hand, honest you couldn't. Aunt Annie cooked them in a lovely pudding, in a pot over an open fire like the gypsies. And we slept on straw. And I picked hops into a big umbrella, and Aunt Annie gave me a shilling. Did you know that when you pick hops your fingers go all black and funny-tasting? Sort of bitter. Nice, though—"

"How old do you be to go hop picking?" Meg asked ungrammatically. "When can I go?"

Molly shook her head. "Oh, well, I really don't—"

"*Girls* wouldn't be any good at it," Danny interrupted scornfully, conveniently ignoring the fact that half the children in the hop gardens had been just that. "There's spiders and beetles and great big green caterpillars that you don't see until you've squashed them in your fingers . . ."

Kitty, within the circle of her mother's arm, flinched.

"Aunt Annie goes," Meghan said firmly. "She told me she'd been every single year since she was a baby. And she was a girl."

"Aunt Annie's different," Danny retorted.

"Aunt Annie," said a new voice from the doorway, "is very pleased to hear it. Some'd probably mean it less flattering.

Hello, young Danny. Recovered, have you?" She grinned down at the boy who had run to her, tousled his hair with her long, bony hand. "You've got a real worker here, you know, Moll. Fingers to the bone stuff." She winked down at Danny, who flushed hotly. Aunt Annie's one and only defect was her tendency to sarcasm.

"I found one or two things of Danny's packed in with ours," she said, dumping a paper parcel onto the table. "Thought I might as well bring them round straight away. Didn't actually expect to find you here, though. I thought it was your day at the office. Isn't Nancy supposed to be here on Mondays?"

"Yes it is. And yes, she is," Molly said a little shortly. "But our Nancy had other things to do today. The sooner I can get something sorted out the better—" She gestured at the open books on the table.

"You haven't mentioned it to Jack, then yet?"

"No."

"You'll have to, you know, sooner or later. You never know, he might jump at the idea: nice, big house in Plaistow."

"He'll say we can't afford it."

"And can you?"

"With the money the Agency's earning, yes."

"Ah." Annie flopped into a chair. "I see the problem. And where's Nancy? Marching up and down with a banner somewhere?"

"Something like that. Gone to listen to one of the Pankhursts, I think."

Annie arched fine-drawn eyebrows. "She's really been bitten by the bug, hasn't she?"

"To the exclusion of almost everything else, I sometimes think. I expected her ages ago. With her away I'm stuck with this—" she flicked at the page she had been working on "—and the children as well. I feel like writing a nice polite little note to the Prime Minister asking him please to give women the vote so that I can have my assistant back!"

Annie, smiling her wide smile, drew Kitty up onto her knee. "All seems like a lot of hot air to me. Votes for women? That'll be the day. The old world's run by men for men, isn't it, Danny boy?" She poked the boy in the ribs. "They're not about to give any of it up just for the askin', are they? Stands to reason. Waste of time, all this talkin'."

"Oh, I wouldn't go as far as that." Molly leaned back in her chair, one hand absently fondling Meghan's mass of hair. "I agree with them. I hope they win, though I don't think it'll happen until the majority of men have the vote. I just wish that Nancy hadn't joined the Cause quite so wholeheartedly. I've a business to run, and with John Marsden retiring it's going to get worse. I need more help, not less."

Annie looked closer at the tired face, the harassed eyes, then asked, indicating the paper strewn on the table, "You trying to work now?"

"I am. Some hopes."

"Right." Briskly Annie clapped her hands. "Come on, kids, get your things. You can come and give your Aunt Annie a hand in the shop. How'd you like that?"

The girls' faces lit with pleasure. "Yes, please!" said Danny.

Molly shook her head, protested half-heartedly, "Oh, no, Annie. I couldn't let you do that."

"Rubbish," Annie said cheerfully. "We'd love to have them."

"Well, if you're sure?"

" 'Course I'm sure. Go on, Danny love, get the girls' coats."

"I haven't even made you a cup of tea."

Annie stood up. "Couldn't have stopped anyway. Charley's all right on his own for a little while, but I don't like to leave him for too long."

"It's incredible how he manages." Molly buttoned the impatient Meghan into her sailor-collared coat; Kitty stood quietly holding hers, waiting her turn.

"He's a game lad, my Charley," Annie said softly, her eyes upon the bright faces of the children.

"Are you certain he won't mind this lot descending on him like a plague on Egypt?"

"No. He won't mind."

Molly did not miss the undertone of sadness in the simple words. The fact that Annie and Charley had no children was not, she knew, of their own choosing. "Well, there they are," she said. "If you're sure?"

"Right. They can stay to tea. What time's Jack due?"

"I'm not sure. These last weeks they've had to go down river for work – Tilbury, Northfleet. He's back at all times."

"Well, at least you'll get some peace and quiet. Come on, troops, quick march—"

Molly watched them down the street. Only Kitty turned to wave. The other two danced around Annie, laughing and shouting as they hurried through the autumn rain.

The tiny house, as she shut the door, sang with blessed quiet. The tick of the clock was clearly audible in the silence. Peace. For a few hours at least.

With a breathed prayer of thanks to Aunt and Guardian Angel Annie, Molly went back to her books.

It was almost three hours later and close to the time when Jack might reasonably be expected home that Molly heard the back door open and close quietly. She leaned back in her chair, stretching cramped muscles, guiltily aware that in her absorption she had not finished the preparations for supper.

"Is that you, Jack?"

"No. It's me." Nancy's voice. Molly breathed a small, relieved sigh. She got up and walked to the door of the scullery.

"Where on earth have you been? I thought—" she stopped, her eyes wide. "In God's name, Nancy, what's happened to you?"

Nancy half-leaned, half-sat upon the kitchen table. She was soaking wet, in her hand she held a shoe, the heel of which was missing. Her coat was muddy, her hat gone, her hair, obviously very hastily repinned, was tumbling untidily around her coat collar. The thin face was flushed, the dark eyes bright as candles in the dim-lit room.

"It's started, Molly, started at last. They won't stop us now."

Molly stared. "Nancy, what are you talking about? Where have you been? What have you been doing? You look as if you've been in a fight—"

"I have. I did this," she said, brandishing the broken shoe, "on a policeman's helmet. They're harder than you'd think, those helmets."

"A policeman's – you've been fighting with a *policeman*?"

"A squad of them. An army of them. Oh, Molly, you should

255

have been there. It was wonderful! We got into the Central Lobby of the House of Commons, and Mrs Pankhurst and a couple of others jumped up onto a settee and started to speak. That was when the police came, and tried to throw us out."

"Oh, my God." Molly sat down hard on a painted kitchen chair.

"They wouldn't allow us to speak. They evicted us by force, carried us out. But we didn't go easily, I can tell you. Ten women were arrested. They should have arrested us all! I've a mind to—"

"Nancy!"

Nancy seemed for the first time to register that Molly's reaction to her story was not one of wholehearted admiration.

Molly stood up. "I'm expecting Jack at any minute," she said, "I've been working all afternoon and I haven't got supper ready. The children aren't home from Annie's yet and are going to be late for bed. Jack isn't going to like any of those things. And tonight I have to talk to him. About John's retirement. The house. The business. Oh, Nancy, how could you?"

"You haven't asked him yet?"

Molly shook her head. "It has to be tonight. I've put it off too long already. John Marsden needs to know if we'll take the house, or if he has to give notice to the landlord to find someone else. And if Jack walks through that door and finds you in this state, and guesses where you've been—I suppose the story's all over London by now?"

"I should think so."

"—then there will be Hell to pay, and me to pay it. I'm sorry, but you know it's so. God knows what he'd say if he saw you like this. You'll have to leave before he comes."

"Of course. I'm sorry. I know Jack doesn't approve of the cause. To be honest with you, I just popped in to ask if—well, if I could just tidy up a bit before I went home? I don't really want Mam to see me looking like this." She had the grace to look a little shamefaced, and Molly, relenting, laughed and pushed her towards the door which led to the stairs.

"I should think so too. You look like something the cat dragged in. Upstairs. Our bedroom, in the front. But do, please, be quick."

She was peeling potatoes with ink-stained fingers over the big, chipped sink when Nancy reappeared much tidier and with most of the more obvious damage either hidden or repaired. Nancy dropped an impulsive kiss on her sister-in-law's cheek.

"Thanks, Molly. Sorry to have bothered you. Good luck with Jack tonight." She lifted a gentle finger to Molly's black hair and wound a silky tendril around her finger. "Not that you need luck. Not with our Jack. He's still as soft on you as the day you married. A bit of Irish blarney and we'll all be living in that nice house before you can say 'knife'."

Molly lifted cold, water-roughened hands. "I wish I could be so sure."

The austere, boyish face broke into a smile, but Nancy said no more. She pulled her shabby coat round a frame that had thinned to gauntness; the garment hung loose as she buttoned it. Nancy could never be persuaded to spend the money she earned on herself.

Molly dropped a potato into a pot that was now, thankfully, almost full. "See you tomorrow then."

"Yes. Oh, by the way—" halfway to the door Nancy stopped, "I almost forgot. Mam said that a gentleman was down home looking for you the other day. That lawyer. I've forgotten his name. The one who dealt with Sam's Will?"

"Mr Ambler."

"That's it."

"What did he want?"

"He wouldn't say. Anyway, Mam gave him this address, so I expect you'll be hearing from him. Do you think Ellen's found a way round the will after all this time?"

"I wouldn't be surprised. It would please her spite. Well, she's welcome if she has. I can afford it if they want me to give it back. I wouldn't mind at all. It would be as if Sam had lent me the money to get started and now I was paying it back, and that would be the end of that. I almost hope she has."

From the front of the house came the sound of a key in the lock. Molly hastily flung salt into the potatoes and swung the heavy pot onto the stove. Nancy, finger to lips, slipped through the back door and shut it quietly behind her.

Molly untied her grubby apron and patted her hair which had

grown long now and coiled demurely and fashionably at the nape of her neck, though the wild curls still refused to behave entirely properly, wisping around her face and neck no matter how hard she combed and pinned them. Then with lifted chin and bright smile she prepared for battle.

The small, smoky room was quiet. The only sound was the rhythmic ticking of the clock, the only movement that of the pendulum and the leaping flames in the hearth. Jack sat, pipe in hand, in the big chair opposite her on the other side of the tiny fireplace. Neither had spoken for several minutes. Silence shrouded the room, yet it seemed to Molly that she could still hear the passionate echoes of her own voice, arguing, reasoning, pleading. Jack had brought against her every single argument that she had expected and prepared for, and a couple that she had not.

Now, with no more to be said, she waited.

Jack stirred. In the restless light of the fire his hair and moustache gleamed gold. His eyes, shadowed deep in their sockets, she could not see.

"It's a lot of brass, lass," he said quietly, "to be found, week in, week out."

"I know it." How many times had she heard it this evening? At least he hadn't yet said an outright no. Molly leaned eagerly forward. "But we wouldn't be paying for this place, remember. And if The Larches goes to someone else, Nancy and I would have to find other premises for the agency, pay rent on them—" or give it up. She would not say it, would not think it. "And if Nancy takes the attic rooms I told you about – the housekeeper's rooms – then she'd pay her bit. Oh, Jack, think how convenient it would be: Nancy and me under one roof, the house, the business, the children – everything. It would be so much easier. We wouldn't be far from your Mam, or Charley —" She had been determined not to start again, but she could not stop. "Just *look* at this place! 'Tis the size of a tea caddy! Isn't it just stupid to stay here when we could afford something better? Even if it's a bit of a struggle at first? We'd have a parlour, a proper one, and a dining room, and a kitchen that's bigger than this room and the scullery put together! The children could have a bedroom each. And the office and typing pool are completely separate. You wouldn't be bothered by it. If we don't take the house – if someone else does—" The thought of what might happen then had been scurrying around her head like a caged mouse ever since John Marsden had finally made the definite announcement of his retirement. Not that his plan to leave the business and join his sister in Southend had been any great surprise; he was no longer young, and the work as the Venture Employment Bureau had grown beyond all expectations was demanding. It had been one of those inevitables that had been pigeonholed in a busy life to be thought about tomorrow; and now tomorrow was upon her. Only Jack's agreement stood between her and the fulfilment of an ambition that had been born on the day that John Marsden had shown her to her first box-room of an office. She had long outgrown that room. Now, she shared the big office with John, was only a step away from making it her own entirely.

Jack leaned forward and tapped his pipe out into the fire. He sat for a moment, elbows on knees, frowning thoughtfully into the blaze. "It's a lot of brass," he said again, "a lot."

"I *know* it is!" Frustration and anxiety curdled to anger. She tried, only partly successfully, to keep the wild impatience from her voice. "But we can afford it, Jack. It isn't as if John were asking me to buy him out of the business – that would be more difficult. But he isn't. All we have to do is to take the tenancy of the house and pay him an agreed percentage of the agency's profits each year. And it's such a lovely house. I know we'd be happy there." She stopped. Jack had turned his head and was watching her intently, the sharp blue eyes roaming her face, studying it, feature by feature. Red light flickered and danced on the deep scar that ran from cheekbone to jaw on the left side of his face. She could not fathom the thoughts behind that suddenly intense gaze, yet some hope, some small excitement lifted, "Please, Jack," she said.

He looked at her for one long moment longer, then said heavily, "I can't pretend I like the idea of using your money."

She could have cried. "Our money. *Our* money. What does it matter who earns it? I don't think you realize just how well the agency is doing."

"Oh, I realize it all right. I'm not daft, nor blind. And I'll tell you something else. I'm proud of it. Proud of you."

She could not believe her ears. "Jack—"

"And I suppose that if John Marsden's posh house in Plaistow's what you want, and the chance to run the whole shooting match on your own, then by God we'll have to see if we can manage it."

"Jack!" Molly launched herself across the space between them, wound her arms about his neck, kissed his mouth, his nose, his scarred cheek.

"Hey up! Wait a bit, wait a bit. There's a condition."

"Condition?" Her head came up sharply. "What condition?"

"You'll have to give me your sworn word that you'll keep our Nancy and her half-witted suffragist friends away from me."

She laughed. "I will."

"Then we'll try it."

She was on his lap, curled into the big chair on top of him; she buried her hands in his thick hair and kissed him, long and slow, felt the ripples of it through his body.

"Thank you," she said. And as she tried to lift her head his arms went around her, forcing her to him, his mouth hard on hers. His fingers were at the pins that held her hair, then, more impatiently, at the tiny buttons of her bodice. His big hands took her shoulders, held her a little way from him so that he could look at her in the firelight. She shook her head sharply and her hair fell about her naked shoulders. She was trembling; the hard skin of his hands was rough on her smooth, warm body. She slipped from his lap and down to the floor in front of the fire. He towered above her, the bulk of him dark, highlights of bone and muscle lit by the dying flames.

She held up her arms, smiling.

Later, in bed, she remembered Nancy's news about Mr Ambler, the lawyer, but listening to Jack's deep, even breathing beside her it did not seem necessary to disturb him. Whatever the man wanted it could wait till the morning.

Jack stirred, moved closer to her. She snuggled to him.

"Moll?"

"Hmm?"

"Downstairs, just now—"

She smiled in the darkness. "Yes?"

"You didn't—" he paused, "you didn't – do anything. Anything to—" he stopped.

"I didn't have to," she said. "It's the time of the month when it's all right."

Something in his silence warned her. She forced herself not to stiffen, not to move away from him.

"If we had a bigger house," he said after a moment, "do you think that you might change your mind?"

No! No, no, no. "Is that another condition?" her voice was very quiet.

"Of course not, lass. I just—"

"We agreed. Both of us. After the twins. Remember?" Remember the pain? Remember the agonizing time it took? Remember the solemn, sombre faces of midwife and doctor? Remember the exhausting struggle against death?

"Yes, I know we did. I just wondered – well, if perhaps in a couple of years or so you might feel differently?"

"No."

Silence lay between them in the dark like an iron bar. "We have two daughters," she said at last, and then with greater emphasis, "and we have a son. Isn't that enough?"

He took a long breath. "Aye," he said, "of course." And he turned from her to settle down to sleep.

CHAPTER TWENTY-FIVE

NANCY SAT IN the small outer office that was now her own, The *Daily Express* spread before her, her face thunderous. When the door opened she did not immediately look up.

"Morning, Nancy."

"Oh – 'morning, Moll. Have you seen this? 'Raucous hooligans'? 'Ill-behaved persons'? 'Screeched'? 'Yelled'? How *dare* they? This damned thing isn't worth the paper it's printed on, you know that? By God, if we don't make them eat their words one day—" For the first time Nancy noticed the expression on Molly's face. " – Molly? Is something wrong?"

"Yes." Molly walked through into the main office, taking off her hat and coat as she went. Nancy followed, stood leaning at the door.

"What is it?"

"I had a letter from Mr Ambler, the solicitor, this morning." Molly paused. Her voice was expressionless. "Ellen Alden's dead."

"Dead?"

"A street accident a couple of weeks ago. She was knocked down by a motor car." Molly seated herself at the desk. She was very pale, her mouth a tense, unhappy line. She spread small hands on the battered leather top of the desk. "She died intestate. As Sam's legitimate son – Ellen's grandson! Danny is her heir." She hit the desk suddenly with a clenched fist. "I won't take it. I won't! I don't want it. I don't want her money anywhere near my son!"

"Is it a lot?"

"Mr Ambler wasn't certain. The house. A few hundred pounds in the bank. A few pieces of jewellery. About a thousand pounds, Mr Ambler said."

"A – *thousand* – pounds?"

"Yes."

"And it all comes to Danny?"

"Yes."

"But the family – Ellen's family – won't they fight it?"

"Apparently not. There's only Uncle Thomas. Mr Ambler was very careful to tell me that he had advised him that he probably had a good case if he cared to fight it, but Uncle Thomas said he wouldn't." For the first time she smiled, a small, grim smile. "Aunt Maude and Cousin Lucy must have thrown fits."

"Why did he refuse?"

Molly shook her head. "I don't know. I suppose he thinks he's doing me a favour. He was the only one of them all – apart from Sam – who liked me."

"A thousand pounds! It's a small fortune! Lucky Danny, eh?"

"I tell you I won't let him take it!" There was real violence in the words.

"What? But why?"

"I don't want any part of her. I don't want her money – and I especially don't want it for Danny. She hated him." The smoke-blue eyes were clouded with something close to fear. "She cursed us. Both of us. I want nothing of hers near my son."

"Oh, Molly, now don't be silly. You can't prevent Danny from taking the money because of something like that! Think of the future. His future. Think what it could mean to a young man to have a nest egg like that!"

"I know. I know. That's what Jack says. He thinks I'm being stupid. Perhaps I am." Molly stood and walked restlessly to the window, stood rubbing her hands nervously on her skirt. "Why in God's Name didn't the woman make a will? She must have known what might happen if—" She stopped, her eyes blurred. Behind her stretched an Irish childhood filled with superstition, with haunts and hobgoblins, ill-wishing and mischief.

"Oh, don't be daft, love. You're getting quite overwrought. Anyone'd think you were frightened of the money! I'm damned if I'd say no to a thousand pounds – not if the Devil himself left it to me!" She checked herself as she turned to leave. " – Oh, by the way, John Marsden's been in looking for you this morning. Something to do with a letter."

"Oh Lord. I've had one letter too many this morning already.

I can't believe that anything good could possibly come from another—"

"Well, you'd be wrong, young lady. Not for the first time, I daresay." Neither of them had heard John Marsden's approach. He stood behind Nancy, his habitual scowl on his face, an opened letter in his hand. "Are you running a business here or a pesky female gossip-shop?"

"Don't be so crotchety. We both know you don't mean it." Molly went back to her desk. "Thanks, Nancy, I'll see you in a minute."

Nancy returned to her own office, grimacing at John Marsden's back before she slammed the door behind her.

Molly regarded her senior partner composedly. "What is it? An offer to take over the staffing of Buckingham Palace?"

"Not far off it." He handed her the letter, watched with a mischievous twinkle in his eyes as she read it.

"But – this is marvellous! Expansion – new offices – completely new staff and organization – and they're hoping that you'll do it all for them!" She looked up. "Stowe, Jefferson and Partners. I think I recognize the name. Have we dealt with them before?"

"I've had some dealings with them in the past, yes. They're a good, reputable, go-ahead firm. They've done very well this year past. Import, export, that sort of thing. Young Jefferson has big ideas. Spends a lot of time in the United States, I believe."

"But this is exactly the kind of thing we've been hoping for!" Molly glanced at the swirling, picturesque signature. "Adam Jefferson. We must get Nancy to write back straight away and confirm the appointment. Next Thursday is all right for you, isn't it?"

"No," John Marsden said peaceably, "as a matter of fact it isn't."

"Oh – well, when would be? We don't want to keep them waiting too long."

He produced a wheeze that might have been a chuckle. "If they wait for me, my lass, then they'll wait for ever. I'm not going." He paused, for effect. "You are."

"But they specifically ask for you."

"So they do. Well, you aren't going to let a little thing like that put you off, are you? Not when they're offering those kind of terms? I'm retiring, remember? Didn't you once tell me, full of fire, that one day they'd come to you?"

"But they haven't," Molly pointed out, not unreasonably. "They've come to you."

John Marsden limped to the door, smiling wickedly. "You'd better go to Mr Jefferson and point out his mistake, then, hadn't you?" He left without waiting for her reply. "Well, young Nancy," she heard him say, "still rioting in the streets with those tomfool hysterical friends of yours, I hear?" This was the recurring theme of acrimonious argument between them. To each of them the beliefs of the other were anathema. John Marsden was and always had been a true-blue, full-blooded Tory. The overwhelming Liberal victory in the elections earlier in the year had been, to him, just another sure sign that the country was going to the dogs. That more Labour MPs than ever before had also been elected simply reinforced this conviction. The reforms that the Liberals and their allies were embarking upon appalled him; but it was the growing agitation for votes for women that was the red rag to the bull. And Nancy – never one to ignore a challenge – was, as he well knew, ready to argue with him every time he opened his mouth. Molly, Adam Jefferson's letter in her hand, heard the inevitable wrangling begin and marched to the door.

"Some of us," she said, "have work to do."

John Marsden waved a testy hand. "Just trying to sort out young Nancy's muddled thinking for her, that's all. Oh – got a bit of advice for you, too, if you want it."

Molly could not help laughing. "Do I have a choice?"

"Doll yourself up a bit for Mr Jefferson. He's got something of a reputation with the ladies, or so I believe. And you don't look half-bad, sometimes, when you try." Nancy snorted. John Marsden ignored her. "Might as well take every advantage that you can, eh? All's fair, as they say—"

"Why John Marsden!" Molly said severely, "I'm surprised at you! And you not one for the ladies, either. Or so you're always trying to tell us."

He chuckled. "Don't greatly care for horses either. But I never walk when I can take a cab."

The girls looked at each other in exasperation as the door closed behind him and they heard his irregular steps, punctuated by his breathless laughter, take him across the hall and into his parlour.

"I swear he gets worse every day," Nancy said.

"He does it deliberately." Molly laid the letter she held on Nancy's desk. "Would you answer this for me? Agree the date they suggest. By the way," she said pausing at the office door, "someone was here looking for you last night, after you'd left. Lad with an accent straight out of Berkeley Square. He had a message."

"Yes, he found me. Mrs Edmonton's son." Nancy smiled suddenly. "The *Honourable* Mrs Edmonton's son, actually. There's a meeting tonight. She wants me to go along and help with the teas." She looked up, slyly. "Care to join us?"

"Lord, Nancy, what do you think I am? A miracle worker? I've enough work, one way and another, to keep me going for a month! I've no time for tea parties!"

Nancy's good-natured laughter followed her into the large, shabby office that, no matter what she did to it, still bore indelibly the print of John Marsden.

She looked around. Soon it would be entirely hers New wallpaper, she thought. New curtains. And a smaller chair. I'll have a telephone installed – John thought them new-fangled contraptions and would not have one in the house. The filing system needs reorganizing. She thought of the opportunities that might be opened up by the Stowe, Jefferson letter. Her first big job, and her most important to date. If she were going to make a success of it she had a lot of hard groundwork to do before she met Mr Jefferson. And she was going to make a success of it. Of that she had no doubt.

She did not, however, feel quite so confident on the following Thursday, the day set for her meeting with Adam Jefferson. The appointment was for eleven o'clock. Molly, determinedly businesslike, and with her nerves, she hoped, well buried beneath a cool exterior, took a Hansom, which ploughed through the November streets in losing competition with electric trams and trolleys, with motor cars and buses that roared and clattered and jammed the muddy streets, creating chaos. Molly watched the new machines through the window with an odd mixture of awe, admiration and irritation. Despite young Edward's frequent attempts to explain the workings of the internal combustion engine – his main passion in life since he had packed away his wooden soldiers – it remained a total mystery to her. These bright, mechanical monsters might as well be worked by magic. Yet she could not deny a certain fascination, despite the noise and smell, and it was exasperatingly true that they moved faster than the horse-drawn traffic.

She was going to be late.

She fidgeted with the wide collar of her smart, grey wool coat, pulled off her gloves, patted her straying, November-damp curls, checked the long pins that secured her feathered hat with its flattering upswept brim. She knew from experience that if this interview were to be a long one those vicious skewers, and the tight-pulled hair in which they were anchored, might give her a headache that could last for hours. She wriggled in a corset too new to be comfortable. "*No one's* that shape" Jack had roared, laughing, when she had shown him the picture of the 'celebrated straight-fronted corset'. Well, he knew differently now. She was that shape – with the help of whalebone, an iron will and grim determination. She just hoped that she would be able to breathe, and prayed that no one would offer her anything to eat or drink. She pulled her gloves back on, picked up her long umbrella – an extravagance of grey silk to match the coat – and tried to cultivate patience in the stony soil of nervous apprehension and near-panic as the minutes slipped by. She had, after all, followed John Marsden's advice, and taken great care with her appearance. The smart coat, the matching umbrella and the flattering hat were new. Unfortunately, the shabby skirt and flounced cotton blouse she wore beneath it were not. With the move to The Larches imminent she had not felt it wise to spend too much money. She just hoped fervently that Mr Jefferson did not believe in the luxury of an overheated office. She straightened her back, tucked her well-polished but about equally well-worn shoes beneath the hem of her skirt, rehearsed in her mind all the details that were set out neatly and efficiently in the documents she carried in her small, businesslike case. Not that she needed such written reminders – every name, every qualification, every penny was as clear in her mind as her own name.

"A big day, this," John Marsden had said, as cheerfully as he ever said anything. "Don't go making a mess of it, now. Large, modern company is Stowe, Jefferson. And getting bigger all the time. Expanding."

Which was, she reflected, more than could be said for this God-forsaken corset.

" 'Ere we are, Miss." The cab had rocked to a final standstill. The driver watched her climb out into the bitterly cold, dirty street. "Number sixteen. That'll be ninepence."

"Thank you." After she had paid him, he touched his tall hat, pulled his heavy muffler up round his mouth and chin, and clucked to the old horse.

"Oh, *wait*!" She almost screamed it.

"Yes, Miss?"

"My case! I've left my case in the cab!" Stupid. Stupid!

The man spat into the road, reined in the horse. With barely concealed impatience he waited while she scrambled inelegantly back up the muddy step and retrieved her case, catching the snap lock on the shabby upholstery of the seat as she did so, nearly spilling the contents upon the dirty floor. Stepping down from the cab she banged her head on the swinging door, knocking her hat askew and nearly tearing her hair out by the roots in the process. She slammed the door in a spurt of temper that nearly tore it off its hinges. The cabby muttered something, then pulled away, leaving her alone on the draughty pavement before the shining, brass-trimmed entrance to the offices of Stowe, Jefferson and Partners.

She gathered together the shreds of her self-possession, straightened her hat as best as she could, took as deep a breath as the wretched corset would allow and marched in.

Mocking her fears, she found she was early, and the office into which an elderly, sourfaced man showed her was empty. She stood just inside the door, where the man had abandoned her, clutching her case and umbrella and taking stock of her surroundings. Mr Jefferson, she saw with mild surprise, lived – or at least worked – in some style. The room was large and – she noticed with sinking heart – extremely warm. It was also very comfortable indeed. With its big desk and the well-stocked bookshelves that filled almost the whole of one wall it seemed to Molly more like a gentleman's private study than a place of business. At one end of the room several large armchairs were grouped around a blazing fire and nearby was a small round table upon which stood a decanter and two slender-stemmed crystal glasses. Upon the floor was spread a rug whose glowing colours echoed the exotic Orient, and that, for its beauty, might as well have hung upon the wall.

She stood looking about her for some minutes, collecting her wits and her thoughts before she carefully set down her case and umbrella and advanced into the room, warily skirting the lovely rug, mindful of her muddy shoes. At the bookcase she stopped, intrigued by the rows of leather-bound, gold-leafed volumes. She ran a small finger along the shelf closest to her. *Business Methods in the United States, Cold Storage, Its Principles and Applications, The Export of Fruit, A Guide to Shipping* and a slim, slightly battered volume entitled *Success in Business*. Daringly, she slipped it from its place, but before she could open it she heard light, brisk footsteps coming along the corridor towards the door. Flustered, she tried unsuccessfully to push the book back. Behind her, the door opened.

"My goodness," said a voice – light, distinctive, a little husky. "What have we here?"

Book in hand she turned to face a slight, elegantly dressed gentleman. His dark eyebrows were curved expressively in surprise, his bright eyes were undisguisedly appreciative. He tilted a smooth dark head in question, waiting for her to speak.

Molly felt like a guest caught in some unspeakably ill-mannered act. "I have an appointment with a Mr Adam Jefferson," she said with as much dignity as she could muster.

"I'm Adam Jefferson. But—" he gestured gracefully, " – I'm afraid that there seems to have been some mistake. I don't recall having an appointment with you. And I'm absolutely certain that I should have remembered if I had." He smiled, suddenly and startlingly. "Shall I relieve you of that?"

For a second she could not think what he meant. She had been clutching the book so tightly that it seemed to have become welded to her fingers. "Oh – I – yes. Thank you. I'm sorry –

I—" her own mortifying incoherence infuriated her. She felt her cheeks grow hot.

"Please don't apologize." He came lightly towards her, a narrow hand outstretched. "I can never resist other people's bookcases, either." He glanced at the title before laying the book upon the table. "I approve your choice, at any rate." He stood waiting politely, "Miss—?"

She found her voice. "Benton. Mrs Benton."

"You believed you had an appointment with me, Mrs Benton?"

"Yes. That is – you got in touch with the Venture Employment Agency—"

"Ah, of course. John Marsden's new undertaking. An extraordinarily good idea, I thought. I admire Mr Marsden's enterprise. You have—" he paused, his expression slightly puzzled, " – a message for me from Mr Marsden?"

Her tiny spurt of irritation served to steady her nerves. "No, Mr Jefferson. I've come to see you about the work that you offered us. The Venture Agency is not Mr Marsden's enterprise, it is mine. Mr Marsden is my partner, but since he is retiring within the next couple of weeks it seemed more sensible for me to assume responsibility for your business from the start. I hope you don't find that – inconvenient?" She allowed herself the slightest of pauses before the word, and saw his long mouth twitch in acknowledgement. "I'm sorry, my assistant obviously omitted to inform you whom to expect when she replied to your letter." Her confidence was returning; her voice was cool and businesslike.

Adam Jefferson was watching her speculatively, a new interest in his dark eyes. He inclined his head gravely. "Please accept my apologies, Mrs Benton. The mistake is mine. I should have checked your letter of reply myself. However, now we have that settled, before we begin—" again that flashing, charming smile, " – let me take your coat. You must be extremely warm."

An understatement. She was decidedly hot. But underneath the smart, silk-lined wool was crumpled, sugar-water-starched cotton and a skirt with a tendency to remain seated when its wearer stood up. "No, thank you."

"As you wish. Now, if you'd like to sit down and make yourself comfortable—?" He waved a hand towards the armchairs by the fire.

"Thank you." She looked around and discovered a prim, straight-backed chair near the desk at the cooler end of the room. Collectedly she walked to it, picking up her case on the way. As she sat down, bolt upright – there was absolutely no other way to sit in the ridiculous corset – the case flew open and paper cascaded across the polished floor.

She took a long, slow breath, and with a control that she had not herself known that she possessed refrained from an exclamation both forceful and unladylike.

Adam Jefferson was making a wellmannered but unsuccessful attempt to keep the amusement from his face. "Please – allow me—"

She had in fact no choice. The iron constriction of the corset ensured that. She could no more have bent down to retrieve the papers than she could have spread wings and flown. And she had the awful conviction that he knew it. Cursing herself, she sat rigidly as he went easily down on one knee and picked up the scattered documents. Her efficient plan of campaign came back to her in unrelated disorder, some of the pages upside down or back to front. Her colour high, she tried to sort them as he handed them to her. In doing so half a dozen more slipped from her lap. He sat back on his heel, laughing openly at last.

"I have a suggestion to make."

She looked at him.

"Why don't I go out and come back in again? It might be a little less flustering for both of us?" It was said easily, a graceful gesture to ease her embarrassment.

She did not smile. "There really isn't any need for that, Mr Jefferson," she said grimly, without thought. "I think perhaps the best thing would be to get on with our business?"

He watched her for a moment longer before, with a single, swift movement he stood up. "Of course." She heard the slight, chill edge in the odd, attractive voice and knew she had made a mistake. Mentally she shrugged. It seemed to her that she'd made so many that morning that one more could hardly make any difference.

He seated himself behind the desk, laced exceptionally well-cared-for hands together on the shining leather top. "Well, now, Mrs Benton," he said, his quiet voice still degrees cooler than it had been, "convince me that the Venture Employment Agency can handle our business."

She fiddled with the papers for a moment under his uncharitable gaze before, impatiently, she put them on the desk without looking at them. "I've been over the information you gave us very carefully. And I think that, in at least one case, you have your figures wrong." She ignored the quizzical quirk of his eyebrows and ploughed on. "I don't believe that you need separate employees for the import and export work. You could form a pool to serve both departments, and then use agency staff – temporary staff – for any extra work. You don't need to employ people permanently for jobs that involve seasonal or other fluctuations. It will keep money in your pocket—"

" – and put money in yours," he finished gently.

"Of course. We aren't a charity, Mr Jefferson. But it will still be a lot more economical from your point of view. Our staff are fully qualified – you'll have no complaints, I promise you." She riffled through the papers, pulled out a slightly crumpled sheet. "I have figures here, projected for six months – as accurately as I could with the information you gave us – that I think will prove that my idea will save you a considerable amount of money—" She held out the paper and he took it, scanned it quickly.

"Well, well," he said softly, "so you have. Tell me more, Mrs Benton."

An hour later she collected her papers together, packed them into her case, snapping the damaged lock firmly, and looked up to find him leaning, elbows on desk, fingers steepled before him, his eyes on her face.

"Mrs Benton," he said into the sudden silence, "I believe that, as they say in the States, we have a deal. And," he added, "that's the first time you've smiled since I walked through the door. I was just beginning to wonder if you could." He leaned back relaxedly.

There was grace in every movement he made. Though not in the absolutely strict sense of the word handsome, he was a disturbingly attractive man and the disarming warmth in his eyes was flattering. Molly remembered what John Marsden had said about this man's reputation with women and did not for a moment doubt it. Despite herself euphoria overcame caution and she laughed. "Smiles come extra in business hours."

"You'll make a fortune in no time."

"Not unless I can persuade you to change your mind about who pays for the advertising, I won't."

Laughing he held his hands in front of him in a gesture of defence. "*Pax*! Business is finished—"

"Half and half," she said composedly, "then it's finished."

He hesitated for only a second. "All right. Done. I might have guessed you wouldn't let me get away with it. You drive a hard bargain, Mrs Benton. Now, I insist – a small toast to our future collaboration."

She stood up as he came around the desk towards her. Although he was several inches taller than she he did not tower above her as most men did. His shoulders were narrow, his body neat and spare beneath well-cut, expensive-looking clothes. The high collar of his shirt was perfectly set and edged knife-sharp, his dark cravat was of chocolate silk and sheened in the light as he moved. "Are you sure that you won't let me take your coat?"

Wild horses could not have torn it from her. "No, thank you." She followed him to the table where stood the decanter and glasses.

"Madeira," he said as he poured, "the very best. I trust it's to your taste?"

She had never tasted Madeira in her life – was not indeed certain what kind of drink it might be. "Perfectly," she said.

He handed her the glass, toasted her with his own. "To the new venture."

"To the new Venture." She gave the words a slightly different emphasis and, laughing, they drank. The rich wine glowed in her blood like fire. She could, she decided, grow very accustomed to Madeira – it was indeed very much to her taste. The thought made her smile again.

"I beg your pardon?" Adam Jefferson had spoken and she had missed his words.

"I asked if you would care to lunch with me?" he asked easily. "Our negotiations seem to have given me an appetite." There was quiet humour in the words.

Molly stared at him, her brash confidence draining from her. Adam Jefferson, she was absolutely certain, would not lunch where one could reasonably keep one's coat on. And anyway, the treacherous stirrings of excitement that she was experiencing at the very thought could not be put down entirely to the effects of the Madeira. Quite suddenly she felt a small, strange shock of alarm. "Thank you, but no." To her own surprise her voice was brisk and showed no sign of regret or wavering. "I have two other appointments today." One with a typewriting machine and another with a pile of ironing, she added to herself, wryly. "I rarely have time for lunch."

"Another time perhaps. Tell me, Mrs Benton," – amusement lurked in his eyes and she had the uncomfortable feeling that he had divined the real reason for her refusal and was entertained by it – "are you always so dauntingly busy?"

"I have a business to run, Mr Jefferson."

"Indeed you have. And on the evidence I've seen today I'd say that you run it very well." The words were absolutely sincere, and Molly flushed. "But remember what they say about all work and no play . . ." He took the glass from her hand and, without asking, refilled it. He handed it to her with a smile. "You may have guessed that I admire attractive ladies, Mrs Benton. But in particular I admire attractive, clever ladies—"

"Which," she found herself saying a little recklessly, "is more than can be said for many of your sex, Mr Jefferson."

"Regrettable, but undoubtedly true. But then you have to understand that some gentlemen feel threatened by a clever lady and their only defence is to tell themselves that they dislike her and her kind."

"And you don't? Feel threatened?" The words were light but contained enough true curiosity to make him smile again.

"I feel threatened by no one," he said simply, and beneath the charming surface Molly glimpsed something diamond-hard and cold as ice.

"I wish I could say the same—" It was out before she could stop herself.

He studied for a moment the golden liquid in his glass, then lifted thoughtful eyes to hers. "But then I think we both know that it isn't feeling threatened that matters. It's what one does about it." He raised his glass very slightly. "I salute you, Mrs Benton."

Her heart was pounding absurdly. She had the distinct feeling that the occasion was slipping beyond her control. "I really think I should go." She drank the Madeira far too quickly. It sang in her head and thickened her tongue.

"But of course." He was immediately, attentively polite and the odd, intimate moment was lost. "I'll see you downstairs and get you a cab."

At the door of the building he shook her hand, held it for a moment in his own. "I do apologize again for the slight misunderstanding, Mrs Benton. Next time, I promise, I'll know whom to expect."

The Madeira, the cold air, and the touch of his hand combined to vanquish caution. She grinned a sudden, impish grin absolutely at odds with the businesslike grey wool. "I – and my profit margin – forgive you, Mr Jefferson. If you're really unhappy not to be working with John Marsden, I'll try scowling and smoking a pipe next time?"

His laughter was a shout of enjoyment. "Something tells me, Mrs Benton, that we're going to work very well together. Very well indeed."

Later, in the Hansom, she remembered that future tense and felt a small twinge of pleasurable anticipation.

And it was not, she realized, with some misgivings, entirely due to the promised profit margins.

CHAPTER TWENTY-SIX

JOHN MARSDEN MOVED out of The Larches in mid-December. Two days later, in damp and drizzling weather, the Bentons moved in. An hour after the cart carrying their furniture had pulled up outside the door Molly stood in near despair in the middle of a chaos that seemed to have no great intention of allowing itself to be sorted out, wishing that not quite so many people had felt it their duty to help. Even Edward had gleefully taken an illicit day off from school and was alternately tripping over things – at twelve he had lost the neat prettiness of his early years and was becoming a gangling, clumsy adolescent – or chasing Danny and the twins around the new house until they were all worked up to such a pitch of excitement that one of the younger ones, usually Kitty, ended up in tears.

"Edward!" Arms piled high with linen, her smudged and dusty face a picture of exasperation, Molly stuck out a foot and barred the way into the empty parlour. "For heaven's sake, stop dashing round like a maniac and make yourself useful. Those books over there—" she nodded her head at a pile of books that had tipped and spread themselves across the floor of the hall – "they're Nancy's. Take them up to her rooms for me, please. Before someone breaks their neck. And, please do try not to drop them on Meg's head on the way. . . . Oh Jack, no! Can't you get some of this stuff into the rooms before you unload more? We're getting in a terrible muddle."

Jack swung the heavy box to the floor as if it had been full of feathers and several small brass ornaments fell from it with a crash and scattered across the floor. He did not bother to pick them up. "We're paying the carter by the half-hour, lass. Sooner we get unloaded, sooner it stops costing us." He cocked his head, listening. "God Almighty, what are those kids doing?"

"God Almighty's the only one who knows." Molly, muttering, dropped to her knees to retrieve the fallen ornaments. At the street door she heard Jack greet someone. She sat back on her heels. Surely, oh surely not someone else who felt duty-bound to 'help'? She scrambled to her feet to find herself face to face with a completely strange young man who was obviously as taken aback at their sudden confrontation as she was. He was rather tall, painfully thin with a pale, sensitive face that was badly marred by the spots and eruptions of late adolescence. Molly judged him to be about seventeen years old.

"I'm – I'm most dreadfully sorry," he said, his precisely accented voice cracking miserably in mid-sentence. "I didn't realize—" He gestured at the mess, jumped as Jack banged through the door carrying single-handed a load that might have made a mule kick.

"It's our Nancy he's looking for." Jack made to dump the box on the floor.

"Jack! That's the best china! Careful—" Molly flew to him, helped him lower the box, then turned to find the young man standing awkwardly where she had left him. "Nancy?" she asked.

"Miss Benton, yes." He blushed. "I have a message for her. From my mother." And then she recognized him. The Honourable Mrs Edmonton's son.

"Oh, I'm sorry. Of course. You came once before, didn't you? Things are a bit muddled, I'm afraid. Nancy's upstairs. It's probably best if I show you the way. Can you squeeze through?"

They left the noise and the chaos behind them as they mounted the stairs. From the foot of the narrow flight that led to Nancy's two attic rooms they could clearly hear her voice and Edward's.

" – and you think this Mr Jones'll give you a job when you leave school next year?"

"He's already said he will. I'm better with engines than he is already. Just imagine. Working all day in a garage. And getting paid for it!" Edward's voice sounded as if he had seen his personal vision of Heaven.

Molly ran up the last few steps and tapped on the open door. Nancy was sitting on the floor amidst a spreading muddle of books. Edward was perched on an armchair, his feet pulled up out of Nancy's way. As they both turned expectant faces to the door Molly's heart tightened a little to see how alike they were. Apart from Edward's still-golden hair he was the image of the girl who had borne him.

"You've got a visitor."

Nancy looked beyond her, saw the young man and smiled. "Oh, hello, Christopher. Come on in."

Christopher Edmonton followed Molly into the room. He seemed to be having some difficulty in managing his lanky frame, his feet and hands were awkwardly big, his straight brown hair flopped forward over his forehead and into his eyes almost every time he moved and he had a little, nervous habit of jerking his head sideways in a vain attempt to flick the straying strands back.

"I've a message from Mother." He handed her a note. Nancy tore it open, glanced at it swiftly, then tucked it into her pocket. "Thanks. Tell her I'll let her know tomorrow, would you? Oh—" She seemed suddenly aware of her duty as a hostess. "Sorry, you haven't been introduced, have you?" She nodded in Molly's direction. "My sister-in-law – and landlady – Mrs Benton. And this is my young brother Edward. Christopher Edmonton."

They murmured how-do-you-dos. There was an awkward silence. The boy, despite his obvious nervousness, showed no inclination to leave. Molly shifted from one foot to the other.

"Well—" she began.

Christopher Edmonton hardly seemed aware of her. He had eyes only for Nancy. "Please, Miss – Miss Benton," he blurted, "may I stay and help? It wouldn't be any trouble, honestly." Nancy's rooms, while not as disordered as the rest of the house, since some of the housekeeper's furniture had been purchased and left in place, were nevertheless in some turmoil.

"Well – I—"

"Please. I'd very much like to."

Molly stared. Could it be that Nancy did not hear the desperate eagerness in the young voice, see the wistful ardour in the eyes? "I'll leave you to it, then," she said.

Nancy was back among her books. "Thanks, Moll."

Christopher perched on the arm of Edward's chair, leaning forward, his straight hair tumbling across his forehead.

He looked a child himself. His eyes did not for a moment leave Nancy's face.

Molly closed the door and went thoughtfully downstairs.

Molly heard from Adam Jefferson only once before the New Year – a brief, polite note inviting her to take luncheon with him one day during the week before Christmas. The note made no mention of business, and Molly knew that she should not go. She mentioned it to no one, carried the note around with her in her pocket for four days, being as determined one moment to refuse as she was the next to accept. She did not doubt that the invitation was a personal one, and experienced a stirring of excitement at the thought. She had found Adam Jefferson both provoking and attractive – a dangerous combination at the best of times. He had about him an energy, a compelling life-force that fascinated her. She had, she knew, never met anyone like him, and the memory of his undisguised interest more than once tempted her to ignore the plangent voice of common sense. But in the end common sense – and propriety – prevailed and a week after receiving his note she sent a stiff little refusal, allowing herself the luxury of regretting it almost the instant it left her hand.

It was as she came back into The Larches after posting that letter that she almost cannoned into Christopher Edmonton who was standing, alone and forlorn-looking at the foot of the stairs, awkwardly clutching an enormous pile of books.

"Hello," she said in some surprise. "You look like an abandoned bookshelf."

He coloured. "I hope you don't mind. Your little boy let me in."

"Nancy's still in the office. Are the books from your mother? You can leave them if you like." She knew her own tactlessness the moment she had spoken. His ears and the back of his neck glowed uncomfortably pink, his hair fell forward, and in flicking it back he dropped two of the books.

"They aren't from Mother, actually. They're a few things I promised Nan—Miss Benton, that I'd lend her." He was struggling to pick up the fallen books without losing the rest.

"Let me do that." Molly picked up the books and balanced

them on top of the pile in his arms. Byron. And an anthology of poetry from the nineteenth century. She took mercy on the lad's embarrassment. "Look, why don't you go upstairs? I'll tell Nancy that you're here."

"Thank you. Thank you very much." His face scarlet, he turned and mounted the stairs. Molly watched him, her face pensive. Poetry? Since when had Nancy been interested in poetry? And had she yet realized that the mere mention of her name was enough to produce a look of quiet devotion on the young – the very young – Mr Edmonton's face? Molly doubted it. She considered for a fleeting moment the thought of some sisterly advice, but dismissed the idea almost as soon as it formed. It was none of her business. Christopher Edmonton's puppy love would die its own death, probably without Nancy ever realizing that it had existed.

Christmas came and went; one of the best, they all declared, that they had ever spent. On Christmas Day the whole family were at The Larches and the still-sparsely furnished rooms rang with laughter and talk and the tinkling sound of the Polyphone that Molly, to the children's delight, had bought. But while the two days were certainly a pleasant break Molly was aware of an impatience to begin the new year, an eagerness to get back to work. There were occasions when she found herself taking little active part in the celebrations, her mind was busy, her thoughts elsewhere. Once or twice she caught Jack's sober eyes upon her.

With Christmas past and the New Year safely launched she threw herself wholeheartedly into the job of staffing Stowe, Jefferson's new offices. More and more she left the routine work of the agency to Nancy, who was more than happy to assume the responsibility. Only the occasional ripple disturbed the peaceful surfaces of their lives; Jack and Nancy were increasingly at loggerheads about Nancy's commitment to the suffrage movement – 'the cause' as she insisted upon calling it, to Jack's irrational irritation. Molly was careful to stay out of their arguments. In fact, she was becoming aware that she habitually went to absurd lengths to avoid argument with Jack, for if the tension between Jack and his sister could be acknowledged, accepted and to a certain extent eased by the occasional outburst, the inexorably growing strain that was making itself felt between husband and wife had no such outlet, for neither of them would admit to its existence. To an outsider, however close, their relationship seemed warm as ever. Only they knew that they made love now only on rare occasions, that the long evenings spent in the parlour were quiet with a silence that grew not so much from companionship as from a gradually widening distance between them. Jack had taken to visiting Annie and Charley once or twice a week; invariably Molly was too busy to go with him. She would not complain, would not, from pride, point out that she too had worked a long hard day and that the washing and ironing, the housework that took up so much of her time in the evening were arduous chores that tired her sometimes to exhaustion. Jack was a strong and kindly man. He loved her, she knew that beyond doubt. But he did not, could not, understand her. He was torn, she knew, between pride at her achievement and unacknowledged resentment of it. Other men's wives were satisfied with house and children and responsible, caring husband. Why must she be different? Since Molly herself hardly knew the answer to that question they never discussed it. And so the words that might have eased, might have led to understanding, were left unspoken and the seeds of estrangement were sown. And beneath the everyday tensions, the hurts, the resentments lay something of which neither of them spoke. Jack wanted a son. He treated Danny as his own, doted upon the girls, would profess utter satisfaction to anyone who enquired, but Molly knew too well the thought that gnawed at him, knew it and could not soften. No more children. They had agreed it, and she would hold him to it. The twins' premature birth had been a nightmare never forgotten. She resented fiercely, if silently, the fact that Jack could apparently dismiss it now and expect her willingly to go through it again. She would not admit, even to herself, that there were other, more selfish and more practical reasons why she did not want another child. And so, as the first weeks of the year flew by, Jack and Molly slipped into habits of coolness that were well disguised to all but themselves.

She was hardly herself aware of how often Adam Jefferson crept into her thoughts until the afternoon that she lifted her head from the papers she had been studying to find him conjured whole, elegant and sure of himself, in the doorway of her office, just as she had imagined him so many times, just as she had known he would come. Nancy hovered uncertainly behind him.

"Mr Jefferson to see you," she said, her surprised eyes on the elegant back.

"Since lunch is a meal that obviously doesn't impress you very greatly," he said, with no preamble beyond a smile, "I've come to take you to tea."

Molly stood up. "I really don't think—"

"Nonsense." Adam Jefferson walked round the desk, drew the chair from behind her as if he had been an attentive servant. "We've business to discuss. And I've no intention of discussing it here."

"But—"

"You surely aren't going to argue with your biggest and most important customer?" The dark eyebrows lifted, the hard, straight mouth smiled just a little.

"No, of course not," Molly said tartly. "I wouldn't dream of it."

"Good. Then get your coat and hat. I've a motor car outside. I'll go and get her started. Wrap up well. It's cold." He was back through the door before she could answer.

"Bring the file on the new staff with you," he called over his shoulder, "we'll look at them over tea. . . ."

Tea at the Royal Hotel was taken in the Palm Court. Molly stood in some dismay by Adam Jefferson's side at the top of a flight of wide marble steps that led down to the spacious tea room, chandelier-lit, in which potted palms and plants were patches of jungle-green and silver tea services and cutlery gleamed on dazzling white tablecloths. Above the clatter and hum of conversation the strains of Strauss rose lilting from behind a discreet screen of living green on the far side of the room.

"But I'm not dressed for a po – for a place like this!" Molly was humiliatingly aware of her smart, businesslike, deadly dull grey wool, her windblown hair.

"Mrs Benton," the oddly distinctive voice, close in her ear, was warm, "you look absolutely stunning. There isn't a woman in the room to touch you."

She surveyed the splendour of feather and fur, of stones that sparked fire in the electric light, and took miserable leave to doubt it.

The waiter indicated a table by a tall window that looked out onto the busy winter street. "Will that be satisfactory, sir?"

"Perfectly. Thank you." Adam Jefferson stood back, waiting for Molly to precede him.

The table looked a mile away, a gamut of eyes to be run before she reached it. She hesitated but since the only alternative to following the waiter was to ask to have tea served on the steps where they stood, with head high and a back like a ramrod she threaded her way to the table by the window. As she settled herself in the high-backed chair, the silver and china, the tea and a great plate of fancy cakes was laid ceremoniously before them by a pretty waitress in neat black and white.

Molly could find absolutely nothing to say. She stared at the steaming water jug and tried to marshal words that were light, intelligent, entertaining.

None came.

She stole a look at her companion from beneath her lashes. He was watching her with something of the same attention that she was lavishing on the water jug, and a spark of laughter lurked in his eyes. In nervous silence she poured the tea, managing predictably to splash too much milk into one cup and too little into the other.

"Sugar?"

"No, thank you."

She passed him a cup that rattled humiliatingly in its saucer as she held it. He put it down, toyed with his spoon. Around them conversation ebbed and flowed like a tidal sea; no one else, it seemed, was dumbstruck.

"Are you—"

"Do you—"

They began in the same breath, broke off, laughing.

"After you."

"Do you want to talk about the work I've done so far? Oh, no—!" Her hand went to her mouth.

"What is it?"

"The file. I've left it in your motor car."

He threw back his head and laughed. "Don't worry. The car's been garaged. I daresay that I can find someone to go and rescue your file." He looked around for a waiter.

"Well, actually," she said diffidently, "I can probably do without it. If you have a pencil and paper? I've all the names and figures in my head."

"Are you sure?"

"Yes." More confidently, she took the proffered pencil and notebook, pulled her chair closer to the table, cleared a space on the spotless tablecloth. She sat for a moment chewing the pencil thoughtfully. "I've been looking at those extra figures you sent over, and it seems to me that it might well pay you to employ someone to concentrate on the North and South American business. Someone who'd specialize in the day-to-day running, and leave you free for the more important projects. . ."

The tea grew cold in the pot and, still absorbed, they hardly noticed it. The orchestra played, broke for an interval, came back and played again. The tables around them were vacated and reoccupied. The buzz of conversation died a little, the tired steps of the waitresses were less hurried.

"So you see, I'm sure you'll find that in some cases you'll find it better to pay a little more for well-qualified staff. The pool, I'll look after – if that's satisfactory. And of course we'll always have replacements if you're short-staffed, or if there's a real panic." Molly put down her pencil.

He watched her for a moment, smiling, then extended his hand across the table. "Congratulations. You've done a splendid job." Molly hesitated before offering her own hand, all the confidence engendered by the last hour draining from her as she became mortifyingly aware in the pale, glittering light of red knuckles and rough skin. He took her fingers in his, squeezed them lightly, held them for noticeably longer than a handshake would warrant. She tried, half-heartedly, to disentangle herself. He lowered his arm so that their clasped hands were resting on the shining starch of the table cloth.

"Thank you for coming."

"Thank you for making me come."

"And has it been such an awful experience after all?"

She laughed at his perception, wrinkling her eyes and shaking her head. He released her hand.

"Good. Now. I propose a toast." He lifted his teacup. "To our continued association," he said solemnly, sipped and pulled a face. "Damn me, the pot's gone cold. And you haven't eaten a crumb! Come along, now, this will never do. I'll get some more——"

As he waved the waitress over and ordered a fresh pot of tea Molly looked around her, astonished to discover that all of those things that had seemed so alien, almost frightening, when first she had arrived now had the reassurance of familiarity. The emptying room no longer threatened. She found herself thinking of the waif who had wandered down Regent Street, just a stone's throw from where she was sitting now, remembering too the girl who had gone to tea in that same street with Harry, Charley and Annie.

What would she have thought of the young woman who sat here now?

"Penny for them."

She shook her head. "Nothing much. I was just thinking about the way things change. The way people change. Without ever really noticing it. One day you open your eyes and look around you and – bang, there it is. Different."

He tinkered with his spoon, watching her. "Not for everyone. It depends. On who you are, what you are, what you want. Most of all what you do about it. Some people can live a lifetime in a prison they have built themselves on the instructions of others, and never know what they have missed. Such people never open their eyes and look around. Never find anything is different. Because they are afraid. Narrow. Grey people in a world of colour. Cardboard people. Not worth bothering with."

"Isn't that a little unkind, Mr Jefferson?" she asked softly. She was aware that over the past hour an intimacy had grown between them that was at odds with the brevity of their acquaintance. She had the strange feeling that she had known this man, and he her, all of her life – and was aware enough to recognize if not to resist the practised talent that induced the feeling.

"Adam," he said, as if he had read her thoughts.

She hesitated, then quietly amended her words. "Adam."

"It may not be kind, but it's true. And I think that you know it. You can't spend your life worrying about what's kind and what isn't. You'd drown in a sea of sentiment. Life is to be lived, to be taken and wrung of every drop of enjoyment, every experience to be had. It offers nothing free. And if, as you say, the world is not kind – who really wants it to be? It's exciting. And beautiful. And often a little perilous. You won't try to tell me that you don't prefer it that way?"

She did not reply.

He leaned forward. She thought she had never seen anyone in whom the flame of life burned brighter. The incisive, sharp-drawn face drew her eyes like a magnet. She realized with something of a shock that she could sit so for hours, simply listening to his voice, watching the hard, sensual mouth, the quick-moving, expressive hands. In that moment it came to her beyond doubt that her first impulse had been right: she should not be here. The man who faced her, smiling so peacefully, could mean only danger.

She poured tea, sipped it slowly. When she spoke she was astonished to find that her voice was as collected as she could wish. "Do you always get so passionate over tea?"

"Only on Tuesdays and Fridays. Or when I see something or someone that I want very badly."

"Today's Thursday," she said.

"Yes."

There was a very small silence. "I see. I'll say one thing for you, Mr Jefferson. You don't beat about the bush."

"I thought it was Adam?"

"And I thought that this was a business meeting?"

"Business is over," he said, his voice very soft. "This is pleasure. Pure pleasure."

"An important ingredient in your life, I gather?" She tried to keep her voice light, to keep the treacherous note of excitement from it.

"Of course. The pleasures of success. Of battles won, and battles lost. The pleasures of love. What would be the point of life without these things? We're on this earth just once. If we don't take what's offered and enjoy it to the full, then we've no one to blame but ourselves."

"And if someone else gets hurt in the process?"

The curt movement of his head held slight irritation, but he laughed nevertheless. "Kindness again? Molly, my dear, people are getting themselves hurt all the time – you, me, the other fellow. You can't waste energy crying for the world. I ask no quarter, but neither do I give it." He leaned forward. "Don't let the world fool you into obeying its piffling rules, Molly Benton. You aren't that kind. Follow your own path. Be yourself. Every moment is precious, and there are no second chances. Do you see yourself, in fifty years, as an old lady looking back and saying, 'I wish I had done'?"

She saw the gleam of gold on his lifted left hand. Oddly, it was a shock.

"Does your wife agree with your – unusual philosophy?" she found herself asking coolly, well aware that it was none of her business.

He released her hand. "In her own way, yes."

"Oh?" She let the silence lengthen.

He sighed. "My wife Caroline married me with, I assure you, very few illusions and with a very clear understanding between us. Each of us had something that the other wanted, and in the way of such things, we struck a bargain—"

"You make it sound like a business deal."

"I suppose you could call it that. Aren't all marriages, in a way, however prettily they're wrapped up? Caroline wanted me—" there was no trace of vanity in the words " – and I wanted a partnership. My wife's maiden name was Stowe."

Stowe, Jefferson and Partners.

"I see."

"I'm perfectly certain that you don't." He relaxed suddenly, smiling again, the slight edge gone from his voice. "Don't waste your concern on Caroline. She's more than capable of looking after herself, I assure you. Now, shall we order more tea—?"

The room had almost emptied. Nearby a waitress hovered, watching them.

"I—" Molly reached for her gloves. " – I think perhaps we should go?"

"Of course." He signalled to the waitress. "My bill, please."

She pulled her gloves on, tried not to watch his strong hands, which rested in tense stillness on the table. She was aware that during the afternoon a strange, half-antagonistic excitement had built between herself and this man whom she barely knew. She was certain that he felt it, was not sure indeed that he had not deliberately engendered it. As he assisted her politely from her chair they barely touched, yet his nearness disturbed her and she stepped sharply away from him.

As they drove to Stratford in the windy half-darkness of the late afternoon they talked of the interesting impersonalities of business and of money. As they pulled up outside The Larches Molly found herself mentioning the bequest that had come to her son, and that Jack had insisted Danny keep.

"I suppose I should do something with it for him. The solicitor is being a little – unhelpful." It was hardly the word, she thought, for the unpleasant Mr Ambler.

"I'd be pleased to advise you. You could do a lot worse for your son than investing it with us. The return will be good, I promise you."

"Oh, I don't really care about that. I just want to be rid of it." She blushed a little in the darkness, aware of how silly that must sound. "I just want it kept safe for Danny until he's twenty-one."

"Don't worry. I'll take care of it. I'll be in touch some time over the next week or so."

Had she known he would say that? Was that why she had brought up the subject? She did not know.

"Thank you. And thank you for tea."

He jumped down from the driver's seat, leaving the engine running, moved round to the passenger side to help her down.

"I'll see you soon, then?" Her hand was fast in his, his voice was serious.

"Yes."

"Promise?"

She took a slow breath. "Yes."

He ran back around the car, swung himself back up into the driving seat, lifted a hand in farewell.

She watched the noisy, gleaming machine nose its way down

the street beneath the lamps and turn the corner at the end, stood still until the sound of its engine had been swallowed by the darkness and the noise of the other traffic.

The house, though lit, was surprisingly quiet. She took off her coat in the hall, fluffed her hair, braced herself for questions and opened the door of Nancy's office.

Christopher Edmonton turned as she entered. His hair was dishevelled and his face chalk-white.

Molly stared. "Christopher? What are you doing here? Where are Nancy and the children?"

"The children are at the shop with your sister-in-law. She says not to worry, Mrs Benton – she'll keep them for the night if necessary—" He stopped, fidgeting with his hands, his knuckles cracking.

"Keep them? Why should she keep them? Christopher, what is all this about? Where's Nancy?"

"She – bit a policeman," the boy blurted miserably. "She's been arrested. She's in prison."

CHAPTER TWENTY-SEVEN

"No sister of mine is staying in gaol. Not for any – cause." Jack, his voice shaking with anger, invested the word with heavy sarcasm. "Not if I can help it."

"But Jack, it's up to her, surely? If she doesn't want her fine paid—" Molly knew it was useless to argue, but was equally certain that she ought to try.

"I don't give a damn what she wants!"

Sitting bolt upright in a fireside chair Sarah winced at the violence in her eldest son's voice.

"Has she given a single thought to anyone else's feelings in all of this?" Jack continued, stationing himself in the centre of the room, his raised, pointed finger sweeping from one of his listeners to the other. "Has she? What about Mam?" The finger jabbed. "How in Hell is she supposed to feel with a daughter in prison?" Sarah stirred but did not speak. "And what about you two? Fine gossip in the shop, eh? What to say to a customer who asks how your sister's liking it in Holloway?"

Charley lifted his head. Molly, as always, felt a pulse of shock at the painful contrast between the strong, clear-featured face and the blank and lifeless eyes.

"No, Jack." Charley's voice was gentle, it almost invariably was. The rage that had first accompanied his disability had gone, subjugated by necessity and courage. "I'll not have that. The lass is going her own road. I'll not go against her for my own sake, nor for Annie's. What worries me is what conditions in prison might do to her. Six weeks can be a long time, and our Nancy's not been strong since—" He stopped.

"Aye. That's what's on my mind." It was the first time Sarah had spoken.

"But to Nancy, to all of them, it's a matter of *principle*." Molly could not keep a quiet tongue; she could still see Nancy's inspired face as she had stood in the dock with the other women and girls who had been charged with her. "They *want* to stay in prison. That's the whole idea. To draw attention to their cause."

Jack turned on her, his face thunderous. "It sounds as if you'd like to be in there with her? You've done nothing but defend the girl. Don't you think there's enough to fight for, enough to suffer for, without inventing senseless and futile 'causes'? If they want a fight, I'll give them something to fight for! A decent living wage for every family. Housing. Medical care. Security in old age. Votes for women?" His voice cracked in his effort not to shout. "When we haven't been able to get the vote for most working *men* yet? When up and down the country wages are being cut, men are being thrown out of work, locked out, tossed into the street to starve, kids and all, so that the masters can keep their profits? What's the matter with our Nancy? Has she gone clear off her head?"

"That isn't fair." Anger lifted like a sudden, bright pennant and despite herself Molly marched into battle – the last thing she had intended to do. "Nancy cares every bit as much about those things as you do. More, perhaps. My God, I should know – between you two I get more lectures than a working man's club! Nancy just has a different way of going about things, that's all. Why can't you see that? Can you blame her? You men have had your chance over the years, haven't you? With your Parliaments, and your armies, your Unions and your wars and revolutions? And what's changed? Nothing. Who are you to get on your high horse because someone – a woman – dares to try something different? In every city in this country Unionists are in prison at this moment for doing *exactly* what Nancy and her friends have been doing. For going against the established order of things. For trying to make their voices heard, trying to get people to listen, trying to change things. I don't hear you calling them lunatics. You raise money to defend them. You support them. You treat them as heroes. You'd *be* one of them if it came to it, you know you would. And, tell me, what would you expect us to say if it came to that? Would you expect us to consider it a disgrace? If they tried to lock you out of the docks tomorrow and it came to a fight, what would you do to a policeman who stood in your way? Ask him politely to step aside?"

"At least," Annie said into the furious silence, "I don't think Jack would be reduced to using his teeth. Not with fists like his."

Charley chuckled. Jack and Molly eyed each other like fighting cocks, both aware that Nancy was not the only, nor even the basic, cause of hostilities. Jack took a breath that visibly lifted his massive chest, ran his fingers through thick and tangled hair. "Fighting amongst ourselves isn't going to get us anywhere."

"I'm not fighting," Molly said promptly. "I'm defending someone who isn't here to defend herself. If this matter is to come to a vote—" she glared into Jack's exasperated face " – then I vote 'no'. Nancy doesn't want the fine paid. She's a grown woman, she's entitled to do as she sees fit. Six weeks isn't a lifetime. If you pay her fine and get her released while her friends stay in prison I doubt if she'll ever forgive you."

Jack let his bright gaze rest on his wife's rebellious face for a long moment before he turned to Sarah. "What about you, Mam?"

"I want her out of that place," Sarah said quietly. "It isn't that I don't understand what Molly's saying. She may even be right, for all I know. But, as Charley says, my lass isn't very strong, whatever she may think. I can't bear the thought of her in—" Her voice broke at last and tears came. She bowed her head.

Jack threw a sidelong glance at Molly, turned to Annie and Charley. "What do you two think?"

Annie didn't hesitate. "Nancy's a birdbrain ever to have got herself involved with the coppers in the first place. Take it from me, jug's no place for a girl like our Nancy. Enough of my lot have been inside. Anyone who doesn't want to get out has got to be touched in the head. Pay up. She'll be so glad to get back to decent, normal people and a hot bath she won't be able to stay mad long."

"Charley?"

Charley did not speak for a considerable time. Jack watched him, as he always did, with unassuageable pain in his own eyes. Seeing it, Molly's anger drained from her like water from a cracked jug. Nothing that anyone, including Charley, could say or do, would ever enable Jack to forgive himself for something that had been totally beyond his power to prevent.

"Charley?" he said again, gently.

Charley shook his head. "No," he said, and then, into the surprised silence, "No," again. "Molly's right. It's Nancy's choice. We shouldn't make it for her."

All eyes turned to Jack. He looked from one to the other. Two for, two against. His the casting vote.

"I'm paying it," he said at last, "and if our Nancy doesn't like it she can kick me when we've got her home."

"I'd like to kick his head in," Nancy said viciously, "that I would."

"Oh, come on, Nancy, he's only done what he thinks is for the best. And you did agree, in the end." Molly poured the tea.

"What else could I do? To hear our Jack talk you'd think Mam was suicidal, and Annie and Charley and you going broke because of me." She stared moodily into her cup, then lifted her head, smiling a little. "I'm a pig, Molly. I haven't even thanked you for coming to meet me. I'll bet Jack didn't know you were setting foot – almost – in the unhallowed halls of Holloway?"

"No, he didn't."

"Well he might tomorrow."

"Oh, Nancy, don't!" It was Molly's turn to frown. "I didn't dream those men were reporters when I gave them my name and address. I thought they were prison officers or something. It wasn't until they actually took the photograph—" She stopped. "– They won't publish it, will they? I mean, two women walking out of a gateway: hardly big news, is it?"

"A prison gateway. And one of them as good-looking as you? Don't bank on it."

Molly discovered that Nancy was right the next evening when Jack came home from work.

She heard him come through the front door, gruffly greet the girls who had, as always, rushed to meet him.

"Daddy, I made you a pie. An apple one. You've got it for after supper. The crust is all lovely and hard—"

Molly smiled at Meghan's shrill voice, waited for Jack's laughter. It didn't come.

"I peeled the apples—" Kitty was hanging on her father's

hand as they came into the kitchen, " – and I didn't cut myself at all. Only nearly."

Molly turned from the stove to greet him, paused at the look on his face. Danny, drawing at the kitchen table, looked up.

"I'm drawing a motor car, like the one Edward showed me at the garage." Jack did not answer. "Dad? What's the matter?"

"Nowt's the matter, lad. I want a word with your mother is all. Take the girls in the parlour for a minute, will you? Here. Share these." He handed over a sticky twist of paper full of sweets.

"Cor, thanks," Danny said. "Humbugs!"

"And gob-stoppers? Are there any gob-stoppers?" Meg, jumping up and down, made an impatient grab for the sweets.

"Do as Daddy asked. Take them into the other room. *Quietly*. Meghan, don't snatch. And Danny, don't tease her. And don't eat them all, you'll spoil your supper. One each, the rest later."

Molly watched them squabble through the door. "There's no gob-stopper here big enough to stop your gob," Danny said with brotherly rudeness. Jack closed the door behind them.

"What is it?" asked Molly.

In answer Jack tossed the paper he had been carrying, folded, upon the table. Molly stared with sinking heart at one of the clearest pictures of herself she had ever seen. Over her shoulder Nancy's face was blurred and fuzzy.

"Oh, Good Lord," she said.

"Read it."

In the silence the clock ticked loudly. "I'll sue them!" Molly said with some violence. "I'll damn well sue them! Why, the cheek of it. They imply that I—that *I*—"

"What were you doing there for God's sake? What were you doing there?"

"I went to meet Nancy. Well, I couldn't leave her to come home alone, could I? As if no one cared?" She tossed the paper angrily onto the table. "How dare they? Just look at the offensive way it's written: 'two valiant Amazons who found that action is harder than words . . . predictably ready to pay up when the going gets tough'. I hope Nancy hasn't seen this."

Jack sat down heavily in the chair by the range, pulled off his heavy boots. "If she hasn't then she must be the only one between here and the riverside who hasn't. The lads went to town on me today, I can tell you. Very funny they found it."

"Oh, Jack, I'm sorry." Molly laid a hand on his shoulder. "Truly I am. Is there anything we can do about it?"

"It's not worth it, lass. Leave it. If you kick up a fuss it'll likely make things worse. It can't be helped now."

"And you aren't angry?"

He shook his head. "It wasn't your fault. Even I can see that. Though I was spitting rivets at first, I can tell you. Why didn't you tell me you were going to meet our Nancy?"

"Because I thought you'd try to stop me."

To her surprise he laughed, throwing his head back in real amusement. "Molly, you're worth a guinea a box! Stop you? Me? When have I ever actually managed to stop you from doing something that your heart was set on? When has anyone? I'd as soon try to stop the sun from shining." He reached for her, drew her to him, rubbed his face gently on her breasts. It was months since he had made such a gesture. Stirred, she touched his hair, ran a finger down his dirty, scarred face. They stayed so, in silence, for a long moment.

"Lord, girl, I can be a fool sometimes," said Jack unexpectedly, his voice muffled by her dress, "I know it. Stiff-necked lot, the Bentons, the whole damned lot of us. Always were. I suppose – it's just that—" He ran out of words.

"–Just that you should have married a little thing who would cook and clean and mend your shirts and care for your children, with no nonsense?" Molly asked very quietly. "Who'd never fight with you, nor make a decision on her own? Who thought her own two feet were there for someone else to step on?

He leaned back, looking up at her with eyes that were crinkled with laughter. "And look what I got landed with – a self-willed hussy who argues with me every time I open my mouth, runs my house in her spare time, adds insult to injury by earning more money than I do, and caps it all by getting her picture in the paper as she walks out of Holloway. Bit of a come-down from the paragon you just described, isn't it?"

Her fingers, that had been playing with his tangled hair, buried deep and tugged.

"Owch! And an Irish temper as well." He stood up swiftly,

imprisoned her with arms that well knew their own strength.

"Supper's spoiling."

"I don't give a damn." He kissed her, hard, then again, longer, quieter.

If it could just always be like this. . . . The very thought seemed treachery. She tightened her arms around him.

"Mum, Mr Ed—" Danny, bursting through the kitchen door, stopped wide-eyed " – monton's here," he finished composedly. "He wants to see Aunt Nancy. Can I take him up?"

Molly disengaged herself from her grinning husband's arms. "Yes, please, Danny. Then wash your hands. Supper's ready."

From the hall beyond the open door Christopher Edmonton had seen the little tableau, had stood abashed, unable to look away, an uncomfortable prickling warmth rising in his body. He could not conceive what it would be like to be a man like Jack Benton. He could not take his eyes off him. The man was enormous; he radiated strength, sheer physical power. His scarred, striking face might have been chiselled from rock. He drew the eye and the attention; people listened when he spoke. Christopher admired him, envied him, was frightened of him – as he was frightened of so many things. He was even afraid of Molly: of her sharp tongue, her energy, her bright, determined eyes. Her very beauty frightened him. He could rarely speak to her without stammering.

"Mum says I can show you upstairs," the little red-headed boy was standing in front of him, head tipped back, looking at him with no trace of shyness or fear. By God, even the children in this house were terrifying.

"Er – thank you."

Christopher trailed up the stairs behind Danny, his heart thumping like a traction engine. Now what? Would Nancy be angry that he had disturbed her? Would she be busy? Or tired? Should he have come?

"Here we are." Self-importantly Danny bashed hard on the door. "Aunt Nancy. A visitor. I can't wait," he added to Christopher with a man-to-man smile, "supper's ready and my mum's got a temper on her like a bee-stung cat if we're late."

Christopher watched him down the stairs with some admiration. He could not somehow visualize young Danny Benton in ten years' time trembling before a woman's door.

"Come in." Nancy's voice was oddly flat. "Door's open."

She was sitting, staring out into the rain, her shoulders slumped. It was bitterly cold in the little slope-ceilinged room. At the sight of the insubstantial frame, the light-boned boyish face, which was highlighted by the single lamp that burned on the table, Christopher felt a twist of physical pain. She looked absurdly vulnerable, hopelessly miserable.

She looked up. "Oh, hello, Chris. Come to see the conquering heroine, have you? The—" she pushed a crumpled newspaper with her foot " – 'valiant Amazon'?" Her voice was choked with self-disgust.

Christopher found his voice. "You aren't letting the *Express* get you down, are you? You know how they feel about the Cause. Why, Mother says that to get your name in the *Express* is the next best thing to making a speech at Hyde Park Corner—"

That brought a very small smile. "Tell Molly that: I don't expect she's exactly over the moon about having her face plastered all over London."

"She seemed all right when I saw her just now."

"Wait till our Jack comes home."

Christopher flushed. "He's home. They were – together. I'm sure your brother wasn't angry."

"Oh well, that's a relief anyway." Her voice was listless.

Christopher shivered. "It's freezing in here. Why haven't you lit the fire? Have you had anything to eat?"

Nancy shrugged, shook her head.

The dim light, the miserable droop of the slight figure in the chair brought stirrings of confidence. "How silly. You'll do no good sitting here in the freezing cold and pretending you're back in prison, you know." He surprised himself with the briskness of his tone. "There's a meeting at home tomorrow—"

Nancy moved her head vaguely. "I'm not sure I can make it tomorrow . . ."

"Nonsense. If you're afraid of what the others will think, or that they'll look down on you because your brother paid your fine then you don't know them. They understand, of course they do. Mother's delighted you're back. She said so. Now, where are the matches? Look at you – the fire laid and ready and you're shivering with cold. Here, put this round you—" He picked up a shawl that was draped over the back of a chair. "No, don't move. Just sit there until I get the fire going. Then I'll make us a cup of cocoa and some toast. Have you any eggs?"

Bemused, Nancy nodded.

"Good. Because scrambled eggs are all that I can do that's edible."

"Scrambled eggs?" A gleam of amusement lit her brown eyes.

More than anything he had ever known he loved every line, every expression on the tired face. "I may be one of the fairly-idle almost-rich," he said with unusual lightness, "but a few years ago I fagged for the most awful chap named Wellington. He had the strongest right arm in the school. And he liked scrambled eggs. Therefore I learned to scramble eggs."

Nancy laughed. "Very sensible."

Christopher winced. "Yes, I suppose that's what I am. Most of the time anyway."

He busied himself with the fire, watched the first unwarming yellow flames lick wood, catch, sputter, dance around the as-yet-untouched coal. Sparks, a puff of smoke; he coughed, blew into the glowing wood, felt the early stealings of warmth.

"There. That'll be going marvellously in a minute. Come closer. That's it. Now stay there and get warm while I get some supper."

He worked at the little stove, quietly happy, whistling softly and tunelessly between his teeth, glancing every now and again at the still figure beside the fire. Nancy had extended her thin hands to the blaze, and the flame glowed bloodily through her fingers.

"Eggs au Edmonton coming up." With a flourish he scraped the golden mixture onto the plate. "Oh, cripes, the plate's cold. It's a good job you aren't Wellington Major." As he laughed the firelight caught his young face, drawing its fine and sensitive lines, sharpening angles, hardening the jaw, mapping the future. "Eat it quickly before it gets cold."

The first mouthful showed her how hungry she was. She ate every scrap, wiped the plate with a crust of toast while he looked on delightedly.

"Cocoa," he said, handing her a mug. "Strong and with lots of sugar, just as you like it."

She took it, cupped her hands around the warmth. "When I was a little girl," she said, "Jack used to smuggle cocoa up to me in bed when I was supposed to be asleep—"

Christopher stared into the glowing coal-cave. "You think a lot of Jack, don't you? For all that you fight a lot?"

There was a long, thoughtful silence. "Yes," said Nancy, faint surprise in her voice. "Yes, I still do. The problem with us is that we look at things from different angles. We both see the same things. But we both see something totally different. And we're both stubborn as mules."

"But you're both right."

She laughed, "Or we're both wrong. And neither of us would admit that."

"He frightens me." An evening of surprises. How had he brought himself to admit that? And to Nancy of all people? She was watching him, waiting for him to go on. "His size, I suppose. His strength. He has a – potential for violence."

"Jack isn't violent. Never deliberately so."

"I didn't say he was. It's a feeling, an impression. I wouldn't want to cross him."

"You'd be right."

Christopher leaned forward and poked the fire. A flurry of sparks flew up the dark chimney. "Jack," he said thoughtfully, "is a symbol of his kind – of his class if you like. Something is changing. There is an impatience, a self-confidence growing in men who work hard and who know the value of that work. But there is violence too, just beneath the surface. It's what makes a policeman heft his truncheon when he sees two or three working men talking together on a corner. It's what brings the troops onto the streets of Wales. It makes fingers jumpy on triggers." His young voice was very serious now.

Nancy looked at him curiously. "It sounds as if you're talking of revolution?"

"Perhaps I am."

"Don't be silly. Revolution? In England?"

"It could happen."

The atmosphere between them had changed. For a moment

neither of them spoke. Then Nancy, in an effort at lightness, said, "What a strange boy you are," and could not miss the sudden, angry lift of his head, the irritation in the movement as he tossed his hair back from his eyes.

"What have I said?"

"Nothing."

"Come on, now, what is it?"

"Don't you know? Don't you really know?" His voice was low.

"Would I be asking if I did?" a faint impatience threaded the words. "Perhaps I should light another lamp—" She made to move, found herself imprisoned by his hands.

"No, don't. Please."

She looked down at the hands that, though trembling, determinedly held hers. "All right." She tried to disengage herself. His cold grip tightened.

"Chris, what is it?"

"I'm not a child. Please don't treat me like a child."

"But I don't—"

" 'What a strange boy you are'," he repeated. "Would you say that to – to Jack?"

She did not answer.

"Would you?"

"No, of course not. But—"

"I'm not a boy, Nancy. I'm a man. A man. And I love you."

The echoes of his raised and desperate voice died into the silence. Gently Nancy pulled her hand from his. His brief courage burned out, he could not look at her. He rested his elbows on his knees, buried his face in his hands.

"You don't mean that. Not the way you said it." Nancy kept her tone level. "You can't. You *are* too young. Not a child, certainly not that. But a boy of how old? Seventeen?"

He nodded.

"And I am twenty-eight. *Twenty-eight*. An old maid. Almost old enough to be your mother." Agonizing thing to say with Edward never far from her mind.

He moved violently. "You're deliberately exaggerating. Eleven years: it isn't that much. If it were the other way round; if you were a man and I a girl – who'd care then? Oh it's stupid! Stupid! I love you, Nancy, truly love you. It isn't fair—" He knew himself how those words, the eternal cry of the child, damned him. He turned away from her.

Into the flickering silence she said, "I think you should go."

"No!" With a movement so sudden she could not prevent it he slipped to the floor at her feet, burying his head in her lap. "Oh, no. Don't send me away. Please don't." It was the cry of a desolate child.

Her hand hovered an inch from the fine, straight hair. "I'm not sending you away. I'm not. But it's late and it really is time for you to go. I'll see you tomorrow at your mother's. But you must promise me something—" He lifted a stricken face, tear-marked in the firelight. Her own eyes blurred at the sight of his distress but she kept her voice calm. "– You must promise never to mention this again. We're friends. We always will be." His breath was catching in his throat; she had to use every ounce of self-discipline she could muster to prevent herself from gathering him into her arms as she might Edward or Danny. "Don't be unhappy. Please don't. These things don't last. It's perfectly natural to – to feel something for someone who is older than you. But you'll see – you'll meet some pretty girl, and the next thing you know you'll be inviting me to the wedding—"

He sat back, ungainly, on his heels, his head moving slowly back and forth. "No," he said.

"Christopher—"

"Please don't say any more." He had almost gained control of his voice. "I know I love you. I know how much. It doesn't matter that you don't believe me. I know I'm not good enough for you," he said, ignoring her involuntary, protesting movement, "I'm weak, not strong like you, and Jack and the others. I'm a coward. But I'll prove to you that my love is the best part of me. I'm sorry if I've embarrassed you. I haven't spoiled things, have I? We are still friends?"

Nancy swallowed. "Of course we are. How could we be anything else? I've no one else to read Mr Byron to me with such feeling. No one else to make me cocoa and scramble me eggs when I'm sick of myself. Ah, that's better—" A tremulous smile had shown through the fiery, glittering tears. "Friends," she added softly. "When you think about it, it's a better word than 'lovers'. More—" she smiled " – comfortable. We'll be friends,

Christopher. Until some young lady takes my friend from me—"

He shook his head, struggled to his feet, brushing the back of his hand across his still-wet face. "I'll see you tomorrow, then?" His voice was almost normal.

She watched him shrug his coat untidily on, fling his scarf about his neck. "Yes."

"You promise?"

"Yes."

"Goodnight, then."

"Goodnight. God Bless."

In the quiet after his departure Nancy leaned a weary head on her hands and stared into the slowly dying fire

CHAPTER TWENTY-EIGHT

ON THE 15TH March 1907 the new offices of Stowe, Jefferson and Partners were to be officially opened. Two days before the event Adam Jefferson arrived in person at The Larches to deliver an engraved invitation card.

"We're making quite a splash of it. I think you might enjoy it."

The physical attraction of the man was almost tangible. Molly put the width of the room between them, "Oh, no, I don't really think that—"

"Of course you'll come. After all the hard work you've put into the project? Miss Benton is, I am sure, more than capable of holding the fort for a day. Aren't you, Miss Benton?"

Nancy smiled, and Molly noted with some surprise that even she did not appear entirely immune to Adam Jefferson's distinctive charm.

"A day? Oh, no, I certainly couldn't manage a whole day."

"Nonsense. There'll be people there whom you should meet. Nothing like personal contact, Mrs Benton, nothing at all. Especially with a smile like yours. Sacrifice a single day on the altar of the Venture Employment Agency's future prospects; you won't regret it, I assure you."

"Must it be for the whole day?"

"But of course." His voice was bland. "You could hardly walk out half-way through? I'll bring you home at about six? Good. That's settled then. I'll be passing this way, I might as well pick you up. About ten-thirty? Good day, Mrs Benton, Miss Benton. I'll see myself out."

Molly pulled a face as the door closed behind him. "Personal contacts? I reckon I made enough of them at the start to last me a lifetime! I wonder if anyone at Stowe, Jefferson's will remember the girl with the blistered feet who pounded on their door with a boxed-up typewriter in one hand and a thinly disguised stick of dynamite in the other?"

*

Nobody did, not that Molly found that surprising. The surprise came a little later when, after a few pleasant, politely applauded speeches, a few glasses of champagne, a few cut ribbons, the guests began to depart and the workers to settle at their new desks.

"I don't know what else you do exceptionally well," Molly said to Adam Jefferson repressively, "but you're certainly an extremely good liar. Is it too much to ask what you have planned for the rest of the day?"

"I thought a trip into Essex. Luncheon at a very quiet and rather pleasant little inn that I know. A few hours together. A chance to talk."

"Business?"

"No. Definitely not."

"And if I won't come?"

He watched her with unsmiling steady eyes for several seconds. "Then I promise you I will not bother you again," he said simply.

Molly tucked a straying curl beneath her hat. "Well, we can't have that, can we?" she said tartly. "Think of the profit margins."

They drove through pale spring sunshine into the lanes and byways of Essex. Epping Forest was mantled in new green, the dark, leaf-smothered earth putting up brave and tender spears of life into the chill air.

"You're very quiet?" Adam raised his voice above the rhythmic chug of engine.

Molly smiled and nodded, nursing the memory of a lifted, laughing face, a warm hand in hers. Harry had been dead for nearly nine years. But the forest still held him, still echoed faintly with the sound of his voice.

The woodland gave way to farmland, to new-sprouting hedges and wide fields. The sky was washed blue and streaky with high cloud. Molly found herself relaxing, exhilarated by the rush of wind, the unaccustomed speed. She was here now, it would be stupid not to enjoy it.

They lunched at an ancient and rambling inn, alone in a room with a low, beamed ceiling, tiny deep-set windows and a fire, very welcome after the sharp March air, in a great inglenook fireplace almost as big as the room itself. The innkeeper treated Adam with that mixture of deference and familiarity reserved for a very special customer.

"Good day, Mr Jefferson. A fine, fine day for a spin in the country. I trust the journey was enjoyable? Some of the roads round here—" he lifted his eyes exaggeratedly to Heaven. "Well, it's just a good job it isn't raining! Will you eat straight away, sir, or will you take sherry first?"

"Sherry, please, Paxton. We'll take them in the little bar. We'll eat in half an hour."

"Certainly, Mr Jefferson, certainly."

"He was expecting us," Molly said.

"Yes, he was."

She did not comment further. She was coming to know Adam Jefferson.

"Come, sit by the fire. You must be chilled. Does the sherry suit you?" He settled himself into a deep, rather battered leather armchair. He was watching her intently.

"Perfectly, thank you." She drank the sherry rather too fast; on top of the champagne and an inadequate breakfast the effect was a little alarming, though not altogether unpleasant.

"I'm sorry?" She had missed something that her companion had said.

"The money we spoke of. I take it you are happy to invest it with us?"

"Oh yes."

"I promise you won't regret it." He spread his fine hands in a characteristic gesture. He used his hands a lot, Molly noted. He knew how attractive they were.

"I'm sure I won't."

"Clever girl. An astute businessman never leaves his money lying useless in the bank. He gets it working for him."

"Quite," she said intelligently.

He leaned forward. "I believe – I really believe – that you're going to make a great success of your agency."

"So do I," she countered promptly.

He laughed. "You, my lovely Irish Molly, are someone I've been waiting a very long time to meet. If there's one thing I enjoy it's being proved right."

"About what?"

"About you. I recognized a kindred spirit the moment I met you. Oh, you may not recognize the likeness yourself as yet. You may not even like the thought. But it's there. So be careful."

"Of what?" She was caught again in that silver web of fascination that the man wove so apparently effortlessly around her. She could not take her eyes from his face.

The distinctive voice was pitched to reach her alone. "Success, Molly, is like a drug. Or like love. If you have never had it then you can manage very well without it, but the first taste, the first touch, and you're in danger of addiction." He watched her for a long moment, the corners of his mouth tilted in a half-smile. Then he called, "Paxton, two more sherries if you please."

She sipped this one more slowly, savouring it as she found herself basking in the warmth of the fire, the attentiveness of her companion, the enjoyable strangeness of the place and situation. A slight recklessness seemed to have overtaken her. And why not, she reasoned silently. Was it such a crime that just for a few hours her life should not be bounded by the office and the kitchen, by Jack's dirty shirts and the children's sticky fingers? Where was the harm? She looked up. Paxton was at her shoulder.

"Lunch is served, Madam."

"Thank you." As if to the manner born she allowed the man to conduct her deferentially to the small room where their table was laid, firelight sparkling in tall wineglasses.

With the landlord gone from the room Adam lifted his glass in grave salute. "How is it," he asked, "that all women are born actresses? It is the one overwhelming advantage that you have over poor, unimaginative men. I drink to you all."

She had never enjoyed herself so much. He talked nonsense, he deferred, he flattered, he made her laugh. The minutes flew, became an hour, two. Paxton served port. Adam, still talking, played with the stem of his glass with long, strong fingers. She watched them in fascination. Then something that he had said jolted her to reality.

"America?" she repeated, aware of an unreasonable dismay. "You're going to America?"

"That's right. The United States. My favourite place. I'm off next week. Have you ever been there?" She shook her head. His face was lit with enthusiasm. "That's where the real opportunities are, Molly. America's the place for a man of ambition."

"You mean you're going for good?" she asked blankly.

He laughed. "Good Lord, no. Three or four months, that's all. I've some people to see, a couple of deals to set up——"

"I see."

There was the smallest spark of victorious amusement in his eyes. "Dare I suggest that you don't seem too happy at the idea?"

In that moment it came to Molly that perhaps the introduction of the subject of the trip had not been quite as casual as it had appeared. "And you try to tell me that women are actresses?" she asked.

"That's no answer. It's very sharp, but it's no answer."

Her face was flushed with wine and the heat from the fire. She laid the back of her hands against her cheeks, not looking at him. "It would sound silly to say that I'll miss you. We hardly know one another."

"It doesn't sound in the least silly." He reached across the table and took her hand. It seemed the most natural thing in the world for him to do. "Some people you can know for years, yet they never touch you, never get close to it. With others – very rarely, but it happens – an hour is enough. A minute. There's a bond, you *know* each other. No matter how you might try to deny it. Such people make the best of friends, and occasionally the worst of enemies. Such people can love while others are still saying 'How do you do'."

"Not a conventional view," she said as lightly as she could manage.

"To hell with convention." He reached a hand, traced the line of her mouth with one finger. She shivered. "We're doing no one any harm," he added, her own thoughts of a short while before, the simplicity of the words infinitely seductive. "When I come back it will be summer. Summer . . ." He made the word an invocation of magic. "Then we'll see." As he bent towards her, without thought or volition she lifted her head. His mouth was just as she had known it would be; the pleasure it gave, greater. Much greater.

"Time to go," he said softly. And she could not, for her life, say if she were relieved or disappointed.

She did not see him again before he left for America. He telephoned her once, to say goodbye, but it was an awkward and unsatisfactory conversation. Molly had still not quite mastered the telephone; she suffered from an urge to shout, to speak in words of one syllable, as if the instrument had reduced her own and her listener's capacity for understanding. On the day of his sailing the thought of his going was in the back of her mind all day, a small misery, scarcely acknowledged. How could she miss someone she hardly ever saw, barely even knew? But she did. She missed the possibility of his coming, discovered that she had listened for his voice on the telephone, or in the outer office greeting Nancy. He had enlivened her life disproportionately, and now he was gone. Three months seemed like an eternity. Yet as the weeks flew by and he had been gone a fortnight, a month, six weeks, the memory of him faded, unable to compete with the realities of a busy life, and their relationship – such as it was – took on a slightly unreal atmosphere. And, too, there were doubts, and guilt. As one month turned into two and the sweet soft smells of May drifted in The Larches overgrown garden she listened to the voices of the children calling through the long, light evening and found, to her relief, that the distinctive tones of that other voice had almost slipped her memory. It was only a step from there to coming to believe that the whole thing was absurd, a moment's aberration best forgotten, as Adam Jefferson had no doubt done by now. She had trouble enough, she reflected wryly, with one man, without getting needlessly entangled with another. Jack's involvement with the troubled Dockers' Union, his stubborn resistance to the growing power of the dedicated revolutionaries who lost no opportunity to ferment discontent and violence were making him harder to live with by the day. His temper was short, his absorption in his own hard, man's world complete.

The matter came to an inevitable head one evening in June.

Three nights out of six Jack had come home late, tired, out of temper.

"I don't know why you agreed to go on to the committee if it makes you so mad," Molly said. Not best pleased herself Molly set before him yet one more ruined supper.

"It isn't the committee that's the problem," Jack said, eyeing the plate with no great enthusiasm, "it's the bloody Shipping Federation. It's the Cement Combine downriver that's refusing to use union labour, or to abide by union terms. It's the paper people with their own wharves downstream who're doing the same. They've undercut wages till it's got to the point where organized firms are having to ask us to lower our rates so that they can compete for contracts. It's no bloody wonder that membership's falling. I'd think twice about joining myself at the moment. What the hell good are we to anyone? It's opportunity on a golden platter for the agitators, the syndicalists who'd rather smash things than alter them."

"What about the Dockers' Union? Are they in as bad a state?"

"Worse, if anything." Gloomily Jack picked at his dried-up meal. "Ben Tillett's got the right of it. He wants an amalgamation of waterside unions."

"Will he get it?"

He shook his head. "Shouldn't think so. Memories are too long. There's still bad blood between the Dockers and the Stevedores from way back. There's many on our executive wouldn't give Ben Tillett the time of day. And the Lightermen, too – independent buggers, they are, they'll have nothing to do with the idea of amalgamation with anyone. Christ, no wonder we're in such a state. The Federation must be laughing their damned socks off."

Molly seated herself opposite him, weighing the moment against the seething anger in his eyes. "Jack?"

"Hmm?" He did not look up.

"Had you considered – would you consider leaving the docks? It's hard and thankless work. Dangerous too. And we could—" He lifted his head and she knew with sinking heart that the moment was wrong.

There was a long moment's quiet. Jack stopped pretending to eat, pushed his plate away.

"What do you suggest? Jobs are growing on trees nowadays are they? P'raps I should run errand boy for Charley and Annie?"

"There's no need to talk like that. It was a suggestion, that's all."

"A bloody silly one."

"Keep your voice down. You'll wake the children."

"Keep your own down, you'll wake the street."

Molly, in stony silence, began to clear the table.

Jack rubbed a harassed hand over his stubble-grown chin. "I'm a skilled man. The docks are all I know. It's where I earn my living. Our living."

Molly opened her mouth, had enough sense, on the edge of temper, to shut it again without saying anything.

"And it isn't just that, either."

Molly clattered the plate she was holding into the sink, rolled up her sleeves. "And don't I know it," she muttered.

His head turned sharply. "What's that supposed to mean?"

She turned on him, her sudden rage impossible to contain. "It means that three times this week I've wasted time, effort and money in cooking a meal that I don't want and it's spoiled in the oven – not because you're working late, but because you're chasing round on business for a Union you just yourself admitted is doing no more good than none. You march in here like a bear with a sore head and expect me to put up with your bad temper. And if I do show some concern, if I try to make a constructive suggestion you bite me head off. I've had a bad day meself, Jack Benton." She was aware of her carefully educated vowels slipping into pure Irish.

"Well, that's easy fixed." He was glaring at her, his strong face mottled with anger, the scar standing white and welted, a raised gash on his cheek.

"What do you mean?"

"If you find it so bloody hard to cope with the business and your husband and children then there's just one way out, isn't there? You give up the business."

"No!"

" – And you concentrate on doing what every other self-respecting woman I know does – with no great effort."

"Jack, no."

"You cook and you clean and you talk over the back fence to

your next door neighbour—" He ran out of steam. His voice echoed in the deathly quiet kitchen.

She looked into his baffled, angry eyes and divined at last the real reason behind the outburst. "And have babies, Jack? Is that it?"

He turned from her, smashed his fist down onto the table hard enough to make the cups rattle in their saucers. "Is it so much to ask? Is it?"

"You know it is."

Visibly his shoulders slumped. He took a slow, deep breath. When he spoke his voice was almost pleading. "I'd look after you. I'd help you, I swear it. You wouldn't have to give up the business, of course you wouldn't. I didn't mean that. I know how much it means to you. But our Nancy could manage for a few months, couldn't she? It was bad last time, I know. But that was twins, Molly, twins. It wouldn't happen again."

"But why risk it, Jack? Why?"

"You know why." His temper was rising again, and with it his voice. "Is it some kind of crime for a man to want a son?"

"You have a son."

"No! No, Molly, I don't! *You* have a son."

The silence that fell was awful. Molly turned from him, stared blankly at the wall above the sink. She heard him fling violently from the table, grab the coat that he had thrown across the back of a chair, heard the front door slam hard enough to shake the house.

In the small bedroom above the kitchen, Danny through half-closed, blurred eyes made inconsequential pictures of the light and shadow that dappled his ceiling from the lamp that illuminated the lane outside.

When Jack came home, much later and staggering a little, Molly was already in bed, albeit far from sleeping, in a makeshift bed in the twins' room.

CHAPTER TWENTY-NINE

THE ATMOSPHERE AT The Larches remained strained. For days Jack and Molly barely exchanged a word, except when necessitated by the everyday business of the household. And although Molly, realizing the stupidity of sleeping uncomfortably in a makeshift bed, moved back into their shared bedroom, they slept like strangers, and the few cold inches that separated their backs might have been a mile. The evenings that Jack spent on Union business, or with Charley and Annie, or visiting Sarah grew even more frequent; Molly neither commented nor complained.

It was nearly two weeks after the row that Charley came, accompanied by Edward, on a warm June evening that was overcast and had a hint of thunder in the air. Molly kissed him with real pleasure. "Charley, how nice to see you. Come in. Jack isn't home yet."

"I didn't think he would be. There's a meeting tonight, he told Mam. It's you I came to see." He used the word easily, as if completely unaware of painful irony. "What's the point of having a gradely lass like you for a sister-in-law if I never get a kiss from her?"

Molly laughed, pecked another kiss on his cheek. "You should have been born an Irishman for your blarney. There. But don't tell your Annie or she'll have my scalp. Sit yourself down, I'll put the kettle on. Tea, Edward?"

Edward glanced at Charley. "No, thanks. Danny about?"

"In the garden with the girls. They've a house in the branches of the apple trees."

"I've made him this." Edward held up a little model motor car, carved in wood, beautifully detailed and with spoked metal wheels that turned.

"Why, Edward, it's lovely! Run and give it to him now, he'll love it."

Edward tried not to look too pleased. "Aw, it's nothing really. But I know how much Danny likes cars."

"Almost as much as you do." Molly watched the boy down the long garden path. "Hasn't he grown? He's a proper young man."

"That he is."

"It doesn't seem possible does it?" The kettle sang and Molly made the tea, waiting. Whatever Charley had come to say he would say it in his own good time. "Is he still as happy at the garage?"

"As a sandboy. I've never known a lad so well suited."

Silence fell, broken by the tinkle of their spoons as they stirred their tea, the sound of the children from the garden.

"Molly?"

She sat a little straighter. Here it came. "Yes?"

"Are you all right?"

"I'm grand, thanks. Yourself?"

The corners of his mouth turned down in clear exasperation. "Don't be daft, woman, I'm not making polite conversation."

"I know it."

"There's something wrong between you and our Jack."

The silence was longer this time.

"It's none of my business," he said.

She relented. "It isn't that, it's just, oh, we have our ups and downs, like anyone else. This is a down, that's all."

He felt for the table with a careful hand, placed his empty cup precisely upon it. From experience Molly did not offer to help him.

"Annie's worried about the pair of you."

"Annie worries about everyone, doesn't she? Has Jack said anything?"

"No, of course not. Though we do seem to be seeing rather a lot of him lately."

"It's up to him what he does with his time." She had not intended to sound quite so sharp. "I'm sorry, Charley, I know you want to help, but you can't, believe me. It'll blow over, I daresay. We've just hit a rough patch, that's all."

Charley turned his head, his sightless eyes directed towards the open door through which faintly floated the sound of the children's voices.

"How's Danny?" he asked, a little surprisingly.

"He's fine."

"Can I ask you something?"

"Well of course."

"Does what's come between you and Jack have anything to do with Danny?"

"No." It was too quick, too sharp. "Whatever makes you think that?"

"He hasn't been – misbehaving?"

Molly placed her cup tidily on the table. "Don't you think that you'd better just tell me whatever it is you came to tell me?"

He sighed. "There's no easy way, Molly. I have to say it straight. Danny's been stealing."

Molly's breath seemed to have stopped. "From *you*?"

Charley nodded. "A couple of times. At first it was just stuff from the shelves. When Annie caught him at it she read the Riot Act good and proper. Annie was upset – you know the kids can have anything they want from the shop if they only ask—"

"Did he take much?"

"Quite a bit, yes. Anyway, the lad cried, swore he'd never do it again, begged us not to tell you, and we agreed. But it's money this time, Moll. From the till."

"What!"

"Yesterday afternoon. Young Danny forgets that though I can't see I can hear things a dog wouldn't't."

"Oh my God."

He leaned forward, reached blindly for her hand. "Now listen, it's a childish mischief, that's all. But he's got to be told, for his own sake. He doesn't know that we know. Annie thought you'd rather speak to him yourself?"

"You are absolutely certain?"

"Would I be here else?"

"No, no of course not. But I don't understand. Why would he do such a thing?"

"You'll have to ask him that. I'm sorry, I really am. But you had to know."

"Yes, I'll speak to him. But Charley—?"

He waited.

"Don't tell Jack? Please don't. I'll sort it out, I promise." He smiled gently. "Why do you think I came when I knew our Jack

314

would be away? Now, is there another cup of tea in that pot?"

It did not take much to get the truth from Danny, the boy was no practised liar.

"But why, Danny, why? And from Aunt Annie and Uncle Charley, of all people! Aren't you ashamed?"

He hung his head determinedly, would not look at her.

She gazed at the bent red head. "Why did you do it?"

"I don't know."

"What do you mean, you don't know? If you don't, who does? You must know——"

He shook his head.

"Look at me. Will you look at me!"

Obdurately he kept his eyes on his dusty boots.

"Do you know what they do to little boys who steal?"

Silence.

"They take them away and put them in prison. Is that what you want?"

His head moved again; his lower lip trembled and he sucked it fiercely.

"Why did you do it?" she asked again, helplessly. "Will you for God's sake say something?"

"I don't know."

She held her temper with difficulty, tried another tack. "You wanted to go hop picking with Aunt Annie again in the autumn, didn't you?"

That brought his head up. "Yes."

"Well, do you think they'll want you with them now? How can they trust you? How can I trust you? Even if they would take you, how could I let you go?"

That broke him. Sobbing, he flung himself upon her. "I don't know why I did it. I don't! I knew I shouldn't, but – Oh, I promise I'll never do it again. Cross my heart I promise——"

She held him from her, her own heart breaking at the desperation in the tear-drenched blue eyes. "Have you still got the money?"

"I spent sixpence," he whispered, his breath hiccoughing in his throat.

She shook him, very gently. "All right. Now stop it. Come on, stop it." She waited until the sobs had subsided. "Now listen. I'll lend you the sixpence – you'll have to pay it back, mind, penny by penny, as you get it – and you can take the money back to Aunt Annie. Tell her how sorry you are. And promise it will never happen again. Is that clear?"

Tears slid down smooth, rounded cheeks.

"Well?" asked Molly sharply.

"All right." The woebegone voice was tragic.

"If you do that – and do it right now – then I don't think we need to tell your father about it—"

Danny turned and walked away.

"Danny!"

He turned, his cherubic face alabaster pale, the tears quite gone. "I'm going to see Aunt Annie. To give her the money and tell her I'm sorry." He walked composedly to the door, "and to ask her if I can go hop-picking with her again," he added, and was gone before his mother could remonstrate.

"Oh, think nothing of it, love. Storm in a teacup. We've all done it, as kids, haven't we? Pinched things? Crikey, I know I did. It's over and done, and now we'll forget it, eh? 'Course Danny can come hopping with us. We're banking on it. And I was going to ask – what about the girls this year? Would you let them come too?"

"What? Oh, Annie, are you crazy? *Three* of them?"

"Why not? The more the merrier. If we'd had six of our own we'd have taken them, wouldn't we?"

"But that's different."

"Too true. If they were ours we'd probably be dying for a few weeks away from 'em!"

"Yes, but—"

"I'd take good care of them I promise. You wouldn't have to worry." Annie's voice was casual, her eyes were pleading.

"Well of course, I know that—"

"It'd give you and Jack a bit of a break. A bit more time together."

Molly averted her eyes, busied herself with the button she was sewing onto Meghan's dress. "Yes."

"You could p'raps come down for a weekend? Nothing like

those Saturday nights – a walk through the fields to The Chequers for a drink, a pudden left over the fire to cook while we're gone. I sometimes think I should have been born a gypsy, that I do. I love the old Kentish fields. Bin every year since I was a nipper. Let 'em come, eh, Molly? It's good for them, you know. Open air, bit of hard work, plenty of freedom. Teach 'em to look after themselves. Danny loved it last year."

"I know he did. He hasn't stopped talking about it yet. I'll see what Jack says."

Annie bent to pick up a cotton reel that had rolled from Molly's lap, tossed it to her. "Talking of the lad," she said, "how is he?"

Molly stabbed the needle with some force into the material. "All right."

"Only all right?"

"Yes. Only bad-temperedly, pig-headedly, self-centredly all right."

"Whoops. Sorry I asked."

Molly pulled a face, half-laughing. "No you aren't. And now you know. Here, make yourself useful—" she tossed a small pair of trousers across to Annie, " – unpick those hems, will you? My son's growing like a weed."

Adam Jefferson finally returned in July, and the first that Molly knew of it was one afternoon when Nancy, after her usual peremptory knock, threw open the office door with the words "Visitor for you" and stepped back to allow a smiling, suntanned figure past her.

"I – Good afternoon, Mr Jefferson." The unexpected sight of him was a shock to shorten her breath. How could she have forgotten the slender, physical beauty of the man?

"Mrs Benton. I'm just back from the States. My senior partner suggested that I should call and express our satisfaction with—"

Nancy shut the door.

He crossed the room, dropping his hat and stick on a chair as he passed, his eyes not leaving hers. She watched him come, a helpless excitement sharpening every nerve-end. He bent and kissed her. She did not move, made no attempt to touch nor to stop him. No mouth was like his. None would ever be. His teeth were very sharp. His hand ran the length of her throat, cupped her breast. Then he straightened, smiling, happy.

"I have thought about doing that," he said solemnly, "for four months."

"Liar."

The spreading, long-fingered hands. "I have. I swear. Constantly." He took note of her expression and qualified the word, laughing. "Almost constantly."

She had to laugh with him. "Or 'on and off'?"

"Unkind." He perched on the desk. They looked at each other, smiling, for a long time.

"How was America?"

"Wonderful."

"And successful?"

"Very."

"You seem to have been gone a long time."

"A bloody lifetime." The warm intimacy of his voice brought blood to her cheeks.

"I've come to take you to tea," he said. "And no arguing."

"My coat's in the hall."

They had tea at the Royal, absurdly an old acquaintance of a place now, holding no terrors at all. Adam spoke with enthusiasm of America, made her see the teeming streets of New York, the almost incomprehensibly wide spaces of the West.

"I've a brother there," she said, "and a father too I think."

"I'm not surprised. I sometimes think there must be more Irish in the United States than are left in Ireland. Do you know where they are?"

She shook her head.

"That's a pity. I could have looked them up when I go back."

"You're going back?"

"Not until October."

"But that's—"

" – months away," he finished for her gently. "Don't think about it. That's for tomorrow. This is today."

She looked pensively into her teacup. "That's how you live, isn't it?"

"There's no other way."

As he helped her into her coat he asked, quite suddenly, "Next Thursday?"

She hesitated. "Here?"

He fussed with her coat a little, settling it on her shoulders. "Do you like strawberries and cream?"

"Yes."

He smiled. "Then somewhere else."

"Where?"

"It's a surprise."

The week passed in a pleasant dream. Nothing it seemed could put her out of sorts, things that just a short while before might have sent her into a rage hardly touched the bright surface of her happiness. She would not analyse it. It was simply as if a window had been thrown open in a cold and dark room and sunshine, warmth and the song of birds had flooded in.

On Thursday, however, she discovered herself to be nervous. She was aware for the first time of deception. She had to lie to Nancy about where she was going, had arranged with Adam for him to pick her up in the High Street by the station. Now she stood fiddling nervously with her gloves half-wishing that she had not agreed to go.

"I'll be back by six. Before probably."

"Fine." Nancy did not look up. "Don't worry. If Jensons telephone what shall I tell them? Can they have Miss McPherson for another week?"

"Yes. And if Miss Johnston comes in tell her we've placed her with Tate's, will you? She starts on Monday."

"Right." Nancy looked up as Molly still hovered. "Off you go then. Hope the meeting isn't too much of a bore."

The discomforting feeling of guilt pricked her as she hurried down the busy street. Then she saw him, saw the bright welcome in his eyes and her scruples dissolved like mist in sunshine.

"Where are we going?"

"Wait and see."

They drove through the dense and decaying East End of London to the City. Molly shivered in the warmth as they passed the malodorous alleys, seeing in every face the vicious shadow of Johnny Cribben. "Must we come this way?"

"It's the shortest. But no – we'll go the long way round next time if you'd prefer." Neither of them commented on that 'next time'.

From the City they drove through the crowded streets to the West End. She expected him to stop, as he had before, somewhere here within the fashionable area of shops and hotels, but they chugged on through ever-increasing motor traffic and the chaos of horse-drawn vehicles into the charming and comparatively quiet streets and squares of Kensington. No noisy markets or narrow, crowded pavements here, nor yet that busy, beehive feeling of the City. Elegant mansions, tall, impeccably kept town houses, discreet and very expensive-looking hotels stood in peaceful tree-lined streets or edged the spacious green squares. The car turned into one of these squares; tall-windowed Regency buildings looked out onto a charming garden of lawns and shrubberies and well-established trees. Beyond the decorative iron railings nursemaids wheeled their smaller charges along the winding paths in perambulators, or sat upon the slatted benches talking while older children played together on the grass. Adam rolled the car to a halt at the foot of a flight of marble steps that led to a grand-looking door set between white-painted pillars.

"Where are we?"

He touched his fingers to his lips in a gesture of mystery. "I believe that Madam likes strawberries and cream?"

"Oh, Adam, don't be silly. What's that got to do with—"

"Do you, or don't you?"

"Yes, but it's August. You can't get strawberries and cream in August. Not even," she added glancing up at the tall façade of the building, "in a place like this."

"We'll see about that."

He handed her from the car, led her up the steps and into a lobby, cool and marble-floored, with on one side an enormous, sweeping staircase beneath glittering chandeliers and on the other the open-work wrought iron doors of a magnificently appointed lift.

"Good afternoon, Mr Jefferson sir."

Molly jumped as a small man, smartly uniformed in mulberry

and blue, appeared as if by magic at Adam's elbow. He preceded them to the lift, conducted them into it with a proprietary air, closed the door with a clash, pressed the button. The brass-trimmed monster rose with a muted whirr; floor after floor floated silently past.

Molly looked at Adam. "Where are we?" she asked. And this time her voice brooked no pleasantries.

He was still ready to try. "We are in one of the few places in London where you can get prime strawberries and cream, in copious quantities whatever the time of the year. Well, almost." The lift, with the slightest of jolts, came to a halt and the man slid the ornate doors open onto a small landing whose polished wooden floor showed sign of neither footprint nor dust. There were two doors, imposingly solid, and with brass fittings that were, like those in the lift, shone to gold. Adam waved Molly courteously to one of the doors. The man touched a cap trimmed with more gold than an admiral's, crashed his gates and was gone. Adam fitted a key to the lock.

"This is my home," he said and pushed the door so that it swung easily open to reveal a large room, expensively and tastefully furnished, its long velvet-draped windows looking onto the sun-gilded treetops of the square. It was a pleasantly masculine room, furnished with leather and shining well-polished wood. By the window stood a small table at which were set two chairs and upon which, bright in silver, was laid an enormous dish of crimson strawberries.

Molly did not move.

"Are you coming in?" Adam asked politely, his eyes tranquil, "Or would you rather that we eat our strawberries on the landing?"

She followed him through the door. In the ordered and comfortable main room of the apartment she could detect not the slightest sign of a feminine hand, even the large vase of flowers that stood in the empty summer grate were somehow too perfect, too mathematically arranged.

As he did so uncomfortably often, Adam detected her thoughts. "I said 'my home'," he emphasized quietly, "not 'ours'. Mine. George – the gentleman in the lift – looks after it for me."

"You have your own apartment?" Such an arrangement was far beyond any lifestyle she had ever known.

"Yes. Caroline prefers the country. During the week I live here. It's more comfortable."

"And more – convenient?" She could not quite keep the sharp edge from her tone.

"Yes," he said. "More convenient."

She had not moved. "You play games, Adam. All the time. Charades."

He had stepped very close to her. The beating of her heart was suffocating her. All the laughter had gone from him, the ruthless, shadowed bones of his face were clearly drawn in the golden light.

"No, Molly. Charades is a game for children. My life isn't in the least like that. Do you want me to take you home?" The question was purposely, cruelly blunt.

She could not answer.

"Well, then, stay awhile." The lightness was back, veiling the arrogant core. "It would be a shame to waste the strawberries, wouldn't it? They taste much better at this time of the year, did you know?"

"Because no one else is eating them?"

He took off his jacket, tossed it on a chair. "Exactly. Clever girl. Please, do take off your coat. It's very warm this afternoon."

She let him slip it from her shoulders; beneath it she was wearing a flounced blouse of lawn so fine that it frothed at throat and wrist like foaming water. She had bought it specially, though she had not admitted as much, even to herself. He dropped her coat on the same chair as his own.

She watched him go to the window.

"This is a nice part of London," he said over his shoulder, "quiet."

"Yes." Outlined against the light he looked extraordinarily slight, almost boyish.

"Have you – lived here long?"

"Two years." He turned. "Do you like it?"

"Very much." Other words, other meanings beneath the conventional exchanges hung in the air between them.

"I thought you would." The atmosphere of the closed room

was heavy. "Perhaps I should open a window?"

"Yes. Please. It's a little airless—" She was only vaguely aware of what she was saying. Her nerves were strung like wire.

He made no move to open the window. "Molly?" Musical voice, soft in the quiet room.

She did not answer, fixed her eyes upon the massive cloud of flowers in the grate.

" – You're very beautiful." The words drifted into warm silence.

She shook her head, sucking at her lower lip. She should leave now. Now. She knew it. She sensed his coming, tensed against it.

A sharp-nailed finger ran along her arm, scratching her skin beneath the fine material.

She shivered, but did not move nor look at him.

The caressing finger moved from her arm to her shoulder, the skin of her throat, down to her breast, rubbing the rising nipple gently.

She closed her eyes.

"Beautiful," he said again. His other hand was moving on the tiny buttons.

She tried, half-heartedly, to move away from him. His arm prevented her.

"Please," he said.

She neither helped nor tried to stop him. The blouse dropped in a soft drift of frills at their feet. His fingers were in her hair, drawing out pins and combs. Her shoulders were naked, her breasts half-bared, swollen, the dark nipples jutting through lace and ribbon. He kissed the hollow of her neck. His hands were at the fastenings of her skirt. At last she came to herself and tried to pull away.

"Adam, don't. You mustn't!"

He held her from him, his grip on her shoulders bruising, a dark flash of anger in his eyes. "Mustn't?"

She turned her head away, unable herself to tell where fear gave way to excitement and both to wild hunger.

He shook her, not roughly but insistently, until she turned back to him. "Look at me. That's better. Now listen. I have never – never, do you understand? – taken a woman against her will. Speaking of games, that is one that I will never play, neither to ease a conscience nor to satisfy an ego. I take nothing, I want nothing that is not freely given. Tell me now that you don't want me and I swear I'll not touch you. Tell me."

"I—" Looking at him she could not lie.

"Tell me." His fingers no longer gripped her shoulders; he had opened his hands and was caressing her bare arms with the flat, hard palms.

"I can't. You know that I can't."

He lifted her chin with his finger. "Don't be afraid. We're harming no one."

"I am afraid. I can't help it."

"There can be no child, if that's what's worrying you." He said it simply, with no embarrassment.

"It isn't just that." But she could not deny the lift of relief in her heart.

"I love you," he said.

"Now you do, at this moment."

"Yes. Now. At this moment. What else can you ask? You're lovely, little Molly, lovely." He caught her wrists, drew her to him.

Her eyes held his intent, unsmiling face. She wanted him. Wanted his body, his mouth, his hands, suddenly had to admit to herself that she did not care what he was. Just once. The phrase that has eternally been the precursor to addiction. Just this once. Or for the rest of her life regret it.

He brought his mouth down hard on hers. She lifted her arms, held him; the light-muscled shoulders bunched beneath her fingers. Her skirt and petticoat slid over her hips; she felt him smile against her mouth as his long fingers tangled in the ribbon of her corset. He lifted her, naked, to the smooth, cold leather of a deep couch.

"Bed later," he said, "and later again. And then strawberries. The best you've ever tasted, I promise."

CHAPTER THIRTY

SHE FELT THAT it must, surely, be written all over her – the happiness, the change. She was astonished to find that she could live her life as if nothing had happened. The world around her was absurdly normal. She lived two lives; as wife, mother, businesswoman she continued as she always had, while another Molly lived for the sight of Adam, the sound of his voice, the touch of his graceful, practised body. The sensible Molly, recognizing infatuation, was aware that a flame so fierce was inevitably dangerous. She suffered pangs of guilt at her deception, moments of near-panic at the thought of discovery. But for the moment that other surprising self was in the ascendancy and happiness more than counterbalanced misgiving. They met, when they could, in Adam's apartment. It was not easy, and their meetings were infrequent, a fact that only served to sharpen the hunger that each felt for the other.

In September Annie and Charley took the children to Kent, and while there was never any question that Adam should come to The Larches, Molly found herself more frequently able to visit him. The weeks moved on – October loomed. Adam was going away again. She tried not to think about it, found herself dwelling on the thought more and more often. He would forget her. He would decide to stay in America. She would never see him again—. Adam laughed at her fears, but, typically, was not reassuring at the cost of honesty.

"Who knows about tomorrow? Why ask? Haven't we agreed that it's now that counts? This very minute?" As he spoke the first gust of autumn rain hit against the bedroom window and slid down the glass like tears.

Strangely enough her relationship with Jack improved during this time, perhaps because, due to a strange combination of happiness and guilt, she herself was kinder, less touchy, more considerate than she had been for some time. She still loved Jack; that was one of her earliest and most surprising discoveries

– not in the wild, almost obsessive way in which she loved Adam, if indeed the feeling that she had for Adam could be described as love, but quieter and with roots that went into a shared past that no one else could displace. Jack's presence, his strength, his support, were things she had taken for granted; the knowledge that she might, through her own actions, forfeit them, frightened her. She found herself trying to please him – small, and not entirely selfish attempts to ease her conscience. Their relationship steadied and regained some of its harmony. Above all she knew that she did not want to hurt him.

But she could not, would not, stop seeing Adam.

In early October, two weeks after Adam had left for America, the twins started school, joining Danny, and Molly, with some relief, found her days entirely her own and her energies channelled once more into the agency. There was plenty to keep her busy.

She walked into Nancy's office one day to find her sister-in-law absorbed in a magazine.

Nancy looked up. "Seen this?"

"What is it?"

"First edition of *Votes for Women*. Good cover, isn't it?"

Molly considered the front page. The enormous, thoughtful figure of a seated woman, chin in hand, brooded over the dwarfed Houses of Parliament. "Yes, it is."

" 'The Haunted House', it's called. Clever, mm?" Nancy had wandered to the window. "It isn't raining, is it?"

"No. Why?" Molly looked up sharply. "Oh, Nancy, no. You aren't going chalking again, are you?"

Nancy looked over her shoulder, shrugged, did not reply.

"Where's the meeting?"

"East Ham Town Hall. Tomorrow."

"Well why on earth don't you hand out bills, or stick up posters or something instead of chalking all over pavements and walls?"

"Cheaper," Nancy said succinctly.

"Not very dignified."

"You sound like Jack."

"Is it legal?"

"I don't know."

"Shouldn't you find out?"

"I expect I will one day, one way or another." Nancy, at the door, paused and looked back. "Coming to the meeting?"

"Nancy, I haven't a spare minute tomorrow. You know it."

"Fair enough. What about next Tuesday?"

"Another meeting?"

"Sort of. A get-together at the Edmontons'. In the evening. She particularly asked me to take you along."

Molly shrugged. "I should think I could manage that, at least."

She was amazed – and amused – on that following Tuesday to find herself, as a woman who had started her own business and was making a success of it, something of a celebrity.

"I think it's absolutely splendid, my dear," said Mrs Edmonton, a tall, imposing figure with untidy greying hair that refused to stay neatly in the bun that its owner's maid had composed for it. "A few more like you and we'd have won the battle long ago."

"Oh, I hardly think—"

"Nonsense. You're a pioneer, young woman. Living proof of the stupidity of a society that keeps half its population unproductively in chains. Or tries to. Congratulations. You've done wonderfully well. And Irish too," she added with tactless forthrightness, "my goodness."

"Oh, Mother!" Christopher squirmed with embarrassment.

"What? What's the matter, boy?"

Molly, stifling laughter, left them.

Winter swooped, in gales and rain; Christmas approached.

The children decorated The Larches with paper chains and sprigs of holly. Sarah arrived with considerate and very welcome gifts, the cakes and puddings that she guessed that Molly had not had time to make. Molly hugged and kissed her warmly. "How many more times are you going to save my life, Mam?" She thought for a rare few minutes of Christmasses at home, with her own mother's cakes and puddings, Mass at midnight, the boys and her father sober as judges until the Child was safely born, then off to celebrate and endure thick heads for three days.

On New Year's Day, as she and Nancy tried to organize

themselves for the new year in the slightly hungover atmosphere of the old, the telephone rang.

"Hello?"

"Happy New Year."

She recognized the voice with a jolt of pleasure that was close to pain. "And to you. How long have you been home?"

"A week or so. I came back for Christmas." The line hissed and crackled. "Molly?"

"I'm here."

"Could you make it next Thursday afternoon? I've so much to tell you—"

As soon try to prevent a swallow from flying south. Half-formed resolutions crumpled like paper. "Yes."

And so it began again.

The dark early months of the year passed quickly. Green buds appeared on the dingy plane trees of Plaistow and in the leafless winter garden of a Kensington square. And in March, with daffodils showing a golden promise in the green and the north-moving sun bringing a temperate early warmth, Nancy Benton was arrested again. She and Christopher had been out chalking notices and had been caught by an unsympathetic policeman. Nancy had stood her ground stoutly, refused to rub out the notice, refused to allow herself to be moved on. The policeman had grown abusive; Nancy had given as good as she got. The scene had drawn a crowd, good-humoured, ready to enjoy a show, and Nancy had given them one, delivering a speech that would have been a credit to one of the Pankhursts. The police-man, at the end of his patience, had tried to arrest her. Nancy, to the crowd's delight, had resisted tooth and nail and size five boots.

Christopher Edmonton had run away.

It was very like visiting someone in hospital, Molly thought, seated opposite a Nancy almost unrecognizable in rough, dark arrow-marked dress, coarse pinafore and cap. Conversation was awkward, next to impossible. And the smell . . .

"You and your damned chalk," Molly said, trying to smile brightly.

"Yes." After only a few days Nancy's face was painfully angled, the hollows beneath her eyes were like bruises, yet the strength of her spirit shone through, defying pity. She leaned forward, her face intense. "Molly, we don't have long. There's something I want you to do for me. Go and see Christopher. Tell him not to worry. There was nothing he could have done. Nothing. I don't want him to be unhappy, to think that he let me down."

Molly did not speak, but her expression was enough.

"Please, Moll. Do it for me. Don't let him think that I blame him for—" she hesitated.

"For running away," Molly said bluntly.

"For being sensible and saving himself while he could. You can't fight a war with all your soldiers in prison, can you?"

"You can't fight one by running away, either."

"You don't understand." She ignored the sardonic movement of Molly's mouth. "He'll be terribly upset, I know. Please, go and see him. Tell him what I said. Please, Molly."

"All right. I'll tell him."

Nancy relaxed, sat back in the wooden chair. "Thank you." She smiled, wryly. "I'm sorry. I've done it again, haven't I? Left you in the lurch. Are you managing?"

"I'm saving my nervous collapse for next week, don't worry."

"Is everyone—" Nancy paused, corrected herself with painful honesty. "– Is Jack mad?"

"As a hornet."

"I thought he might be."

"No fine-paying this time."

"I didn't expect it. I just wish that Jack would try to understand, that's all." Nancy made a sudden, exasperated movement; the sombre-looking wardress who stood close by moved a sharp step nearer. "If he'd just come and *see*. That it isn't play. Who'd put up with this for nothing? You'd think, of all people, that my pig-headed brother'd see what it's all about, wouldn't you?"

"He'll come .round," Molly said unconvincedly, "eventually." She was crushed by the oppressive atmosphere, the massive walls, the ugly hostility of the place. "I don't know how you can do it," she admitted softly, "I couldn't. . . ." Then, impulsively, she said, "Nancy, are you sure? I could raise the money. You could be home tomorrow—" She regretted it almost as soon as the words were out, seeing the stubborn pain in Nancy's eyes.

"No. Absolutely no. A couple of weeks. It isn't a lifetime. I'll be all right. Don't pay it. But Molly—"

"Yes?"

"See Christopher for me. Tell him. Anyone can swing a fist. There are other strengths."

"I'll tell him."

"Time's up." The wardress's voice matched her face: closed and sour.

Nancy stood up docilely, flashed a small rebellious smile at Molly and was gone.

A fortnight later she was released, several pounds lighter in weight and totally unreformed. This time Molly was not the only one there to meet her.

"God bless yer, girl," called one of the women who had gathered by the gate, many of them with rosettes and ribbons of white, purple and green pinned to their lapels or decorating the wide brims of their hats.

"Splendid, my dear, splendid. We're all so very proud of you." Mrs Edmonton shook Nancy's hand fiercely. There was no sign of Christopher.

"I did see him, yes," Molly, a little uncomfortably, said later in reply to Nancy's question, "and I told him what you said."

Nancy, hearing the reservation in Molly's tone, eyed her sister-in-law reproachfully, but said no more.

She did not see Christopher until nearly a week after her release, when he came, finally, one soft spring evening, to a house that was empty of everyone but Nancy, Molly having taken the children to visit their grandmother and Jack not yet arrived home from work.

Nancy opened the door to him, greeted him with easy friendliness, ignored his stammering awkwardness, preceded him up the stairs. In the little, slope-ceilinged room he slumped into a chair, not looking at her, his clasped hands dangling loose between his knees, his shoulders drooping.

"I thought you wouldn't let me in. Wouldn't want to see me. I wouldn't have blamed you."

She did not answer, but he would not lift his eyes.

"I told you I was a coward."

"You've told me a lot of things."

"Do you hate me?"

"Christopher Edmonton," she said, softly exasperated, "will you look at me?"

He kept his head down for one more stubborn moment, then lifted it. Tears glinted, slid down his face. "I'm sorry, Nancy, sorry, sorry—" Shame racked him. "I was afraid. Panic-stricken. I ran away. Left you to—" His voice choked to silence.

Nancy stepped closer to him, put her hand on his head and drew it gently to her, as she might that of a distressed child.

"Chris, dear, don't. Please don't. Didn't Molly tell you what I said?"

"Yes. But I could tell what she really thought."

"It doesn't matter. It doesn't matter what anyone thinks. We know. We know each other, and we know the truth. You're kind and you're gentle. That's better than being brute-brave. You're afraid of physical pain—" his head moved against her " – you can't help that. And one day you'll learn to fight it. That's what real courage is. Not lack of fear, but learning to accept and then to face it. To do the things you know you should do in spite of fear. You'll come to it."

"No." He tried to pull away from her.

"Yes! Yes, you will."

Downstairs a door opened and closed.

"I won't! I'll never be able to. I'm a dis – disgusting coward!" He wrenched himself free, flung himself from the chair, away from her.

She caught his arm. "A coward wouldn't be here now."

"It isn't strength that brought me here." He was trembling violently. "It's weakness again. I couldn't stay away. I tried, I knew I should, but I couldn't. I had to see you, even if you hated me, even if you despised me, as I do myself. Why don't you? Oh, Nancy, why don't you?" He was sobbing now, his hand covering his face.

"Christopher," said Nancy, quietly, helplessly, "how could I despise you? How could I?"

His sobs died. He stayed for a long moment half-turned from her, his face still hidden. Then very slowly he turned to face her.

She looked up at him, steadily, compassion in her eyes. "Silly boy," she said, teasing gently.

Blood suddenly suffused his face. "Don't say that! *Don't.* I'm not a boy—" Before she could move his arms were around her, clutching her to him; clumsily he kissed her, with a roughness born of desperation and total inexperience. She felt his tears on her face, tasted their salt. When he released her abruptly, appalled at his own action, she stood stock-still.

"God, Nancy, I'm sorry. I'm sorry."

She reached a cool, thin hand to his face. "Don't be."

The moment was suspended in space, a drop of time, enclosing them in silence and in love. It was Nancy who lifted her face to him. Unbelievingly he bent to her, uncertain, afraid. His kiss was soft, his mouth unsure. She put her arms about his thin frame, drew him to her, feeling the young body tremble against hers.

He caught her to him, hard. "Nancy, Nancy, Nancy—" he said against her mouth.

"*Jesus Christ!*" The voice came from the door that neither of them had heard open. Jack's face was savage. "What in Hell's name's going on here?"

Christopher, his face a sudden, deathly white, released Nancy so sharply that she staggered. His breath rasped in his throat. He stared at Jack's massive, angry figure in a terror that was almost palpable. The tears had not dried on his face.

"You whipper-snapper." Jack advanced on him, fists bunched by his side, his voice shaking. "You snivelling, sneaking little bastard—"

Nancy stepped between them. "Jack—"

"Shut up and get out of my way. I'll deal with you later."

"It wasn't his fault! Jack, please—"

Her brother was holding his blinding rage by the frailest of threads. "Wasn't his fault? Whose, then? Yours? I believe it, Nancy, I believe it. Is this what's been going on up here all this time? In my house – *my house!*"

332

"No!"

"Who else have you had up here, eh?" He caught her by the shoulders, shook her roughly. Christopher watched in petrified anguish. "Jake Aster scared you off men, did he? How many other boys—" he laid disgusted emphasis on the word "have you treated to tea and buns? And what else? Bed?"

Christopher made a small sound and turned away, his shoulders hunched and his eyes tight-closed against the rise of nausea.

Nancy was staring at Jack in angry, desperate pleading. "Jack, don't. Please don't. It isn't what you think."

He let go of her. "Isn't it? Tell me what, then. Parlour games? Poetry? What kind of lessons is our well-educated young friend here giving you? Or you him?"

"Mr Benton." The words were a whisper. Christopher's eyes were sick. "I swear it isn't as you think. And it wasn't Nancy's fault, it was mine. If anyone's to be b – blamed, it's me. I took advantage of her. It – it was a despicable thing to d – do—" He seemed almost to have forgotten in his fear and humiliation how to breathe. The words were gasped.

"Oh, aye, lad. We're agreed on that at least." Jack's voice was held dangerously quiet, hard as stone. The scar stood livid on his cheek. "Nancy, get out. I'll speak to you later."

"No."

"Out, before I throw you out."

"These rooms are mine, Jack. I pay for them. You had no right to come in without knocking."

"This house is mine. *Mine*. And if I choose to ask my sister where my wife and children are, should I knock on a door to do it? Get downstairs." He stepped forward and Christopher Edmonton flinched physically from him.

"You're not to touch him! Don't you dare." Nancy moved protectively between the two.

"Get out of my way."

"No."

Brother and sister glared at one another. "Then get out of my house," Jack said softly, the memory of another such occasion bitter in his words.

"Don't worry. I'm going, Nancy said."

333

CHAPTER THIRTY-ONE

IT WAS FROM Jack that Molly heard the story, a Jack subdued but not ready to admit that he had over-reacted.

"Edward. Jake Aster. Prison. And now a boy of seventeen. She isn't fit to have in the house, Molly. We've the children to consider. She's a bad influence."

"I don't believe that." Molly's voice was quiet.

"You want the girls growing up like our Nancy?"

"They won't. They don't have Nancy's problems."

"If Nancy's problems include a yen for a snivelling, spineless child, then we can thank God for that."

"Jack, I have to say it: I think you're being utterly unreasonable. Apart from anything else I can't possibly manage without Nancy in the office—"

"You must go your own road. But I'll not have her living in this house. And neither will I have that — that perverted whipper-snapper set foot in the door."

Molly looked up sharply. "That's a bit extreme, isn't it?"

Jack's face was closed. "No. It isn't. Now I want to hear no more about it."

Nancy found lodgings a few streets away with a friend. The arrangement was not as convenient as before, but it caused no insurmountable problems as far as the agency was concerned. A couple of months after she had moved out the newspapers announced the engagement of Christopher Edmonton to Felicity Randal, the daughter of one of his mother's friends. The engagement, said the paper, would be a lengthy one, due to the couple's youth. The morning the announcement appeared, Molly eyed her sister-in-law's unresponsive face, but made no comment. In more than two months Jack and Nancy had spoken not a word to each other, and nothing that Molly could do or say would heal the breach. Nancy, in fact, flatly refused to discuss the matter at all, offering neither excuse nor explanation. The little attic flat stood empty. Molly, her own life not exactly simple, gave up arguing about it with both of them and left it to time to bring them together.

In July, and for the first time in London, the Olympic Games were held at the White City Stadium. It had been built especially for this prestigious occasion, and the whole city went Olympics mad. Edward, Jack and Danny were among the crowds that lined the streets from Windsor to the White City to watch the marathon runners, and throughout the event Londoners in their thousands turned out to cheer the home country's fifty-six gold medals. Such success diverted the mind from unemployment and rising prices, from marked and growing unrest.

"Bread and circuses," Adam said idly to Molly during one of their snatched afternoons at his apartment. "It works every time."

Molly's temper, that afternoon, was strained. Two days before she had seen Adam's car draw up outside Stratford station. Impulsively she had hurried forward, to see Adam, smiling, swing a pretty, laughing girl to the ground and escort her into the booking hall. Neither of them had noticed her. All this afternoon she had been on the brink of asking, of demanding, but had so far said nothing.

"Not every time," she said now, shortly. "The whole world isn't stupid, you know."

"Isn't it?" Adam was still good-tempered. "You surprise me."

"Don't be smug."

"What else can I be when the whole of London appears to have lost its senses over some idiots who are willing to kill themselves in this heat in order to run faster or jump higher, or whatever, than anyone else? It's madness."

"Especially when they don't get paid for it."

"Quite."

"I thought that'd get in somewhere."

"So you were right. So now you can feel smug too." The merest edge of irritation had crept into his voice. "What's got into you this afternoon?"

"Nothing," she said. "I'm tired, that's all. We've been very busy, and I've been single-handed for most of this week—'

He laughed. "What's Nancy campaigning about now?"

"Sweated labour. Women and children. She's got friendly with an organizer of something called the National Federation of Women Workers. They're doing some kind of survey—"

Adam, lying on his back naked beside her, his arms folded behind his head, made a derisive sound.

Molly came up on one elbow, "You've heard of them?"

"Heard of them? I should say so. I doubt there's anyone who employs women between here and John O'Groats who hasn't. A bigger set of interfering biddies I've never come across. When it comes to business they don't know their—" he paused, grinning, " – their rear ends from their elbows. But needless to say they don't let that stop them from telling those who do how to run their affairs."

"That isn't what Nancy says." Molly reached for her clothes, her mind only partly on the conversation.

"No, I don't expect that it is."

"They're trying to stop the exploitation of women and children in the sweatshops."

"Fine words. What do they mean?"

That needled her to sharpness. "You know as well as I do. There are women and children working, living – and dying – in conditions that a decent man wouldn't keep a dog in. And not a million miles from here, either. Slave labour. In one of the richest countries in the world? Living off the lifeblood of people too weak to fight for themselves? It's a disgrace. You don't have to be a Suffragette – or a Union man – to know that."

He looked at her in some amusement, but the expression in his eyes was wary. "Has Nancy made a convert?"

"She didn't have to. No sane person could defend the sweated labour system. Women are blinded, children die of diseases born of filth. If the miners can win an eight hour day, who's to say that these poor souls must work all day and half-way through the night in terrible conditions and for next-to-nothing?" Molly wrestled with a tangled ribbon on her petticoat. "D'you know what a girl gets paid for matchbox making? Twopence farthing a gross. A gross! And they have to buy their own paste. How would you like it? Working sixteen hours out of twenty-four to bring in a wage of a few shillings a week?" She buttoned herself into her dress, her movements angry.

Adam said nothing. He swung his legs over the edge of the bed, reached for his shirt, pulled it over his head.

"Do you have any idea of the cost, in suffering, of that fancy shirt?" Molly was watching him.

"No," he said, unruffled.

"And you don't care, either."

He looked up, anger very close. "There you go again. If you're trying to pick a fight, then for God's sake try to find something more plausible than my bloody shirt."

Her colour high, she turned to the mirror and began tidying her hair.

"Molly? What's wrong?"

She stared, seeing not her blurred reflection in the mirror, but the pretty face, the small, proprietary hands upon Adam's shoulders. "Nothing," she said. She had to be fair. He had never said, never pretended, that he would be faithful. Faithful? What a word to use.

There was movement in the mirror. Adam had come up behind her and was watching her, over her shoulder in the glass, his face hard. "I've told you before that I don't play games," he said. "If you didn't want to come this afternoon you had only to say so."

Miserably she tugged at her hair.

"No one is forcing you to come. Not now. Not ever."

Her heart had begun to thump – a heavy, slow beating that seemed to fill her body, making her breathless. Still she fiddled with her hair.

He reached for her wrist, held it still. "Well?"

She shook her head. The fingers that wrapped, long and strong, around her arm were not gentle. Without releasing her he turned her to face him. "Do you want to finish it?" he asked very quietly, "Is that it?"

"No!" The denial was involuntarily and humiliatingly violent, cutting across his words. "No," she said again, more quietly.

"What, then?"

She avoided his eyes. "Nothing. Nothing, truly. I told you,

I'm tired. I'm out of sorts this afternoon. I – I have a headache."

"Then why didn't you say so?" He was not placated.

"I didn't want to – make a fuss." It did not sound convincing, even to her. "It's the weather I expect. It's so hot and sticky—"

He watched her for a long moment, then let go of her wrist, the anger clearing from his face. He dropped a light kiss onto the top of her head. "Silly girl. You should have told me. I'll find something for your headache before I take you home."

On a sunny August day Molly, as a favour to Nancy, conducted a representative from the National Federation of Women Workers in a short and pre-arranged tour of some of the Venture Employment Bureau's clients. She did not include Stowe, Jefferson and Partners in the itinerary.

Ellie Boston, an abrasive and tactless young woman with plain, aggressive features and unfashionably short dark hair was, despite her obviously preformed opinions, favourably impressed.

"But then, conditions in offices have always been better than those in the factory or the shop, both for men and women," she said. "It's the sweated labour problem that I'm most concerned with. Are you coming on Wednesday?"

"Wednesday?"

"I'm taking Nancy to see some of the sweatshops. You can't campaign unless you know, first hand, what you're campaigning for. Or against. Coming?"

Molly's heart sank. "Oh, no, I don't think—"

"We aren't going till four. You can leave the office for an hour or so, can't you?"

"Well—"

Ellie smiled an unpleasant smile. "I see. You just give donations, do you, Mrs Benton? Leave others to stick their noses in where they aren't wanted? Actually to try to do something? Can't say I blame you. You and ninety-nine per cent of the rest of the world. But Nancy'll be disappointed. She seemed to think you'd want to come."

Molly was stung. "I didn't say I wouldn't come. I just said it was difficult, that's all."

"Wait for easy and you'll wait for ever. Come with us, Mrs

Benton. I'll show you things that you haven't read about in the papers. You're an employer yourself, after all. You should know about these things."

The garret was an oven, a squalid and filthy oven beneath bare, cobwebbed rafters and broken slates. In the winter, blood would freeze. A half-naked baby crawled on the floor, tethered by a piece of rope to the leg of its mother's chair, for the narrow stairs that led directly from the lower room were not banistered, the stairwell was an unguarded and dangerous edge, a sheer drop to the floor below.

Molly held her breath. The stench was appalling. And familiar. The hateful smell of poverty, of hopelessness, of dirt and disease. She loathed it, as she loathed the defeated look on the worn face of the woman, the scabs and scars on the baby's skin, the rat's tail, unwashed and obviously lice-ridden hair of the two small girls who sat at the table with their mother, bending stiff cardboard with sore, calloused fingers, pasting, making boxes.

Ellie Boston, her brusque tongue gentled, laid a few pence on the table and said, "There you are, Bet. Not much, I'm afraid, but the best we can do this week."

"Thanks, Miss." The woman did not stop working, hardly looked up.

In the comparatively fresh air of the street Ellie looked at Molly and Nancy. "You two had enough?" There was painful, frustrated fury in her that needed, it seemed, to be vented in rudeness. "You looked pretty sick up there."

"Of course not," Nancy said stoutly before Molly could open her mouth. "Where are we going now?"

Ellie turned and trudged off down the dirty streets. "Whitechapel," she said over her shoulder. "I've got a message to deliver."

Molly's heart turned over. "Nancy!"

Nancy stopped. "Yes?" She looked tired. Ellie was a long way ahead, hurrying.

"Nothing."

The streets were not familiar; ten years is a long time, and during her stay with Johnny Cribben Molly had seen very little of her surroundings. Whitechapel. The very name had terrified her. Yet here she was, and it was, after all, just another place. There could be nothing to fear. Not now. Not after all this time. But even as she thought it she found herself scanning anxiously every face, every window that they passed.

Ellie stopped outside a decaying clutter of buildings. "Here we are," she said, leading the way into the same depressing dereliction of peeling walls, rickety stairs, doorless holes draped with ragged curtains of dirty blankets that they had seen so often this afternoon. Somewhere a child shrieked, a man's voice was raised in anger. An unappetizing smell of cooking hung on the air, competing with other even less savoury odours. A lavatory door in the yard outside stood permanently jammed open. Even Ellie pulled a face as they passed it.

She led them up several flights of dark stairs, stopped at the bottom of a short run of steps that led up to a curtained doorway. "Dolly? You there? All right if we come up?"

Molly was surprised and uneasy; for the first time today she detected in their guide the faintest air of caution.

A girl's head appeared above them. "If yer quick. 'E'll be rahnd later. But we've got 'alf 'our or so."

Ellie led the way up the steps and into a long narrow room in which were several women and children, heads bent over their work, needles flying. None of them bothered to look up. Battered trestle beds were stacked at one end of the room, indicating that several people lived as well as worked here. Scraps of material littered the floor, were piled into heaps in corners, stuffed into broken window panes and in wide cracks in the walls. Near where Molly was standing lay an old newspaper, the edge shredded and torn. Rats. Molly shivered.

The girl called Dolly was as thin and dirty as any of the other women, and her eyes showed the same overstrained exhaustion. Her speech was almost unintelligible. Yet there was something in the intense, haggard face, in the ugly voice, that caught the attention. Beneath the brutalized surface was a sharp intelligence.

"What did yer fink of it?" she asked Ellie tersely, with no preamble.

"It was marvellous. Just what we were looking for. Have you managed to do any more?"

The girl went to a corner, delved into a pile of scraps, pulled out a couple of grubby sheets of crumpled paper that were covered in untidy writing. "Sod them rats. Little bleeders. Look at that." She smoothed out a nibbled corner. "This'll 'ave ter be yer lot. 'E nearly caught me at it the other day. It'll be me fer the chop if 'e does."

"That's the first sensible fing you've said in weeks," said a woman of indeterminate age who was sitting nearby, without lifting her reddened eyes from her work. "Bleedin' trouble-makers the lot of yer."

Dolly spat, accurately, "Shut yer mahf."

Ellie took the paper. "Thanks, love. The other will be in next week's edition, this'll make the week after. It'll stir things up if anything can. Here." She handed over a couple of silver coins.

The older woman looked up sharply. "D'yer mean ter say yer've been scribblin' that bleedin' stuff fer the *papers?*"

Dolly pocketed the coins. "What if I 'ave?"

"You out yer bleedin' mind or somefink? Yer fink the boss can't read? Jesus, girl, I wouldn't want ter be in your shoes when 'e sees that. Silly cow."

"We've changed the names," Ellie said soothingly. "No one's going to find out who wrote it."

"Why don't yer write yer own rubbish?"

"Because Dolly's stuff is authentic. No amount of study can make up for experience."

Molly moved away from the argument, found herself near the window which looked down into a narrow alleyway, four stories below. The light was fading. With a shock she remembered slippery, crumbling roofs and wet lamplit cobbles, and her stomach stirred. As she stepped sharply back a small boy with an armful of garments cannoned into her.

"Sorry, Miss."

"It was my fault." She watched him throw back a stained blanket from a stack of clean cardboard boxes. For a moment the significance of the lettering on the boxes did not strike her. Carefully the boy folded intricately tucked and embroidered blouses and laid them, one by one, in a square, tissue-lined box. Upon whose lid was neatly stencilled the words "Stowe, Jefferson and Partners."

From a distance Molly heard Dolly saying, "You'd better be orf. 'E's due back any minute. 'E really 'ates you do-gooders." Her smile was mirthless.

The boy threw the blanket back across the boxes to protect them from the dirt of their surroundings, and glanced out of the window. "Bit late," he said, laconically. " 'E's 'ere. Comin' up now. Wiv a friend."

"God Almighty. There's only one staircase. You'll 'ave to 'ide. Not 'ere. There's not room. Dahn the steps. Door to the left. Storeroom. 'Urry, fer Christ's sake—"

"Molly! Come on!" Nancy grabbed Molly's arm, hauled her towards the doorway. As she passed the window Molly looked down. Two men were walking briskly towards the door below, one short, fat, balding, the other much taller, dark, wide-shouldered. "Come *on!*"

She ran down the short flight of steps behind the other two, heard Dolly's voice behind them, sharp and vicious, presumably to the older woman. "One word out of you, one word, and I'll 'ave yer eyes."

The store room was little more than a cupboard, and the door did not shut properly. They squeezed in, stood with pounding hearts listening to the approach of footsteps on the creaking stairs.

"Isn't this a bit silly?" whispered Nancy.

Ellie shook her head grimly. "Not from what I've heard of Bernie Anderson it isn't. Sssh!"

The steps came nearer. Molly tried not to think about the wide-shouldered, striding figure she had seen from the window. It couldn't have been. There must be thousands of big, dark men in this part of the East End. Yet she trembled, strained her ears as men's voices came very close.

"Yer drive an 'ard bargain, I'll say that fer yer." A cracked and wheezing voice, short of breath, making heavy weather of the stairs.

"The only kind." The words were easy, quiet. And familiar? Was the voice familiar?

Their footsteps passed the storeroom door, went on up the steps to the room above.

" 'Ello, girls. Workin' 'ard? That's the ticket, that's the ticket—"

Finger to lips Ellie led the way onto the dark landing and the three girls fled down the stairs to the street.

She faced him in fury, the shock and the fear still sick in her.

"How could you? Adam, how could you? Why didn't you tell me when we were talking about it?"

"Molly, you're being totally unreasonable. I run a business. I leave others to run theirs."

"A business! You make it sound like a respectable tailor's shop! Have you got any idea what those places are like? Have you?"

He shrugged. His mouth was a harsh and angry line. "Of course not. Why should I have? I wouldn't get within five miles of them. And neither should you. You're being quite ridiculously emotional about the whole thing." Adam stood up, the movement abrupt. "Why the Hell did you go if you couldn't take it? You can't tell me that you didn't know what it would be like? Nor that you were naive enough to believe that a firm like ours didn't use sweated labour?"

"Women, little children, working for ha'pennies. Living in squalor. Starving. Bullied by brutes who exploit their weakness so that you and I can make a handsome profit." She did not know if it had been Johnny Cribben who had passed so close to her on the stairs. The mere possibility was enough. "Adam, how could you use them so?"

"Me? You make it sound as if I personally stand over them with a whip! Have you gone crazy or something? You've lost all sense of proportion—" He was really angry now. They faced each other, blazing, ready to hurt. "I buy and I sell. Full stop. Where the stuff comes from, how it's made—that isn't my problem. If people are stupid enough to let others exploit them, then I'm not crying for them. We're all exploited, make no mistake about that. But some of us have the guts and the intelligence to do something about it. I'm not in business as a charity, for God's sake! If you're going to turn into a Joan of Arc at this stage then you can take your banners elsewhere. You won't convert me. I work, and I work damned hard. I'm in business to—"

" – make a profit," she finished for him contemptuously.

"Damned right. Who are you to shout? Your money's in it too, isn't it? You didn't enquire too closely when I doubled your investment in a year—"

She stared at him. "My money? Danny's? Invested in that despicable business?"

He said nothing.

She made a short, bitter sound, almost laughter. "I might have known it. That money. Ellen's God-forsaken money. What good can come out of it?" She picked up her gloves. "I want every penny of it back. No profit. Just the original investment."

"As you wish." His voice was the crackle of ice.

"I want any profit that has been made given to Ellie Boston to help those women."

"That you will have to do yourself. I'll have no part of it." He might have been speaking to a stranger.

"Very well." She walked to the door.

"Molly," he said, very quiet and very cold.

She stopped.

"Don't ever try to interfere with my business life again."

She reached the door, opened it. "Adam," she said with fierce clarity, "I promise that I will never interfere with any part of your life again. Ever." And she shut the door, quiet and sharp, on his disbelieving face.

CHAPTER THIRTY-TWO

THE FOLLOWING MONTHS saw, thanks to Molly's efforts, growing success for the Venture Employment Agency, even at a time of growing industrial problems for the country as a whole and of rapidly increasing and chronic unemployment. She channelled every ounce of her energy into the agency, determined in these difficult times not to see it fail. But even she, preoccupied as she was, could not ignore the growing tension around her.

Month by month during 1909 the political temperature of the country rose feverishly as the Liberal Government under its new leader Herbert Henry Asquith battled through its programme of social reform, fighting both Lords and Commons, facing bitter and acrimonious opposition from those with most practical power in the land: that small percentage of people who controlled the vast bulk of the nation's wealth, and who were not prepared to see the price of the reforms come from their pockets, no matter how well-lined. At the Treasury, David Lloyd George tried to push through his so-called 'People's Budget'. Old age pensions had been introduced for the first day of the new year – five shillings a week for people over seventy years of age. It meant security in old age, independence for many who had lived in the shadow of starvation and destitution. But the scheme had to be financed. The Government set about the task of convincing the Lords that reform was inestimably preferable to revolution. Labour Exchanges were planned in an attempt to alleviate the ever-increasing employment problem, but as the dole queues lengthened, bitterness seeped through idle hours and the mass of the working people were stirring.

Nancy was jubilant when, later in the year, the Trade Board Act established boards with powers to fix minimum wages for workers in many sweated industries. At political meetings up and down the country the old order and those who were attempting to challenge it clashed, sometimes violently. And, obstinately in the thick of the disturbances, often at the heart of them, were the Suffragettes. Because of their success in disrupting political meetings women were banned from attending them; they therefore resorted to subterfuge and disguise, to any ruse that might lead to their voices being heard. They hid overnight in halls that had been hired for political meetings, and interrupted the proceedings from cupboards, from lavatories, from beneath the boards of the stage, denouncing Asquith, their sworn enemy, questioning Liberal politicians. They gate-crashed political gatherings dressed in their husbands' or their brothers' clothes – quite frequently with the men's connivance and approval; they waylaid Asquith's Ministers wherever they might be found, at home, at work, on holiday. They threw bags of flour, rotten fruit, eggs and, occasionally, stones. They were physically ejected from meetings, lampooned, ridiculed, arrested. Yet for all that, more and more people were ready to listen. On occasion a crowd, instead of shouting down a disruptive woman, would cheer and encourage her. But the face of authority was turned implacably against them. Deputations were sent to the Prime Minister, who refused even to see or speak to them. They held meetings of their own, campaigned against Liberal politicians, all to no good effect. So action was stepped up as the year wore on, and the voices of those who still favoured orderly and peaceful protest were drowned in the growing militancy of women determined to be heard at all costs. They mounted an assault on the Houses of Parliament, smashed the windows of government offices; many were arrested and, on non-payment of fines, imprisoned. Refused the status of political prisoners they went on hunger strike and gained early release. They broke more windows, disrupted more meetings, threw stones and bottles. Feeling against them hardened. Their actions now constituted a public menace rather than mere nuisance. The next Suffragette hunger striker was forcibly fed. The uproar that ensued came not only from the women themselves, but the authorities, mistakenly convinced that no woman could endure such torture for long without breaking, continued the barbaric practice. Nancy embraced the new and more aggressive tactics wholeheartedly. In the course of the year she was twice arrested, once goaled and released when she went on hunger strike, before the introduction of forcible feeding. The family, necessarily, resigned themselves to her activities. Nothing anyone could say would stop her. The rift between her and Jack widened; they were coldly polite when they had to meet, never spoke unless it was forced upon them by circumstance. When, in the late months of the year, the constitutional crisis deepened as the 'People's Budget' was thrown hook, line and sinker out of the House of Lords and an early General Election became inevitable, each threw themselves into their separate campaign with a shared fervour.

Molly simply drowned herself in work. It was the only thing that came near to defeating the pain of the break with Adam. As the general demand for labour slackened she made certain that her girls were the best trained, the most efficient, the most likely to be chosen for a post. She drove herself hard, and as a reward saw the Venture Agency established, prospering and secure. She persuaded Jack to allow her to send the children to small local fee-paying schools, and she could never suppress a small lift of pride as they set off each morning, soaped and scrubbed and smartly uniformed, hair slicked down and books tucked tidily beneath their arms. Their reports were predictable: Danny, very bright but distressingly lazy and totally uninterested in his lessons; Meghan as clever as her brother but with an application and far-sightedness that he lacked, and a desire to shine that kept her always half a step ahead of her nearest rival; and Kitty, gentle, popular with the vast majority of the people about her – which could not always be said by any means of the other two – and hardworking.

As another Christmas approached, the last of the decade, an air of excitement and festivity filled The Larches. On a shopping expedition Molly passed the Royal Hotel. She stopped a little way along the road, the strains of Strauss hurtful in her ears, staring into a toy shop window in which had been set up a miniature theatre, the flat, bright, cardboard figures blurring behind the rain-wet glass. This would be the second Christmas since she had seen Adam Jefferson. Surely the pain could not last much longer? Despite herself she still thought of him, could not prevent in quiet moments the assault of the memory of his aggressive vigour, his laughter, his loving. The wound had not healed cleanly. The separation had been too sudden, had come too soon. The festering ache was still there, more than a year later. Recovery was a slow business.

They had a quiet Christmas. With Nancy staying with Sarah and Edward, only Charley and Annie were at The Larches for Christmas Day. While the women washed up after an absurdly enormous meal and the twins and Danny played absorbedly with a cardboard toy theatre, Charley and Jack sat with their feet stretched to the hearth in the parlour discussing the coming elections.

"How do you rate Will Thorne's chances in the election, then?" Charley asked.

"He'll get in all right. Not much doubt about that. Though it's been a dirty campaign, one way and another. But they'll not oust Will from West Ham."

Jack stirred the fire with the poker.

"Word is," Charley said after a moment, "that there's trouble stirring. And that you aren't the most popular lad in the world up some Union alleys."

Jack shrugged. "You could say that." Charley waited. "I've never made any secret of my views, Charley, you know that as well as anyone. I don't hold with violence, political or otherwise. I'll not be ruled by thugs, and I'll not join them in ruling others. There's no advantage for the ordinary working man in that lot. Revolution? They just want to exchange one tyranny – that's their favourite word – for another. I'll campaign for Will Thorne, a good Labour man, and by Christ I'll see him elected. What we need is a strong Labour Party in the House of Commons. But I'll have nowt to do with using strikes for political ends, nor with encouraging violence. They want the troops on the streets, those fellers; they'll see their mates shot down. The ends justify the means. Not for me they don't."

"There's a lot who feel differently."

"I know it."

"If you two can't find something better to talk about than that on Christmas Day," Annie said disgustedly from the door, "then you can come and do the washing up while Molly and me sit with our feet up."

"Ask Jack to open the port," Molly called from the kitchen. "The glasses are in the sideboard. I've just got some rubbish to take out to the dustbin."

A blast of wintry air met her as she opened the door. Head down against the cold, sleety rain, she ran through the dark afternoon to the corner where the dustbin stood. As she turned from it a flash of movement caught her eye and her heart jumped to her throat as a figure loomed from the shadow by the side of the house. Before she could move or cry out a hand was clamped over her mouth and a strong arm had encircled her shoulders and upper arms.

"Be still." The man's voice was gruff. He smelled foul, and his breath was bad. After that first, stunned moment, she struggled fiercely, kicking, biting, tossing her head to free her mouth. It was a full minute before she realized that her captor was calling her by name.

"Molly, Molly. Little wildcat. You always were. Be still, me darlin', be still." The soft accent of Ireland. She stopped struggling and stood quiet, breathing heavily, her back still crushed against his chest.

"That's better, now. That's a good girl." He spoke as if gentling an animal. Warily he took his hard, dirty hand from her mouth. "I'm sorry, girl, I didn't want to frighten you. But God's Truth, I'm enough to frighten anyone the way I look, and if you'd screamed—"

She turned to face him. A tall man, lean, emaciated, his black hair a tangle, curly as her own, wet with winter rain. In a dark, unshaven face, his eyes were bright and wild. He was bigger than she remembered him, and with harshly bitter lines etched in the face she had known. She had last seen him twelve years before, his blood seeping into the gutters of a village street on a day that sometimes returned in nightmares.

"Cormac?" she asked.

Her brother's teeth shone, white and wolfish in the half-dark. "Himself. Large as life and twice as hungry."

She reached a trembling hand to touch him. "But – where have you come from? How did you find me?" Like twins they had been, only eleven months between them and in and out of mischief together all their young lives. "Cormac! Oh, Cormac!"

She was in his arms; he held her clamped to him, his face clenched against tears of his own.

"I need help," he muttered at last. "Food. Shelter. Can you hide me, Moll?"

"Hide you?" She pulled away from him, looked up into his face. "What now? What have you done?"

"I'll tell you later. Just get me in, girl, out of this cursed rain. I feel as if I've not been dry for a week."

"But it's Christmas Day. I've people in – family. Will I tell them—?"

"No!" He caught her arm, roughly. "No one. You'll tell no one. It's a hanging this time for sure if they catch me."

"But—"

"No, I say. They're English, aren't they, this – family of yours?"

"Yes."

"Then I'll not trust them. Have you not a shed – a cellar – anywhere where I'll be dry and can sleep?"

She thought swiftly. "I've better than that. But we'll have to be careful. Go round to the front door. Wait in the porch. I'll come as quick as I can. When I let you in go straight up the stairs, along the landing, up the steps at the end. There's rooms in the attic. Comfortable rooms. A bed."

"Jesus," he said, and the heartfelt thankfulness in his voice brought stinging tears to her eyes.

She watched him, listened to his uneven footsteps as he limped quickly into the gloom. Then she ran to the small flower bed that edged the path, pushed her hands into the cold, clinging mud, wiped them down her already bedraggled dress.

Jack and Annie stared as she opened the parlour door. Jack half-rose from his chair. "Why, Molly love, what's happened?"

She wiped her wild hair back with a muddy hand. "It's all right, nothing to worry about," she laughed shakily. "Daft ha'porth I am. I fell over, in the garden. Danny left his toy engine on the path."

Annie hurried to her. "Are you sure you're not hurt? You're white as a sheet."

"No, truly, I'm all right."

"Here," Jack said handing her a glass of port that had been

standing ready on the sideboard, "drink this."

Thankfully she sipped it. As warmth from the fire and from the drink crept through her body, her hand steadied. "Well, now," she said, almost calmly, "I'd better go and change. I look like something the cat dragged in."

"I'll come with you." Annie was at the door.

"No!" Molly saw Charley's head move as he registered the sharpness of her tone. Wild with impatience she forced herself to smile. "Honestly, Annie, I'm not hurt. Stay and drink your port. I'll be down directly. I've just to wash my hands and face and change my dress.

The long hall, with the lamps not yet lit, was shadowed and dim. From the closed door of the dining room came the sound of the children's voices, raised inevitably in argument. Molly shut the parlour door firmly behind her, listened for a moment then sped to the front door. Cormac was propped against the side of the porch, shivering, his eyes closed.

She pulled him into the hall, jerked her head silently at the stairs, closed the door painfully slowly to prevent its creaking. He was halfway up the stairs, swinging his stiff leg with practised speed. She hurried after him, shepherded him along the landing to the bottom of the short flight of steps that led up to the attic rooms.

"Go on up. I won't be a minute."

She grabbed an armful of spare blankets from a chest in the girls' room, ran up the stairs. Cormac had found the bed, which was stripped to the bare mattress, and had toppled onto it like a fallen tree. Already he was almost asleep.

"Cormac, get up! You can't sleep in those things. You'll catch your death!" Desperately she dragged him to a sitting position, helped him to pull off his shabby coat and wet trousers. "Here, wrap yourself in this. I'm sorry it's so cold up here. But I can't light the fire—" She wrapped him in the thickest, softest blanket and as soon as she was finished he fell sideways, drew his knees up to his chest like an exhausted child. She tucked the other blankets snugly around him.

He moved his head, without opening his eyes, muttered into the pillow.

"What?" she leaned closer.

"Don't – tell anyone."

"I won't. I promise I won't. I'll come back as soon as I can with some food. I'll have to lock you in——" That brought one eye open. His body tensed. "I have to, Cormac, the children play up here sometimes."

The thin frame relaxed again. "Whatever you say," he said, and slept.

She smuggled food up to him, later, before she went to bed, and a glass of whisky. For a moment as she bent over him in the darkness it seemed that he must be unconscious, or dead, so still was he. Then she felt his warmth, heard the light, shallow breathing. He was sleeping the sleep of utter exhaustion. She set the food on a small table near him. In the light of her lamp the lines of his unshaven face were softened, almost he looked again the boy she had known.

It was the next afternoon before she finally contrived to be alone in the house with him. With Jack and the children packed off on an errand to Sarah's she flew up the stairs and unlocked the attic door. Her brother was sitting on the bed, his tousled head in his hands. As he jerked upright there was a wildness about him that made her think of a hunted animal.

"Come downstairs," she said. "There's food, and a fire. We're safe for a while. The others won't be back for a couple of hours."

He sat in Jack's big chair before the fire, his head back and his eyes closed. "You've done all right for yourself?"

"Yes. Here." Molly handed him a glass with an inch of golden whisky in the bottom. "Make it last. If I take any more Jack'll think I'm hitting the bottle."

He toasted her, tossed it back in one gulp, grinned at the look of exasperation on her face. "Learned a long time ago to make the most of what I've got while I've got it." He held the empty glass on the flat, filthy palm of his hand.

"All right. Just one more." She poured it, handed it to him. "Now, let's hear it. What's happened? How on earth did you find me? Who's after you?"

"In that order?"

"In any order."

"Let's start at the end, then. Who's after me? The police, the

Army. God and all His angels for all I know. You call it, they're all after Cormac O'Dowd." It was said with no bravado, tiredly.

"Why?"

He leaned forward, elbows on knees, stared into the fire. "Because I got tired of their hospitality."

"You escaped from prison?"

"I did."

"And?"

"And killed one of the bastards on the way out. Maybe two." The bitterness in his voice and face had returned.

Molly let out a long, slow, unsurprised breath. "I don't understand how you found me?"

Without looking at her he dug into his breast pocket, pulled out a much-folded and tattered piece of newspaper, held it out.

Molly stared at it. "Good God," she said.

"It's a good likeness. And coming out of Holloway, too. A chip off the old block after all, eh, Moll?"

"I wasn't – oh, never mind. Where on earth did you get it?"

"In an English gaol you get English newspapers. Even in Ireland. Oh, yes, I can read as well as yourself now, thanks to the English. At least I've something to show for twelve stinking years."

"You mean you saw this, how many years ago? Two? Three? And recognized me?"

"Look in the mirror, girl, and then look at me. I'd recognize you with your head in a sack. You knew me yesterday, didn't you? Even with this," he said rubbing his black-stubbled jaw.

"If you knew where I was, why didn't you get in touch? Why didn't you write?"

He looked at her quietly for a long time. "Would you have wanted me to?"

She got up, fetched the bottle from the sideboard. He extended his empty glass in silence.

"How did you get this far?" Molly tipped the bottle and the rich liquid splashed.

"I got out with a mate, Paddy Butler. He had contacts in the docks at Dublin. We stowed on a boat for Liverpool. Plan was that we should contact an organization there that arranges passages to America for—" he smiled acidly " – us Irish patriots."

"What went wrong?"

"What always goes wrong? Someone got themselves bought. Or scared. The Army was waiting for us. I got away. Paddy didn't."

"He was caught?"

"He was shot. Dead. They saved themselves the rope. Damn their putrid souls." His fingers round the glass were bone-white.

"So now what?"

He shook his head. "You tell me, girl. I've no friends and no money. I took a chance on this—" he indicated the faded newspaper picture. "It's taken me near two weeks to find you. I'm finished."

Panic rose. Every moment he spent in the house meant danger; danger to the children, danger to Jack, danger to herself.

"But this organization you spoke of—?"

"You joking? After what happened? I'd have to be crazy to go back to them. No."

"I've some money," she said, "and some clothes of Jack's. They'll be a bit big, but they're better than the ones you've got—"

He lifted his head. "You're right, girl. I know what you're thinking, I shouldn't have come."

"I've children, Cormac, three of them—"

"So I'm an uncle, am I?" Beneath the tired smile was defeat. And fear. She could not bear to see it.

"I can give you money," she said again.

He laughed, short and sharp. "And I'll be takin' it to the nice man at the ticket office, will I? And askin' him politely for fast passage to America? Me feet wouldn't touch the ground. Not for long, anyway."

The germ of a disturbing idea moved in Molly's mind. She pushed it away.

"So what will you do?"

He buried his head in his hands. "I don't know, for Christ's sake! But I'll tell you this. I've not come this far to be taken easy. And I'll not be dragged home to hang. When it comes I'll go down fighting, and take as many of the bastards with me as I can."

"Don't talk like that."

"What else? If I can't get out of the country they'll nab me sooner or later. We both know it."

And possibly me, Jack and the children with you. She did not say it. She looked at the thin frame, the hunched shoulders, thought of a childhood shared. Against the stakes at hazard here personal pride counted not at all. If she had to beg Cormac's life from the only man she could think of who might be in a position to help, then so be it. Standing up she walked to the window, stood staring into the garden. "Supposing," she said at last into the silence, "that I said that I might know someone who could help you?"

"Help me?"

"To get to America."

"Who?"

"You don't have to know that. I'm not even promising that I can – persuade him. . . . " The pause was fractional. "I haven't seen him for some time. Are you willing for me to try? There's obvious danger in asking someone else's help."

"There's danger in breathing for me. Do you trust this feller?"

"Trust is a funny word," she said drily. "Let's just say that I don't think it would be to his advantage to betray you. Even if he can't help, I don't think he'd tell on us."

Cormac was watching her closely, his eyes her own smoky blue in spiked, soot-blacked lashes. "You're an O'Dowd to your boots, girl, however much you might try to deny it. The poor feller doesn't stand a chance."

She turned to leave and with a fleeting, crooked smile said, "Don't bank on it."

The ornate lift clanked upwards wretchedly slowly. George, dapper as ever, stared straight ahead as the landings slipped past, his face expressionless. Molly marshalled her nerve; Adam's voice on the telephone had been cool, – it was New Year's Eve, he had arrangements—

Molly, who had been trying unsuccessfully for some days to get in touch with him had been reduced to pleading.

"Adam, please. It's very important. I wouldn't trouble you otherwise, you know it—"

There had been an interminable and nerve-wracking pause. "Very well. This afternoon. My apartment. Four o'clock."

She looked now at the little enamelled corsage watch that hung from her lapel. Ten past. The traffic had been awful. Supposing he hadn't waited? The lift lurched to a stop. George, his eyes impersonal, slid the gates open. She stepped past him, high colour in her cheeks, knocked on Adam's door feeling the little man's gaze still on her. The lift remained stationary. George was making certain that her visit was a welcome one.

"Come in. It isn't locked."

The lift gates clashed behind her as she turned the polished brass door knob.

Adam was standing with his back to the fire, his head up, watching the door, the smoke from a thin, aromatic cigar wreathing about him. It was impossible to discern anything in his closed face. She shut the door carefully, waited by it. Adam's hat and coat were lying across the arm of a chair and he was dressed formally, ready to go out.

The sight of him hurt her more than she could possibly have foreseen.

He stood, unhelpful, waiting for her to speak.

"Thank you for seeing me, Adam. I realize that the time is probably very inconvenient." Outwardly she was calm, businesslike.

"It is." He did not smile; nor did he make any move to welcome her. A light impatience, held more or less politely in check emanated from him, a feeling enhanced by the travelling clothes tossed waiting on the chair.

"I'm sorry." Over the past eighteen months she had contrived to convince herself that absence had exaggerated his graceful good looks, that indefinable attraction that was a physical shock to her each time she saw him. She was dismayed now to discover that she had been wrong.

"Will you sit down?"

"Thank you, no." There was no disguising the animosity that charged the air between them. The stubborn months of separation were a chasm. Yet she watched his eyes, saw the tension in him, sensed that Adam Jefferson was not as cool as he would have her believe.

A quiet moment ticked by.

"You did not come, presumably," Adam said, brutally polite, "to stand by my door in silence? I am, as you know a busy man—"

She held the spark of anger in check. "I have – a favour to ask." Where were all her carefully prepared phrases?

"Oh?" Unfeigned, sardonic surprise.

No way now but to say it, bluntly. "I need passage for someone on one of your ships. To America. I know Stowe, Jefferson have their own runs to New York. I want you to take someone for me—" In her nervousness it had come out all wrong, the words had sounded more a demand than a plea. "Please," she said, hoping it would soften the edge.

"I see." Very deliberately he stubbed out his cigar. "Can you give me one good reason why I should do anything for you? Let alone anything that sounds as – shady as this?"

She had for the moment exhausted her courage and her self-control. She did not answer.

He moved with sudden, violent swiftness to where she stood. His face was pale, tight-drawn with anger. "You have your fair share of gall, haven't you? What in Hell makes you think I'd lift a finger for you?"

"I'm not asking you to do it for nothing," she said quickly. "I'll pay. As much as you want, within reason. Everything I have, if that's what it takes." There was no point in trying to hide her desperation. Every moment that Cormac remained in hiding at The Larches meant danger for the other occupants of the house.

Her tone cut through his anger. She saw the stiffness in him. "Who is it that needs to get to America so urgently and so 'unofficially'?"

"I don't think you need to know that." She tried to walk past him into the room, wanting – needing – to put a physical distance between them. He caught her arm as she passed. She stood still under the bite of his fingers, not looking at him.

"I thought you'd given up this Irish rebel stuff, Molly O'Dowd?" he said softly.

"You're jumping to conclusions."

"Maybe. Now give me one reason why I shouldn't go straight to the authorities with this strange tale of an Irish girl who needs 'unofficial' passage for someone on Stowe, Jefferson's cargo ship to New York? As a patriotic Englishman should?"

"Would you do that?" There was a sharp pain in her arm where his hand encircled it. She felt rage rising in her blood.

"Why shouldn't I?"

The blaze was uncontrollable. "Because there are things in your own dealings, Adam, that you would not care for the authorities to hear about. Nor your wife or father-in-law, if it comes to that. You could get my brother hung, put me and probably Jack, too, in gaol. But I'd see you ruined for it, I promise. Is it worth that, the satisfaction you might get from betraying me because I hurt your pride?"

They were standing as close as lovers, each roused to a storm of rage. She tried to pull away from him and he caught her with his free arm. In a sudden flash of blinding temper she lashed out at him and to her own surprise, before he could prevent it, her hand cracked hard against the bone of his cheek. With a furious exclamation he pinioned her, burying his hand in her hair, dragging her head back. Appalled, she watched the bright stain bloom on his cheek. She had never seen such anger in him before; she felt it wild in his body and in his strong hands, recognized, too, that other blood-fire that matched her own, despite their blazing hostility. Then he released her, almost throwing her from him. She could not take her eyes from his marked cheek.

"I'm sorry," she said, lifting a hand.

He jerked his head away from her touch as if from red-hot metal.

"I didn't want this," she said, unable to control the miserable trembling of her voice, "I didn't want to quarrel. Truly I didn't. I know what I'm asking. I didn't mean to threaten. I need your help, Adam. Please. I don't know anyone else to ask—" Cormac's face was in her mind, bitter, frightened.

"You have an extraordinarily strange way of begging a favour." His fingertips brushed his bruised face.

"Please, Adam. Please help us." There was neither dignity

358

nor pride in the plea. She knew it and did not care.

He heard the change. She saw it in the lift of his head, the dark, narrowed gaze.

"What price would you put on this ticket to freedom that you needed so badly that it brought you to me?"

"Anything I have." Her cheeks burned.

"And what makes you think that you have anything that I want?"

She bowed her head, closed eyes that were suddenly hot with tears. She had lost. Through her own stupid, hot-headed fault she had lost. Now what? She turned blindly towards the door.

"Molly." There was no trace of softening in the savage voice. She stood with her back to him, her shoulders tensed as if against an expected blow. "We've a cargo loading in three days. I'll let you know the arrangements."

She could not believe her ears. She turned.

"It will cost you nothing." His eyes raked her. "Leave now. If you really want to."

She stood as if rooted to the spot. He gave her time, then came quietly to her, anger still in him, bent upon punishment.

She shook her head miserably. "Don't, Adam. Please don't." But there was no conviction in the words. She had known the danger of coming here, of seeing him again, had given herself credit for more strength than she actually possessed. She had been ready to blackmail, ready to use any means to gain his help. And now the jaws of a trap of her own making held her firm.

"Go," he said, before he kissed her, "if you can. I won't stop you." But he said it knowing, as she herself knew, that she could no more have left him in that moment than she could have flown, unharmed, through the window.

Three days later the S.S. *Caroline J.* steamed down river from the Port of London fully loaded for New York. A couple of weeks after that a cryptic telegram was received at the offices of the Venture Employment Agency.

– Cargo N.Y. safe and sound. Thanks for life. COD. –

CHAPTER THIRTY-THREE

"Post," Nancy said, holding out a bundle of letters. "And Mr Danbury's waiting to see you."

"Danbury? George Danbury?"

"That's right. He looks worried."

"Everyone looks worried," Molly said as she took the letters, "it's the expression of the age."

George Danbury was tall, stooping, kindly-faced. He was one of Molly's original clients, and a favourite of hers. This morning he was apologetic. "I have absolutely no complaint about Miss Brown's work. It's quite simply that I can no longer afford to keep her. Business has been very slow these last months. Competition from motorized vehicles has almost destroyed the horse-drawn trade."

Molly dropped the unopened post on her desk. She genuinely liked George Danbury. He was an honest, gentle-natured man who had run a small carting business, which he had inherited from his father, more or less successfully for thirty years before the revolution of the internal combustion engine had overtaken him.

"Couldn't you buy or hire motor vehicles of your own?" she asked. "It's a dreadful shame that a firm as well thought of as Danbury's should go to the wall."

The old man smiled sadly. "The day when goodwill was as good as cash in the bank has long gone, my dear. You can't spend goodwill, nor will a man take it as collateral for a loan. I just don't have the necessary capital now to invest in modernization."

"You don't mean that you might have to close down altogether?"

"It will almost certainly come to that, yes. Though I shall be sorry to see the old firm go." He stood up. "This dog's too old now to learn new tricks, Mrs Benton. New blood's what the business needs, and with the two girls off and married I've no one to help me."

Molly extended her hand. "It was kind of you to come and tell us."

"Not at all. I felt it only right. I've never had the slightest complaint about your young ladies. I didn't want you to think I was starting now."

Molly saw him out.

Moments later she reached for her coat.

Charley sat in thoughtful silence.

"Well?" Molly asked.

"You want me to persuade our Jack to take up carting?"

"No. Not exactly. I wanted first to know what you thought of the idea. It's time for a change, Charley, and if Jack doesn't do it now he never will. He isn't happy; we all know it. He's a moderate man; he hates the way things are going in the docks. In a couple of years there'll be no place for him. We both know there's more to Jack than a strong back. He's clever, and he's good with men. He deserves a chance to prove what he could do. There's no future where he is."

"Aye. No one would argue that."

"Oh, Charley, isn't it just exactly the kind of thing that Jack could do? Isn't it?"

"He'll say he doesn't know the business."

"He can learn, can't he? How much did I know when I started the agency? George has been in the business all his life, he knows it well enough for two. What he needs is a man who can handle the men, a man with strength and common sense. Jack. I've got money in the bank doing nothing. It should be working for us. It would buy lorries, hire men. There'd be a job for Edward, wouldn't there, as our mechanic?" The idea that had germinated as she had listened to George Danbury had grown, budded, burst fully into bloom. It was as if the seed had always been there, waiting. She was passionately convinced that she was right, impatient to convince everyone else. She was not blind to her own motives; she had faced them squarely as she had hurried through the busy streets this morning. To give Jack this opportunity was a way to make amends. For the child she would not give him. For the fact that she could never be the wife that he had expected. For Adam. Above all for Adam.

"Tell me truthfully what you think."

Charley nodded. "You're right. It is a good idea. Our Jack could do it. If you can convince him."

"That's why I want you to talk to him. Will you, Charley. Please?"

"I'll try."

"Thanks." Molly kissed him lightly on the cheek.

In rising, happy excitement she hurried back to the office. Back to the bombshell of an unopened letter.

"Expelled?" Jack looked from the letter to Molly's face, in disbelief and dawning fury. "Danny? There must be some mistake."

"There's no mistake. I went straight to the school this morning, as soon as I heard. Danny is to leave at the end of the week." Molly was drained. She had neither tears nor anger left.

"For *stealing*?"

"Yes."

"Where is he?"

"Upstairs."

"Fetch him."

"Jack, wait. Wait till you've calmed down. Don't get him down here while you're this angry—"

"Angry? I'm—" Jack ran a hand through his hair. "I just don't believe it! Stealing? Stealing what?"

"Money. A watch. Some other things." Molly's voice was expressionless. "There isn't any doubt. When they found the things in his desk he owned up."

"Get him down here."

"Please, Jack, leave it till tomorrow. I know you're angry. You've every right to be. But—"

"But nothing." Jack strode from the room to the foot of the stairs. "Daniel! Get down here! Now!"

He came, small, red-eyed, defiant. Molly's heart sank as she saw the look in his eyes.

"What's this, then?" Jack slapped the table hard with the letter he held in his hand.

Danny did not speak.

"Well?"

The child looked at his mother.

"I'm asking you a question. What's this?" said Jack roughly, shaking the paper in front of Danny's face.

"It's what it says." White-faced challenge. Molly winced.

"It is, is it? It's a report that my son's a thief is it? That he's been expelled from school. Is that what it is?"

"Yes."

"And what have you got to say for yourself?"

The boy lifted a bright head, stared sullenly.

"Jack—" began Molly.

"Leave this to me."

Danny sucked his lip, took a small step backwards.

"Well? Nothing to say?"

He shook his head.

"You took those things?"

A pause. "Yes."

"Why? *Why?*"

The words stuck for a moment, then tumbled in a torrent: "They had more than me. All of them. More money, more nice things. I hated them. Hated them!"

"And you think that gives you the right to thieve from them? To take things that aren't yours?" Jack's voice was heavy with disgust.

Silence again.

"A good thrashing's what you deserve. By God, I've been too soft with you."

"Jack!"

At the sound of Molly's voice Danny's panic overcame him and he tried to run to her, but tripped, knocking a chair flying, almost falling himself. Jack's hand fastened on his shoulder before he could regain his balance.

"Let me go! Let me go! I want my Mum!"

"I'll bet you do."

The child lashed out with his feet. "Get away from me! You can't touch me! You can't! You've no right. You're not my father. I know you're not!" He was crying hysterically, his breath sobbing in his throat. Molly and Jack stood staring at him as if paralysed.

"What did you say?" Molly dropped to her knees beside her

son, caught him by the shoulders, shook him gently. "Danny, stop it. Calm down."

"He isn't my father. I know he isn't. I heard him say. He doesn't want me. I don't care." He flung himself, sobbing, on to Molly's shoulder. "I don't care. I don't care."

Very carefully Jack righted the chair that Danny had knocked over, sat on it, his elbow on the table, his mouth resting on a huge bunched fist.

Molly rocked the child, holding him to her. "Come now, my Danny, come now."

"I'll run away. And you'll never find me. You'll be sorry then." The words were barely coherent.

She lifted his chin with her finger. "Don't be silly now, we'll have no talk like that."

He glanced at Jack from the corner of his eye. "I'm not going back to that school tomorrow. I'm not, so there. He won't make me. I don't care what he does. He's not my father. He can't make me."

Jack's slight movement was one of sharp, physical pain.

Molly sat down, lifted Danny onto her lap. "You must stop saying that, Danny. It isn't true."

Brilliant, sullen eyes met hers, absolutely unconvinced. Harry's eyes.

"I heard him say—"

"You misunderstood," she interrupted. "You aren't grown up enough yet always to understand what grown ups are saying. If – Dad – isn't your father, then who do you think is?"

Tears ran down already tear-drenched cheeks. "I don't know."

"There you are, then." Molly was having difficulty in controlling her own voice. "Now off you go to bed and we'll talk about it in the morning. No one's going to thrash anyone, and no one's going to run away. You know, don't you, how wicked it is to steal?"

He hung his head. "Yes."

"And you know, too, that when you're wicked you hurt not those you hate, but those who love you?"

"I s'pose so."

"Then will you promise me faithfully that you'll never take

anything ever again that doesn't belong to you?"

"Yes," he whispered.

"Then off you go. I'll be up to tuck you in later."

He slid from her lap, walked to the door, his eyes on the carpet, and then they heard his light footsteps mounting the stairs.

"Bloody Hell," Jack said tightly as soon as it was quiet again.

Molly was crying openly now. Slowly Jack stood up and encircled her shoulders with his arm. "There, lass, there."

"I told him a lie," she said.

The arm tightened. "No, you didn't. Everything you said was absolutely true," he said laying his face against her curly hair, "If I'm not his father, then who is?"

In that moment Molly realized that they were closer than they had been for a very long time.

It took a lot of persuasion to get Jack to go and see George Danbury. Molly, encouraged by Charley, had gone before and prepared the way and George Danbury had been delighted at the idea of a partnership. Talking Jack round was taking rather longer, as Molly had known it would.

"I'm a stevedore, Molly. What do I know about carting?"

"As much as I do. Which is enough. I'm not suggesting that you get out there hauling with your bare hands. It's a manager that George needs. Someone with a bit of common sense, someone who can handle men. Someone who can negotiate with Unions without causing a riot. The carters are well organized. George seems to think they run rings round him."

"More than likely. What makes you think I'd be any better?"

"Oh, Jack! You know how the men think, know what they need, understand their language. Think about it. Are you going to spend the rest of your life in the docks? What future is there in that? Are you going to wait until a cargo slips, or you fall and cripple yourself for life? Or worse still, wait until you're too old and they throw you on the scrap heap? You're thirty-five years old. Now's the time. If you don't take this chance you never will."

"I'll think on it."

One evening, with the children in bed and the house quiet

Molly tried a last effort. Jack listened to her in silence, sucking an empty pipe.

" – it isn't today I'm thinking about, but tomorrow, the day after. Danny's future. The girls'. And especially yours. Oh, Jack, are you even listening?"

"Aye, I'm listening." He took the pipe from his mouth and regarded it, Molly thought irritably, as if he had never seen it before. "I was at a meeting yesterday," he added, apparently irrelevantly.

She watched him, waiting.

"Clever young feller, the lad who was speaking. Syndicalist. Just back from France, or some such. Very fiery. Very persuasive. The democratic process is too slow for these lads. They want—" he paused, quoted wryly, " 'a dictatorship of the proletariat'."

"Jargon," Molly said.

"Dangerous jargon." Very deliberately he filled his pipe, tamped it down.

Knowing him, Molly held on to her patience, fetched a box of Swan Vestas from the mantelpiece. "So?"

He lit his pipe, watched the flame of the match burn down almost to his fingertips before he shook it out. "So it wouldn't have taken much to make me turn my card in there and then."

She said nothing, afraid to push him.

"You're really keen to see me try this job at Danbury's, aren't you?"

"Yes."

He tapped his finger thoughtfully on the table.

"Something's still bothering you," she said.

"Aye."

She knew the stumbling block, had known it from the start. "The money? You don't want to use 'my' money?"

He leaned back in a cloud of fragrant smoke.

"Well, if that's what's worrying you, then borrow it, for Heaven's sake. Take it as a loan. A business proposition."

His smile was slow and wide. "It took you a long time to get there, lass, but you made it in the end. That's what I've been waiting to hear. You've got a deal." He extended his hand across the table.

Delightedly she grasped it. "Oh, that's marvellous! Let's celebrate. A glass of port—"

"Wait on." She was about to pull excitedly away, but he held on to her hand. "All legal, mind. Contracts. Interest, going rate—" she made a negative gesture " – and I say *yes*. Or no deal. We'll do this my way or not at all."

"Yes, Jack."

"We'll go to the bank tomorrow. And then to George Danbury."

"Yes, Jack," she said again demurely.

"Enough of your cheek, woman. Get us that drink."

In May Molly went, as she always did at this time of the year, to visit John Marsden in Southend. This trip, to keep the old man in touch with the business, had become a formal yearly ritual that they both enjoyed enormously.

As Molly looked from the train window across the placid, sunlit waters of the estuary, she reflected with real pleasure that the report she had to deliver today was the best ever. And John would no doubt still treat her as if she were a precocious child with ideas above her station. The thought made her smile.

Through the open window came the acrid smell of steam, a drift of salt air from the sea. A child in a full-skirted sailor suit danced down the platform of a station they passed swinging a bucket and spade, face alight with excitement. Molly leaned back comfortably. It wasn't often that she had the chance to sit still for this length of time at a stretch. On the narrow shingle beaches children played, paddled in the high, lapping water. She remembered the day they had brought Danny to the beach as a very little boy, remembered his fear of the vast, moving expanse of the sea. Jack had carried him into it, dabbled his toes in the creaming waves. Molly's fingers drummed lightly on the small portmanteau that rested on her lap. Danny was settled at a new school now. He had never again mentioned the subject of his relationship with Jack. The shattering episode might never have happened. But it haunted Molly. Often she looked at the child and realized that, for all her love, she barely knew him. His behaviour at the new school was impeccable, for the first time in his life he was working to his full capacity, apparently enjoying it and certainly getting very good results. To all intents and purposes he had learned his lesson. Molly stirred a little in her seat. Why did she have misgivings?

The train slowed and, hissing, steamed to a stop. Doors slammed like an irregular volley of rifle fire, and Molly joined the gay crowd shuffling along the platform towards the ticket office.

John Marsden's delight at seeing her was, as usual, well-disguised beneath crotchety gruffness.

"Train late, was it? Been expecting you for the last hour." He had changed very little over the years, the craggy face, brown and weatherbeaten from his daily walk along the pier, was a little more lined, his movements stiffer, his wheezing, death's-door cough exactly the same as it had always been. Molly had come to the conclusion long before that he would outlast them all.

She delivered her report in his pleasant little sitting room that overlooked the front. Even John Marsden could find no complaint to make about the cheque with which she presented him. Business over, they took tea. Sun streamed through the window. Far out in the estuary great ships steamed past, the occasional sailing barge, graceful in the lifting breeze, beat her way upriver, little cockle boats from nearby Leigh carried their tasty loads to the sheds to be cooked and hawked all over East London. In the tiny walled front garden beyond the window a small mounted telescope testified to John's interest in the passing sea-trade.

"Yes, I like it well enough here," he agreed grudgingly to Molly's comment. "Though it's better in the winter, when the blessed trippers stay at home."

Molly suppressed a smile.

"You can't take a step in the summer without falling over someone sucking a stick of rock or looking for what the butler saw. Can't blame them, I suppose," he added, gloomily. "They might as well enjoy themselves while they can. How about a breath of air? The little lad down by the pier saves the papers for me. I always pick them up about now."

Molly strolled beside him in the sunshine amongst the other promenaders. "What did you mean 'enjoy themselves while they can'?" she asked curiously. "What do you think is going to stop them?"

He looked at her sideways, in pure disgust. "Another one who never reads a paper."

"Indeed I do."

"Then you don't understand what you read. I'm disappointed in you, girl. Thought you had a bit of perception."

"There's no need to be rude," she said mildly.

"Tell that to the German Navy," he said, waving an arm in the direction of the peaceful waters, "when you see them riding at anchor out there. Invading people is rude," he added sarcastically.

"Oh, John, don't be ridiculous. You don't believe in all this war-monger talk, do you?"

He made a dismissive noise, half-grunt, half-snort. "You'll see. The Kaiser isn't building dreadnoughts for fun. He's hell-bent on war, that's what. And he doesn't need a Navy to get to France, does he? If the Russians hadn't been so gutless we'd have been at war already, over Turkey, you mark my words."

"But I can't believe—" Molly stopped. "What's going on? —There's a terrible crowd. What is it?" Around the newsstand was gathered a crowd, solemn, quiet, passing newspapers from hand to hand. A woman was crying quietly.

John pushed testily through the crowd.

"Mornin' Guv'nor. Managed ter save yer a couple. Bit of a job, though. Could've sold 'em ten times over, that I could. The old King's up an' died. Poor old Teddy. Read all abaht it—" The newsboy, a scrap of a child in a cap several times too large for him raised his voice, "– read all abaht it."

On a hot early summer's day in 1910 King Edward VII was laid to rest; enormous crowds of his affectionate subjects lined the route of the procession. In the cortège were nine of the crowned heads of Europe. And on that sad day, royalty and commoner had something more than usual in common. Neither was aware that in mourning "l'Oncle de l'Europe" they were also mourning the passing of an age.

CHAPTER THIRTY-FOUR

To NO ONE's surprise but his own Jack Benton took to running his own carting business like a duck to water. As summer moved into autumn he was able to look with justifiable pride at the results of his hard work as, slowly, the Danbury accounts moved from losses to small profits and he was able to start repaying the money he had borrowed from Molly. He and George Danbury worked well together; they were two of a kind – honest, hard-working, straightforward. Molly breathed a sigh of relief and restrained herself with some difficulty from saying 'I told you so'. Jack's relationship with Nancy improved a little as well – in a close-knit family like the Bentons it was impossible to remain entirely at loggerheads. But still it distressed Molly that there was, constantly, the feeling in the air that hostilities were suspended rather than ended, and that their relationship had never got back onto the old footing.

On a dull and cheerless Friday in November Jack tried to warn his sister against attending a Suffragette meeting at Caxton Hall that day. It was planned to send a deputation of respected and distinguished women to Parliament to protest against the vetoing of the Conciliation Bill, which, if passed, would have given at least a small proportion of women the vote. Inevitably Nancy resented what she saw as her brother's interference.

"There's going to be trouble, Nancy. Big trouble. There are rumours that Churchill's given orders that no woman is to be allowed near the House. There'll be massive precautions. . . . He's got enough trouble with the Welsh miners – he'll not let a few women plague him. He's for stopping you once and for all, by all accounts."

"He won't stop us."

"He will. This time."

"If we let ourselves be intimidated we're beaten before we start. And that's just what they want, isn't it? We're simply exercising our democratic rights. We were promised this Bill—"

"For God's sake, girl, can you see no further than the ends of your noses? Do you think the government has engineered a constitutional crisis and called another general election just to spite you? Anyone would think that your precious Bill is the only thing that's suffered—"

Molly recognized the short-fused impatience that any conversation with Nancy seemed to produce in Jack and tried to head off trouble. "Jack, didn't you say you had a meeting—?"

"We're not letting them get away with it." The familiar, stubborn vertical line creased Nancy's forehead. "They've had nearly a year. We've kept the truce. We've not disrupted their wretched Parliamentary games, and now they're backing down. Asquith's got to be shown that we mean business."

"Two elections in a year, the Lords and the Commons at each others' throats, Churchill mobilizing troops against the miners of the Rhondda, and you march on Parliament in support of a lost Bill that would only have given a tiny minority of women the vote anyway. You're touched in the head, the lot of you. Can't you see the country's falling into anarchy? And all you can do is—"

" – That's why we want the vote, stupid!" Nancy snapped. "Fine state you men have brought us to!"

Jack strode to the door, barely containing his anger. "Just take my advice and show a bit of sense this time. Stay at home. There's going to be trouble."

"Not from us," Nancy said obstinately.

Into the silence that followed Jack's irate slamming of the door behind him, Molly sighed. "I think on balance," she said, "I preferred it when you two weren't talking. It was more peaceful."

Molly spent that afternoon in the office. With Nancy away she had plenty to keep her occupied. The children dropped in to see her when they came home from school.

"Can I cook some crumpets for tea?" Kitty asked.

"You'll burn them," Meghan protested.

"I won't!"

"You did last time."

"That was your fault! You wouldn't—"

"Why don't you both go out and come back in again?" Molly asked with some self-restraint. "And Meghan, what in Heaven's name have you done to your hair? It's all over the place again."

"Oh, I don't know." Megan flicked at the mass of fair curls that tumbled across her shoulders. "I just can't seem to keep the clips in. If she's going to do the crumpets, can I make some fudge?"

"No."

Meghan pulled a face. "Oh, go on."

"Meg, I have absolutely no intention of spending my Friday evening clearing up a fudgy mess after you. Now, off you go. And don't fight about the crumpets!" she added before the door slammed shut behind them and they clattered down the hallway in an avalanche of noise.

A couple of hours later she said goodnight to the departing typists, locked the door of the darkened office and prepared hopefully for a half-hour of peace. Jack was not yet home, the children were quiet, the kitchen was warm, silent and empty.

The urgent knocking on the front door came before she had even sat down.

"Oh, no!" Irritated she hurried along the hall, threw the door open. "What – Nancy! What's happened?"

Nancy was supported by Christopher Edmonton. In the faint light her face, the eyes closed and purpling, blood smeared and dribbling from her nose, was all but unrecognizable. She was nursing her left arm in her right. Her clothes were torn and covered in mud and blood.

"Bring her in. Quick."

In the kitchen Molly bathed and tended the battered face, eyed Nancy's twisted arm doubtfully. Danny had already been sent flying for the doctor. "What on earth happened?" she asked Christopher who, himself dishevelled and with a large bruise on his cheek, had so far said not a word, but was sitting at the table watching with anxious, angry eyes.

"She was thrown under a horse," he said in a shaken voice.

"*Thrown?*"

"A policeman punched her in the face and then pushed her

down. 'Ride over her,' he said." He shook his head as if still unable to believe it. " 'Ride over her'!"

"I hope the bloody horse broke its leg," Nancy muttered through swollen lips and drew a sharp, pained breath as she tried to move her arm.

"Sit still, And don't talk. The doctor won't be long. Meghan, Kitty, get away from that door. Aunt Nancy isn't a peepshow."

"O – oh, but—"

"Out!"

They went.

"Jack'll be here soon," Molly said.

Christopher lifted his head. "Will he mind my being here? I'd like to stay. Until I know that Nancy's all right."

"Christopher was very brave," Nancy mumbled. "He could have been hurt himself, hauling me out from under that animal."

Molly smiled at him. The young face had firmed since last she had seen it, the shoulders broadened. "Of course you must stay."

The doctor arrived on the doorstep in the same moment as Jack. Jack erupted into the kitchen.

"What's happened? Who's – Good God!" He stared, shocked, at Nancy's battered face.

"You were right, our Jack," Nancy said, attempting a painful grimace that might have been a smile. "There was trouble, six hours of it."

The doctor stepped past Jack. "Hot water, Mrs Benton, lots of it. And Dettol But first let's look at this arm." He spoke around Nancy as if she were not there. "Has she had a cup of tea? Hot and sweet, please. And she should get to bed as soon as possible after I've dressed this. Where does she live? Is there someone to look after her?"

Nancy opened her bruised mouth. Jack forestalled her. "She'll stay here," he said gruffly. "She's got rooms upstairs. Danny, run and light your Aunt Nancy's fire—"

And so Nancy moved back into the attic flat at The Larches. At first they all pretended that it was a temporary arrangement, until her injuries had healed, but as time went on it became perfectly obvious that for all her protestations about inconveniencing everyone she had no more desire to leave than Molly had to see her go.

In December the general election saw the Liberals once more in power, but still dependent upon the forty-two MPs of the Labour Party and the eighty Irish Nationalists for their majority. Molly 'persuaded' Nancy to stay for Christmas, and then into a new year that began, perhaps prophetically, in dramatic and violent fashion for Londoners when seven hundred and fifty policemen and a detachment of Scots Guards with a machine gun were used in a battle in Sidney Street, Stepney, where three anarchists, who had taken refuge there after killing three unarmed policemen, were killed.

"Getting into practice for the next Suffragette march," Nancy said and laughed a little shakily.

So far Jack had made no comment about his sister's continued stay, and Molly, racking her brains for a diplomatic way to bring up the subject decided it was best left well alone. There was enough trouble about without stirring up more. In Wales the miners were out solidly now, in support of a national minimum wage. Prices were spiralling. Jack gave Danbury's carters a rise, after months of argument with George Danbury, a penny an hour over Union rates.

"They've families to keep," he said, "rents to pay. We want the best; what good are dissatisfied men to us? We're a small outfit. The men's goodwill and loyalty is as important to us as the customer's. They can make or break our reputation." But still he said nothing about Nancy. Until, one day, he bumped into her in the hall.

"Enjoy the party last night, did you?"

She looked at him blankly. "Party?"

"Wasn't that what it was? It sounded like it."

She flushed. "I'm sorry if we disturbed you," she said stiffly. "Some of my friends called. I did ask them to keep their voices down." It was dark in the hall, she could not see her brother's face. He stepped past her to the parlour door.

"It wasn't their voices," he said, placidly, "it was their blessed feet on those floor boards. If you're going to settle in, happen we should see about a nice bit of carpet for that living room of yours. That'd help the noise, I daresay."

"Jack!"

He turned.

She ran to him, flung her arms about his great frame. "Jack, oh Jack!" She could say nothing else.

"There, lass," he said gently, holding her to him. "Where else would you go, in the end?"

A year after the death of King Edward, through a spring that promised a blazing summer, the preparations for the coronation of King George V went on against a background of unrest at home and heightening tension in Europe. On a bright May afternoon Molly stood at the window of Adam's apartment looking out to where the foliage of the trees was already looking a little dusty, a little tired.

"Molly?" Adam's light voice, lazy with pleasure. "What are you doing over there?"

"Thinking. I thought you were asleep." She pulled the silk coverlet that she had taken from the bed around her body. "Adam?"

"Yes?"

"Do you think there's going to be a war?"

"No. Take that thing off."

"How can you be so certain?"

"Economics. No one can afford a war, not even Kaiser Bill. Take it off."

She turned, a halo of light silhouetting her body and her cloud of hair. "I ought to go." The sight of him, the sound of his voice, still made the blood race in her veins.

"Come here." He pushed back the bedclothes, held out a demanding hand.

She came.

On the 22nd June 1911 King George V was crowned in Westminster Abbey. Two days before there had been rioting and fire-raising in Hull by striking seamen and 'coalies'. It was not an auspicious start to the new King's reign.

Worse was to follow.

Within two weeks of the coronation the country was in the grip of yet another war scare, as, flouting British wishes and

375

policy, the German gunboat *Panther* lay off Agadir intent upon securing German interests against French expansion in Morocco. Most of the rest of the massive and menacing German battle fleet steamed in the North Sea, uncomfortably close to the British coasts. At home the hottest summer for seventy years was well set in; London, Liverpool, Manchester sweltered. Tempers frayed. In Wales, the miners, on strike now for nearly ten months, were close to being starved back to work. But the seamen had won, and the hopes and expectations of other Unions were raised.

On 25th July the British Foreign Secretary warned the Admiralty that the British Fleet might be attacked at any time. But the bogey had been brought from the cupboard once too often, and to the ordinary man in the street there were more pressing problems. Wars happened in other places, to other peoples. The Army and the Navy coped with them, that was what they were there for, wasn't it? Empty bellies and emptier pockets were something else again. This time the impetus for change was coming not from the militant extremists but from the mass of the workers.

On a sweltering first day of August – ironically, the same day that the Welsh miners were finally broken – dockers all over the country began to strike. Other Unions followed – carters in Liverpool and London, other associated workers. In the British Parliament a critical battle was being fought to ensure that the second House could never again baulk the wishes of the Commons. In the country as a whole services and transport ground slowly to a halt. Shortages were soon felt as food rotted on the quaysides in the incredibly hot weather. Butter, meat, piles of perishing fruit and vegetables. As day after steaming day passed in the strangely silent, strike-bound cities, rail, road and river transport was stopped. A real threat of famine grew. In Wales and in Liverpool the Riot Act was read, there was fighting in the streets and four men died, shot down by soldiers who sweated, confused, in the heat facing rioters and fire-raisers who might have been their fathers, their brothers.

"How long will it last, do you think?" Molly, Nancy and Jack were in the kitchen of The Larches, every door and window propped to its widest to gain advantage of the slightest stirring of air. With trade and industry virtually at a standstill Molly had closed the office for the duration of the troubles. Jack's carters were out. Jack himself had insisted on it. "We're not strike-breaking. I wouldn't ask my men to do it. We'll stick it out with the rest."

"How long?" he asked now. "God only knows. There's no sign of a break on either side."

"The shops are running out of food," Nancy said, fanning herself, "and prices are sky-high. Strikers broke into a shop in Silvertown and beat up the owner for profiteering."

Molly, frowning, was studying her husband's face. "What have you done to your cheek?"

"Nothing."

"Nothing? It looks as if you've walked into a door."

"Oh, that. Yes, that was what happened."

"Where?"

"What?"

"Where did it happen?"

He moved uncomfortably, "I don't remember."

She got up and marched round the table for a closer look, "Oh, come on now, that's a fresh bruise. You can't have cracked yourself that hard without knowing you'd done it?"

Jack lifted a hand to his face, then too late remembered and tried to cover it.

"Ah!" Molly caught his wrist, stared in disbelief at the scraped knuckles. "*Fighting*?" she asked, faintly.

"Not exactly." He paused. "A difference of opinion."

"This morning?" Light dawned, slowly. "You mean you went to that meeting after all?"

"I wanted to hear what Ben had to say. Lord, Molly, it's only a year since I was one of them—"

"And they showed you that now you aren't? What did you expect, Jack? In their eyes you're a boss now. The enemy."

"It was only a couple of them. There was a scuffle. There were some rough words used." He could not quite keep the hurt and bitterness from his voice.

Molly touched his shoulder. "Then what happened?"

"Ben Tillett saw it. He stepped in, called me up onto the platform. Got me making speeches."

377

"But Jack—"

"They're my mates still. They deserve my support. Sixpence they won, twelve years ago. The docker's tanner. And nothing since. It isn't good enough."

In the office across the hall the telephone rang.

"Blast the thing," Molly said.

"Leave it." Jack wiped the sweat from his face. "It can't be anything important."

"Shall I answer it?" Nancy asked, making no move.

Molly stood up tiredly. "No, I'll go."

The telephone shrilled again as she opened the office door. She picked it up. "Hello?"

"Molly?" Adam's voice came as a shock; it was the last one she had expected to hear.

"Yes."

"Can you talk?"

She pushed the open door with her foot. She could hear the murmur of Jack's and Nancy's voices from the kitchen. "Yes."

"I want to see you about something. Can you get away?"

"It would be difficult."

"It's important. Very important. It wouldn't take long, I promise. Will you meet me in the park by the station, later this afternoon?"

"I can't, Adam. It's too—"

"Oh, come on, Molly darling. For me. Something very important. Please?" Familiar, warm tone, intimate, physical as a touch.

She let out a sighing breath. "What time?"

"Say, four?"

"All right. I'll try. The seat by the big tree." She put the phone down.

"Trouble?" Nancy asked as she walked back into the kitchen.

Molly shook her head. "Tate's, to say that they've closed down completely. Nothing's moving. They want us to hold on to the work we're doing for them."

Nancy yawned. "I thought they rang yesterday about that?"

"They did. This was just confirmation."

"You'd think they'd got something better to do, wouldn't

you? Here, drink your pop before I do. Blessed weather. I could drink the Serpentine.

He was waiting, watching for her. She was nervous.

"I can't be long," she said. "I'm supposed to be going down to see Annie. She hasn't been feeling well."

Playing children shouted, the only ones who seemed unaffected by the enervating heat. Dust shimmered, the streets around the park were strangely still.

Molly sat down beside him, glancing around her. "What was so important?"

He caught her hands, drew her round to face him and kissed her. "A favour," he said. "A very special favour."

She waited.

"Am I right in thinking," Adam asked softly, "that Jack is a close friend of Ben Tillett's?"

"They've known each other a long time, yes. They were quite close at one time. Jack admires Ben—"

Adam's long fingers drummed on the back of the wooden bench. "Didn't you tell me that Jack is already paying his carters over the Union rates?"

"Yes."

"Nothing moves in or out of the docks without Tillett's say-so, right?"

"Adam—"

"And Jack's men must owe him allegiance, rather than their Union? They've nothing to lose by breaking the strike, have they?"

"What cargo of yours is stranded in the docks?" she asked flatly.

"Clever girl. I knew you'd see it. Butter. Tons of it. It'd be running out of its barrels if I hadn't – persuaded –" he smiled, "someone to slip it into cold storage for me. It must be worth a fortune now, in the hotels and restaurants of the West End. Butter's like gold. I've lamb in there too. There's big money to be made, if we're quick, and Jack will get his share, I promise you. If he can get round Tillett, persuade him to – Molly! Where do you think you're going?"

"Get away from me," she said.

He caught her arm, angrily, before she could walk away.

"Molly, be reasonable. I'll cut Jack in for fifty per cent. What he gives Tillett out of that is up to him. Think what he could do with what he'll have left. It'd set his business up for life, and no strings."

She turned on him. "What makes you think, Adam Jefferson, that every man in this world is for sale to the highest bidder? You want to buy Ben Tillett? Well, go ahead and try, but do your own dirty work and don't ask others to do it for you. And I hope to see it when they scrape the pieces off the pavement."

"There's a price for every man. Don't fool yourself."

"But Ben Tillett's is not in money, thank God. And neither is Jack's."

He caught her by the shoulders, pulled her close to him, his fingers moving on her arm harshly caressing, "And yours?"

A child nearby giggled, and fled as Adam glared.

She dragged herself away from him, "My price is paid, Adam. It's finished."

"I've heard that before. Until you want something. Need something."

"No. Not this time."

"Be careful what you say." His anger was barely contained. "No woman walks away from me twice."

She looked at him through the shimmering haze of heat. Fine beads of sweat stood on his brown skin, fury fired the lines of a face that she knew she would not forget to the end of her days.

She turned from him.

"Molly." The voice behind her was quiet, and threaded with rage. "I mean what I say."

A child with a hoop clattered past, shouting. Another almost ran in to her as she walked steadily, blindly, towards the park exit.

The streets were extraordinarily quiet. Men gathered on corners, leaned on walls. Plastered all over the Bentons' shop window were notices – no butter or eggs – no bacon – tea rationed to two ounces per customer.

Charley, as always, raised an alert head as the shop bell tinkled. "May I help you?"

"It's me, Charley. Is Annie around? Nancy said she wasn't feeling too well."

"She's in the back, resting. Molly? Something wrong?"

"Nothing. The heat, that's all. It's getting me down."

"You and the rest of the world." He lifted the counter flap. "Come on through. She'll be pleased to see you."

"What's wrong with her? Is she ill?" She spoke automatically. She hardly remembered getting here, did not know what to do to ease the wracking pain. She only knew that, no matter how much she wanted to she should not cry. The death of secret things must necessarily be mourned in secret.

Charley laughed. "No, not ill. Just – well, go on in. Let her tell you herself."

Annie most certainly did not look well. She was sitting in a deckchair in the little yard beyond the open windows, her feet resting on a stool, her always pale skin translucent and sheened with sweat.

"Annie? Aren't you well?"

Annie's lovely face lit like a lamp. "I feel sick," she announced with something very close to pride. "I feel very sick. Oh, Molly, isn't it bloody marvellous?"

"Sick? What are you talking about?"

Annie laughed. "You're slow today, Moll! I'm expecting a baby! Didn't you guess? I thought everyone had. Oh, Molly, I'm so happy – Moll? Don't cry, love. It's me that's supposed to weep, isn't it?"

But Molly could not stop now. She dropped to her knees beside a surprised Annie, and in her bony arms sobbed as if her heart would break.

PART IV

Spring 1913

CHAPTER THIRTY-FIVE

ANNIE'S SECOND CHILD, Michael Harold Benton, was born in the early spring of 1913, a brother for Arthur Charles who had arrived almost exactly a year before.

"Easy as falling off a log," Annie said with panache. "Now that I've started it's like a penny-in-the-slot machine. You watch – I'm going to finish up like the Old Lady Who Lived in a Shoe."

In the year between the two births the divisions in the country had deepened. Strikes and lockouts had paralysed not only the capital but the whole of the country. British soldiers had been used against British workers and seeds of bitterness had been sown that would not easily be rooted out. They had flowered in more strikes, in fire-raising, in riots and in sabotage. Women too, urged on by the WSPU, embraced a new militancy. They broke windows, set fire to buildings and to letter boxes, assaulted politicians and policemen, and when arrested promptly went on hunger strike. The means used forcibly to feed them revolted even those who agreed with neither their aims nor their methods. Yet stubbornly the banners were raised, stubbornly the stones were thrown, stubbornly the women got themselves arrested again.

A little while after Michael's birth, in mid-March 1913, John Marsden died. It was not unexpected, his health had been failing for some time, yet still it saddened Molly painfully to know that she had lost such a friend. She knew the debt she owed the man, of help and encouragement. She attended his funeral in Southend, one of only half a dozen mourners, and afterwards was informed by John's solicitor that the Venture Agency was now entirely hers.

She sat that evening in the train that clattered and rocked its way back to London, staring unseeing from the window, her mind's eye a kaleidoscope of memories; above all she remembered that first day in John Marsden's office, could almost feel the pinch of those awful shoes, see John's craggy face as he glowered at this latest female to invade his privacy. As she walked from Stratford station out into the bustling Broadway she realized suddenly that she could not face the thought of going straight back to The Larches. She needed a walk, someone to talk to, to shake off the oppression of the occasion. She turned her steps towards Danbury's, and Jack.

She heard the commotion, saw the billowing, acrid smoke that rose into the pastel spring sky long before she reached the yard. Her footsteps quickened. A horse-drawn fire engine rattled past her, bell clanging with strident urgency. She began to run.

The street in which the yard was situated was cordoned off. Excited crowds were gathering, shepherded by policemen. Panic-stricken, Molly pushed and shoved her way through the crowd, ducked under the rope:

" 'Ere, wait a minute, Miss. You can't go down there—"

Danbury's buildings were ablaze. The street was clogged with people, with firemen, with fear-crazed horses.

"Sorry, Miss." The policeman's hand was firm on her arm, "You can't—"

"My name is Benton. Mrs Benton. My husband runs Danbury's. Where is he? Jack Benton. *Where is he?*"

Nearby one of the great carthorses reared, massive forelegs flailing. Even in her distress she could not help but see that only very few of the horses were there. And none at all of the new vans and lorries.

"Well – I'm not sure, Madam. Perhaps you'd better—"

Molly was gone, threading her way through the fire-fighting appliances that lined the road. She tripped over a hose. A fireman grabbed her arm and almost threw her out of the way. The hungry flames roared into the clear evening air that shimmered with the heat as the fire licked on ancient woodwork, crept around old, patched roofs and windows. A cloud of dense smoke, driven by a gust of wind, rolled into the street. Molly doubled up, coughing and choking, her eyes streaming. As they cleared she saw that a familiar figure sat on an upturned box not far from her, his head bent almost to his knees as he struggled for breath. She flew to him.

"George! George, where's Jack? *Where's Jack?*"

He lifted his head, could not speak. His eyes were red and running with water; his breath was coming in great, wheezing gasps. A big policeman bent to touch his shoulder. "The ambulance is here, Mr Danbury. I think you'd better come."

"WHERE IS JACK?" she screamed it against the vicious crackle of flame, the shouts and commotion around them.

"You Mrs Benton?" the policeman asked, sympathy in his eyes.

"Yes," she shouted above the pandemonium. "Yes, I am."

"I think you'd best come with us, Mrs Benton. Your husband's already been taken to the hospital. He was trapped on the top floor, and had to jump. Hurt his legs—"

"Look out!" With a fearful crash the roof of the biggest warehouse caved in, sending a sheaf of flying sparks into the air and causing a red-hot blast to swirl around the street. Somewhere a horse was screaming, an awful, almost human sound that tore the nerves. The firemen had given up the unequal fight for the stables and warehouses. Their hoses were all turned on the dilapidated building that adjoined the stable block and had been Danbury's offices, with storerooms beneath. Steadily the water played upon brick walls that were already scorched where the fire leapt hungrily from shattered windows and loading-doors, curling around the cracking brickwork, gay as red and yellow bunting in the evening sunshine.

It was some hours before she was allowed to see Jack for any length of time. Molly walked the waiting room floor, unable to rest. The others came in turn – Sarah, Annie, Nancy, Edward – but it was as if she could see no one, hear no one until that moment the doctor appeared in the waiting room door.

"Mrs Benton?"

She was on her feet in a moment. "Yes."

"Your husband has recovered consciousness, Mrs Benton. He's still in some pain, of course, but that should ease soon. We've given him something for it. If you'd like to see him for a very few minutes—?"

"Is he going to be all right?"

The doctor patted her shoulder. "Yes, Mrs Benton, he is.

Though the left leg is broken in two places and the right in one. We have removed some splinters of bone. I have to say that, in the circumstances, he's come off comparatively lightly. He'll be off his feet for some considerable time, of course. Some considerable time."

"And Mr Danbury?" she asked, quietly.

The doctor hesitated for a moment, then shrugged. "Very bad, I'm afraid. His chest was weak to start with – I fear he will be an invalid for the rest of his life."

"I see." She followed him along the antiseptic-smelling, cream-tiled corridor and into the ward where Jack lay, his thick hair singed and frizzed, an ugly burn bright against his cheekbone, crossing the old scar. One of his hands, resting on the white cover, was bandaged.

"Well," Molly said taking his free hand with her own, "here's a mess."

His usually bright eyes were blurred with pain and medication. "How's George?" he whispered. .

She hesitated. "Not so good, I'm afraid."

He turned his head on the pillow. She squeezed his hand. "This is quite like old times. Last time you lay in a hospital bed you asked me to marry you, remember?"

He smiled.

"Jack, how did it happen? How did the fire start?"

He shook his head, tiredly. "I've no idea, lass. Have you been to see how much is left?"

"No."

"Not much, I guess. Christ, I never saw anything go up so quickly. Was anyone badly hurt?"

She shook her head. "Only you and George."

"And the animals?"

She looked down at their clasped hands. "They saved some. But most are gone, I'm afraid. The firemen were too busy trying to get you out to save the horses."

"What about the new lorries? They'd been put away for the night in the empty stables—"

"Yes."

"All gone?"

"Yes."

He closed his eyes. "All gone," he said, his tone of voice different.

"No!"

The blue eyes opened and she thought she saw the faintest quirk of a smile at the vehement word, but soon it died. He drew a long, sighing breath. "We have to face it, lass. With no lorries, no horses and no buildings there's no Danbury's. Not even you can conjure something from a pile of ashes."

"What about the insurance?"

"We don't have any."

"What?" She stared at him, appalled.

"Not enough to make any difference, anyway. A few hundred. That'll have to go to George. We can't leave him destitute."

"I have absolutely no intention," she said, trying to keep the sharpness from her voice, "of leaving anyone destitute. Least of all us. Why weren't we adequately insured?"

His eyelids closed wearily again. "I didn't think we could afford it yet—"

She bit back the obvious reply. Behind her a nurse hovered. "I really think we ought to be getting some rest, Mr Benton."

Molly stood up. "Well, it could be worse." Her voice was bright. "The doctor says you'll be all right. Just get yourself well. Concentrate on that. We'll get Danbury's on its feet again before you are, you see if we don't. One way or another—"

Those words of bravado seemed doubly empty the next day as she stood with Annie surveying the still-smoking wreck of Danbury's yard. The sodden heaps of ash smelled horribly, the skeletal buildings mocked any hope of repair. Only one small hut remained unscathed, and one of the smaller store houses whose roof was damaged but whose walls still stood. The two women stood for a long time in glum silence, which Annie broke with an optimistic but misguided, "Perhaps you could sell the land?"

"Oh, for God's sake." Molly turned from her impatiently. "What good would that do anybody? It looks as if George Danbury will never work again. He needs an income. He won't get that if we let the firm fold. What's he going to live on if we give up? And Jack – Jack *needs* this place. He was beginning to make a success of it. Selling the land won't give Jack the incentive he needs to get his legs working again, will it? No. What we need is to turn this shambles to at least some advantage. What we need is *money*. Even with the improvements that Jack had managed to make the yard was outdated, the buildings were falling down, the whole set-up was uneconomic. If we could just lay our hands on enough money we could start again – new equipment, new buildings—" She stopped. Annie was regarding her sardonically, head on one side.

"You got that kind of spare cash?"

Molly shook her head. Every spare penny she had had already gone into Danbury's.

"Then you got a fairy godmother stacked somewhere?"

"There are such things as banks you know," Molly said a little acidly, "And they're there to lend money."

"They are?" Annie rolled her eyes. "You could have fooled me, love."

Jack put the same sentiment a little differently. "No chance," he said, shifting in his hospital bed, "no chance at all. I tried them before, Moll, when we were hoping to expand. We're already up to our eyes in debt – you of all people know that – and they wouldn't even consider lending us more. It's no good, Molly, you're going to have to face it. Danbury's is finished. We'll be lucky to get out of it with a whole skin." He looked drawn and dispirited.

Molly appeared not to have heard him. "If I could get the money," she said, slowly, "if I could just get enough to rebuild and get the transport we need – the place could be just about ready for when you're on your feet again."

Jack smiled something like his old smile. "You never give up, do you?"

She shook her head. "I never have yet. And I won't now."

"You won't get it, lass. I'm telling you."

"I might," she insisted stubbornly. "And I certainly won't if I don't try. I know some people – quite a lot of people – through the agency. At least let me *try*." She tilted her chin cheerfully. "I'm not giving up on the money I lent you without a fight, Jack Benton! I didn't come down with the last shower of rain. I'll make the bank see what a good proposition it is. You see if I don't."

He laughed, tiredly. "No harm in trying."

She kissed him lightly on the cheek. "You just concentrate on getting better. Don't fret. Everything will come right, you see."

She kept her head high and her step brisk until she was out of the ward.

A week later Jack had a second operation. The doctor was very satisfied; the prognosis was good. "There's no reason to believe, Mrs Benton, that your husband won't make a complete recovery. But it's going to take some time, I'm afraid. Rest is what he needs, rest and care. And we must stop him fretting if we can. It does him no good at all."

Molly smiled. "Don't worry, doctor, I think I have some news that will do him as much good as medicine. I'll stop him fretting."

Her news did more than that. Jack, and Annie who was sitting on the other side of the bed, stared at her in total disbelief.

"*How much?*" Jack asked.

Molly grinned.

"Molly – oh, you're an absolute wonder!" Annie cried in admiration, then lowered her voice as she drew a reproving "Ssh" from the Sister who sat at the desk at the end of the ward. "How on earth—"

"Not all in one go, of course," Molly said a little hurriedly. "But it's a start. We can invest in a couple of lorries and a couple of smaller vans and get back into business. We can use the undamaged warehouse. The hut will do for an office just for now. And once we get the rebuilding started, there won't be a better-equipped or more up-to-date outfit in the area than Danbury's. It's an ill wind that blows no good at all. What we have to do is to make certain that we don't lose too many customers and find ourselves having to start back at the beginning—"

"And who's going to do that?" Jack asked.

"Why, I am, of course. Nancy's offered to take over the agency for me, just while you're off your feet. We can't let the clients go, Jack, you must see that? We'd never get them back, bank loan or no bank loan. Now, what do you think about horses? Is there any point in—?"

"How did you get the loan?" asked Jack quietly.

"I went to the bank."

"So did I."

Silence stretched a little awkwardly. Annie looked from one to the other.

"I – well, as a matter of fact I didn't go to our usual bank. I went to a bank manager whom I knew, someone who'd used the agency in the past. It seemed more sensible. He was very sympathetic. He—"

"Sympathetic? A bank manager?" Jack's tone was frankly disbelieving.

"Oh, for God's sake, they are human, you know. What's the matter with you? I thought you'd be pleased—" Molly let irritation show clearly in her tone. Across the bed Annie quirked her eyebrows.

Jack reached for her hand. "I'm sorry, lass. I was surprised, that's all."

On the way home in the bus Annie looked at her intently. Molly pretended to be absorbed in the scene outside the window. Annie dug her in the ribs, none too gently.

"All right, then, come on."

"Come on what?" Molly was defensive.

"How did you do it? You don't fool me with your wide Irish eyes, love. Where did you get the money?"

"From the bank, as I said."

"And?"

Molly turned on her in a quick flash of anger, held the sympathetic green eyes for a moment and then looked away. "I put up the agency."

"What!"

"I borrowed the money on the agency. It was the only thing I could do. The bank wouldn't think of lending it to Danbury's without collateral. The agency was all I had to offer. They've made it a – a transferable company loan, or something. It means that they've lent the money to me – to the agency if you like – and I lend it to Danbury's."

"And if Danbury's fails?"

"It won't."

"But if it does?"

Molly looked back through the window. "Then the agency goes too, I suppose. But it *won't*, Annie. I'll see that it won't. If I have to work twenty-five hours a day I won't see it fail. I've done it before, and I will again. I'll talk every damned firm from Silvertown to Wanstead into using us, see if I don't!"

Annie shook her head. "Jack won't like knowing that you borrowed the money on the agency."

"He isn't going to know!" Molly was fierce. "Not from me, and not from you either. And neither is anyone else. Nancy knows, and so does William Baxter our chief clerk – he had to, for he handles the books. But as far as the rest of the world is concerned I've borrowed the money on Danbury's, and that's that. And if I want to work like a lunatic to get the place going again, it's maybe because I *am* a lunatic. No one will be surprised at that. Don't dare to say anything, Annie. I'll never forgive you."

"I won't," Annie said peaceably, and then after a short silence added, "You're right about one thing, though. You are a lunatic." She turned a laughing face to Molly. "But then aren't we all, one way or another? I can talk."

"Something in particular?" Molly asked interested.

Annie grinned. "Something very particular. I'm pregnant again."

CHAPTER THIRTY-SIX

THE CARTING BUSINESS, Molly discovered with no great surprise, was even more than most a man's world. A world of warehouses and cold stores, of docks and railway sidings, a world of cut-throat competition and tough business methods. Within a couple of weeks of the fire, armed with a list of Danbury's customers that had been supplied from Jack's and William Baxter's memories, for all their records had been destroyed, she began the thankless and dispiriting task of visiting each one in turn, explaining, arguing, cajoling, all but begging. As she had feared, a lot of their business had either gone or was on the point of going to other carriers. Frozen meat could not wait while Danbury's rebuilt, nor could cargoes of butter, tea, coffee, spices remain stacked in warehouses. Stubbornly she persisted, salvaging a little here, extracting a half-promise there, finding herself confronted by a variety of attitudes that ranged from the faintly sympathetic to the downright scornful. Her small, smartly-dressed figure was to be seen on the wharves and quaysides, in the warehouses and the railway sheds. She ran the gauntlet of rough and picturesque appreciation that her appearance in these traditionally male-dominated strongholds provoked with cool self-possession, she risked life and limb as she climbed steep flights of rickety steps in her restricting hobble skirt to sit in a dirty, paper-strewn office and try to convince an overworked and impatient transport boss that Danbury's was not wrecked, that the new lorries would be on the road in days rather than weeks. Some took her seriously, most did not. The disparagement and thinly-veiled ridicule, the impatience, the sometimes sympathetic but always firm refusals to believe that a woman could possibly handle such a business, predictably made her more determined than ever not to give up. But it was hard at the end of an exhausting and often unsuccessful day not to worry, not to remember that every day that went by meant interest to pay, wages bills to be met; harder still to push to the back of her mind the fact that every penny wasted, every shilling unearned was a threat to her own business that she had fought so hard to establish. She saw little of the children – Sarah and Annie, with a minimum of fuss, had stepped into that particular breach – and she fell into bed each night, her aching brain still whirling with activity. She would admit to being discouraged to no one. She visited Jack, watched his steady progress, greeted with a bright, deceitful smile his enquiries as to how her efforts were progressing.

" – William Baxter's been grand. He's working for two to get the books in order. He's never wrong. His memory's amazing. I never find myself anywhere without every fact and figure I need at my fingertips. Lestor's? Well, no, we didn't get that one back, actually. But then, there was never any great profit in it, was there? We're probably better off without them—"

And so, through a May that drizzled like November she trudged, and talked, and tried to ignore the spectre of ruin that marched at her shoulder. At the end of the month Jack was allowed home. The parlour was converted into a cheerful bedroom for him, and on Sunday afternoon the family gathered, bringing books and flowers and advice for the bed-ridden:

"He's trying to do too much," Molly said severely. "Tell him, Charley – if he doesn't behave himself he'll never get well."

"She's right, lad."

"Aye. Mebbe so. But they'll not keep me here for ever. Good as new I'll be in no time."

Later, Charley cornered Molly. "Don't worry, our Moll. We'll keep him still for you. You carry on. How's it going?"

Her momentary hesitation was not lost on his sensitive ear. "Fine. Just fine."

There was a good deal more bravado than truth in the words. As summer approached and the weather improved, in the same but lighter lady-like hobble skirts, sweeping hats and toe-constricting boots she continued to storm square mile after square mile of dockland, acres of railway yards. Hot, nervous, determined, she talked until she was hoarse, learned to swallow pride and strong sweet tea in the same gulp. But in that clear-seeing recess of her mind that she tried, most of the time, to ignore, she knew that she was not winning. Despite Edward's enthusiastic help in the buying of the best and most adaptable transport that they could afford, despite William Baxter's earnest help, despite her own back-breaking, soul-destroying efforts, Danbury and Benton, Carters were slipping inexorably towards disaster, and with it the agency.

"You'll wear yourself out," Nancy said worriedly one night.

"You could be right at that." Molly pulled her boots off and lifted her tired feet to a chair. "God, I'd give anything to go straight to bed."

"Why don't you?"

Molly rubbed her fingers through her tangled hair. "I can't. I've got some figures to go through. Tomorrow's a big day."

"Oh?"

"Tomorrow I beard a Mr Joseph Forrest in his den."

"And?"

"And I either get a big contract for carting Mr Forrest's frozen meat from London to all points north and south or—"

"Or what?"

"Or I admit that I'm neither use nor ornament to Danbury's and quietly shoot myself."

"Are you expecting to get it?"

"To be honest, no." Molly yawned. "But don't tell the Good Lord that. He's on the side, so they say, of those who help themselves. Well, I'm trying at least."

"No one," Nancy said with feeling, "could deny that."

Mr Joseph Forrest's office was large and comfortable and reflected perfectly the temperament of its tenant. It was warm, businesslike, friendly. After the cold, partitioned, rubbish-strewn offices to which she had become accustomed, Molly found the comfort a relief. She liked both the room and its occupant on sight. Joseph Forrest was a grey-haired, portly gentleman of late middle age. His face was a kindly contoured map of fine lines and folds, his skin the burnished colour of a man who spends a good deal of time in the open air. His dark eyes were very shrewd.

"Well, Mrs Benton—" he said steepling his hands before him, "I have to be honest with you. I'm really not sure. It doesn't sound to me as if you actually have the organization—"

"Mr Forrest, I—"

" – to cope with our volume of work. We have a very particular problem, as I'm sure you will appreciate." He studied for the space of a second the small, strong, disappointed face with its wide, smokey eyes and its halo of curly dark hair. "However," he added.

Molly was used to 'howevers'. She looked up with a caustic gleam in her eye. "However?"

"However, we do have a contract that has not yet gone to tender. One that might interest you."

She waited.

"It is not such a big one, nor so profitable as the meat," he said, spreading well-tended hands before him, "but it would be easier for a firm such as yours to cope with."

Molly, with dignity, stood up. She had heard this before, many times. "Don't tell me," she said, "baby's bottles. Embroidery silks? Something, anyway, that you consider fitting for a carting concern run by a woman?" She was at the door before his voice stopped her.

"Fruit," he said. "From the docks to the retailers. Small amounts, short distances. Small profit margins, too, but plenty of them if you're ready to work."

She stopped, turned. "I'm sorry, Mr Forrest. That was unforgivable."

He shook his head.

"May I sit down again?"

"Of course."

An hour later they were established friends. She knew of his young wife and their adored baby daughter, the house they owned in Westcliff-upon-sea, his passion for sailing and the outlines at least of the fruit contract.

"It's my partner whom you need to see, really. A very go-ahead young gentleman, just back from the United States. He has the facts and figures of the fruit side of things. Could you come tomorrow? Say – ten thirty?"

Molly mentally rearranged her day. "Of course. I'll see you then."

She was ten minutes early. She walked the dirty, busy streets, for those minutes, determined not to seem too eager. She walked through the ornate revolving door at exactly twenty-nine minutes past ten and then took the lift to Mr Forrest's office. He was delighted to see her.

"Mrs Benton! Come in, come in. Would you care for tea?"

"Yes, please." She glanced round. The office was empty.

"My partner will be along in a moment. As a matter of fact I've only just managed to contact him. He's been in Liverpool, on a matter of business. But I left a message—Ah." There had come a sharp rap on the door. " – This will be him. Come in."

She lifted and turned her head, froze as the door swung open to reveal a slight, smiling, sparely elegant figure poised in the doorway. She would have recognized him anywhere.

"Adam," Mr Forrest said, "Come along in. How was Liverpool?"

"Liverpool, as always, was dirty," Adam Jefferson said, "but profitable, I'm glad to say." Not by a flicker did he betray the slightest emotion or recognition.

"Well, I'm glad to hear that. Come and meet the young lady I told you of. I didn't mention her name, did I? Mrs Benton, Adam Jefferson, my partner. Adam, this is Mrs Benton."

They looked at one another. "As a matter of fact," the light, husky voice said quietly, "we've met. Mrs Benton and I are old friends."

Molly stood up with considerable care. Her legs were trembling. She extended a perfectly steady hand. "Mr Jefferson."

He moved into the room with all the grace she remembered, yet something about his step was different. His face was hard as stone, the faint, polite smile did not reach his eyes. He took her proffered hand for the most fleeting of moments, the very least that good manners required, and then let it go. She clasped both hands firmly before her and sat down again, very straight.

Joseph Forrest did not seem to notice anything amiss. "Mrs Benton is running her husband's carting business at the moment, Adam, while he recovers from an accident. There was a fire. Nasty business. You may have heard?"

Adam shook his head very slightly. He had moved to a chair

and stood leaning gracefully against the high back, his eyes and attention upon Joseph Forrest. "I didn't, no."

Joseph Forrest shook his head, tutting. "Terrible thing. Terrible. Still—" he said, smiling in fatherly fashion at Molly, "it could have been worse. Your husband, my dear, must feel he is a very lucky man to have such a woman as you behind him. Very lucky indeed."

Molly felt the beginning of a mortifying rise of colour into her cheeks. Adam turned his head and the dark glance flicked over her, sardonically, just once. He almost smiled. Molly sat very still, her every effort bent upon resisting the temptation to march over and slap him, hard. Then the memory of the time that she had done just that washed over her and her cheeks flamed again.

"I thought, Adam, that you might show Mrs Benton over the store? With your agreement I intend to let the fruit contract go to Danbury's—?" He waited for a moment. Adam lifted a narrow, nonchalant shoulder in agreement. "Adam's our expert, Mrs Benton. That's why I poached him away from several other interested parties, eh, Adam?" He turned jovially to Adam. "Don't forget to show Mrs Benton the loading bay that Danbury's will be using."

"I hardly think, Joseph," Adam said quietly, "that Mrs Benton will be driving the lorries herself." He let a small silence develop before he added, the slightest acid edge of sarcasm in his voice, "Or will you?"

She met the goad of his eyes, and for one fiery moment the spark of her temper flared at his unpleasant smile. "No, Mr Jefferson," she said coolly. "Someone taught me a long time ago to let others do the job that they do best. My – our – drivers are extremely competent. I've no intention of doing a hard-working carter out of a job." She stood up. "Goodbye, Mr Forrest. And thank you." She turned to Adam. "Shall we go?"

Adam turned and walked to the door, and Molly, following him, realized suddenly the difference in him. He was limping, very slightly. He still carried himself straight and gracefully, but there was a marked irregularity in his step. On the carpeted landing he pressed the button for the lift and the machinery whirred efficiently. He stood staring straight ahead. Molly, beside him, found herself suddenly bereft of words. She watched the smooth action of pulley and cable through the latticed gates as the lift moved up the shaft towards them. The silence between them was tangible, stony. As the lift car stopped before them with a gentle jolt Adam threw back the gates, stood waiting for her to precede him, perfectly mannered. She stepped inside. He followed; the gates clashed. As they moved smoothly downwards she glanced in the ornate mirror that decorated the side wall of the lift. Multiple reflections of herself and Adam receded into infinity. For one second she allowed herself to study him – the set of his head, the sharp clarity of bone, the straight, hard mouth. She turned away. The lift came quietly to rest. They stepped into the main entrance hall of the building, an impressive marble hall, carpeted and furnished as much like a hotel as a place of business.

"This way." Adam's voice was clipped and cool. He took her lightly by the elbow and steered her through the busy hall to a small swing door at the rear of the building. Once through they were in a narrow, dirty alleyway, unevenly paved between high, blackened brick walls. Adam let go of her arm. Despite his disability he walked very fast. Molly hurried beside him, taking two steps to his one, stumbling awkwardly in her high-heeled boots on the uneven ground, gritting her teeth against asking her escort to slow down. The alleyway led them into one of the main commercial thoroughfares that skirted the docks. The wide road was a chaos of horse-drawn vehicles, trams, motor lorries, porters with carts and with barrows. Adam plunged straight across. Perforce, Molly followed. Halfway across she hesitated a little nervously as an enormous horse plodded in front of her, pulling a heavily loaded cart.

"Come on, Missis," said an impatient voice, "what the 'ell you doin'? You can't stop there."

A tram bell clanged noisily. Molly felt her heel slip into one of the tramlines. She lifted her skirt and disengaged her foot, noticing as she did so that her best leather boots were badly scratched. She muttered fiercely beneath her breath. A firm hand took her elbow and Adam propelled her with some force to the other side of the road. Once there she shook herself free, exasperated. "Is there a fire somewhere?" she asked, with asperity.

He eyed her for a moment, his face expressionless. Around them as they stood the current of humanity swirled. Nearby a group of men, all dressed alike in shabby clothes, flat caps and mufflers, their feet encased in the enormous protective boots of the docker, leaned against the dock wall, smoking and talking. There were few smiles, no laughter, as these casual labourers, shoulders slumped, waited for the noon call-on in the faint hope that they might be luckier than they had been that morning. Somewhere a ship's siren sounded. A long, clanking line of railway trucks pulled slowly past them and the traffic slowed as the trucks crossed the road towards the depot.

"You have to move fast round here," Adam said in that distinctive voice she remembered so well, "or you're dead. Or crippled."

She glanced sharply at him, wanting to ask, knowing that she could not.

"No," he answered the unspoken question easily, "I didn't fall under a train. I had a motor accident, in the United States. Last year. Now – do you want to see the store or not? I haven't much time, I'm afraid. I've an – appointment at twelve." She did not miss the fractional hesitation and came to an immediate conclusion as to the nature of his appointment.

"If you're too busy—" she said, stiffly.

"Oh, for Christ's sake." He was mildly impatient. "If you're going to work for us, as Joseph said, you'll find it helpful to know how we operate. You'll need to instruct your drivers. Are you interested or aren't you?"

She pressed her lips very firmly together and nodded.

He led her through the great dock gates, where the policeman on duty touched his helmet respectfully. "Mornin', Mr Jefferson."

"There it is." Adam pointed to an enormous, windowless brick-built building that stood like the fortress of a giant by the waterside. A great arch in the lower wall showed glimpses, in the electric-lit, cavernous darkness within, of bustling activity. Railway lines led from the arch out through the dock gates.

"There's a station in there!" Molly said wide-eyed.

"That's right. A lot of our stuff goes out by rail. The docks are connected directly to the railhead. This way."

He strode ahead of her. Men greeted him respectfully, eyed Molly with some curiosity. Of necessity she paused at the foot of the very steep steps that led up to the door of the building, cursing once again, silently, her fashionable but totally unsuitable hobble skirt. Adam turned and saw her dilemma. For the first time since they had met in the office, his smile was genuine. He came swiftly back down the steps. "Hold on." Easily he bent down and lifted her bodily onto the first and highest of the steps. "There you are." He turned from her and walked into the great, cathedral-like building, leaving her to follow.

Molly stared after the straight, arrogant back for a moment, truly hating him. Hating him for the cool, businesslike briskness, for his apparent lack of any emotion but impatience at this unexpected meeting that had shaken her to her soul, for having hands so strong and warm that it was as if they still held her. The bells of danger were ringing loudly in her mind. She hesitated. There was nothing to prevent her from leaving right now, forgetting about the contract. For herself, she knew surely, it would be the best and most sensible thing to do. But for Danbury's? She had worked hard for this contract. Joseph Forrest liked her; she sensed it. Who knew what other work he might put their way if they handled this one well? If she walked away now, turned down the fruit contract for no admissible reason, what would he think of her? Of Danbury's? He'd never use them again, that was certain.

Adam had stopped and was talking to a large, red-faced man who was dressed in a rag-bag of clothes over which was spread a huge, stained apron. He towered over Adam's slighter figure – as indeed did almost every other man in the place. Why, she asked herself in irritation, didn't that make Adam look insignificant? He looked back at her now, waiting with scarcely disguised impatience for her to join them. Now or never. Stay or go?

She lifted her chin and marched into the noise and activity of the loading bay.

When she got back to The Larches Jack had visitors.

"Charley brought them," Nancy said.

"Union?"

Nancy shrugged. "I don't think so. How did it go?"

Molly tossed her hat onto the desk. "We got it. The fruit carting contract. Good terms, too."

"Marvellous! Jack'll be pleased."

"Mm. I'll tell him later, when his visitors have gone." Molly stood fiddling with the pens and pencils that were stacked tidily on the desk. "You'll never guess who Joseph Forrest's new partner turned out to be?"

"No?" Nancy was only mildly interested.

"Adam Jefferson." Molly, with sinking heart, realized with what pleasure she spoke that name again, despite everything.

That brought Nancy's head up. "Good Lord! I thought he'd gone to America or something?"

"He did. But he's back. About to make a fortune in cold storage, or so he believes."

"Well, well. You'd better keep your wits about you if he's got a finger in the pie—"

When Molly joined Jack in the parlour later he was lying propped up against his pillows, surrounded by bits of paper. His enforced inactivity had caused him to put on a little weight. His singed hair had grown again, the burn on his face was just a slight pinkness against the ruddy skin. His eyes were bright and clear, and they lit up when Molly walked through the door.

She smiled. "I've brought you a present."

"Oh, aye?"

She leaned close and kissed him lightly. "A contract to haul all of Joseph Forrest's fruit imports within London and Essex."

He opened his arms wide and caught her in a bear hug, rocking her back and forth. "You're a clever little lass, and no mistake."

She looked around for the first time at the papers scattered over the bed. "What's all this?"

"Just something I'm working on with a mate of Charley's. I'll tell you later, if anything comes of it." He leaned back on the pillows. "Are you at the yard tomorrow?"

She stood up, smoothing her dress. "As a matter of fact, I thought that I might just pop back to see Joseph Forrest. Nothing much, just a few details to be worked out—"

Later, seated at her dressing table with her hands to her burning cheeks, staring at herself in the mirror, she asked herself for the dozenth time why she had spoken the words. Why she had even thought them. There was no earthly reason for her to go near Forrest's. Of course she would not go. Of course not.

CHAPTER THIRTY-SEVEN

She sipped her sherry, felt it slide down her throat, warming her, calming her nerves. "Have you known Mr Jefferson for long?" she asked, very casually, and for all the world as if this were not the one and only question she had come to ask.

Joseph Forrest leaned back in his chair. "Oh, yes. We're old friends. I've been after him to join me for years. He's a very astute businessman, Mrs Benton, as you probably know. Very astute."

"Yes," she said.

"He has great hopes of the cold storage industry. He's been to the United States, seen how the big fellows work—"

Curiosity still nibbled. "You knew him when he was at Stowe, Jefferson, then?"

"Oh, yes, of course. Worse day's work old Stowe ever did was to let Adam go. The business world needs men like him. Men with drive, enthusiasm, ambition, brains."

"He certainly has those." She fiddled with her glass for a moment. "Why did he leave the company, do you know?"

Joseph Forrest cleared his throat. "Hrrmp." Molly looked up. To her surprise the older man's face was tinged a faint pink. She looked at him enquiringly.

He was obviously acutely uncomfortable. "I'm not sure – under the circumstances—"

"Circumstances?"

"The – the divorce . . ." He spoke the word as if the very taste were unpleasant. "Caroline was old Stowe's daughter, you see—"

"Yes, I did know that. You mean—" she paused, "you mean she divorced him?"

"Er, yes. That's right. But really, Mrs Benton, I hardly think—"

"And Adam left the firm and joined you?"

"Not just like that, no. He went to America, as you know, and when he came back it was my suggestion that he should join me. As I say, I've always admired Adam—"

"I am absolutely certain, Joseph," the light voice came from the doorway, "that Mrs Benton has not the slightest interest in my doings, past or future—" Adam stood, leaning slightly, at the open door. Beside him, a narrow hand possessively on his arm, stood a very pretty young woman whom Molly recognized immediately from the picture on Joseph's desk as Etta Forrest, Joseph's wife.

Joseph stood up. "Etta, my dear. Come in, come in, both of you. Where did you come across one another?"

Adam laughed as he escorted the girl into the room. She was dressed simply and elegantly in fawn and brown, which emphasized her shining brown hair and creamy skin. She walked gracefully to the desk, accepted her husband's kiss on a smooth cheek, then moved back to where Adam held a chair for her.

"We met outside the bank." Although he addressed himself to Joseph, Adam's cool eyes were still upon Molly. She blushed furiously, wondering how much of her catechism he had heard. "I persuaded Etta to a cup of coffee with me before handing her over to you, Joseph. I hope you aren't going to horsewhip me?"

Joseph laughed, jovially. "Good Lord, of course not, my boy. I have little enough time to give my Etta such little treats myself. Delighted. Absolutely delighted."

Molly stared at him in disbelief. Adam, as on the day before, had not sat down. Molly suspected that, with his damaged leg, it was an action that he could not yet manage with his customary ease. He leaned now behind Etta Forrest's chair, his hand on the chair back, his long fingers just brushing her shoulder. The young woman leaned a little towards him, eyes bright, a faint flush of colour in her pale cheeks. Molly could sense the attraction between them. Surely Joseph Forrest could not be so blind that he could not? Doting he might be; stupid, Molly already knew, he was not. Yet as he gazed at Etta his face showed nothing but pride and utter happiness. My God, thought Molly, the things love can do to us. She darted a look of pure dislike at Adam, who took it, unperturbed. She stood up, putting her glass on the desk.

"Not going, surely?" Adam asked politely. "Please don't let

us chase you away. Not before you've got all the information that you came for—?" The double meaning in the words was for no one in the room but Molly.

"I came to finalize some of the details of the contract," she said stiffly. "I really must be on my way now. With two businesses to run my time is very limited."

"Well, we're delighted that you could spare some of it for us, aren't we, Joseph?" Adam was laughing at her; he had not missed her tart tone, nor the flick of her glance at Etta.

"We most certainly are." Beaming, Joseph came out from behind his desk, his hand extended. "Delighted to do business with you, Mrs Benton," he said warmly. "I'm sure that we're going to suit each other very nicely."

She murmured her thanks, nodded to Adam and to Etta Forrest. The girl looked at her with some curiosity, called out "Goodbye, Mrs Benton."

As the door shut behind her Molly heard Etta's bright voice, pitched quite normally, so that it carried out on to the landing. "Good heavens! Was she serious? Does she really run a business? How extraordinary." It was clear that the words were not meant as a compliment.

Molly heard the sound of Adam's voice, could not hear what he said. She slammed the lift doors behind her hard enough to jam them for a week.

On the day that Jack managed to walk his first half-a-dozen steps alone, Nancy had disappeared on one of her Suffragette missions. When she returned late in the evening to be told the good news, she grinned delightedly. "I'll go and see him in a minute. I'd better get changed first."

Molly studied her. "Yes, I should think you'd better. Nancy, what in the name of Heaven have you been doing?" Nancy's clothes were splattered with scarlet paint, her hands were smeared with it, as was her face. The hem of her dress was torn and her hair was wild.

"Been painting the town red," she said lightly. "Unfortunately a couple of coppers took exception and we had to climb over some railings."

Molly opened her mouth, closed it again as the door opened.

"Hello, Aunt Nancy." Kitty regarded her with astonished eyes but, typically, did not comment.

Meg, just as typically, did. "Gosh, Aunt Nancy, what have you been up to now? You look like the wreck of the *Hesperus*. We just met Effie," she added to her mother without pausing for breath. "She says she can start on Monday. I said it'd be all right. Going up in the world, aren't we? Servants, and all—" She threw her head back and laughed. The twins grew more unlike each other with each day that passed. Meghan, tall and slender, with her mass of fair hair and clear, knowing eyes in a face that displayed her father's strong bones, looked by far the older of the two. "Come on, Kit. Lucy's expecting us – I told her we'd be there by four."

Smiling, Nancy watched them tumble from the room. "What a handful. And who's Effie?"

"Effie Price. You know – the family that lives on the corner of Sarah's road? She's coming to help me in the house."

"Well, it's about time you had someone." Nancy looked down at her ruined dress. "I'd better go and get myself cleaned up before I visit with brother Jack."

His first steps taken, Jack appeared to improve rapidly. His enormous strength and stubborn determination to get completely well drove him to greater efforts each day. Within a couple of weeks of those first steps he could walk with the aid of a stick but inevitably, he overdid it. The doctor tutted, shook a grey head. "Back to bed for a few days, Mr Benton. If you don't get off your feet and take some rest then I'll certainly take no responsibility for the consequences."

So poor Jack, seething and frustrated, had to submit to becoming an invalid again, fussed over happily by Effie Price, a tall, stringy girl with buck teeth and a soft voice who within a couple of days had made herself indispensable to the Benton household. She worked uncomplainingly, swiftly made friends with the children. For Molly she evinced a kind of astonished respect, while Jack she quite openly adored. His uncomplicated, straightforward kindness won her completely. Her own father was a shiftless, brutal man as likely to cuff her as to speak to her.

"Me Dad's a pig," she said frankly to Molly as she washed the breakfast dishes. " 'E's always threatening to up and go. Best thing that could 'appen for all of us, if you ask me."

Meg, still sitting at the table, giggled.

It was Saturday morning and Molly was due at Danbury's offices, where she hoped to catch up on some paperwork. She reached for her coat. "I'm sure you don't mean that, Effie."

"Don't I though?" muttered the girl with feeling as she attacked the pots and pans with more than usual vigour.

As Molly hurried into her coat, Meg jumped to her feet, as if she had been waiting for a signal. "You said we could come," she said.

"Come where?"

"To the yard. You said we could come and see Daisy's new foal."

"Oh—" Molly hesitated, " – not today, love. I'm very busy."

"You're always busy." Meghan's voice was flat. "So when? The foal will be a horse by the time we get to see it." Her lip pouted in an expression that Molly knew all too well. "You promised."

"I know I did, but—" Vague feelings of guilt stirred within her. "All right. Fetch Kitty, quickly. But you'll have to be good, and stay out from under my feet."

"We will." Meg scurried into the hall, shrieking for her sister. A little glumly, Molly followed.

Danbury's was still a long way from being out of trouble. Molly sat in the office poring over figures, leafing through files, nibbling her thumbnail, a straight line of worry between her brows. She sat back, sighing. The crippled carting firm was still on a knife edge. Fortunately the agency was doing well; but for how long could it bring in enough to subsidize Danbury's? How long before the agency, too, began to suffer?

"There's a gentleman here to see you, Mrs Benton." William Baxter put his head round the door. "A Mr Jefferson, from Forrest's. Says it's important."

Molly's lips tightened. She had not seen Adam since that embarrassing day he had overheard her asking Joseph Forrest about him. To have him see Danbury's, now, in chaos, was galling. "Send him in," she said, grimly.

Adam, personable as ever and looking a little out of place in the working yard and untidy temporary office, doffed his hat politely as he came into the room. Molly saw the swift look of appraisal that took in the cracked and hastily taped window, the patchwork roof, the cramped and uncomfortable office.

"It's temporary," she said, shortly, indicating her surroundings with a wave of her hand. "The fire destroyed the offices as well as the stables and a lot of the warehousing. It's more important to get them rebuilt first."

Adam glanced through the dirty window, but with some restraint forbore from pointing out that at the moment nothing at all was being rebuilt. "I guess it must be something of a struggle," he said pleasantly. His eyes on her were surprisingly warm. Molly was aware of her own ink-stained and dishevelled appearance. With as much dignity as she could muster she removed the pencil from the tangle of hair behind her ear, where she had thrust it while she was working.

"Business is picking up quite well now. It could have been worse," she said, coolly. The very last thing that she needed from Adam Jefferson, she thought savagely, was his sympathy. "You wanted to see me?"

He looked at her speculatively for a moment, and almost she could see his mental shrug. The tiniest sprig of olive branch had been offered and refused. "We've a shipment coming in on Monday," he said, his voice now brisk and businesslike, "and one of our clerks made a mistake when he sent the documents through. I was coming in this direction – I've brought the correct ones." He held out the envelope he carried.

"Thank you." She rummaged in a drawer. "Is it the Australian shipment?"

"Yes."

"And do you need the other documents back?"

"Yes, we do, I'm afraid." Still the very polite tone.

Molly waved a slightly harassed hand, "Won't you sit down? I'm not quite certain who had them. I haven't been in the office for a couple of days and— I'll have to ask Mr Baxter."

William Baxter looked up as she put her head round the door. "The documents for the Australian shipment? Yes, Mrs Benton, I know where they are. I'm sorry. I should have told you. I gave them to Smithson, to be ready for Monday. Would you like me to get them for you?"

"Yes, please." Molly managed to keep the relief from her voice. She shut the door and turned to find Adam, still standing, watching her with a totally unfathomable expression on his face. They looked at each other in silence. "Oh, for Heaven's sake," Molly said, suddenly nervous, "won't you sit down? It is all a bit silly, isn't it, this 'Mrs Benton' and 'Mr Jefferson' stuff? We're grown up people, after all. We should be able to behave in a civilized fashion. There's no law that says we can't be—" she sucked her lip, looking for the word.

"Faintly friendly?" Adam was laughing. He reached for the chair that Molly had offered. "I must say that the same thought had crossed my mind. It would certainly be less wearing than the present hostilities." With some care he lowered himself into the chair. "This beastly leg still gives me gyp sometimes," he said, and Molly found herself noting that it was the first unguarded thing that either had said to the other since that first time they had come so unexpectedly face to face in Joseph Forrest's office. She perched on the cluttered desk, watching him.

"How did it happen?" she asked straightforwardly.

"I was driving to the exhibition in Chicago, last autumn. A truck coming the other way ran out of control and hit me head on."

"How horrible."

"Not something to make a habit of. There was too much damage to make a complete repair—" he laughed easily " – to me or to the car. So they scrapped the car and did their best for me. It won't always be this bad, so they tell me."

"Does it hurt still?"

He held her eyes for a long moment. "I don't for the life of me know, Molly Benton, why I should tell you something that I rarely admit to anyone, but, yes, it does. Like Hell."

"You don't show it," she said.

The old derisive gleam was in his eyes. "Would you expect that I would? Of all the emotions that I might excite in others I think that sympathy is my least favourite. I will not have the world pity me."

She remembered the spasm of pain that had crossed his face as he had sat down. "It must be hard sometimes?"

He laughed. "Save your concern, Molly. Pure unadulterated pride is the key. And neither vanity nor a perfected talent for self-preservation are qualities particularly to be admired, except in oneself."

"You haven't changed a bit," she said.

He tilted his dark head, looking up at her. "But you have."

She said nothing, waiting for him to go on, but he did not. He stood up, and it was obvious that he had much more difficulty in doing this than he had in sitting down. Unbalanced and awkward, he had to turn, holding on to the back of the chair to prevent himself from falling. He quirked his dark eyebrows at her. "You see?" He walked to the window and stood looking out into the sunshine.

"Mr Forrest told me that you were divorced," Molly said quietly.

He turned a little, stood outlined against the light. She could not see his expression. "Yes." The single syllable gave absolutely nothing away. He stood stone-still, for a moment. Then, in the sunshine she saw the sudden flash of his smile. "Serves me right, don't you think? Would you sell the yard to me?" The last sentence was said with the same lightness as the first. Molly stared at him. In the office beyond the one in which they stood there were sudden, girlish shrieks of laughter.

"Kitty, you idiot! Wait till I tell Mum—" The door burst open to reveal Meghan, scarlet with laughter and beautiful as a poppy, and a rather downcast-looking Kitty.

"Mum! Guess what Kit just—" Meghan stopped, her eyes wide on Adam. "Oh. I'm sorry."

Adam smiled, his eyes appreciative. Meg blushed even brighter.

"Meghan, Kitty, how many times have I told you not to burst into a room like that?" Molly was conscious that her irritation was not just with their bad manners.

"Don't worry on my account." Adam was laughing. "Far be it from me to object to being interrupted by two such beauties! Your daughters, Molly?"

"Yes." Molly made the introductions brusquely. "This is

Kitty. The noisy one's Meghan. Girls, this is Mr Jefferson, of Forrest and Jefferson."

"Adam," said Adam easily, as he held out his hand.

"Hello," Kitty said shyly.

"How do you do, Adam." Meg was pert. She glanced up at him from beneath long lashes as she shook the proffered hand delicately.

Adam's look was openly admiring. "Well, thank you," he said formally.

"Now out," Molly said succinctly. "We're talking business."

Meghan tossed an affronted head. Since she had come into the room her whole appearance had subtly changed. She had fallen through the door a laughing, shouting child. Her poise now was that of a girl much older, her voice was composed. "We'll wait for you outside. It's nearly time to go home. You promised Dad you'd be back for lunch. He's got Mr Langton coming."

"Meghan, I don't need you to organize my life for me, thank you. Just go and play for half an hour. I'll be ready then."

As the door closed she turned back to Adam. "Did I hear you right? Did you just offer to buy the yard?"

"I did."

"Why?"

"Because I want it."

"Why?" she asked again.

He hesitated.

"Did you walk around before you came in?"

Again, the slightest hesitation before he nodded.

"Then it can't have escaped your notice that we haven't exactly got ourselves back on our feet yet?" She dismissed his ironic glance, reading into it exactly what he was thinking. "All right. I know what I said earlier. What else do you expect? You aren't the only one with—" She smiled suddenly, her eyes crinkling with laughter. "What was it? – 'vanity and a perfected talent for self-preservation'?"

He laughed with her, but his eyes were wary. "I'll give you a good price. I'm not trying to get something for nothing."

"That makes a suspicious change." She sobered, shook her head. "No."

"You drive a hard bargain. A very good price."

"No."

"You haven't heard what's on offer."

"I don't care. Danbury's isn't for sale."

He lowered himself into the chair again, looked up at her with thoughtful eyes. "Why not?"

"I don't have to tell you that, any more than you have to – or intend to – tell me why you want it."

This time he threw back his head and laughed in genuine amusement. "By God, I was right when I said you'd changed! The old Molly wouldn't have come back at me that smartly!"

"Don't be patronizing," she said, unruffled, "it doesn't become you at all."

Into the watchful quiet he asked, "Do you mind if I smoke?"

"Not at all."

She watched as he took out a cigarette case that glimmered dull gold in the sunlight. He extracted a cigarette with some care, tapped it on the case and then in sudden interested afterthought offered the case to her. "I'm sorry. Do you?"

She shook her head. "Not one of my vices."

He lit the cigarette, watched the wreathing smoke lift into the air. "I'm thinking of going into business myself, in a small way."

She waited, and when he did not elaborate asked, "Not carting, I assume?"

"No. A very small, very modern cold store."

"But Forrest and Jefferson have their own cold stores."

"Of course. And I'm not thinking of leaving Joseph. This would simply be an extra venture of my own."

"So you need land," she said shrewdly. "Land that is fairly well situated, close to the docks and—" she hazarded a guess, " – and near the rail terminals, as we are?"

"Almost right. But there's another consideration. I'm looking for something that is close to the heart of London. I have in mind a very exclusive trade."

"A piece of land like that would be fairly hard to come by. Most of it is built on already."

"So I have discovered."

"And that's why you want to buy Danbury's? To close it down and build this – exclusive cold store of yours?"

"Yes."

She shook her head. "No."

"Why not? I told you I'd pay a good price. There's a lot of land here, counting the odd bit beyond the stables."

Irritation stirred. "You really did have a good look round, didn't you?"

"You don't think I'd have made the offer if I hadn't, do you?"

"I suppose not."

"Well?"

She walked round behind the desk and sat down. "Adam, Danbury's is not for sale. I'm sorry, but there it is. The answer is no. Jack needs this place. I've worked my guts out for it. I'm not selling out, and that's that. We aren't beaten yet."

He was looking at her in an oddly calculating way. "What exactly have you been doing here for the past couple of months?"

She looked at him in surprise. "Me?"

"You."

She shrugged. "Selling, mostly. Convincing people that we aren't finished. Drumming up new business."

"As you did when you first started the agency?"

"Much the same sort of thing, yes. Why?"

He struggled to his feet. "I'm not sure. An idea, that's all. Something I need to think about." He nodded to the door. "The fairy princess out there said that you were expected home for lunch?"

"The fairy—? My God, don't let her hear you call her that. You'll turn her head completely. Yes, I do have to go." Oddly reluctant she walked before him to the door. "I can't think where Baxter's got to with those – Ah." As she opened the inner door William Baxter entered from the outer door, waving triumphantly a rather grubby envelope. "Here they are."

She handed the envelope to Adam. "And thank you for taking the trouble to come," she said, a little formally.

"I happened to be passing, as I said."

"And it did give you a chance to look over a piece of desirable property?" She could not resist the gibe.

He laughed. "Something like that."

As if by magic Meghan and Kitty appeared at the door. Meg sent her brightest and loveliest smile in Adam's direction. Adam smiled back.

"Time to go, girls," Molly said brusquely. "Say goodbye to Mr Jefferson."

Kitty whispered something.

"Goodbye, Adam," Meg said, and danced before her mother down the path towards the road. Just inside the gate stood a shiny motor car, dark green, its shiny chrome flashing in the sunlight. "Is that Ad – Mr Jefferson's, do you think?" Meg asked, darting a look at her mother from under her eyelashes.

"Undoubtedly," Molly said.

"Don't you think he might give us a lift home if we asked him?"

Molly turned repressive eyes onto her daughter, "I have no intention whatsoever of asking him so we'll never know, will we?" she asked, sharply.

Before they turned out of the gates she glanced back. Adam was standing, hands in pockets, in the middle of the yard, his eyes ranging the burned-out buildings, the derelict, weed-choked spaces. Molly turned away and hurried home.

"Ee, that was champion." Bernie Langton's north-country accent was as pronounced as Jack's had once been. He leaned back in his chair. "Reet champion," he repeated with some satisfaction.

"I understand you're in the building trade, Mr Langton?" Molly said politely.

"Aye. That's reet. There's a lot of brass to be made in the building just now, Mrs Benton. A lot of brass. And I'm makin' it." His tone indicated total satisfaction with himself and all his doings.

"May we leave the table?" Meg asked demurely.

Molly nodded. Danny and the girls rose with a great scuffing of chairs. At the door Danny paused. "I'll be out for the rest of the day," he said, too casually.

Molly looked at him sharply. "Where are you going?"

"Oh, just to meet someone—" he said vaguely, and was gone before she could remonstrate.

"Boys will be boys, Mrs Benton." Bernie Langton was

smugly expansive. "Can't keep the lad tied to your apron strings for the rest of his life, eh?"

With great difficulty Molly resisted the temptation to tell him to mind his own business. She had taken what she was certain must be an unreasonable dislike to Bernie Langton the moment she had met him.

"Will you take a glass of port, Langton?" Jack asked.

"Port? Oh, aye, I can always manage a drop o' that." The builder was a chunky, red-faced man with few social graces. Molly found that the surprised lift of his eyebrows as he saw that Jack was pouring not two but three glasses of port irritated her out of all proportion to the action. The interview with Adam that morning had disturbed her strangely. She could still hear his voice, still see that sudden characteristic lift of his head. Bernie Langton's boorishness seemed to rasp on nerves already laid bare.

"I'll tell Effie she can clear the table," she said, and stood up. Jack, at the sideboard and standing without his stick, took a step and staggered a little. She was by his side in an instant, supporting him with a now-practised shoulder. "You're doing too much, still, Jack. Remember what the doctor said."

"That's right, Mrs Benton, you tell him." Langton slapped his solid thigh jovially. "Got to get him back on his feet, eh? The sooner you can do that, the sooner you'll like it, eh?"

Molly had had enough. "I beg your pardon?" .

Jack's strong arm squeezed her shoulder, gently warning. "I think what Mr Langton's trying to say is that the sooner I'm better the sooner you can get away from the yard."

"Reet you are," the other man said. "Not that I don't think that you're a plucky little woman, mind, doin' what you have, but speakin' plain, it don't seem fitting to me. Women and business don't mix, to my way of thinking."

"Oh really?"

The challenge in Molly's voice went completely unnoticed. "That's reet. You'll never convince me that a woman wants anything but this—" he tapped the polished table complacently. "That's the way it's always been, don't see any reason why it should change now on account of a few hysterical females that need a good thumping. No, Mrs Benton, you stick to what you know. Them's fine kids you've got there, and this is a fine house. A credit to you. You're not going to tell me you need anything else?"

Molly saw Jack wince, his eyes on her face. She took a deep breath; the man, after all, was Jack's guest. "I believe you gentlemen have some business to discuss?"

Jack nodded.

"In that case I'll leave you to it. I've business of my own to deal with. I'll be in the office, Jack. I've some reports to go over. Effie will clear away and bring you coffee. Have her bring one in to me, would you? Goodbye, Mr Langton." And with barely a glance at their decidedly sobered guest she picked up her port and left them.

CHAPTER THIRTY-EIGHT

THE MESSAGE THAT Molly received a couple of days later asking her to meet Adam at his office on the following Friday was not, in view of their previous conversation, unexpected. With the object of remaining as unruffled as possible she ran to the extravagance of a cab, and so arrived some minutes early for the appointment. She took the smooth-running lift up to the fourth floor and was walking along the thickly carpeted corridor towards Adam's office when the door of that office opened, and Etta and Adam stood framed in the doorway.

"I told you, Etta. I have a business meeting." Adam's voice was firm.

The pretty mouth pouted. "Couldn't you—?"

"No." They were almost of a height. His hand was on her arm. She turned to him, tilting her shining brown head a little. Adam looked past her and saw Molly. "Mrs Benton," he said.

Etta drew back. Molly saw a flash of ill-temper in the suddenly narrowed eyes and the stiffened body. "My goodness," Etta said lightly, "so it is. Good morning, Mrs Benton. Still busy?"

"Yes." Molly made little attempt to keep the brusqueness from her own voice.

Etta turned back to Adam. "Well, I mustn't keep you from your business, must I? You'll be at dinner tonight?"

Adam inclined his head in assent.

"Good. About seven-thirty. Do come a little early, darling. We've got those *boring* Allingtons coming. I'm counting on you to keep me sane. Oh, dear, now look." With a fluttering gesture she had dropped one of her gloves, which landed at Adam's feet. "Silly me." She made no attempt to retrieve it herself, but stood looking at Adam, waiting.

Molly gritted her teeth.

Adam, very carefully, bent to pick up the fallen glove. It was a painful manoeuvre to watch. Etta's eyes flicked from Adam to

Molly and back again. When Adam straightened his face was pale and his mouth hard with pain. He handed the glove to Etta who accepted it with a small challenging smile, her colour high.

"Thank you. Don't bother to see me to the lift. I'll see you tonight." She swept past Molly with a bare inclination of the head.

Adam led the way into the office; Molly followed, closing the door firmly behind her. Adam stood for a second at the desk, his back to her. Knowing him Molly guessed at the rage he was fighting. But when he turned, his face was peaceful and completely unforthcoming. Their eyes met, and there was an odd silence that lasted a moment too long before Molly broke it.

"You wanted to see me."

The strange tension eased. "Yes." Adam lowered himself into a large and comfortable chair behind the desk, waved Molly to a similar one. "I apologize for asking you to come here, but I thought that my office might be a little more—" he smiled – "comfortable than yours. I'm sure you've guessed why I wanted us to meet?"

"You've decided to take me into your confidence regarding your new project," she said bluntly.

"More than that. I want you to join it."

She stared at him. She had been so absolutely certain that this meeting was to be an attempt to coerce her into selling Danbury's, she had come so ready to defend herself and the business from any incursion, however devious or subtle, that she now found herself completely at a loss. She said nothing, but watched Adam suspiciously.

He leaned forward, on his face an expression that she remembered well – totally absorbed, intense. "Let me explain. Don't say anything until I've finished. And don't go off the deep end. Don't decide until you've heard all that I have to say and until you have given yourself a chance to think about it." He took out a cigarette and lit it, studying it thoughtfully for a moment as he marshalled words. "As you know I've spent a good deal of time over the past few years in the United States. I've stayed in hotels from New York to New Orleans, from Pittsburgh to San Francisco. I've eaten in restaurants in Chicago, in St Louis, and in Miami. In none of these places have I ever been offered a drink without ice. I've eaten seafood a thousand miles from the sea, I've eaten Californian grapes in the depths of a New York winter—"

"You can do that in London," she said.

"Of course you can. In the top class hotels. The Savoy. The Ritz. Those that have their own cold-storage equipment, their own ice-making machines." He knew that she had readily grasped the thought behind his words. He watched her.

"Anyone can buy ice, from the Norwegian ships," she said, "There's no difficulty in that—"

"Natural ice. Cut straight from the fiords and ice-fields. Cloudy. Difficult to handle. Machine-made ice is clear, easier and more attractive to use. Molly, listen to me. The luxury use of ice and cold storage is an industry about to boom. The Americans already have the ice-habit. It can only be a matter of time before it spreads over here. We can be in at the start. Oh, I'm not thinking of competing with the big fellows – the Australian frozen meat men, the fruit exporters. I'm not interested in the bulk markets. What I have in mind is a small, exclusive trade. Little hotels and restaurants in London who don't have their own cold storage or ice-making equipment but who can be persuaded to see the advantage in using ours. We'll offer them a luxury service. We'll show them that they can compete with the top-class hotels. We'll provide them with only the very best, the most carefully selected, quality goods."

"All these 'we's'," she said.

He took no notice of the comment. "It will be a small volume of trade with relatively high profit margins. Our clients will discover that they are getting an excellent service that can only improve their reputations, their clientele, and therefore their profits. We'll provide them with flowers from France for their tables, ice for their drinks, the very best quality meats and fish for their kitchens. All we have to do, Molly, is to educate them. To think ice. To think refrigeration. To think—" he paused, for effect " – to think Jefferson and Benton."

She did not move, nor did her expression alter by a flicker. "That sounds grand," she said, drily. "Now, where's the catch? I have to sell you the yard? Or put up the money? Or both?"

He stubbed out the half-smoked cigarette. "Use your brains,

girl. I've got the money and the know-how. You've got the land. And – well, we'll talk about your other assets later." He grinned like a boy, then sobered. "We could do it, Molly. Danbury's land is perfectly sited. You have the men, the transport, the beginnings of an organization. We'd be partners."

"You and me? Partners?"

"And Jack, of course," he said easily. "And there's some possibility that we might have to go to Joseph for extra finance. He's got wind of the idea and is keen to join. And a lot of my assets are tied up at the moment, both here and in the United States. But to be truthful, I'd rather not call on Joseph."

"Why not?"

"This is my baby. I've spent a lot of time and energy on it. I'd like to run it my way."

She notched that one up to be considered later.

"Well?" he asked, "What do you think?"

"I don't know," she said, honestly.

"What can you lose? Danbury's is failing. You're very heavily in debt—"

She picked that up sharply. "What makes you say that?"

"It's common knowledge," he said flatly. "What isn't common knowledge is that you've mortgaged the Venture Agency almost to the hilt to support Danbury's. You're in danger of losing much more than just the yard, Molly—"

She jumped to her feet. "*Who told you that?*"

He shrugged. "A little bird."

She faced him, glowing with fury. "Only three people know where that money came from. And only one of them has had any contact with you. What did you do, Adam, bribe him?" Her voice was bitter.

He shook his head, watching her.

"He's fired anyway."

"That's hardly fair. William Baxter, my dear, is totally devoted both to you and to Jack. Why make him pay for my sins? The fact is that I already had an inkling. When I spoke to Baxter I spoke as if you had told me yourself. You can't blame the old man for confirming it."

"How had you guessed?"

"By making a few discreet enquiries."

"The religious brotherhood of money," she said, scornfully.

"Something like that, yes."

"I don't think much of your business methods."

"You never did," he said equably.

"We couldn't possibly work together."

"Couldn't we? Are you absolutely certain of that? It would be a pity if it were so. For I haven't yet told you of what I consider to be Danbury's biggest asset."

"What's that?"

"You. Molly Benton, and her persuasive Irish tongue. To say absolutely nothing of her pretty Irish face and the cheek of the devil."

She nibbled her lip. The silence lengthened.

"Why don't you sit down again?" Adam suggested softly, "and I'll tell you what I had in mind?"

"And just what does he expect you to do?" Nancy asked.

Molly curled and uncurled the lock of hair that had fallen onto her forehead. "He wants me to sell the idea. To go around to the hotels and restaurants and persuade them to use the service. As I did with the agency when we first started. As I suppose you could say I've been doing with Danbury's. He's got it all worked out. He puts in the money and the contacts, we supply the land and the men. He's the financial wizard, Jack handles the men and the day-to-day running of the place, I do the initial selling and the research into who wants what and when."

"What do you think? Do you fancy it?"

Molly hesitated. "Yes. It's no good pretending that I don't. I wouldn't admit it to Adam Jefferson, but it's a gift from the gods, really. Danbury's isn't going to make it, Nancy, though I've not admitted that to anyone else. This is an opportunity for a fresh start. And it's a damned good idea. With a bit of effort, a bit of hard work, it could take off." She hitched herself onto Nancy's desk and swung her feet, her head bowed in thought. "Two things worry me. One of them, I think I can sort out – and Adam himself has handed me the means." She smiled, a little grimly. "He isn't going to like it one bit. The other – well, the solution to my other problem depends upon you."

"Oh?"

"Well, you must see? I can't be in two places at once. It means leaving things as they are here for longer than we originally agreed."

" – Place runs itself—" Nancy said laconically. "You've got it going like clockwork."

"Nonsense. I couldn't possibly do it without you."

Nancy, smiling, shrugged the words aside. "What is it that Mr Jefferson isn't going to like?"

Molly slipped from the desk, her expression pensive. "I think," she said at last, "that I'm going to insist on a fourth partner. Joseph Forrest. I trust him," she added obliquely.

"And you don't trust Adam Jefferson?"

"I don't trust myself, or Jack, to be smart enough to match him. Neither of us has eyes in the back of our heads. However small a share Joseph takes I feel it will be some kind of safeguard. Adam, I dare say, won't like it – but then, let's see just how keen he is to lay his hands on Danbury's. I've quite made up my mind. And for the fourth shareholder Joseph is the obvious choice. In fact, from Adam's point of view, he must be the best. Joseph will go along with almost anything Adam wants to do, I'm certain. It's just that – well, if Adam wants to cut corners, then he's bound to do it openly, that's all. Joseph's enthusiasm for Adam will be our safeguard."

Nancy shook her head admiringly. "Goodness. Who's been teaching you such tricks?"

Molly laughed a little. "You'd be surprised. Now comes the hardest part. I've got to convince Jack; we can't do anything without him. Let's hope he's in a good mood."

"He's in the parlour," Nancy said. "That awful Langton man's been with him for the best part of the afternoon, but I think he's gone now."

Heading for the door, Molly held up crossed fingers. "Wish me luck."

He was, as Nancy had said, still in the parlour – alone. His legs were getting stronger by the day, there was a new look of vitality about him.

"Well, lass," he greeted her before she could open her mouth, "You can stop worrying. It's all sorted, and I start back at the yard on Monday."

"Sorted?" she asked, taken aback.

"That's right. It'll mean a bit of a change of course, but there you are, things can't stay the same for ever and if Danbury and Benton have to become a glorified builder's yard to survive, well, I suppose it could have been worse—?"

"A *builder's* yard?" She looked at him in total incomprehension. "Jack, what are you talking about?"

"The deal with Langton. Oh, I know you don't care for him love, but there you are — 'Where there's muck there's brass', eh?" His laughter was a little strained.

"What have you done?"

"I told you. I've done a deal with Langton. He's got this big contract for the new worker's estates east of here. Thousands of houses. Back-to-backs. You know the kind."

"I know them."

"I've got the contract to haul his supplies. Bricks, timber, cement, tiles, the lot. And storage, too. We won't make a fortune. Drives a hard bargain, does Bernie. But it'll tide us over, any road. It'll be years before those estates are finished. It won't make millionaires of us, but by God it'll keep our heads above water. What do you think of that?"

Molly found her voice. "Have you actually signed anything?"

"We don't need that, lass. A word is a bond among friends."

"Something like that will take up almost all the yard."

"Aye, it will. Molly? You don't seem overpleased?"

"It didn't occur to you to tell me?" she asked quietly. "Even to mention it to me?"

He frowned. "Do I expect you to tell me what's going on in the agency?"

Caught in her own trap she said, "No. Of course not."

"Well, then. From now on you can stop worrying your head about Danbury's. I'm back. If you ask me you should take a few days off. You've been working too hard. Come on, lass, how about a smile, eh?"

She lifted her head and smiled tiredly. "I'd best go and see Effie about dinner."

She walked the floor of Adam's office, her boot heels clicking sharply on the polished wooden surface. Adam watched her in silence. She reached the window and stopped, staring sightlessly into the busy street, her arms crossed tightly before her, her small hands gripping her elbows.

"And you didn't even tell him?" Adam asked at last.

"I couldn't." She spun on her heel, began her interminable restless pacing again. "How could I? What could I have said? – 'Oh no, Jack dear, I've got other plans'? You don't know him. You don't know what it would do to him."

"But you do – 'have other plans'"? Adam's voice was soft.

"Not any more." She turned from him.

"But you did think about my proposition? You did like it?"

She stood with her back to him, drumming her fingers on the windowsill. "Yes." The word was barely audible.

"You would have gone ahead with it?"

She swung around to face him. "Adam, I *can't*. Don't you see? Danbury's isn't mine to dispose of as I see fit. It's Jack's responsibility—"

" – it's your money—"

"He doesn't know that. And he isn't going to know."

"Is this building contract a viable proposition?"

"I suppose so, yes." She dropped dispiritedly into a chair, "It's worth years of good, steady, quiet work. And Bernie Langton has wrung blood out of Jack for pennies. But, as Jack pointed out—" she pulled a wry face " – it'll keep our heads above water."

"But it isn't what you want?"

"You know it isn't."

"Then you have to tell Jack about our plans. Make him see that we have a better proposition. Show him the money he'll make – the independence it will give him—"

Very slowly she lifted her head, looked directly into his face, her eyes sombre. "You still don't see, do you? After all this time you *still* don't understand the kind of man Jack is? He has accepted Langton's proposition. He has shaken hands on it. To Jack that's sacred. It's more binding than a dozen contracts, signed and sealed. You could show him the crown jewels and it wouldn't change his mind. Expediency might be your watchword, Adam. It may, even, sometimes be mine," she added,

426

honestly, "but Jack doesn't know the meaning of the word. I tried to explain that to you once before."

"I remember."

She held out her hand. "At least, this time, we can say goodbye in a slightly more civilized way."

He hesitated a fraction of a second before taking her proffered hand. "You won't even try to talk him out of it?"

"You have to take my word that there would be no point."

She walked to the door, turned as he opened it for her. "From now onwards you'll be dealing with Jack, of course. On the fruit contract. He's taking over again, from Monday. I – don't suppose we'll bump into each other again."

"Possibly not."

"Goodbye, then."

He smiled.

"Au revoir."

CHAPTER THIRTY-NINE

THREE DAYS LATER the storm broke. Molly walked into the kitchen of The Larches to find Effie in tears, the twins watching her, wide-eyed, Kitty doing her best to comfort her. "Oh, Missis," Effie sobbed, " 'E swore at me! *Swore* at me! 'E 'ad no call ter do that, now did 'e? I was only tryin' to 'elp—"

"Who? Who swore at you, Effie?"

The heartbroken sobs redoubled. "Why, Mr Jack did. Swore 'orrible, 'e did. *An'* shouted. Oh, Missis, 'e's in a terrible takin', I can tell yer. All I did was to offer 'im a nice cup o' tea. I thought it might do 'im some good! 'E 'ad no call to yell an' shout like that. Gawd knows, I get enough of it at 'ome," she added aggrievedly. "I don't 'ave to put up with it 'ere."

"No, of course not, Effie," Molly said soothingly, "and I'm sure there's been some mistake. I'll find Mr Jack and sort it out for you. Where is he?"

"In the parlour," Effie sniffed, then lifted her head and added, repressively, "drinkin'."

Jack did not turn as she opened the parlour door, although he must have heard her. He stood at the sideboard, his back to the room. She heard the clink of glass on glass, saw his head thrown back as he emptied the tumbler in one go.

"Jack? Is something the matter?"

Still he did not turn, nor did he answer. He poured more whisky into the glass, stood staring down into it. He looked massive in the fashionably cluttered room and something in his stance, in the tension of the wide and powerful shoulders made Molly hesitate. He looked – she paused at the thought – dangerous. "Jack?" she said again, uncertainly.

He turned very slowly. As composedly as she could she walked to him. "Jack, love, what is it? What's happened?"

"Why – didn't – you – tell – me," he said, spacing his words very carefully and slowly, his voice a little whisky-blurred, "That – the money – that you borrowed – was lent – not to

Danbury's – but – *to your bloody agency?*" The last words were roared, and he slammed a violent hand on the sideboard, making the glasses jump and tinkle.

She clasped her hands before her. Patently there was no point in denial. "I didn't think it necessary. What difference did it make? We needed the money, and that was the only way to get it."

"What difference does it make?" Jack laughed, harshly. "I'll tell you, my girl, what difference it makes. It makes me look a bloody fool. It makes me look like a ninny who's tied to his woman's apron strings." He glared at her, drained his glass again. "Happen that's what I am, eh? Happen they're right?"

"Jack, for Heaven's sake, what's this all about? Yes, I did borrow the money using the agency. What would you have had me do? Let Danbury's go? I didn't tell you because – because I thought you might be unreasonable about it. And I wasn't far wrong, was I?" she could not resist adding. "But, Jack, no one knows. No one but Annie, and Nancy, and––" She stopped at the sudden worm of recollection that slithered through her mind.

He turned on her savagely, his eyes lit bright with rage.

"No one knows, eh? Well, let me put you right there, lass. Everyone knows. The whole bleeding world knows. Everyone, that is, except me."

"But––"

"Let me tell you what my friend Bernie Langton thinks of it all." He spoke in a venomously conversational tone. "My friend Bernie doesn't care overmuch for a grown man who can't manage his own affairs. Or his own woman. Who doesn't know what's going on behind his back. Who doesn't wear the trousers in his own business, let alone his own home. He feels he can't see his way clear to dealing with a woman. Doesn't seem right somehow, he says, though he knows some might think it old-fashioned––"

"Jack, stop it."

" – but since it's obvious that you're going to have a finger in the pie – any pie – he reckons 'appen he'd best take his custom elsewhere. He won't deal, he says, with a concern run by a woman."

"More fool him," she snapped, her control breaking. "The man's an idiot. And what about words and bonds, Jack? Doesn't this teach you something?"

He muttered something. She turned away. "You're drunk. I'm not going to stand here listening to you. I'll speak to you when you can talk sensibly."

He had her by the arm before she could take a step. "Oh, no. You'll bloody stay here and you'll bloody listen." His fingers curled, cruelly painful, around her wrist. "Danbury's is finished. Do you hear me? Finished. Without this contract, we're dead in a couple of months. We haven't got the work. I hope you're satisfied. If you'd told me, if you'd been straight with me, I might have been able to explain to Langton. I might have persuaded him—"

Infuriated, she found herself shrieking back at him. "It has nothing to do with him where the money came from!"

"Any road," Jack ploughed on, ignoring her, "I wouldn't have been left standing there like some wet-nosed school kid kept out of the grown ups' secrets." He threw off her arm and reached for the bottle.

Breathing hard she watched him for a moment, her mind racing, trying to gauge the extent of his anger, the unreason brought on by drink. "We don't need Bernie Langton," she said.

"Hah!" He threw his great head back in scornful laughter, staggered a little as he turned and toasted her sarcastically with his full glass. "Happen we don't. With Molly O'Dowd in charge, who needs anyone?" It was said brutally. He lifted the glass to his lips.

She stepped forward, reached for his arm, "Jack, please, don't drink any more. We have to talk reasonably about this."

"Let go of me!" She was no match for his strength and he flung her from him. Hampered by her skirt she could not keep her balance; she cannoned into a small table covered in ornaments, hit the wall with a bruising crash that knocked the breath from her body, and fell. Two tiny china figures flew from the fallen table and splintered on the floor, the other ornaments rolled and clattered amongst them. She huddled for a moment, head hanging, her hair in her eyes, her shoulder thumping with pain, trying to control the red mist of pure fury that threatened

o envelope her. She was trembling violently with rage and
reaction.

"Molly—" Jack took a step towards her.

She lifted a blazing face. "Stay away from me!"

"Oh, Jesus." Sobered a little, Jack slumped into an armchair,
buried his head in his big hands.

Very carefully, very slowly, Molly stood up. She shook the
tiny coloured shards of china from her skirt, sucked her bloody
finger briefly where one of the sharp pieces had slit the skin. Her
shoulder and neck hurt.

From outside the door Effie's frightened voice called. "Missis?
Mr Jack? You all right?"

"Mum?" Kitty's voice, high and strained.

Molly walked to the door and opened it a little. "It's all
right," she said steadily, only the faintest tremble of emotion in
her voice. "There's been a slight accident. Something got
broken. Nothing to worry about."

Effie peered over her shoulder to where Jack sat, hunched in
the chair. "Is Mr Jack all right?"

"Perfectly." The word was clipped. "He's had a little too
much to drink, that's all."

Effie nodded and backed down the hall, dragging the worried-
looking Kitty with her. Molly shut the door and leaned against
it, looking at Jack. Something in his stance – his bowed head and
shoulders silhouetted bright against the light, his strong fingers
buried in his hair – reminded her of something, of someone she
had seen just like this in the past. And then, with a shock, she
had it. Harry had looked exactly so in that moment that she had
flung open the bedroom door to confront him in fury. The day of
Danny's conception. Almost, now, as Jack moved she found
herself half-expecting to meet the brilliance of his brother's eyes,
to see the painfully bleached, beautiful face. Her anger drained
from her. In passion and in obstinacy she had almost destroyed
her own and others' lives that day. She would not let that
happen again. The passing years must surely have taught her
something? Giving him time to collect himself she righted the
little table, went down on her knees to gather the broken
ornaments.

"Leave it." His voice was hoarse. "Effie will do it."

431

She did not still her busy hands. "They might get trodden into the carpet."

"Molly—"

She sat back on her heels, regarding him, her hands full of broken china resting in her lap.

" – I'm sorry."

"I'm sorry too. But, Jack, I did what I did for the best. Danbury's desperately needed the money, and I had the means to get it."

He leaned back in the chair. "And now, with Langton backing out and the yard in trouble again the agency goes down the drain with it? Fat lot of sense that makes."

"It isn't going to be like that, Jack." She leaned forward, her face intent. "We aren't going to let an unpleasant, prejudiced article like Bernie Langton do us down, are we?"

"Do we have a choice?"

She laid the shattered china carefully on the table and stood up, smoothing her shirt into her waistband, tidying her hair. "Oh yes. We have a choice." She walked to where the bottle and glasses stood, splashed a very little into the bottom of two glasses, handed one to Jack and kept the other for herself. "Let me tell you about it."

She deliberately put off going to see Adam for two days. If she saw him any earlier, she knew, she might incline to physical violence. She did not ring, made no appointment. When she got to the building that housed Forrest and Jefferson in such style it was to discover that Adam was not there.

"He won't be long, though, my dear." Joseph Forrest was beaming at her. "He's gone over to the store. He'll be back in an hour or so. If you'd like to wait in his office I'm sure he'd have no objection – or you could stay, perhaps, and take a cup of coffee with me—?"

But the two days of self-imposed waiting had strained her patience and her temper beyond endurance. The thought of another hour's idleness was too much for her. "Thank you, no," she said. "I'll go and find him."

He was, the cold store manager respectfully told her, up on the roof where the cranes were unloading a cargo from a ship locked behind the store. A wheezing lift, its scrubbed wooden doors and sides stained and battered, took her up the five stories to the wide expanse of the roof. She stepped into sunshine and a hive of activity. Stacks of crates littered the open space, brawny men in stained white aprons trundled great trolleys piled high with bales and carcasses. The twenty lifts that served the building and dispersed the newly-delivered cargo into the various cold-storage chambers that honeycombed the store below flashed and hummed with industry. Adam stood, talking animatedly, with two other men not far from the lift in which Molly had arrived. As she stepped from it he lifted his eyes and caught sight of her. She saw the slight stilling of his movements, the wary look that flickered across his face. She stood still, waiting for him, uncaring of the attention she was attracting. Adam said something to his companions and one of them guffawed loudly. Then, with his light, slightly unbalanced walk, Adam came towards her.

He artlessly spread beautiful and absolutely clean hands. Nemesis has found me."

"I want to talk to you."

"I rather thought you might."

"I want to know—"

"But not here."

"Adam, I'm not playing games. I want to know—"

Very firmly he caught her arm beneath the elbow. "But not here," he repeated with tranquil insistence. "I may deserve castigation. Not surprisingly, I refuse to accept it in public. You should have waited for me at the office."

She blazed. "Don't tell me what I should and shouldn't do!"

He steered her to the lift, shut the doors behind them firmly, pressed the button, then turned to survey her furious face. "Oh dear," he said.

Her temper, finally, seemed to have slipped its leash together. "Do you know what you are?"

He appeared to consider this as the lift crawled down the building. On each floor as they passed she could see activity as the newly arrived shipment was stowed away. "Yes, I think so," he said at last.

"You're—" With a jolt that made her stagger they hit the

433

bottom. Adam made no attempt to steady her. He was out of th
car and striding away across the floor of the railway loading ba
before she could recover. Infuriated she hurried after him. H
did not wait. At the dock gates he was a dozen yards ahead
her. The policeman touched his helmet. Adam nodded bru
quely. Molly caught up with him as he stood waiting to cross th
busy road.

"*Adam Jefferson!*" she shrieked, over the roar of the traffic.

He bent to her ear. "Fisticuffs in the street? I always suspecte
there might be a fishwife hidden in that pretty little frame
yours somewhere." There was the slightest gap in the traffic. H
caught her hand and almost dragged her through it. Sh
clamped her mouth shut and followed him along the road, dow
the narrow alley and back into Forrest's building. Once insid
the busy foyer not even she had the face to stand and bawl at hi
in public. They went up to the fourth floor in frigid silence. On
there Adam led the way to his office, let them in, waved her to
chair, which she refused with an impatiently shaken head. H
walked to a polished table where stood a decanter of sherry an
some glasses, poured two, without asking, and offered one t
Molly.

"No, thank you," she said, coldly.

He shrugged, put the glass down near her on the desk, sat hin
self in his chair, placed his own glass, untouched, before hin
steepled his fingers thoughtfully and looked up at her with n
the slightest trace of penitence on his face.

"Yes, it was I who told that boor Langton where the mone
came from to prop up Danbury's. And yes, I knew very we
what I was doing and what he would be likely to do. No, I do n
apologize. Does that about cover it? May we talk about som
thing important now?"

"You're despicable."

"Probably. But practical, you must admit. Infinitely pra
tical."

"Jack was shattered."

"More fool him."

"How *dare* you say that! You – he——"

"You're becoming inarticulate. Drink your sherry."

She took a deep breath. "Don't think I don't know wh

you're trying to do. You know you're in the wrong so you goad me into losing my temper, because the only way you can win is to make me look a fool. Well it won't work. Not this time." She leaned over the desk towards him, her eyes blazing. "You'll sit there, and you'll listen to what I've got to say."

Something in his face subtly changed. The dark sweep of lashes flickered, the jaw hardened, yet, oddly, he said nothing. He was watching her intently, his eyes moving over her angry face feature by feature. But for once Molly was beyond observing the unpredictable shifts in this man's moods.

"You had no right – no right whatsoever – to do this. You have taken advantage of one man's good and trusting nature to obtain information to which you had no right, and you have betrayed my confidence in telling others, against my clearly stated wish. You have acted dishonourably and in self-interest. You have brought embarrassment – humiliation – to a proud man who, of all people, doesn't deserve it at your hands. Nor at mine." Her voice was now trembling very slightly. "You are the most – the most unprincipled and – detestable person that I've ever met. If I thought you knew the meaning of the phrase I'd tell you that you should be ashamed of yourself." She stopped, at a loss that he had allowed her such free flow of words.

He sat still, elbows on desk, watching her. With a long, sharp thumbnail he traced the line of his mouth, back and forth. His face was deadly serious. "You're very probably right," he said.

Into the silence she asked, "What game are you playing now?"

He smiled, very slightly. "I hardly know myself."

"You mean that you aren't going to offer some clever, twisted defence for what you did?"

"Oh, come now, I didn't say that exactly. It was simply that in a rare moment of honesty I was agreeing in general with your assessment of the situation. And of me."

Anger still sparked in her eyes. "It's all very well to agree that what you did was wrong after the event. After the damage is done."

"Oh, but of course. I know that very well," he agreed readily. "What's more, I am not for one moment suggesting that if I could turn back the clock that I would act differently—"

She stared at him in astonishment. "But you just said—"

"I just said," he spoke with equable patience, "that you were largely right in what you said. That's all. The way I acted probably was, in some people's eyes, both unprincipled and despicable. I happen to believe that the end justifies the means. And I," he added quietly, his eyes hard upon her, "at least, am honest about that."

The inference of that was not lost on her. She flushed.

"How many times have I said it?" His voice was gentle. "Make excuses to the world, to your family, to your friends, to God Himself if you must. But never, never make excuses to yourself. There is a danger that you might believe them. You told Jack about our plan." It was not a question.

"Yes, I did."

"And?"

She hesitated, nursing her cooling anger. Then she shrugged, accepting the change of subject. "I'm not sure. He wants to talk to you about it."

"Well, we'll have to arrange a meeting, won't we? And you and I will have to combine our persuasive powers to convince him. If we can't do that, we don't deserve anything. How about tomorrow afternoon?"

"It sounds all right. I'll telephone and let you know."

"Fine." He picked up his glass. "A toast. To Jefferson and Benton."

She hesitated. "How about Jefferson, Benton and Forrest?" she asked.

He sipped his drink, his eyes wary. "I told you that I didn't particularly want Joseph in on this."

"Yes. But I do."

"Why?"

She did not reply. She did not have to. She saw the beginnings of mirth in his face. Suddenly he threw back his head and laughed in genuine amusement.

"Has poor Joseph been elected as shepherd to protect two little lambs from the big bad wolf?"

"Something like that."

"He won't side with you against me."

"I know that. Except, I'm sure, in the most extreme circumstances. And it is to prevent such circumstances from arising that I propose that he should be invited to take ten per cent of our shares." She was gaining in confidence. "Otherwise we have no deal."

He was still amused. "An ultimatum, no less." He held up his hands in mocking surrender. "Very well, you win. But tell me something—"

She looked a question, warily.

"While Joseph is protecting you from me, who is to protect me from you?"

"The Good Lord," she said collectedly, "and all His angels."

"I'd better have another case of best brandy delivered to my friend the Bishop at once then."

She had to laugh. "You're impossible."

He moved in his practised way out of his chair and around the desk, stood leaning gracefully above her. "I always have been. I seem to recall that it hasn't always worried you."

She thought that her heart must have stopped at his nearness. He reached for her hand and pulled her to her feet only inches from him. She could feel the strong bones of his hand, the light from the window sheened the brown skin of his face.

"Speaking of honesty," he said, very softly, "tell me something. Cross your heart and hope to die."

"What?" She struggled to quieten the thumping of her heart, to keep her breathing light and even.

"Can you tell me, truthfully, that you aren't glad that I told Langton about the money? That I betrayed you, tricked Baxter, humiliated Jack? Can you tell me that you would rather have had our project fall through? That you and I had never seen one another again?"

She said nothing.

"Well?" His voice was very soft, belying the charged excitement that had flared suddenly between them. His gaze was fixed upon her mouth in a way that she remembered with a pang of almost physical pain.

Her face flamed. "I—"

Right beside them on the desk the telephone shrilled. Without releasing her hand Adam reached for it. "Hello?" His voice was impatient.

"Adam, darling? It's Etta." From where she stood Molly heard the high, clear voice distinctly. She pulled her hand from Adam's, backed away from him. Adam half-turned from her, talked into the instrument quietly but with considerable force.

"I'm busy."

The female voice rustled in the silence.

"No," said Adam, "I can't."

Molly picked up her neglected sherry and drank it in one grim gulp, then gathered together her small handbag and gloves.

"I don't know. I told you – it's difficult. Look, I have to go, I have someone with me. Yes – all right. Goodbye."

Very precisely he cradled the telephone on the hook.

"I have to go," Molly said brightly.

"Of course. I'll see you to the lift." He picked the mood smoothly from her, made no attempt to recreate the odd intimacy of a moment before.

In the lift car Molly looked at the receding images of herself blindly, hardly seeing the hectic colour in her cheeks, the faint glitter of tears unshed.

On the subject of honesty, Adam, she thought with miserable savagery, are you having an affair with your best friend's wife? And, if you are, is it any of my business?

CHAPTER FORTY

THE SUMMER AND autumn of 1913 passed in a blur of hectic activity. Once Jack had been persuaded to the cold storage plan – and in the absence of any reasonable alternative that had proved to be easier than Molly had feared – Adam set to work with his usual single-minded vigour to set it up. Within days the building had been started; the yard swarmed with activity every moment of daylight as the workmen slaved to gain the handsome bonuses Adam had promised for meeting almost – but not quite – impossible deadlines. Jack and Adam worked surprisingly well together. Jack openly admired Adam's acute mind, sharp wits and apparently never-flagging energy while Adam had a perfectly genuine regard for Jack's transparent honesty and his capacity for sheer, bone-breaking hard work. Despite this, however, it was inevitable that sometimes they should clash. Inevitable, too perhaps, that the first of these clashes should occur very early in the project and should concern Molly's part in the new company.

"It's no job for a woman," Jack said, stubbornly, for the third time.

"For God's sake, man!" Adam's hand hit the table, lightly, irritably. Molly was silent, her arguments already voiced. "Your wife is a born saleswoman. Can't you see that? Man, woman, what does it matter? It's what she does best. She went out there and sold the Venture Agency to men who had never until that day given a thought to employing a woman. She traipsed the streets for Danbury's while you were flat on your back – selling something that she knew very little about. And doing it damn well. If you're going to get anywhere in this dog-eat-dog world, you *have* to let your people do the things they do best. Molly's face and blarney-stone tongue'll get her into places where you and I wouldn't stand a chance, make no` mistake about that." His tone, Molly noticed, was slightly irritable and strictly practical. He might have been talking about one of the carthorses. "To begin with, Molly will be the kingpin of the operation. If we can't sell our service then we're finished before we start. Who else is going to do it? Do you fancy the job?"

If Jack's final capitulation was a little grudging, Molly noted with relief it appeared to be complete. And when, dressed to kill and with knees that trembled beneath her fashionable skirts, she began her first trips to the restaurants and hotels that they were hoping to interest in the project, he made neither further comment nor objection.

The company of Jefferson and Benton was set up with Adam as the major shareholder, with forty-five per cent of the shares, Jack and Molly holding between them another forty-five per cent – this being in its turn split twenty-five per cent to twenty per cent in Molly's favour in recognition of her greater part in the setting up of the company – and, as Molly had insisted, with Joseph Forrest, jovially determined to be part of the new venture, being invited to take up the last ten per cent. The first step that the new company took was to pay off the debt that Molly had incurred on the agency, thus ensuring Venture's independence from any possible failure of the new project. Molly's relief on the day that she walked from the bank with the debt finally cleared was akin to euphoria. She had not herself realized how the danger to the agency had weighed on her mind. She now threw herself into the new challenge with heart and soul, confident that the agency was thriving in Nancy's capable hands. She learned every aspect of the new operation, she haunted the docks, the big cold stores, the meat and fish markets. She drank iced lemonade in the Savoy and in the Ritz, her eyes everywhere. Usually on these 'scouting expeditions', as Adam dubbed them, she was accompanied by an uncomfortable Jack, occasionally by Nancy – who was, she discovered, a slightly difficult companion since there was always the likelihood that she might climb up on a chair and make a speech – or, very infrequently, by Adam, who watched with admiration and amusement her efforts to discover where the flowers on the table had come from, or the fruit in the dessert, or the shrimps in the hors d'oeuvre. She and Adam during these months were like old adversaries who unexpectedly found themselves fighting side by side, each ready to admit his need for the other, each appreciating the other's qualities as an ally, yet each watching the other like a hawk for the slightest sign of danger. Since that day in Adam's office he had made no move towards her. Did he know, she wondered, that no matter how hard she tried to prevent it, the sight of him still brought that sudden quickening of her blood? That the oddly attractive sound of his voice affected her no less now than it ever had? She thought, probably not, and told herself, firmly, that it was best so. There was no place in her life for the lies and deceits, and no future at all in any relationship with Adam but a business one. On those occasions that she saw him with his head bent attentively to a pretty girl, or when she caught the occasional flash of antagonistic emotion that she recognized so surely between him and Etta Forrest, she assured herself grimly that she wanted no part of those emotional storms that blew about the man. And she drove herself to work harder than she ever had in her life. She was determined upon success. Adam had called her the kingpin. She would be nothing less. Others might battle on softer territory, she would take him on, on his own ground.

She soon discovered, to her delight, that she actually enjoyed her task. These were not the streets of Stratford and West Ham, the shabby roads of dockland, that she was walking now, but the golden, beckoning thoroughfares of the fashionable West End of London that had first lured her from her home and that still, despite all, held that glamour. Her confidence – at first assumed – grew daily. The metamorphosis that time had wrought in her struck her most forcibly on the day that she pushed her way through smoothly revolving doors into the lobby of a small hotel that she had not visited before, in a side street whose familiarity she had not bothered to try to pin down in her mind. She struck the bell sharply, and a young man with slicked-down hair and supercilious eyes appeared from nowhere.

"I have an appointment with the manager," she said, briskly, smiling. "Mrs Benton."

"Ah yes, Madam. He is expecting you. If you wouldn't mind waiting just a moment I'll tell him you are here?"

She glanced around a lobby that seemed at first sight, beneath its Christmas decorations, exactly like a dozen others she had been in during the past few weeks. Tall potted palms, shining brass fittings, the inevitable patterned mirrors lining the walls – she paused for a moment as she caught sight of herself. She was dressed in blue, still her favourite colour, knee-length tunic over ankle-length, very narrow skirt, smartly-cut jacket, the V-neck revealing a demure, high-necked cream blouse. High on the side of her head her dark blue velvet hat adorned with cream feathers swept upwards, adding inches to her height. She tucked a small wisp of hair behind her ear. The swing door to the dining room opened and a couple came out, the man glancing at her with some interest as they passed. Molly's hand, still raised to her hair, stilled as if it had been frozen. Clearly in the mirror she saw a small, dirt-smeared face, frightened and angry, black hair gypsy wild, ragged shawl clutched around thin shoulders. How had she not realized? This was, she was certain, the very hotel in which she had tried to take a room that day – how many years ago? Fourteen? No, fifteen – the day that she had arrived in London. She could see now the raised eyebrows of the clerk, hear his sneering tones: "We don't buy off the streets—"

Behind her someone cleared his throat politely. "Er – Mrs Benton?"

Very slowly she turned. It was not the same clerk, she was certain. This one was too young. But it was, undoubtedly, the same place. The same shining bell stood still on the counter. She had rung it herself a moment before, without a thought.

"Mr Pearson is waiting, Madam. He asked if you would care for tea?"

She smiled her best and most dazzling smile. "Yes, please, I would." And she glanced just once more at her reflection in the mirror before following him into the inner sanctum of the manager's office.

A couple of hours later, in the comfort of the cab that carried her back through the streets of London to the railway station, she tucked the tiny notebook and pencil that she had been using to record this, her latest success, into her blue velvet bag and sat back to enjoy the view from the window. She had taken particular satisfaction in this day. The other, younger Molly, had sat at her shoulder all afternoon, urging her on, measuring her success with a knowing and happy eye. Outside it was dark already, and

itterly cold. The streets and shops were decorated for Christ-
as. People hurried through the biting wind, lights and lanterns
wung, gaily festive.

"'Ere we are Miss." The vehicle had stopped. The cabby was
t the door.

Molly drew her small purse from her bag to pay the man, and
s she did so her fingers touched a stiff card, an invitation from
oseph Forrest to join him at a New Year's Ball at a large and
shionable hotel, a function designed to usher in the new year of
914 with some style.

Sitting in the train that rattled through the dingy East End
ums, Molly thought again of that small ghost with whom she
ad kept company that afternoon: and again she smiled. But as
he stood at Stratford station half an hour later in the bitter
ind, stamping her small booted feet on the pavement in an
fort to keep them warm, some of her good temper deserted her.
here was not a cab to be had. Then, realizing the futility of
aiting in the cold when ten minutes' brisk walking would take
er home, she turned up her collar, tucked her hands into her
arm, fur-lined muff and set off into the dark evening.

The Broadway, too, was thronged with Christmas shoppers.
here were ghosts here, as well, – ones that she would rather not
member. As if it had been yesterday instead of fifteen years
efore she heard Sam Alden's soft, uncertain voice, saw the
arsh set of Ellen's mouth. She hurried on, almost running,
oking neither to left nor right. Ahead of her a barrel organ
nkled outside a public house; she crossed the road, head down,
o avoid the crowd of youths who were gathered around it,
nsteady on their feet, rowdily drunken. One of them whistled
dmiringly. She bent her head further into the sting of the rising
ind and ignored them.

Young Danny Benton, with still enough of his wits about him
o ensure self-preservation, ducked away from his noisy friends
nd slipped into a dark doorway, while the others continued
o call coarsely admiring remarks at his mother's fast-
isappearing back.

olly leaned a little nervously to the mirror, inspecting her
mooth skin for the slightest blemish, wishing that her unruly

hair would stick in a more disciplined way to the centre parting that she had contrived for it. The soft, ice-blue silk of her gown shone almost silver in the light.

"Oh, Mum, you look lovely," Kitty said from the doorway.

"How clever of Mr Forrest to discover that you were wearing blue," Meghan said. She had picked up the corsage that had arrived at the house just a few moments before and now waltzed around the room, humming beneath her breath, holding the flowers to her own bleached cotton blouse. "I shall wear a lot of blue when I grow up," she said, posing in front of the mirror, the flowers set against her fair hair. "It suits me, doesn't it?"

Molly took the flowers from her. "There'll be nothing left of that by the time you've finished with it. Help me pin it on, Meg, would you?" She stood still while her daughter's quick fingers fastened the delicate thing to her gown. Then finally she surveyed herself, the finished article, in the long mirror. "There. What do you think?"

"Very nice," Meg said nodding.

"Absolutely wonderful!" Kitty said, and then, as the door opened, "Oh, Dad! You look *marvellous*."

Jack, a little red-faced, was attired, as Nancy had put it earlier, a sardonic sisterly twinkle in her eye, 'in full fig', his dress shirt and tie as white as snow, his elegant black coat and trousers showing off his width of shoulder and length of leg. Molly surveyed him with some satisfaction, "You look very handsome."

"Aye, well as long as no one asks me what I feel like. You don't look so bad yourself, lass, I'll say that. Are you ready? The cab's here. Though what in God's name we're doing celebrating the New Year with strangers is beyond me. Family's always been good enough before."

"Oh, Dad!" Meghan's voice was utterly disgusted.

Molly ignored a plaint that she had been hearing ever since Joseph Forrest's invitation had first come. In reality she knew that Jack was every bit as pleased about it as she was. "I'm ready," she said.

The ballroom of the Royal Palace Hotel was everything that Molly had imagined and hoped it might be, and then more. The Forrests had had it sumptuously decorated for the occasion with

444

treamers and garlands of silver and gold, on each table an
rrangement of silver and gold artificial flowers. As their party
ntered, ushered by an efficient gentleman dressed every bit as
esplendently as the male guests, the orchestra had already
aunched into a Strauss waltz that made Molly want to dance to
he table. The air was perfumed and filled with talk and
aughter. They were greeted from all sides by others who were
lready in the swing of celebration. Ice buckets in which nestled
ottles of champagne were upon every table. Molly smiled in
heer delight at the atmosphere, and found herself looking with
omething of a shock directly into Adam's dark eyes as he
egarded her with obvious amusement from where he stood
eside Joseph and Etta Forrest. Etta, dressed in the fashionable
Oriental style with the soft, bright colours and 'harem' skirt that
Molly, regretfully, had had to eschew because of her height, or
ather the lack of it, looked stunning. Her colour was high, her
all, slim figure in the exotic almost stagey outfit demanded
ather than attracted attention. Her eyes, Molly noted, widened
ractionally when they rested upon Jack, whom she had never
net before.

They settled themselves at the table, introductions were made
there were several people in the party whom Molly had not
net – and the orchestra moved smoothly and sweetly into
nother waltz.

"The evening is yours, my friends." Joseph Forrest's benign
ace was already a little flushed, his eyes twinkling with enjoy-
ient. "We'll launch 1914 with an evening to remember, eh?
Vaiter, another couple of bottles of champagne, please."

A rainbow glitter of chandeliers sparkled like diamonds above
he laughing, dancing, chattering crowds. Beneath her chair
Molly's feet moved, her body swayed slightly to the music.
oseph Forrest leaned towards Jack. "I say, Mr Benton, would
ou have any objection to my dancing with your charming
vife?"

Slightly confused, Jack shook his head and Molly found
erself led, a little ponderously, onto the floor. As her partner
teered her into the crowds she saw Etta lean to Adam, saw him
nen stand and offer her his hand. Later, in between avoiding
oseph s none-too-adept feet she saw Adam and Etta dancing

and could not but admire the smooth way that Adam moved. Lately she had noticed that his limp had become considerably less. He exercised with iron resolution, she knew, in order to strengthen his leg. She wondered, wryly, how much effort had been put into preparing for this moment. As the last strains of the waltz died Joseph, laughing, extended his arm to her to lead her back to the table. " – Not as young as I used to be, eh?"

"You dance very well," she said warmly.

He patted her hand. "Nice of you to say so, my dear. Not very honest, eh? But nice."

By the time she reached the table the orchestra had struck up yet again, and this time it was Jack who led her onto the floor to execute a dashing if inexpert two-step. The great ballroom was full now, very warm and full of happy noise. Molly danced again with Jack, and then with a young man whose name she had not caught, who looked at her with admiration, held her much too close and did not seem to notice that she spent two dances calling him 'Mr Er—?' At length, laughing, she had almost to beg him to take her back to the table where Jack was deep in conversation with Joseph Forrest. She reached for her neglected glass of champagne and the narrow hand that she would recognize anywhere touched her wrist lightly.

"I have your husband's permission," Adam said solemnly "to dance with you. May I have the pleasure?"

The musicians, happily, were back to Strauss again. As Molly turned into Adam's arms she caught a swift glimpse of Etta Forrest's wide, challenging eyes fixed upon them both. Just before they were lost in the swirling stream of dancers she saw the other woman tip her head back and drain her glass to the dregs. Then she was alone with Adam in the whirling maelstrom of the waltz, the glittering, spinning, colourful couples around them a mere backdrop to his eyes, his smile, the movement together of their bodies.

"You're enjoying yourself," he said in that odd way he had of turning a question into a statement.

"Yes."

"You should do it more often. It suits you marvellously."

She smiled. She had drunk just enough champagne to be able to admit to herself honestly how much she wanted to be with him, to feel his arms about her if only like this, in public as they danced. What was more, she did not at this particular moment care if he sensed it, as she knew he would. They said not another word to each other as they dipped and whirled, their bodies moving perfectly together, she adjusting without thought to the slightly unbalanced step of his damaged leg. As the music died and the supper bell rang they stood close for a moment, still without words, until Adam, with a smile, offered her his arm to escort her to Jack.

Supper was a noisy affair. Jack and the young man whose name Molly still did not know launched into a deep discussion of the industrial troubles that had plagued the old year, and wondered, pessimistically, what the new one might bring. The two other couples in the party seemed to have their own personal celebration going on at the other end of the table, while Adam had excused himself and was talking to a man on the other side of the room. Molly stood by herself for the moment, surveying the luxuriously loaded table, trying to decide which delightful dish to try and wondering, with professional interest, if the grapes had been stored in redwood sawdust when she became aware that Etta Forrest had come to stand beside her. She looked up into a pair of flatly unfriendly eyes.

"Hello," she said, brightly, "are you enjoying the party?"

"I can't say that I am, no." The younger woman was swaying very slightly, and with a shock Molly saw that she was very drunk. "I find these things an awful bore, actually."

"Really?" There seemed little else to say. Molly moved a step away.

"Have you known Adam long?" The question was blunt, and much too loud.

Taken aback, Molly answered as bluntly, but her voice was quiet. "Yes, I have."

"I thought so." The hostile eyes swept her critically. Infuriatingly, Molly found herself blushing. "Do you find him – easy to work for?"

"I don't work for him," Molly said shortly. "I work with him. And the answer to your question is no, I don't find it easy."

"But easy to dance with," the other woman said very softly.

"Mrs Forrest," said Molly, very coolly, "if you have nothing

447

better to do than to watch others dance, easily or otherwise, then I'm not surprised that you 'find these affairs boring'. Now, will you excuse me, please?"

Jack and the unknown young man seemed pleased to have her join them. Inwardly fuming, outwardly gay, she steered their conversation into lighter channels. From the corner of her eye she saw Etta walk, relatively steadily, to where Adam stood, saw his careful smile, noted the way that with some insistence he propelled her to a chair and then came to the table to fill a small plate of food for her. His eyes met Molly's and, with the slightest of shrugs, he raised his eyebrows, drolly. Suddenly, and for no explicable reason Molly's ill humour deserted her as quickly as it had come. She had come here tonight determined to enjoy herself, and that she would do, Etta Forrest notwithstanding.

The dancing began again, and midnight crept nearer. Just before it struck Molly found herself once again dancing with Adam. This time he talked, lightly and amusingly, as she remembered that he used to. The champagne, she knew, had gone quite thoroughly to her head. She laughed at everything, smoke-blue eyes glittering and shining with pleasure from behind dark lashes. The room blazed with silver and gold, a transient treasure house of celebration. She was aware suddenly that Adam was no longer smiling, no longer talking. His arm around her had drawn her closer to him, the hand that held hers had tightened abruptly, possessively.

"Adam—" she said, and the music stopped. In a moment she was swept away from him by an enthusiastic crowd, one hand in Jack's the other held by a stranger. As the noise died the decorated clock at the far end of the ballroom began to strike twelve, and on the last note a great cheer arose as the figures 1914 were unfurled above it in silver and gold. Jack kissed her, Joseph Forrest kissed her, chastely on the cheek, the nameless young man kissed her, not too chastely, on the mouth. Rings formed around the room – "Should Auld Acquaintance be forgot—?"

She looked for Adam. He was making his way through the crowd, smiling, laughing, kissing the ladies, shaking hands with the men, having his back slapped and his hand pumped, but slowly and inexorably making his way to her. She knew that

448

with perfect confidence. She waited for him, her eyes following his progress. When he reached her she lifted her face for his kiss perfectly naturally, and knew her mistake the moment their lips touched. With a shock as sobering as cold water she felt his desire and her own, and could not pull away. In the end it was he who lifted his head, but not before she had felt in the harsh pressure of his mouth his answering emotion. She stepped back from him, her colour high, her heart hammering. A sweep was making the rounds of the ballroom floor kissing the ladies for luck, shaking the hands of the men, leaving smears of soot on skin and clothes to everyone's uproarious amusement.

"Molly—?" Adam said.

"Good Lord, you two, why so sober?" Joseph Forrest swept up behind them, put an arm about each of them. His hands were covered in soot and his white head was wreathed in a silver streamer. "I can't have that at my party, indeed not!" He steered them towards the sweep. "Here's two you've missed—"

Molly submitted to a sooty kiss. Over the dirty shoulder she saw Etta move close to Adam and lift her lips to his.

Outside, all over the city, the bells rang joyfully, ushering in the new and hopeful year.

CHAPTER FORTY-ONE

IN JANUARY 1914, a couple of weeks after the ball, Adam Jefferson went to the United States to study new cold store techniques and buy new equipment. In the six months that he was away, the newly but already strongly established firm of Jefferson and Benton built steadily on strong foundations. Jack kept the yard and the now-completed cold store running efficiently and well. The sales of ice, both manufactured and natural, were steady. Molly, her initial efforts now bearing fruit, turned her attention to tracking down, haggling over and ordering the high-quality supplies that the business demanded, and found herself enjoying the tasks immensely. Her brisk figure became well-known in the docks as she hunted down her small cargoes in person, watching their handling like a hawk – for fruit and flowers particularly could be easily damaged by careless treatment – persuading their passage with smiles and a quick tongue through the customs, always the first to have her trucks loaded and away. She persuaded Jack that their transport, both motorized and horse-drawn, should be smart and distinctive. Blue and chocolate brown were the colours she chose, with golden, decorative lettering proclaiming to the world that Jefferson and Benton were purveyors of only the highest quality luxury items. She used the information that Adam fed her back from America to good advantage, and for the day-to-day problems she had Joseph Forrest to advise her. They now had an established circle of customers whom she visited regularly armed with a tempting list of the new delicacies that she could, at a price, provide. By April the Jefferson-Benton store was working to capacity. As the spring sunshine strengthened in promise of a glorious summer, Molly surveyed their order books with justifiable satisfaction.

"You should buy an ice-making machine of your own for the summer, you really should," she said to Annie one day. "You can get small ones, you know, specially for shops like yours—"

"And what do we use for money? Buttons?" Annie said, he

voice full of laughter. Her new baby, born in February, had been another boy, Robert Edward – she intended, she had informed Molly, to produce the whole of the West Ham football team for the nineteen thirties.

"They aren't all that expensive." Molly, smiling, dangled a piece of ribbon for the baby to reach for. Aware of silence she looked up. Annie was standing, grinning at her, hands on hips.

"You and your big ideas, Molly girl. I remember saying to Charley the first day I met you – remember, the picnic, that hat with the cherries? – that girl, I said, is going places. And I was right, wasn't I? But we aren't all on our way to our first million, you know love. Some of us are quite happy with what we've got." The words were spoken lightly and certainly not intended as criticism, yet they startled Molly. Walking back to The Larches she thought about them. Ever since the day that she had walked in, footsore and determined, on John Marsden she had believed that she was working for one thing and one thing only, to establish for herself and later for her family some kind of security in a frighteningly insecure world. Now, she suddenly realized, she had that security. Yet still she worked, still she planned, and Annie's quiet content was beyond her. Ambition, she mused, was a strange thing. It might, as in her case, start as a driving necessity, an essential to keep body and soul together in a grim world, but who could tell when it took over as a force in its own right?

Wasn't it Adam who had once told her that success, like love, was an addictive drug? She smiled a little ruefully. Of course it had been Adam. Who would know better about either?

As she turned, her mind abstracted, up the path of The Larches she almost bumped into a tall young man whom she did not at first recognize and who surprised her by doffing his hat politely and murmuring "Good evening, Mrs Benton," as he passed her.

"Was that young Chris Edmonton I saw leaving just now?" she asked Nancy.

"Yes, it was. They're organizing a march for Saturday. He had some leaflets for me to deliver."

"He's married now, isn't he?"

"Yes he is." Nancy's voice was expressionless.

"What's she like?"

"Felicity? Oh – young, pretty, I suppose. Well-connected. A bit stupid."

Molly laughed. "I don't suppose Christopher thinks so." She paused and then added in face of Nancy's dour expression, curiously, "Does he?"

Nancy stood up. "I'm sure I don't know. It isn't anything we discuss. Here – these are the notes on a couple of girls I interviewed today." She tossed a file on the desk and then stood looking down at Molly, her face uncertain. "Moll, I'm sorry, there's something I have to tell you. If I don't then someone else will."

"Oh?" Molly shuffled through the papers. "What is it?"

"It – concerns Danny."

That stilled the busy fingers. Molly lifted her head. "What about him?"

Nancy spread helpless hands. "There's no easy way to say it. He's been playing truant. And now – he's started to steal—"

"*What!*"

"I've known he's been playing truant for some time. I should have told you, I know. But he promised—" Nancy stopped. There was a long, tense silence.

"You'd better tell me it all."

Jack sat in silence in the dark parlour and listened to Molly's tale, told in an even, drained tone that spoke more of her distress than any histrionics might have done. Nancy's revelations had hit her like a bombshell. "He's been playing truant for months. Nancy caught him several times. And others have seen him. He always had an excuse when Nancy mentioned it – you know what he is – she didn't know what to do for the best. He kept promising her faithfully that it wouldn't happen again. She didn't want to cause trouble. But now – stealing again! From Nancy. From the girls' pockets and purses. And from God only knows where else—" Her voice cracked a little.

Jack's face, the still-vicious scar gleaming high on his cheek bone, was rigid with anger. He slammed his hand violently onto the arm of his chair. "By Christ, that's enough! I'm going to take the hide off that lad!"

She shook her head. "What good will that do? This is my fault. My fault!" She buried her dry face in her hands.

"What are you on about?" Jack's voice was rough, but not unkind. "Your fault?"

She lifted her head. "Yes. My fault. I should have known. I should have spent more time with him. I should have remembered—" She stopped. Jack watched her. The sounds of the house were loud in the silence. Above them, in Nancy's rooms, the girls' laughter pealed. In the hall outside the door a floorboard creaked, but neither of them noticed it. "Well," she went on, more composedly. "Now I know, and now I will do something. I want him to leave school. If he wants money so badly, then let him earn it. At the cold store, under your eye. He didn't want to stay on at school anyway. It was I who insisted. But I'm not having him leave to run wild with these – friends – of his. I want you to take him on—"

Jack moved violently from his chair. "Damned if I'll—"

"For Harry's sake, Jack. And for mine. Please."

Jack ran his hands distractedly through his hair.

" – And then – there are things I should tell him, aren't there? We can't keep quiet for ever. Apart from anything else, there's the money. He comes into it on his twenty-first birthday. What will we tell him? How will we explain—?" She stopped, and her expression changed as she stared over Jack's shoulder at the opening door.

Danny leaned against the jamb, one hand negligently in his pocket, his eyes veiled. "Secrets?" he asked.

No one spoke.

The boy shut the door behind him and walked with a kind of tense grace into the room. Fury suddenly suffused Jack's face. "You little – you've been listening at the door!"

"Yes, I have." Danny did not flinch from Jack's sudden movement towards him.

"Jack, no!" Molly moved between them, her hands flat against Jack's huge chest. He stood for a moment, breathing heavily, glaring at the tall, slight figure of the boy over Molly's head. Then he turned from them both, his hands bunched, his jaw corded with anger.

Molly turned to face her son. "I think you'd better sit down."

"I'd rather stand." His voice was pure insolence.

"Sit down." She did not change her tone. "I've no intention of talking to you until you do."

The fragile veneer of his arrogance cracked a little. He stood uncertainly before his mother's iron composure then, with bad grace, dropped into the nearest chair.

Molly remained standing, looking down at him. "I assume that what your Aunt Nancy has finally brought herself to tell me about is true?"

The boy shrugged.

"Answer your mother," Jack snapped.

Danny threw him a look of sheer hostility.

"Well?" Molly asked.

Silence.

"That's answer enough, isn't it? You heard, I assume, what I was saying just now – about your leaving school and working at the cold store?"

The red head lifted then, and he looked at her, a blaze of malice in his blue eyes. "That's not all I heard."

"I didn't imagine that it was." Molly struggled to hold her temper, saw Jack turn away, sensed the effort he was making to contain an impulse to violence. "Very well. Since you are obviously determined to make this as painful as possible for everyone, then I suppose that's the way it has to be. Though these are hardly the circumstances that I would choose—"

"Well, it isn't your choice, is it?" The words were curtly rude. "I heard you say something about money. Money that's coming to me when I'm twenty-one. I want to know about it. I've a right to know about it—"

Molly's voice when she spoke was expressionless. "A few years ago you were left a sum of money. A little over a thousand pounds. The bank has invested it for you. You will come in to the capital sum and any profit that has accrued on your twenty-first birthday. You may not touch a penny before that day."

He waited to see if she were going to continue. When it became apparent that she intended to say no more he made an impatient gesture. "And?"

"And what?" she asked, very hard.

"Where did it come from? How is it that I have money?"

There was an edge of violence in his voice. He narrowed his eyes, watching his mother. "Who's Harry? Did he leave me the money? What had he to do with me?"

Molly bit her lip, her hard-held composure shaken. "Danny, believe me, this isn't the time—"

The boy leapt to his feet. "*Tell me!*" Slowly the pale young face, hard as bone, turned towards Jack. "Why don't you tell me – *Dad*?" The cruel emphasis on the word was blindingly deliberate and left no doubt as to its meaning. Danny was standing very close to Jack, looking into the square, scarred face as if purposely goading the man to force. "Who was Harry?"

Jack was as still as stone. "He was my brother. And your father." Molly flinched from the pain in his voice.

"Aah," Danny said softly. "That explains it." He lifted a hand to his own face. "I never could understand why I should look like you, yet you never wanted me."

"No!"

"That isn't true!" Molly and Jack spoke in unison, Jack's voice passionate.

"Oh yes." Danny kept his eyes on his mother. "Oh, yes it is. I heard him say it. Heard him. Not my son, he said, but yours." In the stunned moment of silence that followed his words he smiled, and turned to where Jack stood, his face shadowed. "What should I call you from now on? Uncle Jack?"

Jack used a vicious and explicit word. Danny lifted a provoking chin, staring at him. Molly saw, suddenly, the hurt in the full, young, downturned mouth. She put a hand to her son, who pulled back from it as if it had been a burning brand. "Well?" he asked Jack.

"Go to hell." Jack stormed past them and out of the door. Mother and son were left looking at one another in the quiet room.

"I'd like to hear the rest," he said. "Did the money come from my father? From Harry? I thought none of the Bentons had any money until you came along?" The words were not kind.

Molly took a breath. "The money was left to you by a woman named Ellen Alden. I married her son, Sam. He died. When Ellen was killed in an accident, the money came to you as her grandson—"

He frowned. "I don't understand." He glanced at the doo[r] through which Jack had left. "I thought you married him?"

"Afterwards." Molly was aware of how badly it sounded, bu[t] could do nothing about it. "Sam was a good man," she added[.] "He accepted you as his own. He—" she swallowed "– loved u[s] both very much."

Not a trace of sympathetic emotion showed on the boy's face[.] "So, let me get this straight," he said with an exaggerate[d] interest. " – You must admit it's a little complicated. Penniles[s] Irish girl gets herself in the family way. Then what? Why didn'[t] Harry marry you?"

"Oh, Danny, it's all so difficult—" She stopped at th[e] derisive expression on his face. "Harry went to South Africa,["] she said, stonily. "He died there."

"What of?"

"Dysentery."

His mouth twisted. "That sounds about right. So then yo[u] married – what was his name? – Sam. Who conveniently uppe[d] and died. That would be about the time you started the agency[,] wouldn't it?"

"Yes."

"I've often wondered," he said softly, "where the capita[l] came from to start it all."

"Sam left me a little."

He looked at her in flat admiration. "Well, well. That was [a] happy chance, wasn't it? And then you were free to marry *him*.["] Again the jerk of the head, the refusal to speak the name. "I'[ll] say one thing. At least we know now where I get it from, eh? [I] may not be his son, but I'm sure as hell yours—"

She slapped him, open-handed, with all her strength. Th[e] heavy ring she wore caught his lip and blood sprang, bright a[s] rubies. He did not move; only the hard face changed. Th[e] bloodied mouth trembled. After a moment the long lashes swep[t] down as the boy squeezed his eyes shut to prevent the tears[.] Bright lamplight haloed his head, glinting like flame in his thic[k] hair. The hurt of years showed suddenly in his face.

Molly spoke his name, very softly. He shook his head fiercely[,] rejecting her, rejecting the love in her voice. Then, abruptly, h[e] broke. He bowed his head into his cupped hands and sobbed lik[e]

456

he child he was. Molly sank to her knees on the floor, drawing
im gently with her. He pillowed his head on her lap and cried as
f his heart would break, while her fingers moved in his hair,
moothed his damp forehead. At last the tearing sobs eased, and
e lay in silence, his hot, wet face turned from her.

"Danny, I'm sorry," she said. "Sorry that it seems that we
ried to deceive you. But there's something that you must
nderstand." She lifted his face with his hand. "What Jack said
hat day he said in anger. Anger not at you, but at me. You'll
nderstand when you're older. For now you must take my word
or it. He didn't mean it. Not the way it must have sounded. He's
een a true father to you. He loves you as his own. Don't make
im suffer more than he already has. He doesn't deserve that
rom you. Truly he doesn't."

Danny sat back on his heels, sniffing.

"Growing up is always a painful business," she said quietly.
I'm sorry we've made it even more difficult for you. Tomor-
ow's a new day. You start work, start your life as a man. Look
orward, not back. You have your life in front of you. We'll help
ou all we can."

He did not answer, but, resting his head again on her lap, lay
ke a tired child, his eyes closed, the tears still marking his
heeks. "What was my real father like?"

She looked down into the wilful, handsome young face with
omething like foreboding. "You're his living image."

Adam arrived back in London in the first, sun-gilded days of
une, a week or so after the clash with Danny. Molly met him,
riefly, at Forrest's offices and the sight of him, as always,
roused those conflicting emotions that any contact with him
nevitably did. He looked bronzed and healthy; his limp was
onsiderably lessened. They had no private communication
eyond that they conveyed by a certain capricious gleam in his
yes when he looked at her, and she was happy to leave it so. She
ad long since dismissed their moments of intimacy on New
'ear's Eve as being the product of too much champagne and too
ttle self-control, an impression that was reinforced on this
ccasion when Etta monopolized both his attention and his

conversation and he did not, as far as Molly could see, put u[p]
any great defence.

"Well, my dear," Joseph said expansively to Molly, "you'll b[e]
at our little house party next weekend?"

"Yes. I'm looking forward to it."

"Good. Good. If the weather holds, then I think you'll find [it]
all quite pleasant. I'm looking forward to having you cheer u[s]
on. Adam's crewing for me—"

"And if anything will ensure that you lose the race, then tha[t]
will—" Adam's face was alight with laughter. Molly foun[d]
herself recoiling from the physical impact of his sudden appea[r]-
ance at her shoulder.

"How uncommonly modest of you."

He was still laughing. "I thought we agreed at least that [I]
knew my own shortcomings?"

"Excuse me a moment." Joseph moved away from them.

"I've a lot to tell you." Adam said to Molly.

"And I you. The 'Grand' in Regent Street has joined us, di[d]
you know? And I've found a firm in Scotland whose salmon is [of]
much better quality than the people we've been using." Sh[e]
knew her own perversity, and could not prevent herself. H[e]
raised his eyebrows.

"Adam," Etta called sharply from the other side of the roo[m]
where he had left her. "A moment, please. The guest list f[or]
Saturday—?"

He frowned. "You look as if you've lost a little weight, Moll[y.]
Is something wrong?"

"Nothing. I'm perfectly all right."

"Adam—" Etta moved elegantly between them, smilin[g]
brilliantly. "You really mustn't monopolize him, Mrs Bento[n.]
Adam, Joseph is asking for you."

Adam eyed her coolly. Her look challenged his. Molly turne[d]
away from them both.

"Will you be joining us at the weekend, Mrs Benton?" Ett[a]
asked smoothly.

Molly tried to keep the pure dislike from her voice. "Yes, [I]
will. Thank you for the invitation."

Etta tucked an arm through hers and steered her away fro[m]
Adam. "All these awful things that are happening in Irelan[d]

my dear. Tell me, aren't you absolutely worried out of your life about your people? I've heard talk of civil war."

Molly carefully extricated her arm. "There is always talk of civil war, Mrs Forrest," she said, very clearly. "And as for Ireland, she has my heartfelt sympathy. She can ill afford to lose more blood. But my own people are well able to look after themselves. The O'Dowds always could. Now, if you will excuse me—?" Brusquely she turned away, reaching for her wrap.

"Going already?" Joseph called from the other side of the room.

"There's work waiting for me at the office," she lied. And with the thought of the coming weekend heavy in her mind, she escaped.

CHAPTER FORTY-TWO

MOLLY STOOD WITH her daughters on the tiny balcony of the room that Joseph descriptively called his "Crow's Nest", looking out over the wide, glittering expanse of the estuary as the late evening sun turned the calm waters into molten gold and the sky to rosy splendour. The evening air still held the warmth of the day; the slightest breath of wind drifted across the water, refreshingly cool. Beneath them, grassy slopes, known in this flat locality as the cliffs, dropped to the road and the beach. Out in the estuary a stately barge, red sails glowing in the sun, cut through the lucent waters headed upriver on the flowing tide to London. Inshore, smaller craft dipped and flew like graceful water birds, or rocked on the wash of the barge's passing. On the beach left by the rising tide children played, their happy shouts lifting to the lofty look-out above the slap of the waves.

Meghan leaned dangerously far out over the wooden rails.

"Do be careful, Meg," Kitty said nervously.

Meghan ignored her. "Where's this Yacht Club place that we're going to tomorrow?"

Molly pointed. "Down there. See? The building halfway up the cliff, just before the pier. The one with the flag flying. And we aren't actually going in it, you know." She pulled a mock-severe face and added in a deep voice, "Ladies isn't allowed."

"Oh, what rot. Still, a garden party should be fun." Meghan's restless eyes darted back and forth across the colourful scene. "What are they?" she said raising a pointing arm. "The big ships, out there beyond the pier?"

"That's the Royal Navy. The Third Battle Squadron, Joseph said. The gentlemen of the Yacht Club have been invited aboard one of them, so I believe." Molly suppressed firmly the feelings of misgivings that the sight of those great grey battleships, so incongruous amongst the bright sails, stirred within her. All too well she remembered John Marsden's grim prediction about the German Navy. "Yet another function that we ladies don't get invited to," she added, keeping her voice bright.

Meghan grinned cheekily. "I'll bet I could get myself invited aboard if I really tried."

Molly did not rise to the bait. Her attention had been attracted by a big, green, open-topped car that was nosing its way through the crowded street towards the house.

"Oh, look!" Meghan had caught sight of the approaching car. "That's Adam, isn't it?" She leaned out above the street, waving.

"Meghan, be careful!" Molly's voice was sharp.

The car rolled to a halt beneath them. "It is Adam, look! Oh, why doesn't he look up?"

"Meghan, will you come back here? Not even Mr Jefferson, with all his talents, would be able to catch you if you fell."

"It might be worth a try," her daughter grinned irrepressibly. She watched as Adam's foreshortened figure reached into the back of the car for a small case and then ran swiftly up the wide steps to the front door, four floors beneath them. "I do believe he's quite the most gorgeous man I've ever met."

"Meghan!" Molly said, turning to stare at her daughter. But Meghan took no notice. With her elbows on the rail she leaned her lovely chin on her spread hands and gazed out across the glittering sea, an exaggeratedly dreamy expression on her face.

"He's so *handsome*, and so – so arrogant, too."

"You're remarkably perceptive," Molly said tartly.

"Oh, but that's the way he should be. The way any man should be. They aren't worth having, are they, if they don't put up a fight? There's no fun in a man who lies down and lets you walk all over him."

"There is such a thing as a happy medium," Molly said, drily, "and honestly, Meg, I hardly think this a suitable subject for—"

"Oh, don't be such a spoilsport, Mum dear, I was only pulling your leg. It was a joke that's all."

"If your father hears you joking like that, you'll be back home before your feet can touch the floor."

"Oh, poof," Meg said, and turned back to the rail.

Molly eyed her repressively but said no more.

"What are we doing tonight?" Kitty asked.

"Dinner's at seven thirty. And then, I believe, Joseph ha invited some friends in to play whist."

"Oh, may we play?" Meg, her good humour immediately restored, moved in her swift, restless fashion back to them. "And may I wear my pale blue tonight? I've been *dying* to wear it. I looks so pretty, and I haven't had a chance to wear it yet. And oh please, Mum, may I put my hair up?"

"Yes you may, and yes you may, and certainly not. In tha order."

"Oh, but—" Meg took note of her mother's expression and shrugged. "Oh, all right."

In the street below the car door slammed. Meg leaned over t look. "That's Mr Forrest's chauffeur garaging Adam's car What a marvellous house this is! How stupid of Danny not t want to come. What on earth's the matter with him lately?" Sh did not wait for an answer. "There are almost more people her to wait on you than there are people to be waited on, have yo noticed? Wonderful. Kit and I have a marvellous room. We'v our own wash-basin, with running water! And a maid run round behind us clearing up." She grinned engagingly at he mother's laughter. "Come on, Kit. Let's go and say hello t Adam." Fair curls flew as Meg danced through the open doo followed, more staidly, by Kitty.

In the peaceful silence left by their going, Molly leaned o the rail and looked out to sea, breathing the clear air, narrowin her eyes against the glitter of sun off water. Beyond the long pie and the small, swooping sails, the great battleships moved wit the suck and swell of the turning tide, while above them gul wheeled, giving voice to their empty, mourning cries.

The next day dawned with sparkling promise. Breakfast at Cli End was served in a large and airy room overlooking the sunli sea. Molly and Jack came downstairs to discover that the gir were already halfway through a hearty breakfast. "We're a going for a walk," Meg announced with no ceremony as he mother and father sat down. "To Leigh. Etta says that there ar sheds there where you can watch the fishermen boil cockles an things. Oh, it's all right," she added ingenuously, catching he mother's eye, "she said we could call her Etta. Didn't you?" she appealed to Etta.

Etta nodded, laughing. "I couldn't possibly have two such grown up young ladies call me 'Aunt Etta'. Her mildy malicious glance flicked to Molly and away. "It would make me feel positively ancient!"

So later that morning, at Meg's insistence, the whole party but Joseph – who had to ready his cutter *Water Baby* for the afternoon's race – set off to walk along the coast of the small village of Leigh-on-sea.

They strolled through the holiday crowds, past beaches on which children and young people played, making sandcastles, or playing ball in the sun. Gentlemen in resplendently striped swimsuits that covered their persons, as was proper, from neck to knee, showed their prowess in the water, whilst their young ladies, the most daring clad in bloomered suits of every hue, paddled, shrieking, in the shallows. The party stopped for a moment to watch the feckless violence of a Punch and Judy show, and then from a gaily painted ice-cream cart Adam bought huge ice creams for the twins, and it seemed to Molly, presented Meg's to her with an especial flourish. Nor did she miss her daughter's pretty blush and fluttering lashes.

Afterwards, as Adam and Etta sauntered on ahead of the Bentons, Molly, despite herself, found herself watching them. They made a striking pair. Etta carried herself well, very straight and gracefully. One of her hands rested lightly on Adam's arm, while in the other she carried a small parasol, coloured to match her dress of palest green, trimmed with cream. It outlined to perfection her smoothly curving hips and breasts. She walked easily, her long legs matching Adam's still slightly uneven stride step for step. She was talking animatedly, and Adam appeared utterly absorbed in her.

Molly averted her eyes. Nearby a paperboy bawled, "Crisis in Ireland". His placard proclaimed, "IS IT CIVIL WAR?". She stared at the scrawled words for a moment before turning away. The warships still rode at anchor off the coast.

At Leigh they found a spot on the grassy cliff-top slopes to eat the fresh-cooked cockles and mussels they had bought. The tide was right out now, and the great stretches of mud glistened in the sunshine. Flocks of birds fed in the shallows; small boats lay on their sides, stranded, waiting for the next lift of the tide to refloat them. Adam, by accident or design, had seated himself beside Molly and lay back on his elbows, his eyes on the heat-hazed distance. Molly followed the direction of his gaze. Two of the Navy ships were sailing majestically up the deep channel that led into the heart of London. He stirred, and caught her eyes upon him.

"We're going to install some more ice-making plant," he said unexpectedly.

Molly could see Etta watching them, and resented it fiercely. Perversely she found herself taking it out on Adam. "Whatever for? We don't need any more. We've spare capacity as it is."

His face changed subtly at the shortness of her tone, and he lifted his shoulders in a shrug. "We may not need it now, but I've a feeling that we may soon." His narrowed eyes were still on the battleships. "If war comes and they stop the North Sea convoys—"

"War? What nonsense!" Etta dismissed the word with a wave of her hand. "The closest you'll get to war, Adam darling, is the race this afternoon. Joseph is quite appallingly determined to win. And the closest we ladies will come to it," she added, irony in her voice, "will be, I daresay, at the Commodore's garden party—"

The garden party was held in the grounds of the Yacht Club, which was perched on steep-sloping ground overlooking the stretch of water upon which the gentlemen members were competing for the last of the week's honours in a final day of regatta. The ladies, gloved, hatted and gowned for the occasion, despite the blazing sun, disposed themselves at small tables set on the terraced lawns and watched the afternoon's racing fortified by weak tea and cucumber sandwiches. There was about the whole affair, Molly was surprised to discover, a kind of infectious gaiety that lightened for the moment at least the odd moodiness that had settled upon her. Her wide-brimmed straw hat, trimmed with flowers that matched exactly the delicate pinks and blues of her dress, shaded her eyes as she watched

464

with the other ladies the racing cutters gracefully skim the shimmering water.

"Where's *Water Baby*?" Etta sank elegantly into the chair beside Molly, fanning herself gently with the folded copy of the day's events. "It's the one with the white stripe – ah, there. Gracious," she said, her voice mildly surprised, "don't tell me they're winning! Good Lord, I do hope not. We'll never hear the last of it."

"Now Etta," scolded a plump young woman sitting at an adjacent table, "you know you don't mean that!"

"Don't I?" Etta tapped the woman's arm sharply with the rolled up paper. "Don't be too sure, Mary my dear."

From the verandah of the clubhouse came a rousing cheer as Joseph's *Water Baby* passed the finishing line ahead of the other boats.

"There goes any chance of a decent conversation at the dinner tonight—" Etta said, putting her hand to her head in mock despair as *Water Baby* sailed into her mooring, Joseph's stocky figure obviously jubilant, at the tiller. Jack had a smaller boat waiting for them there and after Joseph and Adam had climbed into it, he rowed to the shore, where the watching women lost sight of them in the enthusiastic crowds.

"Ah, well," Etta said, standing up with a sigh, "I suppose I'd better go and garland them with roses or something?" And with no suggestion that Molly should join her she started slowly and gracefully down the uncertain steps that led down towards the road and the shore.

Molly sipped her tea and watched. She saw the back-slapping crowds part to let Etta's tall figure through, watched as she kissed first Joseph, then Adam. Adam appeared to say something. Etta pointed. Both Adam and Jack waved up to where Molly sat. She waved back, aware at last in that instant, of the cause of her wretchedness. Even from this distance, the sight of the slight figure in his white shirt and flannels, his hair blown wild by the wind, stirred in her emotions that she did not want to analyse. She despised herself for it, refused to accept that she could not, in the end, defeat it. Love, said a mocking voice in her head. The first taste, the first touch, and you are in danger of addiction.

465

Addiction? Very carefully she put the small cup and saucer on the table before her, straightened her back, lifted her chin. Etta, Adam, Joseph and Jack were coming up the steps towards her, laughing, Joseph beaming with pride, Adam's hair still wet with spray. She smiled brightly and went to meet them.

That evening they dined, the guests of the Yacht Club, at the Palace Hotel, a marvellously gilded wedding cake of a building whose tiers of long windows glittered in the evening light. As they sipped their aperitifs in the comfortable lounge before going in to dinner, Adam cornered her.

"Am I imagining it, or are you avoiding me?"

"You're imagining it."

His eyebrows lifted. "I'm surprised. I never give myself credit for much imagination."

She sipped her drink.

He ignored her silence. "I heard an interesting story last evening," he said, his voice lightly conversational, his eyes very sharp on her face.

"Oh?"

"It seems that a friend of mine had a crop of prime West Indian pineapples snapped from under his nose. Apparently someone discovered his agreed price – he admits that he's had a good thing going for some years – and topped it, behind his back. The deal was signed and sealed before he knew what was happening. He was – a little irate about it."

"Perhaps your friend should try getting up a little earlier in the morning?"

"Perhaps he should. I'll mention it to him next time I see him. If I ever do, that is. For the odd thing is that he seems to have the idea that I had something to do with his lost pineapples."

She looked at him with unclouded eyes. "That's possibly because I used your name. It was expedient."

He smiled at the word.

"These colonial planters can be very old-fashioned, I'm afraid. Not all of them are ready to deal with a woman," Molly said.

"Perhaps they find men more straightforward?"

Her eyes on his face, she let a small silence develop before she said, "I doubt it."

"Can we afford your cleverness? It might be a good crop, but it seemed to me that the price you paid was high."

"There's blight on two of the islands. This crop is prime and healthy. When news of the disease gets through the price will rocket. Yes, Adam, we can afford it."

From the impressive double doors, dinner was announced. Joseph appeared at Molly's elbow. "May I, my dear? Adam, Jack has claimed Etta – I should be grateful if you would escort our two charming younger guests in?" A short distance away the twins stood, both their faces bright with the excitement of their first grown-up occasion.

Adam put down his glass with grace. "Of course." As he turned away he paused, looking at Molly with real curiosity. "How did you find out what he was offering? And about the blight? I haven't heard a word."

Molly took Joseph's arm. "Don't worry, Adam. I didn't use your name for that. I have perfectly good ears of my own."

"I think I'll tell the War Office about you," Adam said, laughing. "We ought to be using you on the Kaiser!"

During the meal Molly found herself almost monopolized by Joseph who relived a dozen times his triumph of the afternoon.

" – warned old Bodger that I was going to do it this year, and by Jove I've done it! She's a queen, my *Water Baby* . . ." He paused, regarding Molly with twinkling eyes. "I've said that before this evening, haven't I?"

Molly smiled. Her eyes were on Meghan, across the table, who was thoroughly absorbed in openly flirting with Adam who appeared to be enjoying every moment of it.

"Must have bored you to tears, my dear."

She shook her head. "Of course not."

He patted her hand. "You're very kind."

"I've enjoyed it. I've never met yachting people before."

"Ah well, my dear, like everything else the club has changed since the days when the old King sailed in the estuary. It's to be expected of course, and believe me, in most cases I'm all in favour of widening the membership. To be honest with you, we were a stuffy lot, before."

"Oh, surely not?" She was barely listening, was watching

Adam's head bent attentively to Meghan, his expressive hand
moving rapidly as he talked.

Joseph leaned towards her, and, lowering his voice, said, "Bu
I must say that in some cases it seems to me that the Committe
has gone too far. Take the man at the corner table. John Cribbe
made his money from the sweatshops, so they say. And othe
things, so it's whispered. But he puts his hand in his pocket fo
repairs to the clubhouse, or presents a new solid silver troph
and it's amazing how respectable he can become overnight.
must say I never thought I'd see the day I'd sit at table with th
likes of Mr Cribben, even with the width of the room betwee
us."

The name had jolted her. She turned her head sharply to loo
at the man that Joseph had spoken of. He sat at a corner tab
beyond a group of Naval officers. Riveted, she stared at hin
The big frame had become corpulent, the handsome face wa
blurred with the flesh of good living; but for one dreadfi
moment she felt those brutal hands upon her. The man lifted
hand and mopped his face with a spotless white handkerchie
She caught the spark of diamonds from his fingers.

She turned away. "What an unpleasant-looking man. Do yo
know him well?" Amazingly, her voice sounded perfectly no
mal.

"Good Lord, no, my dear. We don't move in the same circl
at all." He wagged a knowing finger. "It's the railway, you se
Direct from the East End. It brings the workers on their tri
and it brings—" he glanced at Johnny Cribben again "– other
less savoury. Still, I suppose we're all entitled to our breath
sea air, eh?" He laughed in his jovial way. "Now, brandy,
think? Or would you prefer a port—?"

Molly shifted in her chair slightly, setting her back to th
room.

"Brandy," she said a little breathlessly. "Please."

That solitary, shaking glimpse of Johnny Cribben someho
epitomized for Molly a weekend that should, she knew, hav
been very pleasant but that at every turn seemed to conspi
against her, though, in honesty, she recognized that the tr
cause of her restless ill-humour lay not with others, but with

herself. She had to admit that after Adam's long absence she found it intolerable to be so close to him in such circumstances. During the past week her worry over Danny had already stretched her nerves, and now Adam's mere presence was enough to scrape them raw.

It was Sunday afternoon and the weather was very warm. Most of the occupants of the house were resting in anticipation of an early dinner and the trip home, but Molly, unable to relax, wandered into the large and quiet garden in search of air. By a tiny pond she found a small summerhouse overhung with trees and shrubs. She sauntered towards it; from beyond the high hedge came the sounds of the beach, overhead a seabird curled, calling, into the blue sky. The door to the little house stood open and she entered; the interior was dark after the brilliance of the sun. She stood for a moment, blinded, before the rustle of paper told her, too late, that the haven was already occupied.

"Well," Adam said, smiling as he laid aside the newspaper he had been reading. "Hello."

"I – Hello." She was completely at a loss for words. "I'm sorry – I didn't realize you were here . . ."

It was not well expressed. His silence was pensive. "You mean you wouldn't have come in if you had known?" he quietly asked at last.

She did not answer.

He leaned back in his wicker armchair and watched her with a faintly puzzled frown on his face. "I must confess," he said when it became obvious that she was not going to speak, "to being utterly confused. And by a woman, by Christ," he added mildly. "I never thought I'd see the day. I have to tell you, Mrs Benton, that you are by far the most unpredictable, the most——" he spread helpless hands, half-laughing still, " – the most perverse woman whom I have ever met. You advance, you retreat, you're fierce as a tiger one minute, soft as a kitten the next. Does it have something to do with being Irish?"

Her irritation at the world in general boiled suddenly into fury at him. "Don't laugh at me! Don't dare!" She turned towards the door but he was there before her, barring the way, a familiar anger beginning to smoulder in his eyes.

"Is there some kind of law against it?"

"Of course not," she said, a bitter brightness in her eyes. "If there were I guess half the population would be in gaol, and that would never do." She made to pass him but he did not move. "Adam, please let me pass."

He shook his head. "No. At any rate not until you explain to me how it is that we're standing here glaring at each other like wildcats again. How it is that you can dance like an angel on New Year's Eve and act like a stranger the very next time we meet? How two people who have been——" his eyes forced her to look at him " – as close as we have can so constantly misunderstand one another? Why we can't at least be friends?"

She stared at him miserably – Because I love you, the unutterable words rose raw and clear in her mind – because I have discovered that I truly love you. And I hate you for it. I can't stand what you are, what you will always be. I can't stand to look at Jack and to wish he were you. And I'd cut out my tongue before I told you so——

She looked at him expressionlessly, her blue-grey eyes silvered in the gleam of sunshine that struck like a lance through the open door. Dust danced, glittering, in the beam of light.

He shrugged, irritated. "Well, for Christ's sake, if you won't even answer me?"

"There's nothing to say. I don't know what you're talking about." Her voice was perfectly composed. "But there is just one thing."

"Yes?"

"I wish that you wouldn't encourage Meghan to be so – forward. I have enough trouble with the child without your attentions going to her head. She's at a very impressionable age."

"Now you're being ridiculous." Faint colour was rising beneath the brown skin. "You know as well as I do – as well as Meghan does – that it's just a game. What has it to do with us? With you and me?"

"Nothing at all." Molly tried to brush past him.

Very fast, he put an arm up before her, physically preventing her from leaving. He studied her face for a long slow moment.

"And Etta?" he asked finally, a sudden and merciless understanding in his voice. "Aren't you going to lecture me about her?"

"She's none of my business," Molly said coldly. "Meghan is."

He brought his other arm up behind her, trapping her between himself and the doorjamb; then, with aggressive deliberation he bent his head and kissed her, harshly and with clear intent to hurt. She tried to pull away. With no effort he held her. "You're jealous," he said softly, as he lifted his head at last.

She stepped away from him. "And you're a barbarian!" she snapped, beside herself with rage. "Beneath all that urbanity, all those wonderful good manners of yours, you are an absolute savage!" She hurled the word like a stone.

The expression on his face barely altered as he stepped back from the doorway. She stormed past him into the sunshine.

From a small copse of trees by the garden hedge a pair of narrowed, thoughtful eyes followed her as she fled to the house.

They hardly spoke for weeks, except when absolutely essential in the course of business, and then their mutual politeness was rigid. But events, finally, overtook them. No personal quarrel could override the sudden and frightening surge towards violence that began on the day that the Archduke Ferdinand, heir to the throne of Austria, and his wife were murdered by a fanatical young Serbian student and ended in the bloody sacrifice of millions.

In England the assassination was at first overshadowed by renewed threat of civil war in Ireland. The punitive Austrian ultimatum that followed the murders inevitably meant that irrevocable lines were being drawn between friend and foe; but when war was declared between Serbia and Austria it still seemed in Britain less menacing than the fact that the gunmen and the soldiers were once more out on the Irish streets. Hidden behind the smokescreen of Britain's domestic troubles the frontiers of Europe had begun to smoulder. When, however, at the beginning of August Germany declared war on France and demanded the right to march through tiny, defenceless, neutral Belgium in order to launch her attack, Britain in honour could do nothing but stand by her guarantee of Belgian neutrality. Three days later the German armies marched – and amidst an unprecedented wave of jingoistic patriotism, Britain found herself at war.

As an iron hand clamped down upon Ireland, and Trade Unions and Suffragettes alike declared immediate truce and called their workers to the flag, the problem of supplying and feeding a nation at war became paramount. On the day that Jack Benton, like a million of his fellows, donned the drab khaki that was already appearing in every home and on every street, the first escorted convoys steamed upriver to the docks of London, and Molly and Adam found that they had a war of their own on their hands: while at the recruitment centres men queued and jostled fervently praying that the game would not be over before they had fairly joined it, Molly and Adam worked feverishly to set the cold store on a wartime footing and to turn it over from luxuries to essential foodstuffs. Any other consideration seemed for the moment outrageously irrelevant.

The atmosphere in those first days of August was heady. The brutalizing concept of total war had not yet touched the minds of ordinary people, even now, as the machine that was to grind and crush a whole generation came into being.

It would all be over by Christmas, and the boys would be back home. Everybody said so. And everybody, surely, could not be wrong?

CHAPTER FORTY-THREE

MOLLY, HER ARMS full of dirty washing, pushed open the kitchen door with her foot, her face a picture of haste and exasperation. From the offices came the sound of a typewriter, and of women's voices. Someone laughed shrilly. Molly shouldered the door closed behind her, and then stopped, looking in astonished pleasure at the slight, uniformed figure who leaned, waiting, at the table.

"Nancy! Where on earth did you spring from? Why didn't you let me know?" Unceremoniously she dumped her bundle onto the floor and flew to her sister-in-law, enveloping her in a bear hug.

Nancy smiled tiredly. "I didn't have time. I didn't know myself until an hour or so ago."

"How long have you got?"

"Twenty-four hours."

"Is that all?" Molly looked into the worn and bleakly weary face. "You look as if you could do with at least a week of sleep."

The narrow shoulders lifted in a wry gesture.

"I'll make some tea," said Molly.

Water gushed into the kettle. "You look exhausted. What have you been doing?"

Nancy's laugh was short. "Scrubbing floors. Washing dressings. Making beds. Running errands. That hospital must have a hundred miles of corridor, and I reckon I run up and down every inch at least three times a day." She watched Molly for a moment with tired brown eyes. "I've been taking driving lessons, Moll," she said at last. "Nursing's not for me. I've known it for a long time. I want to drive an ambulance. In France. Or Belgium. Where the fighting is."

There was a small silence before Molly asked, quietly, "Wouldn't that be very dangerous?"

"At least I'd be doing something really useful. There are some women drivers already there – France and Belgium – some with

the various Red Cross organizations and some with private
organized and financed groups. If I have to knock on every do
in London I'll get myself out there. I've quite made up m
mind."

"Then there's no point in arguing with you, is there?" Mol
asked gently. "If there's one thing I know about you, it's that.

Nancy grinned suddenly. "Thanks. Now—" she said stirrin
the dirty clothes with her foot, "– what's all this? I thought fro
what I'd heard that you'd be up there at the Admiralty battlin
officialdom, and here I find you playing house—?"

"Even I have to do it sometimes. No one else will. Effie's gon
– she's working in armaments over at the Silvertown factory
and I sometimes think that the twins don't know that clothe
actually have to be washed occasionally."

"Have you heard from Jack lately?"

"Yesterday, as a matter of fact. He seems fine. Quite cheerfu
It's hard to tell, of course. He doesn't really say much."

"I hear he's got his stripes? Sergeant Benton, eh? Mam'
proud as punch."

"Yes." Molly tinkered with her teaspoon, clicking it agains
the saucer thoughtfully.

Nancy watched her sympathetically. "Don't worry, love. It'
take more than Kaiser Bill to clobber our Jack."

"Yes, of course."

"How long's he been gone now? Three months?"

"Nearly four."

"He didn't exactly hang about did he? He must have been on
of the first to join?"

"That's right." Molly lifted a wry eyebrow, "Seems to m
that you can't keep any of the Bentons from rushing int
uniform. Jack. You. Edward in the RFC." Another name hung i
the air unspoken between them.

"Harry," said Nancy, typically outspoken. "Ironic, isn't it?"

"Yes it is. But this is different. This isn't someone else's war
It's ours. I couldn't have expected Jack to stay out of it." Molly
held out a hand. "Come and sit in the parlour in comfort. I'
light the fire. Blow economy for just this once. This is ar
occasion."

Watching the new-born, crackling flames as they danced ir

he hearth Nancy said, "Edward's been posted to Hornchurch. Home defence. He's pretty angry about it. He's talking about trying to get himself posted."

"Doesn't he think the Zeppelins will come?"

Nancy shrugged. "They haven't come yet, have they? In spite of all the scaremongering." She yawned. "I'll bet more people have been hurt falling about in the dark because of the lighting regulations than have been by any marauding Zeps."

"I hope you're right. Chantale was in Antwerp when the Germans bombed it at the start of the war. It isn't a happy thought that it might happen here."

"Chantale? Is that one of your pet Belgian refugees?"

"She's more than that. She's a Godsend. Although she's lived all her life in Belgium her mother was English, so she speaks the language perfectly. She was fed up with her work at the hostel where all they do is knit socks and balaclavas. I thought I was doing her a favour when I asked her if she'd like a job here. As it's turned out the boot's entirely on the other foot. I don't know where I'd be without her. She's virtually running the agency. Which is just as well, since I've got my hands full at the store."

"Does she have a family?"

Molly shook her head sombrely. "Both her parents and her older sister were killed when the Germans went through Belgium. Killed horribly, I think. She rarely mentions them, but when she does she always uses the word murder. She got away, got caught in the fighting at Ypres and then walked on to the coast. She arrived in England, as so many of them have, with not a penny to her name nor a coat to her back."

"Where does she live?"

"She's still at the hostel."

Nancy hesitated for only a moment. "Why don't you have her here? She could have my flat. It would be more convenient for you, wouldn't it?"

"Yes, it would. But Nancy – the flat is your home—"

"Well of course it is," Nancy said briskly, "and it will be again. But it's a bit silly to leave it empty on the offchance of an occasional twenty-four hour pass, isn't it? I can always go to Mam's. Give the lass the rooms. It'll be nice to know they're being lived in. Just make sure that they're ready for me on the day the guns stop firing."

In the sudden quiet that followed the words Molly said, "Over by Christmas. That's what we all thought." A blast of cold wind buffeted against the window. "All I know is that if the government are handling the war with the same efficiency that they're handling the food supplies, then we'll still be fighting next Christmas!"

Nancy looked at her in surprise. "But the papers are saying there's plenty of food?"

"Oh, there is. The docks are chock-a-block. That's one of the problems. We've sixty per cent higher stocks of frozen meat, a hundred per cent of wheat and barley, and nowhere to put it. The sheds and warehouses that the Admiralty and the War Office have deigned to leave for us are knee-deep in sugar, of all things. The wretched Sugar Commission, in its wisdom, has imported a year's supply in the last four months! We're sinking under it. If something isn't done soon to clear the quays and warehouses we won't be able to land another grain of rice. What with that, the War Office – I mean, I know they need the space, but glory! they aren't the most efficient people in the world – and the weather, the port's half-way to chaos. You never know what's going to be requisitioned next. If the War Office doesn't get you, the Admiralty does. Talk about the right hand not knowing what the left is doing—"

"But the convoys are getting through?"

"At the moment, yes. We've not lost a cargo yet. But Adam's convinced that the North Sea convoys will be stopped if the German U-Boat campaign really begins to bite—" She stopped. Nancy's breathing was soft and even, her eyes had drifted shut. "Nancy?" Molly said gently.

"Good Lord! I'm sorry."

"Bed," Molly ordered. "Off you go."

"Well, perhaps I will get a bit of shut eye." Nancy stood and stretched tiredly. At the door she paused, "Oh, by the way, I saw Chris Edmonton the other day. He sends his regards. He's a Captain, pips and all, safely installed in the War Office filling in forms in triplicate, or so he said. And Felicity is having the time of her life feeding the Boys in Khaki at Victoria station from her

476

aristocratic little trolley." Nancy smiled wearily. "She's having a lovely war." She closed the door very quietly behind her.

Molly listened to the slow footsteps moving up the stairs. It seemed suddenly as if brutal visions of death hovered just beyond the firelit corners of the peaceful room. The sound of the guns of France and Flanders could sometimes be heard in the streets of London, streets that were full of young and not-so-young men in uniform – and already it was possible to distinguish between the eager and untried recruits and the shabbier men back from the trenches, with their apparently indelibly mud-marked uniforms and shadowed eyes. Each day in the newspapers fresh casualties were reported, and no front page was without its black-edged pictures of fresh-faced young men in uniform who were lost now to mothers, wives, sisters, lovers.

With an abrupt movement Molly leaned forward and stirred the meagre fire, and the flames, blood-red, leapt up the chimney.

That first Christmas of war passed, marked in the trenches by a bizarre and singular demonstration of goodwill between enemies and at home by austerity and a determined cheerfulness. On Christmas day a German seaplane attacked Gravesend, at the mouth of the Thames, and escaped unscathed. Ten days before, a Zeppelin had been sighted off the East Coast, but had not ventured inland. The incidents, though small, not unnaturally worried the civilian population. For this was a new and totally unknown fear. Never before had a British civilian population been threatened from the air, and reports from Belgium at the beginning of the conflict had been of a kind to conjure horrors in the least imaginative mind.

It was on January 19th in the new year of 1915 that the first Zeppelin raid on Britain finally came. The attack was launched on towns in East Anglia – Yarmouth, Hunstanton, King's Lynn. Two men and two women were killed and there was much damage done to property. The raid was followed by others, in the same area and on Tyneside. London waited nervously. And as the spring approached, they did not wait in vain; the raiders came.

"Where's Edward's precious Flying Corps?" Annie demanded in indignation. She was pregnant again, and her temper was short. "That's what I'd like to know. The damned Huns do as they like and no one's stopping them. What's the matter with our lot? Why don't they do something?"

Molly looked up from the list she was compiling of guests for a charity concert she was helping to organize in aid of the Red Cross. "Be fair, Annie. They try all right, they just haven't managed it yet. They say that the bullets go right through the airships and out the other side."

"I'd give a tooth to see one of them bloody things come down in flames, that I would," said Annie, unusually vicious.

Annie was not alone in her detestation of the Zeppelin raiders. They cast a shadow of fear out of all proportion to their real threat. As the crews grew more practised and the great ships took to the cover of darkness, many an anxious ear was tuned to the sullen thrum of an engine in the night, many an eye scanned the dark skies for the first sign of the monstrous and apparently invincible apparitions. People grew to recognize a "Zep night" as they might the signs of an approaching storm. Dogs would bark, birds twitter in their nests, disturbed by the vibration of the engines. And each time the monsters came they left behind them a trail of death, destruction and injury while a furiously helpless and demoralized population asked again and again the question that Annie had voiced. Why didn't somebody do something? And all the while the echoes of the guns filled the air as, across the Channel on the Western Front, the thunderous barrages further pulverized ground already turned to mud by months of shelling, and in that desolation known as the Ypres Salient the nauseous, creeping, blinding clouds of gas stole wraithlike across a dead landscape.

For Molly these were months of frantic activity. For every day spent in productive action it seemed to her that three were spent wrangling with officialdom, filling in forms, or trying to cope with the difficulties caused by the shortage of able-bodied man-power. As troopship after troopship sailed from the docks the jobs the men left behind were filled by old men, women and girls. Molly had reason again and again to bless Chantale Lefèvre's efficiency as the agency was overwhelmed with requests for workers. She would often work all day at the yard and then come home to work in the evening with Chantale. Nor did her restless energy allow her to stop there; she also threw herself whole-heartedly into fund-raising activities for the Red Cross. She persuaded 'her' hotels and restaurants to stage charity activities, she wheedled donations from anyone and everyone with whom she came into contact, she organized dances, teas, children's shows, bazaars, bring-and-buy sales. She filled every spare minute with activity. She was as at home on a windswept quay, a busy customs' shed or an Admiralty office as she was at a Town Hall function or, more practically, delivering in person a consignment of 'spoiled' foodstuff to the home for Belgian refugees, which was another of her adopted projects. When Adam complained, mildly, that if they weren't careful they would finish up in need of charity themselves – his own pocket having been considerably lightened by Molly's efforts – she asked him sharply, if he had seen the reports in some papers about complaints of war profiteering in food.

"Does it worry you?"

"It worries me that in some few cases it's true."

"But not in ours. Not with public fund-raiser number one on the staff," he said amiably.

She lifted her chin in a characteristic gesture. "That's right," she said, and marched off to her next appointment. The truce between these two had amounted to an almost total suspension of their personal relationship. Of necessity they spent time together, but always under pressure and rarely alone. They never spoke of anything beyond the need of the moment – the problem of moving and stowing incoming cargo, the stupidity of unnecessarily complicated regulations, the pressing necessity to find someone – almost anyone – to help to run and maintain the compressors. Molly knew nothing of Adam's private life, forbade herself to see him in any light but that of an efficient and necessary working partner. Above all she was aware as Adam himself was, that Jack, in his absence, stood between them now more surely than he ever had in physical presence.

She wrote to Jack with dedicated regularity, filling the pages with the cheerful minutiae of her own life, telling him of Meg's scrapes, of Kitty's determined knitting, of her own sometimes hilarious brushes with officialdom, of her fund-raising activities. She did not tell him of Danny's ever-increasing wildness and her concern about it, nor did she mention that a nearby street had been hit and badly damaged by firebombs. She received in return Jack's own letters, and in them she sensed exactly the same evasion of reality that pervaded her own. He was fine. Wet, cold, tired, but fine. He hoped they were all well. He missed them all. The food was terrible. He'd had a bit of trouble with his ears, but it seemed to be getting better. He doubted he could sleep now, without the sound of the barrage to send him off – no, there seemed no chance yet of leave. His company were being moved back to rest camp – to the reserve trenches – to the front again. The letters were written in smudged pencil, in ink, on any scrap of paper that could be cadged or salvaged. He never ever, even in the privileged, rare, uncensored green-enveloped letters, mentioned the fighting.

One Saturday afternoon in May Molly returned home to find Annie, tea cup resting comfortably on her enormous bulge, settled in the parlour with the twins.

"My God, it's like winter out there—Annie! Whatever are you doing here?"

Annie raised pencilled red brows. "There's a welcome."

"Well you know what I mean. What are you doing this far from home in weather as foul as this? You were due a couple of days ago, weren't you?"

"That's right." Annie was imperturbably cheerful. "Day before yesterday, to be exact. Problem is that you know it, and I know it, but this lazy little beggar doesn't." She slapped her swollen belly lightly. Meg giggled. "So I thought a stroll over to see his aunty Molly might shake him up a bit. There's nothing I hate more than just sitting about waiting for something to happen. Even when the something's a baby."

"But Annie, it's wild out there!" Molly glanced through the window at the driving rain, and trees that bent and lashed in the wind. "You mean you've walked all the way round here because you couldn't think of anything better to do?"

Annie grinned widely. "Something like that I s'pose, yes. I'm neither use nor ornament at home at the moment. I can hardly get behind the shop counter – we've got little Rosie Martin in to help Charley – and Sarah's with the children. You know what kids are – they don't want their boring old Mum when they can have Gran – so until I get round to performing I'm spare, and I'm fed up with it. I must admit that I didn't realize the weather was going to turn quite so bad – it is bloody May, after all – I just thought a quick run round here might give the idle blighter the hint, that's all."

Molly put her hands on her hips and gave her a look.

Annie moved a little uncomfortably in her chair. "All right. So it wasn't the best idea in the world."

"You could say that."

Annie threw back her head and laughed. "The rotten thing about being pregnant," she informed Meg, "is that absolutely everyone orders you about. Please, Miss," she teased Molly, "may I finish my tea before you turn me out?"

Molly laughed. "I'll have one with you. Then I'll hunt up a cab if I can and take you home. Where are you off to?" she asked Meg, who had jumped to her feet, pulling Kitty with her.

"We're going up to the hostel with Chantale. Don't you remember? We're helping her to teach some of the little ones English, and there's a lesson this afternoon."

"Oh, of course. Off you go then. Make sure you wrap up well."

Annie accepted a kiss from each of the girls with a smile.

"Doing their bit then?" she said as the door closed behind them and their young voices calling Chantale echoed up the stairs.

"Oh, they seem to enjoy it. Mind you," Molly said wincing a little as the front door slammed enthusiastically shut, "I suspect it's for different reasons. Kitty goes to teach the children. Meghan, I'm very much afraid, goes to make eyes at a couple of rather attractive young men. She's a little hard to keep up with, that one. I can't be behind her all the time."

"She'll be all right." Annie shifted in her chair, and grimaced.

Molly looked at her in concern. "Is something wrong?"

"No, 'course not. But – well, p'raps you're right. I'd better get home—"

"I'll get my coat and see if I can find a cab."

A moment later Molly came back into the room pulling on her still-wet coat, talking as she came: "I have to say that of the three of them, it's Danny that really worries me – Annie! What is it?"

Annie was doubled over, clinging to the back of an armchair, her face ashen. In a moment she straightened, breathing heavily,. "Sorry love. It looks as if you were right. Ah!" she flinched again, her hand going to her back.

"Oh, Lord."

Annie took a step, supporting herself still with the back of the chair. She leaned for a moment, the sweat running from a face that was pinched and sickly with pain. Then her body convulsed and she sank her teeth into her lip.

Molly ran to her, supporting her as best as she could. "They're coming too fast. We'll never be able to get you home. Oh, Annie—!"

"I know." Annie tried a none-too-successful smile. "Prize idiot, eh? – Leave it – a minute – p'raps they'll – ease."

Molly eyed her doubtfully. "It doesn't look much like it." She took her coat off and tossed it across a chair. "Come on, we'd better get you upstairs."

"No." For the first time panic sparked in the green eyes. "I've got – to get home. All the stuff's there. – And Charley—"

"It looks to me," Molly said practically, "as if it's going to be a damned sight easier to bring the stuff – and Charley – to you. Don't I recall that you had young Michael in half an hour or something? We can't risk it, Annie. Just look at the weather. Even if I could leave you there's no telling how long it would take me to find transport. Be a good girl and come upstairs. I'll telephone for the doctor. It may be a false alarm. If it is, then the minute the pains ease we'll get you home. If not – well, we'll manage, you'll see. Come on, lean on me. Let's get you to bed."

And so it was that, just over an hour later, in the chaos of a household turned upside down by his unexpected arrival, Thomas James Benton bawled his way into the world, quite unaware that he had chosen the wrong address.

CHAPTER FORTY-FOUR

THREE NIGHTS LATER, Molly sat curled up in the big armchair in the parlour taking the first opportunity she had had to write to Jack. In the breezy night something clattered metallically in the street outside. She lifted her head to listen. The gate rattled again. She uncurled her legs from beneath her and ran to the window, opening the curtains a bare crack to peep through. The street was empty. The gate swung fiercely in the wind. She let the curtains drop. Where in Heaven's name was Danny? She looked at the clock that ticked on the mantelpiece. Midnight. He had never stayed out this late before.

Restlessly she poked the fire into a heap of quickly-cooling ashes.

Where was he?

She sat down again, picked up the letter, read through what she had written, picked up the pen and dipped it into the little glass inkwell, sat staring sightless at the paper.

Where was he?

The gate rattled again, but this time it clicked shut firmly and there came the clip of footsteps on the tiled path. Molly felt every tensed nerve relax as she heard her son's key in the lock, and then, in reaction, felt a surge of anger the strength of which was in direct proportion to her relief. She slowly laid aside her letter and stood up.

"Danny?"

The quiet footfalls in the hall stilled. A moment later the door opened a little and Danny's tousled head appeared around it. The curly, autumnal hair was wild, and the thin, fair skin had that pallid sheen of someone who had either just been sick or was just about to be. The picturesquely prominent bones promised his father's good looks, but windblown and heavy-eyed as he was at the moment, Molly thought acidly, it took some imagination to see it.

The boy, clinging unsteadily to the door, did his best, with an obvious effort, to focus his eyes on her. "Mum? What are you doing up? I thought you'd be in bed."

"I'll bet you did." Even from where she stood Molly could smell the alcohol and the stale reek of cigarette smoke. "What time do you call this? Where the Devil have you been?"

"Out with my mates, that's all. Look, Mum, it's late – I've got to get up in the morning—"

"It's a pity you didn't think of that earlier. It seems a little late to realize it at—" with precise movements Molly consulted her little corsage watch " – four minutes past midnight? Will you come in for a moment, please? And shut the door behind you."

For a rebellious second he stayed where he was, then with the graceless unco-ordination of belligerent adolescence he came into the room and stood looking at his mother in guilty defiance.

"I asked you where you'd been?"

He shrugged. "Up West. With some of me mates."

"What? The West End?"

"Yes." His mouth was sullen.

"Doing what?"

"Nothing much. Kicking around."

She looked at him searchingly. "Kicking around," she repeated at last.

He flushed at her tone.

"Supposing there had been a raid?"

"There wouldn't have been," he said, on the edge of rudeness. "Not in this weather."

"Let's get something very clear, Danny Benton, right here and now," she said, her voice quiet and ice-hard. "I will not have you staying out until all hours like this. I will not have you 'kicking around' the West End with the likes of Albie Duncan and the others. *I will not* have it. Nor will I have you drinking and smoking and God knows what else besides—" She passed a tired hand across her eyes. "Get to bed, for God's sake, before you fall over."

She did not look up until the door had closed behind him, and not until the sound of his footsteps had faded did she go upstairs herself.

Annie smiled sympathetically as Molly looked in round the bedroom door. The room was warm and cosy; a fire glowed in

he hearth and the rosy light of one small lamp gilded Annie's
ery halo of hair and gleamed on her bared breast where baby
om was suckling contentedly. "They're a lot easier at this
ge, aren't they?" Annie said, nodding down at the suckling
hild.

Molly had to laugh. "There was a time when I'd never have
elieved it, but, yes, they are," she said wryly.

was less than a week before she clashed with her son again. On
e evening before Annie and the baby were due to move back
ome, Danny announced at dinner with a studied casualness
at immediately alerted his mother that he would be "going
ut later".

"Going out where?"

There was a tell-tale moment's thought. "Just out. I might go
the Electric Theatre. They've got *Tess of the D'Urbevilles*
n again at the Boleyn."

"You've seen it once."

"No law that says I can't see it again, is there?" His voice was
nsolent.

"Danny."

"What?"

"Where are you really going?"

He jumped up, making the crockery clatter on the table.
Kitty was watching him with wide, distressed eyes. Meg shot
er brother one sharp, exasperated look and went on eat-
ng.

"Will you stop treating me like an idiot five-year-old? I've told
you where I'm going. Believe it or not. I don't care."

Kitty put a hand to her mouth. Meg did not look up until the
sound of the front door slamming shook the house.

And this time the Zeppelins did come.

Molly was in the bedroom, helping Annie to pack, with the
baby sleeping soundly in his cot when the first gun rumbled and
the first whistle sounded. Annie lifted her head sharply and put
her finger to her lips. Molly stood very still and listened with her.
Very faintly, on the quiet night air, was carried the drone of an
engine. As the two women stood so, looking at each other, the

door burst open and the twins erupted into the room. Litt
Tom, disturbed, began to cry.

"It's a Zep!" Meg cried excitedly. "Quick, turn the lights ou
let's have a look."

"It probably won't come this—" Molly's words wer
drowned in the rumble of a big gun that rattled the window an
shook the glass ornaments on her dressing table.

"There! That's the gun at Wanstead!" Meg said triumphan
ly. "It is coming this way. Oh, come on, Mum, turn the light
out."

"Shut the door then. And put the screen in front of the fire.
Another sound reached their straining ears now, lighter,
wasp-like buzz counterpointing the resonant hum of the airshi
engines.

Annie flew to the cot and picked up the baby, holding hi
high on her shoulder and rocking him, soothingly.

Molly checked around the room before reaching to the lamp
"All right?"

Annie nodded. Molly turned the lamp down and it died
guttering. In the darkness they crowded to the window anc
opened the curtains.

Apart from the uncertainly wavering beams of the searchlights there was nothing to be seen.

"Oh." Meg was disappointed. "Can't we go into the garden
and look?"

"No," Molly said sharply. "You stay here with us."

Meg subsided.

"It's coming closer," Annie whispered. "Listen."

The droning was much louder.

"There it is!" Meg shrieked, and then, "oh, no it isn't. It's the
searchlights on a cloud."

Gunfire grumbled again, like the rolling thunder of a summer
storm.

"Where's Danny, do you think?" Kitty asked in a small voice,
and was treated to a painful nudge and a withering look from her
sister.

"There's an aeroplane, look," Meg said. "It must be searching
for the Zep. Oh, *please*, Mum, can't we go outside?"

"No."

The little black-painted plane, a moving speck in the search-light's beam, buzzed overhead, very high, turned, banked into the cloud and disappeared.

"He can't find it," Meg said, disgustedly. "You wouldn't think they could miss something that big, would you?"

"Quiet a minute, Meg."

They stood in silence. The Wanstead gun had fallen silent, and in the quiet moment before the big guns closer to the river concussed the night, the sound of the enemy engines were suddenly very loud. Someone in a nearby street blew several sharp blasts on a whistle, and a man shouted.

Kitty's hand crashed against the window. "There! There it is!" she shouted, pointing, as in a flickering finger of light a blunt-nosed monster emerged from a light-gilded cloud. The crack of rifle-fire greeted its appearance and a new explosion of noise from a big gun came very close behind. Other searchlights swept across the sky towards the prey, trying to pin it down in meshed shafts of light. In the sudden onslaught of sound the great ship seemed to be moving noiselessly; the enormous, shadowy shape slid across the night sky, lifted, and was gone. The beams of light frantically searched, probing, sweeping the clouds, finding nothing. Fiery shrapnel bursts marked the place where the menacing thing had been.

"Oh, they can't have lost it!" Meg shrieked. "They *can't*."

"They bloody have," Annie said.

"It was heading for the river from the look of it." Molly was straining her eyes into the light-swept sky.

"The docks and the arsenal," Annie said.

"You wouldn't believe that they—What was that?" A violent explosion had shaken the window. Before they could move or speak there was another, and another.

"The bastards are unloading their bombs." Annie rocked the crying baby. "There now, Tommy, love. There now."

Over towards the Thames an ominous glow had appeared, reflecting sullenly onto low cloud. There was another crumping explosion, and another. Flames reared into the night, red and yellow tongues licking at roof and spire. There was no sign of the airship.

"Where's that bloody plane?" Annie asked. There was a

slight, worried crease between her arched brows as she looked towards the fire.

"That's too close to be the docks burning, isn't it?" Kitty asked very quietly. "It's houses. They've bombed houses."

"The guns got too close for comfort I expect. They're just getting rid of their bombs so that they can get away."

"It's over our way, isn't it?" Annie asked.

Molly dragged her mind from the thought of the absent Danny. "I don't think so. It's hard to tell."

The guns further up the river in the heart of London were crashing now, and more searchlights wandered fruitlessly and blindly about the dark skies. There were more explosions, much further away. Flames lit the darkened streets. The City guns boomed. People were outside now, in nightshirts, pyjamas, dressing gowns, apparently oblivious of the cold, calling and pointing.

"It's gone," Molly said. Her eyes were on the ominous red glow, welded to the sheaves of sparks that lit the night air like a devil's torch. "Back to bed girls."

"Oh, Mum, you can't make us go back yet!"

"Bed," she said firmly. "I'll make us all a hot drink, and you can have yours in bed."

Where was Danny? Where?

Annie was still staring out of the bedroom window, the baby asleep across her shoulder. "Beats me how they can do it."

"Who?"

"The fellers that fly them damned machines. Bombing civilians. Women and kids. Fine brave, soldierly thing to do, wouldn't you say? How can they do it?"

"It's war," Molly said, bleakly.

"It's cold-blooded bloody murder, that's what it is. Whichever way you look at it." Tom made a small, mewing sound.

"Put him to bed, Annie. I'll bring you a drink."

The commotion in the street had died. Molly busied herself in the kitchen, listening for the rattle of the gate. In the past minutes she had in her imagination seen her son injured, maimed, dead. She could not prevent the awful pictures forming and dissolving in her mind, fuelled by the darkness and the lonely silence. She rubbed her knuckles into her eyes, then stood up determinedly, the tray of hot drinks in her hands.

She was at the foot of the stairs when she heard the gate open. And then the knock on the door.

She froze. Not Danny – he had a key. The knocker rose and fell again, a discordant sound, inordinately loud in the night-silence of the house.

As she opened the door, the sight of the burly policeman who stood waiting, silhouetted against the red, smoke-smudged night, almost stopped her heart completely.

"Yes?"

He cleared his throat. Behind him another, younger man, also in uniform, shuffled his feet, his head bowed. "Er – Mrs Benton?" the burly policeman asked, "Mrs Molly Benton?"

"Yes." It was Danny, then. Her mouth was dry as ash. She could barely breathe.

"You've got a Mrs Annie Benton staying in the house with you?"

Taken aback, she stared. Annie?

"Mrs Benton?" he reiterated, gently.

"Oh, yes. She's here." Something awful was happening to her stomach. She leaned on the doorjamb to steady herself.

The policeman put out a hand to help her. "I think perhaps we'd better come in, Mrs Benton," he said gruffly. "As I can see you've guessed we've got some bad news. Some very bad news indeed. I have to see Mrs Annie Benton—"

"The bombs?" Molly whispered.

"I'm afraid so, yes."

She did not move. "Charley?" she asked, incredulously. "Not Charley? And the children—?"

"I'm afraid so."

"Hurt? Badly hurt?"

The man's good-natured face mirrored the distress that she knew must be written upon her own. But he hesitated too long. She knew the answer before he spoke. "It was a direct hit, Mrs Benton. No one in the house survived."

From upstairs Tom let out an indignant yell as his mother laid him down and came to the top of the stairs.

"Molly?" Annie called softly, "is something wrong?"

The shock of the deaths of Charley and the children was numbing for everyone and overwhelming for Annie. Molly found it took weeks for the reality of the tragedy to make itself truly felt. She discovered, too, that, perhaps not surprisingly, a new dread of those aerial monsters and their night-time attacks had been instilled in her. Though she never admitted it to anyone, and never betrayed her fear before Danny or the twins, the already nerve-racking 'Zep nights' became for her the worst terror she had ever endured.

Jack's first leave after his brother's death came in August. Neither he nor Nancy, who had been stationed at Ypres now for several months, had been able to get home for the funerals. He stood by the graves, granite-faced. Small bunches of fresh flowers showed that Annie and probably Sarah with whom she and Tom were now living had been there before them.

"Bastards," he said. "Murdering bastards. Isn't it enough for them, what's happening over there? Must the whole world rot before we're finished?"

Molly knelt and laid their own small offering upon the short, green grass. She had learned long ago that there were no words of comfort to offer that could be anything but empty.

In fact, these much-anticipated five days of Jack's leave were not unclouded, and the reason could not be said to be entirely due to the tragic circumstances of his brother's death. Months under fire, months of living with fear and with death had taken an obvious toll of him. He was withdrawn and quiet, grim lines marked his face. He slept badly, spoke little. There was exhaustion in his eyes, which no amount of rest could ease. Often Molly caught him staring into space, as if listening for something, a strange, intent look on his face. They made love with a kind of violence, as though to fill a desperate vacuum with their passion. But though Molly felt that these were perhaps the only times she truly came close to him she could not pretend to herself that their lovemaking was a success for either of them.

On the day Jack was to return to France he and Molly stood together in the acrid-smelling bustle of the vast station hall almost wordless in the deafening commotion, their ears assaulted by bawled, unintelligible orders, the stamp of marching, booted feet, the shriek and hiss of escaping steam. Around

hem were piled seemingly endless rows of stacked rifles and
kitbags. Uniformed men and women hurried past. Molly found
herself going through the motions of farewell in a kind of haze. It
seemed to her, and she was certain to Jack too, that he had
already gone from her, back to that alien world of which she had
no real knowledge and in which she could have no possible part.
In truth, she thought, bleakly, perhaps he had never left it. As
the train departed in a flurry of brave smiles and fluttered
handkerchiefs she recognized beneath the quite genuine misery
an awful edge of relief. And pondered, as she journeyed home,
on the effect such a war as this might have on nations if it could
so divide those who loved and cared for each other.

CHAPTER FORTY-FIVE

THE AUTUMN OF 1915 was, even more than usually, the van guard of winter. The torrential rain that began in September and turned the charnel house of the Western Front into gruesome quagmire that swallowed horses, guns and men with equal ease, swept the streets of London as if attempting to drown anyone with the temerity to venture out of doors, and continued so without a break through a wild and windy Christmas. By the first day of January 1916 the British army in France numbered one million men, a million men living in the worst conditions and under the most atrocious stress that any human enemy could have devised. The great armies were deadlocked, mired in along an arbitrary line, assaulting each other senselessly and ceaselessly with high explosives, mowing each other down with machine guns, watching each other die and decompose on the strung barbed wire that divided Europe. And all for nothing. Not an inch of ground was taken that was not immediately lost again, not a town or village was left in that great swathe of mud that had one brick still standing upon another. Men drowned in shellholes, were blown to pieces in No Man's Land, were scythed down attempting to take yet another useless square yard of ground. In Britain compulsory military service was introduced. The cry, still, was for men and yet more men, and there were not many who thought to question it. In order to justify the losses already incurred, a victory must be won, no matter what the cost in blood.

In February the Germans launched a surprise attack on Verdun, taking the Allies completely unawares, the avowed aim of the campaign to bleed the French army – already very badly battered – to death. Yet, astonishingly, against unbelievable odds, the French held, and the enemy found themselves once more locked into a battle that was to last for months. To relieve the pressure on their almost exhausted allies, the British began to prepare for a push to the north, on the Somme, but while all eyes were turned to France an event took place that aroused passionate indignation throughout the beleaguered British Isles. For while tens of thousands of Irishmen fought and died beside their Welsh, Scots and English comrades in the trenches, a small group of rebels, on Easter Monday, took over the post office in Dublin and proclaimed from the steps of that building an Irish Republic.

Most of the inhabitants of the city were as bewildered and outraged as the rest of Britain. To hear Germany referred to as a 'gallant ally' was too much for most people to swallow, however patriotically Irish they might be, and anti-rebel feelings were strong, even in Ireland itself. In the brief, fierce fighting that ensued Dublin was reduced almost to the same state as the towns of the Western Front as the thousand or so rebels fought from street to street, from house to house. For Molly, more than most, the newspaper reports were harrowing, bringing back as they did memories that she had believed long buried. Ironically, she caught more than one sharp glance upon her at this time as a discerning ear picked up the trace of her accent, met once or twice with a hostility from strangers that she knew to be undeserved. In truth, however, she had little time to worry about such things. It concerned her far more that the German U-Boat campaign in the North Sea and in the Channel was beginning to take great toll of merchant shipping, and that the new conscription laws meant that she had lost more workers than ever, despite the fact that many men in the cold storage trade could have been exempt – in many cases men were reluctant to remain in their safely starred jobs in face of public opinion, of posters that portrayed their children demanding sternly "What did you do in the Great War, Father?" and of the danger of the muttered word 'Conshie'.

She walked into her office late one May evening to find Adam already there, seated at her desk, a slip of paper in his hand. He stood as she entered the room. There was a gleam in his eyes that she recognized.

"They've done it," he said.

"The North Sea convoys?"

"Yes."

"Stopped altogether?"

"As we expected. Yes."

She regarded him reflectively for a moment. "As you ex
pected. So, no more natural ice." She turned away and began t
rummage in a tray of papers.

"The price of ice has already gone up fifty per cent this year.'

"I know it. You'd better give your crystal ball an extra polis!
tonight," she said, still hunting, then, "Damn!" She stood up
looking around the room.

"What is it?"

"I thought I had the documents for the *Southern Queen*. I did
have, I'm certain." She chewed her lip thoughtfully. "I ha
them with me this afternoon, over at the customs' shed on qua
three. Oh, for Heaven's sake! I must have left them there!"

"Leave them. They'll be quite safe. You can pick them up i
the morning."

She had picked up her small handbag and was already at the
door. "I can't. I need the wretched things now."

"Wait." He was shrugging into his coat. "If you must I'll rur
you over there. I—" he smiled faintly " – acquired some petro
this afternoon."

She realized that she had left the bag in Adam's car almost the
moment that he drove away. Standing in the twilit road outside
the great dock gates she almost stamped her foot in rage at he
own stupidity. All her money was in the bag, to say nothing o
her only means of identification, should anyone choose t
question her presence in this security-sensitive area at a slightly
odd hour. Not that she anticipated any problem – she knev
almost certainly that she would be recognized and allowed t
pass by the guard on the dock gates. A far greater problen
seemed to be that unless she was lucky enough to find someon
she knew who might be willing to lend her the fare, she was in fo
a long and dark walk home.

As she approached the gate she smiled in relief as a mar
stepped out and barred her way, peering at her in the gloom.

"Ah, Sergeant Anderson. I was hoping you might be on duty
I wonder if you could help?"

Moments later she was hurrying through the darkenin
evening towards the customs' shed, her borrowed fare safely ir

er pocket. By now she knew the layout of the area as well as she new her own parlour. To save time she turned into a tiny lleyway that ran between two great warehouses, and her breath lmost choked in her throat as unexpectedly in front of her oomed a figure, rifle in hand, a threatening silhouette in the ading light.

"Halt! Who goes there?"

She stopped.

"Out, you, and let's have a look at you."

She followed the soldier into the open. "I can explain—"

"Yes, I'm sure." He held an open hand towards her. "You got omethin' to show who you are an' what you're doin' 'ere?"

"I – I'm afraid I don't, no."

"Is that so?"

"I stupidly mislaid my bag – left it in a car – my name is Benton. I left some documents in the shed on quay three this fternoon. I've come to collect them." Her voice steadied as she ecovered from the shock of his sudden appearance.

"Did you now? Make a habit of it, do you? Mislayin' things, ike?" His voice was not friendly. "Irish, aren't you?"

"Yes – that is, no—" she stuttered, confused. "My husband is English, so—"

"And where's he?"

Her temper flared at the boorishness of the man. "He's in rance, Private. Fighting for his country."

He was not impressed. "Aren't we all? I think you'd better ome along with me, don't you? And with no fuss, neither."

She stood her ground. "Where to?"

He caught her arm very firmly. "Never you mind. Just come long. We can't 'ave you wanderin' around 'ere on your own in he dark, now can we?" His voice was heavily sarcastic. "You ight 'urt yourself. Or you might 'urt someone else, like. You ver bin to Dublin?"

The question caught her off her guard. "No."

"My brother 'as. In fact, it was the last place 'e ever went ied there, 'e did. A month or so ago, fightin' some of your ates. Hear about that little party, did you? Bloody Irish. Now, ou comin', or do I 'ave to carry you?"

With as much dignity as the undignified situation allowed her

she walked beside him, his hand still firm about her upper arm
to a nearby warehouse in whose cavernous depths stood a sma
wooden hut. As he marched her towards it she pulled bac
"What are you going to do?"

"I'm leavin' you somewhere nice and safe while I go and fir
my sergeant. That's what I'm goin' to do."

Somewhere down the river a gun boomed.

"Look, won't you please listen to me? Sergeant Anderson, o
the Barley Street gate knows me. Knows me well. He'll vouch fo
me. He let me in—"

"More fool 'im. Right. In you go." He hustled her into th
hut, and over her furious protests, slammed the door. She hear
the key turn in the lock, and above that the sound of a whistle
shrill and urgent. The guns boomed again. She beat her fist
against the door.

"Let me out! It's a raid! You can't keep me here—!"

"Safe as 'ouses." His voice was caustic. "The silly bleeder
couldn't 'it the side of a barn anyway, didn't you know that?"

"Don't go away—" His footsteps receded. The guns rumble
again, and it seemed as if the world shook about her.

"*Let me out!*"

Silence.

She stood, shivering, listening. Thinking of those airborn
monsters that had slaughtered Charley and the children. Seein
them. Since that night she had dreamed of them, woken tremb
ling and drenched in sweat.

Please, God, don't let them come—

She stood, straining her ears for the drone of an engine. Th
sound of the guns was continuous now, the volume increasing a
the dock guns took up the chase. Panic pounded in her vein
with her blood. She was freezing cold, and shaking.

Don't let them come. Please don't let them come—

Above the sound of the guns came the strong, steady v
brations of an engine.

She flew to the door, pounding on it until her hands stung an
throbbed with pain. "*Let me out! Let me out!* PLEASE!" Panting an
sobbing she leaned against the door, felt it shudder as th
concussion of an explosion shook the world outside her priso
The hut was windowless. She could see nothing. Mindless pan

took her. She was almost choking with terror. She threw herself against the door as the blast of another explosion vibrated through the air.

"*Let me out!*"

When the sound of the key in the lock came to her ears she flung herself at the door at the very moment that it opened and found herself, unbelievably, held in arms that were strong and familiar. Beyond the open doors of the huge warehouse lurid flames flickered. A great shape hovered in the sky, caught for a moment in a swinging pencil of light. With a shuddering sob she buried her face in Adam's shoulder.

"Molly, my darling. Molly, Molly. It's all right. You're quite safe." He rocked her gently, soothingly. "Come on now, my love. This isn't my girl? Isn't my Molly?" His hand came up to cradle her head, fondling her hair.

She sobbed still, convulsively. The airship's engines throbbed and swelled, then diminished as the thing turned and, unscathed, followed the path downriver towards home. One by one the guns fell silent. Still Molly clung. Adam laid his face against her hair and held her very close. A uniformed figure marched to him smartly and stamped to a halt, his eyes fixed on some point in darkness above Adam's right shoulder.

"Is there anything I can do, sir?"

"Thank you, no, Private Johnston, I think you've done quite enough," Adam said pleasantly.

The soldier's eyes flickered. "Only doin' my duty, sir. I wasn't to know."

At the sound of his voice Molly had quietened. She stood with her face still buried hard in Adam's shoulder.

"That will be all, Private. I'll see Mrs Benton home. You can apologize to her – you will apologize to her – another time."

"Yes, sir."

As the man wheeled smartly and left, Adam tried to put Molly from him, to look into her face. She clung to him.

"It's all over, my love. They've gone. You were quite safe, you know. That idiot was at least right about that. These warehouses are built like fortresses. They use them as air raid shelters in some places, you know they do. Most of the bombs missed

their target anyway. They fell into the water." His voice w:
faintly puzzled, "Molly, what's wrong? What is it? You':
shaking like a leaf—?"

"They killed Charley," she said. "And the children. The po
children—"

He pulled her to him, bowing his face to her head. "Go
forgive me, I had forgotten." He held her for a long time, unt
her violent trembling had eased. At last, with a long, tremblin
breath she drew away from him.

"How did you find me? What are you doing here?"

"You left your bag in the car. I came back with it. Sergear
Anderson told me he'd seen you through the gate – I came t
find you and met that donkey in a uniform who'd shut you ir
That's about it."

"Thank you."

"Don't mention it. Any time you get taken for an Iris!
insurrectionist, just call for me."

She could not respond to his gentle teasing. He looked at he
worriedly.

"I'm sorry," she said at last, "I've made an awful fool o
myself. You see, ever since—" she caught her breath, trie
again, "Ever since—"

"Don't think about it." His arms were strong about her. H
lifted her chin, tilting her head. Complete darkness had fallen
Her wet face glimmered in the reflected light of distant flame
They could hear, faintly, the cries of the firefighters, the clang o
bells. Very gently he kissed her. She stood quite still, the silen
tears still running down her face.

"I'll take you home," he said.

The big car nosed through dim-lit streets. At the crossroad:
beyond the docks, Adam stopped. "Is there someone at hom
with your children?"

"Yes. Chantale's there. Adam, where are you going?"

"I told you." She could not see his face in the darkness, "I'n
taking you home."

She was too exhausted to argue. The weariness of month
seemed to be engulfing her, a tide drawn to the flood by th
evening's terror. She lay back on the luxurious leather up
holstery, her eyes shut. She felt drained and lethargic. An

ridiculously safe. Somewhere in her memory those words he had whispered to her as he held her echoed softly.

She woke with a start as they pulled up at the foot of the steps that she had once known so well. The apartment too was the same. Adam settled her in a deep armchair, lifted her feet to a footstool, then went to the telephone and dialled, his eyes on Molly's face.

"Hello? Is that Ma'm'selle Lefevre? Ah hello, Adam Jefferson here. Yes, that's right. She asked me to ring. She's been delayed, I'm afraid – *no*, no, there's nothing wrong. It's just business, that's all. She didn't want you to worry. Thank you. Yes, I'll tell her. Fine. I'll make certain she gets back safely. Good night, Ma'm'selle." He cradled the receiver. "They're fine. I don't think they'd even missed you."

She sat up, swinging her legs from the footstool. "Thank you Adam, I—"

Very firmly he pushed her back into the chair. "Just be still for a minute. Doctor Jefferson prescribes medicine first, talk afterwards."

"Medicine?"

He went to a cupboard, held up a bottle. "The finest French brandy, saved for just such an emergency."

"I don't know how you do it."

"The same as I ever did. Don't worry about it. Just drink it. It isn't stolen, if that's what's worrying you."

"The thought didn't cross my mind." As he poured the drinks her eyes went to the window. "You haven't drawn the curtains."

"I'll do it if it makes you feel safer. But they won't come back tonight. And if they did they won't bomb Kensington. If he wins the war the Kaiser's going to live here."

"That isn't funny, Adam."

He came to her, knelt beside her, put the glass of brandy into her hand. "Don't tell me my Molly's losing her sense of humour?"

"You called me that before, tonight."

"Do you mind?"

She had loved him for so long now that it seemed almost as much a part of her as her breath; she had denied it to herself so long that his bent head, his intent face, the hard, narrow hand

499

that held hers seemed unreal. "No," she said simply, and took a mouthful of the smooth, warming brandy. His hand held the glass insistently tilted, forcing her to drink the rest.

"Isn't that a dreadful waste of good brandy?" she asked.

He took the empty glass from her hand. "Do you feel better?"

"Yes. Thank you." Her head swam for a moment and she lay back in the chair. "Don't I recall that you had an appointment for this evening?"

"I cancelled it."

"I'm sorry."

"Don't be. When have you ever known me do something that I didn't want to do?" He took her hand in both of his, opened the small, curled fingers gently and kissed the palm.

She rolled her head, tear-swollen eyes closed, in a small, protesting movement. "Please. Don't." But her hand remained, open, in his.

"Molly. Look at me." He waited. "Look at me," he said again.

She opened her eyes.

"I think you know that I have never begged a woman—"

She did not reply, because she could not.

"Must I start now?" he asked softly.

"Would you?"

"Yes." The word was unhesitating. "If that is what you require of me."

"At this moment."

"Of course. What else is there? Knowing me as you do would you demand a commitment beyond that? Tomorrow is an illusion. It never comes. There is only now." His shadowed face was unsmiling. "I have never in my life wanted anything as much as I want you at this moment." The room was very still. It seemed to Molly that her very breath had suspended itself. "In what seems like another life you called me a barbarian. Perhaps I am. Perhaps, my love, we both are. It's certain, anyway, that we recognized each other the moment we met. And now, here, at this moment, you have me on my knees. Are you going to take advantage of that?" The line of his mouth was hard as ever She could not take her eyes from it.

She reached both her hands to his face, felt the warmth and

the strength pulsing into her limbs from the simple touch of him.
"No," she said, and as she drew his light weight upon her she
closed her eyes, shutting out the world, the war, the demands of
the people who could lay claim to her and closing in for the space
of a moment the love, the need, the giving that she had denied for
so long.

Far, far away the guns of battle rumbled.

On the first of July 1916 the British attack was launched on the
Somme. On that first day alone twenty thousand British dead
littered the battlefields, and forty thousand more filled the
hospitals and the casualty clearing stations to overflowing. As
news of the losses filtered home, and the magnitude of the
disaster was realized, with whole families of men, whole streets
and villages being wiped out, the stunned nation mourned the
worst day in Britain's long military history. For ten agonizing
days Molly did not hear from Jack. Anxiously she scanned the
casualty lists, watched for the postman, the telegraph boy, and
forced herself to believe that the lack of news was good news. At
last her patience was rewarded, when she received a hastily
scribbled note telling her that he was safe and well, a minor flesh
wound in his hand, now healed, having been his reason for not
writing before. With that she had to be satisfied; the note told
her nothing else. In the next post there arrived a letter from
Nancy, who was still stationed at Ypres, her usual understated
and humorous epistle, though Molly could not help noting that
even Nancy's tough resilience seemed a little frayed at the edges.

The new influx of wounded strained the home-front hospitals
and services to their utmost. Molly launched herself feverishly
into yet another storm of fund-raising, badgering and cajoling,
organizing, demanding. She visited the hospitals to discover their
needs and used every ounce of influence that she, Adam, or anyone else possessed to obtain them. She saw Adam alone on a few
rare and precious occasions at his apartment, time snatched for
both of them out of pressing activity, time out of life that seemed
to neither of them to have anything to do with anyone or
anything beyond themselves.

Late in August, Edward came home on leave before being

posted at last and was swept into the maelstrom of activity a₁
laughingly declared that he would be glad to get back to the w
for a rest. Then, at a hospital tea dance, he met Chantale Lefèv
and a wartime romance blossomed that the whole family watcl
ed with amusement and pleasure.

"Oh, heavens, isn't it *romantic*?" Meg asked, pure envy in h₁
voice, "they can't take their eyes off each other."

The family were sitting at the breakfast table. Molly lifted h₁
head as the letter box clicked. Kitty was out of her chair and in
the hall before anyone else could move. "It's a green one! Dad
writing. Open it, Mum, quick!"

Molly slit the envelope and ran her eyes swiftly over the fe
written lines.

"He's coming home. Leave at last. Next week." In the tumu
of the girls' excitement Danny continued to eat stoically.

The week of that leave was one of the worst she had ever live
through. After the first ecstasy of welcome and excitement ha
worn off it became obvious to the most casual eye that there wa
something very wrong with Jack. He had been quiet before
now he was almost totally withdrawn. He had lost weight
looked ten years older than his age. He jumped at the slightes
noise. His hands shook. And so far as she could tell he slept no
at all. Night after night she woke to find him standing at the ope
window, a shadow in the shadows, looking out into the rustling
darkness. She found his tense silences almost unbearable. H
answered her questions in monosyllables or not at all. H
absolutely refused to discuss the war.

" – Let it be, lass. Talking won't change anything. Won'
explain anything. Won't make sense of anything, come to tha₁
Let it be."

"But, Jack, perhaps if you talked about it, told me abou
it—?"

"No!" The word was spat, savagely. "There'd be no ease i₁
that. Don't think it. I'm tired, lass. Dog tired." His eyes had ₁
worn defeated look that wrung her heart. "Let it be."

Their lovemaking, as before, was desperate to the point o
violence and totally unsatisfactory for either of them. Once, h
cried. She held him, bewildered, as the sobs shook him. Later h

ept, and woke in the middle of the night with a cry that woke
ae whole house. In despair she watched him, feeling his pain,
elpless to aid him.

On the Saturday evening two days before he was due to go
ack, they had an unexpected visitor. Christopher Edmonton
urned up on the doorstep of The Larches, elegant in tailored
niform, his cap tucked neatly under his arm, an expression of
ervous determination on his face. It was the first time any of
1em had seen him for years.

"Oh, please, don't get up, Mr Benton—" he held up a quick
and as Molly, her face a picture of politely suppressed surprise,
ed him into the parlour. Jack, who had barely moved, sat back
1 his chair and eyed the tall, neat figure expressionlessly.

"Won't you sit down?" Molly was at a loss as to how to
address this unfamiliar young man with his adult's face and
he clipped pleasant voice that showed no sign of the stammer
she remembered. To call him Christopher, as she had used,
.eemed entirely inappropriate. To call him Captain Edmonton
vas impossible. "You remember my sister-in-law, Mrs
Benton?"

Annie, who had come to visit Jack, was sitting silently by the
window. She nodded, unsmiling.

"Yes, of course." If Christopher noticed the desperate change
.hat bereavement had wrought in Annie he gave no sign of it,
and Molly warmed towards him. But she was puzzled by him.
He seemed entirely self-composed, yet she saw that the long
1ands that held his cap were clenched so that the bones stood
.tark against the skin.

He looked at Jack. "I heard that you were wounded, Mr
Benton? On the Somme, wasn't it?"

Jack nodded. "A scratch."

"Pretty awful business from what I heard. You're recovered, I
rust?"

"Yes, thank you," Jack said, taking an easy breath, a savage
.park in his eyes, "Sir."

The young man moved his head sharply. The straight brown
1air, shorter than Molly remembered it, fell forward across his
`orehead and he flicked his head sideways in the familiar gesture
:o flip it back. His face was afire, yet he held Jack's eyes steadily

with his own. "I apologize for coming in uniform," he sa
quietly. "Had I known that you were here I promise I should n
have done. I've been meaning to come for weeks. Months.
wasn't sure – wasn't certain – that I would be welcome."

His composure was deserting him. Jack sat, stone-faced, an
watched it happening.

Molly could not bear it. She put an impulsive hand on th
young man's shoulder. "Christopher! Why of course you'r
welcome! How could you doubt it? However you're dressed, an
whatever the time!"

"Thank you." His smile was grateful.

"Sit down." She saw that his eyes were still fixed upon Jack'
still figure. "I'll light the lamps."

"Oh, no, Moll," Annie protested quickly from the window
"not yet. Don't pull the blinds yet." She was watching the wide
still sky.

Christopher stood stubbornly in the centre of the room. "Yo
were at Loos, weren't you, Mr Benton? Before the Somme?"

"Aye. I was."

"Nancy told me. Before she left." The name was spoken a
last. He took courage from it, but not enough to sustain him
entirely. His eyes moved from Jack to Molly. "I came to ask afte
her, Mrs Benton. I don't have her address. She said she'd write
She promised. But she didn't."

"Aye, well," Jack said from his chair, "I daresay that ou
Nancy's got more to do than push a pen and shuffle forms, lad
Her time's well taken, any road." The emphasis, and the insul
to the young man in his pristine War Office uniform wa
unmistakable.

"Jack!"

"It's all right, Mrs Benton." Christopher was turning his cap
in his hands, over and over, but his voice was perfectly steady. "I
know what Mr Benton is saying. And I know that he has every
justification." He smiled, a slight downturn of his sensitive
mouth. "Self-deception is not one of my vices. I understand why
none of you approve of any association between me and Nancy
And I swear that under any other circumstances I would no
dream of enlisting your help in this way. But please—" he
turned in earnest appeal to Jack, " – Nancy and I are old friends

504

simply want to know – have to know – that she's all right. That ∎e's safe still. That she doesn't regret her decision."

"She doesn't," Molly said positively, and taking the matter ∎to her own hands she got up and walked to the sideboard, not ∎oking at Jack. "Here. Her latest letter. It came last week."

Christopher took the envelope, looked at Jack. "May I?" He ∎aused. "Please?"

"If I say no?"

Without a word Christopher extended the letter towards the ∎ther man, not even looking at it.

Jack considered him with hard eyes. "Happen you're more of ∎ man than I gave you credit for, Captain Edmonton," he said at ∎st. "Go on. Read it. Where's the harm?"

Christopher took the letter to the window to gain the last of ∎e light. In the silence the paper crackled. Molly saw that, as he ∎nished reading, his long thumb brushed gently across the ∎arelessly scrawled signature.

"Thank you," he said, handing her the letter and retrieving ∎is cap from the table, "that was what I came to find out. You've ∎een very kind," he added stiffly.

Jack leaned back in his chair. "Oh, for Christ's sake, lad, sit ∎own," he said, a tired note in his voice. "Molly, lass, is there a ∎rop of whisky in the bottle?"

It was much later when the whistle shrieked in the street ∎utside. Oddly, there had been no warning barrage. Annie ∎tiffened. Christopher looked up sharply. "A Zeppelin?"

Faintly, in the distance, a gun crumped. Jack's eyes closed for ∎ fraction of a second longer than a blink. Another gun opened ∎p, quite close, rattling the glass in the window. The whisky ∎lass in Jack's hand jerked. Somewhere above them came the ∎nsect buzz of an aeroplane and, distantly, the rattle of a ∎nachine-gun.

Molly seated herself on the arm of her husband's chair, ∎nobtrusively placing herself between him and the other occu-∎ants of the room. She could feel the force of his trembling ∎hrough the frame of the chair.

The sound of the aeroplane came again, and more machine-∎un fire. The airship's resonant drone beat against the ear-∎rums.

Nancy's letter was still lying on the table. Christopher picked it up and looked at it.

"Keep it," Molly said.

He folded it carefully, tucked it neatly into his pocket.

A strange, reverberating explosion seemed to shake the very air. Sweat sheened Jack's face. In the street someone shouted loudly, excitedly.

"Dad! Mum! They've got the Zep! It's burning! Come and look, oh come and look!" Meg burst into the room in her nightgown. Behind her stood Kitty, plaits wild, eyes wide. The room was bright with light. Annie flew to the door, followed closely by the girls.

Molly hesitated. "Jack—"

"Go and watch the Zeppelin burn," Jack said, in the voice of a stranger.

Outside the street was thronged with people. Except that many were in their nightclothes, it might have been a street festival. Men shouted, women pointed, children danced and shrieked. The sky was a blaze of white light, its centre a holocaust that could have been the sun itself.

"Holy Mary," Molly said, her hand to her mouth.

The great, blazing, cigar-shaped torch drifted slowly across the London sky, illuminating all of the city in its death-glow. Like fire itself, cheering ran through the watching multitudes. Not far from that ball of flame that just a short while before had been an invincible and menacing airship a tiny, black-painted aeroplane looped a wild loop, victorious, and the people below shouted themselves hoarse at the sight. Molly looked at Annie. She was staring, tense as a drawn bow, at the flower of flame that was dipping away to the north. Molly thought of the dreadful charred load that it must carry and, enemy or not, felt sickness rise. Near them a motor bike revved up. "Let's follow it! Let's see the buggers hit the ground. Let's watch 'em fry!"

Molly's stomach turned again.

"Come on, Annie, let's get inside."

"No." Annie's eyes were fixed on the flaming airship as if on a vision of heaven, "Burn!" she said, her voice low and vicious, "burn damn you!"

Molly turned and left her. Going back through the front door

'The Larches' she met Christopher coming out. In the deep shadows of the doorway she could not see his face beneath the peak of his cap.

"Thank you, Mrs Benton," he said, extending his hand.

She took it. "I've done nothing. I'm sorry if—" From within the house came the sudden crash of glass. Molly ran past Christopher, through the hall and into the parlour.

Jack stood, his massive shoulders hunched, leaning against the mantelpiece and staring down at the whisky glass that lay, shattered, in the hearth.

In the sky outside the bloody, murderous glow was dying at last.

Three days later Jack returned to France. With an odd, fatalistic premonition, Molly waited, but she heard nothing from him. The letter, when it came, was addressed in unfamiliar writing. She stood looking at it for a long time before she opened it.

" – it is with great regret – killed in action – greatly missed – a true friend and a brave soldier—"

She laid the letter on the table and walked, blindly, to the window. Outside, it had started to rain again.

CHAPTER FORTY-SIX

It took Captain Christopher Edmonton almost four mont
to get himself posted to Flanders. But over the furious a
obstructive protests of a mother who, however patriotic s
might be, was understandably certain that he had taken leave
his senses, and with the somewhat surprising co-operation o
wife for whom the idea of having a husband on active duty he
much appeal, he at last managed it, and, not without misgivin
but feeling as if for almost the first time in his life he had made
decision of his own and stuck to it, arrived in that b
leaguered few square miles of quagmire known as the Ypr
Salient in the middle of the worst winter that Europe ha
suffered since 1880.

"You'll get used to it," said a sympathetic and very youn
looking fellow officer in the swaying, freezing cold railwa
carriage that trundled them across the frozen fields of Flander

Christopher smiled unhappily. Ever since the troopship ha
docked he had been aware of the rumbling shock of the grea
guns. A small cold fist of fear had clenched in his stomach whe
first he had heard them, and lay there still like something he ha
eaten and was unable to digest. Used to it? He very muc
doubted it. He doubted it from the moment he stepped from th
train at Bailleul. He doubted it more when he saw for the firs
time, with a shock of disbelief, though he had believed himse
prepared, what years of brutal bombardment had done to th
prosperous and harmless little town of Ypres, when he saw th
ravaged land, its quiet fields reconstituted by high explosive int
an unrecognizable and untenable sea of fouled mud. No tre
stood, nor was any building unscathed. The gentle, woode
countryside had been reduced to a desolation of scorche
foot-high stumps and tangled barbed wire. On the slight ridge
that ringed the salient – 'hills' in military terms in this fla
country – the Germans were entrenched, tiered like spectator
above the Roman Circus of death below. From their advar

geous positions they could direct their fire at will within the
asted area beneath them, bombardment that continued
most without a break day and night. The ghost of Ypres stood
the middle of this desolation, a smudge of the landscape
arked only by the shattered remnants of its medieval spires
at pointed jagged, accusing fingers at the leaden skies. Within
ours of his arrival in the flattened town, Christopher heard the
omment that, for him, encapsulated vividly the devastation of
ese flat lowlands.

"If you stand on a chair, sir," said the cheerful cockney
orporal who had been assigned to show him to his quarters,
I've 'eard it said you can see England."

Grimly Christopher set himself to survive. His first experience
the front line did nothing to reassure him. In the scratches in
e usually liquid, but at present frozen mud that were the
ritish trenches – in marked contrast to the solidly-built con-
rete blockhouses on the opposing ridges, – men shivered, the
lood almost freezing in their veins, cursing the war, the
eather, the General Staff, their only hope of relief the uncertain
lessing of a 'Blighty', one that might send them, maimed but
live, back home. Christopher learned to keep his head down, to
ndure sights and sounds that in days past might have driven
im to sickness, to stand like a statue in the night of No-Man's
and while the Very lights swung eerily above him and the
German gunners, made expert from long practise, laid a creep-
ng barrage across the lit, blasted ground, searching for any
emnant of life. He learned to live with fear, to live with the
nowledge that he, too, had taken life – an idea that, a few short
ears ago, would have been unacceptable to the point of absurdi-
y – learned, to his own surprise to eat, drink, sleep, talk, laugh
with others like himself for all the world as if this lunacy were
quite normal, while about them howled the bombardment that
e sometimes felt, if it did not kill him outright, must surely
hatter every nerve and bone in his body by its force.

But he found Nancy. He had written to tell her when he had
first got his posting and they were to meet first, a couple of weeks
after his arrival, at an *estaminet* in a village a couple of miles west
of Ypres, where the possibility of their reunion being interrupted
by a stray shell was at least a little reduced. Christopher reached

the rendezvous first, took a seat by the window, certain that ⟨s⟩he
would not come. But ten minutes later he spotted her strid⟨ing⟩
down the cratered, icy street, trench coat collar turned
around her ears, hands in pockets, her boyish shoulde⟨rs⟩
hunched against the cold. He saw her pause in the doorway
looking round the smoke-filled steamy room. When her ey⟨es⟩
found Christopher, the old, brilliant smile lit them and s⟨he⟩
pushed her way through the crowds towards him.

He stood up.

"Chris!" She extended both gloved hands.

He took them in his own, looking into a face that, behind ⟨her⟩
smile, was lined and tired. She had grown thinner than ever; s⟨he⟩
looked, if anything, older than her thirty-seven years, yet still ⟨in⟩
her dark eyes and in her quick movements was life, vigo⟨ur,⟩
humour. To some this thin, untidy woman in her unflatteri⟨ng⟩
masculine outfit might have appeared plain. To Christopher s⟨he⟩
was nothing short of beautiful. He loved her still, he knew it wi⟨th⟩
certainty. Very swiftly he bent and kissed her cold cheek.

She held him at arm's length, and studied him – the spar⟨e,⟩
hardened face, the mud-stained uniform. "My, my," she said ⟨at⟩
last, softly, "Christopher Edmonton, all grown up."

Over a bottle of harsh local wine she told him, simply an⟨d⟩
steadily, of Jack's death.

He spread his hands. "I'm sorry. Terribly sorry."

She nodded. "It's strange to think of our Jack gone. Of a⟨ll⟩
people, strangely, I never thought it would be him. Stupid, ⟨I⟩
suppose."

"How's Mrs Benton – Molly?"

"Oh," Nancy fiddled with her wine glass, twirling it betwee⟨n⟩
her fingers, "as well as can be expected is the phrase, isn't it?"

In the quiet moment that followed the words the laughte⟨r⟩
around them sounded very loud, drowning the distant sound ⟨of⟩
the guns.

He reached across the table and, absolutely naturally, too⟨k⟩
her hand. "Nancy. I am so very glad to see you."

Her hardened fingers closed about his. "And I you."

On the day in March that the letter arrived at The Larch⟨es⟩
telling of this meeting, Molly arrived at her office at Jefferso⟨n⟩

Benton late in the morning to find Adam waiting for her.

"Working lady's hours, are we?" He shut the door behind her, helped her from her coat and, very lightly, kissed the top of her head. He did not miss the way that she moved away from him.

"What is it?"

"Danny," she said bleakly.

He waited.

"We had yet another blazing row yesterday. Which finished when he walked out. And started again when he walked back in – a soldier."

"But he isn't old enough, is he?"

"Since when did that matter? He lied. They don't count their teeth, you know. He told the recruiting sergeant that he wasn't going to sit at home, waiting to be conscripted. . . . How many of Kitchener's New Army are lads who've had a row with their mothers, do you think?"

"You could get him back. If you told them."

She turned away. "Certainly I could. And then he'd go off and join somewhere else, under an assumed name. He'd never forgive me. And I'd never know if—" She could not go on. She moved round the desk and sat down. "I'm sorry. It isn't your problem. You were waiting to see me?"

He nodded. "The North Sea convoys."

"It's bad?"

"Very. The Channel's infested with U-Boats. They're hunting in packs outside the estuary."

"You think the government's going to divert the convoys?"

"It's on the cards. I'll be surprised if they don't."

"But that'll mean absolute havoc. The western ports don't have the facilities, and they're already overloaded. And what about the railways? They'll be chaotic—"

"You know that and I know that. Unfortunately the little men in peaked caps in the Admiralty don't appear to know it. If they divert the convoys then the people in the south are really going to discover what a food shortage means."

"And for the first time in your life you might find yourself with no profit?"

"I might at that."

The words were not idle. As the ruthless German U-Boat

campaign built up and many thousands of tons of British and neutral shipping were lost, there was an outcry against using the besieged Port of London to import the nation's food. Once again, pressure was brought to bear to divert the convoys. A committee was appointed, to report to the Admiralty. It reported that such a diversion was only practicable to a very limited extent. The west coast ports were already working to capacity. In any case, their facilities were specialized – frozen meat could not be unloaded with equipment designed to handle coal, nor wheat with cranes that normally hoisted steel.

"Thank God for that, anyway," Molly said. "It's about time someone showed some sense."

Adam shook his head. "Advice is one thing. Taking it, quite another. There's a lot of pressure being brought to bear. More and more convoys are being diverted still, report or no report. The problem isn't over yet."

For the man in the street the question was simple. Where were the Navy? Why didn't they just do the job they were supposed to do and protect the merchantmen? And, often, the question was asked in tandem with another: never mind about the Navy, where were the RFC? Where were those who were supposed to protect the skies of Britain? For as the year moved from spring to summer, the raiders came again. They struck at the south coast, the east coast and then, inevitably, at London. But this time it was not the slow-moving airships that terrorized the sky, for the explosive tracer bullets that had brought down that first Zeppelin the September before had made an airship mission over England nothing short of suicidal. By this summer of 1917 new words were on everyone's lips: Gothas, Giants. They came in bright clouds from the sun, the Gothas, small and manoeuvrable, the Giants, as their name suggested, big and ugly. It had been just seven years since the first, to most people incredible, cross-channel flight. Now they came in pairs, in tens, in twenties, attacking docks, railways, arsenals, caring little that these objectives were sometimes impossible to pinpoint in densely populated areas and that, inevitably, most of the casualties were civilian. People slept in the streets, in the parks, in the underground stations. Squadrons that had been diverted to the Western Front were brought back hastily to face this new attack:

nd with them came Edward Benton. He turned up unexpec-
:dly at The Larches one evening, to find Molly gingerly
utting Meghan's fair hair while Kitty and Effie looked on.

"Oh, go on, Mum. Do it shorter than that. I want it –
dward!" At considerable risk to her ear Meg leapt from
eneath the scissors that her mother was wielding and threw
erself on her uncle. Edward grinned widely.

"Hello, everyone. Why, hello, Effie – I thought you'd gone?"

"She did," Meg interrupted, still hanging around his neck,
but she got scared and came back."

Effie was not in the least put out by the bluntness. "So would
ou, young Meg, if the blessèd factory blew up around your ears.
'ou won't catch me near Silvertown again in a hurry, I can tell
ou."

"Edward, come in. I didn't know you were home. Effie, put
he kettle on—"

"Well, actually," the young man said, blushing a little as he
:xtricated himself from Meg's embrace and smoothed down
lready immaculate hair, "I can't stay. I don't have much time.
And – well, I rather hoped that I might see Chantale?"

Molly smiled. "Of course. She's upstairs. Call in and see us
Defore you go, though, won't you?"

In the event he did more than that. He appeared in the
loorway of the parlour looking confusedly proud and happy, the
slight, dark Belgian girl of whom Molly had become very fond
:linging to his arm.

"We wanted you to be the first to know—" Edward began
shyly and was almost smothered by Meg who was across the
·oom in a second.

"You've popped the question! I knew you would! I said,
lidn't I?" she demanded of the room at large. "I said that was
what he'd come for! A wedding! How lovely! When's it to be?"

"As soon as we can make it. There's no point in hanging
around, is there? I mean – in the circumstances—" Molly saw a
shadow pass across Chantale's happy face. "I don't know how
long it will be before they send us back. Chantale agrees. We'll
get a licence, or whatever it is you do— What's the matter,
Molly? Aren't you pleased?"

Molly smiled warmly. "Why, of course I am. I was just

thinking – couldn't you wait just a couple of weeks? Perhaps Nancy will be able to make it home for the occasion?"

Edward shook his head. "It would have been nice, of course, but it's no good, we can't afford to wait on the off-chance. She probably wouldn't be able to get home anyway. A brother's wedding isn't exactly a priority event, is it?" He pulled Chantal close to him. "I'll write and tell her of course, but by the time she gets the letter there'll likely be a new Mrs Benton."

As Edward had surmised, the letter telling Nancy of her son's proposed marriage did indeed arrive a day or so after the event. She read the letter several times over before tucking it into her pocket and bending again to the task of folding a light summer dress and packing it into the small case that lay on her bed.

"News?" asked the plump girl who was sitting on the next bed watching her.

"Yes."

"Good or bad?" asked the other, unabashed by the shortness of the monosyllable.

"Good."

"Makes a change." The girl lay back on the bed and stared gloomily at the stained and peeling ceiling. "Lucky you, eh? Five days' leave and good news too. I should be so lucky. Touch me before you go, will you? It might rub off."

Nancy did not reply, but continued her packing with her neat, swift movements.

"You're very quiet," the girl said, eyeing Nancy slyly. "Are you sure you aren't off somewhere with that good-looking young Captain What's-his-name that's always hanging around?"

There was a faint tremor in Nancy's hands as she snapped the case shut. "Don't be daft."

"Well I—"

"I have to go. See you Friday."

At the busy railhead Nancy stood waiting to join the train and watching the activity. Long lines of khaki-clad men, cheerful in the sunshine, were queueing for everything – for the trains, for the latrines, for a cup of tea. After the taking of the Messines Ridge a month or so before the pressure on the men in the Salient

ad thankfully eased a little. The weather, too, was better, and
ad been for a couple of months, though the warmth did little for
1e mud except to change it into a quaking, stinking bog. Nancy
ad been stationed at a Casualty Clearing Station just behind
1e reserve trenches on that hot June night when they had blown
1e Ridge. The waiting had seemed endless. She had sat on the
unning board of her ambulance, wreathed in cigarette smoke,
:nse as a spring, waiting as it had seemed that the whole world
ad been waiting, while beyond the shaded lamps a host of men
ad scrambled through wreckage-littered darkness to their
ppointed places. At two in the morning the British guns had
uddenly ceased their roar. The silence had been uncanny as,
uspicious but perhaps also thankful, the German artillery, too,
ad fallen silent. And in that silence a bird had sung, the most
peautiful crescendo of sound that Nancy had ever heard. With
housands of others she had stilled, and listened. Then she had
eached for another cigarette, and as she had struck the match
he world had lit and turned as the mines that had been planted
peneath the Ridge blew and seemed to split the world apart.
Within minutes the guns had started up again, and through the
amiliar thunder Nancy had heard the whistles and the shouts as
he infantry had gone in.

It had been more than two days before she had learnt that
Christopher had gone over with the second wave – more import-
int that he had survived those two days comparatively un-
cathed. For her they had been days of ceaseless activity in
vhich she had found herself, sleepless, juddering over all-but
mpassable roads in the warmth of the summer's night or in the
plazing heat of the sun, wrestling with a vehicle that sometimes
eemed to have acquired a malicious life of its own, and praying
hrough gritted teeth that she was not doing more harm than
good to the men that she was carrying.

When, finally, Christopher had managed to find her, having
peen sent back from the lines to have a flesh wound in his arm
dressed, she had unashamedly flung her arms about him,
purying her face in the foul-smelling rough cloth of his uniform
acket. He had been very pale, a trickle of blood had shown at the
oots of his straight brown hair and his arm had been bandaged.
It had been in that moment that she had known that she would

go away with him. He had asked her, often, and each time s
had refused. But in the horrors of that June day she had realiz
that she had been wrong.

Now, as she boarded the train that was to take her to Cala
where Christopher for the sake of discretion had arranged
meet her, that certainty, not surprisingly, had somewhat dis
pated. They were going to a villa on the coast of Brittany, own
by some friends of the Edmontons and shut up for the durati
of the war. When Christopher had written asking if he and
friend might use it for a few days the owners had written to s
they would be only too pleased to do anything to help the 'lads
the front'. As she watched the embattled countryside roll pa
even nervous as she was, she had to smile again at that. Th
letter in her pocket crackled. She turned her mind from
wedding she had missed and settled herself for the journey
Calais and to Christopher.

Beyond the open verandah where they sat, the sea, far below
creamed at the foot of the cliffs and sparkled blindingly in th
evening sunshine. On the table between them was the remains
a simple meal – bread, cheese, and a half-empty bottle of wine.

"Best meal I've ever eaten," Christopher said.

Nancy nodded sleepily. As seagulls wheeled and called an
the red sun dipped low a faint breeze stirred her short hai

"Have you ever seen anything so peaceful?"

"I'd forgotten anything could be."

Silence settled around them, a silence enhanced rather tha
disturbed by the mournful crying of the birds and the shiftin
sound of the sea. They had not, Nancy realized, actually spoke
much since Christopher had picked her up in a borrowed car fu
of black market petrol and they had set off into the green an
miraculously normal countryside. It had hardly seemed neces
sary to speak. It had been enough to savour the fact that th
sound of the guns was fading behind them, to see sunshine o
fields undamaged and peaceful, to see houses and village
standing safe and snug, their roofs whole, the unbroken glass i
their windows reflecting the light.

Behind them now the handsome villa with its quiet, dust

heeted rooms waited for the night. The sea was molten gold in the sunset.

Christopher stretched his long frame lazily. "Cigarette?"

"Please."

He lit two, handed her one. She laughed suddenly.

"What is it?" he looked at her quizzically.

"Well, just look at me. At us. Think back a few years." She lifted the cigarette and let the smoke wreath upwards in the still air. "Not so very long ago this alone would be enough to brand me a scarlet woman, let alone——" She stopped again. "You pick up some bad habits in the army."

Christopher reached for the wine bottle. "Let's finish this off."

They sipped the wine in silence until the sun finally slipped away and dusk washed around them. The evening air was warm and very soft. Nancy became aware that Christopher had turned his head and was watching her. She moved a little, lying back in the deep wicker chair, a sudden and unmistakable stirring of excitement deep in her body. She stretched, languidly.

"I suppose we ought to clear these things away?"

He shook his head. "Not now. Tomorrow will do."

She looked out to where the swelling ocean still lapped, unseen. "I had forgotten that we had tomorrow," she said softly.

"Tomorrow, and the next day, and the next."

He came to her, knelt beside her. In the gathering darkness she studied the lines of his face, lifted a hand towards him, but then did not touch him.

"I've a present for you," he said after a moment.

She watched as he fished in his jacket pocket.

"It's a bit battered I'm afraid. The mud's got to it." He handed her a small, leather-bound book.

"What is it?" The cover was soft, the pages fine, much-worn beneath her fingers. She could not see to read it.

"Byron. Remember? Tomorrow you shall sit all day in the sun and read to me."

She ran her fingers over the cover, sensed the warmth of much loving use. "But it's yours."

"I want you to have it. Please, don't say you won't."

Her fingers laced with his. "Thank you."

They stayed so for a long time, then Christopher, withou
releasing her hand, sat on the floor at her feet, leaning bac
against her legs. The sea whispered in the darkness.

"We really should go in," she said at last, regretfully.

He stirred. "I suppose so."

Neither of them moved.

"Nancy?"

"Yes?"

He rested his head on her knees. She could not see him in th
darkness. "I want you. I want to make love to you."

She said nothing.

"Please," he said.

"You don't have to ask."

She felt him shiver, then saw the dark shape of him above her
felt his mouth on hers, uncertain and soft at first, then harder
more urgent. His fingers found the buttons of her shirt. Hei
breasts were tiny, the nipples small and hard. He brushed them
with his warm tongue. She cradled his head, her fingers
brushing through the fine hair. "Shall we go inside?"

"No, out here. I want you out here, in the open air." A little
way along the verandah was a day bed, set for the sun, he
half-carried her to it, dragged the cover from it.

The air was cold on her warm skin. Naked, she lay beneath
him, taken beyond thought, beyond memory, by his gentle
lovemaking. And later she lay with his sleeping body a dead
weight upon her, refusing to close her own eyes. These moments
must not be wasted in sleep. Time, she knew, could be the
greatest traitor of all.

Their few precious days sped by, as she had known that they
would, lost in the sunshine and the sand, in the wild headlands
and glittering sea. They read Byron on the beach, declaimed
him on the windy cliffs, whispered behind closed shutters in the
loving nights. Against her own convictions she grew young
again in his company, and he, it seemed, changed as she
watched him.

On their last morning, he stood at the door of the kitchen tall
and tanned, love in his eyes, unshadowed, his diffidence and
uncertainty finally gone.

She lifted the basket from the table, looked around for one last me and could not speak.

Looks like another push," Christopher said when they arrived ack at Calais, almost inevitably it seemed to that apparently onfused activity that they had both come to know well. For the ake of propriety he was leaving her to catch a train for the last tage of the journey while he returned the car to its owner.

She caught his hands. "Christopher, promise me you'll be areful—" She bit her lip, shaking her head ruefully. "Damn. I lways swore I'd never do that to a man."

He took her by the shoulders. "Be careful yourself. You'll ever know how much you mean to me. You are sanity in a unatic world."

"Some might put it the other way round," she said, smartly, ler eyes too bright for laughter.

They came together for a moment in the noise and confusion, he trains packed with uniformed men. "Stations are my least avourite places," she said, breaking away. "Please go. You lon't have to wait. I have Lord Byron for company."

In her hand she held the small leather book. He wrapped it, and her hands, in his own, lifted them to his lips. "Remember this: You are more than life to me. You are my whole strength. We'll be together one day, I promise you, no matter what. No one will stop us."

On the railway line that ran past the other side of the platform a long, clanking line of trucks was rolling slowly by, the great, ugly snouts of mounted guns pointed skywards, waiting.

"Take care," she whispered.

"I will." He kissed her, quickly and lightly, and then he was gone.

Three days later the ambulance that Nancy Benton was driving along the desolate track that had once been the Menin Road suffered a direct hit from a high explosive shell.

Nancy was lucky. She died at once.

CHAPTER FORTY-SEVEN

THE AUTUMN AND winter of 1917 were the grimmest of the wa
both for those at home and for those in the trenches. Durin
September there were raids on London on six out of eigl
consecutive nights, bringing human casualties and destructic
of property, fraying further nerves already at breaking poin
The psychological effect of the raids was inestimable: the life
the capital was seriously disrupted, the temper of its populatic
was short-fused, people were angry and frightened. Any shop
business whose unfortunate owner bore a name even slightl
Teutonic was in real danger of being stoned or even burned. An
an additional strain was, as Adam had predicted, that, as th
convoys continued to be attacked or diverted, food failed to ge
through to the capital. With the railways of the south alread
clogged with war materials, food shipments piled up in the west
and Londoners muttered while they queued. They cared less
that in unpredictable Russia centuries of repressive Czarist rul
had come to an end, or that the French army had come
perilously close to open revolt than that the price of butte
continued to rise and that after a long wait all they could get wa
half a loaf.

A few days before Christmas Molly came home to The
Larches to be told that a visitor was waiting in the parlour.

"Christopher! How nice to see you!" Molly's voice wa
genuinely warm.

Christopher, with some difficulty, lowered himself into the
offered chair.

The fire had been lit and glowed rosily, tamped down with
dust to make the fuel last longer. In the corner of the room a
small, decorated Christmas tree shone in the light. Carefully
Christopher propped his walking stick against the chair. His
right leg stuck stiffly out in front of him. He was in civilian
clothes.

"You were wounded," Molly said, gently.

"At Passchendael." He smiled a little, deprecatingly. "A 'blighty' one. Next best thing to a home posting, so they say." The lightness of his tone was painful. "Mrs Benton—"

"Molly."

He smiled. "Molly, yes. I came to offer my condolences—" He struggled for a moment over the name, " – Nancy told me about Jack. And then – to have lost her, too—" His voice trembled very slightly. "I wanted to come, just to tell you—" he spread helpless hands, " – these things are impossible to say. I'm sorry. Totally inadequate words."

"But welcome," she said quietly. "Thank you."

Christopher's eyes had strayed to a new photograph upon the table at his elbow. The tall, young uniformed figure smiled jauntily. "Your son?" Christopher asked in surprise.

"Yes. He joined the army some months ago. He's being sent to France. Next week."

He said nothing.

"I just won't think about it," she said, honestly, and for a moment the strain behind the calm exterior was plain to be seen. Then she stood up briskly. "I'm glad you came. I've been meaning to get in touch with you."

"Oh?"

"I've something for you." She walked to the sideboard, opened a drawer and came back carrying a small book. "Sarah gave this to me, as a keepsake for Nancy. But – somehow I feel that you should have it. It has your name in it."

His hand shook as he took it, his fingers closing around familiar, warm leather. He bowed his head. "Are you sure?" he asked, after a moment.

"Of course. It is yours, isn't it?"

"It was. I gave it to her." He lifted the cover. CHRISTOPHER EDMONTON. 1912. His own writing, faded and smudged. Then beneath it, strong and clear, NANCY BENTON. JUNE 1917. SOFT EYES LOOKED LOVE TO EYES WHICH SPAKE AGAIN—" he stared at the blurring words. "And all went merry as a marriage bell," he said, softly. "Do you know the quotation?"

"I looked it up. It's 'Childe Harold', isn't it?"

He nodded. " 'But hark! – that heavy sound breaks in once more/ As if the clouds its echoes would repeat/ And nearer,

clearer, deadlier than before!/ Arm! Arm! it is – it is –
cannon's opening roar!'"

"Please keep the book," she said, into the quiet, "I think s
would have wanted you to have it. And I have – other things.

"Thank you." Very carefully he tucked the book into
pocket, then with the help of his stick he began to struggle to
feet.

"Oh, please—" Molly stepped forward to assist him, but w
waved away. "Won't you stay for a drink?"

He smiled pleasantly, his eyes distant. "I won't, if you dor
mind. It takes me an age to get anywhere with this, and wi
transport the way it is—" They stood awkwardly, looking at o
another. " – I won't impose on you. I hope you haven't mind
my coming? I simply felt that I had to convey my sympath
And my thanks. I think that in the past you have been a goo
friend to me. And now," he touched his pocket, "thank yo
especially for this. It is far more than I could have hoped for.
had nothing to remember her by. I thought I needed nothin
Now I know that not to be so."

Molly put an impulsive hand on his arm. "If you want he
remembered, truly remembered, by people other than u
you could give me – or rather Nancy – something in e>
change."

"Oh? Why certainly – if I can—?"

"I'm setting up a fund. In Nancy's name. A memorial to her
A fund for the education of bright, working class girls. Fe
paying scholarships to schools and colleges – perhaps, wh
knows, if I can get enough support – even to universities. But it'
difficult, as you can probably guess. This kind of thing at th
moment is bound to come a long way behind the Red Cross, th
refugees – oh, the million and one worthy calls on people'
charitable pockets. But I'm determined to do it anyway."

"It's a wonderful idea. A perfect memorial to Nancy."

"That's what I thought. But if it's going to get off th
ground—"

"How much do you need?" he asked, simply.

"I'm starting it with a thousand pounds. May I count on you
for—?"

"The same," he said.

"Oh, but that's too much." She was quite genuinely taken aback.

"A thousand," he said, firmly. "And money as well-used as any I have ever spent. I'll approach my mother, too. I'm certain she'll help. She was very fond of Nancy."

After he had taken his leave the girls found their mother staring pensively into the fire. "He was a lot better looking than I remembered him," said Meg.

"You think anyone who's male and over twenty good-looking," retorted her sister, with unaccustomed asperity. "I thought he looked terribly sad. Sort of battered."

"You make him sound like an old tin mug."

Their voices washed over Molly unheard. She was remembering the time, in another life, when a gangling youth had walked into the chaos of moving-in day at The Larches; trying – and failing – to discover any resemblance at all between that remembered, sensitively youthful face and the hardened, damaged face of the young man who had just left.

A couple of days after Christmas – a Christmas spent very quietly with the twins, Sarah, and Annie and little Tom, and inevitably haunted by absent faces – Molly and Adam dined in his apartment. Adam, as always, had contrived gracefully to rise above such things as shortages and rationing and provide something approximating a pre-war meal.

"You're impossible," Molly said, regarding her inch-thick steak. "Poor Effi's 'doin' somethin' with mince'. I feel as if I ought to put this in a bag and take it home."

Adam, smiling, opened the wine. Outside the window a London pea-souper wreathed ghostly fingers in the darkness; the best defence of all for the city against the Gothas and the Giants. There had been no raids since Christmas Eve.

Molly picked up her wine glass and looked through it at the flickering candlelight. It glowed like rubies.

Adam leaned across the table. "You're looking particularly beautiful tonight."

She lifted cool eyes. "And you're looking particularly pleased with yourself."

He laughed. "It's the temporary security afforded by the fog.

And it might have something to do with the company I'r keeping." He half-bowed across the table.

"I see." Very composedly, Molly sipped her wine. "I wouldn't, of course, have anything to do with the fact that you'r bribing and corrupting half the city of Liverpool to ensure ou cargoes' precedence over everyone else's?"

The silence was telling.

"I've known for a week," she continued pleasantly. "Yo really should be more careful what you say in front of Willian Baxter. He works for me, Adam. Not for you. You've got the poor man quite worried with your – unorthodox methods o business."

Adam laid down his knife and fork, laced long fingers togethe and regarded her gravely over them. In the fog-bound silence o the room the flames crackled in the hearth. "Are you going to read me the Riot Act?"

She shook her head, and saw the gleam of surprise in his eyes. She had thought about this long and hard. "No. The shipments are getting through, and that means that people are getting badly needed supplies that they otherwise might not. If anything needs to take precedence – by whatever method – it's our foodstuffs. If I insist that you stop——" she paused " – oiling hinges, then someone else will start and London might find itself with a fine supply of cotton reels or flannelette nightdresses." ·

He regarded her with absolute and undisguised admiration. "How very practical of you."

"But—" she said.

"Ah."

"But I'm not happy about the excess profits we're making. You've made a lot of things of me in the past, Adam, but I'm damned if even you are going to turn me into a war profiteer."

"That's an emotional phrase."

"I'll say it is."

For a long moment he did not speak. Then he said, "It's too much to expect, of course, that you haven't already decided what you think should be done about it?"

This was her moment: she had planned it for a week. She leaned forward, her small face intent. "It's really very simple. Marvellously so. I want us to donate the excess profits to

ancy's funds. Oh, Adam, don't you see – it's the perfect thing
to spend the money on—"

He remained silent and unsmiling. Her heart sank. She had
lost. If she could not persuade him, she knew there was no way to
force him.

"By Christ," he said at last, quietly. "I must be going soft in
the head. All right. It's a deal. But only what you can prove to
me are excess profits, mind. I'm not finishing up in the poor-
house for you or for anyone else."

Molly laughed wrily. Beneath her triumph, a thought lay,
still and heavy, like a stone in a bright pool of water. A few years
ago Molly O'Dowd would not have come to such an arrangement. She would have been storming into the street looking for a
policeman. Ends and means. Where would it stop?

Adam did not notice her odd change of mood. He stood up
and came to her, offering his hand. She came to him and he
kissed her, his mouth hard, familiar, infinitely exciting. "You'll
make an honest man of me yet, Molly," he said into her hair.

And, even if she had seen it, she might have misinterpreted
the thoughtful gleam in his eyes.

At the beginning of March 1918 Danny came home on leave.
Molly was never more pleased to see anyone in her life, nor more
astonished to see so great a change in such a short while, for the
boy who had left came home a man.

"Why, Danny-oh," Meg crowed, swinging on her brother's
hands, "how *handsome* you look! I swear I could fall for you
myself!"

"You must have grown an inch," Molly said.

"Two," he grinned. "Hello, Kit."

Kitty clung to him in silence.

"If you'd let a fellow breath for a minute," he said, "then he
might be able to lay his hands on a couple of things that you
ladies might like." Even his voice was different, Molly noticed;
the words were clipped and clear, the sloppiness of enunciation
that she had used to scold about completely gone.

In the parlour he dug into his kitbag. "Here, pussy cat," he
said, tossing a small packet to Meghan.

"Oh, Danny, what is it?"

"Open it and see."

He stood watching, a smile on his face as his sister's eag
fingers shredded the paper. The last traces of awkward ad
lescence had left him. He was as tall as Jack had been, but w
built, like Harry, his true father, spare and graceful. The bur
ished red-brown hair, even shorn as it had been by an army barb
curled crisply away from a face that Molly saw with some m
giving would undoubtedly charm most women into ignoring t
flaws that were inherent in it – a certain hard selfishness abo
the mouth, a jauntiness that promised arrogance in the tilt of t
well-shaped head. He stood easily, his eyes on Meghan, a look
such confident expectation on his face that Molly, too, turn
her face to her daughter.

"Danny! Oh, Danny, how marvellous! How on earth d
you—?" Meghan's face was brilliant. "Look oh look what I'
got!" She held up a slender, glittering chain of gold from whi
depended a perfect golden rose whose heart was set with a sing
stone that winked fire as it swung from her fingers.

Molly looked sharply at her son. With the air of a magician
produced another little package, the twin of the one he had give
Meghan. "Here, Kit. This is for you."

With trembling fingers Kitty carefully opened her gif
smoothing the pretty paper into a neat square before she opene
the tiny box. "Oh, Danny, it's lovely!" She too had a golde
chain, from which hung a tiny locket edged with glowing stone
blood-red, which turned it, as she held it up, into a heart of fir
"But Danny," she said, aghast, "it must have cost *pounds*!" an
then, abashed, "Oh, I'm sorry, I didn't mean—" She stoppe
blushing as red as the rubies in her locket.

"And now—" this time Danny's hand went to his pocke
"– for what our gallant allies across the water might call the *piè
de résistance*—" He pulled from his pocket a small twist
rustling tissue paper. "For you," he said to Molly.

The ring glittered on the palm of her hand like a capricio
moonbeam trapped in metal and stone.

"Does it fit?" His young voice was anxious.

She slipped it on her finger. "Perfectly. What a lovely thin
Thank you." She stood on tiptoe to kiss him. "Have you give
up eating or something?" she asked, smiling.

Very faintly he flushed. "Of course not. What do you mean?"

"Well, you didn't get these at a sixpenny stall in Petticoat Lane, did you?" She tried to hide the tiny, gnawing doubts behind the lightness of the words.

Danny was digging once more in the bag. "I'm not Tommy Atkins in the trenches, you know Mum. Oh, no. I soon realized that wasn't for Danny Benton. I'm in the Officer's Mess at an HQ just outside Calais. Safe as houses." He grinned disarmingly. "No one's fired a shot at me in anger yet. And with a bit of luck no one ever will. It's a cushy billet, with the chance to make a few bob on the side."

"What exactly do you do?"

"Oh," he said, shrugging vaguely, still hunting in the bag, "all sorts of things. Ah, here it is!" As if he were producing a rabbit from a hat he straightened to reveal a bottle in his hand. "Champagne. To celebrate the return of the prodigal."

"Champagne?" said Molly.

"Vintage. And you don't have to worry—" the brilliant eyes were fixed on her face, a cold gleam in their depths, "I – didn't pinch it."

"Danny, I didn't for a moment think that—"

"Didn't you?" The challenge was clear in his clipped voice.

"Oh, for Heaven's sake!" Meg snatched the bottle from Danny and danced around the room with it. "Don't start you two! Danny, hurry! Open it!" She waltzed to Danny and caught his hand, "Champagne! When I'm older and this rotten old war's over I shall drink nothing else!"

Her brother looked down at her, grinning. "That's my girl."

Molly looked at the pair of them, something close to pain in her eyes. There was a restlessness about them both, a bright, intolerant charm that stirred a deep forboding in her.

"The glasses. Come on, Mum, where are the glasses?" Meghan could not stand still

"In the sideboard."

With a sound like a gunshot the cork flew as Danny, expertly, opened the champagne without spilling a drop. Laughing they all gathered round to catch the bubbling fountain of liquid in their glasses. Molly laughed with her children, firmly suppressing her momentary misgivings. Danny was home, and safe That for the moment was enough.

"A toast."

They stopped and turned to her. She raised her glas. She wa looking at her son. "To our Danny. Welcome home."

Danny's leave flew past. It seemed to Molly, in the way of thes things, that no sooner had he fairly arrived than he was packin to leave again; and two days after he had gone, the Germans, in choking cloud of fog and gas on a foul March day, launched th massive offensive that was intended to shatter the Allied de fences once and for all, and to put an end to the war before th intervention of the United States of America tipped the balanc irrevocably. In the initial shock and confusion whole British Commonwealth and French units were overrun and – in som cases quite literally – lost. Yet, astonishingly, the fierce anc unexpected attack found itself faced with tenacious and unex pected resistance put up by men who might have been expected after four years of bitter fighting under atrocious conditions to b at the end of their tether. But to the dismay of the German Hig Command the expected collapse did not materialize and, ex hausted and stretched to the limit, its own homeland now being forced to the edge of starvation by the British blockade, the attacking force ground to a halt, staggered, and then found itself being pushed back. Yet more blood flowed to irrigate ground that must surely be already sodden with it – along the fertile valleys of the Marne, the Somme and the Aisne, in the fields of Flanders and of Normandy. All along that front, that had been for so long static, the conflict raged as a fire will blaze before dying, made more vicious by desperation on both sides.

At home the newspaper reports of the fighting were confusing – only the growing casualty lists could be taken as truth. Yet the ill wind that blew across the Western Front brought some good to beleaguered Londoners, for the German squadrons were needed elsewhere, and the Gothas and the Giants no longer plagued the skies of England. The convoys returned as more escorts became available and the Port of London came to life once more, bringing much-needed supplies to the city. On that day in May when the first American troops disembarked at the

London docks amidst the cheers of the population, their arrival signalled the beginning of the end for war-battered Germany, and, as the Americans continued to arrive throughout the summer and then to leave for France, the scales of power that had been so delicately and disastrously balanced for the last three and a half years tilted at last.

On the day when the news came that the ridge of Passchendael – perhaps the most emotive name in that catalogue of war – had at last been stormed and taken by Australian troops, Chantale Benton, hearing the news from Molly, collapsed in an emotional storm of tears. Molly, whilst comforting her, was surprised. Chantale had rarely shown such open emotion. On the contrary, it had often worried Molly more than a little that a girl naturally as warm-natured and impulsive as Chantale should nurse her grief for her parents and her homeland and her utter hatred for the nation who had killed the first and desecrated the second, in such secrecy and with such little outward show.

"There, there," she said now, "Chantale, my love, don't cry so. It's nearly over, I'm sure. Edward will be home—"

Chantale sniffed and wiped her eyes. "But still they fight—"

"Edward will be all right. You'll see." Chantale's face was very pale. Molly looked at her anxiously. "My dear, are you feeling unwell? You look very peaky."

"Peaky? What is this, peaky?" The girl had regained her composure a little.

Molly laughed. "I'm sorry. Your English is so good that sometimes I forget. I mean tired. Pale. Do you feel all right?"

A smile glittered through the tears. "Only sometimes not. As is to be expected, I think. As are these stupid tears—" she brushed her hands across her face with an embarrassed, half-laughing gesture, "for – did you not guess? – I am to have a child."

In a moment she was in Molly's arms again, both of them laughing and crying together.

From the picture that stood next to Jack's in pride of place on the mantelpiece, Nancy's smiling face watched them both.

CHAPTER FORTY-EIGHT

IN THE DOUR and icy darkness of a winter's dawn on the eleventh of November 1918 in the unlikely setting of a railway carriage standing deep in a forest in France a group of tired and sober-faced men put their names to an historic document. A few hours later, at eleven that same morning, the church bells rang, the maroons boomed and men crawled from the trenches for the last time, hardly daring to believe that it was safe to do so. It was Armistice day, and the war to end all wars was itself finally ended.

At home a tempest of celebration swept the land. People streamed into the streets, laughing, weeping, cheering, singing, the incandescent and insubstantial bubble of victory dancing before them, and understandably on that morning few thought to question it. The years of slaughter had come to an end: that for the moment was enough. And if all the tears shed on that day were not tears of joy, and if not everyone felt inclined to join the roistering crowds who rode in flag decked cars and taxis, danced on bunting-wreathed omnibuses, sang and celebrated their way down streets that were safe at last, it made no great difference to those bent upon carnival.

Molly's first thought, after the initial euphoria at The Larches, was for Annie and Sarah. She hurried through streets where strangers greeted her to the small house the two women shared. As she had suspected, the general happiness was not well reflected in the dark little kitchen in which Annie, with relentless, energetic rhythm, kneaded dough for a batch of bread, her face a sombre contrast to those smiling ones Molly had seen in the streets outside. Little Tom, his nose on a level with the table top, stood on tiptoe to watch the fascinating operation, his dark eyes solemn. Beside the open grate Sarah sat rocking slightly, her veined and knotted hands folded unquietly in her lap.

"Oh, please, won't you come back to The Larches with me?

he girls would love to see you, and we could—"

The dough crashed hard onto the table. Tom jumped, start-
d. Annie shook her head. The bright hair had faded, the mouth
at once had smiled so readily was tight. She had put on a
nsiderable amount of weight, and her clothes, though clean,
ere untidy and dowdy. There was little sign in her of that
ughing girl who had ridden with Charley to Epping Forest.
No, Moll. Thanks all the same. We're all right here. Young
om, you get your fingers out of there!"

Molly looked from one to the other, her heart aching, "Sarah?
Won't you come? At least for tea?"

Sarah lifted her head. In the last two years, Molly thought
ith a pang, she had aged ten. She looked frail and old. "Nay,
ass. Like our Annie says, we'll do all right here, thanks all the
ame. You go on along home. The girls'll be wanting to get out
nd about and 'tis only natural that they should." She smiled
redly. "Thanks for thinking of us, lass."

The atmosphere in the room was oppressive. Heavy net
urtains obscured the one window, the small fire glowed sullenly
n the half-darkness.

"Annie," Molly said softly, "I'm not suggesting that we
hould have a party or dance in the streets. Do you think that I
lon't understand? Do you think that I don't mourn? You know
ne better than that. I came because I couldn't bear to think of
ou here, alone. I want you both to come back with me so that
ve can be together. As Charley, and Jack, and Nancy would
ave wanted us to be. The war – is over." She spoke the words
lowly, emphasizing them. "We have to look to the future
now."

"Yes, well," Annie said, quietly, "we aren't all as good at that
s you are."

The words were not spoken unkindly, yet the bite was there,
nd Molly flinched from it.

"Oh, Hell!" With considerable violence Annie dumped the
lough on the table and gestured with her whitened hands. "I'm
orry, Moll, love. I'm sorry. I didn't mean that the way it
ounded, honest I didn't. Christ knows where we'd have been
without you over these past couple of years. But you have to
understand – we aren't all like you. Do you think I don't see

what's happening to me? Do you think I wouldn't do somethi
about it if I could?"

Alarmed by his mother's tone Tom began to whimper. Ann
was across the room and had him in her arms in a second. "O
there now, Tommy love, what is it?"

Sarah's eyes met Molly's. "There's nowt to do here, lass," s
said kindly. "Go home to your girls. They'll be waiting. It
where you belong."

Fighting misery, Molly hurried through the festive streets
discover to her surprise Adam's car standing outside the door
The Larches.

She ran swiftly up the steps to the front door, which opened a
if by magic as she approached it.

"Oh, Mum, where have you been? You've been *ages!*
Meghan danced around her, soft skirt swinging around lon
legs, the golden rose her brother had given her sparkling at he
throat. "Adam's here. He's come to take us out. To London, t
see the celebrations. In the car! Oh, do come on, we've bee
waiting and waiting. I thought you were never comin
back!"

"I had to see your Grandma and Aunt Annie." Molly looke
over her daughter's shoulder to where, in the deeper shado
beyond the door Adam stood waiting, watching her, smiling.

"Are they all right?" Kitty had joined her sister. Dressed i
dark brown, her fine hair waving softly about a face that wa
bright with excitement, she looked as pretty as Molly had eve
seen her.

Molly hesitated for just a moment before she said briskl
"Yes, they're fine. They send their love."

Meghan was not listening to a word. "Can we go? I'm *dying* t
see what's happening. If we don't hurry it will all be over."

"I doubt that." Laughing, Adam limped down the step
"Your carriage awaits, Mrs Benton."

Suddenly the excitement that the visit to Annie and Sarah ha
quelled bubbled in her again. Meg's mood was infectious, a
Adam had obviously already found. Molly laughed. "Than
you, Adam. What a lovely idea."

And so, in happy convoy with hundreds like them, they drov
through the streets and squares of London, a London gone wil

with delight, packed with revellers, flag-decked, ringing with the sounds of horns and sirens, of whistles and of brass bands. Eventually they left the car and joined the jostling, ecstatic crowds in Trafalgar Square, where Meghan, whose jaunty boater was by now decorated with long streamers of red, white and blue, was swept off her feet by a gangling Australian.

"Give us a kiss, darlin'." The slightly tipsy soldier noticed Adam for the first time and added solemnly. "Beggin' yer pardon, mate?"

Adam, grinning, waved a gracious hand. "By all means." And the blushing Meghan received, to the applause of onlookers, not one smacking kiss but two.

"An' one fer luck," the lanky Australian slurred, rocking unsteadily on his feet. Then, "Tell yer what, darlin' – how about a swap?" His bony hand whipped the tiny boater from Meg's mass of hair and perched it on his own head, while in exchange he set his bush hat at a cheeky angle on her head. "There," he said in some admiration, "it certainly looks a bloody sight better on you than it does on me, darlin'." And before any of them could stop him he had staggered off into the crowds. The last they saw of him was Meghan's boater, in the distance, bobbing ludicrously amongst the sea of heads. Meghan laughed delightedly, knowing very well the pretty and patriotic sight she made in the wide-brimmed khaki bush hat.

At Kitty's insistence they joined the crowds who streamed down The Mall to Buckingham Palace. In the great open space outside the Palace railings the band of the Guards were playing in seemingly endless succession the national anthems of Great Britain and of all her allies. The massive crowds here were a little less raucous. Men and women in uniform stood to attention as the strains of the anthems lifted above the hubbub, and the crowds swayed slightly, listening, many a face suddenly wet with tears. When the long and solemn tribute finally came to an end there rose a deafening cheer, and the Victoria Memorial, high above their heads, reared through a sudden sea of waving, white handkerchiefs.

Adam steered his charges into St James's Park, where the hot-chestnut vendors were doing a roaring trade, their barrows gaily decked, as was everything else, in the Union Jack or in red, white and blue bunting. As the girls hopped hot nuts from one hand to another to cool them down Adam bought three bright favours from one of the costers who had appeared as if from nowhere, his barrows loaded with flags, streamers, hats, balloons. Adam pinned one on each of his charges, kissing each of them on the cheek as he did so. Molly lifted her head, leaning to him, roused as always by the touch of his mouth on her skin however light. Then turned and found Meghan's eyes wide and interested upon her.

On a park bench nearby a soldier sat, unashamedly crying, sobbing into his cupped hands, a sight that stayed with Molly for ever as the true illustration of the strange, bitter happiness of the day.

It was moving towards evening and full darkness before she said, finally and resolutely, "Time to go home."

"O-oh, but Mum—!"

"There'll be plenty going on at home. You don't want to miss that, do you?" The crowds about them were getting more and more rowdy as liquor began to oil the wheels of celebration. Adam, catching Molly's slightly worried eye, nodded.

"Your mother's right, now, Meg. Come on, back to the car."

Stratford, like the rest of London, was *en fête*. Bonfires blazed, street parties, organized from nowhere, blocked off streets and squares. They were astonished to find, just along the road from The Larches that a trestle table had been set up from which beer and sandwiches were being dispensed while people danced to the music of a barrel organ. As the car inched through the revellers many greeted Molly and the girls in friendly fashion, and many an inquisitive stare was bent upon Adam, who endured them with panache, a gleam of laughter in his eyes. Meghan, in her element, and enjoying every minute of this unexpected parade, her peevishness at being made to come home completely forgotten, waved the dashing bush hat in the air.

"Look, there's Lucy Regan. And Betty. Oh, we don't have to go in yet, do we Mum? Can we stay? Can we? We won't be late, I promise."

Kitty said nothing, but her hazel eyes pleaded for her.

Molly smiled. "Of course. But don't be in any later than ten."

As Adam rolled the car to a halt outside the house the girls ran back along the road, calling to their friends. Adam looked down at Molly. "Do you want to join them?"

She shook her head. "No. I don't think I do. I've had enough excitement for one day. I wondered – well, would you like to come in for a quiet drink?"

"I thought you'd never ask."

Effie had left a good fire burning in the parlour with an almost illegible note propped on the mantelpiece informing Molly that she had gone to the party, leaving bread and cheese in the kitchen for supper. Molly drew the curtains. Outside the flames of the bonfire leapt and flickered, a firework zipped and flew in a rain of brilliant stars. With cold clarity she suddenly remembered the night that the Zeppelin had been shot down, and she shivered.

"It doesn't seem possible, does it? That it's over, I mean?"

Adam had come up close behind her. Gently he turned her to face him. Their kiss lasted for long moments, punctuated by the sound of the celebrations in the street outside. As they drew apart Molly laughed, a little breathlessly. "Do you fancy some of Effie's bread and cheese?"

"Later, perhaps. I've got something else for us to try. It's in the car. I'll get it."

He was gone a long time. Restlessly Molly roamed the room. She stopped by the long bookshelf, ran her eyes absently along it, and stopped with a small shock of recognition at the battered and peeling spine of a book that had been the twins' favourite in its time, as it had always been hers. She remembered with a sudden pang the look on her father's face as she had left him staring down at a book that he could not read, saw again a small figure huddled in a chair at Christmas time, shutting out loneliness and fear with a tale of white rabbits and Cheshire cats, recalled the day that Ellen Alden had ripped that same book to shreds in her manic grief. She pushed the book a little into the shelf, straightened the row, moved away, towards the mantelpiece where Jack's and Nancy's photographs stood. Jack, in uniform, looked straight ahead, unsmiling and martial. The photographer, unsuccessfully, had tried to camouflage the scar

on the side of his face. Very slowly Molly lifted her hand an
traced it with her finger, beneath the smooth, cold glass. For
moment the room blurred around her, and, blinking, she turne
away.

She wandered to the door. Adam had left the street door open
through it she saw him standing by the car, trapped in conversa
tion with a group of laughing girls, led, predictably, by Meg, stil
sporting the gallant bush hat. She would probably, thought he
mother drily, want to sleep in it.

Across the hall the door to the darkened offices stood open
On an impulse she moved across the passage and stood in the
doorway of the office that had for so long been Nancy's and wa.
now, ironically, Chantale's, the girl who was the daughter-in-law
that Nancy had never seen, and who was carrying her grand
child. For a moment Molly conjured in her head the memories
aware even as she did so, that day by day the hurt was softening
Nancy, arguing about women's rights with John Marsden
Nancy, battered, her heelless shoe brandished as a trophy.
Molly crossed the room to the door of the main office, switched
on the lights and advanced to the centre of the room. On her big
desk lay the papers she had been working on concerning the
newly-established Nancy Benton Trust. She riffled through
them.

She heard Adam's light, uneven footsteps before he spoke.
"Don't you ever stop working?" He leaned in the doorway, as he
had once before, watching her.

She laughed. "I was thinking. Do you know that it's twenty
years almost to the day since I first walked through the door? I
can see John now, sitting behind this very desk, scowling at me
like the wolf at Red Riding Hood."

"Did he scare you?"

"I don't think so. My feet hurt too much."

He came into the room towards her. Now she could see that in
his hands he held an opened bottle of champagne and two tall
glasses. "You've come a long way since that day. You're on the
way to becoming a very rich lady." He placed the long, fluted
glasses on the desk top and poured the champagne. She watched
as it foamed, sparkling, into the glass.

"Yes, I suppose so." She frowned a little, her head on one

de. "You know just about all about me, don't you? It's all a bit ae-sided, isn't it? There's still so much I don't know about you. 'here you come from? How you started?"

He laughed and picked up a glass in each hand. "That's another story. You only get to hear it if you marry me." Then, ato the sudden silence he added tranquilly, "This seems an appropriate time and it's certainly," he glanced around, a spark of humour in his eyes, "the most appropriate place. Will you aarry me?"

Outside another firework lit the sky with lovely, multi-ploured stars that blazed brightly for a few seconds then fell, ading, to earth.

Molly studied him in the flickering light, smiling. Then, very lowly, she shook her head. Love, she had discovered, was one hing, marriage quite another.

"I won't ask you again," he said mildly.

She moved to him, stood on tiptoe, and dropped a kiss, eather-light, on his cheek. "Oh, yes, Adam," she said softly, "You will."

She sensed his sudden stillness before, despite himself, laugh-er rose: laughter in which she joined as it lifted above the sounds of the world's celebrations outside.

Belva Plain

– the best-loved bestseller –

Evergreen £2.50

The tempestuous story of Anna Friedman, the beautiful, penniless Jewish girl who arrives in New York from Poland at the turn of the century and survives to become the matriarch of a powerful dynasty.

Random Winds £2.50

The poignant story of a family of doctors – Dr Farrell, the old-fashioned country doctor who dies penniless and exhausted, his son Martin who becomes a famous brain surgeon but is haunted by his forbidden love for a woman, and Martin's daughter Claire, headstrong and modern, whose troubled romance provides a bitter-sweet ending.

Eden Burning £2.50

A romantic saga set against the backdrop of New York, Paris and the Caribbean. The island of St Felice holds many secrets, one of which is the secret of the passionate moment of abandon that threatened to destroy the life of beautiful Teresa Francis. A story of violence, political upheaval and clandestine love.

Crescent City £2.50

Miriam Raphael leaves the ghettoes of Europe to become a belle of New Orleans. Trapped in a bad marriage she begins a turbulent, forbidden love affair with dangerous, attractive André Perrin. But the horrors of the Civil War sweep away the old splendour, and Miriam must rebuild her own and her family's life from the ashes.

FONTANA PAPERBACKS

Fontana Paperbacks: Fiction

Fontana is a leading paperback publisher of both non-fiction, popular and academic, and fiction. Below are some recent fiction titles.

- ☐ COMING TO TERMS Imogen Winn £2.25
- ☐ TAPPING THE SOURCE Kem Nunn £1.95
- ☐ METZGER'S DOG Thomas Perry £2.50
- ☐ THE SKYLARK'S SONG Audrey Howard £1.95
- ☐ THE MYSTERY OF THE BLUE TRAIN Agatha Christie £1.75
- ☐ A SPLENDID DEFIANCE Stella Riley £1.95
- ☐ ALMOST PARADISE Susan Isaacs £2.95
- ☐ NIGHT OF ERROR Desmond Bagley £1.95
- ☐ SABRA Nigel Slater £1.75
- ☐ THE FALLEN ANGELS Susannah Kells £2.50
- ☐ THE RAGING OF THE SEA Charles Gidley £2.95
- ☐ CRESCENT CITY Belva Plain £2.75
- ☐ THE KILLING ANNIVERSARY Ian St James £2.95
- ☐ LEMONADE SPRINGS Denise Jefferies £1.95
- ☐ THE BONE COLLECTORS Brian Callison £1.95

You can buy Fontana paperbacks at your local bookshop or newsagent. Or you can order them from Fontana Paperbacks, Cash Sales Department, Box 29, Douglas, Isle of Man. Please send a cheque, postal or money order (not currency) worth the purchase price plus 15p per book for postage (maximum postage is £3.00 for orders within the UK).

NAME (Block letters) _____

ADDRESS _____

_____

While every effort is made to keep prices low, it is sometimes necessary to increase them at short notice. Fontana Paperbacks reserve the right to show new retail prices on covers which may differ from those previously advertised in the text or elsewhere.